InHap♥pily Ever After

Kim DeSalvo

D1713858

DEDICATION

For Mumsy and Pops, who never let me forget that dreams really can come true

Contents

ACKNOWLEDGMENTS

Wow, has this been a different experience. Never in a million years did I expect that my first novel—self-published by an unknown author— would experience the success that Incidental Happenstance enjoyed. I've learned a lot since I first started it; first and foremost, that there are a lot of people in my life who helped to make it all happen. Some were in my face, some worked behind the scenes, and others came from places I never expected to help make this book happen. First and foremost, my wonderful parents, who read every word over and over, let me bounce crazy ideas off of them, and were a constant source of encouragement and support. Next, all of those who read parts or all of the story and put in way more than two cents—my wonderful sister Gianna, Dorothy, Amy, and Sue; who kept asking for more pages and helped me push forward. Thanks to Teri, self-proclaimed InHap junkie turned editor extraordinaire, for her great suggestions and for helping me get commas in all the right places. My appreciation to Nathan, for helping get all my legal ducks in a row, and to Chris, for his help with the back cover. Much love and gratitude to Tyler, for giving up entire days for photo and video shoots, and for always being willing to lend a hand; even dropping his own projects to help me with mine.

As always, I am grateful for my wonderful readers. You kept me motivated, inspired, and upbeat throughout this whole process, and I am incredibly thankful for you. So many of you feel like dear friends, and your kind words and support have meant more to me than you will ever know.

About the Cover

I'll admit; when I published my first book, I was pretty clueless. It was an overwhelming process, and nothing gave me more difficulty than designing the cover. I'll be the first to admit that I'm not a visual artist, and have a tremendous respect for those who are. Not too long after the first book came out, I reconnected with Jennifer Blocker, a dear friend from my own "pinky-swear-friend-days." She had been doing some fabulous modeling, and we started talking about how cool it would be if she could do a shot for my cover. She sent all kinds of pics—and although they were all fabulous, I didn't see one that summed it all up. Until I went and stalked her portfolio, that is. This pic, taken by Tim Hufford of Digital Northern Exposures, jumped out at me right away. I loved how the moon glowed at the top of the guitar, but what really struck me was the confident swagger of the woman—a swagger that Tia was trying so hard to achieve. It captured an essence—a power—and I was thrilled when they both agreed to allow me to use the photo. Thanks, Jen and Tim, for helping me give Tia her swag!

Chapter 1

"Oh Dylan, I can't believe you're here. Am I dreaming?" Tia closed her eyes tightly for a brief second, shook her head, and opened them again, a smile slowly spreading over her face. "I've had this same dream at least a thousand times."

"No baby, not a dream." He pulled her into his lap so that she straddled him and felt his heart melt at the joy he saw in her eyes. All the worry, all the doubt drifted away; she'd never stopped loving him either. He was a very lucky man. "This, my love, is what they call a dream come true."

"Oh yeah," she agreed, tears trailing down her cheeks even as she laughed out loud. "Definitely a dream come true." She raised her hands to trace his features; running her fingers over the shadowy stubble of a beard and through the carelessly unkempt waves of his hair; streaked lighter from his months in the sun. Her thumbs traced the curve of full brows shaped over impossibly blue eyes rimmed in long lashes and down the strong nose to his full lips, curved in a telling smile. He tucked one hand around her lower back, pulling her in close before taking her hands into his own, kissing her palms in turn before returning them to his face.

"Oh, God, I can't believe this," she said, "you really never broke up with me?"

"Not even for a second."

"The email was a fake?"

"Completely."

"And the pictures in the tabloids—all forgeries?" Her voice broke as the realization sunk in.

"Every single one of them." Dylan's lips curled up then; the smile he saved just for her; the one that crinkled the corners of his eyes and puckered a tiny dimple in his left cheek. The one that melted her heart every single time she saw it. "Bloody hell I missed you," he said with a rasp of raw emotion in his voice. He wrapped his arms around her tightly and pulled her in; cocooning her in an embrace that even a few hours ago she believed she'd never feel again. She thought she might shatter with the pure intensity of it all.

"Oh God, Dylan, you can't even imagine how much I missed you, how much I love you..."

"Believe me, I know exactly how much," he whispered. He buried his face in her hair and inhaled deeply, holding his breath for a moment before releasing it on a long sigh. "I love you so much, Tia. Thinking I lost you was the worst kind of hell. I'm so sorry that I let you down..."

Tia pulled back and looked hard into his eyes. "Don't you apologize—you were going through the same thing I was. You didn't do anything wrong, Dylan."

He pressed his lips together, his features contorting. He squinted and cocked his head, and she could read the pain in his eyes. "Yes I did, baby girl." She opened her mouth to protest; to tell him that none of it mattered now that they were together again; but he silenced her with a soft brush of his lips over hers. "Just let me say this, because I need to for my own peace of mind." He took her face in his hands and held her gaze. "I doubted you, love, and I never should have done that for even a second. I knew there was something off about that bloody email—I just knew in my gut that it wasn't you—could never have been you—but I fell for it anyway. Then I doubted Jessa's loyalty, and sent her packing without even giving her a chance to defend herself. Two of the most important people in my life—two people that I trusted without fail—and *she* managed to break it all apart. I let that bitch get into my head, Tia, and I can't stop kicking myself for that."

"Oh, sweetie," she said softly, "I fell for it too. I believed it, even though Lexi said it reeked of Penelope and couldn't have been you that wrote it..."

"Yeah, and then you had the added complication of seeing those damn pictures in the tabloids," he growled. "I don't know if I can forgive myself for not protecting you from that. I should've been more diligent, I should've..."

"How could you have known?" Tia interrupted. "I mean, who would even consider that another person could do something so...so...heartless?"

"But I knew what she was after from the start. I should have seen through her bullshit from the beginning. Why did I even trust her for a minute?" He dropped his eyes and balled his hands into fists.

"Because you're a good person, Dylan," Tia said, gently unclenching his fingers and forcing him to meet her gaze. "You want to believe the best about people; look for the good in them. She knew that, and she used it to her advantage." She put her hands on his shoulders and added, "But she didn't win, baby. We won. We're together, and none of the rest of it matters now."

Dylan ran his fingers roughly through his wavy locks. "I know you're right," he said, pressing his mouth into a firm line, "but it kills me that you spent so much time thinking that I'd abandoned you and given up on us, when nothing could be further from the truth." He touched his lips to hers and let them rest there for a moment.

"It's a drop in the ocean compared to the time we have ahead of us, Dyl, and I'd much prefer to focus on that."

His features softened and he smiled. "Oh God, you're absolutely right—regardless of everything else, this is a happy day. No more secrets, no more hiding. It's you and me against the world now, Tia. Officially and forever."

"I really like the sound of that," she whispered. "Officially and forever. That is really all that matters."

He pulled her to his mouth slowly, their lips and tongues moving in a familiar dance and building to a crescendo that took her breath away. He shifted, laying Tia against the long seat and pressed his body to hers, crushing her mouth with a more demanding kiss. Tia lost herself in warm velvet, wet tongues, the softness of his lips and his touch. She inhaled sharply as his hand slid over her breast, cupping it firmly and giving it a possessive squeeze. Tia squirmed closer, pressing her hips into his and moaning softly when she felt his desire pushing urgently against her inner thigh.

"I can't even tell you how badly I want you right now," he growled into her ear, sending a long shiver down her spine.

"Show me," she whispered back, sliding her hand over to press it to his jeans, stroking him through the soft fabric and pulling another snarl from deep in his throat. There was no "slow and easy" in his eyes or his touch, and Tia felt her own urgency rising to meet his.

Finally, the limo pulled into her driveway and they all but tumbled out of the car. Tia fumbled for her keys as Dylan scooped his bags from the driver's hands. She grabbed his arm and pulled him to the door, finally managed to flip the lock, and then they were inside.

For the briefest moment they just stared at each other, the intensity of their combined gazes speaking what it would take hours for words to say. There were a tremendous number of tangled emotions in them both; relief, disbelief, apologies, forgiveness, joy. A rogue tear spilled down Tia's cheek, and Dylan caught it with his fingertip, then pulled her to him.

"My baby girl," he growled, his lips vibrating against her ear. He nipped her earlobe and slid his tongue along the contour of her neck down to her shoulder, the slight stubble on his cheeks sending shivers along her nerve endings.

"Oh Dylan, I missed you so much," Tia murmured as his hands roamed over her body rough and fast. As she slowly inhaled her heart recognized his scent; dark and animal and masculine and woodsy; and a thousand delicious memories rolled over the back of her closed eyelids. The ragged echoes of their breathing slithered off the walls and then his mouth was on hers and she surrendered to pure sensation. Dylan caught her just as her knees went weak and pressed her against the door, her soft body molding itself around every line of his hard frame.

Dylan couldn't think of a time he'd wanted anything as badly as he wanted Tia at this moment. His girl; his everything; was looking at him with such desire, such trust, such intense need. He was suddenly transported back to the first time he and Tia had made love.

He'd wanted her so badly that night—there was something about her and the way she made him feel that he couldn't explain at the time. But as badly as he'd wanted her, he was filled at the same time with an intense desire to protect her. He was only in Chicago for a few days; and because he'd believed that he'd have to walk away, his lustful feelings fought savagely against those compelled to respect her honor. In the end, though, it was beyond their control—wanton desire had claimed an undeniable victory over chivalry, and the spark that would become their love had burst into flame in an instant. He could feel that same heat singeing him right now.

They'd been there and done that since that opening night; fumbled through the first touches, bumped heads and teeth going in for kisses, seen each other with too little sleep, too much to drink, and with noses red-rimmed and running from head colds. They'd had a crash course in each other that summer in Europe, and had grown closer and more comfortable with every passing day.

He thought at the time that he couldn't possibly feel a more desperate need to be joined with this woman, but the blood coursing through his veins in this moment was a fire that could only be cooled by sexual release. She was his drug of choice and he was way overdue for a fix. He hooked his thumbs in the shoulders of the jacket she'd worn that day and pushed it down,

Kim DeSalvo

bunching it at her wrists and holding her fast. With his other hand, he tore open her blouse, buttons skittering across the wood floor, and bent to bury his face in the swell of her cleavage. He kissed and nibbled his way around the curve of each breast, then skimmed his lips over the fabric of her bra, nipping at her hardened bud through the lace.

"Ah!" she cried on a sharp intake of breath. "Oh Dyl, I've dreamed this so many times…"

Dylan's response was a look that contained so much fire that Tia thought she might actually burn. There was no tenderness there; just raw and primal hunger as he unhooked the front clasp with one quick motion and greedily sucked one hardened nipple into his mouth, rolling the other between his thumb and forefinger. The sensation was pure ecstasy, and Tia arched her back as every nerve ending in her body pulsed with electricity, each streak of current connected to the spot directly between her legs that swelled and throbbed in anticipation. She felt a floodgate open, and pressed her hips into him insistently.

"No dream could feel this good," Dylan snarled, moving his free hand to unbutton and slide her pants down in one swift motion to pool at her feet. She whined in the back of her throat as she stepped out of them and kicked them aside, trying to wriggle her arms loose. She was overcome with the depth of her need; more than anything she wanted to touch him; to rake her fingernails down his naked back; run her hands over every inch of his body and pull him deep into the place inside her that only he could fill. She groaned in protest as he tightened the grip at her wrists, but then moaned with pleasure when he pinned her to the wall with his body, put his hand behind her neck, and kissed her with undeniable urgency.

Dylan took a small step back and ran his gaze slowly up and down her body, chewing seductively on his upper lip. Goosebumps popped up on her flesh despite the inferno that burned inside. She'd lost the power of speech and perhaps even the ability to form cohesive thought, so lost was she in the intensity of his stare. Her breath came in ragged gasps until Dylan finally settled his eyes on hers and took in her own longing.

"You're so fucking beautiful," he said, his voice rough and raw.

"Oh Dyl," she whispered, "I just want to touch you. Please let me touch you." She tugged at her bindings once more, but she had little strength to resist.

"Soon," he croaked. "Very soon."

Dylan gently stroked her cheek with the back of his hand, then raised his index and middle fingers to her lips and pushed them inside her mouth. Tia groaned, running her tongue along and between his fingers while fighting the urge to wiggle free. With his eyes blazing into hers, he slid his moistened fingers inside her panties, gliding them slowly over her sex before spearing her with them. Tia arched into him and cried out as he pushed them deep, nearly lifting her off the floor. She threw her head back as the entire focus of her being centered on the place where they were connected, on the heat and the wetness and the sensations that were rising up more quickly than she could control. "Look at me, baby," Dylan commanded, "I want to see everything I make you feel."

"Mmm," she moaned and forced her gaze to his; no easy task as Dylan swirled and scissored his long fingers, slowly stroking the place deep inside her that sent waves of pleasure rolling over her entire body.

A slow wail was all she could manage as he slid them out ever so slowly, nearly making her come by running the length of one slick finger along her swollen core.

Dylan held her eyes as he lifted his now glistening fingers to his own mouth, sliding them inside. Tia moaned when his eyes lidded and clouded with desire as he licked her juices from them. "God, I missed the taste of you," he hissed as he slowly pulled them out, running his tongue over his lips before finally releasing her arms.

"Oh God," Tia shuddered quickly shrugging out of her jacket and ruined blouse and tossing them to the floor. "I need you inside me right now," she pleaded, her voice guttural. She'd never in her life felt such intense need—a physical ache to have their bodies joined. She shoved her hands underneath his shirt and pushed it roughly over his head while he snaked out of his jeans and finally, they were flesh to flesh.

"I like the way you say that," he growled as they crushed together; their hands moving possessively over reclaimed territory. "Tell me again."

"Now, Dylan, please!" she insisted, desperately needing the space inside her filled. He bent and scooped her up and they fell together onto the couch, frantically tossing pillows to the floor. Dylan shifted his weight and lifted her hips, plunging himself into the slickness of her; planting himself to the hilt in one swift motion. She came instantly on a strangled cry, and he forged a rhythm that was rough and hard and fast as wave after wave of delicious pleasure ebbed and flowed through her entire being.

It was too much for him to bear...simply being inside her again brought him to the edge immediately, but her face—her beautiful face—threatened to toss him off the cliff from which he barely clung. He held her gaze as he watched the pleasure he was bringing her play out over her features; her eyes hooded as she crested the wave, then rolling back as she tumbled over into ecstasy; the muscles of her legs quivering against him where they were wrapped around his waist. She held her hands under her hips to give him deeper access and the passionate sounds that slipped through her swollen lips echoed off the walls. She was heat and velvet and sweet, sweet, slickness and he could feel her clenching around him as he pushed urgently toward the precipice from which he was now desperate to plunge.

"Oh, Dylan, yes!" Tia hissed as she felt his climax swelling inside her, and rode it with him as he came on a snarl and a curse. He thought that he'd never heard a more beautiful sound than her crying his name in the throes of passion, and as the muscles that surrounded him tightened their grip he felt a second orgasm building inside him and quickened his pace. He watched her eyes go wide as she felt it too, and she threw her head back in pure carnal bliss as they rode the next wave together until he fell on her, completely spent and breathing in gasps.

Reaching blindly over the back of the couch, Dylan pulled a blanket over them and wrapped it tight to ward off the drafts wafting over their slick bodies. He rolled onto his side, pulling her close and taking her hand in his, interlacing their fingers and bringing it to his lips as he smiled down at her. He'd never seen her look more beautiful, he thought as he drank in her sex-flushed face, her disheveled hair, and the smudge of mascara at the corner of one eye. He disentangled his fingers and pushed them through her twisted locks, tucking them behind her ear.

"I'm so glad you came back for me," she whispered, reaching up to stroke his face.

"Oh, baby, I never let you go," he smiled, placing her palm on the center of his chest. "You were always right here, Tia." She spread her fingers, sifting them through the soft hair there and absorbing his warmth and the still-frantic beat of his heart. He lifted the Eiffel Tower charm from where it rested on her chest and turned it so the tiny diamonds caught the light. He'd given it to her the night he first told her he was in love with her as a reminder of just that—that she'd always be in his heart, no matter how much physical distance was between them. How he wished that there hadn't been so many moments of great doubt during that separation...how he wished he could have spared her that pain.

"I took it off," she admitted. "When I thought you were finished with me I couldn't bear to wear it—couldn't stand to have it shining at me in the mirror when it felt like all the sparkle was gone from my life. But I didn't tell anyone we broke up, and people started noticing I wasn't wearing it, so I had to put it back on. I'm glad that I did."

Dylan smirked and raised an eyebrow; a simple gesture that she'd missed horribly over the past months, but that seemed to mock her in the moment. "You didn't tell anyone we broke up?"

he asked, with what could only be described as a laugh in his voice.

"No, I didn't," Tia said defensively. "My parents booked a cruise when I told them I wasn't going to be here for the holidays, and I didn't want them to feel guilty about leaving me here all alone; or worse, insist that I go with them. Plus, I'd gone over our last phone conversation in my mind at least a thousand times, but I couldn't remember anything that even hinted at us breaking up. That was the day you told me that Jessa was working on my plane ticket, and we were both so excited about seeing each other again. Maybe it was denial, I don't know, but I kept hoping maybe you'd miss me..." she watched as his smirk turned into a grin, and wished she could put her hands on her hips and stare him down. "What's so funny about that?"

Dylan kissed the end of her nose. "I didn't tell anyone either."

Tia's eyes narrowed in surprise. She'd kept Dylan a secret from everyone she knew; except for Lexi of course; but Dylan's family had known about her pretty much from the start. They were expecting her to join them for the holidays...how could he not have told them that she wasn't coming? "No one? Not your parents? Not even the guys?"

"Not a soul," he smiled.

"Why not?"

"I guess I just couldn't accept that we were done either," he said. "No matter how much evidence was staring me in the face, I kept wracking my brain trying to come up with something that would've changed your mind about us." He shook his head. "Believe me, I picked apart that conversation too, but I couldn't think of a single thing that raised even the smallest red flag. I, of course, assumed that you had the plane ticket, and hoped that maybe you'd show up anyway so we could talk things through. And if you didn't, I was going to skip the holiday and come find you..." The corners of his lips turned up in a sardonic grin, "...to convince you to stay with me. I can be quite persuasive, I think," he said, walking his fingers softly over her breast.

"I'll never be through with you, Miller," she smiled back. "Better get used to that right now."

"Music to my ears," he said.

Tia took his hand and gave it a squeeze while she assimilated what he'd just told her. All the weeks of mourning, all the tears—her decision to give up on men completely because she knew she'd never be able to feel for anyone else what she felt for Dylan—none of it mattered now. He'd never stopped loving her as she'd never stopped loving him. God, when she'd woken up this morning, thinking that she should've started packing for her trip to Australia but instead believing that she'd be facing a lonely weekend and one more unbearable week before the most miserable Christmas of her life...she never for a moment considered that she'd be here; in his arms again and full of new hope for the future. It was a really good place to be, she thought as she snuggled against the man she loved.

Chapter 2

The thought weaved in and out of her consciousness before taking root and growing quickly. The future. 'Officially and forever,' he'd said. Although she'd considered at least a million times what would happen when she and Dylan went public with their relationship, it had always been that—in the future. She realized suddenly that the future was now, and that over the course of the next few days, she'd be facing the reality of stepping out of her completely ordinary life and into the public eye without any time to prepare. The 'whole talk show circuit' comment still hadn't been discussed, but 'going public with their relationship' meant that she'd be expected to make some sort of an appearance, at the very least, which did nothing to settle her heart.

Then another thought crashed into her brain with just as much force. If they were going to be gone next week—she'd already decided that it would be pointless to go back to school for just the last two days before the holiday break—she needed to introduce Dylan to her parents. Her coworkers had already met him, and although all she wanted to do was hide away from the world and keep Dylan to herself, she had a very small window in which to share him with her friends and family. She couldn't possibly let any of the people she cared about find out about their relationship from a television show; especially since she felt so guilty about lying to them all along.

Nervous energy flooded her system and she crawled out of her warm cocoon, grabbing another blanket from the back of the armchair and wrapping herself in it. Her thoughts were flying in a hundred different directions at once and she couldn't seem to nail any of them down. "Oh God, it's going to get crazy real fast, isn't it?" she asked rhetorically.

Dylan stood and wrapped his arms around her. "You could say that," he said simply.

Tia took a deep breath and exhaled slowly, trying to make sense of it all. It was a hell of a lot to take in within a couple hour time period.

"OK," she said, sounding more confident than she felt. "I can do this, right? I mean, it's not like I didn't know for a long time that it was coming. I thought I'd have a little more lead time, but it is what it is." She pulled in a deep breath and looked him in the eye. "So what's next, Dyl? What should I expect? Tell me about 'the whole talk show circuit.'"

The fierce protective instinct he felt only for her kicked into high gear, and Dylan felt stopped. Part of him wanted to lie to her; to tell her that the changes that were coming wouldn't alter her whole perception of reality. He wanted to protect her from all of it; shield her from what he knew was coming.   If things had played out normally,--if he'd come back after shooting the film and they'd simply gone public as a couple—it might have been a little blurb on the celebrity pages and a few pictures in the tabloids; maybe a talk show appearance or two because of his "sexiest man" title. The whole thing probably would have blown over in a few weeks without too much fuss, and they could have built their life together in the relative cocoon of anonymity he worked so hard to protect. The whole Penelope factor, however, completely changed the game. He'd never been at the center of a media firestorm, but he knew plenty of people who had; and none of them came out of it unscathed. America's obsession with celebrity news and the vast number of outlets dedicated to delivering it were overwhelming, and anything involving a scandal of this magnitude was going to be a big story. He'd had a bad feeling in the pit of his stomach from the moment he'd contacted *Person to Person* about running his story, and he certainly wasn't feeling any easier since Jessa had texted him that the requests for interviews had quickly started pouring in. It was going to be a bloody avalanche, and once it started rolling, nothing was going to stop it.

"I wish I could tell you that it'll be no big deal," he finally said, "but I can't. I promise you complete transparency though, even though some of it isn't going to be what you want to hear." He took her hand and kissed the back of it. "You're going to have a whole new life, love. A very different one than the one you've been living up to now. Some of it'll be really great—a lot of it will—but being under public scrutiny is a really mixed bag, and I just don't know how it's all going to play out."

"I'm already freaking out about being on television," she said. "Putting myself out there in front of millions of people isn't exactly something I ever thought I'd do. I do really well in front of ten-year-olds, but with adults...not so much." She dropped her eyes and her voice fell to a whisper. "What if they don't like me, Dyl?"

"Oh baby girl," he said immediately, pushing a strand of her hair behind her ear. "You are the most loveable person in the world; I know this from personal experience." He planted a supportive kiss on her forehead. "I truly believe that most people will love you, because you are a good and genuine person— but in the end, who cares what other people think? There are always going to be haters no matter how wonderful you are, but they won't know the real you. None of them will. Some people will adore you, and others will just be plain out jealous that you've gone from "rags to riches," for lack of a better term."

"And I'll bet there'll be quite a few who are just pissed off that I took you off the market," Tia tossed in.

"There may be a few of those," he answered honestly. "But if you just be yourself, who could help but love you? One of the toughest challenges will be staying true to your values; trying to protect who you really are on the inside, even while people judge you without knowing anything about you." He shook his head and took her face in his hands, bringing her up to meet his eyes. "Do you remember the first night we met?"

"Every single detail."

"You asked me that night why I couldn't just be a normal guy. I told you that I was a normal guy; I just wasn't in a normal situation."

Tia's eyes widened in understanding. "I get it Dylan, I do. I'm not going to change, but people's perceptions of me will."

"Unfortunately, yes," he said sadly, wishing again that he could protect her from the spotlight and all its glaring accusations. "I wish I could tell you differently…"

"Oh, some of it just sucks, doesn't it?" she said in frustration. "I'm nobody. I'm not trying to hitch a ride to fame on your coattails, but some people will see it that way, won't they?"

"Some will," Dylan said. "But you know who your true friends are—the ones who've loved you all along. You'll have to be much more careful about the people you choose as new friends; because not all of them will have your best interests at heart. It'll be an adjustment, obviously, but I intend to make it as easy on you as I can. I'll be by your side every step of the way."

"It's funny, in a way," she said. "I see it in my students all the time; the big dreams of living the lives of the rich and famous. So many of them want to be movie stars or sports heroes—they idolize celebrities even when they don't deserve it."

"We're a bit backward, aren't we?" Dylan mused. "Sometimes I feel guilty that I get paid so well for what I do; for making music or pretending to be someone else in films. The real heroes are the ones who give of themselves to make our world a better place; but they're too often undervalued. Being a teacher is noble thing, Tia. You've made a real difference in people's lives. That'll play into how the public sees you, too, I think. I'm pretty sure your cheering section will be much bigger than you think it will."

His comment caused Tia's mind to make yet another leap. How would her students see her once she'd been in the spotlight? Once they'd seen her on television and on the covers of magazines? What about the parents and her coworkers? She wasn't naïve enough to think that she was just going to be able walk back into her classroom after the holidays and teach reading and math like nothing had happened. It'd only been a couple hours since she walked out of school, but she already felt as if it were a distant memory; as if she'd walked away from that part of her life as soon as she'd stepped out of the building.

"I'm not going to be able to go back, am I?" she asked, already knowing the answer. "To teaching, I mean."

"We'll cross that bridge when we come to it," Dylan replied, "but I don't think so, Tia. I'm so sorry." He watched a momentary shadow cross her face as the reality sank in. He hated what Penelope had done on so many levels, but none so much as how it affected Tia's life. It was likely that even if they hadn't been thrown into this shit storm; even if they had been able to go public on their own terms; that Tia's teaching career would have ended. But it would've been her decision; she would've had time to come to accept it instead of having it forced on her. She was smart, though, and he knew she would have already contemplated the possibility, and hopefully that would help her now.

"I pretty much figured that," she said softly. "I'll miss it, of course, but I'm so ready to start the new chapter of my life that includes you, Dyl. I've wanted that for so long, and as much as some parts of this whole situation suck beyond belief, the end result is that we finally get to start a real life together, and that makes me happier than anything else in the world could."

"It's about time we get our happy ending," Dylan said. "And it will be happy, Tia, I promise you that."

"Alright then," she sighed, "tell me what the next week's going to be like; and don't try to spare me the gory details. I need to know what I'm in for."

Dylan's stomach rumbled. He hadn't eaten since the international flight, and even though they'd put a fairly decent meal in front of him, he'd been so worried about what would happen when he arrived; so worried that the rejection might have been real; that he'd barely touched his food. He pulled the blanket tighter around him to ward off the chill and looked out the window at the snow that fell in giant flakes. "Can we do it over lunch?" he asked. "I'm bloody starving."

They threw on some clothes and Dylan poked his way through Tia's cabinets, putting on water for tea and pulling mugs from her cabinet. He frowned when he saw the paltry selection of food in her fridge.

"I know," she said, interpreting his frown. "I kind of haven't been eating too well lately, and I've been avoiding the grocery store…"

He was reminded again of what she'd had to go through the past weeks, being bombarded with the forged photographs of him and Penelope that made them look like the couple of the freaking year. "I haven't exactly been the poster child for healthy eating lately either," he admitted. "But I think my appetite is finally coming back." His stomach grumbled again in agreement.

Tia looked at the clock, and saw it was just past 11. "How about I order us a pizza?" she suggested, reaching for the phone.

"Brilliant," Dylan replied. He'd missed a lot of comfort food while he was in New Zealand, but perhaps none more than a greasy Chicago-style pizza dripping with cheese and slathered in pepperoni. "And while we're waiting, you may as well start packing. I've got a room in the city, and I think we ought to stay there tonight. I don't know how long the secret will hold, and we don't need to deal with a mess of paparazzi just yet."

To emphasize his point, Tia turned on her phone to find twenty-three missed calls and seventeen voice mail messages. As she scrolled through the numbers, she saw that most of them were either from other schools in her district or from work friends. Apparently Ned's warning to keep the information quiet didn't keep people from passing it along. She couldn't blame them, really, it was too juicy a story to keep—she knew it all too well.

She ignored the messages and called for the pizza, then went and pulled her suitcases from the hall closet. Damn it, she thought, as she rummaged through her closets and drawers, trying to decide what to pack. Her plan had been to shop for some new clothes to wear in Australia; her teacher clothes didn't even come close to fitting the bill; but since they'd allegedly broken up, she'd never gone. She had precious little that would work for meeting Dylan's parents, and even less that would be appropriate for going on national television as Dylan Miller's girlfriend. She pulled things out and then put them back, tossing things into drawers and frowning all the while.

"Tia," Dylan laughed, pulling her from her concentration as she hauled out all the clothes she'd bought at Harrods when they were in London; the only things in her wardrobe that even came close to being worthy of taking with her. "Sit down for a second. You're like a bloody tornado."

She sat on the edge of the bed and he rested his hand on her knee. "I've got nothing, Dylan. Nothing worthy of being on television, nothing for meeting your parents..."

"Don't worry about that," he said. "We'll take care of it later. I'll have Jessa get a few things for the early interviews, and the two of you can go shopping between appearances." She opened her mouth to protest, but he silenced her with a kiss. "Hey. What's mine is yours now, love," he said. "One of the things you're going to have to get used to is that you don't have to worry about money. I have plenty to share and I would love nothing more than to spoil you a little."

Tia scowled, but then threw her hands in the air in surrender. "Well, I don't see that I have much of a choice. Most of the stuff I bought in England doesn't exactly project the image I want to put out to the public, I'm afraid."

Dylan smiled, remembering the smoking hot red dress she wore the night in Northampton when his friends realized, before he even did, that he was hopelessly in love with her. "I agree. That red dress should be for my eyes only," he teased. "Just worry about the basics, then." He watched with interest as she opened a drawer and started pulling out panties and bras; leopard print, pink with lace accents—and had visions of taking them off of her slowly, maybe with his teeth… "Damn," he said, shaking his head. "Imagining you in those makes *me* want to get down to basics."

"Yeah, you like?" Tia teased, holding up a lacy purple bra over her faded Bears sweatshirt. "It'd only take me a minute to change."

"Nothing would make me happier," he said, "but we have a lot of details to work out in a short amount of time. I think you should put that near the top of the suitcase, though," he added, waggling his eyebrows, "for later." Tia pulled out some matching panties, and tucked them into a pocket of the bag. "Ah, I so wish it didn't have to be like this…I just want to hole up with you for about a week and ravage you non-stop, but we're going to have a very busy couple weeks, I'm afraid."

"Tell me something I don't know," she said sarcastically.

"Ha ha," he replied with just as much sarcasm. "But let's put things in perspective, shall we? Before we even worry about talk shows or interviews, we have some business to take care of here. First and foremost, I need to meet your parents, Tia. I need to thank them for raising such an incredible woman, and let them know my intentions are pure. Then we need to make appearances at as many of your hang-outs as we can. If you don't make personal introductions people will be insulted, and that can cause a lot of negative backlash."

"Grrrr," Tia growled, sucking in a deep breath. "God, I know," she said, drawing the words out in exasperation. "Oh Dylan…I do want to tell everyone—I've been wanting for so long to tell the whole world who I'm in love with—but I just want to keep you to myself, too. I know those two worlds can't coexist, but still…"

Dylan raised one eyebrow at her. "You know, it was pretty hard not to notice that no one you work with knew I was 'your Dylan,'" he said. "I think Lilly about had a bloody heart attack when I walked into the office." He smiled, remembering the school secretary's confused expression as she matched the face in the photograph tacked to her wall with the one on the man in front of her. "Does anyone know?"

Tia looked down at their joined hands and shook her head slowly. "No," she confessed. "After what happened at the airport in Italy, I was afraid to tell anyone. I'd kept you a secret for so long already; I just figured it would be easier to deal with all the changes when we were together."

He raised her hand to his mouth and kissed it. "I don't know whether to be impressed...or insulted," he teased. "Seriously...no one knows?"

"No one but Lexi," Tia said, adding, "Can you believe she's kept the secret all this time?"

"I have to say that I'm definitely impressed about that," Dylan chuckled. "I'm really glad that you waited actually—I would've been worried sick being on the other side of the world and thinking of you dealing with the media all alone, even without the whole...other situation. Plus, it's given you a lot of time to think things through. I bet you're more ready for this than you think you are. You'll be brilliant."

"Oh, I don't know if *ready* is exactly the right term," she said with a smirk. "But I can say with complete confidence that I'm ready for that part of it to be over."

"This'll be the fun part," he smiled, "meeting your family and friends."

Tia was lost in her own thoughts for a moment before she responded. "Wow, I have so much to tell everyone," she whispered "especially my parents. It's been horrible having to lie to them. None of them know about Paris, or Wembley, or the songs you wrote me...I've only been able to share a few pictures; and now I can finally tell them everything! That part of it's going to be amazing...it'll be like reliving the whole thing over again now that I can finally talk about it."

"And I'm excited to share that with you," Dylan said. "So let's think about this. We're leaving Sunday for California. I promised my good friend Tony that I'd give him the exclusive, and he's worked out a Sunday night special for our little 'coming out party.' He's sending his private jet over..."

"Tony Granger?" Tia asked. It was the only Tony she knew of who had that kind of pull—he had the number one late night talk show on television. She realized that she and Dylan still had a lot to learn about each other—she hadn't known that the two of them were friends.

"The very one," he said. "He was one of the first people to give InHap the stage and an interview, and we've been friends ever since. I called him during my layover in San Francisco and he had it set up within a couple of hours. I don't know the whole schedule yet—Jessa's working on it—but I do know that we'll do that on Sunday, and a couple other smaller shows on Monday. We'll head out to New York sometime during the week to do it all over again on the East Coast, and Jessa'll change our flight so we can leave for Australia from there. That means we only have today and tomorrow to make all the introductions..."

"Oh no," Tia said. "Not today. I'm going to have to share you with the whole damn world way sooner than I want to—I'm keeping you all to myself today."

"Absolutely agreed," Dylan replied. "But that means tomorrow's going to be really busy." He took a deep breath before continuing. "I know you probably don't want to hear this, but I think maybe we should meet your parents at the country club. I know you don't hang out there much anymore..."

"I don't hang out there at all," Tia sighed, "but I had a feeling you were going to suggest it. Most of those people don't mean anything to me. Why there?"

"Well, first of all, we should really do as many personal intros as we can before we hit the air waves," he explained, "and a lot of people there know you. I know the place might not mean anything to you anymore, but it does to your parents. This'll be a huge story, and they'll be part of it too, especially in their social circles. You said yourself that your mother loves her gossip. She'll be at the top of the pecking order with this one—her only daughter will be at the center of a big media circus, and she'll get to be one of the stars." Tia looked at him from the corner of her eye, contemplating, and pressed her lips together in reluctant consent.

"I thought that might be a selling point," he continued, "but I'll admit that I have a bit of a selfish reason too…" he paused, and Tia turned to him, furrowing her eyebrows. She'd never seen Dylan do anything selfish. "I'd be lying if I didn't admit that I'd like to have the chance to get a look at that Jace character. Call it my jealous nature, or maybe it's just a man thing, but I'd love to see the look on his face when he sees us together. It might just teach him a little humility, or something."

Tia smiled at the thought. It was hard to believe that Dylan Miller, Sexiest Man on Earth, could be jealous of someone like Jace. She certainly didn't relish the thought of seeing him again, but the thought of *him* seeing *her* with Dylan gave her a bit of smug pleasure. It wasn't even the celebrity factor that made her feel that way—it was more Jace's cocky assumption that Dylan wouldn't be faithful to her because he was a musician. If ever there was a person who deserved to be put in his place, it was Jace; especially after the way he'd treated Bitsy. And if ever there was a person who could put him there, it was definitely Dylan Miller.

"Oh, all right," she sighed, "that's what we'll do."

"It can just be a hit-and-run, you know; we can go somewhere more private after we make an appearance. We're kind of making this up as we go along; this is a first for me too, remember."

"I'll have my dad get the DND. The guy who built the country club had this one table in the restaurant built in to be totally private—it's kind of tucked in the corner and surrounded by high walls, and there's even a private hallway that leads to other exits so we can make a quick getaway if we need to. A lot of business deals go down over dinner and drinks at that table, so it's kind of labeled, 'Do Not Disturb.'"

"Brilliant," he said. "Sounds perfect."

Tia's eyes brightened and a smile split her face. "Oh my God, I can't believe I can finally introduce you to them! I've wanted to for so long…"

"I really can't wait to meet them, Tia, but I'd be lying if I said I wasn't nervous." He pressed his lips together in a half-smile. "Do you think they'll like me?"

Tia's heart nearly melted. She was privately thrilled that he'd be anxious about meeting her parents—especially since she was downright petrified about meeting his. But she knew better than anyone that Dylan didn't put himself on a pedestal…he didn't assume people would like him just because he was famous. And he was just down to earth enough not to realize that pretty much anyone would like him just for being himself. It saddened her that not enough people gave him that chance.

"They'll love you Dylan, don't worry," she said sincerely. "They'll see in you what I see in you—they'll get to know the real you, which is at least ten times more amazing than the celebrity you."

He was struck speechless by the honesty in her words. He was one incredibly lucky man, he thought. All he could do was pull her close and whisper, "Thank you," into her ear.

Tia inhaled deeply and slowly released a long sigh as she considered the dark side of the introductions—fessing up to her blatant dishonesty with the people she cared about the most. "Did I do the right thing, Dyl?" she whispered. Dylan raised an eyebrow in question. "Wow, I guess this is a little more overwhelming than I thought it would be…" she swallowed hard around the lump that was forming in her throat. "…I mean, you know I wanted to tell everyone, right? And I want to tell everyone now, but I still want to keep you for myself…Aurg. It's just really short notice—I thought I'd have time to ease into it, or at least go into it with some sort of plan."

"You did the right thing, baby," he assured her. "Life would've been very different for you if you had told people. Especially when the tabloids started printing all that rubbish."

"But it means that we have to practically go on tour to introduce you, and I have to admit to everyone I care about that I lied to them."

"They'll understand," he said softly. "Don't be surprised if some of them seem a little put out at first, but once they've had time to think about it, they'll see your dilemma."

"Even my parents?" she croaked. She was most worried about them being hurt that she didn't trust them with the biggest news of her entire life.

"Especially your parents," he said. "They raised you to be strong and independent, and to know what's best for you. They'll know you didn't make the decision lightly."

She took a deep, cleansing breath; a huge weight suddenly lifted from her shoulders. "You're pretty remarkable, you know that?" she whispered, grabbing his hand and giving it a squeeze.

Dylan squeezed back, and pressed his lips to her forehead. "As are you, my love. It'll be fabulous, don't worry." He rested his forehead against hers and smiled. "So now that we've got that sorted out, how about we go to the pub tomorrow night, then? I've got a couple bottles of Tully in my bag for Paddy that I picked up in Ireland. Do you think you could get some of the same people who were there that first night to show up last minute?"

"Most of them practically live there on Saturday nights," she said, "but I'll text Sean and have him put out the word." She shook her head, smiling wryly. "Damn, Miller—we're really going to freak out some worlds tomorrow!" She thought back to that first night at *Paddy's*—the very first night they had met—when Sean had played a few of Dylan's songs on the pub's stage, completely unaware that Tia's escort was actually Dylan Miller himself. She'd spent a fair amount of time at the pub over the past four months, and had really reconnected with her old friends. Dylan had made a great impression on them—not just because he bought a round of Paddy's favorite whiskey for the house, but because they all knew how Tia had suffered after Nick's death and they were genuinely happy to see her smile again. They credited Dylan with that and they were completely right; but they still had no idea that the two of them had just met earlier that night.

"I really look forward to seeing Sean again," Dylan said. "All of them, actually. They are your true friends, you know, and they'll be the ones you turn to time and time again. I hope they'll be my friends, too."

"I do know, believe me. And I think they'll be pretty cool about it. As cool as anyone can be, I guess. It's going to be quite a surprise no matter what—I think we'll need to be prepared for a little shock and awe."

"Yeah, I'm pretty sure it'll be a bit of a stunner," he said smirking, "but that's another reason why it's good to hit places with a bunch of people. It'll be "shock and awe," as you so eloquently put it, for the first bit, and then things will calm down. It beats doing it over and over, believe me."

"It's weird to think that after tomorrow, my life will never be the same."

"No, Tia, not the same. But what fun is a life that just stays the same? It'll be a whole new adventure that we'll embark on together." He paused for a moment, a melancholy look casting a shadow over his eyes. With everything in his life there was a give and take; a sacrifice to be made. He was torn between wanting to shield her from the changes his celebrity would bring to her life and being incredibly grateful that that same celebrity would make sure she never wanted for anything.

"So," he said, changing the subject. "Any other places we need to hit? Do you belong to any clubs, or groups, or church or anything?"

Tia shook her head. "No, that's pretty much it. I'll text Lilly and have her invite my work friends to *Paddy's* so we can do that all in one shot. I have a pretty pathetic life, huh?"

"Not at all. And even if you did, I'm making it my personal mission to make sure you have only the best from this point on."

"I've got *you*, Dylan. It's already the best." He wrapped her up in his arms and held her tight.

"Well, that'll make for a pretty crazy day, I think; and after that, a bloody typhoon. It'll be much quieter when we get to Australia—we'll need do an appearance or two, but we'll be able to enjoy the holidays in relative peace."

"How long before the typhoon moves off to calmer waters?" Tia asked, almost afraid to hear the answer.

"We'll just have to take it day by day."

Tia stopped and looked around her little bedroom while another thought gained clarity in her mind. She turned to Dylan. "I'm not coming back here, am I?"

Dylan bowed his head and looked at the ground, unwilling to meet her eyes as he delivered the news. "No," he said, "not to live on your own, Tia, I'm sorry. Once your identity is public knowledge, this house won't be safe enough for my comfort level, and I won't compromise when it comes to your safety. I'll have Jessa look into some apartments in the city while we're on holiday."

Way to go, he thought as he watched Tia's face. She continued packing, but her eyes darted around the room, taking in the familiar scenes that would no longer be part of her life. So far he'd told her that she'd likely never return to her job, that she'd have to be very careful about making new friends, and that she would never again live in her own house. Saying it out loud made him realize just how much she was going to have to give up to be with him. He was damn sure going to make certain it was worth it. "Bloody hell," he said, standing and pulling her into his arms. "I feel horrible about the sacrifices you're having to make—I promise I'll make it up to you, Tia."

Tia sighed and took a long look around her little bedroom. She'd once planned to make a life here; in this little slice of suburbia. It seemed like a lifetime ago now that she stood in this room with Nick, the walls bare and white as they taped up color swatches and planned out how they'd make a home; and someday a family; in this little house. But this wasn't her life anymore, and hadn't been in quite some time. She'd just been going through the motions of that simple existence—even though she'd maintained the façade fairly well it was still just that—a cover that masked the changes that had come into her life the minute she'd met Dylan.

She leaned into him and wrapped her arms around his neck. "This is just a building, Dyl, not a life. My life is with you now, and any little sacrifices I have to make now will be more than worth it in the end. It's no big deal, really—just something I have to get used to."

She looked around again and realized that she meant every word she'd said. Aside from a couple pictures on the walls, she really wasn't attached to anything in the house. Most of the furniture was hand-me-down, as she and Nick had planned to furnish it after they'd gotten married. Tia hadn't had a bridal shower before Nick died, so she had no china or matching bath towels or anything else that she felt she needed to take with her. They hadn't lived in the house together; planning instead to wait until after they'd married to move in, so they'd made precious few memories here. It wouldn't be so hard to walk away, especially now that she had the promise of a new life with Dylan. "Really, it's not a big deal—don't look so sad," she said, smiling and pulling his arms around her. "How can I be anything but happy when I have you?"

The doorbell rang, and Tia jumped, her eyes widening for a second before realizing it was probably just the pizza delivery man. Here was something new too, she thought, paranoia. She realized she'd be looking over her shoulder a lot more in the coming days. Dylan pulled the curtain aside and peered onto the front porch. "Oh good, food's here," he said. "Be sure to look through peepholes before you open doors from now on."

"I don't have a peephole," she said, looking over his shoulder at the man standing on the porch holding a pizza box. She recognized him immediately and sucked in a breath. "Dylan, that's not a pizza delivery guy...it's the limo driver who brought us here..." She looked into the street, and saw the car parked there. Footprints in the snow led from the car to her door.

"He's just security, sweetheart," Dylan said. When she turned to him, he continued. "They've always been there, Tia. I usually keep them way in the background, but at times they're a necessity, and this is one of those times. Management gets downright pissed when I go out without an entourage but most of the time, people don't spare much more than a second glance, especially when it's out of context. When they see someone they think they recognize, they do a double take and think, 'that really looks like so-and-so,' but they don't really believe it. When they do recognize you, sometimes they're happy with a smile and a wave. Some feel compelled to come up to you and tell you how they've enjoyed your work, or even, in some cases, how you've changed their lives." They both smiled, remembering how Tia had first approached Dylan and told him something along those lines. She too had questioned whether or not the man sitting across from her at the little dive bar could actually be Dylan Miller. It was his tattoo that had given him away, but if it weren't for that identifying symbol, would she have approached him at all? She thought not. "But this is a game-changer," he continued. "Now that you're going to be out in the open, they're going to have to be a much more visible presence, at least for a little while."

Tia shrugged. It was just one more thing she'd have to get used to in her new life, and she had much bigger things to worry about than a security detail. She greeted the guard when she opened the door and offered him a slice of pizza, then she and Dylan sat down to their little makeshift feast.

Chapter 3

Tia hooked the clasp on the purple bra and opened the door. The place was just as she remembered, and she was beyond thrilled that Dylan had thought to get the same room that they had stayed in the first time they'd made love. She never would've guessed back in May that she'd be here again all these months later under such different circumstances—she'd been so afraid that night that it would be the last time she'd ever have with Dylan. She'd certainly changed a lot since that evening, she thought as she grabbed the bottle of wine that sat chilling in the silver bucket and two glasses. It was much too cold for the hot tub tonight, so instead Dylan had started a fire in the gas fireplace and laid some blankets and pillows out on the floor before it. He was sitting, shirtless, leaning against the couch strumming absent-mindedly on his guitar, and she stopped to just look at him for a moment and say a silent prayer of thanks that this incredibly beautiful man had come back into her life. Tomorrow they might belong to the whole world, but tonight, no one existed except each other, and she had every intention of making the most of it.

"Even better than I imagined," he said, looking appreciatively at her nearly naked body and leaning the guitar against the couch. Tia poured the wine, handed him a glass, and stretched out beside him.

"Very happy to exceed your expectations," she purred, swirling her fingers through the soft hair on his chest.

"About bloody time we really get this reunion officially started," he teased, pushing her hair behind her ear and bringing his mouth down to meet hers. The kiss was tender, soft, and left her wanting more. "A toast, then," he smiled, touching the rim of his glass to hers. "I don't think there's ever been anything I've wanted to celebrate more than having you back in my life."

"Officially and forever," she smiled. "Do you have a new song to play for me?"

He grinned at her and ran his gaze up her body. "Really?" he asked. "You come out here dressed like that, and think I can concentrate on anything else but how amazingly sexy you are?" He grabbed her ankles and pulled so that she was lying before the fire and rolled atop her. "That's for later," he said, pressing his body against hers and finding her mouth once again.

The kiss started tenderly; sweet and soft; but soon grew more insistent. He moved to her neck, the stubble of his thin beard tickling as he nibbled his way down to her collarbone. She tilted her head back to give him more access, and he ran his hands down the length of her body.

Oh, how she'd missed his hands! The rough callouses on his fingertips caressed her skin, throwing shivers everywhere. She drew her breath in sharply as his fingers swirled over her back, then over to her stomach, where they headed north. He unhooked her bra with one quick motion, and then they skimmed over her nipples; tracing circles there as she moaned, pushing herself into his touch. "Slower this time," she smiled. "Deliciously slow. I want to savor you."

"Deliciously slow, you say," he murmured as his lips trailed further down her body. "I can do that. We have plenty of time."

"Mmmm hmmm," she hummed, unable to articulate anything other than the pleasure she felt at his hands on her skin and his mouth at her breast.

He took his sweet time with her, running his fingers softly over the silky fabric of her panties and then back up to cradle her breasts. Her hands explored as well, exalting in the feel of his skin and his intoxicating scent, running her hands slowly and reverently over the familiar contours of his body.

"God, you're beautiful," he whispered as he rolled her over, sliding off his jeans while she shrugged out of her panties. He spread himself over her, pressing his body to hers and separating her legs with one of his own. He shifted so that he lay next to her, and found her slick opening with the tip of his finger. "So beautiful," he breathed as he felt just how much she wanted him.

"I could do this forever," she murmured.

"Forever's not nearly long enough." He slipped his finger into her slowly, then pulled it out, swirling it over her nipple before taking the bud into his mouth, gently sucking the hardened flesh. "I need more of that," he said, running his tongue down her stomach until he skimmed it over her swollen core.

Tia moaned in pleasure, and raised her hips to meet his mouth. Slowly ceased to apply when he was swirling his tongue in and around the most sensitive and aching parts of her, but too soon he shifted his focus upward, nipping his way up to her stomach and planting soft kisses at her hips.

She wanted to beg him to continue; she needed him desperately; but his hands moved achingly slowly over her curves and valleys, sending shock waves of bliss that shorted out her ability to form any rational words. He skimmed her thighs with the tips of his fingers, purposefully lingering at her opening but refusing to enter, even as she pushed her hips into his caress.

"Mmmnnn," she mumbled, "more."

"Oh, I've got more for you, baby girl. Much more."

She tried to protest, but then he pulled her nipple between his fingers and tightened the grasp while massaging her breast. She thought she might come right there, so connected was every part of her to the throbbing between her legs. Biting her lip to slow the building momentum, she arched her back to press herself against him and took his need into her hands, stroking him firmly.

This, Tia thought, *is the purest definition of making love.* It was beautiful and magical and amazing and perfect and every cell in her body pulsed with the beat of her heart. They took pleasure in giving pleasure and explored each other without inhibition, whispering tiny sentiments and finding pure joy in the connection of their bodies. The past months and the coming days fell away as they made their way slowly to the crescendo, the outside world ceasing to exist in moments of the sheer beauty of true love.

When he finally slid inside, she felt filled with light, and he smiled down at her until he had to throw his head back with release and pure ecstasy. "I love you," they said in unison as they slipped over the edge together.

They held each other silently for a few moments, smiling and touching and kissing before Dylan grabbed their wine, handing her a glass and touching the rim with his own.

"I think that was the perfect pace," Tia smiled, putting her hand to his cheek and nuzzling against his chest. "Just exactly right."

"Mmmm. Couldn't agree more." He fluffed up a pillow and tucked it behind him, leaning against the couch.

Tia sighed, smiling comfortably. Dylan watched as she stretched out on the floor; propping her head up on her arm. Her eyes drifted over to the guitar still leaning against the couch, then back to Dylan, and back and forth again as she motioned toward the instrument with a toss of her head.

"Now you want a song?" he teased. "I'm not even sure my fingers will work to play them after the way you took advantage of me."

Tia let an easy grin slide over her face. "You have to remember that I was in love with your music long before I knew you. Long before I ever even entertained the idea that you could possibly be part of my life, your songs were a huge part. They'll always be my first love, I'm afraid." She leaned up and planted a tender kiss on his cheek. "Did you write any for me?"

"They're all for you, love," he smiled, "ever since the minute I met you they were all for you."

"That's so sweet. How many new ones do you have?"

"Quite a few, actually. There's going to be a lot of variety on the new album, I think. In the beginning I wrote a few fun ones and a couple ballads; but I went through so many emotions over the past few months that I'm not even sure what genre we'll be in after this...there's a little bit of blues, some mushy love songs, some seriously pissed-off stuff...I don't know what'll make the final cut, but it ought to be interesting. I may have to do a solo album to get in all the love songs I wrote for you." He leaned over and grabbed the guitar, slung it over his neck, and strummed a few chords. "I think I'll play a sad one for you first; it'll give you a little glimpse into how I was feeling when I thought I'd lost you. I do like how it turned out in the end, though, but I'm really glad I'll never have to feel the way I did when I wrote it."

"Oh Dyl," she sighed as he plucked the first notes. She remembered all too well the crushing sadness she'd felt when she thought she'd never see him again, and had to remind herself that he'd been feeling the same way, all alone on the other side of the world.

Even the guitar sounded as if it were weeping as he wove around the intro, humming in the back of his throat. He looked into her eyes and sang; his voice soulful and melancholy.

The veil hangs over midnight and I'm sitting here alone...
Can't see you; touch you; face to face can't even get you
on the phone...
The moon hangs heavy as my heart blocking stars out
from the sky...
Alone and dark without you and I can't figure out just
why

You know you are my heart...
I feel all torn up and broken whenever we're apart...
Can't seem to do the simplest things can't even start...
I need you back I need you near...
There's just this veil of midnight when you're not here

A restless night of broken dreams the images of you...
Come flashing back consuming me there's nothing I can
do...

I left you back so far away oh how I miss your smile...

Can't face the coming morning...
Guess I'll dream of you a while...
You left me lost and broken, oh how I miss your touch...
The mere thought of life without you ...Is asking way too much

You know you are my heart...
I'm all ripped up and broken since we were torn apart...
Going on without you—I don't know where to start...
I need you back I need you near...
There's this crushing veil of midnight when you're not here...

"Oh, baby," Tia whispered as the final chords wept from the strings. She wiped a tear from her cheek and moved to him. He tossed the guitar onto the couch behind him and she climbed into his arms; wrapping herself around him. "It's beautiful and perfect but I so wish you never had to write it. That you never had to be that sad..."

"Never again, that's for sure," he said softly. "I'll never let you be so far away from me again."

"I'd follow you anywhere," she smiled. "I'm your biggest fan, you know."

"And the only one that matters." He pulled her to him, curling her into the nest of his body. They slept there, before the fire; the best sleep either of them had had in months.

✶✶✶✶✶

The car rolled up to the valet area, and Dylan pulled her hand up and kissed the back of it. "You ready, baby?" he asked, the confidence in his voice settling a few of her butterflies. "I'll be by your side every step of the way. This is going to be the fun part."

She smiled. "As ready as I'll ever be," she said with as much conviction as she could muster, her voice only faltering a little.

She took a deep breath and held it, hoping it would calm her shaking.

Ricco, the valet, opened the passenger side door as the security guard hopped out and stood at the ready. When Dylan stepped out of the car Ricco's head tilted and his eyes slanted as he tried to place the face. Recognition dawned on him then and his eyes widened; filling instantly with the look that she and Dylan called, "star struck."

"Whoa," he said, "aren't you that guy who was on the news this morning?"

Dylan had turned on the television while they had their morning coffee, to see just how much buzz the story had generated in the media. They flipped through channels, and it was just as Dylan had feared. It was really big news. Anytime a Hollywood starlet got arrested the story seemed to jump to the top of the headlines, but since the whole fiasco was being called a "love triangle," and it involved two celebrities and a mystery woman, it was positively viral. "Experts" were making guesses about who the mystery lady might be, and one station was asking viewers to name the woman they thought would be Dylan's perfect match. Tia Hastings, fifth grade teacher and ordinary citizen, did not appear on the list. The media was quick to demonize Penelope, as well, wondering aloud whether her disastrous break-up with Jason Whitten "threw her over the edge."

Person to Person was on the store shelves, featuring Dylan's own words; which reporters were quoting in their segments. On the cover was a huge triangle with all three corners cut away. Dylan's picture was in the top angle; a perfect smile on his face, and his gaze focused on the question mark that filled the lower left section. The lower right portion featured a rather unflattering picture of Penelope, scowling and looking up toward the picture of Dylan. In the center read the headline, "Accused!" and beneath that, "What Really Happened Down Under—in Dylan Miller's Own Words."

Dylan reached out and shook Ricco's hand. "I'm Dylan Miller; nice to meet you," he replied kindly.

"Oh man, my wife's not going to believe this!" he exclaimed. "Please, sir, can I get a picture with you so I can send it to her? She's a big fan of yours!"

"Absolutely," Dylan said graciously. "But first I really think you need to open the door for my lady."

Ricco caught himself quickly. "Oh...oh my gosh! Of course, I'm so sorry!" He ran around the car and opened the other door, extending his hand to assist the passenger. When he recognized Tia he stopped, squinting his eyes and shaking his head in disbelief. "Uhh...Miss Hastings?"

"Hi Ricco, how are you today?" she asked, flashing a shy smile. He stared at her for a moment, brow furled, trying to connect the dots. He'd worked at the club for several years, and had always liked Tia. She always had a smile and a kind word, and even though he knew she was a school teacher, and had a lot less money than some of the other club members, she never once stiffed him on a tip. Ricco had known about her fiancé's death, and had seen the shadow behind her eyes when she tried to pretend for her parents and her friend, Lexi Summers, that she was OK. Tia was so down-to-earth...low-key...and seeing her with this big celebrity guy was just not computing.

As he followed Tia around the back of the car, scratching his head, another vehicle pulled up to the valet station. Tia heard a shriek as the passenger recognized Dylan and jumped from the SUV, rushing toward them. As Tia was taking aim with Ricco's phone, the door to the club opened and a trio of girls walked out. They saw the commotion, and made their way over, pulling their own phones from their pockets when they realized who was standing there. *So it begins,* Tia thought, as she snapped the picture and another phone was thrust into her hand. The others hadn't even realized she and Dylan were together—in fact, they paid her little mind as Dylan turned on his full rock star charm; shaking hands, signing scraps of paper, posing for pictures, and exchanging kind words with everyone for a few minutes. He waved away the next approaching group, apologizing and saying, "Listen mates—I appreciate the warm welcome, but it's bloody cold out here." They giggled a bit too enthusiastically. "It's been nice meeting all of you, but I'm here to meet my girlfriend's parents for the first time, and as you can imagine, I'm a bit nervous, and just need to get on with it, you know?"

Eyes darted around and shoulders shrugged as they looked right past Tia, who just stood back with a knowing smile. When Dylan reached over and took her hand, planting a soft kiss on her forehead and heading for the entrance, their eyes widened and their mouths formed little "o's." Most of them knew who Tia was, and they were more than a little surprised the see her on the arm of a rock star. The crowd chuckled and nodded as they approached the entrance, but the befuddled wave of people followed them anyway, pressing ever closer; their tasks forgotten, some leaving cars idling along the curb. They bottlenecked at the door, and Dylan was swept through by the crowd, his hand yanked from Tia's, leaving her at the back of the wave.

All eyes in the well-appointed lobby turned toward the commotion as the chattering group pushed in. From her seat on the long couch where she eagerly awaited the arrival of her daughter and her first chance to meet the man who'd essentially brought her back to life, Danielle Hastings recognized the tall, commanding figure that was the center of attention and rose to her feet. "Oh my goodness, Will," she exclaimed as she stared at the face of the man she'd seen on television just a few hours earlier. "I think that's Dylan Miller!"

"Who?"

"He was all over the news this morning, remember? He's the actor who's part of that scandal with Penelope Valentine." She shook her head at the look of confusion he threw her way. "Remember, the love triangle? What's he doing *here*?"

Will merely shrugged...he hadn't paid a whole lot of attention to the story this morning, being wrapped up, as usual, in the morning paper. But the excitement was palpable, and they watched the group with interest, especially when Tia finally made her way through the door. They watched as Dylan spotted her and reached across the crowd to grasp her hand. He pulled her in close and draped his arm protectively over her shoulder, ignoring the rest of the crowd and letting her take the lead.

"Oh my," Danielle gasped as she watched her only child walking toward them with a huge smile on her face and her arm around the celebrity. "Oh my!"

"Wait a second; is Tia…" Will asked, suddenly interested. His voice trailed off as Tia waved and led Dylan to where Danielle steadied herself on the back of the couch and fanned her face with her pocketbook.

"Oh goodness…I think so!" she exclaimed.

Tia's heart thumped in her chest and she fought to control her breathing. Damn, if she didn't gain some control of her body functions, her heart was going to give out. It was as if the world was moving in slow motion—she was hyper-aware of every detail, and yet felt as though everything in her peripheral vision was floating in clouds. She could hear the sounds of the crowd, but was completely focused on the surprised faces of her parents as she and Dylan approached. She swelled with pride at having Dylan by her side, and was beyond thrilled to finally introduce him as her boyfriend, but she was still incredibly anxious about how they'd take the news that she'd lied to them for months. Quickly, she glanced around and took in the stares of the other patrons; shock, awe, and downright incredulousness. *Damn it*, she thought, *I know exactly how they feel.* She pursed her lips and inhaled deeply, releasing the breath slowly as she reached her parents.

"Mom, Dad," Tia said in a rush, "Oh God, I have a million things to tell you, and at least that many apologies to make, but I'm so happy to finally introduce you to Dylan!"

Her parents' mouths practically hung open as she hugged them both, and they stared openly at the couple, the shock plainly evident on their faces. Dylan took it in stride, as he always did, and planted small kisses on her mom's cheeks, then enthusiastically shook her dad's hand. "I'm so pleased to finally meet both of you," he said. "Tia's told me so much about you."

There was a heartbeat of uncomfortable silence, but then her dad recovered, shaking his head and smiling. "It's such a pleasure to meet you, Dylan," he said. "Tia's told us a lot about you too, of course, but she didn't tell us that you were a celebrity. Forgive us if we're a little bit shocked." He extended his hand again, more consciously. "I'm Will," he said, "and this is my wife, Danielle."

"I'm pretty used to that kind of reaction, believe me," Dylan smiled, taking Danielle's hand. "No problem at all."

"You may be used to it," Will said, "but you certainly shouldn't have to deal with it in a situation like this. Please, accept my apologies." He glanced around at the curious onlookers that were filling the sizeable lobby and turned to Tia. "Well, I guess I know why you insisted I reserve the DND. Shall we?" He took his still-speechless wife's hand and led the way into the dining room, where even more patrons turned their heads and gawked openly. The foursome simply smiled and waved, and retreated into the sanctity of the little alcove at the back of the room.

Chapter 4

The DND lived up to its name. Up a couple steps and separated from the rest of the room by a beverage station and a private section of the bar, it was the perfect place for the group to chat out of the prying eyes and ears that sought to be part of their introductions.

They sat down, and Danielle finally found her voice. "You have to forgive me," she croaked. "Obviously, this is a bit more than I was expecting," she added, her fingers on her throat, "but I'm so happy to finally meet you too, Dylan. We have heard so many wonderful things about you. You've made our little girl very happy, and for that, I'm incredibly grateful." She reached across the table and squeezed Dylan's hand.

"That is completely mutual, believe me," he smiled, draping his arm over the back of Tia's chair and tossing her a wink.

"I saw the story on the news this morning, but I had no idea...OK," she said, trying to make sense of the situation, "this whole thing obviously has a whole new meaning—I'm afraid you're going to have to fill in some of the gaps for us." She turned to Tia. "How in the world is our only daughter in the middle of an international scandal and a celebrity love triangle?"

"Oh, Mom," Tia said, "I really wanted to tell you everything..."

Dylan interrupted. "First of all, please let me clarify one thing. There is no *triangle,* and there never was. Everything that horrible woman did was complete rubbish—a total pack of lies— and I intend to see that she pays the price for what she did." He turned to Will. "There was never a moment when I stopped loving your daughter; or one where I was unfaithful to her."

Tia leaned her head on Dylan's shoulder and addressed her parents. "This whole thing hit like a tornado. Dylan just got back to the States yesterday, and he showed up at school to..." She paused, unsure what to say next. This was completely new to them, and they had no background knowledge to help make sense of any of it. "I don't even know where to start," she said. "I've only heard bits and pieces of the story myself..." She looked at Dylan, turning her palms up and shrugging her shoulders.

"Well, I guess it's best to get that out in the open right away anyway, since it's the news of the day," Dylan started. "I want you to know that I take full responsibility for Tia being hurt, and I plan to spend the rest of my life making it up to her." Tia smiled up at him and squeezed his thigh, where her hand was resting. "I really don't know the whole story myself—I only found out what she'd done a couple days ago, and left as soon as I could to come and find Tia—but I'll try and fill you in on what I've pieced together.

"Penelope actually showed up right after Tia and I met, to tell me that she'd be my co-star in the film. I'd literally just met Tia the day before, but she'd already made a huge impression on me, and the last thing I wanted was to have our time together interrupted; especially since I was only in town for a couple days and thought that would be all the time we'd have. Miss Valentine made some crude comments about her and me having 'chemistry,' or some rubbish like that, and at the time I was really feeling the chemistry with Tia. I told her to leave, and put her out of my mind completely."

Tia wanted desperately to interject...she had so much to tell her parents; she wanted to share all the good things that had happened in her and Dylan's relationship. She hated that they had to start the conversation with the Penelope story, but since her parents saw it all on the news, they had to get it out in the open right away. They'd completely avoided the topic last night, but, as much as she didn't really want to know, she had to hear it before it was broadcast to the entire world. She bit her tongue, and let Dylan continue.

"It wasn't until September that I saw her again; once I got to New Zealand. Unfortunately, the way they'd set things up, we were living and working in smothering proximity. I kept trying to get her to make some friends, I spent weekends hanging out with the crew, and I was crystal clear that I was in love with Tia. She seemed to accept that, and we built a rather tentative friendship. I never really trusted her, but I did believe that she was trying. Obviously, though, she had an agenda all along and I was too stupid to see it."

Tia jerked her head at him, and addressed her parents. "Now I need to interrupt. I have to tell you that Dylan is the kind of person who always looks for the good in people. He trusted her, to a certain extent, because that's the kind of person he is. It's one of his best qualities." She turned to Dylan. "I don't fault you for that; and neither should you," she said firmly.

"Thank you," he said to her, "but I'll still be kicking myself for that for a long time, because you ended up hurt by it." He took a deep breath before continuing. "From the information I got—mostly from the assistant who was bribed into helping her carry out her plan—Penelope had some crazy idea that if we were a couple, she'd be back in Hollywood's good graces and would live happily ever after. When I didn't return her affections, she hatched this huge, elaborate scheme to make it appear that Tia had broken up with me, thinking I would turn to her for comfort. Of course, she also had to make Tia think I'd broken up with her." He looked at Tia with pain in his eyes. "And it worked."

Now it was Danielle's turn to interrupt. "Wait a minute," she said, looking back and forth between them, "are you saying that you thought Dylan broke up with you?"

Tia nodded, unable to meet her mother's gaze.

"You never mentioned anything about that at all!" Danielle exclaimed. "Why wouldn't you tell me that, honey? You must have really been hurting—you know I would have been there for you."

Tia sighed. "Of course you would have been, Mom, I know that. But you would have been there at your own expense, and that would've made me feel even worse." Her mother's eyes narrowed in confusion and she continued. "You had your holiday trip all planned, and I didn't want to ruin that—I figured either you'd cancel if you knew that I didn't really have anywhere to spend the holidays—or you'd ask me to go with you and I'd ruin your trip anyway by being depressed the whole time. Plus, I kept hoping that I'd get that ticket eventually, and that Dylan and I could work things out. No matter how much evidence was staring me in the face, there was always a part of me that refused to believe that it was over—what we had was just too strong." She turned to Dylan and smiled. "I'm so glad I was right about that." He leaned over and planted a soft kiss on her lips.

"Oh honey," her mother whispered. "I'm so sorry you had to go through all that alone! I'm sorry you had to go through it at all!"

Tia smiled at the genuine caring in her mother's eyes, and knew that she was the luckiest person on Earth for so many reasons. None of it mattered anymore, and she refused to dwell on anything negative on this incredible day. She looked from her mom to her dad to the love of her life and felt an incredible sense of peace and joy bubble up inside her. No matter what happened in New Zealand, she knew beyond the shadow of a doubt that Dylan had never once forgotten about her, and that he loved her with his whole being.

Now it was Will's turn to butt in. "What did she do, Dylan? How did she break you up?"

"Well," Dylan continued, "we were on the other side of the world, obviously, and our internet and phone reception was sketchy at best. We lived in this little village unto itself; we were a good distance from the nearest town, and kind of our own entity. She used that to her advantage. It started, as far as I can tell, after she had her assistant take Jessa...she's my assistant...to Auckland for the weekend and convinced her to buy some sort of unique scarf. Then she bought another one just like it, and paid an actress that apparently looked a lot like Jessa, to hand out my mobile number at the airport. My phone started ringing off the hook—suddenly fans were calling to chat, and Penelope convinced me to ask one of them how they got the number. When they described Jessa to a tee, right down to the damn scarf, I started doubting her." He shook his head, remembering his rage that day, and how he sent Jessa packing without giving her a chance to explain anything. One more thing he'd suffer for a very long time to come.

"This woman, Angela—who was Penelope's assistant—managed to play it up so that I believed it, and I fired Jessa on the spot. Angela was full of apologies, and volunteered to be my assistant for the rest of the time we were there. It didn't leave me much of a choice, really, which was their plan all along. That started the domino effect." He took a deep breath. It was all still very fresh in his mind, and Tia was hearing it for the first time. He knew he couldn't shelter her from the truth, but he certainly didn't relish the idea of telling her the details, either. They had a relationship built on honesty, though, and he wouldn't lie to her. It would all come out eventually in court, and he didn't want any surprises when that fiasco got rolling.

"I had no choice but to change my mobile number, and Angela volunteered to take care of it for me while I was away from the village for a few days filming some scenes out in the wilderness. She changed Tia's number on the SIM card so I couldn't reach her, and they sabotaged my computer. They hired some teenager to plant some sort of virus and sent both of us emails, supposedly from each other, saying that we were done with the relationship and wanted to sever all ties."

"We both believed it," Tia sighed. "Even though in the back of our minds we didn't think it could be true, there was no other explanation at the time and we weren't able to get a hold of each other to figure it out."

"I was beside myself," Dylan continued. "I had sent Tia a ticket to join me in Australia for the holiday. I wanted to introduce her to my parents and show her where I grew up—but the next part of their plan cut off our only remaining form of communication—letters. I wrote Tia just about every day—

sometimes twice in a day. I put in pictures of our summer with every one; to remind her of the time we spent together, and to hopefully keep the idea of 'us' in her mind. I was begging her to call me; to come to Australia so we could work it out. I knew it took weeks for the letters to reach her, but it was all I had at the time. Angela, in the guise of being my assistant, was taking care of the mail, and it turns out that Penelope was stealing all the letters I wrote to Tia." He turned to her, and pulled her in closer, taking her hand with his free one and looking her in the eye. This was going to hurt her, he knew, and there was no way to shelter her from it. Not for long.

"She was erasing Tia's name on the letters and writing in her own; cutting Tia's face out of the pictures and putting her own photos in their places. It was all part of some obsessive, sick, and twisted fantasy that we would be a couple."

Tia swallowed hard. So far, they'd waved away the waitress, who was hovering just out of earshot, waiting for her chance to wait on Dylan Miller. Now Tia motioned her over and asked for some water, and she returned in seconds with an icy pitcher and four glasses with lemon wedges perched on the rims. Each of them took a slow drink, letting what had been said so far sink in. It was only the tip of the iceberg, Dylan knew, and Tia's parents were only now finding out that they were a couple. There was the whole summer to share with them yet. It was a lot to take in, and Tia hitched in a breath.

"Sorry," Tia muttered, after downing nearly half her glass. Dylan poured her some more, leaning over her and whispering, "It's me who's sorry, love. I hate that you have to hear any of this." He pressed his lips to her forehead.

"I know, baby," she said. "But it needs to be said, and I need some time to process it anyway. Go ahead."

He winced, but he continued. "A few nights ago—bloody hell, I can't believe it was only a few nights ago—she faked the death of an aunt who didn't even exist and had a meltdown in my trailer." He paused, deciding to leave out the part about her trying to seduce him in her own trailer. "She inadvertently left her phone behind, and I found it later that evening. I figured it would be best to bring it to her, and I walked in on her putting together scrapbooks already full of pictures and letters I'd sent to Tia. I saw some of the tabloids, too—her agent was sending her copies of all the magazines that boasted pictures of us—pictures from rehearsals and filming that their teenaged hacker had doctored to make it look like we were on dates and holidays. I also found the plane ticket I'd sent to Tia in the piles." He paused to let everyone take it in.

"It all started to make sense to me then—the lost phone number, the computer crash, the change of assistants—and I called the director immediately, and told him to call the police. I had him wait with her while I barged in to Angela's trailer—I just knew she had to have had help keeping the whole thing together. She caved pretty quickly and told me everything I've told you; of course saying that Penelope forced her into the whole mess. I found out that night that Tia hadn't dumped me at all—in fact, even though she'd been told to burn them, Angela had kept Tia's letters to me in a shoebox, and she finally handed them over. I tell you, it was like holding a treasure when she gave me that box. I realized, of course, that Tia had been going through the same kind of hell, and that she was still in the dark; thinking I'd dumped her. The only thing I could do was to find her right away. I spent most of that night in the police station, giving statements, and the rest of it reading all of Tia's letters. I met with the director the next day, and refused to do one more scene with that horrid woman. We filmed a few scenes with a double the next morning, after I got in touch with Jessa and begged forgiveness. Thankfully, she'd suspected all along that Penelope had been behind the whole mess, and said that she'd be thrilled to make her first order of business helping me and Tia get back together, and she worked on tickets to get me back here. I just arrived yesterday morning."

There was a collective quiet at the table as each tried to assimilate the information. Danielle looked at Tia with pity in her eyes.

"This is the first time I've heard it, too," Tia said. "We didn't want to talk about it yesterday...we were just so happy to be together and didn't want anything to spoil the only private time we're going to have for a while."

"I can't believe that anyone could be so...damn, I don't even know a word for it!" Will growled.

Danielle took in the look on her daughter's face. "I shouldn't have even asked. I'm so sorry, sweetie."

Tia reached over and took her mom's hand. "I'm the one who's sorry! None of this bad stuff matters now... we have a happy ending—a happy new beginning—and today is for celebrating! I can't tell you how horrible I felt keeping all this from you guys. I'm just sorry I never told you!"

"What?" Danielle asked. "You mean about who Dylan really is?"

"I wanted to tell you so badly at least a million times," she said. "But I was afraid of how people would react and how my life would change, and Dylan was so far away, and then I thought we'd broken up..."

"Oh sweetie, you're absolutely right!" her mother quickly agreed. "Don't you feel guilty for one minute—I can't even imagine what a struggle that was for you. Of course you did the right thing. Now no more talk about that horrid woman... let's change the subject to happier things, OK? Let's start at *your* beginning. This is all new news us, so you have to tell us everything! How in the world did you two meet, anyway?" her mother asked enthusiastically. The tone at the table changed completely as they spent the next hour talking about their relationship, the places they'd visited on the tour, and their love. Tia felt so relieved to be able tell her parents the happy things, and was thrilled as they fell into an easy conversation. She knew that her parents would love Dylan, and soon they were laughing together and sharing stories like old friends. They could all feel the presence of the people who looked on—Tia couldn't help put peek over the barrier once to see that every table in the restaurant was full and many others stood around the edges, but as anxious as the atmosphere was in the room, no one trespassed on the sanctity of the DND.

They all scooched around to the same side of the table, lining up their chairs so Tia could share some of the pictures and videos that she hadn't been able to show before. Her throat tightened as she sat with the people she loved the most; sandwiched between Dylan and her mother. She hadn't felt so much peace in a long time, and she was overcome with emotion. This was ending up to be a great day.

When they got back to the present and had answered what seemed a million questions, they all stopped and took a collective breath. It was a lot to absorb in one sitting, and Dylan could almost see their minds spinning. In a normal situation, they would have gotten this information over the course of months. However, he thought wryly, introducing a popular celebrity at the middle of an international scandal as your boyfriend would never qualify as a normal situation. He needed to give them some time to catch up with it all; and to catch up with each other. He took advantage of a lull in the conversation to give them just that. "I'm sure you have a lot to talk about as a family," he said, standing, "Tia told me that there is a back entrance here—do you think I could make it to the men's room without being noticed?"

Will pulled out his wallet and handed him a card. "You can head outside through that door," he said pointing, "and turn left. You'll see the outside entrance for the locker room a few doors down and you can swipe the card to get in. Considering half the membership of the place is in the dining room and it's only twelve degrees outside, I doubt you'll run into anyone."

Dylan pressed his lips to the top of Tia's head. "I'll give you all some time to catch up, and be back in a bit." He donned his coat, pulled a hat over his head and slipped out into the December day.

Chapter 5

The entrance to the locker room was well marked, and Dylan stepped inside. The room appeared empty, and he took a seat on a long leather couch that spanned the back wall across from a marble vanity top that held four basin sinks. He picked up a magazine, disappointed that there wasn't a copy of *Person to Person* on the coffee table—he hadn't yet had a chance to see his story in print—and settled in to wait.

He flipped mindlessly through pages filled with yachts, exotic cars, private planes and other indulgences, but he stopped and stared at a Harry Winston ad toward the back of the magazine, finally tearing it out and folding it into his pocket. As he reached for another magazine, he heard the whoosh of another door opening and then voices and the slam of locker doors. A short time later a shower went on, and then a man about his age walked over to the counter and spread shaving cream over his face. He took one swipe with the razor before catching Dylan's reflection in the mirror. He jumped, startled, and turned toward Dylan.

"Whew," he said, "you scared me, man!" Dylan watched the recognition dawn on the man's face as his brows furrowed. "Oh shit, aren't you Dylan Miller?"

Dylan stood. "I am. Good to meet you."

"Wow! My pleasure, man. I'm a fan of your music!" He extended his hand, and Dylan shook it.

"Thanks a lot—I appreciate that."

He shook his head. "This is too crazy! Do you have a show in town tonight or something? I don't remember hearing about one."

"No, not tonight," Dylan said. "I'm in town on personal business."

"Wow," he said again, "this is too weird to be standing here talking to you!" He stroked his chin and realized his face was still covered with shaving cream. He reached behind him and grabbed a towel, swiping his cheeks. "Are you thinking of joining the club? It's a great place; I'd be happy to sponsor you!"

Dylan could almost see the wheels turning in his head. It was the same story—this guy didn't know anything about Dylan except that he was a celebrity, but he'd be "happy to sponsor him." The guy figured that being Dylan's friend would mean invitations to parties, celebrity outings, access to lots of women...he'd been down that road before.

"I'm sorry," Dylan said. "I didn't get your name..."

"Oh shit, I'm sorry," he chuckled. "I just freaked out a little bit—I'm Jace. Jace McIntire." He reached out his hand and shook again by way of introduction.

Dylan's eyes narrowed as the name registered in his mind. What were the chances? First, that there was more than one Jace in this particular club, and second, that he'd run into him like this, when there was no one else around except for someone that just turned on a shower somewhere out of his sight? Incidental happenstance, once again, perhaps? He clenched his teeth and forced calm over his features. Part of him wanted to flatten the guy; Dylan knew that he'd tried to make Tia doubt his own intentions; but that wasn't his style. It didn't mean he couldn't have a little fun with him, however.

"I'm not sure if I'll be looking to join," Dylan said, contemplatively. "I'm just here as a guest today. It seems like a nice place, though."

Jace nodded enthusiastically. "Oh, it is! We've got a great golf course—do you golf? I'd love to get you out there sometime. We've got a great restaurant, a full service spa, an Olympic sized pool, racquetball, tennis...you name it. Has anyone taken you on a tour? I could show you around, if you have some time. It'd be great to have you as a member, so if you need anything—want to play a little racquetball, need a dinner reservation, anything at all—I've got some pull around here, and I'd be glad to help you out with anything you need, brother."

This had to be the guy, Dylan thought. His arrogance was obvious, and he was blatantly sucking up for his own advantage. "Well, now that you mention it," he said casually, "there is something you could help me out with," Dylan said.

"Just name it," Jace replied eagerly. "Anything at all!"

"I appreciate that, mate, thanks. I'm looking for a person, actually; a member here, but I think it's only fair to tell you that I'm not looking for him because he's a friend."

Jace nodded, contemplating. "OK by me," he said. "I know pretty much everyone here—what's his name?"

"That's the problem see; I don't know his name," Dylan said smoothly. "What I do know is that he's some sort of hot shot lawyer who thinks the world revolves around him—a serious prick from what I understand."

Jace laughed. "I'm an attorney myself. Believe me, I know a few guys like that. Why, do you need representation for something? If so, I'm your man. Seriously. I dabble in a little bit of everything."

Dylan smiled. "That's not it, but thanks. No, it's purely a personal issue. This particular asshole was trying real hard to steal my girlfriend, and I'd love to have a few words with him, if you know what I mean." He tilted his head conspiratorially and Jace returned the gesture, nodding. *Right where I want you*, Dylan thought.

"Why would anyone think they could take a woman away from you?" he joked.

"Well, that's where it gets interesting, Jace—you see, he didn't know that *I* was her boyfriend, only that she had one. But what difference should that make, right? What kind of wanker would try to steal anyone's girlfriend?" He glared directly into his eyes, making sure his displeasure was coming through loud and clear.

Dylan's lips curled up slightly when he saw the quick drop of Jace's eyes, the slight falter of his perma-grin. But so far, he was doing a passable job of maintaining his cool.

"I agree," Jace nodded, "that's pretty low, man."

"Damn fucking straight it is." Dylan gave him another hard stare, and waited just a beat too long before continuing. "Obviously, I travel a lot for work," he smiled, "and for the past few months I've been filming a movie in New Zealand..." he paused for effect, and smirked inwardly when he saw the realization sinking in. Jace swallowed hard, and his expression did more than falter; it started to visibly crash. His eyes widened, and the corners of his lips started to quiver.

"This bastard knew she was in love with someone," Dylan continued, his voice more menacing, "but he had the fucking audacity to tell her that because I was a musician I wouldn't be faithful to her, and probably wouldn't ever come back. Then, the asshole actually suggested that she give *him* a shot since I was so far away and would never know the difference. Can you believe the nerve?" He tried to keep his face serious, but inside he was having incredible fun watching the man start to squirm.

Jace just shook his head, and tried to paste a look of disgust on his face. Shit. Tia was fucking dating Dylan Miller? No wonder she rejected him! Who could compete with that? He couldn't blame the guy for being pissed off, either, but he was becoming increasingly aware of the look in the dude's eyes. Did he know—was Miller just toying with him?

"That sucks, man," he replied nervously. "So, you want to have it out with this dude, or what?" His fight or flight response was starting to kick in as adrenaline pumped through his veins and he was feeling particularly edgy. He needed to know what to expect. He rolled his weight to the balls of his feet and shifted his center of gravity back and forth while willing a look of composure to cover his nervousness.

"I'm not entirely sure yet," Dylan said. "The gentleman in me just wants him to see us together, so he has a face to put with my girl that isn't his." Jace exhaled slowly through clenched teeth. "But I have to be honest with you mate, the gentleman in me is kind of taking a back seat. The caveman in me wants to wrestle him to the ground, put my hands on his cocky little throat, get right up in his face..." he took a step closer to Jace, just a touch into his personal space, and glared into his eyes. He had a couple inches on the prick, and the fact that Jace was cowering just a bit, unnerved by the lack of comfortable distance between them, gave Dylan the definite advantage. "...and tell him, 'Never again, asshole. Never. Fucking. Again. You never stood a chance in hell, but you made my girl uncomfortable, and if you so much as go near her again, I will take extreme pleasure in seriously kicking your ass.'" He waited a couple beats and smiled warmly, then took a step back, relaxing his posture. He patted Jace on the arm and he jumped back nearly a foot. "As you can imagine, there's a pretty big part of me that does just want to kick his ass and be done with it. I'm trying real hard to keep that part under control, but who knows?" He shrugged his shoulders and smiled again. "I'm not entirely sure what I'll do until I'm face-to-face with him, I guess, but I'd like to have the opportunity to find out."

Jace tried to keep his face calm and his voice steady, but he was failing miserably at both. His hands were shaking—he saw the malice in Miller's eyes and was positive now that the dude knew exactly to whom he was speaking.

Jace looked down at his watch with an exaggerated motion. "Shit," he stammered, "I'm sorry, but I'm meeting my girlfriend for lunch," he said, emphasizing the word *girlfriend,* "and I'm already late. I've...got to go. I, ah, I'll see what I can do about your...um...situation." He didn't ask for the girlfriend's name or how to get in touch with him if he did find something out, and Dylan smiled, knowing the message was received loud and clear.

"Oh, sure, I understand. I hope you do, as well. I am glad I met you, Jace," Dylan said in a much less pleasant voice, drawing out his name with a snake-like hiss.

Jace turned once more, the discomfort clear in his eyes. "You too," he managed, but the door was already swinging shut.

"Hey Jace," Lexi said as he rushed past her on his way out the door. "Is Ryan in there?"

He glared at her and kept walking, his cheeks still smeared with shaving cream and a towel hanging around his neck. "What's up with you?" she called to his fleeing figure.

Then the locker room door opened again, and Dylan walked out, a huge smile on his face.

"Dylan?" she asked incredulously, stopping and staring. "Holy shit! It is you!"

"Hey, Lexi!" he smiled. "Great to see you!" He pulled her into a friendly hug.

"Oh my God, Dylan, what are you doing here? So you're what all the buzz around here is about—that explains a lot," she continued, without waiting for an answer. "Wait a minute, are you and Tia...?" She couldn't seem to find the rest of the words.

"We are!" he said, his smile growing. "She rang you last night—didn't you get the message?"

"Shit, I had to go to a freaking opera, and I lost my phone in a taxi, and I...but who cares, you and Tia are back together? For real?" She squealed the last words, her excitement mounting.

His smile said it all, and she threw herself into his arms and gave him another huge hug. "You have a hell of a lot of explaining to do, but I'm so happy for both of you!"

The door opened again, and Ryan stepped out. The first thing he saw was Lexi, his *fiancé*, in the arms of—holy shit, Dylan Miller? He stopped, frozen in place, watching her jump all over the guy. They obviously knew each other better than a backstage meeting at a huge festival somewhere, which was the story he'd been told. Anger and jealousy boiled up inside him, and he finally found his voice.

"Lexi, what the fuck?" he exclaimed, raising his palms in disbelief. He couldn't believe she was actually standing right there, her arms around his neck! Ryan sucked a breath in through his teeth and tried to keep his head from exploding. He knew that Lexi'd met Miller when she was over in Europe in July—Tia's boyfriend's band was playing at some festival; or so he'd been told—and the girls had all access passes. Dylan Miller was her fantasy..."Mr. Sexiest Man in the World"...and Ryan had basically given her carte blanche to sleep with the dude—'without guilt or repercussion,' they'd declared one night while watching a bad horror flick over even worse wine. "My pick is definitely Dylan Miller!" she'd said without a second's hesitation, her smile lighting her face in the most lascivious of ways. "That man is so hot that hell wouldn't be able to hold him," she'd added.

Ever since she got back from that damned trip with Tia she'd been secretive and elusive; but really? She brought him here, to his country club, and was rubbing it in his face? The edges of his vision went white, especially when she untangled her arms and laughed right at him.

He'd put two and two together after she got back and guessed pretty quickly that she'd slept with Miller. Hell, the dude was a celebrity who could probably have any woman he wanted, and Lexi wasn't exactly tough on the eyes. Seeing them standing there together, shit-eating grins on both their faces, pretty much confirmed his suspicions...but since he'd been asinine enough to give her fucking permission to do it, there was precious little he could do or say about it. This was pretty heartless, though, flaunting the damn rock star in his face at *his* country club.

Lexi curled her arm around Dylan's waist. "There you are!" she said brightly. "Oh my God, Ryan, I can finally tell you everything! I'm so excited to finally introduce you to..."

"I know who he is," Ryan snapped. "You want to tell me what the hell is going on?" He couldn't believe she was standing there, with a fucking smile on her face, introducing Miller as if he'd be happy to meet the man!

Lexi interpreted the look on Ryan's face and immediately guessed what he was thinking. "Oh Ry," she giggled. "He's *Tia's* Dylan, you *idiot*," she said, moving to wrap her arm around Ryan after giving him a pretty good punch on the arm. "He's here because..." she looked at Dylan. "Why are you *here*, exactly?" she asked, frowning toward the direction in which Jace had just fled.

"Meeting the parents," Dylan smiled, extending his hand to Ryan. "Nice to meet you Ryan—I've heard quite a lot about you."

Ryan took a deep breath, recovered his composure and shook Dylan's hand. "Really? Tia's Dylan?" The relief was evident on his face. "Shit. I've heard a lot about you too, but not..."

"I know," Dylan interrupted. "Not who I actually was, right?" Ryan looked to Lexi for an explanation, but Dylan provided it. "That's been the general MO," he said. "Tia swore Lexi to secrecy—it wasn't easy for her, being the only one who knew about us. Even Tia's parents just found out exactly who I am a couple hours ago."

"Unfuckingbelievable," he smirked, exhaling a relived sigh and looking at Lexi. "You actually kept a secret like that?"

She gave him a little shove. "Yes, I obviously did since you thought Dylan was here to see me."

"Whatever," he joked back, but he found he had to swallow around a sizeable lump that had formed in his throat.

"Wait," Lexi said, turning back to Dylan. "So you already met Will and Danielle? What are you doing hiding out in the locker room, then?" Her eyes got wide. "Oh crap, did something go wrong?"

"No, no," Dylan quickly reassured her. "Everything's great. We did the meet and greet, filled them in on the last seven months in one breathless tornado, and I figured that they could use a little time to talk about me behind my back," he smiled. "It was a bit of a shock, as you can imagine, so I figured they needed to do some family regrouping. I'm going to go sneak out the back door and head back over there now, actually," he added. "I just wanted to catch a glimpse of my new friend's retreat with his tail between his legs first." He turned his eyes in the direction Jace had fled, and Lexi understood immediately.

"Now that they've had a little time for this all to sink in, I need to give her dad a chance to get to know me a little and explain that my intentions are pure—why don't you give us a half hour or so and then join us?"

Lexi looked at Ryan and he shrugged, turning the corners of his mouth down in agreement. "See you in a bit then!" she said. "And Dylan? I'm so glad you're back, but I'm not kidding—you really do have a lot of explaining to do!"

"Go get a copy of today's *Person to Person*," he suggested. "It'll tell you a lot, and then I won't have to rehash the whole story again—we can just fill in the gaps." She looked confused for a moment, then turned and headed for the girls' locker room to see if she could scrounge up a copy.

Dylan made it back to the DND without incident and dropped a kiss on Tia's head. "I just saw Lexi and Ryan," he said. "I think maybe the sight of me stopped his heart for a second or two when he saw her hugging me, but she managed the introductions. They're going to join us in a little bit."

"I completely forgot that she never called me back!" Tia answered.

"Something about an opera, a taxi, and a lost phone," Dylan said. "I'm sure she'll fill you in. She obviously kept the secret; he didn't have a clue."

"I have to tell you," Tia smirked, "I definitely had my doubts that she could actually pull it off. She did so much better than I expected!"

Dylan turned to Will. "How about us guys get to know each other a little bit? I imagine you must have at least a million questions for me. Can I buy you a drink?"

"Absolutely," Will replied. "I could definitely use one." He stood, excusing himself, and led Dylan over to the little private section of the bar.

As soon as the men left the table, Danielle lit up. "Oh my goodness, Tia, he's gorgeous! I didn't want to say with your dad here, but...wow...yummy!" she giggled like a schoolgirl and Tia smiled.

"Well, he is the Sexiest Man on Earth as voted by Person to Person readers," she said. She never got tired of saying that.

"Oh, and the accent—it's like melted chocolate. I could never get tired of listening to him talk."

"I know, right? I'm so lucky, Mom; I don't even know how I could be so lucky."

"But most importantly, it's pretty obvious that you make each other happy. I can't believe my baby's in love."

"I know, Mom," she said, unable to tramp down the huge smile on her face. "He's just the most amazing guy..."

"Oh, I'm just so happy for you!" she exclaimed, squeezing Tia's hand. "I was so worried after Nick died..."

"Me too," Tia confided. "Oh Mom, you know how I was! I really didn't think I'd ever be able to fall in love again. But Dylan is so..." she searched for the right words, but only one came to mind. "...perfect." She glanced over to where he and her dad were in deep conversation. She'd never seen Dylan look so serious; it had to be disconcerting to be meeting your girlfriend's father for the first time in an ordinary situation, but this one was beyond extraordinary. Her stomach fluttered at the thought that he was so nervous. People tend to think that celebrities are just oozing with confidence, but she knew better. He caught her eye and smiled, tossing her the look he reserved just for her.

"Well, he's obviously an Adonis," she said, "that goes without saying. But now you need to tell me all the things you can't say in front of your father—girl talk!"

Tia's eyes brightened and her smile split her face. "There's so much I've been wanting to tell you that I don't even know where to start! He wrote me a song...oh God, first I have to tell you about my birthday! It was the most romantic night of my life, Mom! We were in Paris..."

They rested their heads affectionately together, and Tia was thrilled to finally share all the stories she'd wanted to tell her mom for months, punching up pictures and videos on her iPad to help her tell the tale.

A few feet away, Dylan and Will touched glasses in a toast at the bar. "I want you to know I'm an open book, Will. Ask me anything you'd like. You must have a lot of questions." Dylan opened as they sipped their drinks.

"Probably," Will replied, "but none of them seem to be coming to me right now. I'm still trying to reconcile the fact that my little girl is at the center of an international celebrity scandal, I guess," he said with a chuckle.

"I want you to know that I encouraged Tia to tell you who I was, especially after the summer ended. I'm sorry if you feel blindsided by all of this. It was never my intention to..."

"Oh no, it's not that at all," Will interrupted, dismissing his concerns with a wave of his hand. "Tia explained why she didn't tell us, and we completely understand her reasoning. She made the decision that was best for her, and it was probably the right one under the circumstances. It would have been really tough on her if the media descended and she had to deal with it alone. She did tell us a lot about you...it just never even entered our minds that you might be a celebrity. She talked about you like you were a prince, I'll tell you that, but not like you were famous. It's just a little more to take in, that's all. We'll get over it, I promise you," he said with a wry smile.

"That's one of the things that drew me to her in the first place," Dylan explained. "She never put on an act for me because I was a celebrity, and that doesn't happen to me very often. She was real from the first time we met, and she got to know me as a person. I felt comfortable with her from the start."

Will smiled. "That's my Tia," he said. "She's about as down-to-earth as they come. Always has been."

Dylan shifted in his seat. He couldn't remember ever being so nervous—not even in front of 100,000 people at a concert venue—but then, he'd never before even contemplated asking the question he was about to ask. "Listen, Will," Dylan began, his voice faltering just a bit. "I need you to know that I am completely in love with your daughter, and that this whole experience has shown me that I never want to be without her again. I know you just met me, and that you don't know anything about me as a man. I'm a celebrity, yes, but I don't revel in that. I live in Colorado, far away from Hollywood and all its crazy bloody drama. My main job is music, and I do it because I love it with a passion I can't even begin to explain. I'd do it even if I wasn't famous or didn't make a lot of money..."

Will simply nodded. He could sense that the man had something big to say, and that he was more than a little nervous about saying it. He'd pretty much already guessed it, just after seeing them together for a short time and hearing their story, so he maintained his calm demeanor even as he smiled on the inside. Dylan breathed deeply and continued. "Tia and I have had a wild and crazy relationship, and thinking that she didn't want to be with me these past couple months about tore me apart." He paused, stroking his chin with his fingers, feeling the tremble in them. He swallowed hard before continuing, placing his shaky hands in his lap and feeling the sweat on his palms.

"I know this is far from the perfect circumstance, and in an ideal situation I would have met you months ago and given you a chance to get to know me, but..." he paused, taking a sip from his drink since his mouth had just gone as dry as a desert, "... I want to marry your daughter, Will. I know it's too much to ask for your blessing, since you just met me a couple hours ago, but the couple weeks we'll be in Australia will be the quietest we'll have for a while, and I was hoping..."

Will held up his hand to interrupt, smiling. "Take a breath, Dylan," he chuckled.

Dylan inhaled deeply and took another sip of his whiskey with visibly shaky hands. "OK," he said, smiling back. "Guess I'm a little nervous. I've never done this before."

Will patted him on the back affectionately. "Tia is our only child, as you know, and all we've ever wanted is for her to be happy. When Nick died, we had our doubts that she ever could be happy again, and we worried about her constantly. When she met you, she started coming back to life, and we couldn't have been more thrilled. You brought her back from a dark place, Dylan, and we'll be forever grateful for that." Dylan looked at him and nodded, hope slipping into his eyes.

"You've already proven that you love Tia. Just the fact that you're here, that you resisted the advances of a beautiful movie star out of loyalty to our daughter, and that you immediately jumped on a plane to find her again when you found out how you'd been played proves that.

"We trust Tia completely, and know that she has good feel for people. If she loves you, and it's pretty obvious that she does, then I'd be proud to call you my son. You absolutely have my blessing."

Dylan smiled wide, and shook Will's hand, his breath rushing out in a whoosh. "Thank you sir, you don't know how much that means to me! I promise you that I'll spend the rest of my life making her happy."

Will smiled back. "I trust that you will, Dylan. It's pretty obvious that you mean it."

"I'm planning to ask her on New Year's Eve," Dylan said excitedly. "I'm working on a little side trip to Sydney after Christmas, and I'm going to come up with something really special."

"Your secret is safe with me," Will said, smiling. "I think we both know what her answer will be, so I guess I can just go ahead and welcome you to the family."

"Thank you sir, thank you very much!" Dylan replied enthusiastically. He felt lighter suddenly, his breathing settled, and he felt as if the final piece of the puzzle that was his life had finally fallen into place. He could see only happy endings in his future, and the thought made him smile wide.

"I don't need to tell you not to tip off Danielle, right?" Will smirked. "Tia may have told you that her mother has a love of gossip. She'd never purposely spoil the surprise, of course, but…"

Dylan nodded. "I definitely want it to be a surprise, so my lips are sealed."

"Mine too," he said, locking his lips with his fingers. "Now, son, shall we get back to the ladies before we raise too much suspicion? The look on your face alone is enough to give it away. Besides, I see Lexi dying to come and join us."

Chapter 6

Tia felt much better about everything as they pulled up to the curb next to *Paddy's*. The introductions at the club went better than she'd hoped, she'd been able to introduce Dylan to most of her family at her parents' place afterward, and she was looking forward to now being able to share the real Dylan with her true friends.

Ryan's Mustang pulled up across the street just as they were getting out of the car, and Lexi opened the door before he even stopped, causing him to have to slam on his brakes.

"This is so exciting!" she yelled across the street as she came running over. "I mean, the looks on the faces of the people at the club were absolutely priceless, but I can't wait to see how all these guys react—I mean, they've actually met Dylan before—this is going to be crazy."

"Yeah it is," Tia said excitedly. "I was nervous about the club, but I seriously can't wait for these introductions."

Dylan turned to Ryan. "That's a really sweet ride," he said, looking at the Mustang. "Great paint job."

"Thanks," Ryan said proudly. "I had it done at Midwest Craft Motors...you know the place that has the TV show? They actually featured it on one of their shows."

Lexi rolled her eyes. "Oh yeah. That was Ryan's fifteen minutes...or should I say fifteen *seconds* of fame. He actually got to be on television when he went to pick it up."

"Really?" Dylan said. "That's pretty awesome, mate. They did a great job. I've never seen anything like it."

"Ten coats of clear over that baby," Ryan added proudly. "And the engine's bored thirty over, so she rides like a dream."

"Sometimes I wonder if he loves that car more than me," Lexi smirked. "But hey, I look good in it, so I don't complain. Not too much, anyway."

Tia pulled out her phone. "I'm going to text Sean and have him meet us at the kitchen entrance around back," she said as she tapped out the message. "I want him to "meet" Dylan first," she said making air quotes with her fingers, "and maybe let him do one big introduction on the mic so we can get that out of the way and just mingle."

Lexi shrugged. "We'll go in the front, then, and meet you inside. We're on the list, right?"

Tia nodded. She'd asked Sean to close the place for a private party, telling him that she had a surprise for him and that she wanted to be surrounded by her friends when she shared it. She really wanted the night to be just about the people she cared about, and he was happy to oblige. It wasn't like the usual crowd wouldn't pack the place, anyway.

"Hey, it's about time you showed your face again, my friend," Sean said as he opened the back door. "About damn..." He stopped short when he saw who was standing there, his mouth still forming the next word and his eyes widening.

"Sean, you remember Dylan," Tia said slyly.

"Great to see you again, mate," Dylan said smiling.

"Oh, fuck me man!" Sean exclaimed, blinking his eyes to make sure that what he was seeing was real. "No way!" He grabbed Dylan's hand in an enthusiastic shake and pulled him into a tight embrace. "Seriously?" When Tia told him she had a surprise for him, he'd been sure that she was going to announce that she and Dylan were engaged. He was thrilled for her; knowing how hard it had been to recover after the loss of his cousin, Nick. Tia had shared a lot of information about their relationship over the past few months, but had never hinted that her new love was Dylan Miller. Oh yeah, this was a surprise, alright.

"Holy shit," he said again. "Dylan effing Miller. I knew there was something...I knew you looked familiar...I should have known!" He shook his head and raked his fingers through his hair. "I'm such an idiot. You even told me you worked in the entertainment industry, but I never put it together..." He punched his fist into his open hand. "This is just so crazy...you and Tia..."

"Sean," Tia said, a warning in her voice. "Chill out. You're the one I'm counting on to stay grounded with this whole thing."

Sean shook his head vigorously, as if trying to make the pieces fall into place. "Of course. Absolutely. Just let me have my little freak-out minute of shock here, will you? It'll be cool in a sec. I mean, you can't spring something like this on me and not expect a reaction." He turned to Dylan. "Am I right?"

"Take your time," Dylan teased. "We'll just stand here and wait for you to get your head out of your ass."

"Screw you," he teased back, giving Dylan a friendly shove. "This is just...completely unexpected. I can't believe..."

"Believe it Sean, and shut the hell up already," Tia joked. "You're making an ass of yourself. Not that that's any different from a normal day, but still..." she grinned.

Sean put his hand over his mouth in an exaggerated gesture of self-imposed silence. Before Tia could say another word, he parted two fingers and muttered through the gap, "You've got some 'splaining to do, though—and I'm all ears."

Tia sighed, and pulled Sean into a hug. "I owe you an explanation *and* an apology," she began, "and I need to get the apology out of the way first. I'm so sorry I lied, Sean," she said sincerely. "I hated not being able to tell anyone the truth." She took a deep breath and exhaled slowly. "No one except for Lexi knew about me and Dylan before today. The night you met Dylan? That was the first night I met him, too." A look of confusion crossed Sean's face. "I have a big confession to make, Sean," she said sadly, looking down before continuing. "I was so afraid to come to the memorial that night. So scared, in fact, that I had no intention of coming. I was so worried that you'd all be mad at me for not being around, or even worse that you'd pity me...just when I was feeling like I could actually move on." She caught the look on his face, and spoke before he could. "I know it was stupid," she said quickly. "I should've known then, too, but it was all so much..." Sean pulled her to him, and gave her a reassuring squeeze. "I was convinced that I had to do it alone, and that's how I met Dylan. He was at this other pub in disguise, trying to have a normal night for a change, and through a crazy bunch of circumstances we ended up hanging out together and kind of accidentally ended up here..."

"Wow," Sean said, bewildered. "I had no idea, guys."

"Of course you didn't," Tia said. "And neither did we. At the time, I didn't think I'd ever see Dylan again after that night; and certainly not after the weekend. He was only in town for two shows, and then he was doing the summer tour in Europe...I knew that if I told everyone who he really was, I wouldn't have the chance to get to know him. We were getting on so well, and I was completely blown away because I thought it would take so much more time before I felt that comfortable with another guy...and so I kept him to myself. Plus, his original plan was to have a normal evening out, and he was having so much fun just hanging with everyone without the celebrity thing getting in the way..."

Sean turned to Dylan, who quickly agreed. "I don't get too many chances to just hang out with people, as you might imagine," he said, "and it's one of the things I miss most about having a normal life. I really appreciated being able to do that. I couldn't remember the last time I was just able to blend into a crowd—to play some darts, have a couple beers, and let someone else play the music..."

Sean blushed, remembering that he'd played some of the band's music that night, and that Dylan had complimented him on his performance and his song choice. He smirked as the memory sharpened. "Shit. I asked if you were a fan of InHap, and you said something like you'd followed them from the beginning. How did I not figure that out?"

"Guess you're not terribly observant," Dylan joked, inciting another smirk from Sean.

"Or maybe the mullet just looked so natural on you..."

Tia put her hands on her hips and addressed the boys sternly. "Can we get on with this, please?" They both snapped to attention, facing her and trying to tamper down their sarcastic smiles. When she was sure she had their attention, she pushed back her own smile and continued. "Truth is, I kept the secret from everyone—Dylan just met my parents for the first time earlier today. But now that he's back, we're going public with our relationship. We leave for California tomorrow, and—holy crap, this scares me to death—we'll be on all the talk shows and radio shows and God knows what else."

"That's awesome, really! Congratulations!"

"Thanks mate," Dylan said. "But before we go tell the whole world, we wanted to make sure we told our friends. We want them to be the first to know. I just got back yesterday, and we have bloody little time, so here we are."

Tia added, "Judging by the number of cars in the street, I'm guessing it's pretty crowded tonight..." Sean nodded. "So I thought that maybe the easiest way to reintroduce him would be to do it in one shot—tell the story once, and then just hang out so Dylan can get reacquainted with everyone. Do you think you could get on the mic and get it done?"

"Oh, I can totally do that," he grinned. "I'd be glad to."

His enthusiasm gave Tia pause. "No celebrity stuff, Sean, OK? That's not what this is about."

"Don't worry, I do have some class. I have to call it up from the very depths of my being, but I can pull it off, don't worry."

"Not worried at all, my friend," Dylan said with confidence. "The thing is, Tia and I are serious about each other, and I want her friends to be my friends—not because I'm a fucking celebrity, but because I'm part of her life." He smirked, and added, "And because I'm a hell of a guy."

"I get it," Sean confirmed with an uncharacteristic seriousness in his voice. "Really. Consider it handled." He shook Dylan's hand again. "Really good to see you again, man."

"You too," Dylan said sincerely.

"You still owe me a poker night, you know," he grinned.

"As soon as I possibly can," Dylan smiled back.

Tia jumped in. "Why don't you send Paddy and Siobhan back so we can say hi to them in private, too, before we do this whole thing."

Dylan held up a paper shopping bag. "Good idea. I got a little something for Paddy that I picked up over in Ireland on the tour."

Sean smiled. "If that's what I think it is, then you're fucking golden, man. I'll go get them."

"Young Master Dylan, I'm so glad to see you again!" Paddy exclaimed when he entered the kitchen. The two men shook hands, and Paddy pulled him into a rough hug. Siobhan hugged Tia and then Dylan in turn. "It's been much too long since our paths have crossed. I must say, though, that with as much as Tia talks about you, it's almost like you've been here all along."

Dylan smiled. "There are few places where I feel so welcome, that's for sure. It's really good to be back."

"I think this calls for a little celebration drink, don't you?" Paddy said. "Still have a taste for the Tully? It kind of gets under your skin, doesn't it?"

"That it does," Dylan grinned back. "And I know it's your favorite, so I picked these up for you when I was in Ireland a few months back..." he placed a bag on the counter top, and Paddy reached inside, holding up a bottle with a glint in his eyes.

"This is the liquid gold!" he said. "When were you in Ireland?"

"It was one of the early stops on the tour," Dylan answered. "One of the stops Tia missed, unfortunately." Paddy's head turned in question, and Sean was quick to make the clarification.

"Uncle Paddy, this is *Dylan Miller*...you know...Incidental Happenstance?" Sean added, "That's Dylan's band!"

The recognition dawned on his face. "Well now, that name I definitely know! That was my Nick's favorite group—I think I probably know all of your songs, too—they're played on my stage all the time. Now that definitely calls for a shot of Tully!"

"At least one," Dylan winked. "Once we get the introductions done I want to get another round for the house; but keep the good stuff for us, right?"

"This boy's got to have some Irish in his blood somewhere!" Paddy exclaimed, smiling at Tia and pouring a round for the little group huddled in the kitchen. Sean downed his and headed out into the bar to make the announcement.

"Here Here!" Sean said into the mic, in his usual *Paddy's* greeting.

"Where's here?" came the standard answer from the patrons.

"Listen up, everyone," he started. "I have some news to share with you and I need you to all pay attention!" Something like a moan came up from the crowd. "Seriously," he continued, "it's important." He paused to be sure he had everyone's eyes on his. "I called a lot of you today asking you to come tonight. I said I had a surprise, but at the time, I had no idea how big a surprise it would actually be." He scratched his head, trying to put together the right words as the crowd mumbled under its collective breath.

"I'm sure you remember when Tia brought Dylan here for Nick's memorial. You all made him feel incredibly welcome, and he made an impression on all of us, especially because he was the one who made Tia smile again. I, for one, considered him a friend after just a few minutes of knowing him—he was a genuine guy." A murmur of agreement rose from the ranks. "And God knows we've heard enough about him since then—even though he hasn't been able to get back here, whenever Tia's around, it sure feels like he is!" A few glasses were raised, and Tia couldn't help but smile as Dylan pulled her close while they hovered at the entrance to the pub.

"Well, Dylan's in town, and for some strange reason, he wanted to come hang out with you crazy people!" More glasses were raised, and few whistles sounded from the floor. Sean held up his hand for quiet.

"What none of us knew; what I just found out, actually, is that they'd only just met that night, the night of the memorial, and that the Dylan you met that night isn't the same Dylan you're going to see tonight. I mean, he's the same guy on the inside, but the outside is very different."

Someone yelled out, "Please tell me he got a haircut!" Giggles of exaggerated approval rose up from the group, and Dylan and Tia shared a knowing glance.

Sean waited for the laughs to stop, then he continued. "Yeah, yeah," he said. "You'll be thrilled to know that his hair is different..." more mock cheers filled the room. "...but that isn't the first thing you'll notice—trust me." He waited for the room to quiet before continuing. "Maybe some of you saw the news today, about how everybody's favorite singer, Dylan Miller, is involved in a sordid love triangle with a bitchy Hollywood starlet who shall remain unnamed and a mystery woman who has yet to be named..." Murmurs rose again. "Well, I might not have believed it if I hadn't just seen it with my own eyes, but..." he paused for effect, "...our very own Tia is that mystery woman, and they're here tonight. They're going public with their relationship in a big way tomorrow, but they wanted to come here first, so Tia could formally introduce him to her friends. Apparently, you clowns made some sort of impression on him, and he wants to count you as his friends, too." Heads turned, scanning the room, most of them not putting it past Sean to stage an elaborate hoax.

"One of the things Dylan appreciated the most about that night, because he was disguised when he and Tia first met, was that we all treated him like one of the family. He's the same guy on the inside, and he wants it to stay that way. He doesn't want to be treated any differently than you treated him then, so don't make asses out of yourselves, OK? So I'm going to let them say a few words that'll be easier to say once to all of you rather than a thousand times over." He turned to the entryway, where Tia and Dylan still stood. "Shit, I feel like a fucking talk show host here, but I'm happy to be the one introducing them as a couple for the first time—Tia Hastings and Dylan Miller!" He stepped aside as the couple mounted the small stage and stepped up behind the mic. Thundering applause and catcalls bounced off the walls, and the couple just smiled, waving them away.

"Wow. This isn't awkward at all," Tia said sarcastically into the mic as a hush fell over the room and she took in the wide-eyed looks of her friends. "First off, I need to say that I'm incredibly sorry I kept all of this from you—you are my dearest friends, and I felt horrible lying to you all. Like Sean said, the last time Dylan was here was the night of the memorial, and we'd just met a few hours before that. At the time I had no idea that things between us were going to progress like this—in fact, I didn't think I'd ever see him again after that night. It was a fluke that we even met, and then he was heading off to Europe for a tour, and I didn't see how...anyway, that's a long story; one that I'm sure I'll be telling at least a thousand times in the next few weeks.

"Much to my obvious delight things did progress, and Dylan invited me to Europe. But after the tour, when Dylan had to go film the now infamous movie in New Zealand, we agreed that it would be better if we waited to make the announcement until we were at least on the same continent. No one knew who he really was—except for Lexi..." She pointed to her best friend, who was doing a fine job on her own of calling attention to herself. "Even my parents just met him earlier today." She paused and took a breath. "But finally, after a whole lot of time apart and an incredible amount of bullshit courtesy of the..." she looked at Sean. "What did you call her? The "bitchy Hollywood starlet?" we are back together and ready to tell the whole world.

"Dylan wanted to come here tonight because he counts you as his friends, and I hope you'll do the same. He really is the nice guy you met back in May and, well," she said, the grin stretching across her face, "he's also the man I love, and neither of us could think of a better way to celebrate than with all of you incredible people....the most important people in my life."

Applause rang through the pub, and Dylan stepped up to the mic.

"It's so good to see you all again," he said. "I have to tell you that the last time I was here, I had the best time meeting all of you and seeing the love you have for my girl here. I had no idea that night that she'd become the love of my life, or that I'd feel guilty for deceiving you." He paused, taking in the sea of faces that were staring at him, dumbstruck. "Bloody hell, this *is* awkward," he said smiling at Tia and tucking his long hair carelessly behind his ears. "I can't really add anything to what Tia just said—I do count you as friends, and I hope to get to know you all better. So, I'm just Tia's boyfriend, OK?" Nods of agreement filled the room. "Alright, so at the risk of it becoming 'my thing,' I'd like to buy a round of Tully for all of you—the traditional friendship drink to mark the start of an honest and true friendship."

Cheers rang out through the bar, and the patrons lifted their glasses to the couple. Tia and Dylan clasped hands and bowed slightly, accepting their congratulations, and when someone in the crowd started clinking silverware against a glass in the old wedding tradition, others joined in. Dylan obliged them by pulling Tia into his arms and tipping her back for a kiss, to the delight of the crowd. Then he hopped off the stage and made his way to the bar to help Paddy and Siobhan distribute the trays of shots.

When everyone had a shot glass in their hands, Paddy stepped up to the mic. "I'm going to take the liberty of making this toast, because it's my damn bar," he said laughing. He held up his glass, and the others followed suit. "Here's to happiness, love, friendship, and second chances," he said. "In life you can't ask for anything more, but should never settle for anything less."

He raised his glass to Tia and Dylan, and they stepped up to toast with him. Then they raised their glasses to the rest of the crowd, and the shots were downed, glasses clunked, cheers raised.

Tia turned to Siobhan and whispered, "I promised Dylan that you make the best corned beef brisket sandwich in the world, and that he could have one. I need one, too."

"Oh," she smiled, "I can definitely handle that request!" she said as she hustled back toward the kitchen.

They made the rounds of the tables, greeting everyone and sharing bits of their story. They would have liked to have stayed longer—Tia was truly impressed with the way her friends treated Dylan. There were some star struck looks, some nervous giggles, and plenty of batting eyelashes; but that was par for the course whenever Dylan was in a room, and she'd have to get used to it. Time after time Tia looked around the room and smiled—she considered most of the people here family, and she relaxed and actually enjoyed herself. This was how she'd envisioned going public with Dylan...a gathering in a safe place full of her friends and family...the genuine pleasure of introducing the people she loved to each other and building friendships. Her work friends mingled with her pub friends; Lilly, her school secretary, took charge and introduced everyone, and Lexi rode on the high of being the only one who knew about the relationship from the start. Sean, Dave, and Tim dragged Dylan into a dart 'rematch,' and she joined friends at a group of tables to 'dish scoop' and share pictures and videos from her incredible summer; finally able to put it out there. It was reminiscing and new beginnings, and more than once Tia glanced over at the table where she and Dylan had sat that first night, remembering when Sean had strummed the first chords of *Pull You Up* from the little stage on the other side of the room and Dylan had asked her to dance; singing the song that had been so instrumental in her healing into her ear. She'd felt something incredible that first time he took her into his arms, but never imagined then that she was on the verge of the most amazing journey of her life. It felt strange. She was the same person, but she felt so *different*, and even her closest friends saw her differently. She could see it in their expressions; hear it in their voices as they sat entranced, waiting to hear the story of how she won the heart of the "Sexiest Man on Earth." Things wouldn't be the same and Dylan was right—what fun was a life that never changed; never offered challenges and makeovers and do-overs? Paddy was right, too. You couldn't ask for anything more, and shouldn't settle for anything less. She was at home here with these people, and Dylan would be too. These were her true friends and she was lucky to have them.

Ryan sat by himself at a small table at the back of the pub, sipping a Harp and watching Lexi flit about the tables chatting and telling anyone who'd listen how she'd been the only privileged one in on the secret of Dylan's true identity. He smiled to himself as he watched her over-exaggerated gestures and the pure joy on her face as she shared her own versions of stories about the couple; clearly enjoying the spotlight thrust upon her. She'd been waiting for this day for a long time, he realized, and although it wasn't her who slept with Miller, she was certainly thrilled to talk about her connection to him...and to the rest of the band. He still felt like a bit of a fool when he remembered how he'd first reacted when he saw his fiancé in the arms of the rock star; and although he was relieved that it wasn't Lexi that Miller had come to see, part of him was kind of pissed off that she'd kept the information from him—that she'd not shared with him that she was on tour with one of the world's biggest bands over the summer instead of just hanging out with her friend and engaging in the usual tourist rituals.

These weren't his people. Back in the day, when Tia and Nick were dating, he and Lexi would hang out here occasionally; mainly for St. Patrick's Day parties and when Tia was singing on the little makeshift stage with her fiancé's band. They were nice enough, but most of his socializing over the past few years was with stuffy old lawyer types; going to operas and tremendously boring dinner parties or hanging out at the country club in his constant effort to make partner at his firm so that he could truly enjoy the finer things in life and provide a good future for himself and the family he would one day have. Lexi seemed in her element, however, pausing to wave at him periodically from across the room as she moved from group to group, sometimes lacing her arm through Dylan's and encouraging him to help her tell a story.

Aside from that, he may as well have been invisible. All attention was focused on the happy couple and on Dylan in particular—especially from the ladies, he noticed. They couldn't seem to take their eyes off of him, and batted their eyelashes while regarding him with coy smiles whenever he tossed a glance their way. He was obviously used to this kind of attention and smiled warmly at everyone, accepting hugs from the ladies and hearty handshakes from the men as he and Tia mingled with groups and Dylan tried to laugh off the many requests for him to take the stage and sing something for the patrons.

Ryan looked at his watch and frowned when he realized they'd been here just shy of an hour. No way this party was going to be breaking up anytime soon, so he leaned back, sipped his beer and watched from a distance, the brew bitter on his tongue and the isolation chewing on his ego.

Chapter 7

Tony Granger was one rich motherfucker, as Dylan eloquently put it. He not only hosted the most popular late night talk show on television but was also a shrewd businessman, and he was seriously loaded. His home was a sprawling estate north of San Diego, and his private helicopter flew him in to work each day. He had an obsession for classic cars, owned an entire island in the Caribbean, and had several private jets; one of which Dylan and Tia boarded late Sunday morning for the start of what Tia had coined their "media blitzkrieg." Tony also happened to be one of Dylan's closest friends outside of the band, and was the reason that they were making the West Coast the first leg of their trip—he'd apparently jumped at the opportunity to be the first to satisfy the public demand for more of the "love triangle" story that was still big news, especially when Dylan offered Tony their first public appearance as a couple.

They flew into a little airport near San Diego, one often used by celebrities who want to avoid the constant paparazzi that camp out at LAX, and were quickly hustled onto the helicopter that would take them directly to Tony's estate. Because Tony had offered the station the shot at an exclusive—the answer to the big question, "who is the mystery woman who stole Dylan Miller's heart and sent Oscar nominee Penelope Valentine over the edge?" he'd been given a Sunday night slot and time was of the essence. Tony also wanted to make damn sure that the news broke on his show, and not in the social media universe. He'd been fretting since yesterday, worried that pictures of the mystery woman would show up on the internet—and they had— but since there were literally thousands of pictures of Dylan with different girls on the web, with many of them claiming that they were the "mystery woman," even Tony's crew hadn't been able to figure out which one might actually be Tia.

When he got the call from his pilot that the chopper was in the air, he poured himself two fingers of scotch. It was way early, but he was ready to do some celebrating—he was looking forward to seeing his old friend, and was adding up the dollar signs that his appearance would add to Tony's own bank account.

Tia had had an amazing time at *Paddy's*, and considered the first hurdle of her new public relationship with Dylan a success. Being with her friends, it was fairly easy to push the next one to the back of her mind, but as her first appearance on live TV loomed closer, she was freaking out a little. Maybe more than a little. Never in a million years had she imagined that she'd be the subject of anything that had the word "international" in front of it, and she certainly never dreamed that she'd be the much-anticipated guest on a television show that was expected to have viewers in numbers on par with the Super Bowl.

Thankfully, Jessa was already in LA, and was working on putting together enough of a wardrobe to get Tia through the first few appearances. The plan was to prep at Tony's house—normally the producers would be in contact with upcoming guests over the course of a few days to go over the questions that would be asked during the interview, but since they didn't have that luxury, the producer would meet them at Tony's and they'd do a crash course there. They were scheduled to arrive around 11:30 (thank goodness for the extra two hours the time zone difference would afford them, Tia thought), and they had to be at the studio by 5:00 for hair, make-up, and prep before going live at 6:00.

Tia was also thankful that Jessa was handling their schedules; which would be nothing short of insane, in her opinion. During the week there would not only be a frenzy of appearances, but shopping trips to buy even more clothes—God knew you couldn't make a public appearance in the same outfit more than once. Dylan had also scheduled a preliminary meeting with his attorney to discuss their part in the upcoming legal proceedings against Penelope and potential civil suit as well as sit-downs with record producers and tour managers to finalize the band's studio time and dates for the fall tour. Since she didn't want to think ahead any farther than the next item on her to-do list, Tia was more than happy to put it all in Jessa's capable hands.

They were both looking very forward to seeing her again, but they weren't going to have much time for a reunion—their public commitments were going to more than fill their waking hours. Wednesday morning they were off to New York to do it all over again, and then to Sydney on Friday, where she'd meet Dylan's entire family. *Could I fit a few more things in a week?* she thought wryly as she stared out the window at the landscape unfolding below her. *Maybe I could climb Everest, or win the Nobel Peace Prize.*

"You OK?" Dylan asked, taking her hand and pulling her from her nervous thoughts.

She looked at him and smiled. "I'm good," she said, leaning up to kiss him tenderly. "I'm just coming to terms with a few things, I guess." She sighed, and leaned into him. "It's kind of hard to believe that my whole life is going to change in just a few hours."

"I know," he said, shaking his head sadly. "I'm sorry."

She looked at him, her eyebrows raised. "Don't you for a minute be sorry! It's going to be different, is all, and you," she said, squeezing his hand, "are more than worth it." He smiled down at her, and rested his lips on the top of her head. "Really, Dylan, I knew this was going to happen eventually. I hoped for it even, because it would mean that we could really be together. I just didn't expect that there'd be so much freaking hype about the whole thing, you know? I kind of thought it would be like a little burp; a quick story and maybe my fifteen minutes of fame. It's just a bit more than I expected."

"A burp?" Dylan chuckled. "That's an interesting way to describe it. But you're right; if it weren't for the damn Penelope situation, it would've been a lot simpler. She really fucked this up for us."

"I know," she sighed. "I've thought about it a lot, but in the end it really doesn't matter because you are what I want, Dylan, no matter how crazy it all gets. Those months without you..."

"Are behind us, and are never going to happen again," he promised, pulling her closer.

"I know that, and I know it'll be easier when you go back to Colorado because..."

"Tia," he whispered, "I don't want a long-distance relationship. The last thing in the world I want is distance between us. I want you to come and *live* with me in Colorado."

"Oh!" she gasped. It wasn't as though she hadn't considered the possibility of moving to be with him—she'd dreamed of it over the past seven months actually, a lot—it was just that things were happening so quickly in the past couple days that she hadn't had time to really think about what came after Australia. She felt a huge bubble of joy rise up inside her and surface as a smile.

"After you left me in Europe I felt like I'd lost a part of myself. No matter how small, and believe me, the bed in that trailer was small, every bed I slept in felt empty without you beside me. I don't want that feeling ever again."

"Oh Dylan," she said, unable to find the words she wanted.

"You don't have to decide anything right now—I didn't mean to put another thing on your plate when it's already so full—you have plenty of time to think about it..."

"Are you serious?" she exclaimed, pulling away to look at him so he could see the conviction on her face. "I don't have to think about anything! I've already been dreading saying goodbye to you again. I'd go anywhere to be with you."

"That's what I was hoping you'd say," he said with a smile. "I meant it Tia, when I said I never want us to be apart again. I mean, there'll be traveling for me, sure, and we'll work that out, but I never want permanent distance between us again."

"Me either."

"All the next steps we take together."

She pulled away to look up at him. "You know the funny thing?"

"What?"

"I still haven't decided if I'm more nervous about appearing on TV in front of millions of people or about meeting your family. I don't really care what the rest of the world thinks of me, but I care a lot about what they think. I really want them to like me."

"They're going to love you, trust me. Not just because I do, but because you're an amazing person. All you need to do is be yourself. My parents are very down to earth and easy going. You should be a lot more nervous about meeting Tony. Now that guy's a trip!"

Jessa was there, waiting on the tarmac, when the copter touched down on the massive estate. Tia stood back and let Dylan embrace her first, her heart melting as she overheard the apologies he whispered into her ear.

"I know," she said, stepping up on her toes to kiss his cheek as an uncharacteristic tear fell down her own. "I'm sorry too, but it's behind us now and I intend for it stay there. There'll be a little bit of time for a reunion later and you can tell me how much you missed me and couldn't live without me; but right now, we have a lot to do."

"Bloody hell it's good to have you back."

"It's good to be back." Jessa threw her arms around Tia next. "I can't even begin to tell you how sorry I am," she whispered. "I can't believe that bitch got the upper hand on me! I'm so glad you're together again."

"I'm glad we're all together again," Tia replied honestly. "And she fooled all of us, so you have nothing to be sorry for—seriously."

Jessa hustled them onto an oversized golf cart and they drove the winding trail to the main house. As they pulled up, Tony sauntered out the front door and smiled. "Dylan Miller, you crazy bastard!" he said. "Guess Hollywood finally caught up to you, eh?" Dylan grinned as Tony pulled him into a quick embrace. "Your assistant is a bit on the fiery side, isn't she?" he said quietly before releasing him. Dylan smirked and nodded slightly.

"Good to see you, mate!" Dylan replied. He stepped back and looked Tony over. "You're looking pretty fit for an old man!"

"Yeah, well, divorce agrees with me, it seems," he said lightly. "Although the alimony payments are a serious bitch! But," he shrugged, "what can you do? None of them seem to be able to keep up with me."

"What was this, number four?" Dylan mused. "Did I even meet this latest one? What was she around, a couple months?"

Tony smirked. "Number three, and eight months," he said, "but can I help it if it just wasn't meant to be?"

"Yeah, well I'm sure the right one's out there somewhere," Dylan joked.

"That remains to be seen," he said, "but you know I'll have a hell of a lot of fun looking."

Jessa stepped up to them and cleared her throat loudly. "I hate to break up your little reunion," she announced, "but we have a lot of details to cover in a very short time, and we really need to get to work."

Tony rolled his eyes at Dylan and strolled toward Tia. "So, you must be the beautiful mystery woman the world is dying to know about!" He took Tia's hand and lightly kissed the back of it.

"Tony Granger, meet Tia Hastings—number one and only," Dylan said proudly.

"Very nice to meet you," Tia said shyly. Dylan was right—this guy was a trip. He was an imposing figure; Dylan was six foot two, and Tony had at least another couple inches on him. His overall demeanor dripped with confidence and self-assurance, his voice commanded an audience, and he carried himself with an easy grace that made it seem as if the world were his for the taking. His smile, however, was genuine, and she knew that if

Dylan called him a friend, he had to be the real deal. She met his eyes and tried to smile confidently.

"The pleasure is mine," he beamed. "It's good to see Dylan Miller serious about something in his life," he joked. "Now maybe I can be at the top of the most eligible bachelor list for a change!"

He swept them inside and into a comfortably furnished room that was about the size of Tia's entire house. A huge spread of sandwiches, salads, and desserts was laid out on a long table, and Tony poured wine from his own vineyard into crystal glasses. For the next two hours, they went over the format of the show and the information they wanted to cover in the hour time slot. As much as Tia loved reliving the happy details of their relationship, especially since she had to keep them hidden for so long, she was becoming increasingly aware that soon the stories would no longer belong to her, Dylan, and their inner circle of friends and family; but to the whole world. Their private lives would be discussed over water coolers and in break rooms everywhere, and the thought made her a bit uncomfortable. As much as she tried not to think about it, she wondered what her life might be like if the public didn't find her worthy of Dylan Miller—if they were disappointed in his choice.

"What do you say, Tia?" Tony prodded, pulling her out of her own melancholy thoughts.

"What?" Tia said, shaking her head. "I'm sorry, I didn't catch what you said," she murmured apologetically.

Dylan moved closer to her on the couch and took her hand. "Tony asked if you feel comfortable with the "spontaneous introduction,"" he repeated.

"Oh, sure, fine," she said, trying to pull herself back into the present. The spots the network was running to advertise the show planted the seed that they might just fill in the question mark in the "love triangle," and wanted to make the audience wait until the second half of the show before bringing Tia on stage. If nothing else, it gave her another half hour to calm her nerves and practice with Jessa and a coach from the show. There was no turning back now, so she really just wanted to get through it; hoping that each subsequent appearance would get easier. "I'm up for whatever you decide," she said, forcing a smile.

"Excellent!" Tony said, clapping his hands together. "I really appreciate you giving me the first shot, both of you. The ratings are going to be through the roof, I promise." Then, turning to Tia, he added, "Don't worry though, darling—the audience will be fairly small. Just ignore the cameras and pretend we're sitting here, a few friends sharing a conversation..."

"Just picture them all in their underwear, right?" Tia joked, taking a deep breath and a small sip of the Chardonnay.

"Something like that," Tony smiled, reaching over to pat her hand. "Don't worry about a thing, really. It won't be as hard as you think. You'll be great!"

Tia had to spend a lot more time in make-up than Dylan, so he and Tony moved to their shared dressing room to catch up; avoiding the self-important TV execs and managers that buzzed around the Green Room texting and barking orders into their cell phones.

"It really is damn good to see you, Dylan," Tony said sincerely. "It's been too long."

"You too, mate," Dylan replied. "These damn crazy lives we lead don't leave much time for some of the things that really matter, do they?"

"You can say that again," he agreed. Tony waggled his eyebrows. "So, as long as we're on the subject of things that matter, I have to ask...and this is friend to friend—not for the show."

"Shoot." Dylan raised his eyebrow and tilted his head.

"I have to tell you, the two of you are really adorable together, and I don't say that very often—I mean, I can't even believe that the word "adorable" just came out of my mouth. Is this thing between you and Tia pretty serious?"

Dylan smiled, and decided to let Tony in on the secret. "Serious as a bloody heart-attack, my friend. Tomorrow, while the girls are shopping, I'm meeting with someone from Harry Winston. I'm going to ask her to marry me on New Year's Eve."

"No shit!" he said, standing and pulling Dylan into an embrace. "Congratulations in advance! Spectacular man, really, although a lot of hearts are going to be breaking around the world when that announcement comes out!"

"I've never given a damn about the rest of the world Tony, you know that," he said with a grin. "But it is big. It's going to keep us in the spotlight for longer than I feel comfortable, that's for sure. But she's the one, there's no doubt about it, and I don't want to waste any more time not having her be my wife."

"I'm thrilled for you, man, I really am. When do you think you'll do the deed?"

Dylan laughed. "I haven't even asked her yet! But, seeing as she's already agreed to move in with me, I'm pretty confident that she'll say yes." When Tony looked at him intently, he shrugged and continued. "As soon as possible, I guess. I know it takes some time to plan these things, but I'm hoping for Spring. Maybe end of May, if we can get it together. We met on Memorial Day weekend, so it would already be an anniversary of sorts."

Tony's face skewed for a moment, and his face twisted up in contemplation. "Give me just a minute in my own head, will you?" he asked, getting up and pacing the room without waiting for an answer. Dylan watched his facial expressions shift as if he were in deep thought. He could almost see Tony's mind working, especially when he started texting furiously and jotting notes on a little spiral pad he pulled from the inside pocket of his jacket. Dylan heard the swooshes and blips of incoming and outgoing texts, and watched with amusement as Tony mumbled to himself while scribbling figures on the pad. Finally Tony got one more text and smiled wide as he sat down across from Dylan. When he spoke, his face was completely serious.

"Dylan," he started. "I have a proposition for you. It may sound crazy at first, but hear me out, OK?"

Dylan raised an eyebrow. "OK..." he said, his tone cautious. He had no intention of getting married on live television, or subjecting their wedding day to hoards of media, if that was what Tony had in mind.

"It's a win-win situation," he said. "Actually, you can throw about a dozen more wins into the mix. Of course it's up to the two of you to decide, and my feelings won't be hurt if you don't accept..."

"Just spill it, Tony," Dylan said suspiciously.

"I was just thinking about what to give you for a wedding present," he said. "And I decided; what better gift could I give you than your wedding?" A slow smile crept over his face.

"I'm listening," Dylan replied.

Chapter 8

"Welcome to a special live edition of *After Dark*," Tony grinned into the camera. "I'm really glad you could all join me tonight for what promises to be a very special show, and I want to take a minute to thank our producers for allowing me to put all the rumors to rest and answer the questions you've all been asking over the past couple days." He paused, giving the audience a knowing wink. "Now, unless you've been living under a rock for the past week, I know you've seen the news, or read *Person to Person* magazine, and you know that my special guest tonight is none other than Dylan Miller; he's been named, "Sexiest Man on Earth," "Rock's Most Eligible Bachelor," and is a huge star of both stage and screen.

"I won't waste a lot of time with introductions—you know that he's been the subject of a media frenzy involving a bizarre love triangle..." he held up the *Person to Person* cover and waited a beat for the cameras to zoom in, "...numerous criminal activities, and a mystery woman who stole his heart and triggered the alleged jealous rage of Penelope Valentine, Oscar nominated actress and co-star of his latest film." He waited for the applause to die down before continuing.

"Here to tell his story in person for the first time, and to announce to the world whether or not he's found his mystery lady and can fill in this question mark..." he pointed to the lower left corner of the magazine cover and waited again for the extreme close up that filled the monitor, "...is my very good friend. Ladies and gentlemen, Dylan Miller."

The impromptu crowd that had filled the studio rose to their feet and cheered, and would have, regardless of the little electronic sign that signaled them to do so. Dylan strolled confidently out onto the stage, shook hands and shared a man-hug with Tony, and took a seat on the couch at Tony's right after bowing and waving to the audience.

"It's so great to have you here, Dylan,"

"It's great to be here; thanks for having me." He bowed to the audience and Tony had to pause as the applause erupted again.

"Well," Tony started, "I know it's a bit of an understatement, but it seems you've had yourself a little excitement recently."

Dylan smiled. "Understatement indeed...it's been a bloody roller coaster, if you want to know the truth."

Tony once again held up the issue of *Person to Person*. "This says that the article is in your words, but you've always been kind of media-shy and very vocal about avoiding anything that's considered a tabloid. So, did you actually write this?"

"Yeah, I did," Dylan replied. "I pretty much threw it together on the plane on the way back to The States."

"You mean, when you pretty much abandoned your film contract in New Zealand to come back and find your lost love? Why the tabloids?"

"I didn't have much of a choice, really," Dylan replied. "It was the medium she used to fabricate a relationship that didn't exist, and I had to clear that up. I had to do it fast, too, and they were more than happy to accommodate me."

"I bet they were," Tony smiled wryly. "There's some pretty powerful stuff in here." Tony summarized the story, throwing in all the requisite "allegedlys" in order to stay in compliance with the law. "So you're claiming that Penelope Valentine knowingly sabotaged your relationship by cutting off all your communication, so she could have you for herself."

"I can't say exactly what her final intentions were," Dylan said, "but that about sums it up based on what I do know. I'm sure there's a lot more to the story that I don't even know about yet."

"So all the pictures and the stories that appeared in the previous issues of the tabloids—you're saying they were doctored to make it look like you were romantically involved?"

"I haven't seen them all, but I can absolutely tell you that she and I were never on a tropical beach together and that we never did anything that could be considered a date. There was never anything romantic about our relationship, so anything portrayed in that way is complete rubbish."

They chatted for the next fifteen minutes or so about the ordeal, or at least about what Dylan could legally discuss of it. Tia watched nervously from the monitor in the dressing room, gratefully accepting a cup of ice chips from Jessa and crunching them between her teeth in an attempt to control her breathing and keep her mind focused, waiting for the moment they'd rehearsed—the moment when she would walk out of her normal life and into the limelight. She still found it hard to believe that she was the mystery woman they were talking about; the ordinary girl who'd stolen the heart of one of the world's most eligible bachelors. In just a few short minutes the whole world would know that Tia Hastings was more than a mere curiosity. She was a headline.

"Wow, it really has been a roller coaster," Tony said. "So, Penelope's still in New Zealand, sitting in a jail cell and waiting for extradition to the US?"

"I don't give a bloody rat's ass where she is," Dylan spat, "but I hope she's still keeping track of the tabloids she loves so much." He smiled wryly, thinking that some small justice might be done if Penelope had to endure what she'd forced Tia to go through—being alone and without any possible contact with him and being bombarded with pictures of him and Tia pursuing their happily ever after. He knew that this show was being syndicated all over the world, and although he'd never considered himself a vengeful person, part of him hoped she was watching right now.

"What would you say to her, if you had the chance?" Tony prompted.

"I have absolutely nothing to say to her," Dylan said. "Not a single word."

"Well, there you have it folks, right from the man himself," Tony said to the camera. "We here at *After Dark* will keep you posted on the newest developments as they become available, and hope that whatever happens, justice will prevail." The audience cheered, and Tony again waited for the applause to die down.

"After the break, we'll get to the question everyone is dying to have answered. Did Dylan find his lost love, did she take him back, and are they still together? Stay with us—this is sure to be the news that'll have everyone talking! Be right back!"

The light announcing the commercial break came on and Tony sat back in his chair and took a swig from his coffee mug. One of the assistants ran out to let him know that Tia was ready, and that she seemed as calm as could be expected given the circumstances. Dylan breathed a sigh of relief; although the average person thought it would be incredible to be on television, especially in this capacity, he and Tia knew all too well that it was much different than most imagined. He turned to Tony and excused himself, jogging back to the dressing room and throwing open the door. Tia came directly into his arms.

"How you doing, baby girl?" he smiled.

She looked up at him confidently. "I was having a minor cardiac episode, but I'm better now," she mumbled, pulling him close. "This helps."

He pressed his lips to her forehead, careful not smudge the stage make-up and was glad to see Jessa give him a thumbs-up when he caught her eye. "I'll see you in two minutes, then," he said. "We're in this together, OK? You're going to be absolutely brilliant, I promise you."

She smiled back. "You're a pretty easy guy to love, you know that Miller?"

"I love you too," he whispered as an assistant rushed in to wave him back to the stage. "Always and forever." He blew her a kiss, and whisked through the door.

"Welcome back to a very special edition of *After Dark*," Tony said to the camera. "My guest tonight, as you well know, is none other than Dylan Miller, and I don't think I can wait another minute to ask what's on everyone's minds." The audience inhaled, and moved to the edges of their seats.

Tony turned to Dylan. "At the end of the *Person to Person* article, it says that 'you have to go and find her—try to make it right.'" He paused for effect, and could almost feel the anticipation fill the room. Tony leaned in and almost whispered, "Did you? Did you find her?"

The audience held their collective breath. Tony did a great job laying the foundation, leading them up to this question. It was what millions of viewers had tuned in to see—did love prevail in the end?

Dylan let his famous smile slide slowly onto his face for the camera. "I left New Zealand and went to find her straight away," he said. "And I did. Just a couple days ago—on Friday."

The crowd cheered, their hands clutched in anticipation.

"And?" Tony prodded.

Dylan looked down shyly and his smile told the story before his voice did. "Well...I'm very glad to say that there is a happy ending in all of this mess, Tony. Turns out she never stopped loving me either."

The crowd rose to their feet as Dylan's eyes lifted to meet them and his smile grew even bigger. "That's how I felt, too," he told them conspiratorially. "Times about a million."

Tony waited for the cheers of the crowd to die down before asking, "I'm thrilled to hear it! So where does it go from here, Dylan?"

"It only goes up from here," he said with a smile. "I've got the woman I love, so no matter what else happens, I win." The applause from the small audience was almost deafening.

"Now, this had to be quite a shock for her, too," Tony said. "I mean, her life was stolen away as well—allegedly—and she had to feel pretty hopeless at the time. What does she think about the whole thing? I mean, it's pretty unbelievable—this is like the stuff of romance novels. How did she react when she saw you? Obviously she'd seen the tabloid pictures, and thought you'd moved on…" Tony prompted.

"It's been quite a whirlwind, as you can imagine," he answered. "It's a lot of ups and downs, and it doesn't help that it's been a crazy couple days and that she's been thrown into this media blitz. She's not a movie star or a public figure, so she's not used to the kind of attention that's been thrust upon her. She's incredibly strong, though, and holding up as well as can be imagined—better even." He looked toward the stage entrance before turning back to Tony. "We're going to plan a future together, and we…" he paused, and looked at Tony. "You know, actually, maybe you should ask her."

The crowd indicated that they indeed wanted to hear it from her, whether Tony wanted to or not. It was exactly the way he had wanted it to play out, and he had a hard time keeping the surprised look on his face.

"She's here? Really? Well, I don't think there's any question that the world is dying to meet her." He paused for effect, then looked at Dylan. "Why don't you make the introductions?" Then he turned toward the audience and shook his finger at them, adding sarcastically, "And you be nice—I know there are more than a few of you out there whose hearts are already broken that the man's no longer available!"

The audience agreed.

"It would be my absolute pleasure," Dylan said, turning toward the audience and the camera. "I'm proud to introduce you to the most incredible and beautiful woman in the world, the woman I love, Tia Hastings."

The audience rose to its feet yet again as Tia walked onto the stage and the world got their first glimpse of the woman who'd won Dylan Miller's heart. Dylan vaulted deftly over the back of the couch, catching her in an embrace and tilting her back for a kiss; part for the audience, part for moral support. "They love you already," he whispered as he led her over to where Tony was standing. Tony took both her hands in his and kissed her cheek, and she sat on the couch with Dylan's arm firmly around her shoulders. The audience applauded long after the sign went dim, giving Tia another moment to catch her breath. She looked out at the audience and smiled, amazed at the grins, waves, thumbs-ups, and even a few tears being directed at her by total strangers—it was both incredible and disconcerting at the same time.

Tony looked surprised. "You weren't kidding, Dylan, she's beautiful!"

Dylan smiled and nodded his agreement, gesturing toward her and getting another approving roar from the crowd.

"Hello, Tia."

"Hi Tony."

He shook his head as he waited for the audience to quiet. "Wow. I don't even know where to begin. I've known Dylan for a lot of years, and I can honestly tell you that I've never seen such a huge smile on his face. Someone might want to put that face on a magazine cover or something, I'm just saying," he joked. He waited a beat for the laughter to die down and turned back to Tia. "This whole thing must be a little overwhelming for you."

"Yet another understatement," she smiled. "I'm still pinching myself, actually. It's been a really crazy couple of days."

"I can only imagine what it's been like for you. I mean, you pretty much went from zero to sixty faster than a Ferrari...can you take us through what's happened?"

She took a deep breath and cleared her throat. "Wow, I'm not sure I even can! Dylan described it pretty well; it's kind of been like riding a roller coaster or a really big wave. It's been so crazy I have to remind myself to breathe sometimes." She took a big breath to emphasize the point. "Everything's happened so fast, like you said, that I'm still trying to make sense of it all. Two days ago I was still trying to figure out how I could live without him; we hadn't had any communication at all for months, and I'd given up hope that I'd ever even see him again. Then all of a sudden not only is he back, but I find out I never really lost him in the first place. That in itself is a lot to take in; and then you add all this..." she swept her hand across the audience, "...and it becomes too big to even describe with words. But I do have one thing I really want to say."

"The floor is yours."

She looked at Dylan. "I am absolutely, positively, in love with this man, and it's not just because of his pretty face. He's an incredible person—he's warm, funny, generous, caring—when I thought I'd lost him, I was devastated. Having him back in my life is more incredible than I can begin to tell you." She choked on the last words, and Dylan buried his face in her neck. Her mic picked up his soft whisper, "God, I love you, baby girl," and Tony smiled. *Media gold*, he thought as the audience burst into applause.

"All this media stuff is new to me, and to be honest, I never expected it would be such a big deal, so forgive me if I'm a bit overwhelmed. It's a lot to take in at one time; especially since I really want to focus on being back with Dylan."

Tony pressed his lips together and nodded in understanding. "Oh yeah, we can definitely be overwhelming. I imagine you felt that way when Dylan suddenly showed up again, out of the blue, after being gone for so long. He said in the *Person to Person* article that he rushed back from New Zealand, maybe even breaking his contractual obligation with the studio, with the sole purpose of finding you. How did that happen?"

Tia smiled, amazed that she was able to push out the cameras and the audience and just focus on the conversation. Dylan's arm was securely around her shoulder, and his other hand crossed his body and rested on her leg. Tony was a friend, and knowing that Dylan trusted him was enough to help her relax. She cocked her head, searching for the right words. "It was...surreal I guess would be the best explanation. I was at work, actually—I'm a teacher—

and we were in a staff meeting when our secretary came in and made a big deal about no one hassling the man she was about to introduce. It happened so fast that I didn't even have time to imagine that it might be Dylan; and even when he was standing right in front of me, it took me a minute to process that it was really him."

"How about your coworkers? It's got to be a bit unusual to preface an introduction like that...did some of them guess it might be him?"

"None of them knew the truth about who Dylan really was, actually," she admitted.

Tony looked truly surprised. "Wait a minute," he said, "you were dating Dylan Miller, one of the most sought after bachelors in the world, for months, and your co-workers didn't know it? How is that even possible?"

"Nobody knew his real identity," she said, "except for my best friend, and only because she was going to the InHap show with me the night after we met."

"Wait, are you saying that not even your family knew?"

"Nope," she smiled. "That's been another big part of the whirlwind the past couple days. I finally got to introduce him to my family and friends; and share all the stories I couldn't tell them before."

Tony snapped to attention, and turned to one of the producers before coming back to the camera. "My producer is reminding me that we need to take a commercial break," he said. "We'll hear more about this when we come back. Stay right where you are."

The woman behind the camera signaled that they were off the air, and a shaggy-headed teenager scurried over with a couple bottles of water. "You rock," he whispered as he handed Dylan the chilled bottle. He ran off before they could even thank him.

"Spectacular!" Tony exclaimed. "You're a natural, Tia; they're in love with you already."

"I agree completely," Dylan added, pressing a kiss to the top of her head. "Brilliant."

"It's easier than I thought it would be," she admitted. "I was so nervous at first, but I'm actually feeling OK." An audience member answered her with a "Go Tia!" which earned him a round of applause.

"On in ten," the camerawoman announced; counting down. "Three, two," and a point of her finger signaled they were back live.

Tony shook his head. "Welcome back," he said, "if you're just joining us, you've missed out on some startling revelations. Tia informed us, just before we went to commercial, that up until yesterday, her best friend was the only person in her life who knew that she was dating Dylan Miller." He raised his eyebrows at Dylan. "Were you bothered by that?"

"Actually, I was impressed," Dylan said. "I have to say it's one of the things I love best about her. For Tia it was never about being involved with someone famous. They all knew she was in a relationship; they knew I played in a band, knew my first name; but that was it. She never wanted to flaunt it, because she knew she'd lose some of her individuality once it was out there."

"It was so hard," Tia admitted. "Again, not because he was famous, but because I wanted so badly to tell the whole world who I was in love with—especially my friends and family. I hated not being able to tell them everything."

"So why keep it a secret, then?" Tony asked honestly.

"When we first met, I thought I'd have a weekend with him, at the most," Tia started. "He was playing in Chicago for a couple nights, going on to Cleveland, then heading to Europe for the summer, and of course to New Zealand to film the movie. The first couple nights he even kept telling me that he couldn't make me any promises, and that it might be easier if we just walked away before things had a chance to get too intense. I wanted to keep him to myself then, because I knew we'd only have a short time together. I didn't want to share him with anyone."

"So, you only knew him a couple weeks before he invited you on the tour, then?"

Tia and Dylan shared a smile, and he interjected. "I only knew her a couple *days* before I asked her to go to Europe, Tony. It all happened so fast—neither of us expected it, neither of us was even close to looking for it, but we both felt something pretty powerful. Bringing her on the tour was the only way we could explore it further, because it would've been nearly a year before I'd even be back in The States again."

"Luckily, my job gives me summers off."

"That's for sure," Dylan agreed. "It dawned on me on what I thought would be our last night together—it was Memorial Day, and I had to fly out the next morning for a gig. I tried to put the situation out of my mind; tried to chalk it up to an amazing chance encounter, but I just couldn't imagine letting her walk away."

Tony's eyes were wide and he shook his head slowly in contemplation. "Wow, this has to be one of the best stories I've heard on my show, and I've been doing this a long time. Almost sounds like a little bit of, at the risk of being cliché, incidental happenstance?"

"The very best sort," Dylan agreed.

He turned back to Tia. "So, what's next for you, then, Tia? I have a very strong feeling that your days of anonymity are behind you...there are a lot of changes in your future, my dear. Do you think you'll be able to go back to your job? Do you even want to?"

Tia sighed. "I can't even think past today, to be honest with you," she said. "The rest of this week is full of interviews, and then we're going to spend the holidays in Australia with Dylan's family. I'm having a hard enough time wrapping my head around that."

"Oh yeah," Tony said, "meeting the folks—that's always an adventure!"

"I think I was less nervous about being here than I am about that," she admitted. "But we haven't had much of a chance to really discuss what comes next. Right now, we're taking it day by happy day."

"Am I right, though, in saying that this isn't the first time you've been in front of a big crowd?" he asked slyly. "Would you be the Mystery Wembley Girl? The one who took over singing harmony for Ty Waters when his voice wasn't up to scratch at one of the London shows?"

Tia smiled huge, remembering. "Yup, that was me alright."

"I understand there was a big to-do in the British tabloids about that," he said.

"There was, but they got my name wrong, and the pictures were too fuzzy to identify me, so I was still in the clear."

"So I have to ask, how did the two of you meet? You have to admit, a school teacher and a rock star are a pretty unlikely match."

Dylan looked at his watch and smiled. "I don't think there's enough time left to tell that story; it could fill a whole show."

Tony looked at his own watch. "You're right—I'm afraid we are running out of time, which is too bad, because I've got so many more questions!"

Dylan pulled Tia close. "I'll tell you this, Tony. We have a lot of future plans to discuss because I plan a future with this woman." The crowd broke into applause. "Right now, though, I'm just so happy to have her back in my life, and we're taking it one day at a time. I'll keep you posted though."

"I'm counting on it, and expect to see you back here again soon. But on that note, we are out of time, so until then, I wish you both a little luck and a lot of happiness!"

He closed the show, and then the three of them walked down into the audience, shaking hands and receiving well-wishes from the crowd.

*****

Ryan and Jace sat at a table in *Smitty's Sports Bar*, nursing Fat Tires and glancing occasionally at the Packers /Vikings game that dominated the huge televisions spread around the pub. It wasn't one of their usual hang-outs by any means, but they were sick of driving and parking only to walk into a place and see a sign that advertised that they'd be showing the *After Dark* special airing at 8:00. Although Tia's name wasn't yet public knowledge, it seemed that enough folks in town either knew that it would be Tia on the program or that the mystery woman was a local and had convinced their usual hangouts to air the show.

He'd begged off Lexi's numerous requests to attend the viewing party at the pub, much to her chagrin. "It's a once in a lifetime event, Ryan. How could you not watch Tia's television debut?" she'd asked.

Ryan had gotten more than his fill of Tia's "debut" the night before, spending several hours sitting alone and watching Lexi bask in the limelight cast by her best friend. He'd spent the whole damn day on the fringes of it all, actually, first at the club and then at *Paddy's*. He watched all the country club people fawning all over Tia, acting like she was suddenly everyone's best friend even though most of them had barely spared her a polite hello prior to her attachment to Dylan Miller. The last thing he wanted to do was to spend his Sunday night there, too.

He and Jace had met first at the club, but it didn't take long to determine that they were setting up for an event. Turned out that they were hosting a viewing party for the show too, complete with a buffet and full bar. They took one look at each other and without saying a word, walked out to find a different venue at which to spend their evening.

The game was tied at 10 and the Packers were on the 30 yard line with three minutes to go in the half when they heard the announcement. "Ladies and Gentleman, if I can have your attention, please!" one of the servers bellowed. "We've just found out that there's going to be a special edition of *After Dark* starting in a few minutes, and that they're going to announce on the show that Dylan Miller's mystery girl is from right here in Chicago! A number of you have asked if we can tune in, and since some of it'll be during half time, we're going to show it on the televisions in the bar section. We'll keep the game on in the dining area, so if you want to move, you should settle up with your server and make your way—it starts in ten minutes."

"Seriously?" Jace asked incredulously as Ryan just shook his head. He glanced around the room and saw the African-American woman who'd been at the pub last night—the school secretary, if he remembered correctly—followed by a little entourage of teachers from Tia's school. He and Jace simultaneously picked up their mugs and drained their beers, grabbing their coats and wordlessly heading for the exit.

*****

"Hey Fancy Pants," the guard said to the woman in the cell. "Got somethin' here you ought to see. My cousin in America sent it to me."

"Fuck off," Penelope said unenthusiastically.

Madeline ignored her and set her laptop outside of Penelope's cell, turned up the volume, and struck a key. And as much as Penelope didn't want to look, didn't want to know, Dylan was on the screen, and she couldn't turn away.

Madeline watched with interest as Penelope's facial expressions went from elation to devastation when the host, a good looking guy named Tony Granger, asked Dylan Miller; who was absolutely smokin' hot in Madeline's opinion; if he had found the girl he was looking for.

""Well...I'm very happy to say that there is a happy ending in all of this mess, Tony," the beautiful man said. "Turns out she never stopped loving me either."

For a moment, silent tears streamed down the prisoner's face. Then, he said that his woman was there with him and introduced her, slipping her a juicy kiss right there in front of the whole world. That's when the prisoner went off the edge.

Penelope had remained stoic during her detention; refusing to speak to anyone unless absolutely necessary, eating only enough of the absolute shit they tried to pass off as food to keep her alive, and trying to maintain her dignity in her less than dignified situation. Once again, she pulled from her Oscar nominated acting skills to show the peons who ran this place that they couldn't touch her—couldn't break her. Surely, she thought, Dylan would come to his senses at some point and realize that what she'd done, she'd done for love. They'd shared too much over the past few months for him to just walk away and leave her.

Damn it, it only took a couple *days* for him to fall for that *bitch*, and she had so much more to offer than that Tia chick could ever give him.

But now she watched them on the screen, unable to turn her head away even though it crushed something inside her to see them together; her eyes locked on Dylan's smiling face as he pulled Tia into his arms...

"AAARRRUGGGG!" she screamed, the strangled cry exploding from somewhere deep inside her and bouncing back and forth off the bare walls of the tiny cell, echoing and mocking her. Her features contorted and she lost her hold on self-control. She started flinging things at the wall—magazines, her smelly, flat pillow, the blanket off the bed. There was precious little in the room to hurl, however, and none of it crashed, broke, or made her feel even the slightest bit better. What she wanted to do was to smash the laptop—to watch Tia's smug and smiling fucking face disappear in a spider web of broken glass; shattered just like Penelope was shattered. But the guard had it just maddeningly out of her grasp, and the fat cunt laughed when she tried desperately to reach it. Instead, she flashed Penelope an evil grin and leaned over to hit the replay button; Dylan's mellow voice now echoing with her own moans. She howled in sadness and broke into huge racking sobs, pushed her palms against her ears to block it all out and slid to the floor, defeated.

She'd kept hoping that she would wake up from this nightmare, but apparently what she'd done—little things really—intercepting a few letters, fiddling with a computer and a phone, selling some slightly doctored photos—was being blown way out of proportion. And because she'd been in this godforsaken country there were charges stacking up on two continents, and they couldn't even tell her when she'd be able to go home. Not that she had anything to go back to.

She'd thought that if she could explain things to Dylan; just talk to him, he'd understand, and maybe even forgive her eventually. She kept waiting for him to show up here, but obviously he'd left at the first opportunity and run straight to *her* and he wasn't coming back. He'd actually said, on national television, that he had nothing to say to her. Not ever.

The hopelessness of her situation drowned her—if Dylan and that damn teacher were on national television, it was only a matter of time before her fucking mother and sister would see how she'd screwed up her life. Again. She could just picture the bitches and their smug faces with their 'I told you so's and their 'she deserves it's.' All hope gone, she curled into fetal position in the corner of the room, tucked her head in the crook of her elbow, and let the tears come.

Chapter 9

Tia felt like she'd been tossed around in a tornado by the time they got to the studio on Tuesday morning; not a good place to be right before a photo shoot for an international magazine; the name of which she didn't know and didn't really care. She'd been moving so much the past couple days that she was actually looking forward to sitting in the make-up chair and closing her eyes for a few minutes.

"Mr. Miller, Miss Hastings, we're so happy to be working with you this morning!" said a heavy-set woman wearing too much eye makeup. A small troupe of others rushed up to shake their hands as they were swept into the room. There were several different areas set up with a variety of themes; a garden, a street scene, a park, and a cozy room with a stone fireplace and a red velvet chaise lounge.

A young girl with hoops in her ears, lower lip, and right nostril rushed up to greet Dylan. "I don't know if you remember me," she said, batting her lashes, "but I worked with you about a year ago on the shoot for 'Remember Yesterday.' I did your hair and makeup..."

"Of course," Dylan said, flashing his celebrity smile. "You did a great job."

"Oh, well, you're so easy," she breathed, "not much work needed at all. I'm so excited to work with you again."

Tia rolled her eyes as the woman flirted with her man. Dylan caught her look and rolled his back.

"You're so lucky," Sarah, the makeup artist told her as she smeared creams into Tia's skin. "He's just so dreamy..."

"Don't I know it," she answered as Sarah swirled a large makeup brush over her face. "On both counts."

"You've got great cheekbones. And I just love the color of your eyes. We can pretty much go in any direction you want—this is your chance to reinvent yourself. Or, invent yourself, I guess, since you're kind of new to the whole celebrity scene. We can go completely glamorous or...oh! How about 50's starlet? We can do an updo, add some lashes..."

"I don't think so," Tia smiled. "That just isn't me. And if I have to be thrust into all of this, I at least want to stay true to myself. I'm not really the glamorous type."

Sarah sat in the swivel chair next to her and turned Tia's to face her. "I totally respect that, really. So why don't you tell me a bit about yourself so I can get it just right. Describe yourself in three words."

Tia raised her eyebrows. "Three words?"

"Yup. The first ones that come to mind that describe you best."

"Hmmm. I guess the first one would be "Earthy." I'm pretty down to earth, and I love nature...you know, hiking, bird watching, that kind of thing."

"OK, what's next?"

"Honest. And then..." words bounced around in her head; it was so hard to narrow yourself down to three adjectives. Finally, she settled on the one that had and would see her and Dylan through any situation. "Loyal."

"I can do that." Sarah opened a drawer and pulled out some pallets of color. "Close your eyes and trust me. We can always wash it off and start over if you hate it, but I'm pretty sure I've got you down."

It was some time before Sara spun Tia's chair around to face the mirror. When she got a look at herself, she sucked in a short gasp. Never in her life had she had so much product on her face—not even the makeup people for the TV shows they'd already done spent so much time, but somehow, she still looked natural. A soft gold shimmered under her eyebrows, and her lids were covered in shades of green that got progressively darker as they reached her temples. The colors made her eyes pop, and her newly-shaped brows looked full and natural under a variety of pencils and powders. Her lashes swept high and dark, and there was just the slightest emerald green line curving below each eye. Sarah had somehow managed to make her skin look flawless, and her lips appeared plump and pouty, with just a touch of color and sparkle. "Wow, you mean I could look like this every day?" she asked. "I absolutely love it!"

"You could if you hired me as your personal makeup artist," Sarah smiled. "It's hardly an everyday application process, but if I do say so myself, you look earthy, honest, and loyal. You two make an adorable couple, by the way."

"Thank you," Tia said in response to the compliment and the job well done.

"We'll get to the kissing pictures later," Marlon, a man in obnoxious orange crop pants and an even more ridiculous flowing paisley shirt, crooned when Dylan pulled her into his arms as she emerged on the set. Dyl just laughed, and planted a gentle kiss on the tip of Tia's nose.

"OK, now look into each other's eyes and give me a soft smile," Marlon, said for about the hundredth time. "A natural one—you love each other!" Once again, Tia smiled for the cameras that clicked softly all around her. Never in all her life had she taken so many pictures at once; six outfits, two makeup 'fresheners,' and four scenery changes had her head reeling and her lips quivering—she didn't know if it was even possible for her to smile anymore. Her entire face felt like it had just undergone a Zumba class and a weight training session...her cheeks and jaw were physically aching. But when Dylan looked at her the way he only looked at her, she couldn't help but smile back.

After the hustle of the photo shoot, the interview was a piece of cake. Bryn Simmons fawned over Dylan for longer than necessary, but when she started asking questions, she was all business. Tia had figured that she'd be answering all the same questions she had on Tony's show and the morning news program and radio talk show they'd done the day before, but Bryn surprised her.

"So, Tia, what's been the hardest part for you in all this?"

"Wow. I guess I'd have to say dealing with all the attention. I'm not used to having people be so interested in the things I do. It's a really awkward feeling, and it's kind of disconcerting, if you want to know the truth."

"Because you want people to like you?"

Tia took a second to think about how to answer the question. Since the airing of Sunday's show, their story had indeed gone viral. Social media was buzzing—Facebook pages had been started in their honor, they'd earned several hashtags on Twitter… *#Dylentia* and *#Frstcouple* were trending regularly. As Dylan had predicted, most of the talk was positive—one blogger had even dubbed her "America's Princess Ti," likening her situation to Diana's rise from the humble beginnings of a school teacher to that of royalty. In this case, Dylan was dubbed, "The Prince of Rock."

But as Dylan had also once said, there were haters, too. "Free Penelope" campaigns were springing up as well, and they called Tia a "poser," a "gold digger," and a "wannabe." Tia was glad that there was precious little time in her schedule these days to dwell on any of it; because she didn't really deserve either status, in her opinion; but as much as she tried to let it roll off her back, some of it stung. OK, a lot of it stung. Not because they said harsh things, but because they said them for reasons Tia couldn't begin to understand. None of them knew her—none of them knew Dylan or Penelope either—but that didn't stop them from boisterously making judgments and calling names. She was reminded of one of her favorite authors who, after writing an incredibly successful children's series, published her first book for adults. The author had taken a holiday when the book was released, presumably because she was smart enough to know that the critics would be out in force because the book wasn't about her beloved character. She was right, too. Initial reviews were terrible, and people who hadn't even read the book were writing scathing posts. Soon, however, it was at the top of the charts, because she's a terrific writer and the real fans soon out spoke the haters.

"I want to be very careful about how I answer that question, because I'm not sure I can make it come across the way I mean it to. As a human being, of course I want people to like me. We're social creatures, and we certainly don't aspire to be *unliked.* But more than that, I don't want people to hate me because of who I fell in love with, or for any other reason outside of my control. I mean, if I've done something to you personally, you can choose not to like me; but the people making these comments don't know me, so I have a hard time with them making judgments, good or bad. I wasn't in New Zealand—I had no part in what happened there. I didn't attack Penelope—to this day I haven't said anything negative about her publicly because I don't really know her, and I don't think it's fair. I certainly don't like what she did—or allegedly did—because of the impact it's had on my life personally; but I don't know what was in her head. That's the double-edged sword of this kind of attention. It doesn't liken itself to developing new relationships because there's always a pre-formed opinion, so it's hard for people to get to know the real you." She took a deep breath and smiled. "I hope that answered your question; I don't really know exactly how to explain it. It's a strange feeling." she said.

"Oh, definitely," Bryn smiled, reaching over to pat Tia's hand. "That's probably one of the most real and honest answers about celebrity I've ever heard. It takes a lot of guts to say it; especially when the jury is still out on your public persona."

"I never wanted a public persona—I just happened to fall for an incredible man who already had one."

"And I think we just got the quote for the cover," Bryn said softly. "You're the real deal, Tia. I have to say I had my doubts, but I really think you guys are going to make it."

"Oh, we'll make it, all right," Dylan smiled. "I have no doubts about us."

It was, without a doubt, the most insane week of Tia's life. Between the interviews, photo shoots, shopping trips, and phone calls, she didn't know whether she was coming or going, and was very glad to have Jessa on her side, especially when Dylan was off taking care of his own business. By the time the week ended, it felt like she'd appeared on just about every talk show in the country, and she wondered if her head would ever stop spinning. She never got tired of talking about her love for Dylan, but she certainly wasn't getting any pleasure out of having to discuss the Penelope situation over and over. Just hearing her name made Tia cringe, but she was part of the story too, and part of every interview they granted. Penelope was still sitting in a jail cell in New Zealand so she wasn't allowed to make any statements, but someone who called herself a "prison director" described a scene in which a very emotionally unstable movie star went ballistic after seeing Dylan and Tia's first television appearance.

News stations were reporting that her lawyers were close to reaching a deal with New Zealand authorities for Penelope's extradition—speculation was that they were willing to settle for an "undisclosed fine," seeing as all the charges applied to US citizens, American tabloids, and mail destined for Americans on both ends. There didn't seem to be any doubt in the lawyers' minds, however, that she'd be facing some prison time if convicted of all charges. And considering that her "former assistant and alleged accomplice" was willing to testify in exchange for a reduced sentence, it didn't look like Penelope was going to be winning any Oscars anytime soon.

By the time Friday night came, Tia felt like a zombie, and she stumbled into the living quarters of the New York suite with just a few hours to pack before they left on a twenty five hour trip to Australia.

Australia. God, she thought, falling onto the bed and throwing her forearm over her eyes. Just an hour, just sixty little minutes to gather her thoughts, and then she could consider packing for a two-week trip that included meeting Dylan's entire family. How would she measure up to their expectations? How could she make any impression at all, with how exhausted she was?

She felt Dylan's presence in the room before he touched her—the slightest brush of his lips against her own. She moaned; part desire, part irritation, and gave herself over to his kiss.

"Mmmm," she mumbled. "I haven't left your side for most of the week, but I still miss you."

"I know," he said sympathetically. "It's really draining, isn't it, being the center of so much attention?" It was more a statement than a question.

"Yeah, kind of sucks," she said. "But you get used to it, right? Oh God, please tell me it gets easier."

"A little bit, I guess," he whispered, sliding his hand beneath her shirt and stroking her nipples with the rough pads of his fingers. "You've been amazing, Tia. Just by being yourself, you've gotten the whole world to fall in love with you."

It was true. In just one short week Tia Hastings, fifth grade teacher, had become a media darling. Bryn put out some of the pictures and excerpts from the interview on the magazine's website in advance of the issue, and it had gotten something like a gazillion hits.

"I don't care about the whole world, baby...as long as you love me, it's all that matters."

"Let me show you how much," he said, nibbling his way down her neck deliciously.

She purred, then grunted. "Look at the clock, Dyl, we've only got a few hours to pack, shower, and head for the airport."

"I can be quick," he smiled against her collarbone.

"I don't want you to be quick," she whispered. "I haven't been able to stop thinking about 'deliciously slow,' and there's not nearly enough time." But when he slid his hand up her thigh, she surrendered. "Oh, I can't say no to you; not when you're doing that."

She wrapped her arms around his neck and pulled him down to her, wiggling beneath him until their bodies molded together seamlessly. He pressed his mouth to hers, and her exhaustion lifted as her pulse quickened and her hands moved down to rest at his waist. "Have I told you today how amazing you are?" he breathed into her ear.

"Not in the past ten minutes," she smiled against his neck. No matter how exasperated she'd gotten at the crazy pace of the week and the breakneck schedule, Dylan was her constant cheerleader and support system. He knew how emotionally draining it was for her to have to rehash the Penelope situation over and over, and made it his personal mission to tell her how incredible she was and how much he loved her every chance he got. It had definitely kept her more upbeat, and she felt good knowing he was proud of her.

"Positively amazing," he said, running his hands down the sides of her body. "Beautiful too."

"I love you so much, baby. I couldn't have done any of it without you."

"And I can't do this without you," he smiled, slipping her shirt over her head and pressing his body to hers.

Chapter 10

Realization finally dawned on her, and it wasn't the kind of dawn that lit up the sky with pinks and oranges and promises of a beautiful day. Hers was the one that crept up slowly behind gray, dark clouds; casting only enough light to cloak the world in perpetual shadow. She was stuck—trapped was a better word, actually—and life as she knew it was over. When she finally cried herself out and the guard had tired of taunting her and left, she felt like she'd been sucker-punched in the gut, taken a right hook to the face, and been dealt a roundhouse kick in the head.

Reality hit like a ton of bricks.

"Get me the hell out of here, Ben," she hissed at the computer screen where her lawyer was taking notes from his spacious office with the incredible view, picking something out of his teeth as if she couldn't see him. "This is bullshit and you know it. They can't keep me here. I'm an American citizen."

"It's not that easy, Penelope. You've gotten yourself into a lot of trouble, and it's going to take some time to get it all unraveled. There are a colorful variety of charges stacking up on two continents, and our legal systems don't work exactly the same way. I've retained an attorney there in New Zealand to handle the paperwork and such on your end, and I'm meeting with the federal prosecutor the day after tomorrow to get an idea of what charges you'll have to face over here. But you need to remember that it's almost Christmas. A lot of people are on holidays this time of year and it might take a little longer to get the ball rolling."

Penelope leaned back in the chair and ground the heels of her hands into her closed eyes. Less than a week ago she believed that she'd be in Australia for Christmas; meeting Dylan's family and moving their relationship to a whole new glorious level. Never in a million years would she have guessed that she would be spending it in a goddamn jail cell instead. "Are you telling me that I might have to spend Christmas here? What about bail?"

Ben dropped his eyes. "I'm telling that you *are* going to be spending it there, I'm afraid, and probably New Year's, too. There are a lot of facets to this situation, and they aren't going to be resolved in a couple days. You're the poster child of a flight risk, Penelope, and you don't have anywhere to go if they let you out. The studio won't take you, and you don't have anyone there who can even post it for you. The bright side is that the New Zealand authorities want you gone; especially since all of your crimes involved Americans; so I think we can get you back here fairly soon. Understand, though, that your troubles are far from over once you get back to the States."

"Jesus Christ! This is being blown totally out of proportion, Ben, and you know it. They're trying to throw the book at me because I'm famous and my case will get them on television. You know, couples break up every day, and lots of them have a little help from a third party. Just plead temporary insanity and be done with it already, so I can go the fuck home." Her eyes narrowed and her voice dropped a couple decibels as she leaned closer to the screen. "I don't know how much longer I can stay in this place, Ben. The people here are downright mean to me—I mean they're really fucking rude. The food sucks, they won't let me make phone calls..."

"You're in *jail*, Miss Valentine, not at Club Med, and when you do get home, you'll be headed for a place much like that one. Look at me." He waited until she finished rolling her eyes and he had her attention. "Insanity isn't even close to being an option, and, unfortunately for you, you can't plead stupid. Not only will there be federal charges, but others as well. The parent company of *Person to Person* is furious that you've made a mockery of their magazine..."

"Yeah right, because everything in the tabloids is the stone cold truth," she said sarcastically.

"What you gave them were stone cold lies, and they need to save face. Be prepared that they will do that at your expense, both in the media and the courtroom; and don't forget that both Mr. Miller and Miss Hastings could sue for personal damages as well. I have to tell you emphatically that you don't have much of a leg to stand on here; legally, that is. The evidence against you is overwhelming; they have the photo albums, all the letters you took, the pictures you altered; they have the hacker you hired to mess with Miller's computer…and believe me, he's talking up a storm; the witness statement from the producer of the movie; and the prosecutor's been talking to your former assistant who's already singing like a canary…"

"I knew that bitch would turn on me. She was the one who did most of it, you know, not me."

Now it was Ben's turn to roll his eyes. "You know I've looked at this from every possible angle, and no matter how many ways I turn it, there's going to be a price to pay. You didn't even try to cover your tracks—you made memory albums out of your crimes, for chrissakes, and those'll be on display in the courtroom if we take this to trial. My advice to you, and what I'll be focusing most of my attention on, is putting together a plea bargain. You'll probably pay some hefty fines, but I think maybe we can keep the jail time to a minimum."

"More jail time—are you kidding me? For doctoring a couple pictures and taking a few letters?"

Ben nodded. "That's not how the prosecutor's going to see it, and it sure as hell isn't the way Mr. Miller sees it. He and his lady friend have been all over the television, the radio, the magazines—social media's going crazy—and they're not exactly singing your praises," he said sympathetically.

"Oh, I'm sure his little babysitter's got all kinds of things to say about me. Lies—all of them."

"Miss Hastings has been playing this thing just right, and hasn't said one negative thing directly against you. I know it doesn't seem fair, but even though they haven't been dragging your name through the mud, you are firmly entrenched as the villain in this situation. I know it isn't what you want to hear, but you need to accept the fact that this could go on for quite a while longer before it's all settled."

Penelope glared at him, and he could almost feel the daggers piercing him from across the ocean. "That's the best you can do? That's what I'm paying you for? To tell me to sit back and accept this?" She stepped back and swept her arm across the bland room.

Ben pressed his lips together and nodded. "That's why I'm going to shoot for a plea bargain. If this is dragged through the media, it'll be a flipping free-for-all. I'm sorry, but it's the truth of the matter, and it wouldn't be right for me to give you false hope."

"False hope?" she said weakly. "Ben, I really need to talk to Dylan. I know he said he didn't want to talk to me, but goddamn it, we were on the verge of something wonderful before all this happened. If I could just have a few minutes with him, I know I could make him see."

Ben shook his head, exasperated. "Absolutely, positively, no way. You need to forget that kind of thinking right now. Under no circumstances are you to make any attempt to contact him, and I'm telling you this not only as your attorney, but as someone who's known you for a lot of years and wants what's best for you." He felt a twinge of pain in his heart when he watched her eyes well up, but she needed to hear it. "He's in love with her, Penelope, and he's not coming back to save you."

"How could he just leave like that? Without even giving me a chance to explain?" The puddles at the rims of her eyes overflowed, and a single tear slid down each cheek.

He could see by her empty stare that he'd lost her; that it was pointless to continue this discussion right now. He was also starting to see glimmers of a potential defense, one that might lessen the punishment she'd have to serve and that might get her some sympathy from the public. "I'm going to get to work on this right now, Penelope, and I'll get you home as soon as I possibly can. You keep out of trouble, and I'll be in touch as soon as I know something."

As soon as her face disappeared from his screen, he leaned back in his chair and chewed absently on the end of his pen. Damn, she really believed that she and Miller had something going on; quite the opposite of what he'd said in the seemingly endless interviews over the past few days. What had Angela said about her former boss? He sifted through the file until he found the dialogue from her initial interview. Obsessed; freak show; unwilling to consider any other outcome than the one she'd written for herself.

Crime of passion, he jotted on his note pad. Well, crimes, in this instance, but all orbiting around the same nucleus—her obsession with Miller and the belief that she could make him fall in love with her. If he played it right, he might be able to swing it so that her time was spent in one of those cushy Hollywood psych hospitals instead of prison. The feds had much bigger things to worry about than a desperate actress with a pathetic crush. It wasn't national security or anything; and aside from the happy couple, no one else was really hurt by the whole thing. He pulled the pen from his mouth, wiped the end of it on the back of his tie, and started jotting some notes.

Penelope recognized the wheezing and the heavy shuffle of the guard coming down the corridor. His name was Eddie, she thought, and he was the only person in this whole damn place who didn't snicker at her every time he walked by; in fact, he seemed to go out of his way to be nice to her. He was a hideous creature; short and stocky with a shock of bright red hair that stuck out from his head in untamable clumps and pock marks all over his blotchy, pinched face. He was also, she realized, exactly what she needed to get a message out to her fans and to make a plea to Dylan. She turned on some tears as he came around the corner and prepared quickly for her next act.

"Ma'am? Are you OK? Aren't you gonna to go to dinner?"

"Please, just leave me alone. Why do you have to be so mean to me?"

Eddie winced. He was one of the only people in this place who wasn't badmouthing the actress. Everyone else seemed to think that it was hilarious how she went from the top of the world to the bottom of the barrel in just a few short days, but he could see where she was coming from. It wasn't like she was a criminal—she'd been in love with someone and had gone to some desperate measures to get him to return her feelings. The way his co-workers were talking, you'd think she offed the other chick or something. Eddie knew all too well what it was like not to have someone return your affections; he'd been there more times than he could count. Why couldn't anyone see that she was just a beautiful, misunderstood woman who needed a friend? He could be that friend to her, if only she'd let him.

"I'm really sorry," he said softly. "About everything. I don't think you're a horrible person. You really loved him, didn't you?"

Penelope sat up and wiped her face. "I still do," she whispered back, putting all the pathetic whine she could muster into her voice. "No one understands what I'm going through; no one cares about my side of the story."

"I do," he said, coming around the corner into her view. "I know exactly how you feel."

She looked up at him and forced a grim smile. "You do?"

He hovered outside the door of her cell and fidgeted nervously. "I really do. I wish there was something I could do to help you, Miss Valentine."

"Oh please, call me Penelope," she said sweetly.

"Um, OK, Penelope. I'm Eddie."

"I know."

"You know my name?"

"Of course I do, Eddie. How could I not know the name of the only decent human being in this whole place? You've always been nice to me, and I appreciate that more than I can tell you. I'm afraid I haven't always been as nice to you, and I'm sorry about that. I just don't know what I'm doing here and I'm so confused, you know? I'm so far away from home and I have no contact with the outside world while they make a mockery of me without giving me a chance to defend myself." She stood up and took his hands in her own, smiling up at him with all the gratitude she could summon. He stiffened at her touch, but recovered and smiled back at her warmly. *God, even his teeth are offensive*, she thought, but she managed to keep the smile on her face.

"It's not right the way they treat you. I keep telling them."

"Would you really help me, Eddie? Because there's something I really need to do, and I can't do it on my own." She batted her eyelashes at him and gave him her best doe-eyed look. "I'd be forever grateful to you."

Eddie took a step back and began wringing his hands. Even without makeup she was a stunning woman, he thought, and even though he knew she'd never give him a passing glance on a regular day, the way that she was looking at him now made him want to turn the whole world upside-down for her. He looked around nervously, very aware that he could get into some serious trouble and maybe even lose his job if he did anything against the rules.

"Oh Eddie, I'm not going to ask you to bust me out or anything," she smiled, laying her hand on his arm. "I'm not even going to ask you to take out Madeline for me, although that would seriously make my day."

Eddie guffawed like a braying mule. "Oh, she's such a bitch, isn't she?" he whispered.

"That she is," Penelope agreed, pressing her palms together as if in prayer and leaning close enough to get a good whiff of the man's BO.

"What do you want me to do?" he asked.

"I need to get my message out there, Eddie, that's all. I need to tell my fans that I'm still the person they've always known and thank them for sticking by me. I need to tell my own story, and get a message to Dylan." She pressed her lips together and looked at him from drooped lids. "I have to say I'm sorry, Eddie," she choked, fresh tears spilling from her eyes, "for the pain I've caused my family, my fans, and especially Dylan. Even if he hates me, I still want him to be happy, and I need him to know that."

She took one look at the indecision on his face, and knew she had to ramp up her game. He could get into some serious trouble for helping her, obviously, but even though his bottom line didn't matter to her one bit, hers was dependent on having an ally. If he gave her get what she needed, she'd make sure he stayed out of it.

"No one would ever know," she whispered, stepping toward him and laying the palm of her hand on his repulsive cheek. She wasn't sure if any amount of soap would wash off the grease and disgust, but she was willing to chance it. She saw his eyes widen for a second, then he leaned into her hand and his face softened.

"What do you need?"

Ten minutes later, she sat in a stinking janitor closet with his cell phone in her hand. She hit the record button, and started to speak.

"Hello my wonderful fans," she whispered. "I want to thank you all for standing by me through this horrible ordeal—you are the reason I wake up every morning in this God-forsaken place. I'm heartbroken by the lies and exaggerations you're being told and I need to tell you my side of the story..."

Chapter 11

It was a balmy 82 degrees when they touched down in Melbourne; a far cry from the cold and snow they'd left behind in New York. They were the first ones off the plane, and were hustled through the entry point by a sandy-haired host who claimed to be a die-hard InHap fan. As they approached the big red sign for the meeting point Tia saw Kelley Miller standing beneath it, a huge smile on her face. Tia recognized her not just from pictures she'd seen, but because she could see Dylan in the color of her hair, the blue of her eyes, and the tilt of her smile. Kelley rushed up and threw her arms around her son, then embraced Tia before Dylan even had a chance to introduce them. "You are an absolute gift, Tia," she whispered into her ear as she hugged her. "I am so glad that you're finally here." Her accent was thicker than Dylan's, and was definitively Aussie, without Dylan's hint of Brit.

"Thank you so much," she said. "I'm really happy to finally meet you. Dylan's told me so much about you."

"And believe me, he's told me a lot about you. I feel as if I already know you, and meeting you is just a formality."

"I guess introductions aren't necessary, then," Dylan smirked. He linked one arm around his mother and the other around Tia. "It's so good to finally have my two best girls together," he smiled, kissing the tops of their heads in turn and pulling them tight.

"Your dad's circling the airport," she said. "Let's get your luggage and head for home. I'm so glad to be able to spend Christmas with my baby! It's been years."

"Too many years," Dylan answered. "It's great to be home, Mum."

"And you've brought us the very best present," she said, squeezing Tia's arm behind Dylan's back.

They'd made no secret of the fact that they'd be in Australia for the holidays, and fully expected the group of photographers and reporters that stood around the luggage carousel, their eyes sweeping over the mass of humanity that paraded through the area. Their host was already directing an attendant toward them with their luggage, and they told the security guard that they were happy to pose for some photos and answer some questions.

"There they are!" a balding, heavyset man bellowed and it was like someone fired a starting pistol. All eyes turned in the direction of the media, and the crowd followed as they approached the couple.

"Dylan! Tia! Could we have a couple moments of your time, please?"

"I'll just go see about that luggage," Kelley smiled, bending her index finger toward the host as Dylan and Tia smiled for the cameras.

"Absolutely," Dylan said, turning on his rock star charm and striding toward them confidently, his hand outstretched. "How you all doing today?"

The flashes of the cameras made them a blur of faces and voices, so Tia just smiled in their general direction.

"Welcome home, Dylan, and welcome to Australia, Tia; is this your first time Down Under?"

"Yes, it is. I've always wanted to visit—I'm really glad to finally be here."

"What are you most looking forward to doing on your holiday?"

"Honestly? After the crazy week we just had, I'm mostly looking forward to spending some quiet time with Dylan, and getting to know his family." She leaned in and smiled. "Of course, it's an amazing country, and I want to see as much as I possibly can in the short time we're here. It probably sounds lame to you, but I can't wait to see kangaroos, koalas, wombats...I just love the outdoors. There is so much I want to see, but a couple weeks isn't even close to enough time to do it all. I'm glad we'll be coming back many times."

"I can't wait to show her some of the places that meant so much to me when I was growing up," Dylan added. "It's so good to finally bring her home."

"Tia, can you tell us what you're feeling right now?"

"Like the luckiest woman in the world," she said, smiling up at Dylan.

"How about you, Dylan?"

He wrapped his arm around Tia and smiled. "I've got my baby girl back...how do you think I'm feeling?" He planted a kiss on Tia's lips and flashed the paparazzi a wink. "I'm positively brilliant."

"You're meeting his family for the first time, right?"

"Yes she is, and I can't wait a minute longer. Tia hasn't had a chance to meet my dad yet, and I'd really like to make those introductions. It's been nice chatting with you all, but I hope you'll excuse us." He grabbed Tia's hand and got only two steps toward the exit before a tall blonde in a short green dress stepped out and thrust a microphone toward Tia's face.

"Tia, Callie Strong from WHO. I'm wondering if you might give us a statement in response to Penelope Valentine's comments about you and her relationship with Dylan."

Tia narrowed her eyes and shot a quick glance at Dyl, who merely shrugged in return. "I'm sorry, but I'm not aware of any comments she's made. My understanding is that she isn't being allowed to make any public statements except through her attorney."

"Well, she somehow got a video up on her Facebook page last night. Oh—you were probably in the air when it came out. I could summarize for you; she said..."

Dylan slung his arm around her protectively and headed immediately for the exit. "Not interested in the slightest," he called over his shoulder as they made a hasty retreat, waving off and apologizing to the onlookers thrusting papers toward them for autographs. "Have a Happy Christmas, everyone—I know I will!" The paparazzi followed them and continued snapping pictures, but the rest of their questions were lost in the din of the crowd.

"Don't think about it," Dylan said. "I know it's hard, but it doesn't matter one iota what she says, and this isn't the time to worry about it. We'll deal with it on our terms and in our own time. Can you do that?"

"I'm going to do my very best," she said, squeezing his hand. They stepped out the door and saw Kelley and the man who could only be Dylan's dad waving at them from a short distance away. She pushed it to the back of her mind and greeted Steve Miller with a smile.

All of Tia's trepidation left her within minutes of pulling away from the curb. Conversation began easily enough, with Steve and Kelley asking Tia general questions about herself, but before long, they fell into the comfortable bantering of a close-knit family that hadn't seen in each other in a while. Tia sat back and laughed as Steve and Dylan joked and made digs at each other while Kelley rolled her eyes in fake exasperation. By the time they rolled down the long driveway of the Miller home, Tia felt as if she'd known them for much longer than the forty minutes they had spent in the car.

The house was comfortable and warm—not huge, but set on a sprawling piece of property that boasted lots of mature trees, a huge deck overlooking an expansive garden full of sculptures and colorful blooms, and huge windows that let in lots of natural light. Every room was tastefully decorated with a combination of Kelley's incredible art and family heirlooms. Walls and tables were dotted with a wide variety of family photos that featured Dylan at various ages as well as his sister, Shelby. Dylan blushed when Steve led Tia into his "office;" a room dedicated to their son's success. "Ah, dads, you know," he muttered as Steve pointed out Dylan's first guitar, tour posters from one of his early bands, "Slingshot," and an entire wall full of articles and magazine covers.

"This is my personal favorite," Tia smiled, pointing to the "Sexiest Man" cover.

"Yeah, I have to say I felt a bit odd hanging that one," Steve snickered. "Kind of hard to think about the feral kid who we could barely force to take a Pommy shower some days as 'sexy.' Now I could tell you some stories..."

Dylan clamped his hand around Steve's mouth. "I'll not have you scaring her away with those old fish stories," he smirked.

"I didn't even understand half of it," Tia giggled. "What's a Pommy shower?"

"Never mind," Dylan said with a laugh. "One thing you've got to know about my dad straight off is that he has a tendency to exaggerate, so you should really only believe about half of what he says. And since you never know which half, you may as well just ignore all of it."

"I don't need to exaggerate when it comes to you," he teased. "You came by it honestly."

"Are you two at it already?" Kelley asked. "Really, let Tia get settled, at least, before you start behaving like a couple of children." She winked at Tia and put out her hand. "Come on. My favorite room to show off is my studio—my incredible son had it added onto the house so I'd have a place all to myself where I could focus my creativity."

"Your work is amazing; I can't wait to see more."

They walked down a long hallway into a large room with a high domed ceiling and five tall windows designed to catch the light from every angle at any time of day. A variety of paintings in various stages of completion were propped on easels and against walls, a large, well-used kiln stood in one corner, and various tapestries were draped over tables. Tia's eyes widened as she took in the incredible pieces, but her breath caught when she saw the painting sitting uncovered atop an easel in the center of the room. "Oh," she breathed, walking toward it. "It's Tuscany!" She recognized the scene immediately, and was instantly transported back. She and Dylan had stayed a couple nights in a little villa overlooking a vineyard, and they'd sat on the veranda one night and watched one of the most beautiful sunsets either of them had ever seen. It was one of their last days together before she returned home and Dylan headed for New Zealand, and the mood had been melancholy as they'd sipped a local wine and watched the incredible colors explode the sky and wash over the fruit of the land. Not only had Kelley managed to capture the perfect colors, but somehow she'd also encapsulated the mood of the evening. Tia stepped closer to take in the details; her eyes gravitating to the clusters of grapes that adorned each lower corner. Vines twisted from each cluster, shifting and morphing along the bottom edge of the sunset to become two hands intertwined at the center of the frame, the tendrils binding them together.

Kelley stood back and let her take it in, pleased that she'd not only recognized the setting but was drawn to the joined hands that were meant to be hers and Dylan's. He'd shared the photograph with her on his short visit before going to make the film, and repeated what he'd told Tia that night— that he was tangled up in her just like the vines were with each other, and that nothing could undo the love they shared.

Tia spoke without taking her eyes from the canvas. She could almost feel the cool breeze that had swirled around them that evening, could almost smell the air; tangy and sweetened by the delicate fruits. "I can't even think of a word to describe how beautiful this is," she whispered. "Breathtaking doesn't seem strong enough, but it absolutely does take my breath away. It's like I could just walk into it and be right back there again."

Kelley slipped her arm around Tia, resting her head on her shoulder. "I'm so glad you like it," she said. "It's your Christmas present, Tia. Grapevines are significant; they've been a symbol of abundance and fertility dating all the way back to Biblical Times. When Dylan stopped here on his way to New Zealand we sat in those two chairs right there," she pointed at a comfortable seating area under a window to the left, "and he told me that he'd found 'the one.' I looked into his eyes and knew instantly that it was true. When he showed me this photograph and shared with me what he'd told you that night, I knew that I had to paint it. I hope that it will bring you joy as you begin your lives together."

"Thank you," Tia breathed. "I don't even know what to say. I've never owned anything so beautiful and truly significant." She brought her hand to her heart and blinked back the emotion that suddenly filled her.

"You are so welcome," Kelley said, rubbing small circles on her back. "In every way, Tia. I hope you know I mean that very sincerely."

Tia wiped away a tear and a small giggle escaped her throat. "I can't believe I was so nervous about meeting you!" she smiled. "Thank you for making me feel so welcome, and especially thank you for raising such an incredible son. I couldn't be happier than I am at this very moment."

Dylan came over and wrapped both his girls in a warm embrace. "Neither could I," he said. "This is going to be the best Christmas ever!"

It was. Tia fell in love with Dylan's family—aunts, uncles, cousins, close friends—and she cherished every minute of the next few days with them as they came in couples and small groups to welcome Dylan home and to meet the woman who'd captured his heart. On Christmas Day she chatted easily with the ladies as they moved around the large kitchen preparing the meal, Dylan strolling in every few minutes to steal a kiss and something off one of the many plates and platters that were filling the countertops; laughing as his mom or an aunt playfully scolded him and slapped his hand away from the food. The day was clear and bright, and Tia reveled in enjoying Christmas dinner outdoors for the first time in her life, and in playing games on the lawn with the children. She felt her heart flutter as she watched Dylan interact with them as well, chasing, twirling, and tossing them into the air as they squealed with delight. Remembering Kelley's comment about fertility, an image of him as a father burst into her mind and burned there brightly. She couldn't help but smile.

The next day was Boxing Day, a national holiday Tia knew nothing about. The Miller family tradition was for all of the men to head over to the Melbourne Cricket Ground for the start of the annual matches, and Tia insisted that Dylan go. After the joyful noise of Christmas Day and the arrival of the other men as they joked good-naturedly about the rivalries among the teams playing, the house was blissfully quiet when the caravan of vehicles pulled out of the driveway.

"Ahh," Kelley sighed, stretching her arms over her head, "peace and quiet at last. It's been such a whirlwind, I feel like we've barely had time to really get to know each other. Why don't we go into my studio so we can chat?" She poured some steaming tea into two mugs and handed one to Tia.

"I'd love that," Tia said, following her into the warm and inviting space and taking a seat on one of the large comfortable chairs.

"Now that the boys are out of our hair, I really want to thank you, Tia," she said sincerely, "for everything you've done for my Dylan."

Tia crinkled her eyes in surprise. "I'm quite certain I can assure you that he's done much more for me than I've done for him."

"I'm glad to hear you say that because that's the way I raised him," she smiled, "but you've done more for him than even he knows, and it goes back a long way. I know he's told you his version of the story, but when Shelby got sick...he had a really tough time with it."

"I know," Tia said softly.

"You of all people do," she said, "and the fact that you share that common bond of loss brings you closer—you can't understand it unless you've been through it yourself. Then it takes on a whole life of its own."

Tia nodded. She knew it all too well.

"They were close, the two of them," she continued. "Oh, they had their usually sibling rivalry moments, of course, but he doted on Shelby, and she just thought the sun and moon set on her big brother." She sighed, her eyes traveling away as the memories came flooding back. "Dylan suffered a lot during that time. Not only was he facing the loss of his sister but we were moving him to an entirely different country and he had to leave everything he knew behind. Plus, Shelby required so much time, so much care, and although he'd never admit it, he felt a bit neglected."

Tia reached out and touched her lightly on the arm. "He has only the very best things to say about his childhood, aside from losing her."

"Oh, I do know that," she sighed, "but he had to grow up pretty quickly once we got to the States. Steve had to find work, and his long hours meant that Dylan had to kind of be the man of the house a lot of the time. I was a wreck, and Shelby needed so much. I just wanted to spend as much time with her as I could; knowing that I'd lose her; but at the same time, it was almost more than I could bear, watching her slip away day by day. It was a lot for a teenager to have to deal with. But he was so good with her, you know? He seemed to know exactly what she needed when Steve and I were at a complete loss. He spent so many hours sitting with her, playing his music for her, and even though I envied it at the time, he was what she really needed to deal with it all. I'll be honest and tell you that too often I wished desperately for the relationship the two of them had—he always knew just how to make her smile while I was floundering around trying to keep a smile pasted on my own face. And then she asked him to write her a goodbye song...

"It was so hard for him, and I hated watching him struggle with it. He wanted it to be so perfect, but he didn't want to finish it, because he didn't want to say goodbye. I know he was in denial a lot of the time, as we all were, and couldn't face the fact that her time was short. She died just days after he shared it with her." She wiped absently at a tear that had spilled down her cheek and Tia leaned over, pressing her hand to Kelley's in support.

"Dylan fought the feelings for so long, and even after years had gone by, he still couldn't really deal with it. He carried it with him, feeling so guilty that he was still here. It's part of what drives him. I think he feels like he has to live up to something; that he has to be successful so he'll be worthy of what she could never be. Like he has to live for them both."

"It's something he'll carry with him always," Tia said compassionately, her own eyes welling. "But it's also something that'll make him stronger, especially now that he's really coming to terms with it."

"You know," she said, reaching over to take Tia's hand. "I learned from that experience that life is short, and that death is so...final. It took me a long time, too, but I finally realized that you've got to love them while they're here, mourn them when they go, and celebrate them once they're gone. It's because of you that he's finally able to do that; celebrate her, I mean; and I'll always be grateful."

"We've been dealing with it together," Tia replied, "and at times it's been hard on both of us, but his strength has been my rock, too."

"I can see how good you are together. I'm really glad you found each other."

Tia smiled. "It almost sounds cliché because I say it all the time, but I really couldn't possibly be any happier."

Kelley stood and wiped the tears from her face. "Me either. So let's get happy then!" she pronounced, smiling. "I hid a bottle of my favorite wine away from the Christmas toasts. How about we grab some leftovers and I'll show you all the pictures of Dylan's awkward years that he thinks he threw away when he thought I wasn't looking?"

Tia chuckled. "I can't think of a better way to spend the afternoon. Lead the way!"

Chapter 12

The boys returned from their cricket game waving flags and oversized sponge hands over their heads; the victors singing their teams' fight songs. Dylan caught Tia's eye right away and a grin split his face. He strolled over and wrapped his arms around her, murmuring, "Ah, now the day is perfect..."

"I missed you, too," she whispered back, "but I had the best time with your mom—she's such an incredible person!"

"I told you that you had nothing to worry about," he said, giving her a squeeze. "I just knew you'd love each other."

"You have an amazing family, Dyl. I love them all."

"They love you too, baby girl. I knew they would."

"This has been the best Christmas—thank you."

"And the fun has only just begun. We'll do the show tomorrow morning, and then we'll head out on the next part of your Aussie adventure. There's so much more I want to show you."

"I can't wait. Are you going to tell me where we're going?"

"I want most of it to be a surprise, but we're going to end up in Sydney for New Year's Eve. It's an amazing city, and the fireworks over the Harbour Bridge are spectacular."

Tia smiled into his shoulder. "I can't wait. As much as I've enjoyed your family, I'm really looking forward to having some time just for the two of us."

"We still have a lot of catching up to do."

"That we do," she agreed.

"There's a lot to do in Sydney, but I'll leave New Year's Eve up to you. We could go down to one of the shows to watch the fireworks with the crowd or do something more private..."

"Private," she said immediately. "I think I've had more than enough public to last me a lifetime, and we're going back to it all in just a week. I want all the time I can have with you. Just you."

"Private it is, then. We'll have a great view of the bridge from our room."

"I was thinking we could make our own fireworks," Tia whispered into his ear.

"I like the way you think," he said, pulling her in and brushing his lips against hers.

They walked into the kitchen and caught Steve and Kelley in a passionate embrace.

"Disgusting," Dylan joked. "Nothing worse than seeing your parents snogging. I'm scarred for life."

"Really," Steve said sarcastically. "Remember the birds and the bees—didn't we have that little talk a long time ago? Maybe now that you've finally found a woman who seems willing to put up with you, we need to have a little refresher course."

Dylan put his hands up to shield his face. "Bloody hell, don't remind me. That's a memory better off forgotten."

"Don't you remember, Dyl?" he joked. "It was the summer before your sophomore year..."

"OK, I'm really going to have to insist that this conversation ends right here..."

Steve grabbed Dylan around the neck and playfully roughed his hair. "It's not you I want to talk to anyway," he said, releasing him and offering Tia his arm. "It's been so crazy around here that we haven't had much time to talk. Will you take a walk with me?"

"I'd be glad to," she smiled, grabbing a sweatshirt off the hook by the door and linking her arm through his.

They walked for a bit in companionable silence through the cool of the evening, under a blazing carpet of stars that seemed almost close enough to touch. The Milky Way—a wavy streak of dark and cloud—split the sky like a river, dotted along the edges by pinpoints of light that blazed and twinkled like jewels.

"There are so many stars here," she said wistfully, looking up at the unfamiliar constellations of the Southern Hemisphere. "It's just beautiful."

"Funny thing about stars," Steve answered thoughtfully, "There are literally billions out there, but only a fraction shine brightly enough for us to see. They overpower the others with their brilliance, and are revered—worshiped even—for the sparkle they bring to the world. But all of them must endure a lot of heat and inner turmoil to maintain that sparkle, or else they'll fade out and be overshadowed like so many others that came before them."

"You're talking about Dylan," she said.

"In some respects," he answered, "but we all have our moments of sparkle; even if no one ever sees them. Dylan is definitely one of the ones shining brightly right now, but fame is a fickle mistress. And goodness knows he's endured a lot of heat and turmoil, especially these days."

"I hope you know that I'm not with Dylan because of his..."

"Oh no, no," he said with a shake of his head and a wave of dismissal. "That's not what I'm suggesting at all. It's obvious to anyone who sees the two of you together that what you have is real and very deep." He took her by the shoulders and turned her so that she was facing the Milky Way. He stepped behind her, took her hand, and extended her index finger; pointing it so that she could follow up the length of it with her eyes to where it rested on one of the most brilliant points of light in the sky. "See that one there, the really bright one?" he asked.

"Yes."

"That's Alpha Centauri. It's actually two stars, close enough together that we see them as one. You've acquired your own brilliance for the world now, Tia, so close to Dylan's that you shine together as a single entity. But you're smart enough to know that it won't last too long. Another big story will overshadow this one, and even though your brilliance won't fade, it will be overpowered."

"I've always preferred to cast a softer glow over a bigger area," she said. "I never had any aspirations to be a star."

"A very wise answer," Steve smiled, and they both watched as a shooting star streaked across the night sky.

"Then there are stars like that one," Tia said. "A bright flash that burns out much too quickly and never gets a chance to truly shine." She knew that Steve would understand her meaning, as she had understood his.

He smiled warmly at her and put his arm across her shoulders, pulling her into a knowing embrace. "There are those," he agreed, "and we know it all too well, don't we? You know, one group of Aborigines believe that when their people, the Yolngu, die, they travel to the spirit land in the sky on a mystical canoe. Once they've arrived at the spirit land, their canoe is sent back to the Earth in the form of a shooting star—it's meant to let the grieving family know that the one who has left them arrived safely at their final destination. They say that the lights along the edge of the Milky Way are the burning campfires of those who have passed on.

"I know that Kelley has already thanked you for what you've done for our son, but I also want to thank you for what you've done for my wife. The night we buried Shelby we dragged a blanket into our backyard and laid for hours, under the stars, just holding hands and watching for that sign from her that she was OK—that she'd made it to heaven. We had no idea that there was going to be a meteor shower that night, and when they started filling the sky, they were more beautiful than any fireworks display." Tia heard the change in his voice, the shake as he recalled the memory, and gave his hand a reassuring squeeze. "We cried together that night, after so many months of holding the tears at bay, and mourned the loss of our daughter."

"I'm so sorry," Tia whispered.

"Between you and me, Tia, Kelley has been hoping for a long time that Dylan would meet someone; so she could have a daughter again. She's worried out loud though, over the years, about him getting caught up in the celebrity scene and making the wrong choice—more than a few times she cringed openly when she caught wind of Dylan dating some actress who she knew didn't have his best interests at heart. But as the years went by, she started worrying that he'd never find the right partner to share his life, and that bothered her even more. I knew that my son had a good head on his shoulders, and that he'd know when he found the right one. I'm really glad it's you."

"Me too. You know, I was so nervous about meeting you—I worried that I wouldn't measure up to other girls he's brought home—that I didn't have much to offer. You've really made me feel like part of the family, and I appreciate that so much. I can see where Dylan gets so many of his best qualities."

"Dylan's never brought anyone home before," Steve said, and Tia's eyes widened in surprise. They hadn't discussed it, but she assumed he had. A little spot in her heart tingled at the revelation. "He's very protective of his mum," he continued, "and he knows how much she's missed having a girl around—someone to share in all those things the way only women can. That's how we knew that you were the real deal, Tia. He'd never bring a woman here if he wasn't sure she had staying power, and that she'd be able to bond seamlessly with our family—especially when it comes to Kelley."

"Thank you for sharing that with me, Steve," she said gratefully. "You have no idea how much it means."

"Which brings me back to the reason I want to thank you. We've celebrated a lot of holidays since Shelby's been gone, but there's been a hole in every one; a shadow that everyone can see but no one wants to acknowledge." He looked at Tia. "She would've been about your age, you know," he continued, "and there's always that wonder about what sort of woman she would have turned out to be if she'd had the chance. Having you here, seeing the relationship that you and Dylan have built despite a lot of complications, has been like a breath of fresh air. You brought a particular kind of joy to our house that hasn't been here in a long time; your sparkle kept the shadows at bay. It's been so nice watching you and Kelley bond; seeing how much she's enjoyed getting to know you.

"You understand, I know you do. When you lose someone, they'll always be there, because they're a part of you. But it doesn't mean that someone else can't still be everything to you; that you can't love someone else just as much, but in a different way. Dylan is that everything for you, and in just a few short days, you're already becoming that to us. I really can't tell you how glad we all are to have you as part of our family, Tia," he said with a bow of his head, "and I couldn't let you leave without telling you. So, thank you."

"I don't even know what to say to that," Tia said, completely at a loss for words. "That is honestly one of the nicest things anyone's ever said to me." She pulled in a deep breath of the crisp air and let it out on a sigh. "Thank *you* for opening your hearts to me. I hope we'll be able to see you again very soon."

"I'm quite certain we will," Steve said with a knowing smile that was masked by the darkness.

"Aren't you chilly out there?" Kelley called from the deck. "How about some tea?"

"Brilliant," Steve and Tia said at exactly the same time. They giggled, linked arms once again, and headed for the warmth— literally and figuratively—of the house.

Chapter 13

Lexi didn't even consider not taking the call that popped up as "unknown caller" on her display. Both Tia's and Dylan's phones showed up that way, and as the crazy time difference and family obligations had prevented them from talking on Christmas Day, she smiled as she tapped the screen.

"Merry Christmas, girlfriend!" she exclaimed enthusiastically. "I'm guessing you were a good girl, and got everything you wanted?"

"Well, I always get everything I want," a man's voice teased. "But to be honest, I probably deserved coal in my stocking."

Lexi sat upright and tried to place the voice. It definitely wasn't Dylan's, but it sounded familiar. For a second, Bo's name flashed in her mind—he had a similar sense of humor, but she pushed that aside quickly. She'd know his voice anywhere, and this wasn't it. "Who is this?" she asked curiously, a smile in her voice, "and why do you deserve coal?"

A hearty laugh filled her ear. "I'm guessing that I'm speaking to Lexi Summers," he said. "Tia told me you had a quick wit." He paused for just a moment. "This is Tony Granger...host of *After Dark?*" He said the last few words as if they were a question, but there was just enough arrogance behind them to let her know that he expected anyone would know who he was—and be honored by the call.

Lexi's heart quickened. The time she'd spent with InHap had pretty much cured her of her star struck affliction, but still, it wasn't every day that the host of the most popular talk show on television called you directly to chat. "Ah, Tony Granger," she replied cooly. "Tia mentioned you might be calling, and she also told me that you were more than *deserving* of coal; you were likely the original recipient," she said with a grin.

"And I doubt you'd find many who would argue that conclusion, Miss Summers," She could almost hear the smile in his voice. "May I call you Lexi?"

"You may," she said, "if I can call you Tony."

"Of course," he said, the smirk easily travelling through the phone lines.

"So, what can I do for you, Tony? I can only imagine that you're calling to beg me to give you the exclusive story about Tia and Dylan's love affair in the early days, when I was the only one who knew about it. I'll tell you, however, that it is my Christmas vacation, and I'm not just going to drop everything and run out to LA to appear on your show," she said with just as much smirk in her tone.

"Oh," Tony replied, as if he were seriously contemplating her words. "You mean it's not enough that the world wants to hear your story, and that you'll be the topic of discussion over every water cooler for days?"

"Tia's already shown me what *that* does for you—and no thank you very much."

Tony took the bait willingly. Tia had already told him that Lexi was willing to do it, and that it wouldn't take much to persuade her.

"Hmmm. Tia told me you might be willing to…"

"Not the day after freaking Christmas I'm not, Tony," she said rather convincingly. "Unless you make me an offer I can't refuse?"

Tony chuckled. "Yeah, Tia told me you'd play hardball, too. But she also said that one word might tip you over the edge. I was hoping not to have to show my hand so early in the conversation, but…"

"OK, you've got me interested. What're you offering?"

"Have you ever been to the after Christmas sales on Rodeo Drive? They're different than they are anywhere else in the world…and did I mention it's a lovely 80 degrees in LA right now?"

"Damn it," Lexi smirked. "You pretty much had me at 'shopping,' but if you throw in some palm trees, a car to use while I'm there, and a decent room, I might just give in."

"Wow," Tony teased back. "You're easy. I guess you'll take care of your own transportation to get here, then?"

"Yeah, sure," Lexi said sarcastically. "And I'll see you sometime in February, then. Do you want to leave me a number where I can reach you when I get there?"

"Touche," Tony said. "Now I guess you've got me."

Lexi giggled. "Just give me the details, Tony. I already told Tia and Dylan I'd do it, as you well know. I will tell you, though, that this really isn't the ideal timing, but that I do have a bit of a weakness for shopping. I will need to be home before New Year's Eve, though."

"The timing can be whatever you want it to be," Tony offered. "I can send my jet to the closest airport whenever you want it—we'll record the show on Monday afternoon. You can leave any time after we're done, although that's going to make for a long night with the time difference and all, or stay until Tuesday morning. I can offer you a room at the Four Seasons and a car with a driver for as long as you stay. Your choice, as long as you promise not to give your story to anyone else before you appear on my show."

Lexi didn't have to roll it around in her mind for long. She told Dylan that she'd give Tony first dibs, and had put off a couple of local news shows that had already called to request interviews. A little sun would give her at least a bit of a golden glow for the New Year's Eve party she and Ryan were attending, and she'd be sure to find something fabulous to wear in LA. "You've got a deal, Tony," she said, already pulling her suitcase out from under the bed. "I'll leave tomorrow morning, and come back Monday night." That would give her a long weekend to shop and see some of the sights, and she'd still be back in plenty of time for the party on Tuesday.

"Excellent," Tony replied. "I'll arrange your transportation immediately and have my assistant call you back in a few hours with the details. I look forward to meeting you, Lexi."

"You too," Lexi said. She cut off the call and began humming to herself as she happily pulled summer clothes from the back of her closet and arranged them on the bed.

"What do you mean, you're going to LA for a couple days?" Ryan demanded.

"I'm going to be a guest on *After Dark*. To talk about Tia and Dylan's early days."

Ryan's face crinkled up in distaste. "As if there aren't enough people talking about Tia and Dylan," he said sarcastically. "They were just on every single freaking TV show in the world last week."

"I know that," Lexi answered with just as much sarcasm. "It's obviously really big news right now, and they're in Australia. The public wants more, and Tony called to see if I'd..."

"Oh, so now you're on a first-name basis with Tony Granger?" he interrupted. "You're not the celebrity, Lexi. Neither is Tia. She just happens to be banging a rock star. So why the hell would the public give two shits about what you have to say?"

His words stung, but Lexi just shook her head. "Obviously Tony thinks they will, or he wouldn't have called," she said evenly.

Ryan rolled his eyes and exhaled in exasperation. "You're just loving every minute of this, aren't you?"

"Geez Ryan, chill out," she groaned. "I'm doing a favor for friends; that's all. I'm going to fly out tomorrow, spend the weekend shopping, do the show on Monday, and be home late Monday night. You're just jealous that I'm getting out of this Chicago weather for a few days."

Ryan's head snapped up. "Did you just say you're leaving tomorrow?"

"That's the plan."

"My parents' annual holiday dinner is on Sunday," he countered. "They're expecting us both to be there."

Lexi cringed. The Stallworth 'Annual Holiday Dinner' was marginally more fun than having a root canal...maybe. It was a hundred people crammed into the banquet hall at the country club; mostly retired lawyers and business types who loved to listen to themselves talk. Only a dozen or so of the guests were Lexi and Ryan's age, and they usually spent most of the evening trying to hang together in an attempt to avoid being subjected to listening to the old-timers giving them advice on everything from how to advance their legal careers to where to vacation on their honeymoons. Although she maintained a stoic face, she was turning cartwheels on the inside that she'd be able to skip out on a year of that torture. "I'm one person in a hundred, Ry. I think the dinner will go on just fine without me for one year."

"That's not the point," he argued. "You're their future daughter-in-law. How's it going to look if you blow off their biggest social event of the year?"

Lexi pretended to ponder the question before answering. "Umm...like I'm in LA soaking up some rays, getting in a shopping spree, and appearing on a late night talk show?"

Ryan grunted and turned away, but Lexi grabbed his arm before he could storm out of the room. "Come on, Ryan, really?" she said. "They'll all wish they were me! You'll get all kinds of bonus points with the living dead because your 'society lady' is taking advantage of a free trip to LA. They'll be positively green with envy. It'll give them something to talk about besides what a nice place Martha's freaking Vineyard is this time of year." He groaned, but the corners of his lips just barely tipped up in a suppressed smile. Ryan was fully aware of her dislike for this annual tradition—he complained about it every year too, but seemed to forget how painful it was until he had to go through it again. "Think about it." she added. "You get to tell them that I got a personal call from Tony Granger asking me to appear on his show. You'll actually get to talk for a change! And they'll listen!"

"OK, you have a point, but it'll suck being there without you," he conceded. "It'll be even more boring than usual." He stuck his lips out in a pout, and she stretched up to kiss them.

"I'll be back before you know it," she assured him. "Barring a Monday-only sale at Jimmy Choo, I'll be back late that night."

"No way I'd let you go if you were missing New Year's Eve," he said grudgingly.

"No way I'd go if it meant missing New Year's Eve," she smiled.

Chapter 14

It was just another talk show; just another morning news program on which to make an appearance. But it came in the middle of her holiday, and damn it; after what she'd gone through the past couple weeks, she deserved a break. Still, it was the only appearance they were making in Melbourne—many of the shows were in rerun over the holiday season—and it was Dylan's hometown. She didn't really have a choice.

Tia had been watching the news program over the past couple days, just so she'd have an idea about the personalities that would be interviewing them. Dylan had also agreed to be their 'musical guest,' meaning he'd play a song or two in front of a live audience outside the studio after the interview was over.

The weather couldn't have been more perfect; a lovely 74 degrees with thin, puffy clouds floating lazily in the sky. Tia donned a bright yellow sundress splashed with purple and orange flowers, a fabulous pair of orange heels, and pulled her hair up into a casual knot; Dylan tossed on a pair of cargo shorts and a t-shirt.

There was already a crowd gathered as the car approached the studio, and Tia giggled when she saw the velvet ropes that hung from brass poles to create an unobstructed pathway from the street to the door. A large platform was set up in the plaza alongside the studio, and a crowd was already beginning to stake claim to the areas closest to the stage.

As she did before each appearance, Tia gave herself a mental pep talk. Dylan, as he did before each appearance, massaged her shoulders to help her relax and then planted a loud smacking kiss on the back of her hand for moral support. She had really unwound over the past few days in the privacy of his parents' house, and the thought of being thrust into the spotlight once again rubbed like sandpaper over the ends of her nerves. *Get over it,* she told herself. *Get through it, smile, be charming, and be done.* God she was looking forward to the next week when they'd have some time alone.

The car came to a stop and Dylan pulled her in. "You'll be brilliant, as always," he said matter-of-factly.

"I'll be the same as always, anyway," she smiled. "I don't know why I'm extra nervous...I guess because it's your hometown and I..."

"It's just another interview, love," he said. "The same as all the others."

The driver opened the door and the excitement of the crowd instantly filled her ears. Dylan stepped out and gave a quick wave before offering Tia his hand and helping her out of the car. He was right, she knew. Just because they were in another country didn't make it any different than all the rest. She put on what she called her "celebrity smile" and stepped out onto the curb.

The crowd whistled and cheered and Tia waved enthusiastically, shaking hands and signing the notebooks and bits of paper being shoved toward her from both sides of the ropes. She and Dylan zigzagged across the walkway, giving equal attention to both sides. "I love you Tia!" "You're so lucky!" "Hey Dylan, I'm your biggest fan!" Many of the shouts and comments blended into each other, but a few stood out and made Tia feel almost giddy. Dylan took her hand and twirled her, putting on a little show for the crowd and Tia laughed—she couldn't help but feel good when she got such a welcoming reception.

They almost reached the door to the studio—had it ever taken so long to walk just a few yards?—when she heard the comment from her left side. "You don't deserve him, you loser! You should've let Penelope have him! Scarlet letter for you!" Tia turned her head, her smile fading, and saw the projectile coming. She put up her hands to block the impact, but it was too late. Something hard smacked her face just under her left eye, and she was showered with some sort of red liquid that got into her eyes, blinding her. Instinctively she opened her mouth to cry out, and the unmistakable coppery taste of blood was on her tongue.

Dylan was at her side in an instant and security an second later, shielding her with their bodies and ushering her toward the door. Another bomb came flying in and exploded at her feet, and she slipped to the ground, landing hard on her knee and scraping her elbow when she hit the pavement. She was pulled up immediately, and another group of guards grabbed the still screaming woman from the crowd, stopping her from hurling yet another of the blood bombs. But the damage was done. A very shaky Tia was hustled into a private room where the door was closed on the cameras that had filmed their arrival and subsequent attack.

"What the fuck?" Dylan yelled as he used his own shirt to mop the offensive slime from her face. "Baby, are you OK?" He turned to one of the security guards who'd escorted them in. "Get me some water and some towels!"

There was a small crowd in an instant, with bottles of water and a large bowl pilfered from a staff lounge. Dylan poured water on her face as she held her head over the bowl and attempted to rinse her eyes. Tia grabbed one of the bottles and tipped it to her mouth, washing out the offensive taste and spitting into the bowl.

"Oh my God, I'm so sorry," Lana, one of the reporters, said. "Are you OK?" Apologies were being tossed around from all directions, and towels were being thrust into Tia's hands. "Are you bleeding?"

"Not my blood," Tia managed, coughing and wiping at her face.

When she finally cleared her eyes and could see, she looked up at the crowd that was gawking at her and wanted nothing more than to close them again.

"Tia, look at me," Dylan commanded, and as soon as she did, she burst into tears. "I'm so sorry, baby girl," he said, taking her into his arms. She sobbed into his shoulder and uttered just one word. "Why?"

The door burst open and another security guard rushed in. "Sheep's blood, according to the offender," he said, "in a balloon weighted with a rock. There's an ambulance on the way. Are you alright, miss?" He tossed a first aid kit onto the table and knelt before Tia. "Where are you hurt?"

Tia sucked up some courage from a deep well she didn't even know she had. She realized that although she was personally attacked, the attack wasn't *personal*. The woman who did this didn't know anything at all about Tia Hastings; she was just a fan of Penelope's. What she did was rude and immature and hateful and a thousand other ugly adjectives, but it was directed at Tia the quasi-celebrity, not Tia the person. She had to understand that; had to *believe* it, or she wasn't going to be able to do this. It was just one step further than those who threw hurtful words, and she couldn't dwell on every negative comment or action that had nothing to do with the person she was on the inside. *The show must go on*, she thought with a sarcastic snicker. She sat up, wiped the tears from her face, and turned toward the officer. "I'm fine. Just a few scratches from when I fell and a bump on my cheek. I don't need an ambulance."

"You'll get checked out," Dylan insisted. "You took a nasty spill."

She raised her hand to her face and felt the tender spot where the rock had connected. "I'd be fine with an ice pack and a couple Band-Aids, I think."

"She'll get checked out," Dylan said to the cop. He turned her face and took her hand from her cheek, his eyes flaming. "Bloody hell, there's already a bruise! Oh sweetheart..." he took one of the remaining clean towels and soaked it with cold water, holding it to the swollen spot just below her eye. "Can someone get me an icepack, please?" He was trying to sound calm, but the frantic anger in his voice was clearly evident. He turned to the guard and hissed between clenched teeth, "Did you get the bitch?"

"We got her. This is a serious offence, Mr. Miller, and you can be assured that all necessary charges will be filed."

"I bloody well hope so."

"I don't want to press charges," Tia said quietly.

"What are you talking about?" Dylan hissed. "You were attacked. Damn right we're pressing charges."

"I'm not pressing charges. I can't take this personally—she doesn't know me." She brought her hand to Dylan's face and tried to smile in an attempt to douse some of the anger burning in his eyes. "I'm OK, Dyl, really."

He pressed his lips together and shook his head. "We'll talk about it later."

"I'd really rather not," she said, "I think I'll just try and forget the whole thing." She turned to one of the producers. "Bring in the cameras. We can do the interview in here."

"Fuck the interview! As soon as the medics get you checked out, I'm taking you home."

She turned to him. "No, Dyl. We came here to do this, and I'm not letting some random person with a Penelope complex scare me out of it. I'll be fine. I've got a scraped knee and a little knot on my cheek. Believe me, I've been through worse." He opened his mouth to argue, but she raised her hand, and he shook his head and let her finish. "Look, she's one of the haters. They're out there. They're always going to be out there. I want to let her and all the rest of them know that what they do has an impact on us. That we're not made of stone, and we're certainly not made of glass. I'm not going to go skulking away because of one crazy person. There are a lot more people out there who came to see you...to see us...and we owe them. Maybe some of the others will figure out that we're real people too. I want to do the interview."

Dylan growled and pushed his fingers through his hair. His face twisted in disgust when he pulled them out; smeared with blood. He pressed his forehead to Tia's. "What am I going to do with you, woman?" he croaked. "You really want to do this?"

"I do."

He tossed his head back in surrender and shrugged at the producer who hovered nervously by the door. "I guess we're going to do an interview, then."

The man jumped up as if he'd been hit by a cattle prod. "Ah, OK, I'll call wardrobe and tell hair and makeup to get ready…"

"No hair or makeup," Tia said. "And no wardrobe. I know the cameras were filming when we came in…everyone saw what happened. There's no sense in trying to pretend it didn't. No sense pretending anything. They're going to get me, plain and simple, and that's it."

She stood up and looked down at her splattered dress. Her hair was soaked from all the water that was poured over her head and even her shoes were completely ruined. She wouldn't normally have even walked out of her house looking like such a wreck, and here she was, insisting they put her on television. Was she nuts?

Dylan looked at her with an emotion that could only be described as complete and total adoration. "You are positively amazing, you know that?"

"Yeah, well, you might be on a short list of people who think so after I get through with this, but the ones on the short list are the only ones who really matter in the end, anyway."

He took her face in his hands and she winced at the contact. "Oh bloody hell," he whispered, "I'm sorry." Tia had never felt a kiss as tender as the feather-light one he placed on her swollen cheekbone. "I love you so much."

The door crashed open and a camera and lighting crew burst in. "It'll just take us a couple minutes to get this set up—it's not ideal, but it'll work." A middle-aged woman, hefting a camera nearly as big as she was, stopped as she was setting up a stage light and turned to Tia. "I just want to say that I think you're so brave for doing this. I saw what happened, and I'm incredibly sorry. I hope you know that there are a lot more people pulling for you than against you."

"Thanks," Tia smiled, pushing her wet hair behind her ears. "That means a lot. Especially right now."

They had the makeshift studio set up within minutes; just a couple lights and three portable cameras. Some folding chairs were brought in, and the news anchors strolled through the door, adjusting tiny microphones clipped to their lapels.

"We've got about two and a half minutes before we go back live," Carole Peppers said. "Are you sure you want to do this?"

"We're sure," Tia said, and Dylan scooted his chair as close to hers as he could and took her hand.

"I applaud your courage," Dan Matheson added, "and we're so grateful you decided to stay. This can't be easy, but I think it's a good message."

"And we're back live," Carole said into the camera. "If you're just joining us, you know we've been scrambling over here. Our guests today, Dylan Miller and Tia Hastings, were attacked by a member of our audience on their way into the studio. We are horrified and embarrassed by the behavior of one of our citizens, and show it to you again only because it will help you understand the courage of one brave woman in the face of adversity. Here's what happened just a few minutes ago." She turned to Tia. "We go live with you in one minute...you doing OK?"

Tia nodded. The cameraman counted down on his fingers, and Carole pressed her lips together as he tucked the last digit. "We offer our sincere apologies to not only Tia and Dylan, but to all of those who had to witness that blatant lack of basic human respect. From what we gather from police, the balloon contained sheep's blood, and was weighted with a rock. Tia was hit in the face, and a second balloon landed at her feet, causing her to slip and fall. We fully expected that the interview was not going to happen, but Tia is insisting we go forward."

"We are moved by her bravery and truly appreciate that she still wants to talk with us," Dan added. "So without further delay, Ladies and Gentlemen, Tia Hastings and Dylan Miller."

The camera man facing them pointed, indicating they were now on live. Tia could hear the wail of an approaching siren in the distance.

Carole began, "First of all, I just have to apologize one more time. As our audience can see, you are still covered with the contents of the balloon used in the attack. Can you tell us why you decided to go through with the interview?"

Tia cleared her throat. "We said we'd be here, and we didn't want to let anyone down. I saw how many people were gathering by the stage to hear Dylan sing and to welcome us; and it wouldn't be fair to them if we just left."

"You'd just been attacked...I'm sure they would understand..."

"I've got a couple bumps and bruises—hardly enough to make me rush home; although, this isn't exactly the look I had in mind for my Australian TV debut." She pasted on a smile and lifted her wet hair, letting it fall back in clumps onto her shoulders.

The EMTs came in just then, toting medical bags and pushing a stretcher. "Ladies and gentlemen, medical help has just arrived. We're going to send you off to Jay for the weather while they check Tia out, and then we'll be back with you. Stay tuned." Dan waited a couple beats before saying, "And we're out."

They continued the interview after the EMTs cleaned Tia's wounds and evaluated her eye. It was quickly determined that she had no serious injuries, so they patched her up and gave her a proper ice pack. Tia steered them away from questions about the attack, and even though she looked a mess, by the end of the interview she was laughing and telling stories about meeting Dylan's parents for the first time, and sharing her favorite observations about Australia.

"What do you mean you still want to perform?" Dylan asked when she suggested it during the final commercial break of their segment.

"People came to see you, Dyl, and they deserve that. I promised I'd sing back-up."

"You don't need to..."

"I know. I want to."

"Damn it woman, you are stubborn. And strong. And freaking sexy, even covered in sheep blood."

"Don't you forget it," she teased. "You don't want to mess with me."

He turned his palms out. "No way," he smiled. "You can win every argument."

"Can I get that in writing?"

The roar from the crowd was deafening as Dylan and Tia took the stage in their blood splattered clothes. Words of encouragement and support washed over them like a blanket and Tia stepped up to the mic first. "I knew that the rest of you were awesome!" she yelled. "Thanks so much for your support!"

"No, thank you!" came a hundred voices amidst thunderous applause.

Tia stepped back and let Dylan take the reins. "That's my girl Tia!" he bellowed. "She's the most incredible woman I've ever met, and today—she's my hero!"

He strummed the first chords of *I'll Pull You Up*, and in light of the situation, it had a whole new meaning. He'd literally pulled her up in so many ways she couldn't even begin to count them. Since this was the first time he'd played it live in Australia, the crowd went wild. She never got tired of singing this song and as Tia chimed in, she could feel her confidence increase with every note she sang. These people didn't know her either, but they were supportive of her nonetheless and weren't shy about letting her know it. She'd always told her students that 99% of the people in the world are good, and looking out over the audience, she could clearly see the truth in that statement.

"Thank you very much," he sang as he coaxed out the final notes. "This next one's a new one, hope you like it." Tia grinned when he started plucking the first notes of her favorite new song, *House Without a Home*. He wrote it in New Zealand, because he couldn't stop thinking about how much they'd both gravitated toward the natural beauty of many of the places they'd visited on the tour. He told her that the whole time he was filming out in some of the wilder parts of the country, he kept seeing things he knew would make her smile; like birds, sunsets, and waterfalls. There was no harmony written for this one yet, so Tia moved to the side of the stage and enjoyed, as she always did, watching Dylan do what he did best. She closed her eyes and let his honest gravelly voice wash over her.

Gravity just let me go, I'm tired of this world you know...
got nothing left to give, and I can't keep takin'...
Even open eyes don't truly see...in our narcissist's society...
don't know how we can live...with this mess we're makin'...

Oh...no...we reap only what we sow...
On this big blue ball...life is precious overall...

Bodies littered on the ground, in the forest there will be no sound...
the white bear cannot live...when his world is bakin...

Oh...yeah...it's time to take a stand...
because on this big blue ball...life is precious overall...

So leave the forest to the trees...keep the fishes in the seas...
we all need some room to roam...what good's a house without a home...

Understand it's got to be...about all of us and not just 'me'...
not hard to tip the scale...when the balance is already shakin'...
Open up your eyes and see...that nothing good in life comes free...
Seems we're on a spiral down...and my heart is breakin'...

Oh...please...you know it brings me to my knees...

you know that on this big blue ball...life is precious overall...

Let's leave the forest to the trees...keep the fishes in the seas...
we all need some room to roam...what good's a house without a home...

Yeah leave the forest to the trees...and the flowers to the bees...
all creatures need some room to roam...can't have a house without a home...

Tia was so mesmerized by Dylan on stage and the passion that he had for his music that she was transported to another place. When he strummed the last chord, she rushed out to throw her arms around him as the audience responded with yet another roar of approval.

"Thank you very much, friends, for coming out to support us today and for helping us heal. I hope we'll see you again soon." Dylan swept his guitar off his shoulder and pulled Tia into his bow. The couple hundred people who'd showed up for their little performance sounded like a couple thousand and that was all the support she needed to know she'd done the right thing. They waved one last time, and jumped from the stage, shaking hands with a few audience members and then with Carole, Dan, and some of the crew before jumping into the waiting car.

She thought she'd break down after the whole thing was over; thought she was just being strong in the moment and that it would all catch up with her and flood her with emotion. But when she jumped into the back of the car, she smiled. "That went well, don't you think?" she said.

"Come here, baby girl," Dylan grinned. She cuddled up to him, both of them still a bit damp and in desperate need of showers. "I am just so bloody proud of you, I can't even form the words." He laughed. "No pun intended. You handled that whole situation with so much class and grace, and you were positively brilliant." He shook his head, at a loss for words, but his smile said it all. "God I love you. More than I can possibly say."

Kelley rushed down to meet the car as they pulled up to the house, and she took Tia immediately into her arms. "I'm so sorry, sweetie, but I am so proud of the way you handled the whole thing!"

The look on Kelley's face and the tenderness in her touch caused Tia's self-control to falter just a bit and she choked back a sob. "I don't think I'll ever understand how people can be so cruel," she said, "but I do know that I did the right thing."

"Come on," Kelley said, "I'm going to draw you a nice bath with lots of bubbles, and then we're going to have some wine and do your hair and go out for a nice dinner. You showed them that they can't break you—let's show them that life goes on."

Tia took a deep breath as they walked into the restaurant. Dylan's arm was firmly around her waist and Steve was at her other side with Kelley at her back. Tia knew that their placement in proximity to her own body were by design, and she was incredibly grateful for the physical as well as the emotional support; especially since her legs felt a bit like cooked spaghetti. It hit her while she was soaking in the tub, the hot water and soap stinging the shredded flesh on her knee and elbow. She had her own little pity party, her quiet sobs masked by the hum of the jets that churned the water and loosened her tense muscles.

The last thing she wanted to do was face the public again tonight; especially with her cheek swollen and turning colors; but the show must go on. She couldn't fathom why a complete stranger would want to hurt her on behalf of another complete stranger—she knew she'd never be able to rationalize the whole thing, but it kept her brain spiraling out in all directions. Although she'd never admit it out loud, she couldn't help but wonder if it might happen again. Apparently not everyone had defected from Penelope's fan club, and they seemed to be really pissed off.

In the end, she knew that she had to do it; she was not going to live her life in fear. She sucked it up, toweled off, and felt considerably better after she fixed her hair and dulled the bruise with some makeup. Slipping into a comfortable pair of jeans and the Cricket Australia training shirt Dylan had gotten her on Boxing Day, she breathed a little prayer that none of Penelope's fans would be at the restaurant.

"Oh wow," the hostess said excitedly when they entered the lobby. "I can't believe this. It's really you."

Dylan extended his hand to the visibly shaking spikey-haired brunette. "Dylan Miller," he said by way of pointless introduction. She giggled and shook his hand.

"I know... I mean, I'm Vanessa...wow...I'm just..."

"Can we get a table for four, Vanessa?" he said sweetly. "Something kind of tucked away in a corner, maybe?"

"Oh, yes, of course. Let me see what I've got available." She turned to Tia. "Can I just say that I really admire how you handled that whole awful situation this morning? I think you showed a lot of class. What a horrible thing to do to someone. I don't think I could've done what you did—is it true you're not pressing any charges?"

"It's true," Tia said, "and thank you for the support—I really appreciate it."

"That just makes you even more of a bigger person. Brave, too, for going out in public right away. Does it hurt?" She raised her hand to her own cheek, indicating the spot where Tia's face was swollen and already turning a lovely shade of purple.

"A little. I think it may have left a bigger bruise on my ego, though."

"Well I think you were great. You both are. The whole world's pulling for you, you know."

"Thanks again. I really do appreciate it."

"I can have them make you up a table in the other room. There's no one in there right now, so it'll be more private."

"That'd be great," Dylan smiled.

Private or not, all eyes in the restaurant were on them as soon as they entered the dining area. Tia tried to hold her head high and forced a smile; which came with the price of a zinging pain; as they made their way to the doorway that led into another room. Whispers swept up from every table and she could feel the stares boring into her. Panic coiled around her lungs and squeezed there so that she could only breathe in tiny sips. Somewhere a glass fell to the floor and shattered, and she cried out; nearly jumping out of her skin as she buried her face into Dylan's chest.

"It's OK, baby," he whispered into her ear. "I've got you."

She sucked in a breath, and heard the resonance of a clap which was followed by another and another. By the time they reached the doorway, the diners were on their feet, nodding their heads and applauding her courage.

"Thank you," she managed, bowing her head as she swallowed hard. Dylan gave a little wave and they slipped into the other room and into a booth that would shield them from prying eyes.

"Good job, sweetie," Kelley smiled. "You did great."

"Brilliant," Dylan agreed, brushing his lips over her hair.

"I don't feel brilliant," she admitted. "I thought I was going to pass out for minute there."

"I know," he said, pulling her close, "but I'll always be here to catch you if you fall."

Chapter 15

"OK, so you guys ready for the semi-weekly update?" Dylan had Jessa on speaker phone as they sat under the shade of a Tasmanian Blue Gum sipping fresh lemonade. "Fire when ready," Dylan said. "We're both here."

"Oh, good. How's the eye doing, Tia?"

She touched the knot that was still swollen and turning horrendous new shades of purple and yellow. "Nothing a little make-up won't fix," she said, adding, "it's sore, but it'll be fine in a few days. Hey...before I forget, I want to thank you again for getting through to my parents before it hit the American airwaves. You saved them a lot of worry. Thanks for listening to me vent, too."

"No problem. And I'm glad you're on the mend. Thankfully you don't have any appearances scheduled for a while."

"Nope," Dylan said. "Just a lot of well-earned R & R."

"You both deserve it. Have a great time. I'll email you if there's anything important, but otherwise, I'll try to leave you guys alone. I'm totally jealous, you know."

"Everything's all set in for our trip, right?"

"Of course. As usual, I was able to make good on all your crazy requests."

Dylan smiled. "That's why you're the best. What have you got for us today?"

"First order of business; the Esther Caglio video." Some savvy blogger had figured out Penelope's real name and snagged an exclusive interview with her mother and sister, who were more than happy to tell anyone who would listen what a horrible person Penelope really was. They were especially vocal about how she'd slept with her sister's husband and dropped the bomb at Thanksgiving dinner, and even provided some photos of Esther in her less-than-glamorous years. "It's gone viral, of course, and she's managed to lose a lot of her support. Did you watch it?"

Dylan turned to Tia, who shook her head. "Not interested," Dylan said, "neither one of us. I assume you did."

"It was a hell of a strain on the eyes, but it does fall into my job description, so I choked it down. It was exactly what you'd expect—a bunch of self-serving bullshit meant to drum up some sympathy from her adoring fans." Jessa's voice got shrill and dramatic. "She claims, of course, that you two were building a relationship, but she forgives you for leaving her in jail to rot. Oh, and she really wants to talk to you so she can explain. There was a really lame apology in there somewhere, but she didn't admit to anything."

"That's what I figured. No comment, right? I don't even want you to say, "no comment." Not one word to her."

"I figured as much. I've gotten a few calls already, as you can imagine. I just hung up."

"Good."

"Well, most of the sympathy she may have gotten pretty much went out the window after the family interview, anyway. It showed up something like three hours after her latest rant, so her elation was short lived."

"That's all I need to hear about that, then. Any good news?"

"It's all good for you. InHap songs are getting heavier than usual airplay and album sales are up—always good right before a new one and a tour. I got a few more sound bites from Bo and Ty; I'll send them over this afternoon. I've also got no fewer than three major magazines who want to pay Tia extraordinary amounts of money for a cover and an exclusive, and a book publisher who wants to know if she's interested in writing a book about her 'rise to fame,' as they put it. What do you think about that, Tia?"

"I think I'll need to do something to earn my keep, but I'm not ready to commit to anything right now. I could maybe handle the magazines, but writing a book? I don't know that I have that in me."

"You wouldn't need to. They have all kinds of ghost writers who would do most of it for you, pretty much. Something to think about, anyway. I told them you'd be out of commission for a little while, but I got the agent's number if you want it. I bet they'd give you a pretty good advance."

"It's crazy, isn't it? Two weeks ago I was worried that the public wouldn't find me worthy of Dylan, and now someone thinks that people would buy a book I wrote?"

Dylan laughed. "If anything, it's me who's not worthy." He picked up her hand and kissed the back of it.

"Well, you know they'd expect it to be full of lots of juicy details about your love life, right? I know I don't have to tell you that the ladies aren't going stop lusting after Dylan just because he's spoken for."

"Oh, believe me, I know that all too well," Tia said, "which is the main reason I don't think I'd do it. Those juicy details belong to me, and I don't want to share them with anyone. God knows they've gotten deep enough into my personal life."

"Then I guess you're not interested in doing a reality show either, huh?—I've gotten a couple offers for that too."

"Oh God no."

"I didn't think so. I pretty much told them that, but said I'd run it by you anyway. Oh—you do know that Tony called Lexi, right? She's going to do his show on Monday night."

"Yeah, she texted me. I think she's pretty excited about it; she said something about going early to do some shopping and soak up some vitamin D."

"I'm sure she'll be great." Jessa paused. "There's just one more thing I think you need to know. It looks like they're close to striking an extradition deal. New Zealand is going to settle for a fine and get her the hell out of their country. Speculation on this end is that there'll be more fines and possibly some jail time. Rumor has it that her attorney is going to push for a psych facility, alleging that her crimes were…" her voice changed to the bravado of an obnoxious news reporter… "'crimes of passion' and that her obsession drove her to the 'brink of madness.'"

"Oh, she passed over the brink. She bloody well threw herself over the cliff."

"Couldn't agree more. Oh, and they're wondering whether you'll both want to sue for personal damages, too. Your attorney called yesterday, once the extradition info leaked out. I told him I'd pass on the message, but that you wouldn't be back in country for a bit yet and you'd get back with him."

Tia wasn't looking forward to that conversation. As much as she hated what Penelope did, suing her wouldn't do anything but bring more pain to everyone involved. She positively dreaded the thought of spending hours with lawyers hashing out the case, and the last thing she wanted was to see Penelope face-to-face in court. As far as she was concerned, losing her career, Dylan, and the respect of the public was more than enough punishment— God knew that Dylan didn't need the money, and she'd just as soon put the whole thing behind them and move forward. She wasn't sure how Dyl was feeling about the whole thing, but she hoped that he'd want to do the same. "I haven't even had a chance to think about that yet with everything else that's going on," she answered cautiously.

"You've got a bit of time yet before you have to decide. Well, I guess that's all I know. No final date set yet, but if it happens while you're gone, do you want to know?"

"Not interested in the slightest," Dylan said immediately.

"Alright then, you guys have a fantastic time, and I'll talk to you when you get to Sydney; unless something important comes up. Love you guys!"

"Love you too Jessa, and thanks again. I really can't believe all that you do. You absolutely are the best."

"Of course she is," Dylan agreed, sending his love before breaking the connection. He turned to Tia and smiled. "So, now that the business is all taken care of, what do you say about taking a little road trip?"

"Ready when you are," she smiled back. "I'm already packed."

***

"I can't even begin to tell you how much I've enjoyed my stay here," Tia told Steve and Kelley as they loaded their bags into the little Audi convertible early Friday morning. "Thanks so much for an amazing Christmas and for making me feel so welcome."

Kelley pulled her into a warm embrace and gently kissed the purple bruise beneath her left eye. "It's been an absolute pleasure welcoming you to the family," she replied. "I'm so happy that you and Dylan found each other, and that we've gotten a chance to know you." She lowered her voice to a whisper loud enough to be heard by the men. "You are exactly what he's been missing in his life—he better know how lucky he is to have you!"

Dylan wrapped his arms affectionately around Kelley. "I do know, Mum, and I'm going to do everything I can to be worthy of her; don't worry." He planted kisses on both her cheeks and hugged his dad. "I'm damn lucky to have the two of you, as well, and promise we'll stay longer on our next visit."

"I'll hold you to that," Kelley smiled as Dylan opened the door for Tia. "Let us know when you have all the tour dates locked in—we'll try and sneak over by you for a few weeks in the summer. Now you guys drive safely and have a wonderful trip—I'm so glad you'll get to see some of the country, Tia."

Dylan couldn't think of a time in his life when he'd describe what he was feeling as 'warm and tingly,' but as he leapt deftly over the door into the driver's seat; the woman he loved tying a silk scarf around her hair in preparation for the windy ride and his parents waving their final goodbyes; the words popped into his mind and made him smile. He tied his own hair back with an elastic band and tucked it into the new baseball cap he'd picked up at the Cricket game on Boxing Day before giving his mum one final kiss and firing the engine.

He was filled with excitement for the next leg of their journey. First and foremost, it would be the first chunk of time that he and Tia would have truly alone, without the commitments of appearances; public or personal. In Europe, they'd had to work around the tour, of course, and in the past two weeks, interviews and family gatherings. He was really looking forward to the down time so they could catch their breath and have a bit of normalcy back in their lives; if such a thing were even possible.

They could've flown into Sydney, but he wanted to show Tia the natural side of Australia that he knew she'd love—the rocky shores, pristine beaches, and lush forests that sprawled along the Southern Coast. Four days wasn't nearly enough time to do it justice, but at least he could show her the highlights, and share some of the places that were so much a part of his early years. Then, in just a few short days, he'd ask her to be his wife. Warm and tingly indeed, he thought as he reached over and took her hand.

"I just love them, Dyl," Tia smiled as they headed out on the highway. "They're really amazing people."

"I told you you had nothing to worry about," he smirked. "They love you too; that much is obvious. I know they've been waiting a long time for me to find you, but it's more than that, I think," he said thoughtfully. "Seeing the way my Mum was with you brought back a lot of memories..."

"I know what you mean," Tia said, recalling for Dylan the conversation she'd had with his dad the night before.

"Sometimes I forget just how big a role she played in the family, even for the short time she was here. I should have known he'd see it too, even though Aussie men are notorious for having tough skins and swallowing back their feelings. And having another woman in the house just lit Mum up, you know? Like she had a daughter again. It was great seeing her so happy. You made one hell of an impression, Tia. I knew you would."

Tia raised their joined hands to her lips and pressed them against the back of Dylan's hand. "Thank you," she said. "I really do feel like we bonded. I know they would've liked you to stay longer, but I'm really looking forward to some time alone."

Dylan turned to her and waggled his eyebrows. "And I've got a lot of plans for you over the next few days—another reason I thought a little road trip would be a welcome break. God knows we've spent enough time on airplanes over the past couple weeks."

"Enough for a lifetime, I think. I'm already dreading the flight home."

They drove for a while in silence, Tia glancing in the rear view mirror to watch the city landscape fade behind them and catching a glimpse of the non-descript sedan that followed behind them. *As alone as we're going to get anyway,* she thought. Two security people, one male and one female, would be escorting them on their trip—they'd keep their distance unless they were needed, Dylan had told her, but they'd be there nonetheless. After the attack in Melbourne, he insisted he wouldn't compromise when it came to her safety; and as much as she hated the thought of having strangers watching them every time they stepped out of a hotel room, she loved that he was so protective of her. After her little panic attack at the restaurant the night of the incident, she did feel a bit safer knowing that there was someone watching her back.

She took a deep breath of the fresh air and pushed out the memory. Instead, she let her mind wander over other events of the past couple weeks, still amazed at just how much had happened. In one sense it felt like a lifetime; the constant activity and sheer amount they'd accomplished seemed incomprehensible as she looked back on it, and yet being so busy had made the time fly by. It felt absolutely wonderful to have no agenda except for spending time with Dylan and she was excited to be at the start of their journey, with eight glorious days in front of her before she had to face reality again.

"How about that view?" Dylan's voice pulled her from her thoughts and she looked out to see the incredible blue of the ocean just peeping over the horizon.

"It's absolutely beautiful," she answered, bringing her attention back to the present and the incredible man at her side.

"I couldn't agree more. The ocean's kind of pretty too," he smiled at her and she knew that as far as the Penelope situation was concerned, she'd already won the greatest victory of all.

"I think maybe I've died and gone to heaven," Tia said, stretching her arms over her head. "I can't even believe we actually have four days in a row with nothing to do except explore the Australian countryside. This is the best part of the trip, you know, with all the anticipation ahead of us. Oh! Oh, wait! Pull over!" Tia squealed.

Dylan jammed on the brakes and pulled to the side of the road. "What's wrong?"

"Kangaroos!"

Dylan laughed. "You about gave me a bloody heart attack! For some kangaroos?"

"I've never seen them in the wild before...oh wow, aren't they just beautiful?"

Dylan watched pure delight brighten Tia's face as she followed the troop with wide eyes until they melted into the brush. "They are when I see them through your eyes," he said, leaning over to brush his lips across hers. "I love how you love the simple things in life, Tia; it's really refreshing."

"The simple things make life more beautiful, because they're beautiful in their simplicity."

"Well said. That was the inspiration for *House Without a Home,* you know. You really *care.* Not just about people, not just about things, but about everything. I admire that about you."

"It's my new favorite song. I just love it."

Dylan found pure joy in showing Tia the natural beauty of the places that held so many fond memories for him. He was constantly amazed by her adventurous spirit and her love for the simplest things; his heart warmed when she squealed in delight upon seeing her first emus strolling across a grassy field and when she stood speechless, eyes wide, when he stopped at a scenic overlook for a breathtaking view of the waves crashing over rocky cliffs far below them.

He felt like a kid again, carefree and far from the chaos they'd experienced in much of their relationship so far. They laughed constantly and fell into an easy rhythm of casual conversation and comfortable silences.

Tia squirmed excitedly in her seat as he drove up to the airport at Phillip Island and approached the waiting helicopter. "Is that for us?"

"It is. Since we only have a short time on this trip, I thought we could at least get a pretty good overview from the air."

"I like the way you think," she said, throwing her arms around his neck.

He probably spent more time watching her reactions to the sites than he did looking out the window as they soared over the scenic vistas. After a thorough tour of the surrounding area, they touched down at Bass Valley Winery and were met by the owner for a tour of the vineyards and a scrumptious lunch before continuing their aerial tour of the rest of the island. That night, as they waited anxiously in their skybox for the start of the daily Penguin Parade, Dylan couldn't take his eyes off her. She quivered in anticipation as the sun dipped into the blue water, awaiting the arrival of the Little Penguins; tiny native birds returning from the sea to waddle up the beach to the safety of their sand dune burrows. He was transported back to the night in Northampton, about halfway through their summer together, and he recalled the lightness he felt when he realized he was in love with her— remembered thinking, *I love this girl!* to himself as they were twirling on the dance floor. Now, the words that came to his mind were, *I'm going to marry this girl!* and he couldn't have been happier.

Seeing his native country through her eyes made him fall in love with Australia all over again, and he couldn't wait to take her to his favorite place. Nicknamed, "The Prom," by the locals,

Wilsons Promontory National Park is a sprawling national treasure encompassing beautiful beaches, rocky outcrops, lush forests, mountain peaks, and an abundance of native wildlife. He couldn't wait to walk with her over Squeaky Beach, take her for a hike through Lilly Pilly Gully, and bring her snorkeling in the beautiful marine reserve. He'd had many a vacation at The Prom, and it was there that they took one of their final trips as a family, him carrying Shelby on his back along the beach when her strength failed her, twisting his feet with each step over the round pebbles of quartz to produce a squeak worthy of both of them. He hadn't been back since that day, but he knew that being there with Tia would make for a healing presence, and that he could re-live some of his fondest childhood memories without the crushing sadness of loss overtaking him. He'd really been harboring this way too long, he thought. About bloody time he enjoyed life again, just for him. And, of course, for Tia.

"Oh Dylan, it just keeps on getting better and better, doesn't it?" Tia asked as they entered the park boundaries and headed for the coast. "This is just the most beautiful scenery I've ever seen, and every time we round another curve in the road, it just gets more breathtaking. Thank you for sharing this with me...I am so glad you decided to come this way."

Dylan pulled off to the side of the road and put his hands on her cheeks. "Bloody hell I love you, woman," he said fondly, bringing his mouth to hers for a soft kiss. "Every day I wake up thinking I couldn't possibly love you more, but by the time I lay my head on the pillow at night, with you by my side, I realize that I didn't even know what love was when I woke up."

"That's got to be the sweetest thing anyone has ever said to me," she replied breathlessly. "We just keep getting better and better, don't we?"

"Indeed we do," he answered with a smile, "and we always will. Always and forever."

"I'll never get tired of hearing that," she said, leaning across the seat to steal another kiss.

Dylan pulled the car back onto the road, the tan sedan pulling out behind them. "We're camping under the stars tonight," he said. "I've reserved us a tent—not rustic in the camping sense, but in a great location, and at night, a lot of the nocturnal animals sniff around the campground—echidnas, bandicoots, opossums...and in the morning, some of the most amazing birds you've ever seen will come and beg for breakfast. I've brought some nuts that they like to eat—sometimes they'll sit right on your arms to eat them."

"Oh, I love it already!" Tia exclaimed.

The "tent" was more like a luxury hotel room, and Tia's breath caught in her throat as they walked in. It had a queen size bed, a wooden deck, and a private bathroom; although it shared a communal kitchen with the rest of the campground. They dropped off their bags and headed out for a hike, Tia clasping her hands in silent reverence under her chin when she saw a dozen or so cockatoos soaring overhead. The scenery took her breath away—lush greenery, blue sky, and wildlife everywhere—she felt a sense of absolute peace here. She couldn't help but rush to the water when they saw a pod of dolphins swimming by as they walked along the beach, and she looked forward to the next morning, when they'd be snorkeling in the marine reserve that encapsulated the entire south side of the park.

They watched the sunset together from the beach, then returned to the campground for a quiet evening of wildlife watching and stargazing. They'd picked up a couple nice steaks and some fresh salad fixings in one of the towns they'd passed through, and they planned to grill out and enjoy dinner outdoors.

"We're going to need some utensils," she said, "to cook these and to eat them. Where was the kitchen?"

"Right down that path," Dylan pointed. "The barbie's over there too, so just grab the grocery sacks and I'll get the cooler. We'll pick up Deb and Michael on the way—I bought some extra steaks, since they're going to be here anyway. And wear your hat."

After the debacle in Melbourne, Dylan insisted that Tia wear an obnoxious floppy hat whenever they were wandering in public. *"It's just hideous enough that most people will turn away rather than stare,"* he'd said when he presented it to her. *"With that and a pair of sunglasses, hardly anyone will recognize you."* She groaned and pulled it over her head, tucking her hair beneath it. It was that or a wig, Dylan had insisted, and she sure as hell didn't want to deal with that kind of inconvenience.

He did have a point though, and it was well taken. It was disconcerting having strangers come up to greet her in random places, and it did happen. The night of the Melbourne incident, when they went to dinner with Dylan's folks, she'd been followed into the ladies room by another restaurant patron. She was a very nice woman who had just wanted an autograph, a picture, and to show her support, but it was incredibly awkward being addressed from the other side of the bathroom stall when she was trying to pee.

The two members of their security detail were staying in the next tent over. Tia knew that it was their job to accompany them everywhere they went—although they'd pretty much stayed out of sight during their little adventures, she'd felt their presence everywhere they'd gone—but she still felt bad about intruding on their evening to have them follow her and Dyl to the barbeque area so they could cook their dinner. She didn't feel comfortable with the fact that they had to drop whatever they were doing to follow their every whim; even though they were being paid well for it. It was simply well outside of her own comfort zone.

They were sitting on the wooden deck of their tent, eating sandwiches from wax paper wrappers and sipping iced tea from paper cups. As soon as they saw the couple approaching, they rewrapped their makeshift dinners and stood. "Heading out?" the man, Michael asked, ready to forgo his own dinner to follow them wherever they went.

"Just over to the kitchen—Dylan got dinner for all of us," Tia said, holding up the shopping bags and motioning to the large cooler Dylan carried. "The grill...I'm sorry, the *barbie*...is just down the road. Come and join us."

Michael was down the few steps in an instant, taking the cooler from Dylan. Tia noticed that he was younger than she first thought; perhaps in his late thirties, with thinning hair and strong arms. "That's very kind; I'm pretty sure whatever you've got in that cooler beats these lousy sandwiches," he said. Deb took the bags from Tia, and followed them toward the kitchen.

"You're sure?" she asked. "We wouldn't want to impose."

"Positive," Tia answered, turning on the path that led to their destination.

"Hold on," Dylan said, "I've forgotten something." He looked at Deborah. "You two go ahead; we'll be right behind you." Michael set the cooler down, and followed Dylan back to their quarters.

Tia looked around the long narrow 'tent' that served as a kitchen. There was a group of people already out in the barbeque area, but they were already cooking and the kitchen was empty. Deb set the bags down on one of the tables and groaned in pleasure as she started pulling out the contents. "Oh, this is just great," she said excitedly. "That was probably the worst sandwich in the history of sandwich making—it got wet in the cooler and the bread was absolutely saturated. Thanks again for inviting us— this looks amazing."

"Absolutely," Tia smiled. "Dylan got enough food for a small army—plenty to share." The kitchen was rustic but well appointed, and she began pulling out some plates and utensils as Deb began scrubbing vegetables. Tia tossed her hat on the table next to the bags and unwrapped the steaks; rubbing some seasoning onto them and piling them on one of the plates. She was digging through the silverware drawer looking for some tongs when the door swung open, and four women walked in, each carrying a bag of their own.

"G'day," one of them said, smiling. "Beautiful evening, isn't it?"

"It couldn't be more perfect," Tia replied.

Their heads turned toward her. "An American, are you?" an older woman with gray hair and crinkly eyes asked.

"Yes," Tia laughed. "Is it that obvious?"

"Hard to hide the accent, love," she said kindly. She walked toward Tia offering her hand to shake, but stopped a few paces away. "Wait a minute," Crinkle Eyes said, her head tilted and her eyes narrowed. "I know you from somewhere." She cocked her head the other way, trying to make the connection as Deb tensed and moved closer to her side.

A slightly younger heavyset woman set her bags on the opposite table and studied Tia as well. "No way," she said, reaching into a huge cloth bag. Tia ducked instinctively and chastised herself for panicking when the woman pulled out a magazine. She looked from the rag to Tia and back again, then held it up for the others to see. "It's you, isn't it?" she asked, turning the magazine toward Tia. It was her face on the cover, all right, there was no denying it. Thankfully, they'd used one of the pictures that had been taken at the airport, and not one where she was covered in blood; although the headline read, "Battle of Hastings." An image in the corner showed the woman who had allegedly hurled the blood bomb. She was wearing a "Free Penelope" t-shirt, and was being dragged away by two security officers. "I can still see the bruise. You're Tia Hastings."

Tia pasted on her best smile and extended her hand. The women looked friendly enough, with open faces and genuine smiles, but she couldn't help but feel her self-preservation instinct kicking in.   The ladies looked at her, eyes wide and smiling. "That's me," she said kindly. "It's nice to meet you."

They shook her hand in turn, chattering all the while and comparing her face to the one on the magazine again and again, as if to make sure they weren't mistaken. Each of them told Tia her name, but the only one she remembered was Agnes, aka Crinkle Eyes, who seemed to be the spokesperson for the group.

"Oh my gosh, I can't believe this," she said. "Can I just say that I'm appalled by what happened to you the other day. I saw the program—but the way you stood tall and handled yourself..."

she whistled through her teeth. "Like a real lady," she finished with a smile.

"Thanks very much; I appreciate that," Tia said graciously. It seemed she was saying those words a lot lately, much as Dylan often did.

"Are you on holiday, then?" another woman asked, "with Dylan Miller?"

"I am," Tia answered, "and I have to say, this is honestly one of the most beautiful places I've ever seen. And with just one exception, the people are lovely, too."

"Is he here too?" the heavy-set woman asked excitedly.

Just then, Michael walked through the door toting the cooler, with Dylan right behind. "Oh my stars, I can't believe this!" Agnes exclaimed. "I never would have thought..." She rushed over to Dylan and took his hand, introducing herself and the rest of her little group. "We're with the Sunshine Seniors," she explained. "We're a travel club that goes...oh who cares?" she giggled. "I've been travelling all my life, but I've never run into any celebrities before! This is our lucky day!"

The other ladies chimed their agreement.

"Oh, won't you join us for dinner?" Agnes begged.

"Oh please do. We've got more than enough, we always do," the heavyset woman said. "It would mean so much to us—please say you'll have supper with us."

Dylan smiled and put his arm around Tia's shoulders. "How can we say no to an offer like that?" he said. "We'd be happy to. We've got some steaks and a few other things to toss in, too." Tia looked at him from the corner of her eye, and he just shrugged, leaning over and whispering, "It's already a party, and it's a bit of harmless fun. We'll spend an hour and they'll have something to brag to their kids about tomorrow."

"OK then, sounds great to me," Tia agreed, and the ladies pumped their hands in the air in a victory cheer. Agnes took Tia by the hand while two others; Beth and Laurel, she tried to remember after they introduced themselves again; flanked Dylan, lacing their arms through his. They led him out the door and around the back of the building, where about six other people were gathered. Several women bustled about, stacking plates on picnic tables and pulling food from coolers. A smaller group of men sat on the fringes, laughing and drinking beer from oversized cans. Michael trailed behind with the cooler, and Deb followed with the stack of plates and cooking tools Tia had gathered from the kitchen.

Agnes cleared her throat loudly. "Ladies and Gentlemen," she began, "we have a real treat here tonight—two real live celebrities have agreed to join us for dinner!"

One of the men looked up and slid a pair of glasses onto his face. "Real life celebrities, huh?" he said doubtfully. "What kind of celebrities?"

"Oh my gosh...I just saw you on television," a brown-haired woman breathed. She rushed up to greet them as Agnes passed the magazine over to the men, who looked over the top of it at Dylan and Tia as they skimmed the story. "This isn't awkward at all," Tia whispered sarcastically from the side of her mouth.

"Wait a minute," one of the men said, "I heard this story—it's the one where that actress tried to break you up, right?" He stood and reached into a cooler, handing Dylan one of the giant cans and extending his hand. "I'm sorry I'm not familiar with your music, but I can tell you that my daughter and granddaughter are both big fans—I had to buy the granddaughter a poster of you last Christmas. I can't tell you how jealous they're going to be!" Several others agreed, and just like that, they were welcomed into the fold.

An hour turned into two, pictures and video greetings were recorded, autographs were signed. It was nearly ten by the time they said their goodbyes, and Tia and Dylan headed for their own tent, trailed by Deb and Michael, whom they'd also gotten to know better over the course of the evening.

"So, your first celebrity excursion," Dylan said. "Kind of weird, huh?"

"At first, yeah," Tia agreed, "but it was kind of fun in the end. Why did you agree so quickly? I mean, I'm not sorry you did, but I didn't expect it, I guess."

"It's a fine line, this," Dylan said, swirling his index finger in the air. "You don't always know which side you're walking, but sometimes it's a no-brainer. This was just about being nice to some people who wanted to rub elbows with celebrity; for whatever that's worth. It wasn't for the cameras, it wasn't a publicity stunt...it was just about making someone's day. We had company anyway, with Deb and Mike, so what's a few more people? Their kids and grandkids will think they're cool, and they'll have a great story to tell on their next trip. Maybe the media will get wind of it and maybe they won't, but that wasn't the point. The point was simply to bring a little joy to people, and that, to me, is the fun part of the fame." His eyes widened, and he leaned down to the cooler that Michael had left on the porch. "Oh damn, I forgot something," he said, reaching inside and pulling out a now crumpled and wilting wrist corsage. He took Tia's hand and slipped it on her wrist.

"What's this?" she asked, looking oddly at the unusual gift.

"We're at 'The Prom,'" he said, "I meant to give this to you much earlier, but then..."

Tia hopped on the first step to their tent and turned toward Dylan. They were eye to eye, and she put her hands on his shoulders, pressing her forehead to his. "Listen," she whispered. "Remember what you said this morning, about not knowing what love was when you woke up in the morning?"

"Yeah."

"Times about a million," she smiled, putting her hands behind his neck and pulling him in for a soft kiss. "You're an incredible man, Mr. Miller. I am so beyond lucky to have you in my life."

Dylan grabbed her around the waist and swept her into his arms. "Why don't you show me?" he murmured against her neck.

"Over and over, always and forever," she replied, as he swept her into his arms and carried her to their bed.

The tour of the coast ended way too soon, with a trip to the summit of Genoa Peak in Croajingolong National Park, a snorkeling excursion with the seals in the crystal blue waters of Montague Island, and a dolphin spotting off the shores of Jervis Bay. As they had in Europe, Tia and Dylan discovered that they were compatible in all the ways that mattered, and each and every night, he kissed her under the stars before they returned to their room to make love; rediscovering the scents, tastes, and contours of each other's bodies.

It was the perfect mix of adventure and down time, and in the many hours they spent in the car they chatted about mundane things like favorite ice cream flavors (Tia, cookie dough, Dylan, rocky road) to favorite books (Tia, The Stand, Dylan, the one Tia was going to write about their romance because he couldn't wait to see how sexy she made him out to be) to Dylan's ranch in Colorado that Tia would soon make her own. She had marveled so many times at how much they still had to learn about each other, but by the time they got to Sydney and she got her first views of the incredible city, she felt as as if they'd known each other all their lives.

Chapter 16

"Hey, good evening everyone, and welcome to *After Dark*!" Tony crooned after he finished his monologue and took his usual place behind the big desk. "I've got a great show for you tonight— the last one of the year. It's all about deception, secrets, and finding lost love."

"Ooooh…" the audience responded.

"Yeah, it's big stuff, right? And speaking of big stuff, the news just came out that authorities are very close to striking a deal with the government in New Zealand to extradite Penelope Valentine. Apparently, they're going to settle for an "undisclosed fine;" I'd hate to have to pay that bill! Now, if you saw my special last week—and I'm sure you did—you got to meet Tia Hastings, the woman at the center of this whole controversy, for the first time right here on this stage. You heard her say that there was only one person outside of the band who knew about her relationship with Dylan Miller—Her best friend, who was sworn to secrecy for almost seven months…" the audience groaned in reply… "I know, seven months! Can you imagine having to keep a secret like that? I don't think I could do it!" He paused to let the audience react. "My first guest tonight is arguably the best friend anyone could have; not only did she keep that secret, but she was there for the early days of their relationship and was the only one Tia could turn to after the allegedly fabricated break-up. Here to share some inside scoop about the story no one can seem to get enough of these days is Tia's best friend…please welcome Lexi Summers!"

Lexi pasted on her best smile as she walked onto the stage toward Tony's outstretched arms, trading the requisite air kiss and light hug before taking her seat on the couch at his right. She soaked in the cheers of the crowd while she tried to settle her heart—she was a lot more nervous than she thought she'd be. She looked damn good though, thanks to the knockout of a dress she'd picked up in a little boutique on her shopping spree yesterday; which helped to boost her confidence a little.

When the "applause" light went out and the audience quieted, Tony smiled and shook his head at Lexi. "Seven months," he stated with disbelief. "You knew about their relationship for more than half a year, and never told a soul. How hard was it to keep a secret like that?"

Lexi answered with a sardonic grin. "Definitely the hardest one I've ever had to keep. One of the first things I said after I found out about her and Dylan was that I couldn't wait to tell everyone, but she swore me to secrecy on the spot."

"Take us back to that day," Tony prodded. "I mean, how do you react to that kind of news? Your best friend...what...calls you up and tells you that she met Dylan Miller last night and that they had a date later that day? Did you even believe her?"

Lexi smirked before answering; she'd rehearsed the questions Tony would ask and how she'd respond with the producers. "Well, that's not exactly how it happened, Tony, and I'm still kind of pissed about it, actually...but looking back, I guess I kind of deserved it."

Tony leaned in anxiously and waited; tenting his fingers under his chin. Automatically, a good number of audience members leaned forward in their own seats, mimicking his stance. "I have a feeling this is going to be good," he grinned.

"It was for her—she really nailed me, that's for sure. So, the Friday night of Memorial Day weekend was the one-year anniversary of the day Tia's fiancé died." Murmurs of sympathy rose up from the crowd. "Tia decided it was time to get her life back on track, and she decided to go to this little dump of a bar; to just kind of be a barfly and get out into a crowd. When she told me where she was going, I pretty much begged her not to go there—it's kind of a shady place, and she hadn't been out alone for a long time." Her mind wandered for a moment as she considered, for the first time now that she'd voiced it, how different their lives would be if Tia had listened to her that night. She took a deep breath before she continued.

"I was worried sick because she said she'd only be out a couple of hours, and she didn't call until around three in the morning—that's when she told me she met someone. I started giving her a hard time about it—told her she could do a lot better than some guy who hung out at that dump. Maybe that's why she didn't tell me. She just let me figure it out for myself."

Tony looked puzzled. "How did she do that?" he asked.

"Well," she said, playing it up for the cameras, "we had tickets for the InHap concert on Saturday night. Tia canceled our dinner plans and told me that she was hanging out with her new guy that day because his band had a gig that night, too. She tried to convince me to come out with them after the show—it was the drummer's birthday, she said, and they were having a party, but I told her there was no way I was going to be a third wheel on their first date. Plus, I still thought they were some grungy pub band, and had a horrible picture in my mind of how that would play out. Then she told me that this guy had an 'in' at the venue and had upgraded our seats—but even while I was sitting front and center of the stage, it never even crossed my mind that her new guy could possibly be Dylan Miller...I mean, how likely would that be?"

"Not very," Tony agreed.

"Tia met me at our seats right before InHap took the stage, and I told her that Dylan had looked right at me and smiled when he was onstage with the opening band—that he'd noticed me in the crowd..." She stopped for a moment and chose her words carefully, "...and she just laughed at me. InHap played a few songs, and it was like Dylan was singing right to us; I even suggested we try to get backstage after the show. The third song they played was *I'll Pull You Up*—the crowd went crazy, because they'd never played it live before—and right then he dedicated the entire show to her in front of sixty thousand people. His eyes never left hers throughout the entire song, and all I could do was stare at them both, my mouth hanging open like a complete idiot. I mean, I was totally blown away! It took pretty much the whole song for it to sink in that he was the guy she met the night before."

"Wow. And she swore you to secrecy right then and there?"

Lexi nodded. "Oh yeah! She made me pinky swear, and anyone out there who still has a friend from middle school knows that there's no stronger bond!" The audience agreed with a smattering of applause.

"Why do you think she did that? I mean, most people would want to announce something like that on the evening news, don't you think? Why the secret?"

"Well, at the time, she figured she'd get to be with Dylan for a day or two at the most—InHap had one more show in Chicago the next night, so it was possible they'd see each other again; but after that they were going to tour Europe, so of course Tia thought that would be it. She was worried about how people would react, and she wanted to keep him all to herself for the short time they did have. So I made the promise. At the time, I figured I'd only have to keep the secret for a couple days, so it seemed doable."

"But then he invited her to Europe," Tony said, "and a couple days turned into a couple months."

Lexi nodded. "You know, it all happened so quickly...it had to. They had an intense connection, and Tia going on the tour was the only way they could figure out if it was real. Dylan wouldn't be back home for a year between the tour and the movie, and lucky for her she has summers off, so she headed off to Europe, where they obviously decided it was the real deal."

"Which meant that you still had to keep the secret while Dylan was New Zealand."

Lexi answered with a smile and a nod of her head.

"And we'll hear more about that when we get back from a commercial break," Tony smiled into the camera. "Stay tuned, folks...we've barely scratched the surface of this story!" The audience clapped, and the camerawoman indicated "cut!" with the swipe of a finger in front of her throat.

Bo sat fidgeting in his dressing room. The video feed was broken so the monitor was blank, and he was flipping absently through a month-old issue of *Rock's Finest,* waiting for someone to come and mic him up for his stint. It had been a fluke that when Granger had called him he'd already been in LA, playing a few gigs with one of his former band mates from the old days. Dylan had more than given him carte blanche to appear on his behalf; in fact, he said he'd be doing them a favor by taking some of the heat off of him and Tia. Finally, the door opened, and a cute little brunette walked in with his microphone.

Tony leaned in and patted the back of her hand. "You're doing great, Lexi—you're a natural at this!" He motioned to an assistant who ran up with a cup of water.

"Thanks," Lexi said, gratefully draining the ice cold liquid. She was really having fun with the whole thing and her heart had settled, but her mouth felt like the freaking Sahara.

"Ten seconds," said a disembodied voice over a speaker. Tony shifted in his chair and turned on his TV smile as the cameraman counted down and then motioned that they were rolling.

"Welcome back to *After Dark,"* he began. "My first guest tonight is Lexi Summers, best friend of America's newest sweetheart, Tia Hastings." He turned back to face Lexi. "So, Lexi," he said, "before we went to commercial, you were telling us about how Tia surprised you with the identity of her new beau..."

"Blindsided me is a better word," Lexi laughed.

"You also said that before you figured it out, you had decided not to join Tia that night for the drummer's birthday party. Was it really his birthday, and did the fact that you'd be hanging out with Incidental Happenstance change your mind?"

Lexi hesitated for a couple heartbeats; they hadn't rehearsed that question, but it wasn't a hard one to answer. "Absolutely!" she exclaimed. "That was a complete game-changer. I was beside myself going backstage to meet them all—I was still in shock, I think. But they're all such nice guys; they made me feel completely comfortable in no time. Especially Bo; the birthday boy."

Tony smiled wide—his surprise question provided the perfect segue into the next segment. "On that note, Ladies and Gentleman, I'd like to introduce my next guest," he said into the camera, watching Lexi from the corner of his eye and catching the slightly confused expression he had hoped for. In the conversations he had with Dylan, he had heard a lot of little sidebars comments about the quirky and unique friendship that Lexi had forged with Bo Collins. He thought it would be fun to bring them back together for the show, without either one knowing the other was here. Bo was probably bored to death by now in the room with the 'broken' monitor and a few old magazines, and he couldn't wait to see how they reacted to each other. "Please help me welcome one of Dylan's best friends, drummer for Incidental Happenstance, Bo Collins!"

There was one split second when Tony saw Lexi's eyes widen in complete surprise; then her entire face just lit up. As soon as Bo appeared from the side of the stage she let out an excited squeal and leapt from her seat, rushing to greet him. Tony turned just in time to see Bo's realization sink in, and smiled as Bo quickened his step while a grin split his face. Lexi threw her arms around him and called out his name. His mic picked up Bo's hushed whisper, "Hey there beautiful! Now isn't this the best surprise!"

Tony watched as the big man picked her up and spun her in a slow circle before putting her down and leading her back to the couch. He stopped for a handshake and man-hug with Tony before taking his place on the couch beside an obviously flushed and flustered Lexi Summers. Bo turned to her and flashed his famous smile, wrapping her hand in his own. Lexi responded by leaning her head on his shoulder and smiling up at him.

"Well, that's quite the reunion!" Tony smiled.

"I can't believe it!" Lexi exclaimed. "It's been ages!"

"It's great to see you too, angel," Bo replied.

"So, how long has it been since you've seen each other?" Tony asked.

They looked at each other. "It was late September, wasn't it?" Bo asked.

Lexi nodded. "It wasn't too long after Dylan got to New Zealand," she said to Tony. "Bo was passing through Chicago and took Tia and me out for dinner."

Tony turned to Bo. "So Bo, Lexi was telling us about how shocked she was when she first found out about Dylan and Tia." Bo smiled, remembering. "How did Dylan share the information with the rest of the band? Was he secretive too?"

Bo chuckled; his deep laughter rumbling in his chest. "Oh no, not Dylan," he said with a grin. "Quite the opposite, actually. We had a lot to do at the arena that day...it was our first show in Chicago and we'd gotten some new electronics that needed to be hooked up, tested, and adjusted, which was going to take some time. One of the trucks carrying some of the stage equipment had broken down on the way from Indianapolis, and then Dylan had a couple interviews to do on top of it all.

"It was about 9:30, and Dyl'd just finished one of the interviews. He comes practically *dancing* into the room with this pathetic grin on his face—I'm tellin' you, it was like that kid in the candy story look, and we all knew something'd gone down. So I ask him, 'What's got you grinnin' like the Cheshire Cat?' and he says, 'you'd be grinnin' too, if you met a gorgeous and amazing woman last night like I did.'

"I tell you, all the heads in that room snapped to attention, and all eyes turned to Dylan. I mean, it's pretty hard not to notice that most women find him fairly easy on the eyes, but he's always seen it as kind of a curse. I mean, the man could have pretty much any woman he wanted, but he didn't want any of them because he couldn't trust that they would be in it for the right reasons. He'd been burned more than once, and it had been a long time since I'd seen him smile like that. But the look on his face that day was like nothing I'd ever seen before, and I've known the man— hell, I've lived with the man—for a lot of years. He had it bad already, and he's not the kind of guy that falls hard for anything so easily."

"Are you saying it was love at first sight?" Tony asked.

Bo pressed his lips together and nodded his head. "He told me a little bit about what happened the night before; how they met, and what they did. He said it was like they went through six months in one night—they'd connected in a way that threw him for a loop, and he was like a schoolboy with a crush. He pranced around the whole morning. That grin never left his face, and when we'd tease him about it, he'd only smile bigger. He kept looking at his watch, and was pretty much useless as far as the work we needed to get done.

"When Tia showed up that afternoon, and I saw them together for the first time, it was like I could *feel* their connection. I got a good vibe from her right away, and it was obvious that she was good for Dylan. There was something in his eyes...and hers too...that spoke volumes."

Lexi sat upright. "I know what you mean! When I saw them together that first night, I said the same thing...I told Tia that I could feel the connection between them like it was a physical thing in the room..."

"Speaking of physical things in the room..." Bo began.

"Penelope Valentine!" they said together.

Tony shrugged his shoulders and tilted his head, indicating they'd lost him. Then, he sat back and let things play out. As Bo was describing the look in Dylan's eyes and the smile he couldn't tame when Tia was around, Tony couldn't help but think he was witnessing a connection between Bo and Lexi that neither of them realized was there. Dylan had said that they had an obnoxious and repetitive flirtation that they all laughed about, but from where Tony was sitting, there was more to it than that. The body language—the way she leaned against him, the way he held onto her hand, the way they looked at each other—said that there was more there than mere flirtation. But who was he to say? God knew he'd been through three divorces...romance wasn't exactly his forte. He was willing to bet, however, that Lexi wouldn't be taking the flight she'd been planning to jump on shortly after they finished shooting. Something told him she'd hold off and fly out in the morning.

Lexi deferred to Bo. "That was the first night she came sniffin' around. She showed up backstage and started demanding to see Dylan, saying she had something important that she needed to discuss with him. He'd just finished playing a song with our opening band, and so we sent out a message that she was on the prowl. Dyl was so wrapped up in Tia, and so confused by how to reconcile the fact that he would have to say goodbye to her in just a couple days even though he was just getting to know her, that they just pretty much hid out in a different dressing room until it was time for us to take the stage."

Beside him, Lexi started to giggle. Bo took one look at her and his eyes went wide. He joined in, and pretty soon they were laughing so hard they were practically keeping each other from falling off the couch. Tony leaned forward, a smile on his own face. Yup, he'd definitely put down money that she wasn't flying home tonight.

They turned back. "Tell him," Lexi prodded, trying to rein in her laughter. "It's such a great story!"

Bo was busting a gut, and managed to squeak out, "Go ahead...you tell it!"

"Well," she started, "after the show, Penelope came bursting into the common room. The guys had just left to get cleaned up, and she comes in and confronts Tia, insinuating that she slept her way into getting a show dedication. She was just plain rotten; I can't think of a better way to describe it. Her face was wrinkled up like there was a bad smell in the room, and she totally looked down her nose at both of us. Tia told her that the guys had gone to shower up and she stormed out of there, determined to find Dylan." She glanced at Bo, and started giggling again. "Turns out," she smiled, "the boys had pretty much anticipated the move, and Bo was actually the one in Dylan's shower. She walked right into the bathroom and Bo..." she burst into another fit of giggles, and Bo took over.

Tony sat back in his chair smiled. His guests had effectively taken over his show, and he couldn't have been more pleased. They played off each other perfectly, finishing each other's sentences, and sharing little bits of stories that wouldn't have come out in a standard interview. It was like they were suddenly the only two people in the room, and it translated perfectly to television. He could imagine people all over the country feeling as if they were sitting with them in their living rooms. He made a subtle gesture toward the producer that said, *Give me another minute...this is too good to pass up.*

"She was just so *fake,*" Bo continued. "Her voice was so sweet, but there was no sugar there, ya know? So I yanked open the shower curtain, and watched all the blood drain out of her face...she was expecting a naked Dylan to be standing there, and instead," Bo stood and turned in a slow circle. "...she got me. I don't have to tell you that as soon she was able to breathe again, she ran out of there so fast she was just a blur!"

Everyone in the studio joined in the laughter as they imagined the shock that Penelope felt when she was surprised by Bo. The giggles continued until Bo's face changed, and he held up his hand for silence.

"That part was funny, but later that night, when we were out celebrating my birthday, she showed up again, at the club, and that's where the whole thing started." Lexi's face got serious as well, and she dropped her head. "That woman practically propositioned Dylan right in front of Tia," he said, his voice low and steady. "She basically told Tia that she wasn't worthy of Dylan—something like, 'If you want to have fun tonight, you should take your chances with someone who's at your level.' I watched the doubt fill Tia's eyes, and saw her face fall. She was unsure of herself—she was obviously feeling something for Dylan that she couldn't come to terms with; especially since she believed that he was leaving the next night. Penelope dropped the bomb that she'd be his co-star, and that she thought they'd have 'great chemistry' together. It was like she was already working on ways to sink her teeth into Dylan even then. Allegedly," he added.

Tony took a sip from his coffee mug and let the two of them chatter on about the trip to Europe. Lexi bragged that she was the one who told Dylan about Tia's birthday and shared the story about the surprise dinner on the Eiffel Tower, and Bo talked about how anxious Dylan was waiting for Tia to show up after the school year ended and she first came to Europe. They kept talking during the commercial breaks—not real breaks as they were filming and not live, but more a chance to catch their breath and grab a quick drink of water—so all he really had to do was ask a few unscripted questions and let them run with it. He hadn't planned to fill the whole show with the two of them, but they were too good to pass up. His assistant could reschedule the other guest.

When Tony made his final comments and wished the crowd a Happy New Year, Bo and Lexi wandered through the audience shaking hands and signing autographs. Lexi was astounded that anyone would actually want her autograph, but she happily scribbled her name on whatever was handed to her. As the last of the audience members drifted out the door, Bo draped his arm over Lexi's shoulder. On their way to Tony's lounge for the 'debriefing,' he asked, "How about dinner, beautiful?"

Lexi was instantly torn. She'd pretty much promised Ryan that she'd be home tonight, but she hadn't seen Bo in months, and it would be great to hang with him for a while. God, she could use some more of his lightheartedness and his humor right about now, and if she didn't take advantage of this opportunity, who knew when she'd get to see him again? What in the world would she tell Ryan, though? He'd been pretty pissed off at first when she told him she was coming to LA. *You're not the celebrity, Lexi,* he'd said; insinuating that she was enjoying a ride on Tia's coattails and looking for attention of her own. And so what if she was enjoying it? She was entitled to her 15 minutes, right? She looked up at Bo and smiled. To hell with the consequences, she decided—she needed a little Bo time. "What do you have in mind, handsome?" she smiled, tucking her hand into the crook of his arm.

His grin widened, making the corners of his eyes crinkle. "Would you be staying at the Four Seasons?" he asked. "I'm assuming Tony puts all his guests there." Lexi nodded. "There's a nice little Japanese restaurant just a short walk away—they've got great sushi, and do a real nice leisurely dinner...we could catch up for a while, then maybe go back to one of our rooms to watch the show?"

The show! What an idiot she was! Not once, in all the planning of this whirlwind last minute trip had she considered that the show would air hours after they taped it—and that she'd be on a plane when it did. It was the perfect reason for staying until the next morning...it wasn't like she'd be able to watch it with Ryan anyway, so it would be perfect to watch it with Bo. "I always have liked the way you think," she said, wrapping her arm around his waist as they entered Tony's lounge to say their goodbyes.

Chapter 17

Lexi leaned back in the comfy leopard print chair in Bo's suite and watched him fiddle with the remote control. "Look, I'm camouflaged," she teased, referring to the leopard print lounge outfit she'd changed into before heading down to Bo's room to watch the show. She'd picked it up in a little boutique during one of her many shopping escapades over the past couple days, and although she'd cringed when she saw the price tag, she'd never felt a fabric so luxuriously silky and simply had to have it. She held the leopard pillow from the chair in front of her face and said, "Can't even see me, can you?"

"Are you even here?" Bo teased back, his head moving back and forth as he pretended to scan the room. Lexi stood up and set the pillow down, raising her hands in the air in a 'ta da!' "Oh, there you are," he grinned, "I was worried for a minute there that I was just imagining I had a beautiful woman clad in leopard print hanging out in my room. The good Lord knows I've had that fantasy before."

Lexi plopped onto the mustard-colored love seat that faced the television and stretched her long legs up to rest on the coffee table. "I'd better sit here then—wouldn't want you to forget I'm here." She took a deep breath and sighed, completely content after a leisurely and delicious dinner, some great wine, and excellent company. With Bo, it was so easy to have fun that she'd forgotten to get nervous about watching her television debut.

Tony hadn't even batted an eye when she told him she'd like to change her departure to tomorrow morning. "Whenever you want," he'd said, giving her a business card with a number on it. "There's someone on call 24/7, so just text after you've called for the car. They'll have the plane ready by the time you get there." Ryan had been less than excited that she was staying, but he really had no argument when she told him she wanted to watch the show when it first aired. She made him promise to wait, though, and watch the recording so they could both see it at the same time since it would be on later in California than it would in Chicago.

"Oh, Mr. Collins," she teased as Bo handed her a glass of wine, "you would be a great catch, you know that?"

His eyes widened for just a split second, and then his easy grin slipped over his face. "Yeah, you think? I'm sure my ex-wives would have somethin' to say about that," he teased back, waiting a couple heartbeats before adding, "What makes you say that?"

"Well," Lexi started, sitting up straighter and raising her fingers to count up the ways, "first off, you're such a gentleman...you really know how to make a lady feel special." She lifted another finger. "Second, you have a great sense of humor. Third, you're one of the easiest people in the world to talk to— people just feel good around you!"

"Don't forget, 'devastatingly handsome,'" he joked. "Most people notice that one first off."

"There is that," she agreed, tipping her wine glass in his direction in a toast. "Seriously, though, Bo—how is it that you're not taken?"

His grin wavered, and his eyes darkened for just the briefest moment, but it was enough to make Lexi wonder what was behind the shadow. Had he been hurt by someone? Bo recovered quickly, though, and tapped his wine glass against hers.

"I guess it's because you're not available, my little princess," he smiled. "Who could hold a candle to you?"

Lexi felt a flush burn her cheeks and lost her breath for just the slightest moment before returning Bo's grin. "Well, we'll always have London," she said, her voice sounding a bit hoarse. The wine was apparently going to her head.

"Indeed we will," Bo answered. Just then, the opening theme song for *After Dark* filled the room. Lexi patted the spot next to her and Bo folded himself onto the love seat and turned up the volume. He turned to her with his glass raised for another toast; a more serious look on his face. "To your TV debut—I'm so glad I could share it with you."

Lexi tapped the rim of her glass against his. "Can't think of a better person to share it with," she said, setting down her glass and settling in. "This is so exciting! I might even be more nervous now than I was walking out onto the stage." Her heartbeat quickened, and she fanned her face with her hand as she watched Tony's monologue and waited anxiously for him to call her name.

She held her breath as she watched herself walk out onto the stage, then let out a little squeak of excitement. It was really strange seeing herself on television; almost like being in a dream. "Damn this is cool!" she exclaimed, wiggling in her seat. They watched her segment excitedly, chatting about how the cameras zoomed in on her best angles and how one seemed to hover a bit too long over the low neckline of her dress. "Well it is fantastic cleavage, right?" Lexi asked, puffing out her chest in an exaggerated motion. "The best," Bo replied gruffly, diverting his eyes back to the television.

Lexi jumped up and refilled their wine glasses during one of the commercial breaks, and checked her phone. She'd missed a text from Ryan wishing her good luck, and saw a second one that read, "U look fantastic! Gr8 job!" She shot him a quick thank you, and heard the theme music starting up from the other room. She fell back onto the couch and said excitedly "Oh, here you come, Bo."

Bo froze as he watched himself walk out onto the set. He was certainly aware that he was a big guy, but seeing how tiny Lexi looked in his arms really took him aback. "Who the hell is that guy?" he asked. "Damn, do I really look like that?"

"What do you mean?"

No wonder people thought of him as loveable old Bo, he thought to himself. He looked like the life of the party, the funny clown who got all the laughs but never the ladies. He patted his stomach and laughed it off, but inside, he couldn't find any humor in it. "I think I need to call Jenny Craig," he said wryly.

"They say the camera adds ten pounds, you know."

"Yeah? It didn't add ten pounds to you—oh wait, I know…maybe it accidentally added your ten pounds onto me; that must be it. It looked like I was going to break you in half when I picked you up—you really did disappear."

Lexi laced her fingers through his and leaned against him. "You're still devastatingly handsome," she purred, her voice vibrating against him as she spoke.

He looked down at her, cuddled up innocently against him, the swell of her 'fantastic cleavage' seeming to taunt him and it was as if an alien life force took over his body. His vision went cloudy, and he could actually see himself reaching over and lifting Lexi's chin, running his fingers along the curve of her neck, and bringing his lips down to meet hers. He shook his head slightly to toss the image from his mind and stiffened; his hand actually raised as if to truly make the move and then…holy shit, he *stiffened.*

He felt his eyes widen, and held his breath. *Dead puppies, dead puppies,* he thought over and over in an attempt to stop the stirring; but she was still pressed against him; the silk of her goddamned-soft wild cat outfit brushing against his arms and her hand wrapped tightly in his. *Dead kittens, dead kittens,* he changed his chant, but it did nothing to slow the flow of blood and he felt a full-blown hard-on coming and coming fast.

Bo nearly jerked his fingers from hers, catching a taunting spark from the diamond that glittered on her left hand. He stood up and turned away from her, grabbing the only thing in the room he could use to effectively hide his embarrassment—the leopard print pillow from the matching chair. *Shit,* he thought. *This is not good.*

Lexi's head tilted and her eyes narrowed in confusion at his sudden move and obvious discomfort. "What's wrong, Bo?" she asked.

"Nothing," he nearly snarled, the words stuck in his throat. He had no idea what to say to her—no excuse for why he'd leapt from her side like she had leprosy instead of looking really sexy in a leopard print outfit. He was saved from saying anything else by the chirp of her phone signaling an incoming text message. She frowned at him once more and rose, walking into the little kitchen area of the suite to to check the message.

"What the hell Is up bw u n the drmmr?" the message said. Lexi stared at it for a minute, wondering the same thing, before texting back, "NOTHING—RELAX."

Bo fell onto the chair and took some deep, calming breaths, putting the pillow in his lap and folding his hands to rest on top of it. Yeah, he needed a little prayer right now. Lexi returned just as the last commercial break ended; a question in her eyes as she took in his new seating arrangement, and returned to the couch, folding her legs under her and crossing her arms over her chest. He forced his best smile, made some lame joke about the way Tony stopped interviewing them and just let them talk, and tried to keep the conversation light; tried to turn on his usual charm; but even he wasn't buying it.

It was impossible not to notice the shift. Bo smiled and joked through the rest of the show, but the atmosphere in the room had changed, and Lexi couldn't help but wonder why. At first she thought it was the weight thing; he was obviously bothered by the way he looked on TV; but she loved him just the way he was and couldn't see why he'd be so flustered by it. He was *bulky,* built like a linebacker, sure, but not overly *heavy.* Would he be embarrassed enough by that little thing to physically move away from her? Bo Collins exuded confidence...she couldn't imagine him being that hard on himself.

The show ended, the final credits scrolling over the three of them moving into the crowd to shake hands with members of the audience. Bo clapped his hands in a round of applause and smiled at her. "Congratulations, beautiful—you absolutely stole the show."

"Thanks, handsome," she smirked. "You were pretty fantastic too. It wouldn't have been nearly as much fun without you. Having you there was the best surprise."

"It was my pleasure." Damn, just thinking the word *pleasure* increased the hum between his legs and he stretched out his arms and yawned, taking an exaggerated glance at his watch. It wasn't that he wanted Lexi to go, not at all, but he felt like a complete ass sitting there trying to hide an erection that wouldn't quit; and probably wouldn't until she was out of his field of vision. Or smell, or hearing, or anything else for that matter.

Lexi was confused, but she was no idiot. It was obvious that Bo wanted her to go. She took the hint, and gathered up her things. "Well, I've got an early flight set up, so I probably should try and get a few hours of sleep. I won't see you before I leave— but I hope I'll see you soon." She walked over to give him a hug, but he didn't get out of the chair...just leaned toward her a bit and gave her back a friendly pat.

"I hope so too," he said, and watched her walk out.

Lexi opened the door and sat on the zebra striped chair that adorned her own room, trying to figure out a cause for the complete 360-degree turn the night had taken. She and Bo had a great dinner, lots of laughs, and for the first three-quarters of the show, were getting on as well as ever. Even if he did get a sudden case of self-consciousness after seeing himself on the television set, it still didn't explain why he'd just all of a sudden purposely put distance between them...it just didn't make sense.

Then another thought hit her as she replayed the events in her mind. Right after his uneasiness, she'd grabbed onto his hand and practically laid on him, telling him he was 'devastatingly handsome.'

Oh God...it was the first time they'd ever been really alone; and in a hotel room no less; and she'd practically pushed her breasts in his face and asked him if he liked her cleavage...holy shit, did he think she was hitting on him? Is that why he moved as far away from her as he could and put a pillow down as a barrier—so she couldn't get that close again? Just the thought that he might have gotten that impression made the sushi she'd eaten earlier feel as if it had suddenly started swimming around in her gut.

She loved her relationship with Bo, and thinking that she'd done something to screw that up made her heart skip a beat. Should she say something? What if she was completely wrong, and ended up creating a problem that wasn't even there? Would mentioning it only make things more uncomfortable? She wrung her hands in her lap, remembering the look on Bo's face when he wouldn't even hug her goodbye. Uncomfortable was an understatement, and she got up and started pacing the room. *Shit,* she thought. *This is not good.*

Ryan plopped on the couch and pulled up the menu on the TV. At first he'd been kind of pissed that Lexi was staying an extra night in LA, but if he were in her shoes, he probably would've stayed too. In the end, Lexi had been right about the bragging rights he got out of her personal invitation from Tony Granger—there were enough of the 'living dead,' as Lexi so affectionately coined them, at his parents' dinner party who didn't know anything about the story. A good number of them had no idea who Dylan Miller was, but they sure as hell perked up when they heard the name Tony Granger. Ryan had been the center of attention for a good chunk of the night, and for the first time that he could remember; he came away from that dinner with a good taste in his mouth. It was holiday vacation, it was nearly New Year's Eve, and his girl was on television. Life was good.

The theme music started up, and Granger walked to center stage. *Must be nice to be that dude,* he thought. The guy had more money than the Pope, and all he had to do was walk out every night, tell a few jokes, and then sit down with the rich and famous and let them brag about themselves. Tough life.

He listened attentively to the monologue in case he mentioned Lexi, laughed at a couple of halfway decent jokes about failed New Year's resolutions, and leaned forward in anticipation when Tony announced who his first guest would be.

Ryan hadn't thought to ask if she knew who else would be on the show with her...but he selfishly hoped it would be someone way more famous than Miller had recently become.

He sat through the series of commercials that always followed the monologue; car insurance, beer, a TV series, a sports car; and perked up when he heard the theme music again. When Lexi walked out onto the stage, his heart nearly stopped. She looked absolutely gorgeous; an obviously new and just as obviously expensive dress draped over her figure like it was made for her, and she wore impossibly high heels that showed off her incredible legs. It was hard for him to believe that this was his girl, his fiancé, walking out onto that stage like she owned it; accepting the applause of the audience as if it was something she did every day.

She was witty, well-spoken, and downright modest about the whole situation, and she had the audience eating out of her hand. *Maybe I was too hard on her,* he thought as he crammed a handful of popcorn into his mouth. He watched with interest and even pride as she handled herself with more class than some of Granger's usual guests exhibited. When the next round of commercials came on, he grabbed a Coke from the fridge, poured some more popcorn into his bowl, and settled back in.

He stopped with the can halfway to his mouth when Granger introduced the next guest and he watched as the band's drummer, a huge black dude with a big white grin, picked Lexi up and called her 'beautiful.' She was so excited to see him that her smile about tore her face in half, and she practically sat in the guy's lap when they got to the couch. A spark of jealousy scissored around in his gut as he watched the two of them talking—it's not like the guy was Lexi's type or anything—hell, he was a far cry from Miller's league, but it was obvious that they'd forged some kind of bond while she was in Europe. *Another thing she neglected to tell me*, he fumed as he slammed down the Coke and went to the fridge to grab a beer. Just one more secret—one more freaking lie—how many more things were there that he didn't know? He took a pull of the beer and watched as they laughed together, telling stories of shared times that he knew nothing about and suddenly wondered if they were watching the show together somewhere; and if he even knew Lexi anymore.

Lexi hit the send button on the text, and checked the bathroom once more to be sure she hadn't forgotten anything. She knew sleep would be impossible, so she figured she may as well go home right now. Maybe the hum of the private jet would lull her into some sort of rest. It was late—well, early actually—but she'd summoned her courage and decided she was going to go see Bo before she left. She just couldn't leave with things between them uncomfortable, so she was just going to say it...tell him that she hadn't meant anything by her behavior, and that she considered him one of her very best friends and wanted to keep it that way. She didn't even care if she woke him up—it was too important to her that his opinion of her wasn't tarnished. He was an honorable man, she knew that, and if he thought she was behaving less than honorably tonight, she had to set the record straight.

With her bags in tow she stepped off the elevator and knocked on his door. She waited a minute before knocking again, in case he was getting out of bed. When he didn't open it, she pulled out her phone and called his room, hearing the shrill ring through the door but getting no answer. Could he have already left, or was he purposely avoiding her? She was about to knock again when her phone vibrated in her hand. Her car was waiting at the front entrance, ready to take her to the airport. Although she hated leaving things this way, she had little choice, and she dragged her bags down to the lobby to head for home.

Bo hadn't sweated this much since...hell, he didn't think he'd *ever* sweated this much. He had a lot of nervous energy—*no, sexual energy, damn it,* he thought...*may as well be honest about it*—that he needed to burn off, and he moved from the treadmill to the weight bench and started doing curls. Maybe once he'd exhausted himself, a cold shower would wash the unwelcomed thoughts from his mind.

Lexi was his friend, damn it, and a good one at that. They had a rapport he'd never had with anyone else, and he wanted to keep it that way. There was no excuse for the images that were suddenly sprouting and growing in his mind...images of her lying on his bed, her golden hair spread around his pillow as he slowly spread her...*Damn it!* He pushed himself harder, adding more weight to the bar and switching to bench presses. Thank goodness the gym opened with his room key—he definitely needed this distraction.

Not only was Lexi his friend, he reminded himself, but she was an engaged woman—forbidden territory. He had no business thinking this way about her, and worried about how she'd perceived his sudden move to the chair. Did she notice his blatantly obvious 'excitement,' or did she think that all of a sudden, for no apparent reason, he wanted to get as far away from her as he could? Either way made him look like a complete idiot. Damn it, would she even care if he didn't want to be close to her? She was the one who'd patted the spot beside her when the show was starting, but if she'd gotten a glimpse of the way the crotch of his pants was vibrating...

Shit. Shit, shit, shit, he thought as he pushed his muscles to the edge of overload. He couldn't leave things like this, he just couldn't. He needed to talk to her before she left in the morning—tell her that she was still his princess and that he was sorry he'd behaved like such a complete ass. He could make a joke of it; make it a typical Bo statement. And if he went while he was still sweaty from the gym, he wouldn't be tempted to pull her into his arms and beg her to stay. Then he could finish off with a cold shower and try and get some sleep, although he had great doubts that he'd even catch a wink.

He mopped the sweat off his face with a towel and took a cautious whiff of an armpit. At least he didn't smell like he'd just sweated out a couple gallons of body fluid.

He made his way to her room and knocked, the door swinging open when he hit it. Total darkness greeted him, and he stuck his head in and called out her name. When he got no answer, and heard no sounds coming from inside, he stepped in and turned on the light; his heart sinking. The closet was open and empty, there was no clutter of toiletries sitting on the vanity, and the bed was neatly made. No suitcase sat on the little valet stand, and a stack of bills sat on the night table—a tip for the maid, presumably.

Obviously he had offended her, he thought sadly, dragging himself back to his room. She couldn't even wait until her scheduled flight in the morning to get away from him. Lexi was gone.

Chapter 18

The cooling evening air washed over them as they sat on the balcony overlooking the bridge and Sydney Harbour, sipping champagne and nibbling on chocolate-dipped strawberries and truffles, and awaiting the start of the New Year's Eve celebration. They looked out over the bustling streets below them, all the crowds heading toward the water's edge for the best view of the spectacular fireworks show that would mark the start of a new year.

The city simply hummed; Tia could think of no better word to describe it. Buildings were ablaze with lights, music of all kinds wafted up to their balcony, and the laughter and celebration of the people in the streets electrified the atmosphere with an anticipatory feel. She smiled and sat back in her chair, more than happy to participate in the party from a distance.

As she did on every New Year's Eve she could remember, Tia reflected on the past twelve months, hardly able to believe all that had happened in such a short time. She recovered from the loss of Nick and made her way back into the world, found Dylan, fell in love again, toured the entire continent of Europe, lost Dylan, and somehow; whether by incidence or happenstance; reclaimed him into her life once again. She was thrust into the media spotlight and hesitantly embraced a new world; a new life with the man she loved. She very likely lost her career—she'd been putting off making a final decision, but she didn't see how she could balance her old life with her new one. Tia Hastings—no doubt about it—was a very different person than she had been just a year ago. She turned and smiled at Dylan and without saying a word, he knew her mind and shared her thoughts. It had been an unbelievable year, but in the end, it had been the best year of her life; and it was all because of Dylan Miller. Sliding her chair closer she snuggled into him, fully embracing the familiarity and comfort level they shared. Just as much could be said in silence as can be said with words, she thought. Even Dylan was quiet tonight; preoccupied, almost; perhaps lost in his own reminiscing over the past 365 days.

He popped the cork on a freshly chilled bottle of champagne as the clock approached midnight and poured two glasses, setting them on the small table that sat on the balcony. He looked at her and smiled; a look in his eyes she'd never seen before—well, maybe once, at the top of the Eiffel Tower the night he first told her he loved her. Rolling the memory around in her mind like a favorite dream, she opened her arms to the love of her life.

They heard the music crescendo in the distance, and the countdown of the crowd below. Ten! Nine! Eight! Seven! Dylan and Tia counted along with them, and kissed right after they said, One! Then came the first *whoosh!* that signified the start of the fireworks display, which started with a bang off the Harbour Bridge; an explosion of color and sparks that filled the night sky with fire. Tia felt them more than she saw them as she was still attached to Dylan, their tongues mingling as they started a new year filled with more promise than either of them ever imagined.

Dylan pulled away and held her at arms' length, looking deep into her eyes. There was so much love, so much intensity in his gaze; that she caught her breath and smiled. "I love you so much," she whispered, her voice as light as the sparks that drifted down from the sky. "Happy New Year, baby."

Dylan swallowed, and smiled back. "I love you too, Tia," he breathed. "I can't even form the words to tell you how much." She leaned into him, but he held her back and kept her captivated with his stare. "This year has been so crazy," he said. "I found you, I thought I lost you, I found you again, and now neither of us will ever be the same. And I don't want us to be the same. You've made me see the world in a whole different light, and my favorite view is seeing it through your eyes. I'm a better man for knowing you, Tia Hastings. My life has been so incredible since you walked into it, and I want to spend the rest of my life making you happy."

"Oh Dylan," she whispered. "You make me so happy. Every day." She smiled warmly, her eyes full of pure and unadulterated adoration.

"This is going to be the year of us, Tia, and it's just the beginning of a lifetime together." He raked his hands through his hair, and reached into the pocket of his jacket, his gaze never faltering. "The next time the tabloids print a headline that says 'Engaged,' I want it to have an exclamation point and a picture of us under it." He pulled his hand from his pocket, and Tia saw the gold-embossed black box that he held and she inhaled on a gasp, unconsciously bringing her hand to her heart as Dylan dropped to one knee.

"I worship you, Tia Hastings. Life without you would have no meaning, and you would make me the happiest man on earth if you would be my wife." He opened the box, but Tia couldn't take her eyes off of his and all the sentiment she saw there. "Please. Say you'll marry me."

A flood of emotion washed over her in an instant, and in that moment, she knew beyond the shadow of a doubt that she was the luckiest woman in the world. "Yes," she croaked, then louder, "Yes!" Her voice dropped to a whisper as she fought tears of joy. "With every cell in my body, yes. Oh Dylan..." She held out a very shaky hand and looked down as he slipped the ring onto the third finger of her left hand. He kissed the ring and her hand before standing up and pulling her into his arms. Their kiss was sweet and tender, and the fireworks in the distance seemed just for them.

"I love you so much!" she whispered. "Oh my God...I'm going to marry you!"

"I'm so lucky to have you," he said, his voice thin. "I can't wait to make you Mrs. Miller."

"Oh...Oh!" she said. "I can't believe this! Once again, I'm going to tell you that you've given me the best night of my life! I don't...even know what to say...except I love you..." The tears spilled then and Dylan kissed them away, picking her up and turning her in a slow circle as she buried her face into his shoulder and wrapped her arms and legs around him tightly. Just as she had shouted from the top of the Eiffel Tower when he first told her he loved her, Tia leaned over the balcony and yelled into the revelry, "I'm going to marry the most amazing man in the world!" A small group of people below heard her shout, and turned their faces up toward them. "Congratulations!" one called out, as the others clapped their hands together and sent up a "Whoo Hoo!" She turned back to Dylan and repeated the words; more quietly this time and only for him. "I'm going to marry the most amazing man in the world." She took his face in her hands and planted a very shaky kiss on his smiling lips. "Oh my God, Dyl," she whispered. "I..." but she could still come up with no words to articulate what she was feeling at that moment.

Dylan finished the sentence for her; "... can't think of anything in the world that deserves a toast more than that," he said, moving to the table to pick up the champagne glasses. Tia raised her shaking left hand to get a look at her engagement ring; the symbol of the love she and Dylan shared. When she saw the fireworks reflected in the crystal clear stone, she gasped out loud.

Dylan turned and saw her staring, gape-mouthed at the ring. "Do you like it?" he asked nervously. "I admit I don't know a whole lot about jewelry, but the guy from Harry Winston said..."

For a second, she could only stare at her hand. The center stone was enormous—she'd never seen a diamond so big. It was an oval shape, and smaller diamonds surrounded it. The band, lined with even more diamonds, seemed insignificant to hold it. Dylan waited anxiously for her approval, and she caught her breath and threw her arms around his neck.

"It's absolutely beautiful!" she breathed. "It's also enormous—*oh my God*—did you rob the Crown Jewels?" she joked.

"They were all big... hell, I've never shopped for an engagement ring before and I had to sneak in the meeting while you and Jessa were out shopping. But you get the best, sweetheart. The best of everything from now on, and I'm so glad that I can give it to you. Are you sure you like it?"

She cradled his face in her palms and kissed his mouth. "It's perfect. You're perfect. I would have said yes if you offered me one of those lollipop rings, but this is...incredible!" She kissed his lips and then each cheek. "Oh my God," she said again, still in shock. "We're going to get married!"

He smiled and handed her a glass of champagne as the grand finale exploded the night sky. "A toast, then," he said, "To the best year of our lives so far and the woman I love; the soon-to-be Mrs. Dylan Miller." He raised his glass and they tapped the crystal flutes together, intertwining their arms to sip the bubbly as the final shower of sparks cascaded down over Sydney.

"I'm so relieved you said yes," he admitted, taking a deep breath.

"Did you doubt it for a second?" she asked.

"Maybe for a second," he smirked. "But let me tell you, no matter how confident I was that you'd say yes, that's a big deal, asking someone to marry you. I've been sweating it all day!"

"Well then, be glad that you only have to do it once, because you're going to be stuck with me forever, mister. I'm never letting you go."

"I'm counting on that," he said, and they slipped into the room to make their own fireworks.

Afterward, as they lay tangled in each other's arms, Dylan could sense Tia's anxiousness. "I'm reading your mind," he said.

"Oh yeah?" she said. "And what am I thinking, besides that I'm the happiest woman on the face of the earth?"

He smiled. "You're thinking about how you want to make some calls to tell a few other people that you're the happiest woman on earth," he teased.

"Can we?" she asked anxiously. "Oh Dyl, I'm so excited..."

"Of course we can," he said. "I want to tell the whole world!" The truth of it was, very soon they would tell the whole world, and they both knew that it would bring even more attention to them. But neither of them minded in this case; not one bit.

They powered up the laptop and pulled up the video chat so they could deliver the news in person. They called Dylan's parents first, since it was already past 1:00 AM in Melbourne. Of course, Dylan had told them of his plan, so they knew the call was coming. The video hadn't popped up on the screen yet, but Tia heard the excitement in Kelley's voice. "Happy New Year! Do we have some good news?"

"She said yes!" Dylan sang as the video feed went through just in time to see their excited faces.

"Congratulations to both of you!" they said together. "Welcome to the family, Tia! We're so glad to have you as our daughter!"

"I can't think of a more incredible family to join," she said, and they chatted for a few minutes before ending the call. Her parents were next on the list. "They don't usually keep the computer on—maybe I should call them first," she said. "It's kind of early there, isn't it?" She'd had the time difference down when Dylan was in New Zealand, but her mind wasn't working at full capacity at the moment; and she was way too excited to dig up some paper and do the math.

"Oh, I'm pretty sure they'll be online," Dylan said with a smirk.

"They know?" Tia asked incredulously.

"Your dad does," he smiled. "I couldn't ask you to be my wife without his blessing, you know."

"When in the world did you get his blessing?" she asked. "You only met them for a few hours!"

"Hell, he barely knew me a few minutes before I asked him," he answered. "I was surprised and glad that he gave it— after asking you to marry me, it was the second most nerve-wracking thing I've ever done. Makes standing on stage in front of a hundred thousand people seem like a piece of cake, that's for sure."

"Oh Dylan," she gushed. "That's so sweet! I'm so glad you did that!"

"Your mum doesn't know, though, so it'll be a surprise to her, remember."

She clicked their number from her contact list, and they answered almost immediately. "Happy New Year!" Tia exclaimed!

"Happy New Year to you!" her mom said. "Although we've got a ways to wait for midnight here. It's not even nine in the morning yet."

"Did you two have a nice New Year's Eve?" her dad asked, the hint of knowing in his voice.

"Oh Mom, Dad...I have the most exciting news!" She paused for a moment to catch her breath. She still couldn't believe she was saying this. "Dylan and I are engaged!"

The look on her mom's face was priceless, and Tia was so glad, that even across oceans and time zones, she could see her mother's face light up when she heard the news. How she wished she and Dylan had this connection while he was in New Zealand, she thought. It could have been a game changer.

"Engaged?! Did you hear that William? Our baby's getting married!!" Tia watched as her mom visibly choked up, and her smile lit up the whole screen.

"We're so happy for you!" her dad said. "Welcome to the family, Dylan. I'm proud to call you my son, and I know you'll take good care of our little girl there."

"The best," Dylan agreed.

"Well, let me see the ring!" her mother urged, and Tia held her hand up in front of the camera. Dylan reached over and helped her steady it—she was still shaky whenever she looked at it.

"Oh my goodness," her mother breathed. "Is that a real diamond? I've never seen anything that big!"

"It better be," Dylan laughed.

"Oh, it's so beautiful! Exquisite!" she breathed. "I'm beyond words right now, you guys—I'm just so incredibly thrilled for you both..."

Dylan piped in. "Listen, I really want to thank you both for being so welcoming to me, especially in light of the...situation. I do promise you that I'm dedicating my life to your daughter's happiness, and that I feel incredibly honored that she's agreed to be my wife..." he turned to Tia. "Damn it feels good to say that!"

They smiled at each other and then back at the camera. "I'm the happiest girl in the world right now," she told her parents, "and I'm so glad you gave Dylan your blessing, Dad. It means so much to me. To both of us."

"You knew?" Danielle's head turned; the surprise evident in her voice.

"He asked for my blessing and I gave it," Will replied, pulling her in and giving her a squeeze. "I knew better than to let you in on the secret," he said with a taunting smile.

"We'll talk about this later," she smiled at him, "and let's just say that you're very lucky that I'm so excited right now; excited enough that I might let you off easy—this time..."

They spent some time catching up on news from home—it seemed that the media had found Will and Danielle, and their phone was ringing off the hook. There was also a small entourage occasionally camped out in the street in front of the house looking for comments, interviews, anything that they could use to fuel the fire. "Barbara Walters's people called me," her mom said. "I told them I wouldn't speak to anyone but Barbara herself, and they said they'd see what they could do! If she calls, can I talk to her?"

"Sure," Tia agreed after getting a nod from Dylan. "But don't spill the news about the engagement until we go public, OK? I don't want any of my friends to find out on the news. We've got a lot of calls to make first."

"Oh, I can't wait to see the look on Martha Granite's face. Do you know she's been trying to hook Dakota up with some pro golfer that her cousin knows ever since the day you brought Dylan to the club? She just can't stand the fact that someone else's daughter is dating a celebrity and hers isn't. She's going have a fit." Her mother especially liked the attention she was getting at the country club, at her bridge club, and pretty much everywhere she went. She was like a movie star, she said, and she was positively basking in it.

"Not yet, Mom," Tia warned.

"Give us 48 hours," Dylan added. "It'll be out by then." '

"Oh, it's going to be so hard! I mean, who doesn't want to brag that their daughter is engaged?" Tia shot her a look with narrowed eyes and pursed lips. "But I'll do it, I promise. I'll be as good as Lexi."

"We better make those calls fast," Dylan smiled after they cut the connection.

Chapter 19

The first two calls to Lexi went unanswered, so Tia tapped her screen again. She was just about to hang up and try once more when Lexi finally came on the line, her voice a barely audible whisper. "This better be the goddamned lottery office calling to tell me I've won millions," she croaked.

"It's way better than that!" Tia sang happily into the phone. "Turn on your computer and pull up Skype—I'm calling back in five minutes with big news!"

"I've only been in bed for like five minutes," she said. "No brain function. Call back later."

Tia laughed. "Oh, OK. I guess you can just read about it in the papers later, with the rest of the general public. Sleep well," she said, hanging up without further explanation. She waited only a couple minutes before the little box popped up at the bottom of her computer screen, telling her that Lexi was online.

Lexi answered the call without video. "This better be good," she grumbled. "And it better be short, too, because I am in desperate need of more beauty sleep."

"You have to have the video on!" Tia said. "I can't continue this conversation until you do."

"Shit," Lexi croaked. "I just got back from freaking California an hour ago; I was there doing an interview for you two, I'll have you know—Bo was on the show with me. I seriously just got into bed, and we've got a party tonight that's going to go late. I look like death warmed over—no way you're seeing me. Video stays off."

"Well, this conversation is pointless then," Tia teased. "I wanted you to be among the first to know, but there's a necessary visual component, so if you absolutely refuse, I'll just call someone else. But I don't want you to be bitching at me later that I didn't tell you first..."

"Ohhhh shit, this better be good," she mumbled.

"Not one more word until you turn on the video. I need to see your face, and you need to see something too."

"Christ," Lexi muttered, but she turned on the video feed. Tia waited a few seconds for the images to load, her heart beating a mile a minute. "What the hell is that?" Lexi asked when the image popped up on her screen. "Holy shit, is that a fucking *ring*?"

"We're engaged!" Tia exclaimed, moving her hand from in front of the screen and getting her first glimpse of Lexi; her normally coifed hair matted down on one side and sticking out in all directions on the other; a raccoon-ish smudge of mascara beneath both her eyes.

"Yikes!" Tia teased. "You weren't kidding about the beauty sleep, honey..."

"Never mind that," she said excitedly, her eyes widening. "Is this for real? You guys are getting married?" Her head turned from the screen and her face pinched. "Crap," she said, trying to tone down the excitement in her voice, "I woke Ryan up. He's going to be pissed." She smiled back through the camera. "I can't believe it—I mean, of course I can believe it, but I wasn't expecting it so soon...oh my God, congratulations!"

Dylan's smiling face appeared on the screen. He took one look at Lexi's image, and his expression morphed to exaggerated surprise. "How much of that beauty sleep are you allowing yourself, Lex? Tonight's New Year's Eve, you know."

"Screw you Miller!" she laughed. "And don't you dare tell Bo you saw me like this...I have to remain the perfect princess in his eyes." She frowned, feeling the sense of loss and confusion from the previous night settling down on her. She may never be anything to Bo again, she thought sadly.

"Not a word from me," Dylan teased back. "I wouldn't even know how to begin to describe it..."

Lexi very purposefully scratched at the end of her nose with her middle finger. "I've seen Tia in the morning too, and it isn't any better."

"I've seen her plenty of mornings," he chuckled, "and she always looks beautiful." He put his palm up to block the view of the camera, and smacked a loud kiss on Tia's cheek.

"Alright, enough talk about my natural attributes," she said. "You're engaged! Holy crap, after all you guys have been through, you so deserve to be happy. I'm so excited for you!"

"Can you believe it?" Tia shouted. "It's been a hell of a year, but this new one's going to be nothing but awesome!" She recounted for Lexi how Dylan had popped the question, and happily granted every request to see the ring.

"That thing is enormous," Lexi said. "Are you sure it's real?"

"It bloody well better be," Dylan said, "Why do people keep asking me that?"

"Uh, maybe because stones that big are usually only found in quarries? Oh my God, when are you going to do it? You think you'll get married this year?" Lexi asked.

"We haven't gotten that far yet," Tia said at the exact same time Dylan answered, "As soon as possible!"

Tia knew instantly what she was thinking. "Not July, Lex, don't worry about that. We've only been engaged a couple hours—we haven't even started that discussion..." It was the month of Lexi and Ryan's wedding, and Tia was the maid of honor. She'd never consider treading on that.

"July?" Dylan interjected. "No way I'm waiting that long."

Tia looked up at him, narrowed her eyes, and shook her head. "Obviously, my *fiancé*..." she said, loving the sound of the word rolling off her tongue, "has no clue about how much time it takes to plan a wedding." She smiled up at him.

Dylan sat down beside her on the loveseat, bringing his face back into the camera's view. "Obviously, my *fiancé*," he said with just as much emphasis, "has no clue about the perks of her new celebrity status. Designers will be knocking each other over for the chance to design her dress, and the same goes for florists, cake decorators, caterers...plus, we have a secret weapon," he added. "Guess what Jessa did before she started working for me?"

"Holy crap," Tia breathed. "She was a wedding planner!"

"That's right," Dylan boasted. "No way I'm waiting until July. I was thinking more like May. I think I could be available on Memorial Day weekend."

Tia sucked in an audible breath. "That would be the one year anniversary of when we met!" she said.

"It would," Dylan smiled before he caught himself. "Oh bloody hell," he said, "I'm an idiot. It would also be the anniversary of Nick's..."

Tia cut him off. "No Dylan, it wouldn't. It wouldn't be the same day. Besides, it would be good to associate something happy with that time of year too. And if Nick could hand pick the guy I'd be with, it would definitely be you. I love the idea!" She turned back to the camera. "Of course you'll be my maid of honor, right Lex?"

"I'd kick your ass if you asked anyone else," she said. "Holy shit, I can't believe you're going to get married before me—I've been planning this thing for over a year!" Her eyes widened, and she looked right into the camera. "Oh, T, it's going to be so much fun doing some of our wedding plans together. Have you thought about where you'll get married? I mean, your family is in Chicago and his is in freaking Australia, for chrissakes. Can't get much further apart than that. It won't be that warm here in May yet, but it's almost winter there, isn't it?"

Tia turned to Dylan. "Wow, that is going to be a tough one," she said to him. "Not only that, but you have friends in England, Colorado and California, too. How are we going to get everyone together in one place?" she asked.

"I have an idea about that, but I'll talk to you about it later," he said.

"What later?" Tia said, punching him on the arm. "You've already considered this? You know you have to tell me..."

"I think this is the spot in the conversation where I check out and go back to bed," Lexi said, "although I don't think I can sleep anymore. You're getting married! I'm so excited for both of you! Happy New Year—love you both!"

"Love you too, Lex—have fun tonight!" They cut the connection, and Tia immediately turned to Dylan, hands on her hips.

"OK, spill. You have an idea about how we can get everyone together for our wedding?"

"I have a great idea," he smiled at her. "It may sound a bit off at first, so listen to the whole plan before you decide, OK?"

"OK," she said suspiciously. "I'm all ears."

"Where to start," Dylan pondered. "OK. So first of all, our wedding is going to be big news—I wish it wasn't that way, but this media circus has gone beyond my wildest imagination, and it is what it is."

Tia nodded. "Yeah, it's gone above and beyond, that's for sure."

"What that means," he continued, "is that the media is going to do everything it can to get access to the wedding— everyone's going to want an exclusive, or a picture they can sell...but if we can control the media, we can still have a private wedding and have the final say in what gets published."

"Yeah, but who can control the media? The tabloids don't take no for an answer, and they certainly aren't polite." She groaned. "Oh Dylan, the last thing I want is for our wedding day to be a three-ring circus."

"Absolutely not," he said. "That's where this idea comes from. Remember, I have a very good friend who is a media mogul..."

"Tony."

"Exactly. His influence runs deep. He made me an incredible offer—one that has the potential to be a win-win-win-win situation. I think he threw a few more "wins" into it when he pitched it to me, but it really could be the perfect solution. But the decision is ours, Tia, so don't feel like you have to take him up on his offer if it isn't what you want. Just hear it all out, and then give it some thought."

"That's an awful lot of 'wins,'" she smiled, "but I'm not getting married on TV, if that's what he's thinking."

"No way. I wouldn't even consider that for a minute. However, we do have a responsibility to our fans, so try to have an open mind, OK?"

"Oh…alright," she said grudgingly.

"So Tony has his own island in the Bahamas…" he paused and let her soak that in for a minute, smiling when he saw her perk up and a smile touch her lips.

"…and he's been developing it, building a very small and exclusive resort for the rich and famous. It's going to be operational sometime in mid-May, if everything stays on schedule, and he's pretty confident that it will. It can accommodate around 150 people, maybe a few more, and he's offered to give us our wedding, on his island, as a gift. We'll have the entire island to ourselves for the whole Memorial Day weekend."

"Wait…are you saying we could get married on the beach, on a private island?" Her eyes widened and then narrowed as she contemplated the idea. Dylan imagined he'd run much the same gamut of emotions over his own face when he first heard the news, and he'd only shown Tia the tip of the iceberg thus far. He smiled, contemplating the next concern she was likely to voice. He had solutions for every single one of them, he thought, as he'd considered them all during his discussion with Tony, as well. "Oh Dylan, it sounds positively wonderful," she started, "but remember, my friends and family aren't rich. How can I ask them to spend so much money to fly out for a weekend? I mean, Lexi and Ryan and my parents could afford it, but my teacher friends…"

"That's one of the 'wins,'" he said. "Tony has a couple planes, and one of them's a corporate jet. He's offered to fly our guests over and back. They wouldn't have to pay anything."

"Whoa," she breathed, her mind racing, "seriously?"

"Our wedding would be the 'grand opening,' for lack of a better term, of his resort, and so for him, it would be a test run of how the whole place will work. He's got a full staff—cooks, housekeeping, groundskeepers, the whole deal—and he wants a chance to fill the place and make sure everything is perfect before he opens it officially. So all of our guests win—they get a free weekend at an exclusive property on a private island—a place that'll only be accessible to people willing to pay big bucks after that weekend. Tony's going to be charging a small fortune to stay there once it opens officially, and our guests will always be able to say that they were the very first to christen the place."

"Oh wow, I'd call that a huge win!" she exclaimed, her smile growing wider.

"And of course we win, because we get a perfect setting for our wedding and the media doesn't have to know about it. We'd keep the location secret—we'd just tell people to save the weekend, and tell them to pack swimsuits. They wouldn't know where they were going until they were on the plane, so the details won't even have a chance to leak out. We can have our day without helicopters buzzing overhead or reporters standing outside the church."

"OK," she said, contemplating, "I definitely like the sound of that. I can't even imagine having paparazzi invade our wedding day—that would be awful. And getting married on the beach...that's been a dream of mine since I was a kid..." her eyes glazed dreamily as she envisioned it in her mind. "But that's two wins—us and our guests. What are the other ones?"

"Well, believe it or not, Tony wins a few times." Tia raised her eyebrows. "He's an investor, and a shrewd one at that. There're a few things in it for him, but none of them impact our bottom line. First of all, he gets the trial run for his new resort and business venture—we do have to be prepared for the possibility that there may some bugs—it'll be the first time the place is up and running, the first experience for the staff; things like that. He doesn't anticipate any issues, because he's got a whole team of people working proactively on the final outcome, but he wouldn't want anything to go wrong if he had paying guests—and like I said, people who stay there are going to pay big.

"Second, and this includes another win for him too, is that he has several big investments in tabloid television. He has his show, obviously, but he also has a controlling interest in a tabloid TV show and holdings in a pretty popular magazine...I forget which one, but it's big."

"Really? I wouldn't have guessed that."

"There's big money in it, apparently, and Tony is the epitome of big money," he smirked.

"That's for sure," Tia agreed.

"So as a businessman, he sees big opportunity here. Obviously, we'll want wedding pictures and videos..."

"Definitely."

"So we'd sequester them, basically. We'd have our own people, or Tony's, and they'd have to agree to give up their cell phones when they arrived. Actually, there won't be phone or internet service on the island except for hard connections in the main house. That way, no one could leak any of the pictures or the location to the press. Then, after all is said and done, Tony would have exclusive rights to the pictures. He'd be the first one to air bits and pieces on his late night show, then the next day he'd have exclusives on his tabloid show and for the magazine. He stands to make a ton of money off of it, but we'd have final say in what gets aired and printed. Or Jessa would," he added. "I'm going to be much too busy with my new wife to worry about those kinds of details." He leaned over and planted a tender kiss on her lips.

"So the public wins in that deal too," he said. "They'll get an inside look at our day without anyone intruding on it. Oh, and Tony has a deal with the Travel Channel to do a documentary about his resort, so we'd agree to let some of our footage be part of that show too. We may do a couple little interviews along the way, and maybe some of the guests who'd like to be on television would do a couple as well. That's another moneymaker for Tony—it'd be great advertising for him that we were the first guests." He paused, and let her soak it all in for a moment. "So, a lot of wins, and no real downside, from what I can see." He pulled her close and nuzzled the top of her head. "It's pretty crazy, but it could just be the perfect answer for the perfect day. Think about it…"

"I don't know that I need to think about it much at all, Dyl. It does sound absolutely perfect, and it may be the only way we can have our day to ourselves! But what about your parents and your London friends? It's an awfully long way for them to go…"

"My parents are overdue for a holiday anyway, and they have an anniversary coming up. I'll get them and the rest of my family here and send them on a cruise or something afterward. Considering that our wedding is being given to us, the least I can do is get our guests here. I can charter a plane from London for those guys pretty easily. The wedding'll have to be fairly small, though, Tia. Remember, the resort only has room for about 150 guests."

"That's not a problem for me—I don't have a big family, and I'd much rather have a small and intimate wedding anyway. Oh my gosh…we'd be able to spend the whole weekend with everyone we care about. Do you know anything about the island? I mean, will there be activities for the guests?"

"Oh yeah. It's going to be a full service resort, so there'll be beach activities, wave runners, hiking, zip lining, snorkeling, diving, and a whole host of other things to do. I was thinking that we'd fly everyone in on Thursday and Friday—at least a few of them would be able to get an extra day off. My thought is that we'd have a bonfire on the beach party on Thursday night, bachelor and bachelorette parties on Friday, rehearsals on Saturday, the wedding on Sunday, and fly everyone home Monday. Tony's even offered his yacht for the girls' party. You could do a sunset cruise or something."

Tia was nearly climbing out of her skin, and she jumped off the couch and started pacing the room. It was coming together in her mind, and all the pictures in her head were perfect. How could she say no to an offer like that? She would get the wedding of her dreams, and everyone she cared about most would not only be able to share the whole weekend with them, they'd be part of something they could brag about for years to come. What wasn't to love about the idea?

She watched Dylan watching her. She knew he could read her mounting excitement and although he tried to keep a stoic face, the corners of his lips kept twitching where he was trying to tamper down a smile. He was enjoying watching Tia fit all the pieces together in her own mind, and was pretty sure she was going to go for it. She was whispering to herself under her breath as she paced, and her smile was getting close to splitting her face. He waited as patiently as he could for her to reach a conclusion, and he knew the exact moment she decided to say yes—it was like a light came on inside her and she was positively glowing with excitement.

"Let me see if I have this all straight," she said, sitting back down. "I just want to make sure I have all the details correct."

"Absolutely," he mused.

"So, your mega-rich friend is loaning us his private island resort for the weekend, all expenses paid for us and all our guests, including food, drinks, activities, a wedding reception, his private plane and his private yacht..."

"Yup," Dylan said, his own smile growing.

"...and in return, we just have to let him put some of our wedding pictures and videos—pictures and videos that *we* choose-- on his TV show and in his tabloid, and maybe do an interview for a documentary about the island?"

"That about sums it up," Dylan smiled. "So, what do you think?"

"What do I think?" she sang, pulling Dylan up from the couch and dancing him in a circle. "What do I think? I think, how could we say no to something like that? It's absolutely perfect!"

Dylan swung his hands under her legs and swept her into his arms. "I thought you'd say that, and I agree completely. It's going to be brilliant! And to think, I didn't even have to pull out the big guns to convince you!"

"There are bigger guns than the ones you already mentioned?" she asked.

"There's a spa on the property too," he said, smiling. "And all the girls are going to get the full treatment before the wedding. I figured I'd pull that out if I needed to, but…"

"Oh Dylan, I'd marry you any time, any place—I hope you know that. But this setting, and the timing and the…oh, I love you so much, and I just can't wait to marry you!"

He set her down and slid his hands up her hips. "Let me show you how much I want you to be my wife," he murmured in her ear before pushing her back down onto the bed and covering her body with his own.

"Yes, show me," she whispered. "The rest of the phone calls can wait."

Chapter 20

They slept in on New Year's Day, and had a wonderful breakfast in their room before heading out to see the city. After stepping out onto the balcony that faced the Harbor Bridge, Tia opted for a short skirt and a tank top, carefully tucking her hair into the blonde wig Dylan had given her at breakfast. "It's just easier to be proactive," he said as he pulled it from his bag. "This is the big city."

Tia took it in stride. "Should I take this as an insult, Miller? Barely got a ring on my finger and already you're wishing you had a blonde."

Dylan grabbed her from behind and tossed her on the bed, rolling her over and studying her. "Who are you," he teased, "and what have you done with my fiancé?" Tia giggled, and he leaned down and kissed her. "I wouldn't change one hair on your beautiful head; unless I'm taking you out in a crowd. I don't want to share you with anyone."

"Remember our second date?" she asked. "The first time I saw *you* without the wig? I said you'd be wonderful no matter what hair you had." She smiled, adding, "But I don't miss the mullet. Please tell me I don't look like the mullet."

"You would be perfect for me even if you were completely bald," he said affectionately. "This," he said, twirling one of the blonde locks around his finger, "is just to keep the wolves at bay. You're still the woman I love underneath, and I'll never forget it. Neither should you."

They spent the afternoon wandering the city, touring the Opera House, and doing some shopping. After an early dinner, they headed to the bridge to meet with the guide that would lead their climb to the top to see the amazing views of Sydney and the harbor at sunset.

They suited up in their official gray and blue tour jumpsuits, and joined the rest of their group to do some practice climbs and get used to the harnesses that would connect them to the bridge during the climb. Tia had never been afraid of heights, per se, but standing at the bottom of the monumental structure and raising her eyes to the top gave her a bit of a flutter in her stomach.

"You ready?" Dylan asked. Tia could see the flash of anticipation in his eyes, and couldn't help but share in his excitement.

"Let's do this thing," she said confidently, raising her hand for a high five.

It was over two hours before they stood at the top, tiny boats sailing beneath them on their way out to sea and toy cars gliding over the bridge below them. They were rewarded with a magnificent sunset; the huge orange ball sinking into the sea in the distance and setting the smooth waters of the harbor aflame.

"I'm queen of the world!" Tia said, raising her arms in victory and leaning just slightly over the railing.

Dylan wrapped his arms around her waist and took in the view over her shoulder. "Definitely the queen of mine," he whispered in her ear.

Tia did feel on top of the world. She glanced down at her left hand; the brilliant diamond sparkling orange in the fading light of the sun. In the distance, the lights of Sydney came twinkling on, and the glow around the Opera House reflected off the water, casting a soft shimmer on the ripples of the waves. The air was cool, and the sea breeze left a slight taste of salt on the back of her tongue. She'd never in her life been so happy, and she turned toward Dylan, holding her camera in front of them as she puckered her lips for a kiss.

"And you are my prince," she whispered before joining the rest of their fellow climbers for a group shot with the city in the background.

She woke up with a start, sweat beading on her forehead. Throwing off the covers, she slipped gently from beneath Dylan's arm, careful not to wake him, pulled on her robe, and stepped out onto the balcony. The nightmare had left her shaky, and she placed her hands on the rail, leaning on her arms and letting the cool morning breeze slip over her skin and slide into her lungs.

It had been the same dream on and off over the past week, and Tia knew it was her subconscious trying to wake her up to a hard realization. She usually only had school nightmares in the weeks leading up to the start of a new year, and she didn't need an expert to interpret the meaning of this one; it had been clear for a while now, but she had been pushing it to the back of her mind. It was time to face reality, and do what she knew was the right thing, regardless of the teeter-totter effect it had on her heart.

She held her left hand up to the approaching sunrise, devoid of the sparkling diamond that she didn't dare sleep in for fear of injuring herself or Dylan with its sheer size and weight. But already, after just a day of wearing it out in the hot sun of the Sydney summer, she could see the faint line; lighter than the skin around it; that outlined where the ring sat on her finger.

Life had taken yet another turn. A wonderful, glorious turn, no doubt, but it was a sharp one, and it greatly changed the path her life would take in the future. She'd come back from Europe a different person, but she'd worked so hard to hide that new side of herself; to keep up the façade that she was still the same Tia who'd left in June to spend some time 'studying' abroad. Having Dylan so far away and falling back into her old routines made it easier to cope with his absence and to maintain the charade—but this new development changed the game completely, and she could no longer play by the same rules.

It was hard enough to go back to her life as a school teacher after spending the entire summer with InHap; staying at the most luxurious hotels, buying clothes and handbags that cost nearly what she'd make in two weeks at her job, and falling in love with the 'Sexiest Man on Earth.' But there was no pretending anymore.

Some of it she'd miss—Friday nights at Paddy's with impromptu calls to the stage to sing with Sean and whoever he considered part of his "band" at the moment...lunches with Lexi at Spartan's Deli, sitting street side and spending a summer afternoon people-watching...walks through the park with Bonnie, her elderly neighbor's adorable mutt who never got tired of sniffing tree trunks and the back ends of other dogs. The list went on, but there was another list, perhaps nearly as long, of things she'd be glad to put behind her; first and foremost, the country club snobs with their better-than-you attitudes that had irked her from the very first day she went. None of those things, however, came even close to what she felt about giving up her job.

She'd wanted to be a teacher for as long as she could remember, and she believed in the work she did with children...but she knew—had known for some time but had refused to fully admit—that she couldn't just go back to her job and pick up where she'd left off. The time had come to put it behind her and move forward. It wouldn't be fair to anyone involved; including herself; to even attempt to go back to work. School would start back up in less than a week, and she owed it to her kids and her coworkers to make sure that her situation didn't interfere with their primary responsibilities of teaching and learning. She needed to resign from her job, and she needed to do it soon.

She snuck back into the room to look at the clock on the night table. 5:00 AM Sydney time translated to noon in Chicago, the previous day. She'd give herself the morning to prepare what she was going to say, and call Ned at home after she'd had a chance to talk it over with Dylan. She knew beyond the shadow of a doubt that he'd support her decision, but would just feel better about it herself after having his agreement.

Tia had no idea how long she stood there—the sun came up and bathed the waters of the harbor in golden light, traffic increased on the roads below, and voices echoed up from the sidewalks. Finally, Dylan awoke and came out to find her, wrapping her in his arms, his just-woken voice scratching, "I woke up and you weren't there. Not a good way to start the day." He nibbled at her neck and slipped his hand beneath her robe, caressing her stomach. "How long have you been up?"

"A while," she said simply.

Sensing her mood, he turned her toward him and took her into his arms. "What's wrong, love?"

Tia took a deep breath, holding it for a moment before exhaling slowly. "Oh Dyl," she began, "I'm just thinking about some things. Most of them are amazing—marrying you, spending our lives together—but before I can move forward with those things, there are some loose ends I need to tie up." He raised one eyebrow at her. "The most important of which being my job. I need to resign, Dyl. I've known it for a while, but with school starting back up in a few days...it just wouldn't be fair to anyone if I stayed." She hadn't meant to cry, but her eyes welled up and a couple tears made their way down her cheeks.

Dylan pulled her to him. "I'm so sorry, baby girl," he whispered into her hair.

"Don't be sorry," she said. "It's for the happiest reason in the world. I'll miss it sure...well, some of it, at least." She giggled. "I won't miss report card time, or conferences, or meetings, or all the red tape...I'll just miss the kids. Teaching them; watching that light bulb come on when they understand something that I taught them. But it is a job, and you are my life. There will be so many happy things to take up my time, and I wouldn't trade that for anything."

"You'll find something rewarding, I promise you," he said. "Maybe working with kids through the charity, or with the kids that come to the ranch..."

"I know that, I really do," she answered. "But right now, I need to call Ned and get this done. I've put it off too long already, and it'll be easier to look forward when I've dealt with the past."

"Get on with it then," he said, wrapping his arms around her. "You'll feel better once it's done."

Dylan gave her a supportive hug, grabbed the newspaper off the table, and went out onto the balcony. "I'll be here if you need me," he said, sliding the door shut.

Tia punched in Ned's number, her heart racing and her breathing ragged. She knew she wouldn't regret the decision in the long term, but that didn't make it any easier in the moment. Ned answered on the second ring.

"Hi Ned, it's Tia," she said, knowing that her number would've come up as all zeros on his end.

"Tia, great to hear from you," he said. "Happy New Year. Are you home?"

"No, I'm still in Australia. We're scheduled to fly back on Sunday."

"How is Australia?" he asked. "I've always wanted to go there."

"It's amazing. You should make a point of it. It's a spectacular country...Listen, Ned," she said, her voice shaking just the slightest bit, "I really need to talk to you. About my job. I'm sorry to bother you at home, but I didn't see any other way..."

His sigh filled her ear. "I've been expecting your call, Tia. I can't say I've been looking forward to this chat, but I've known it was coming."

"Me too, but I've been putting it off. It's not a conversation I ever thought I'd have to have, but now...something else has come up that adds more complication to the whole situation. The announcement isn't going to be public for another day or so, but I need to let you know. Dylan asked me to marry him, and I..."

"Congratulations!" Ned said excitedly. "I couldn't be happier for you, Tia. After seeing the two of you together, the way he looked at you, I thought that might be the case. I wish you all the best—you know that, right?"

Now it was Tia's turn to sigh. "I do, Ned, and I appreciate it tremendously. I've already called some of the girls with the news, but I know I can trust you not to say anything until we've made the official announcement..."

"Of course. My lips are sealed."

"You know, Ned, my years at Jefferson have been some of the best of my life..."

"But life has a funny way of throwing curve balls, doesn't it?" he finished for her.

"Yeah, and this is a big one."

"I'll say. But it's the best kind, too, and you deserve to be happy. I'm so glad that you are."

"Thank you," she whispered. A few thumping heartbeats went by before she was able to continue. "Listen Ned, this is really hard for me, but I just need to come out and say it. When I started teaching, I totally believed I'd retire at a ripe old age with a lot of great memories and a small pension. I thought I'd do it for life. But with all that's happened...I've got to resign my position, Ned. It isn't fair to anyone for me to stay. I'm so sorry."

"You have nothing to be sorry for, Tia—you should never apologize for finding happiness. We'll be sorry to lose you, that's for sure, because you're a great teacher. But at the end of the day, it's a job. Your life comes first, and you're going to have a really great one. Like I said, I've been anticipating this conversation since you walked out the door on that Friday, and I put together a contingency plan. I talked with the superintendent and the board..."

"I hate that you had to do that over the holidays, Ned," she said. "God knows you deserve a break, too."

"Just part of the job," he said. "I wanted to make sure I had some ducks in a row just in case; and I was pretty sure how things would play out, especially after I saw all the publicity the two of you were getting. You've become quite a celebrity yourself, haven't you?"

"By default," Tia agreed, "and it isn't something I wanted to happen; it just goes with this sparticular territory, I guess. I'm figuring it all out as I go along. A lot of it hasn't been easy."

"I imagine not—I saw what happened in Melbourne. Are you OK?"

Tia unconsciously touched her cheek. The bruise was nearly gone; it had faded to a sickly yellow color that was easily concealed with a bit of makeup. "I'm good," she said. "Almost as good as new."

"I'm glad to hear it. You're strong, and you've got a good head on your shoulders. You handled it perfectly."

"Thanks Ned."

"You're going to be great, Tia. I'll actually get to say I knew you when—a lot of us will, and it's kind of exciting, if you want to know the truth. But you're making the right decision. You wouldn't believe the calls the Administration Building has been fielding ever since your name went public—we're kind of figuring it out as we go along, too."

"I'm really sorry about that, Ned, it was never my intention..."

"Of course it wasn't, and no one blames you. Like I said, it's been kind of fun, in its own way. But you're right, going back to the classroom isn't the best thing for anyone involved; I knew you'd see that too."

"So what happens next?" she asked.

Ned went through the logistics, and Tia jotted notes. "At some point in the near future you'll need to clean your things out of your room and turn in your keys...I'd suggest waiting until we make your resignation public so the media won't be hanging around. I guess you have a top-secret phone number now, eh? It came up all zeros on my phone."

"Yeah, it's a secure number. Weird, huh? I'll call you when I get back, OK? I'll try and get in on Wednesday or Thursday. I'll leave most of my things for the new teacher, so it shouldn't take too long to pack up my personal stuff." She thought of the two pictures of Dylan that she had in her classroom; the one of him in disguise that was tacked to the bulletin board behind her desk, and the 'real' one she'd tucked into her desk drawer way back in August, when she couldn't tell anyone who he was.

"Hey Ned? I'd really like to say goodbye to the kids...I'll call you and set something up. I may bring Dylan with me—I think they'd be excited about that."

"We all would," he said. "I think it would be a big deal for both of you to visit the school—would you consider saying goodbye to everyone at a brief assembly? You'll be missed by all the kids, you know, not just the ones in your class."

"I think we could do that," she said, perfectly comfortable speaking for Dylan on that matter. She knew that he'd be more than happy to do that for her. "I'll be in touch early in the week to set something up. Thank you so much, Ned, for making this easier than I thought it would be, and for your support and guidance over the years. You are exactly where you're supposed to be, and the kids and teachers are lucky to have you."

"Everything OK?" Dylan asked, as Tia stepped out onto the balcony with a fresh cup of coffee.

Tia smiled and sucked in a cleansing breath, releasing it in a whoosh. "Everything's good. Nothing to do but move forward from here."

"I'm so glad to hear that," Dylan said, pulling her into his arms and tipping her back for a kiss. "There's nothing I want more."

Chapter 21

Speed—maybe that was the answer. God knew nothing else was working.

On a normal New Year's Eve Bo would wake up and reminisce over the previous year; proud of what he'd accomplished and excited about the new one to come. He'd say a little prayer of thanks for the job he loved that allowed him to live exactly the way he wanted to, and for the incredible people that filled his life.

This year, though, he hurt all over. After the punishment he'd dealt his body the night before, his muscles screamed at him and he could barely even get out of bed to take a piss. What the hell was he thinking, pumping iron like he did it every day? Then, what he *was* thinking came rushing back like a giant wave, and a whole new kind of pain settled in and took hold. Lexi. Damn it all, he'd behaved like a complete ass and she'd left before he could explain—before he could tell her...tell her what? There really wasn't a way to explain that his feelings for her ran deeper than he'd considered; and telling her would make her run away even faster than she was already sprinting. For a brief moment he considered calling her to at least apologize; although he couldn't come up with a reason that didn't sound like complete bullshit—*I felt a cold coming on and didn't want to give it to you...I was having a hot flash...I wanted to kiss you so bad that if I didn't move away I couldn't guarantee that I wouldn't make the move...*

He thought about going straight home to his place in Big Sur to clear his mind and get his head out of his ass, and strongly contemplated just pulling the covers over his head and staying right where he was for the rest of the day. But it was New Year's Eve, and he'd promised his buddy Benji that he'd bang sticks for him during his set at one of the biggest bashes in the city. Who knew, maybe some pounding bass, the chance to beat out some of his anxiety on stage, and huge quantities of alcohol might just get his mind to a better place. God, he hoped he'd be able to move his arms enough to even play.

He threw off the covers and dragged his tired ass to the gym again, focusing on stretch and recovery, and was pleasantly surprised when his muscled began to loosen. He made a resolution that he was going to get himself into shape, and ordered himself a veggie egg white omelet and a fruit plate for breakfast before treating himself to another arctic shower. No way he was spending the day sitting in the room and dwelling on the night before—he needed to point his mind in a completely different direction, so he wrapped his head in a bandana, slid on some shades, and headed for Malibu Beach.

The party delivered on all promises and then some—whiskey flowed like water, scantily clad women with fake tits and open dance cards flitted among the locals and mostly B-list celebrities who'd shelled out a grand or more per ticket, and the music was just plain hot. It was the one night of the year to indulge without limits; and judging by the amounts of blow and X he saw being passed around and the vacant looks on a lot of faces, inhibitions were definitely out the window.

Bo pushed the nagging thoughts to the back of his mind and threw all his focus into the present. He mingled with other musicians, danced with a handful of models, and did shots with the star of some horror flick that just hit the theaters. He was feeling pretty pumped by the time he hit the stage; a pleasant buzz in his head and his fingers tingling the way they always did when he was about to climb behind a drum kit.

"Thank you!" Benji addressed the crowd. "I've got some special guests playing with me tonight—can you give a warm welcome to Kyle Warrup on bass guitar!" He waited a few beats for the applause to die down. "And, someone you may have seen on television last night—a man who has stood naked in front of

Penelope Valentine and lived to tell the tale—from Incidental Happenstance, on drums, Bo Collins!"

Bo jumped to the front of the stage and waved his sticks in the air, basking in the enthusiastic welcome and the anticipation he always felt just before he hit the stage. He poured himself into the music, crashing out beats with fervor and pounding his frustrations into the snare. After his final bow at the end of their set, he wandered through the crowd buying drinks for beautiful women and shooting whiskey with some cool guys. When the countdown to midnight started, with his head buzzing from the bourbon and the music, he found a tantalizing honey-colored beauty in his arms and pulled her in for a long and lingering kiss as confetti rained down around them and Auld Lang Syne was plucked on a blues guitar.

"Hey Mr. Bo Collins," she purred into his ear. "Want to make this a real happy new year? I'm just three floors up...want to join me for a nightcap?" She looked up him, her espresso eyes lidded in gold and her full lips tinted glossy pink.

There was no question of her willingness—or perhaps intent would be a better word—and although he wasn't a one-night-stand kind of guy, he seriously considered her offer. He let his eyes wander down to where her breasts were trying to push themselves out of the...holy shit, really?...leopard print dress...*well, it is fantastic cleavage, don't you think?* Lexi's voice was suddenly in his head, and the image of her jutting out her own more modest; but definitely more natural; breasts burned in his memory.

It shouldn't have had such a profound effect on him—he thought he'd be able to shake it off and take –what did she say her name was?—up on her obvious offer to rid him of his recent hormonal overload, but despite the fact that she was absolutely gorgeous and readily available, he thanked her for the offer and politely turned her down. He left her standing on the dance floor, and went to find Benji to say his goodbyes. He downed one more drink at the bar and caught a taxi back to the Four Seasons anticipating another restless night full of thoughts he had absolutely no business thinking.

Before he collapsed onto the bed, he fished his phone out of his pocket and listened to the message from Dylan; "Where the hell are you mate? I've been trying to reach you all day...well anyway, hope wherever you are, you're having a Happy New Year. Oh, and I was wondering if you'd consider being my best man— seems Tia's willing to put up with me for a lifetime, and I need you there when it comes time to make it official. Don't make any plans for Memorial Day weekend—it'll be a birthday you'll never forget. Hate leaving this in a message, but I wanted you to hear it from me, just in case. Give me a ring when you can."

"Well I'll be goddamned," Bo said to himself. He got up and splashed some cold water on his face so he could jump start at least enough neurons to have an intelligent conversation. He had no idea what time it was in Australia, and he didn't care. His best friend; whom Bo had believed might be a bachelor to the end; was getting married.

"It's about bloody time," Dylan said when he picked up the call. "Happy New Year!"

"Especially for you, Strummer Boy. Congratulations!"

"Hold on," Dylan said, "let me put you on speaker."

"Hey Bo!" Tia sang. "Happy New Year!"

"You sure you want to put up with that Aussie pretty boy for the rest of your life?" he joked. "He snores, as you well know, and he's got a whole list of other nasty habits that I'm sure he's been hiding from you. We really need to talk."

Tia laughed out loud. "Yeah, I'm pretty sure I can handle him," she said.

"How do you know all those so-called irritating habits aren't just my way of making your life more interesting, Bobo?" Dylan added.

"Yeah, interesting's one word for it. I can think of a few others, but I don't want to offend a lady as lovely as Tia." His voice got more serious. "You know I'm thrilled for you right? I can't think of two people who'll make each other happier. And 'best man' is a role I can easily fill—I'm honored to do it."

"Thanks, Bo. I can't think of a better best man for Dylan. You'll get to stand up with Lexi, of course, so that'll be *interesting* as well. I can think of a few other words too, but none of them seems big enough when it comes to the way you two behave when you're together. I've missed it though, I'll admit. I have so many great memories of our time in Europe. I can't wait for us to all be together again."

And just like that, Lexi was in his head once more; dancing with him at the little pub in Northampton, her blue eyes laughing as he spun her around the dance floor. "I can behave when I have to," he joked, knowing that it would be her fiancé filling the slots on her dance card and not him. He wondered, after the way they'd left things the other night, whether she'd even be able to stomach the requisite best man/maid of honor dance.

"Really?" Dylan asked sarcastically, "because I've never seen that, and I've known you a long time..."

"Maybe I'm just trying to keep *your* life interesting."

"You always do," Dylan replied. "Listen mate, we've just arrived at the restaurant, so I'll be in touch when we're back in country, OK? We'll be back on Sunday."

"Sounds good—congratulations again, guys," he said sincerely. "I'm really happy for you."

"Thanks, Bo. We're pretty damn happy too." Dylan clicked off the line, and Bo immediately felt the emptiness settle in. It went deeper than he cared to admit. He fell onto the bed and threw his arm across his face. "At least someone gets to be happy tonight," he mumbled to himself, letting the alcohol drag him down into a fretful rest.

The hangover was atrocious—he spent the day nursing it over pots of coffee and room service; which was fine with him. The weather paralleled what he felt—gloomy skies and strong thunderstorms that shook the walls and drove spears of lightning into the ground. Hardly conducive to a five-hour road trip on his Harley.

The next day, however, dawned bright and clear, and so did his head; as clear as he could hope for, anyway. The sun dried the roads by late morning and temperatures were expected to be in the low 70's. Bo stuffed his duffel into the saddlebag, pulled on his black leather jacket and helmet, and hit the road, headed for the PCH and some wide open spaces.

Damn, he loved the power of the Harley beneath him. Once he got a fair distance from the city the road opened up and he gunned the engine, paying no attention whatsoever to the numbers on the speedometer and just enjoying the scenery. The Pacific was on his left; whitecaps slapping against rocky shores; and the twisting road brought the blue of the ocean in and out of view. The sleek machine glided over the pavement, its telltale growl drowning out the sounds of the crashing surf. He pulled the salt air deep into his lungs, willing it to sweep away the rest of the cobwebs that clung at the edges of his mind. He tried humming one InHap's new numbers, focusing on where he'd place the beats to give it just the right tempo. A run formed in his head, and he mentally planned out a killer solo that he'd put somewhere in the summer shows; maybe in the middle of *House Without a Home.*

He slipped into auto-pilot; he'd driven this road so many times that he sometimes thought his bike knew the way home. He was just considering adding a bongo to the solo when, without warning, his bike lurched beneath him and he had to cut the handlebar to straighten himself. His stomach lurched in response, and he was instantly snapped back to focus. Just as he glanced into the rear-view mirror to see if he'd hit something, he felt the road go out from under him again. Everything seemed to happen in slow motion then—he felt the knot in his stomach as he realized what was happening. Earthquake. And he was in a bad place; with sheer cliffs on both sides of him. He hit the throttle and hoped to power past the cliff to his right, but the road buckled beneath him and he slowed up to maintain control. His stomach fell as the road twisted, and he turned his head to the right just in time to see a shower of rocks tumbling down the cliff and sailing into the air, pelting him like a hailstorm. Gunning the engine to get past the onslaught, he had to just as quickly pull the break as the concrete split and rose up ahead of him. He heard a crash, and turned his head just in time to see a basketball-sized boulder catapult off a larger rock and go airborne. He watched as it turned end-over-end through the air, knowing in his gut that it was going to make contact long before he heard the sharp *crack*! as it hit him full force in the face. There was a screech of tires, and then, for what seemed entirely too long a time, his ears were filled with the sickening sound of metal slicing hard against asphalt as he went into a slide. The bike was yanked out from under him, and he tumbled over and over, hearing more than feeling the assault on his body. There was one more audible crack, and then blissfully, his world went black.

Dylan got the call on Saturday just as they were sitting down to dinner. "Hey Chloe," Tia heard him say enthusiastically as he picked up the call. "What a great surprise. How's my favorite other mother?"

Tia watched as all the color drained from Dylan's face in an instant. He sat up ramrod straight and shot her a look that contained something she'd never before seen in his eyes—fear. "Oh no," he said, "tell me what happened." He held up his hand to mimic writing, and Tia pulled her journal and a pen from her purse, opening it to a fresh page. She waited anxiously as Dylan scribbled notes on the paper and then chewed on the end of the pen. "Bloody hell. Is he going to be OK?" she held her breath as he paused. "I'm on my way, Chloe. I'll be there as soon as I possibly can. Tell him to hold on."

He ended the call, and turned to Tia with a heartbroken look on his face. "It's Bo," he said frantically. "There's been an accident, and he's in hospital."

"Oh my God." Tia was on her feet instantly, and Dylan tossed some bills on the table and led her out of the restaurant just as the server was arriving with their meals. "I'm sorry," he said as they headed for the door. "There's been an emergency. We have to go."

"What happened, Dyl?" Tia asked as he hustled her out the door and to the car where Mike was sitting behind the wheel. "Is he OK?"

"I don't know. He was heading home from LA on his bike and an earthquake hit while he was driving down PCH. That was his mum calling. She's still on her way to hospital and doesn't know the extent of anything yet—just that he's in ICU..." His eyes were wide and darting around aimlessly as he tried to process the information that his best friend was critically injured. Tia knew they both felt the fear profoundly—they'd both suffered through losing someone they loved, and neither thought they could go through the crushing agony again. She remembered the day of Nick's accident—remembered that the sun was shining, that she'd been wearing shorts for the first time of the season. The foreman from the job found her in the yard, doing some early gardening after a good day at work, and she knew as soon as she'd seen his face that something horrible had happened...

Tia wrapped her hand in Dylan's and pulled out her phone with the other, punching Jessa's number. She relayed the information quickly, and jumped from the car before it even stopped in front of their hotel. "You go check out and I'll start packing." Dylan snapped out of his daze and headed for the front desk as Tia dashed for the elevator.

"Oh my God, what happened?" Lexi asked. Tia and Dylan were on their way to the airport, both frantically making calls to alert everyone they could about the situation.

"We're not exactly sure yet," she answered. "Bo's mom was still on her way to the hospital when she called and we haven't heard back from her yet. We're on our way to the airport right now, and we're hoping to get there in time to catch the next flight out. All we know at this point is that he's in ICU and that he has extensive injuries." She choked on the last words, horrified to associate them with someone she'd come to love like a brother.

"Holy shit," she whispered. "How long will it take you get there?"

"Oh God, it's going to be the better part of a day." Her throat constricted and she swallowed hard. She could really feel the distance all of a sudden, and could feel Dylan's tension in knowing that he couldn't get to his best friend's side any sooner. A lot could happen in that amount of time. "That's if we can catch this flight—it's going to be close."

Lexi was thinking the same thing. "You have to call me as soon as you know something. I'll be sitting by the phone. Day or night, you need to let me know, OK?"

"I will. We're just pulling up to the terminal now. Gotta go." She cut the connection; and Lexi dropped her phone on the table, put her face in her hands, and wept.

"What's wrong?" Ryan asked when he let himself into her apartment a couple hours later and found Lexi sitting on the couch and staring at the wall. "You look like you've been crying."

She had hoped that she'd be able to hide it, but she couldn't stop thinking about Bo lying in a hospital bed and possibly fighting for his life. ICU wasn't a good sign, and she hadn't heard anything else from Tia. She looked at Ryan, dressed in his favorite sweater and a pair of khakis, and her stomach turned at the thought of trying to keep things light over a casual dinner at one of their favorite restaurants. For the briefest of moments she considered telling him the truth, but after the blow up Ryan had after their television appearance, she wasn't about to tell him that she couldn't get Bo Collins off her mind; even if it was for a damn good reason.

She'd washed her face and reapplied her makeup, but nothing could hide her red-rimmed eyes. "I'm not feeling so good," she lied, "I think I'm coming down with something."

"So, no flaming saganaki, then, I'm guessing?"

Lexi put her hand over her stomach and cringed. "Oh God no. I really don't feel like eating anything right now. I'm sorry, I should've called you, but I thought that I'd feel better..."

"How about I pick something up?" he suggested. "We can just chill here and watch a movie or something."

"I don't know," she said. "If I am coming down with something, the last thing I want to do is give it to you. I should probably just try and sleep it off; get some rest and hope it doesn't stick."

Ryan didn't bat an eye, and Lexi felt guilty for lying to him. "OK," he said. "Maybe I'll call Jace and see if he's up for some wings or something. Rest up and feel better—I won't bother you if you're going to try to sleep, but call me if you need anything."

"Thanks, Ry. I think that's what I need to do. Sorry to make you come all the way out for nothing."

"No problem," he said, kissing her on the forehead. "Hmm. You do feel a little bit feverish, actually; you probably should get some rest."

I'm feverish, all right, she thought as she closed the door and grabbed her phone, staring at it and willing it to ring. She opened the fridge, pulling out some leftover chicken and giving it an appraising sniff. Deeming it edible, she dumped it unceremoniously onto a plate and tossed it in to nuke it. She was actually starving, and was glad that her stomach hadn't rumbled in protest as she was turning down dinner in Greektown.

There were twelve seconds left on the microwave when her phone chirped, and she rushed into the other room to grab it, relief and trepidation flooding her when she saw that the call was coming from Qantas Airlines.

"Oh thank God," she said, falling onto the couch and ignoring the beep of the microwave. "Is he OK? What's going on?"

"We still don't know much, but the latest info is that they've airlifted him to UCLA. I guess he's in pretty bad shape right now, and they've got a lot more tests to do before they can assess the damage." She stopped and took a few deep breaths, but they did nothing to cool the fire of fear that was burning in her gut. "The biggest concern right now is brain swelling, so they put him straight in the ICU once they got him there."

"Brain swelling? Holy crap, that sounds horrible. What the hell happened?"

"He was headed for home on his motorcycle, and an earthquake hit. Not a real bad one, but it had been storming the couple days before and the rain apparently loosened some of the rocks on the cliffs along the PCH. From what the witness says, a rock about the size of a soccer ball hit him right in the head and he was thrown off his bike…" she swallowed hard as her throat constricted. "He hit the ground pretty hard and got pelted with a bunch more before the rock slide finally stopped. Thank God he was wearing a helmet, or it could've been…" she paused, unable to finish the sentence, and took a deep breath before continuing. "They do know he's got a couple cracked ribs, a nasty concussion, a broken arm and a punctured lung. Oh, Lex, his mother said she didn't recognize him; he's so swollen and bruised…he's got a fractured eye socket…"

"Oh my God," Lexi breathed.

"That's what looks the worst right now, I guess, but the doctors aren't even going to start looking at most of the injuries until they're sure his brain is stable. It's awful, but the doctors are still saying that he was lucky…it could've been much worse."

"Oh, poor Bo; I just can't believe it."

Tia choked on a sob. "Bo's one of the strongest people I know. He'll be OK, I know he will. Chloe, that's Bo's mom, is at the hospital now, but they aren't giving her a whole lot of information yet. Damn it, I hate that we're still so far away…"

Lexi felt some protective instinct rise up inside her and she felt a desperate need to go there; to hold his hand and tell him that he was going to be OK. She knew it wasn't her place, but she felt so helpless sitting on the phone two thousand miles away. "I know what you mean," she said. "Are all the guys there?"

"Everyone but Tommy—he was on a sailing holiday somewhere around St. Croix with some friends and they weren't able to get a hold of him right away. He's headed for the nearest harbor where he can get a flight out. Bo's sister is on her way there too; she lives out East somewhere. Boston, I think."

Lexi's brain conjured up a picture of Bo's family—she'd never met Ms. Collins, but she imagined that she'd be slightly heavy, with long graying hair, cocoa skin, a warm laugh, and eyes that crinkled like Bo's did when she smiled. "I'm glad you're going to be there too, Tia. Keep me updated, and tell him I love him, OK? Tell him he's too damn stubborn not to pull through just so he can continue to torture the rest of us with his bad jokes." She sniffed back a sob.

"I will," Tia answered. "That's all I know for now, but I'll call as soon as I have any more info. Dylan's going to call Ty for an update in a couple hours, and we should be there by late morning. God I wish this plane would go faster. Poor Dyl; he's an absolute wreck."

"I can't even imagine. Give him a hug for me and let me know as soon as you have some news."

Lexi barely slept; every time she closed her eyes, her mind would conjure up a picture of Bo lying broken in a hospital bed with tubes snaking out of him in all directions. She spent most of the night pacing, and when Ryan let himself into her apartment in the morning and found her curled up under a blanket on the couch, it wasn't hard to convince him that she still wasn't feeling well. She felt even more guilty that he'd brought her some tea and her favorite pastry from the bakery down the street to make her feel better, but in spite of his thoughtfulness, she was grateful that he didn't insist on staying.

It was late morning before Tia called back. "He's stable, but that's all we really know right now," she reported. "Brie and I are running out to get some food for everyone who's here. They're still not letting anyone in to see him, but no one wants to leave."

"Who's Brie?"

"Bo's sister. She's an amazing person; so much like Bo. I love her already—I just wish we weren't meeting under these circumstances. You'd really like her—she's edgy, classy, and has a sharp tongue. She's really holding everyone together; keeping everyone positive. Here she comes now...I'll call you when we have some real news."

Lexi ended the call and sat on the edge of her bed, putting her face in her hands and letting the tears come once again. Helpless didn't begin to describe what she was feeling, but she had no other way to explain it. Better helpless than hopeless, she thought, bowing her head and saying a prayer that Bo would be OK.

Tia entered the room quietly, the soft hum of the respirator hissing and clicking in a haunting rhythm, dotted with the bleeps of the heart monitor. She'd waited a long time for her turn to see him, and she pulled up the stool and took Bo's hand gently in hers. "Oh sweetie, we're all here for you," she whispered. "You have a whole team of people outside pulling for you, you know that don't you?" The only answer was a click from the IV drip, signaling another dose of some yellowish liquid that flowed down the tube and into a vein. Bo's skin felt thin and papery, and despite his bulky frame he looked so fragile that Tia had to hitch in a breath. "Tommy just got here—he'll be in to see you in a little bit; and I talked to Lexi—she isn't here, but she wanted me to tell you that she loves you, and that she's pray..." the heart monitor beeped three times, out of its normal rhythm, and Tia held her breath as she watched it peak twice, then fall back into a normal pattern. She let out her breath and felt her own heart hammering in her chest. "She's praying for you too, and she knows you'll pull through. She says you're too damn stubborn not to, so just get on with it already, OK? Come on back to us, Bo. We all love you."

She found it hard to speak around the tightness in her throat, and she felt the burning sting of tears. Not wanting Bo to hear fear in her voice, if he could hear her at all, she started humming one of InHap's songs while gently stroking his right arm. Soon, there was a light tapping at the window that indicated her ten minutes were up. "We need you Bo; stay strong," she whispered before slipping out of the room.

Chapter 22

Lexi had fully expected to strut into work on Monday in a hot new outfit that showed off her freshly bronzed skin and bask in the temporary celebrity she'd surely enjoy around the office after her TV appearance. Instead, she dragged herself in after an emotionally taxing weekend clad in a tired old pantsuit and sporting some major bags beneath her eyes. Even the crowd that waited in the lobby, applauding and patting her on the back, did little to boost her spirits, and she had a hard time even forcing a smile. Most of them had heard about Bo's accident, and asked if she knew anything about his condition.

Bo was improving, but he still had a long way to go. They were able to cast his arm, but he had yet to regain consciousness and was still in ICU. The doctors were keeping him medicated so both his lung and brain had more time to heal, but the prognosis was good, and they were confident that the brain hadn't swelled so much or been deprived of oxygen long enough to cause any brain damage. They wouldn't be sure, however, until he woke up.

Tia had been keeping her posted, but she still felt out of the loop and wished there was something more she could do besides worry and wait for her phone to ring. She'd sent a big bouquet of flowers, but it felt like an empty gesture. What she really wanted to do was go to him, and tell him how sorry she was for the way she behaved last week.

She and Ryan were on rocky ground; he'd found out about Bo's accident and determined that her alleged illness was faked. He was sick of her lying, he said, and sick of being played for a fool. It was stupid not to tell him—she should have realized that he'd find out eventually and know that she'd already been made fully aware, but she had been in some major emotional turmoil and her brain was barely functioning. Or maybe it was functioning enough to know that she didn't want to deal with the bullshit she was going to get from Ryan one way or the other once he found out. Apparently, he was still pissed about the exchange she'd had with Bo on Tony's show, and he just couldn't seem to let it go. It seemed that it didn't take much to piss Ryan off these days, and she always felt like she was walking on eggshells around him. She couldn't say exactly when it started, but if she had to pinpoint a time, it would be the day he walked out of the locker room and saw her in Dylan's arms. The shit really hit the fan, though, on New Year's Eve, when she got the news of Tia and Dylan's engagement...

"I'm really sorry I woke you up, honey... I didn't want to freak you out by showing up unannounced at four AM, and then I got excited when Tia told me she was engaged, and I couldn't help it," she'd said.

"Oh yeah, the whole fucking world's gonna be turning cartwheels over that news," he'd said sarcastically. "At least maybe now you'll cross *him* off the list of people you want to fuck."

"What the hell do you mean by that?" she answered, her palms up and her shoulders shrugging. "He was the only one on the list, and I crossed him off the minute I found out he was dating my best friend. Months ago. It's not my fault that you don't believe me, but that's not even what's pissing you off, is it—you're not that dim."

"I'm starting to wonder about that," he said, shooting daggers from his eyes. "Where'd you spend the night last night, Lex?"

"At about 30,000 feet, Ryan. On a plane coming back here so we could spend New Year's Eve together. What are you insinuating?"

"Always the smart ass," he hissed. "Let me rephrase that. Where'd you watch the show? Were you with the drummer?"

For a split second she considered lying, but didn't see the point. She hadn't done anything wrong, and had nothing to apologize for as far as that was concerned. "Yes, Bo and I watched the show together. So what?"

"I see. Dylan is no longer available, so you jumped to someone else in the band? The big black drummer? Are you that desperate to get banged by a celebrity?"

Before she could think; before she could even form words in her mind to respond to his ridiculous accusation, her hand came up and cracked him across the face. "How dare you," she hissed. "You have no right..."

"Don't I? Put yourself in my goddamn shoes for a minute here, Lexi. I walk out of the locker room at the club and find you in the arms of the guy I practically gave you permission to sleep with—the guy you said was "hotter than hell," or something to that effect. Then I find out that you not only hid the fact that you knew him, but that the two weeks you spent in Europe weren't just you and Tia shopping and getting your goddamn nails done, but that you were on tour with the fucking band the whole time."

"I had to keep that a secret," she said. "For Tia's sake. You know that, Ryan."

"What about my sake? I'm your fiancé, Lex. I knew you were hiding something the minute you got back from that damn trip. You were secretive and evasive and shared almost no details—I figured that you'd slept with Miller, and that was why you kept telling me you'd crossed him off your list..."

"I know you thought that—you threw it in my face every chance you got!" she yelled. "Do you really have that little trust in me, Ry? I swore to you that I didn't, but you kept getting in your little digs and accusations whenever you could. You don't think it hurt me that you didn't believe me? You don't think it hurts me now that you think I'd jump into bed with Bo just so I could 'bang a celebrity,' as you so delicately put it?"

"How many more secrets, Lexi? It seems like every time I turn around I find out something else you've been hiding from me. What am I supposed to think, especially when I see you on TV practically sitting in the dude's lap—right after he calls you beautiful in front of the whole damn world—and then you call and tell me you aren't coming home and I find out you were with him? You should have told me all of it—we're not supposed to have secrets from each other."

"It wasn't mine to tell. Tia didn't even tell her own parents, Ryan. I wasn't trying to hide something *from* you; I was hiding it *for* her. There's a big difference."

"Not from where I'm standing, there isn't."

Lexi sucked in a deep breath and took his hand. He tried to pull it from her grasp, but she held tight and looked at him hard. "I'm so sorry, sweetie, for how all this has made you feel. But I'm engaged to you because I love you, and I would never do anything to jeopardize our relationship. Bo and I are friends; that's all. We have similar senses of humor and joke around with each other— it's all very harmless, I promise you. He's never once hit on me, and I've never hit on him. I've never been unfaithful to you, and I never will be; you should know me well enough to be sure about that. I've only seen Bo once since Europe, months ago...and before you even say I hid that from you too, remember that I was still keeping Tia's secret at the time."

Ryan dropped his head. "What else? What else do I need to know, because I don't like being blindsided like this, Lexi, and I don't want any more surprises."

"There's nothing else, Ryan, I promise," she whispered, and climbed into his lap to hold him.

He'd forgiven her, it seemed, finally, but there was still this tension between them that she hoped would dwindle with time. God knew her explanations weren't making things any better. The party had been miserable that night, both of them running on way too little sleep and neither in a celebratory mood. They left shortly after midnight, and fell quickly into restless dreams.

And now he accused her again of having something going on with Bo. They'd had another nasty fight yesterday, and she was still reeling. And now, it was Monday.

The welcoming committee felt more like a mob crushing in on her. She could just feel them staromg, and people she barely knew; workers from other offices with whom she'd shared no more than a smile and a nod in the hallway or on the elevator; were hugging her just a bit too enthusiastically and showering her with compliments and well wishes. It was nearly half an hour before she got into her office and shut the door, falling into her chair and powering up her laptop.

Her stomach sank when she opened her email—she had 146 new messages, the subject line of many being, "Congratulations!" and "You were amazing!" She groaned out loud when she saw that a good number of them were from clients, and she knew she'd have to open them and possibly respond. It was going to be a long freaking morning.

The first email on the list had the subject, "Your Invited!" and was from the office slut, Candy Christmas. Lexi wasn't a bit surprised that she'd used the wrong form of "you're;" it certainly wasn't her intellectual skills that had contributed to her rise in the firm. She'd amassed a number of nicknames over the couple years she'd been with *Family Advocates Inc.*, Lexi's personal favorites being "Eye Candy," and "The Gift That Keeps on Giving." Candy was gorgeous in a Playboy model kind of way, and claimed to have a sex addiction. She'd slept with a good number of the men in the firm, some of them married, and Lexi found her deplorable, doing her best to avoid the annoying woman whenever possible. She opened the email reluctantly, hoping it contained an invitation to an office party or a baby shower for Peggy, one of the receptionists, but wasn't a bit surprised when neither was the case.

"...to our monthly Progressive Dinner!" it read, causing Lexi to

shake her head. "Next Saturday, starting at 6:00!!!!! We'll start at my

place for wine and cheese, then move to LaVonne's for appetizers, Allie's for salads, Stella's for main course, and Bailey's for dessert, then finish

off back at my place for cocktails ☺ My guest this month will be Lexi

Sommers, my newly famous friend! (she'll just be a special guest this

time, and can take a rotation next round!) Remember, our theme

this month is Italiano—see you on Saturday!"

"You've got to be kidding," Lexi said out loud, not at all surprised that the woman didn't even know how to spell her freaking name. As she hit the delete key, her door swung open and the spelling disaster herself walked in, balancing some files in one arm and a paper coffee cup in the other.

"Good morning!" Candy practically sang, setting down the coffee and taking a seat in the chair in front of Lexi's desk. "I brought you a skinny mocha latte from my favorite café." She pushed the cup over toward Lexi.

"Um, thanks," Lexi managed. "Are all those files for me?"

"No, none of them, actually," Candy said with a toothy smile. *Crocodile smile*, Lexi thought immediately. "I just wanted to tell you again how amazing it was seeing you on *After Dark* last week, and to see if you got my invitation to our progressive dinner on Saturday. I'm so excited to have you come!" She clasped her hands together in the most fake display of delight Lexi had ever seen.

Before Lexi could even respond, her phone rang. She snatched it up, grateful for the temporary distraction, only to wish she hadn't .

"Lexi, it's Dalia Buchanan, darling, how are you?"

Dalia was member of the country club and a former client. Lexi had helped her successfully slam it to her husband in their divorce after he'd impregnated one of his nurses and spent a good chunk of their marital estate to keep her quiet in a luxury penthouse in the city. She still sung Lexi's praises around the club; and had secured her a fair share of new clients; but they didn't run in the same social circles. "I'm good, Dalia…how about you?" She squinted at Candy, but she just leaned back in the chair and showed no signs of leaving.

"Oh I'm just great, darling, and it's obvious that you are too. I thought you were just fabulous on TV the other night—Danielle Hastings told us you'd be on, and a bunch of us watched you together—you made us all so proud…"

"Well, ah, thanks," Lexi said. "It was an interesting experience."

"I'd love to hear all about it! Listen, I don't want to keep you; you must have a million things on your plate right now; but I wanted to shoot you a quick call to invite you to lunch a week from Saturday. I have a friend who's looking for a good attorney, and of course I gave her your name. She's got a lot of influence, but she hasn't told her husband yet that she's planning to divorce him and take the kids, so I thought it would be best to meet in a less formal setting. She'll pay you for your time, of course."

"I'm happy to do it, Dalia, but I have to wait until a bit later in the week to confirm, is that OK? Tia's may be coming back that week and I…"

"Marvelous—she could join us! It's been such a whirlwind for her the past few weeks; I'd just love to catch up with her and congratulate her on her engagement! She could bring Dylan, too. I could set up a grand tour of the club for him, you know, in case he wants to join. We could talk business over tea, and after he's had a chance to see all the club's amenities, I'll treat you all to lunch."

Lexi saw the situation for what it was—a blatant attempt to be seen in the company of Dylan and Tia. Dalia barely gave Tia the time of day; she wasn't rude or dismissive, she just didn't go out of her way to be friendly. Now suddenly she wanted to buy her lunch? She knew that wouldn't be the case if it weren't for her relationship with Dylan.

Yet again, Lexi had a whole new appreciation for the tough decisions Tia had to make in regard to her relationship with Dylan. She remembered how outwardly frustrated she'd been when Tia swore her to secrecy, telling her that it was too good a secret to keep and that she should be singing from the rooftops; but she now saw the complexity of the whole situation, and once more, had a new respect for Tia's ability to see the whole picture. Tia knew that people would look at her differently; treat her differently; because she was involved with someone famous. She'd chosen to remain as anonymous as she could for as long as she could because she understood that people would "crawl out of the woodwork" for a little piece of that action. And judging by the number of incoming emails that kept her computer pinging, she'd absolutely made the right decision.

"I certainly can't speak for them," she answered. "When they come back they'll have a lot of celebrating to do with friends and family, and I'd guess they'll have a very tight schedule. That's why I'll have to let you know later in the week whether I can do Saturday—it depends on when they get back and what their plans are. Can I call you on Thursday or Friday and let you know? Or, is it possible to get together in the next couple days? I know she won't be coming back for at least that long, and I'll have more availability."

"No, my friend is out of town at the moment, so we'll take our chances for that Saturday, I think," Dalia responded. "You will be sure to invite them, right, just in case?"

"Yeah, sure," she said, more to get her off the phone than anything else. "I'll be in touch."

"So, Tia and Dylan are coming back next week, huh? We don't usually invite men to our dinner, unless they're incredibly sexy, which in this case, is an understatement," Candy said with a wistful smile. "I'd be very glad to make an exception, and I was going to ask you to invite Tia anyway—I've always liked her. Do they like Italian food? Does Dylan have a favorite wine?"

"Candy," Lexi said, getting more aggravated by the minute. Another ping of her computer signaled yet another email; she glanced at the screen to see the subject, "Go You!" and gritted her teeth. Candy looked at her expectantly and smiled warmly. "I'm not going to be able to go to your dinner on Saturday..."

"Well, we can always move it to the next Saturday if that works better for you all; not a problem!"

"It is a problem," she said simply. "It just isn't my thing. I appreciate the invite," she said to be polite, "but my fiancé and I have a standing date on Saturday nights, so…"

"Oh gosh, that's right—a Fourth of July wedding, right? Have you picked out a dress?"

Damn it, she was a sucker for showing off her dress, and Candy probably knew it. Lexi pulled up the picture on her phone and handed it over.

"Oh my gosh, it's absolutely beautiful!" Candy gushed. "I love how the sparkles look like fireworks—it's just perfect! I can't wait to see it in person. You know, a few of the girls and I have been talking about hosting a bridal shower for you…"

Damn it exponentially, Lexi thought. She'd never even considered inviting Candy to her wedding. She sucked in a breath and held it, counting slowly to ten. The last thing she wanted to do was start shit at work, but she also couldn't let Candy think she'd be invited, and then piss her off later. "You know," she started, "Ryan and I are really stymied on how to keep the guest list short. We have very limited space, and he has a huge family…"

Candy wasn't shaken. "Oh, I bet that's hard! Hey, any chance I can sit at Dylan's table? Obviously Tia will be up with the wedding party, and so there'll be an extra seat at his table and I don't currently have a boyfriend…"

Lexi cringed on the inside, especially when she thought about making Dylan sit through her obnoxiousness all night, but held her composure. "Sorry, Candy, but I really have to limit my guest list to my closest friends, and…"

"But we're friends!" she exclaimed. "And I'd be positively heartbroken if I didn't see your big day! You and Brian are just so perfect for each other, and I…"

"Ryan," Lexi corrected. "His name is Ryan."

Candy shook it off. "That's what I meant! Now where did that come from?" she pondered openly, shaking her head. "Of course I know that! And, I have a good friend who does make-up for the Channel 6 News—I'm sure I could get her to do yours on your wedding day. It'll be my gift to you!"

Lexi retreated into her own thoughts for a moment. This is what Tia would be going through for the rest of her life, she thought, wondering if anything that came out of the mouth of someone who wasn't a real friend was genuine, or if it would always be fabricated for their own benefit. It was what Dylan had been dealing with for years, and she had a new understanding of where he came from. No wonder he went out in disguise. He'd never have a second of normalcy if he didn't.

"Wow, Candy," she said. "I really appreciate that you'd want to do that, but really, I have all the details pretty well planned out." She paused, unsure of how to continue. "And I'm really sorry to tell you this, but I'm not sure I can fit you in. We had the preliminary guest lists made over a month ago, and really, we don't hang out socially, or anything, and you weren't on it." Candy looked stricken. "You wouldn't believe how many people are trying to get invited just to meet Dylan," she said, hoping it might ease the situation. "It pisses me off that people who barely know me are trying to get an invitation to my wedding not to see me get married, but hoping to score some time with the 'Sexiest Man on Earth.' I hope you're not offended—it's nothing personal, it's just that I have to keep to my original list, and I had precious little room for coworkers. I'm really sorry."

Candy was very obviously offended—she did a pitiful job of hiding it, but she forced a smile, and stood. "Well," she said, "I could maybe just come after dinner, then? I wouldn't be in the way or anything—I won't even drink—or I'll pay cash at the bar—I'd be devastated if I missed out!"

On the chance to try and lure Dylan into your bed, Lexi thought to herself. She'd go for Dylan first, Lexi was sure about that, but she was just as certain that he'd never even pass her a second glance. Candy wasn't picky though, and she didn't seem to know how to take no for an answer, either. Dylan would never forgive her if he had to sit through dinner in Candy's company. "I'll have to see what the final list looks like and let you know,"

she said to avoid a further confrontation. She'd deal with it later—
she had a feeling she was going to be pissing a lot of people off in
the long run when the invites were actually handed out. But, no
matter what, it was her damn wedding, and she certainly wasn't
going to go out of her way to accommodate people who weren't
even friends.

Candy forced another smile, and tried to appear cheery.
"OK!" she said between clenched teeth before slinking out the
door.

Chapter 23

Bo's hospital room was an explosion of color. There were so many cards, flowers, and gifts flooding in that they quickly ran out of places to put them, so Tia and Dylan started delivering some of the bouquets to other patients. The entire staff all knew that the boys from InHap were hanging around the hospital, and more than a few made it a point to make a quick round of Bo's floor during their shifts. Tia would stop them, and ask if there were any patients on their floors who weren't getting visitors, or who might be cheered up with a bouquet. When one nurse said they'd be even cheerier if the flowers were delivered personally, they each took an armful of vases and made some rounds. This was one of the things Dylan did with his charity, she knew, and they fell into a daily rhythm; spending time with Bo and whoever showed up to keep watch each morning, and strolling through the hospital in the afternoons, delivering flowers and signing autographs or taking pictures with the patients. Dylan left a guitar in Bo's room, and on several occasions played a few songs in the waiting rooms or the common areas on the floors.

It was a great feeling, bringing a little bit of happiness to the people confined to hospital beds or wheelchairs, but the best part for Tia was when they visited the children's ward. Inevitably, they ended up there every day, Dylan stepping easily out of his "cool rock star" mode into the role of "goofy child entertainer;" leading the kids in rousing renditions of songs from Disney movies and classic kids' favorites. They took a trip over to a local toy store after seeing the well-worn pile of board games in crushed boxes stacked helter-skelter on shelves in the activity room, and brought a couple new games to the kids each day. Of course, they ended up playing them, as well.

Tia loved being around the children. Her former students had only been back in school for a week, but she already missed them and found herself wondering if Austin had mastered his multiplication tables or if Ashley had yet found the joy in reading. On any other year she would have welcomed a longer holiday break, but knowing she was never going back gave it a completely different feel. It made her feel good to sit with some of the older kids and help them with their lessons while Dylan played *Old Maid* with the younger ones. Bringing genuine smiles to the faces of the sick children and their bone-weary families was the brightest spot in the ever-growing string of days with no signs of improvement in Bo, and soon the rest of their group sought a bit of solace in the children's ward as well.

Every day, they made their way back to Bo's room hoping for a sign that he was coming back to them, and every day, they were met with a solemn shake of the head by whoever had watch duty at the time. They took turns reading Bo the newspaper or books, singing to him, playing his favorite television shows, and trying to coax him out of the dark place where he dwelled; but they never seemed to be able to manage more than a moan or the slight squeeze of a hand. It was draining them emotionally; trying to keep a positive energy in the room for Bo while communicating the lack of progress with sad eyes and haunting glances; but each one of them crowded into the tiny room every morning, thankful that the hospital was lax with the two-visitor rule where InHap was concerned.

"You're really brilliant with the kids, Tia," Dylan said one afternoon as they headed back toward Bo's room. Tia had done an impromptu history lesson with four upper-elementary aged patients, and Dylan found himself as captivated as the students by her energy and presentation. Having gone to school in Australia, he really didn't know a whole lot about American history, and he was fascinated by her descriptions of the Patriots and the reasons behind the American Revolution. "I can really see what an amazing teacher you are."

"You're pretty amazing yourself," she replied with a smile, "although I would never have guessed that you'd be such a ruthless "Candyland" player. I mean really, Miller, I saw you pull that double-purple from the middle of the deck."

"Prove it," he grinned, raising one eyebrow and lacing his fingers through hers. They got into the elevator to go back up to Bo's floor and Dylan turned to Tia. "Hey. I'm serious when I say that you are amazing with those kids, love. You don't bat an eye at their afflictions and that helps to make them forget about being sick for a while. It might be something to think about—if you wanted to do this from time to time, you could do it through the charity...you could still work with children; even set up some activities or lessons to do with them, if you wanted."

"That same thought is already dancing around in my head. I remember telling you at *Sing Along Cassidy's* how much I respected the personal appearances you made through the charity. I would love to be a part of that; especially with the kids."

"We also have those youth programs at the ranch. Bo helps run one for troubled inner city kids, combining drumming to beat out aggression and taking care of the animals to nurture respect for others. Denny has two-week program for kids with disabilities, and I help out with that one whenever I'm at home. You could jump into those, or even create one of your own if you want to. Just because you can't teach doesn't mean you can't still impact kids."

She pulled him into a tight embrace just as the doors slid open. "Have I told you today how much I love you? I completely agree—it could be amazing."

Brie was rushing toward them as they stepped into the hall. "He's awake!" she blurted, her smile telling all. Tia and Dylan shared an excited glance. It had been over two weeks of standing sentinel over his withering frame, and although none of them would admit it out loud, the hope that he'd come back to them intact faded just a little bit every day. The look in Brie's eyes, however, told them all they needed to know. Bo was back! "The nurses are in there right now, and the doctors will be up in a bit.

His blood pressure's good, his eyes are working, he's able to answer questions about what year it is and who the president is…" a tear fell from her eye, and a giggle escaped with a sob. "…he told them the president was Mickey Mouse, and that it was the year of the rat. A rat named Penelope Valentine." Their smiles grew and they simply nodded to each other; to anyone who knew him, those statements were proof that the Bo they knew and loved was going to pull through just fine. They fell in line behind Bo's obviously elated older sister and rushed back to his room with grins on their faces.

Bo was sitting up in bed for the first time. When Dylan and Tia walked in, he grinned, then winced at the pain the effort brought to his still-puffy face. He'd had moments of semi-clarity over the past couple of days, but this was the first time he was actually awake and alert.

"You look like a hot fucking mess, my friend," Dylan said, his smile wide. "But in this case, I couldn't be happier." He pulled Bo into a gentle embrace, careful not to squeeze too hard.

"Yeah, well only one of us gets to be the pretty boy," he teased back, extending his hand to Tia. "Congratulations to both of you. I can honestly say that I've never known two people more meant to be together." His voice was gruff and scratchy, but Bo's usual quick wit and teasing lightened all of their hearts. He was going to be OK.

Tia leaned over and placed a gentle kiss on his forehead. "It's so good to have you back, Bo. You had us scared for a while there. And thank you. Now that you're back, we have all kinds of reasons to celebrate."

Bo held out his hand to Tia. "Let me see your ring, darlin'." She placed her hand in Bo's and his one good eye popped out of his head in fake surprise. "Damn, Strummer Boy—is that thing real?"

"Bloody hell," Dylan laughed. "Why in the world does everyone keep asking me that?"

Ty gave him a little shove and laughed with him. "I think the last time I saw a rock that big, I was at the Tower of London, checking out the Crown Jewels."

Angelo chimed in. "I'm so sorry guys; we really should have celebrated that."

Dylan shook his head and Tia smiled. "Yeah, well we've had a few other things on our minds, and rightly so. It wasn't a time for celebrating."

"And it wouldn't have felt right without Bo," Tia added.

"Well, it sure as hell is time for celebrating now," Bo said, picking up the remote and punching the call button repeatedly.

Within seconds, the nurse came rushing into the room. "What's wrong?" she said quickly, scanning the scene with her practiced eye.

"We need some champagne in here right away," Bo demanded. "We've got a few things to celebrate, and we just can't do it without some bubbly." He flashed her a crooked grin. "So get on it, will you?"

The nurse, a heavy-set black woman with tight curls and an even tighter expression, put her hands on her hips and glared at Bo. "Mmm hmmm," she said, shaking her head. "Is that so? The only bubbly in your future, young man, is the possibility of a sponge bath. And if you hit the call button like that again, you won't even get that. You'll be so raunchy that no one'll come to visit you, and you won't have anything to celebrate. Is that clear?"

"Oh, I like her," Brie laughed.

Bo stuck out his lower lip in a pout.

"I said, is that clear?"

Bo nodded like a chastised child and mumbled, "Yes ma'am."

She pointed her finger at him. "I've got your number, Mr. Collins, and I won't forget it. Now you behave yourself or I'll have a word with your therapist and make sure you're too beat to be a nuisance." She forced a serious face, but there was a twinkle in her eye that shone with amusement.

Bo dropped his head, and she turned on her heal and marched out of the room.

"Well, she put you in your place, now didn't she?" Chloe said. "And if you give any trouble to these people trying to help you, I'll put you over my knee." Her stern face was belied by her wide smile. Ten years had melted off her since Bo was declared to be out of the woods, and it quickly became clear where both Bo and Brie got many of their best qualities.

"I woke up for this?" Bo said. "Should've stayed in the damn coma."

Two doctors strolled in and kicked everyone out of the room so they could examine their patient. The group paced the waiting room with nervous excitement until Tommy showed up with a huge sack of sandwiches. They fell on the food like a pack of starving wolves; none of them had had a proper meal in longer than they cared to remember, but their appetites had returned with Bo's consciousness. The doctors came to see them nearly an hour later, and gave them the best news they'd had in a long while. There didn't appear to be any brain damage, and, aside from a long upcoming stint with physical therapy and a few lingering effects from his injuries, he was expected to make a full recovery. They breathed a collective sigh of enormous relief, and walked back into his room with smiles on their faces.

"Do you remember anything that happened, Bo?" Tia asked. "The accident, I mean." Bo's immediate and extended family crowded into his room, celebrating his recovery and catching him up on what he'd missed over the time he was in the coma. His mom and sister were able to corroborate his recollections of Christmas; but it seemed that his memories were scattered after that.

"Not a thing. And I don't mind if it stays that way. Doc says I may have some fuzzy memories, or be forgetful for a while, but I'd be more than happy not to relive any of that. Hard enough livin' with the aftermath," he yawned, holding up his casted arm. "Man, those docs put me through the ringer," he said absently, shaking his head. "It's really not so unusual for people not to remember New Year's Eve," he said to his frowning mother. She just put her hands on her hips and pressed her mouth into a thin line, staring him down and giving him the slightest shake of her head. He knew that she wasn't buying it. Neither was he, but that was a worry for another time. Right now he was so exhausted he could barely stay awake.

"You know I love you all, and it's great to be back among the living. I really appreciate y'all bein' here, but I don't think I can hold my good eye open much longer, so I do hope you'll excuse me. I need to rest up for my sponge bath." He waggled his eyebrows, but his eyelids drooped, and they all knew that even though none of them wanted to go, he really did need his rest.

"How about dinner?" Chloe suggested. "There's a little Italian place down the street. Bo's treat, since it's his fault we've been surviving on take-out and cafeteria food for the past couple weeks."

They said their goodbyes to Bo, and gathered their belongings. "Gonna be a chilly one," Brie said as they made their way to the elevator. "Unseasonably cool, the weatherman said."

"Oh, I left my jacket," Tia said, "I'll be right back,"

She tiptoed in—Bo's breathing was already in the early stages of sleep. She plucked her jacket from the chair and heard him whisper. Not sure if he was talking to her, she leaned in. He exhaled slowly and said what sounded like, "Soooo...sorrrry... sexy..." He repeated the phrase again, and Tia tucked the blanket over his casted arm. "You'll be sexy again Bo, I promise," she whispered back, but he was already snoring softly.

"Thank God," Lexi said, falling onto the couch as Tia recounted their afternoon with Bo.

"The old Bo's still there," she said gratefully. "Right now there's some memory loss, but the doctor says that's normal, and they may come back in time. Headaches, dizziness and that kind of thing are to be expected, but they're pretty confident he'll make a full recovery. He didn't remember anything about the accident, but he remembered that Dylan and I are engaged, so that's a good sign, I think."

"And he was cracking jokes and pissing off the nurses within minutes of regaining consciousness? Sounds like Bo to me. Oh, Tia, I'm just so relieved. I've been so worried I haven't been able to think straight. Tell him how happy I am, will you?"

"I will, but it would be even better if you told him yourself. I'm sure your voice would cheer him up."

"You think so?" she asked. She wished it were true, but she was probably the last person he wanted to talk to. "I don't want to intrude—he has his family, and you guys—just tell him for me, OK?"

"OK. Hey, Dylan's flagging me from the table. I think our dinner is here. Talk to you tomorrow?"

"Sure," Lexi said, wishing that she could be there, with all of them, as they celebrated Bo's recovery and Tia and Dylan's engagement. "Talk to you then."

Bo sat alone in his room; an InHap album vibrating in his ear and pictures spread out on the bed all around him. He remembered a lot and for that he was grateful, but there were enough fuzzy bits at the edges of his brain to cause him concern. He was more than OK with not recalling the specifics of the accident—as far as he was concerned, those details could keep to the dark recesses of his mind forever. He had recognized his family; both his biological one and his band one; right away, and he was completely confident that once he had a pair of sticks in his hands he'd still be on top of his game. He'd listened to two of their albums already, tapping out the rhythms with the tips of his fingers.

Another headache started squeezing at his temples like a vice and he pulled the buds from his ears. The doctors said they were to be expected, but a couple had been goddamn vicious and he rang for the nurse in the hope that a little magic juice via his IV drip would knock him out and nip it in the bud. He scooped up the pictures and put them back into the box, saying a little silent prayer of thanks that he wasn't a vegetable who didn't remember his own name. As he waited for the medicine to take effect, he propped his laptop on the little tray attached to his bed and pulled up the video.

He'd watched it at least a dozen times already, frustrated by the haze that covered his memory like an opaque curtain. There were tiny glimpses—shadows mostly— behind the veil, but no matter how hard he focused, he couldn't get any clarity. He remembered Lexi; he had a lot of damn good memories, actually. He saw himself strolling down the red carpet with her at Icon, dancing with her at the little club in Northampton, and clearly recalled the way they shamelessly flirted. He remembered the way everyone around them rolled their eyes at them whenever they were together, and the way they finished each other's sentences. They were all good memories, which is why he had no explanation for why seeing her on the video provoked a profound sadness in him.

Most of Christmas was fairly clear, brought into focus by photos his mother and sister had given him, but his memory was a game of hopscotch after that. Bo had no idea how he spent New Year's Eve, but did remember Dylan's voicemail about their engagement. No matter how hard he concentrated though, he couldn't recall appearing on *After Dark,* despite all the times he replayed it. And for the life of him, he couldn't figure out why watching Lexi jump into his arms over and over again filled him with a deep sense of regret.

The magic juice flowed through his veins, causing the shade to thicken over his thoughts, and he drifted off into a fitful sleep.

Chapter 24

"Hey, Lex, what's up?" Ryan said into the phone as he shrugged into his coat. "I'm just heading over to the deli for an Italian beef. You in the neighborhood?"

"No, just working," she answered, "and I've got an appointment coming in about fifteen minutes. I just wanted to ask if you were getting off at a decent hour today," she said.

"Should be, yeah," Ryan answered. "Just getting some things rolled over for the start of the year...not too much to do. It's been pretty quiet here, actually. Want to do dinner or something?"

"Yeah, I was hoping to. Tia and Dylan invited us out for a little engagement celebration. They just got back this afternoon, and I can't wait to see her rock up close and in person. They've got reservations at the Signature Room for 7:00."

Son of a bitch, Ryan thought, bringing his free hand up to massage his forehead and wishing he'd been more proactive with his social calendar. He'd known they were coming back, and should have figured that Lexi would be itching to spend some time with them. Frankly, he'd rather be fed to a den of starving lions; the past few weeks had been trying, to say the least, with all the buzz about the so-called "royal couple" and he was already sick of it. He'd finally managed to quiet things down at the office—at least all the secretaries weren't asking him on a regular basis how Tia and Dylan were doing—but the club was still buzzing, and he couldn't seem to get the ringing out of his damn ears.

Tia's parents were members, of course, so there was constant chatter about the engagement and speculation about when and where the nuptials would take place. Then there were the guys who kept asking if Dylan was thinking about joining the club, talking about how cool it would be to get invited to concerts and parties and drooling over the actresses they could meet. Of course the ladies were the worst—every time he and Lexi were having dinner or drinks they were constantly popping by the table, asking for updates about the drummer and sucking up to Lexi, who was always happy to be in the know and share the gossip. It seemed that everyone wanted to be her friend these days, and she was getting invited to more parties than a birthday clown. At least she was smart enough to realize that none of them really gave a shit about being her bosom buddy, but she seemed to love the attention, nonetheless.

He was willing to bet that Tia had never even heard of The Signature Room until a few months ago; she certainly couldn't have afforded to frequent the place on her salary. Suddenly, though, she was the queen of the world, wearing a ring with a freaking diamond big enough to be called a rock and having people willing to fall down at *her* feet as well as Dylan's. La dee fucking da.

It was too late to try and come up with an excuse not to go, so he was going to have face another night of being invisible while Lexi basked in the fringes of the spotlight and everyone in the place whispered and stared at their table. He and Lex had been on some rocky ground the past few weeks, especially since the drummer kept popping up in conversations. He'd come to the conclusion that she hadn't slept with the guy—he was hardly her type—but he was getting sick of hearing about the dude. Obviously, that would be a big topic of conversation over dinner tonight. Yup, a den of lions sounded pretty damn good right now.

He really needed to get over this whole thing; had to find a way to make it fit into his life and his life with Lexi or it was going to eat him alive. He'd already spent way too many hours pondering it, and realized that there wasn't going to be a happy ending—not for him anyway. As a lawyer he prided himself on being able to see all sides of the story, and to decipher squarely where to put the blame. Problem was; there really wasn't any blame to place in this situation—it just sucked of its own volition.

Lexi really didn't deserve to be punished because her best friend landed a rock star; and who wouldn't jump at free trip to Europe to tour with the band and live the good life for a while? It was Tia who'd sworn her to secrecy—hell, she didn't even tell her own parents—and Lexi was a loyal friend. He had to give Tia props for not flaunting Miller in everyone's faces the minute she met him; he knew a lot of people who would; and he respected that she kept him on the down-low and went on with her life.

Then there was Miller. In all honesty, he kind of liked the guy; what he knew of him, anyway. He didn't get a bad rap in the press, he didn't seem completely full of himself, and he really seemed to love Tia. She was a good person too, and she deserved to be happy, especially after the shit hand she'd been dealt when Nick died.

As much as the lawyer in him wanted to place blame for his negative feelings somewhere, there really wasn't anywhere to put it except for squarely on his own shoulders. Maybe he needed to suck it up and give the guy a chance, because God knew it wasn't going to be going away any time soon. Or ever. Damn, sometimes he really missed Nick and the simpler days, when they could hang out as a foursome and shoot the shit without anyone asking for autographs.

"You still there?" Lexi asked, pulling him from his thoughts.

"Yeah, sorry, just got an email in," he lied. "I guess we can do that. Pick you up at six?"

"Dylan's got a limo, actually," she said. "They're going to pick me up around six, so you could either meet me at my place, or we could swing by and get you. You can spend the night if you want, in case it goes late."

"It's only Tuesday, Lex, and I've got an early meeting tomorrow, so I can't stay out late. Why don't you just come and get me—I can always catch a cab back home if I need to."

"OK, we'll see you around six-fifteen then. I'll text you when we're close. Oh, and they're planning something at *Paddy's* for Friday night, so make sure you keep that open too."

"Great," Ryan said absent-mindedly. Another night with the rowdy bunch at the Irish bar—he could hardly wait. "Listen, I've gotta go. I'll see you later, OK?"

"OK sweetie, have a good rest of the day…love you!"

"You too," Ryan mumbled before he tapped the screen to end the call. He started toward the door, but decided that if he was going to have an expensive dinner on Miller's dime, he was going to be good and hungry for it. He had some granola bars In his desk; that would tide him over.

Ryan was the last stop, so the three of them were already drinking champagne when he climbed into the limo.

"Hey, congratulations," Ryan said, trying to sound enthusiastic. He planted a kiss on Lexi, hugged Tia, and shook Dylan's hand. "I'm really happy for you guys."

"It's great to see you again, Ryan," Dylan said. "I'm glad you could join us on such short notice."

"Oh God, you've got to see Tia's ring!" Lexi exclaimed, grabbing Tia's hand and holding it out to Ryan. Tia smiled shyly as she allowed her friend to dangle her hand in front of Ryan's face. His eyes widened as he took it in; he couldn't help but notice how ordinary Lexi's ring looked next to the gigantic stone on Tia's finger. It really was a rock.

"Damn," he said, trying to keep his voice light. "Looks like you robbed the crown jewels, or something."

"That's what I said," Tia agreed, taking back her hand and resting it in Dylan's.

"That's what a lot of people have said. I didn't know anything about buying engagement rings. I just took the guy's word for it," Dylan said, shrugging. *Must be nice to have so much disposable cash,* Ryan thought bitterly.

"So how was Australia?" Ryan asked.

"Yes, yes, let's see some pictures!" Lexi exclaimed. Tia pulled out her IPad and started scrolling through photos and sharing stories. Ryan sat back and listened, nodding and smiling at all the right times while Lexi got positively giddy over them. It was going to be a long effing night.

They pulled up to the Hancock Building and were immediately met at the car by a man who obviously held a higher position than valet. "Mr. Miller, sir," he said reverently as he held open the door. "It's an honor to have you visit us this evening."

"Glad to meet you," Dylan said, shaking his hand.

The man reached over to assist Tia, bowing at her as she exited. "Welcome, Miss Hastings, we are so thrilled to have you and your guests here tonight."

He nodded at Ryan, and helped Lexi out of the car, turning back to Dylan. "Begging your pardon, sir," the man said, "I wouldn't normally do this, and would probably get in a lot of trouble for it if my supervisor knew, but could I please have an autograph? My daughter is a huge fan of yours."

"Happy to do it," Dylan said warmly as the man handed him a sheet of hotel stationary. "What's her name?"

"Madison. Maddie," he said happily as Dylan signed the paper. "Thank you so much, it'll really mean a lot to her." He bowed his head again, and led them into the building. "The elevator is waiting for you...please enjoy your evening."

"Thank you, I'm sure we will," Dylan replied.

Ryan couldn't help but notice that a small army of people had somehow managed to gather in the lobby as they walked through, their eyes intently focused on Tia and Dylan, who smiled and waved like they were fucking celebrities or something. *Oh yeah*, he thought, *that's exactly what they are.*

They were led to a semi-secluded table next to the windows, where they had a breathtaking view of the city below, and were quickly greeted by a most enthusiastic server who batted her eyes shamelessly at Dylan while taking their drink orders. Another attendant rushed over to place their napkins in their laps and fill their water glasses. "Anything at all I can do for you, anything at all, my name is Elena," she said breathlessly as she managed to brush her hand against Dylan's while handing him the wine list. Then she turned her attention to Tia. "Best wishes," she said, craning her neck to get a look at Tia's ring. "How excited you must be!"

"I am, thank you," Tia said graciously as Dylan placed his hand over hers on the table. She was more than used to women being drawn to Dylan, and just as used to his automatic reaction of touching her in some way, to reassure her. It had taken some time, but she was finally getting over the fact that nearly every woman they met couldn't take their eyes off her fiancé. Not that she could blame them.

Dylan ordered a bottle of champagne for a toast, and handed the wine list to Ryan. "Would you like to pick a bottle of wine to go with dinner?"

Ryan took one look at the lengthy list and swallowed. He enjoyed wine, sure, but he was far from a connoisseur, especially with this kind of selection. "I'm clueless," he admitted. "I wouldn't even know where to start." He handed the list back to Dylan. "Feel free," he said.

"Do you like reds?" Dylan asked. "I see they have one of my favorites; it's not too dry, not too sweet..."

"Sounds good to me," Ryan offered, shrugging his shoulders.

Elena arrived with a bottle of champagne in a silver bucket, and another server ceremoniously popped the cork and filled their glasses before slipping away. "On the house," Elena said brightly, "a gift from the manager to congratulate you on your engagement."

"My thanks," Dylan said as Ryan's eyes widened. Freaking Dom Perignon?. If there was anyone in the room who could afford a bottle as expensive as this one, it was Miller. And they were giving it to him for free?

Dylan lifted his glass, and the others did the same. "A toast, then," he said, "to old friends and new, and to happily ever afters."

"In this case," Lexi smiled, "I'd say, to '*InHap*pily' ever afters!"

"Oh, I like that," Tia smiled, leaning into Dylan. They touched the rims of their glasses together and sipped the bubbly.

It was a bit disconcerting to Ryan having so many people fuss over him. He'd been to his share of decent restaurants in his day, but this place was a little over the top. Before he even put down his glass after taking a sip of water, someone was there to top it off. The chef paid them a personal visit to deliver a special appetizer he'd made just for them, and it seemed that every eye in the place was fixed on their table. Maybe it wasn't the restaurant, he thought, but the company. It seemed everyone in the place made it their personal missions to make sure Dylan Miller was happy. The other diners watched them with sideways glances or gape-mouthed stares...whatever the looks, they were all very aware that there was a celebrity among them. It made him uncomfortable, but Dylan barely seemed to notice. He probably dealt with it everywhere he went, but Ryan didn't think he could ever get used to it.

"So catch me up on your news," Tia prodded. "Tell me about *After Dark*—is Tony a trip, or what?"

"Oh my God, yes," Lexi agreed. "But his assistant, Malcolm? That guy's an absolute beast!" She turned to Dylan. "Let me just say how lucky you are to have Jessa."

"Don't I know it," he agreed.

"So, you didn't know that Bo was going to be on the show with you?"

"It was a complete surprise," Lexi beamed. "I had no clue until Tony announced his name. I was totally blown away."

That was obvious, Ryan thought bitterly as he listened to her recall their reunion, subsequent dinner, and how they'd watched the show together. She talked as if Ryan wasn't even there, and he still cringed at the excitement in her voice as she talked about Bo Collins.

Ryan sat back as the conversation went on around him. They had a history together, a history in which he had no part. He had precious little to add, and was glad when their meals arrived so he'd have something else to focus on besides his wine glass. He could already feel the buzz in his head; not good when he had an early meeting with the partners in the morning.

They'd barely finished their meals when Ryan saw the woman approaching their table. He recognized her face immediately—she was one of his firm's biggest clients. He didn't work with her personally; she was from old money, and only the partners were allowed to handle her affairs. She approached the table with a huge smile and a wave, and he pulled her name from his memory. Victoria Damon. He hadn't recognized her at first because she never smiled; in fact, the staff around the office called her Victoria 'Demon' behind her back—she had a reputation for going for the balls, and didn't take shit from anyone.

"Mr. Stallworth, isn't it?" she gushed, offering Ryan her hand for a limp shake. "What a pleasure to see you this evening."

Ryan stood to take her hand, surprised she even knew his name. The few occasions he'd met her, she'd barely acknowledged his presence. "Thank you, Ms. Damon," he replied curtly, "You look well, as always."

"This must be your lovely fiancé," she said, offering her hand to Lexi. "Lexi, is it? I saw you on television a few weeks back. Your future husband's firm handles all my affairs; he's got a bright future ahead, this one; you're a lucky young lady."

"Thank you, I think so," Lexi answered cordially.

Victoria turned to Dylan, who rose from the table, and Ryan saw immediately the real reason for her uncharacteristically enthusiastic greeting. She'd wanted an introduction to Dylan, and wasn't above using her influence with his firm to get it. Now he felt as if she had him by the balls.

"Victoria Damon, Dylan Miller and Tia Hastings," he offered as Victoria turned on her high society charm.

"Oh, what an absolute pleasure!" she sang. "I'd like to offer you my very best wishes on your recent engagement; you must be so happy."

"We are," Dylan answered simply, "thank you very much."

"Do you have a date yet?" she asked.

Tia looked at Dylan. "Not yet," she said.

"You know," Victoria replied, turning her back on Ryan completely and taking Dylan's hand, "one of the divisions of my company, Vida International, specializes in high-end event planning. We could help you have the wedding of your dreams, and we take care of all the details. We've hosted events for some of the most influential..."

Dylan interrupted. "That's very kind of you. I appreciate the offer, but we've already got someone working on that."

"Oh, well, of course," she said. "I'll just leave you with my card, if I may. If you have any questions at all, you can contact me directly." She handed Dylan a gold business card, and he slipped it into his pocket. "I'm also the CEO of '4 the Children,'" she added. "We're an international charity dedicated to bringing basic medical treatment to children in developing nations. I'm hosting an event at my home weekend after next, and I'd love to have you as my guest. Perhaps you'd even consider donating a personalized item for our silent auction? It's a very good cause."

"I'm afraid my calendar is bursting at the seams, Ms. Damon, so I won't be able to attend," Dylan said. "But I'll pass on your card to my assistant—I'm sure we can do something as far as a donation. I'll have her contact you later in the week, and I wish you the best of luck with your event. I'm always happy to support a worthy cause." He put out his hand. "It was very nice meeting you; enjoy the rest of your evening." He took his seat, an indication that he was finished with the conversation.

"Call me Victoria, please," she smiled, not taking the hint. She reached into her overpriced bag and pulled out another foil business card. "Here, let me give you another card for your assistant, just in case you decide you'd like to hear about my wedding services."

"All right then," Dylan replied, taking the second card and adding it to his pocket with the first. "Do have a nice evening, now."

She seemed to suddenly come to her senses. "Oh. My, yes...well the pleasure has certainly been all mine," she breathed, batting her eyelashes at Dylan and taking his hand once more. "If you find you have that Saturday open, don't hesitate to contact me. I'm sure I can fit you in, even at the last minute."

Dylan took his hand back, and picked up his wine glass, tipping it slightly in her direction. "I'm afraid it's not possible, but again, I wish you the best of luck."

"Yes, well, do take care...I hope we meet up again real soon. Have a beautiful evening, and again, best wishes!"

She turned and left without a goodbye or even another glance at Ryan, who fumed silently. He was humiliated that one of his firm's clients; someone who barely knew him; would use him like that just to shake Miller's goddamn hand, and then turn her back on him like he didn't even exist. He clenched his teeth as he sat back down at the table.

"I'm incredibly embarrassed and sorry about that," Ryan said. "That was really fucking rude of her, and I'm actually shocked that she'd behave that way."

Dylan waved it off. "Not your fault—don't sweat it," he said. "Happens all the time, unfortunately. So, should we order some dessert? They do a nice little assortment so we can taste a bit of everything."

The only thing Ryan tasted at the moment was bitter. He'd been demoralized in front of his fiancé and her celebrity friends, and the rest of them were just going on with the evening as if nothing had happened. He felt the heat of anger rush to his face and pressed his hands to his water glass, then to his cheeks to cool them. Maybe this sort of thing happened all the time to people like Dylan Miller, but Ryan hadn't been made to feel so insignificant in a very long time; if ever. He sat back and watched the three of them laughing; more private jokes that he wasn't part of.

"So, you don't have a final date set yet?" Lexi asked.

"We do, actually," Tia said; tipping her head in and looking around to make sure none of the over attentive staff were listening. She looked at Dylan for approval, and he answered with a shrug. "We're not planning to announce it publicly for a few more weeks, but it is going to be Memorial Day weekend, and it's going to be so amazing, I can't even tell you!"

Ryan's heart sank. He and Lexi had been engaged nearly a year, and now Tia was going to get married a month before them? Fireworks or no, their wedding wasn't going to be the spectacular gala that theirs would be. This night just kept getting worse.

"Oh my God, where?" Lexi asked excitedly.

"It's going to be a secret," Tia answered, her smile lighting up her face, "to keep the paparazzi away. No one's going to know where they're going until they're on the way there. We're arranging all the transportation for the guests so the media can't figure it out. But I'll tell you this, because I know you can keep the secret. It's going to be the whole weekend, so don't make any plans!"

"A weekend-long celebration? Holy shit, this is going to be the event of the year! And you really think you can pull it together that quickly?" Lexi asked.

Dylan smiled and Tia answered. "We've got Jessa on it," she said. "You know she can do anything."

"Do you really need to do it so soon?" Ryan interjected; instantly sorry he'd said it. All six eyes squinted at him, and he could almost feel the daggers shooting from Lexi's. Dylan regained his composure quickly, and pressed his lips together.

"Pretty much," Dylan answered, either not noticing or not acknowledging his condescending tone. "I only have a couple months between the studio and rehearsals for the tour, and we need to squeeze a honeymoon in there, too. If it were up to me, I'd do it today, but you know women, they want these big weddings..." he smiled at Tia, who pouted out her lower lip.

"Is it going to be huge? Will it be a star-studded affair? Oh, I can hardly wait to go dress shopping!"

Dylan laughed. "There'll be a few celebrities there, but we're going to keep it fairly small, actually. Close friends and family, mostly."

"A whole weekend at a secret location," she said dreamily, "I don't know if I can wait!"

"Me either," Tia said. "We haven't hammered out all the details yet, but I'll give you all the ones I can once I know them."

"Oohh, I'll have to start putting extra money in my vacation fund right away."

"You don't need to—the best part is that it isn't going to cost anyone a dime."

"Are you serious?" Lexi asked, stunned. "How..."

"You'll find out eventually, but for now, it's all part of the surprise."

"Oh my God, this is unbelievable. Are you busy Saturday afternoon? Want to go dress shopping?"

"Actually, I've got a few people sending over some sketches...for all three of us. I'm hoping to get some in the next week or so. Would you be available to go for an initial fitting next weekend if I see one I really like?"

"Oh, I see," Lexi teased. "So you've got people now? Like actual designers? The ones who make dresses for the stars?"

"The very ones," Tia smiled shyly. Dylan had been right—top name designers were calling Jessa every day begging to make her wedding dress, knowing that pictures of it would be all over the news and the magazines. Tia imagined people asking, 'Who are you wearing?' She never in a million years thought that would be a question she'd ever be asked. It was actually a little much, in her opinion—she knew it was going to cost a small fortune and her mind hadn't yet come to terms with the fact that she was now a wealthy woman. She would have been fine with a regular dress from a normal bridal shop, but she also knew that if she went that route, she'd have to deal with a lot of unwanted attention and the chance that someone would snap a photo of her in her dress and sell it to the media before the wedding. In the end, it was just easier and less stressful to put it in the hands of a professional. Plus, it was exciting to know that she'd be wearing a dress that was one of a kind and made just for her.

"I can definitely do that. Just let me know what time."

"Then maybe after that we can shop for invitations—I need to get those real quick. Or at least, "Save the Date" cards."

"Sounds great," Lexi said. "I still haven't found the ones I want yet, and I need to get those rolling too."

Ryan just wanted to sink into his seat and disappear. The longer he sat and listened, the more insignificant he felt in the company of his own fiancé and her former school teacher best friend. Here he was, sitting down to a hundred-dollar-meal and drinking champagne that cost more than that, and no one else was even batting an eye. He made a good living; and it would get even better when he finally made partner, but he'd never be able to give Lexi carte blanche to hire designers to make her dresses or wedding planners to handle all the details. They were paying for the wedding themselves—he was expecting the guests to give *him* money, not providing *them* with an entire weekend of festivities on his dime. A sick feeling sloshed around in his stomach and his forty-five dollar steak suddenly felt like a rock.

Less than a year ago, Tia was scraping and saving just to be able to afford a long weekend in Punta freaking Cana. Lexi often picked up her tab when they went out somewhere on the fancier side, as she knew that Tia was also paying the mortgage on her tiny little house and didn't have a lot left over for extras. Now the tables had completely turned, and he wondered how Lexi would take it when the realization sunk in that he was never going to be able to give her what Tia had. No matter how hard he worked, he was never going to be a multi -millionaire. He felt really out of his league here, but Lexi was looking pretty damn comfortable. He glanced at his watch, wondering how much longer this evening was going to drag on, or if anyone would notice if he just left.

Chapter 25

Ryan barely slept a wink all night. When his alarm went off at five, he could hardly peel his tongue off the roof of his mouth and it felt like someone was using a jackhammer inside his skull. He knew at the time that it was a stupid move to down two more glasses of champagne in the limo on the ride home, but he just couldn't stand listening to Lexi going on about wearing a gown— that's what she called it, a goddamn *gown*-- made by an actual famous designer when he knew damn well she'd gotten her own wedding dress off the rack.

He downed three aspirin and drank about a gallon of coffee, but he just couldn't get himself moving, and was five minutes late for his seven thirty meeting. It was impossible to miss the cold stares from the partners when he rushed in, out of breath. It was all he could do to keep his eyes open much less focus on the discussion, and Wes had to kick him more than once under the table when his eyelids simply refused to stay open and he dozed off. When the meeting finally ended, he rushed to his own office, hoping to lock the door and catch a quick nap so he could make it through the rest of the day.

"Victoria Damon here to see you, Mr. Stallworth," Shannon, the secretary, yelled at his fleeting figure.

Shit, he thought. Since he wasn't allowed to handle any of her legal affairs, he could only venture a guess that she was here in regard to their meeting the night before; and that was the last thing he wanted to deal with at the moment. His head was still pounding, and the coffee had gone right through him—he really needed to take a piss. "Tell her I'm in a..." he opened the door to his office and saw her seated there, a shiny designer bag that matched her outfit centered perfectly in her lap. He turned and glared at Shannon over his shoulder, giving her a look that indicated they'd be speaking about this later. She just shrugged at him, raising her palms in the air to indicate she'd been left little choice in the matter.

He sucked in a breath and pasted on his best smile, willing his bladder to hold out for he hoped would be a very brief encounter. "Ms. Damon," he said as brightly as he could muster. "How nice to see you again." He shook her limp hand and moved behind his desk, taking a seat.

"And you as well," she answered. "I trust you enjoyed your dinner last night?" Ryan noticed that she didn't invite him to be on a first name basis as she had so quickly with Dylan.

Enjoyed wasn't exactly the word he would use, but he held the smile and nodded. "I did, very much, thank you."

"And your company," she added. "I didn't realize you were acquainted with Dylan Miller."

Ryan couldn't resist the opportunity to one-up her snobby assumption that he wouldn't have friends in high places. He tented his fingers under his chin and smiled wider. "Yes, well, my fiancé is going to be the maid of honor at their wedding. They just got back into town, so we were celebrating their engagement." *Pull that out of your high society ass and choke on it,* he thought as he remembered how she'd turned her back on him and refused to acknowledge his presence once he'd made the introduction to Miller.

"Yes, I recognized your fiancé from *After Dark,*" she replied. "Tia and Dylan are such a lovely couple. She's a lucky young lady."

Ryan's bladder was uncomfortably full, and he was in no mood for small talk. "I'm afraid I'm not familiar with your file, Ms. Damon, but if you'd like to give me an idea of what you need, I can be up to speed in a day or two and set up another meeting with you then."

"I'm not here to discuss my file, Mr. Stallworth," she said shortly. "I'm here on more of a personal matter, actually."

Ryan squinted, gritting his teeth. Before last night, there wasn't anything personal in the world that 'The Demon' could possibly want to discuss with the lowly lawyer who wasn't even allowed to peek at her company's files. But suddenly, after seeing him hanging out with Mister Hot Shot Rock Star, she was in the mood for a friendly chat. There was only one possible 'personal' reason that she'd be calling on him, and he was immediately offended. His first thought was that she was going to invite him to the charity auction in the hopes he might convince Dylan to go along with him. He wanted to tell her that they had no personal relationship and that she could feel free to hustle her narcissistic ass out of his office as fast as she was able to move, but she was one of the firms top clients, so instead, he pressed his lips together and said, "I'm afraid I don't understand."

"I'll cut to the chase," she said. Ryan expected nothing less, based on her reputation. She wasn't exactly known for small talk.

"Please do," he said, fighting the urge to squirm in his seat.

"First off, I did a bit of research last night and discovered that Dylan has his own charity dedicated to helping children. I'd like to set up a meeting with him personally to discuss how we could be of assistance to each other and further both causes."

Ryan frowned. "Wouldn't you need to speak to the people who run the actual charity?" he asked. "Obviously he has people taking care of the details."

"I would think you'd know that's not how I work, Mr. Stallworth. I only deal with the people at the top; not the help. I did have some of my assistants look into that this morning, but it didn't seem at all that they'd be able to set up a direct meeting. Since you're such good friends and you can easily vouch for my reputation, you can eliminate the middle man and set something up for me. I can work around his schedule, of course, and would be willing to go to him if he's unable to come to me."

He was hardly good friends with Miller—he barely knew the dude, really. But he wasn't about to let The Demon know that. "I appreciate your faith in me, Ms. Damon," he answered, "but unfortunately, Dylan's got an incredibly busy schedule and isn't looking to put anything more on his plate at this time. He's only going to be in Chicago for a short while before he's due out west to start work on the next InHap album, he's getting married, and then he's got a tour this summer. Plus, the drummer for his band was in a nasty accident and he's been spending a lot of his free time with him, helping him along with his recovery." Ryan didn't know if that was true, but it sounded good, anyway. "I wish I could help you," he lied, "but I really don't see that I can. Dylan's a very busy man, especially these days." As if he'd ever lower himself to the point of begging Dylan to meet with her. Yeah, right.

"I see. Yes, I can certainly understand that he 'has a lot on his plate,' as you put it, so perhaps I'll try again when things settle down for him. There is another matter you *could* help me with, though," she said.

Ryan raised his eyebrows. He could actually feel the walls of his bladder reaching the breaking point, and really wanted to get her out of his office so he could make a beeline for the restroom. "What's that?"

"Well, I would very much like to attend the Millers' wedding," she said with the same expressionless face she'd use to discuss a business merger or acquisition. "Perhaps he'd be more likely to meet with me once we've developed a bit of a social relationship. Surely you could do me that small favor."

Small favor? Ryan could almost feel his mouth hanging open. He stared at her for a moment, wondering if it was actually possible that she'd really just asked him that question and then said, "Excuse me?"

"Since your fiancé will be standing up in the wedding, there'll likely be an odd number at your table. Certainly as such a close personal friend he wouldn't mind if you brought one extra guest." She must have gotten a look at the incredulousness on Ryan's face because she lowered her nose, putting her eyes at Ryan's level, and her voice dropped. "I give a great deal of business to this firm and have never had to lower myself to asking for favors. I don't see any other connection to the families, however, so I'm here to ask for one now."

What...the...hell? Ryan thought. *Is she serious?* But he only had to look at her pinched-up smirk to know that this was no joke. She really thought that even if he was a 'close personal friend,' that put him in a position to affect the guest list for their fucking wedding? He took a deep breath, counted to ten, and hoped to hell that what he was about to say wasn't going to come out the way he meant it. "I'm terribly sorry, Ms. Damon," he said, biting his tongue between words, "but as you know from your own work, people are invited to a wedding at the sole discretion of the bride and groom, and not their guests." It was time to fess up. "I mean no disrespect, but I really don't see any way I can help you. My fiancé and Tia are great friends, but I've really only met Dylan a few times—no one except for Lexi even knew that he and Tia were a couple until a month ago, and then they were only here a few days before they went to California, New York, Australia..."

"I know where they've been," she said. "And now that he's back, I'm sure you'll be seeing more of them both. All you need to do is to ask if you can bring an important guest..."

"It's not my wedding," Ryan insisted. "I have no control over their guest list."

A slight smile turned up the corners of her lips, and Ryan felt the ambush coming before she even spoke. "Ah, well, I guess I should have expected that, and you are correct—it is the bride and groom's decision—you know that well, don't you, as you're no doubt working on the guest lists for your own wedding." Ryan knew instantly that he'd been had. He should have seen it coming, but instead he fell in headfirst. "I assume that Tia will be standing up in your wedding as well, which will leave an odd number at Dylan's table. Can I expect to be seated there?"

Ryan bit his tongue hard enough to draw blood, but it didn't even begin to cover the bitter taste that was already in his mouth. What could he say to that? The Demon actually smiled then, her face seeming to crack where the skin so rarely folded, and he had a vision of reaching across the desk and grabbing her by the throat in much the same way she now had him once again by the balls. She was using him, and had no qualms whatsoever about doing it.

What was with people and their obsession with celebrities? He'd been too pissed off believing that Lexi had slept with Miller to be in awe of his fame when they'd first met, but he was already sick of the way people fell down at his fucking feet everywhere he went and the way everyone else was pretty much invisible. Or maybe it was just him who ceased to exist whenever Dylan Miller shared the same space. Either way, it sucked to be Ryan Stallworth. Anger bubbled up in him and his bladder threatened to explode, but he couldn't let The Demon see how tightly she was clutching his nuts.

"I can't make any promises, Ms. Damon, as family and friends have to be seated first," he said quietly, "but I'll see what I can do."

"I'll look forward to hearing from you then," she said, handing him one of her gold cards. "You can contact me directly at that number," she said, and she stood up and walked out without another word, leaving Ryan dumbfounded and completely pissed off.

He meant to have words with Shannon before he hit the toilet, but he saw one of his own clients seated in the little waiting area, and had to hold his tongue.

"Miss Van Dyke here to see you," she said coldly, giving him a dark stare.

The woman who'd been sitting jumped up and offered Ryan her hand. "I don't have an appointment, Ryan," she said, "but I was in the neighborhood and hope you'll do me the courtesy."

Donna Van Dyke was young, good looking, energetic, and successful; thanks to her parents handing over their company. She had a reputation as a party girl, though, and she spent money like it was going out of style. Ryan had done a lot more than manage her company's finances over the past three years; he'd had to help her with her own, as well. No matter how many ways he laid it out for her, he just wasn't able to make her understand that she couldn't spend the company's cash on her own indulgences. Donna refused to take no for an answer if there was something she wanted; whether it be a car, a boat, a vacation, or a business venture. The fact that she showed up without an appointment probably meant that he was going to have to do some financial juggling—she had that familiar gleam in her eye; the one she got when she locked onto something she simply had to have. He shook her hand, and motioned for her to go into his office. "Of course Donna," he said kindly, "come on in. I've just come out of back-to-back meetings and need to use the restroom. I'll be with you in just a moment." He offered her a drink, then made a beeline for the men's room.

He couldn't believe the exquisite agony as he released the aching muscle and emptied his bladder. *Piss on you, Demon, piss on you,* he thought as he tried to tame down the anger that coursed through his veins at the nerve of Victoria Damon; who did a hell of a job living up to her nickname. He took his time washing his hands, splashing some cold water on his face to ease the burn there and took a few deep breaths before returning to his office and an actual client.

"Ryan," she began, taking a small sip of her mineral water. "I need your help."

"Anything," he said with a smile. "You know that. I'm at your service."

"This is a little unconventional...I have a bit of a personal business proposal for you, actually."

"I'm listening."

"We've known each other a lot of years, Ryan, and you've helped me out a great deal. I want you to know that I consider you a friend."

"I'm glad to hear that, Donna." *A friend?* he thought. *As if.*

"So," she began, "One of my friends told me that your future wife is best friends with Dylan Miller's fiancé. Was she really the only one who knew they were a couple? She didn't even tell you?"

Like he needed to be reminded of that. "They didn't even tell Tia's parents," he said. "It was all very hush-hush."

"Oh, how exciting! Is it true that your fiancé and Tia will be standing up in each other's weddings?"

Shit! he thought. *Seriously? Another one?*

"Yes. They've been friends since middle school," he said, working hard to keep his cool. There was no use lying about it—like everything else Miller, it would be public knowledge soon, if it wasn't already. "She's the maid of honor."

"Oh my gosh; I really, *really*, want to meet him," she said, uncharacteristically capricious. She'd always at least tried to maintain a professional demeanor when she was in his office, but apparently, where Dylan was concerned, it was all out the window. "I've been a huge fan of his for like ever, and I'm prepared to offer you a generous wedding gift if I can attend, and an even better one if I can sit at his table." She paused for a moment. "I'm prepared to offer you five thousand dollars for a seat next to his."

Ryan held his breath and bit his tongue to avoid saying all the nasty words running through his mind. Now he was being bribed? By a client? He couldn't believe the nerve, but once again, he had to maintain his cool even as he was about to erupt on the inside. He exhaled slowly through his teeth before speaking.

"Wow. I'm not even sure how to respond to that, Donna," he began. "We have worked together a lot over the past few years, but we've never done anything socially before, and our guest list is already over the limit."

"Make it ten thousand, then," she countered without so much as a blink. Ryan slowly counted to ten once again in his mind, but it didn't make him feel any less like exploding.

"I'm afraid that money won't affect the outcome of my guest list. I'll also tell you that you're not the first one to make this request, and that I can't possibly accommodate everyone who wants to meet Dylan. Certainly not at my own wedding. " To get rid of her, he forced a smile and added, "I'll see what I can do, but I can't guarantee anything."

"It's one seat, Ryan. You'll pay maybe, what, fifty or sixty bucks a head, and I'll give you ten grand? You'll make out like a bandit. It's good business."

"It's my *wedding*, Donna," he spat, unable to control his frustration any longer, "not business. I'm not selling tickets."

"And *I'll* tell *you*," she said, her smile fading, "that you're going to have party crashers, regardless of whether you invite them or not. And I just might be one of them. So the choice is yours—a generous gift for an invitation, or none at all if I crash." The look in her eyes morphed from friendly to downright menacing, but Ryan refused to flinch. His head was pounding worse than ever and he was in no mood or physical state to deal with this kind of bullshit at the moment.

"Thank you for stopping in, Miss Van Dyke," he said, purposely using her surname. "If I can be of any assistance to you in a legal matter, please don't hesitate to call on me."

She turned on her heel, shot daggers at him with her eyes, and left without another word.

He waited about four heartbeats, then burst from his office to lay into Shannon. "No more impromptu meetings," he bellowed at her. "The next time someone walks into that door unannounced, you make sure you let me know...and you do NOT let someone into my office without my approval!"

Shannon just looked at him wide-eyed, more than a little surprised by his outburst. Hearing the commotion, Wes poked his head out of his office, beckoning with a curl of his index finger. "A word, Ryan?" he said.

Flustered, Ryan stormed to Wes's door and walked inside, falling onto the chair in front of his desk.

"Sorry Wes, but I..." he began, but his boss was quick to interrupt.

"Do you want to tell me what the hell is going on with you today, Ryan?" he demanded. "You drag your ass in late for a meeting, you look like a goddamn zombie, and now you're bitching out the secretary?" Ryan opened his mouth to speak, but was silenced by the look in his boss's eyes and the finger pointed angrily at his chest. He dropped his shoulders and bowed his head, waiting for the verbal beating to be over. "I'll tell you this, Stallworth...anytime Victoria Damon walks into this office and requests an audience with you, you will grant it, and you'll do it with a smile! Same goes for Donna Van Dyke. You better get your shit together, and do it quick."

Ryan took a deep breath and nodded. "I'm sorry Wes, really. I just had a really long night and a miserable start to the day."

"Yeah? Well I'm going all mushy inside," he said sarcastically. "I don't give a shit what kind of night you had; you don't take it out on our best clients. Am I clear?" He took in Ryan's face, and shook his head. "Aw, hell, what's going on?" he said more sympathetically.

"Damn it, it's not that he's a bad guy—he isn't at all. He doesn't rub anybody's nose in it, you know? But this is absolute bullshit." he said after he'd recounted for Wes the demands made by the clients.

"You know, Ryan, you might want to consider hiring some security for your wedding," Wes replied. "Donna's probably right-- you're likely to have all kinds of party crashers showing up uninvited."

"Security? Are you serious?" he asked incredulously.

"I'm absolutely serious," Wes said. "If you have someone you barely know telling you that they'll crash your reception, you think there aren't dozens more who would do it? Miller's big news thanks to this love triangle thing, plus he's some kind of sex symbol, or something. Lots of the ladies are going to want to meet him."

"But he's engaged to my fiancé's best friend," he said, "and she's going to be there. Hell, if everything goes according to plan, they'll already be married! What do they think is going to happen?"

"Who knows?" he smiled. "They just want to be able to say they rubbed elbows with a celebrity and that there was a chance that something could happen. His wife'll be seated with the wedding party, so he'll be all by his sexy lonesome self. Maybe you should just take the money and invite them—you could make a fortune!"

"It's my goddamn wedding, Wes, not a fucking rock concert. I'm not selling front row tickets to the highest bidder, and I'm not hiring a bunch of thugs to keep my reception under control!" He raked his fingers roughly through his hair. "I don't know if you've been to any weddings lately," he said sarcastically, "but the focus is supposed to be on the bride and groom—not one of the guests."

Wes shrugged. "I don't know what to tell you, buddy. It is what it is, so you'd best figure out a way to make it work for you. I'm telling you though, you could really make a lot of dough."

"Shit," Ryan said, "Not only would Lexi kill me, but again, it's my wedding, and I'm not filling the reception with a bunch of people that I barely know."

Wes shrugged. "Who knows? Maybe by that time the notoriety will die down and you won't even have to worry about it. They won't be in the news forever, and things might quiet down. It's just big right now, so it's on everyone's minds."

"That's not going to happen. Tia and Dylan just got engaged a few weeks ago, but they're planning on getting married before us. Like, a little over a month before us. So that means that there'll be pictures of their wedding all over the place right before ours happens. Plus, there's the whole Penelope Valentine thing, and the infamous movie they did in New Zealand will come out..."

"Why are they getting hitched so quick, and why so close to yours? That seems like a shitty thing to do to a friend. Is she pregnant, or something?"

"Ah, he's going into the studio next month to make a new record, and then his band is going to start touring in the fall so he needs to be in rehearsals...I guess they don't have a big window. Plus, they're getting married on the one year anniversary of when they met." He bit his lower lip and shook his head.

"Pretty shitty timing for you," Wes agreed.

"The thing is? I don't really fault Miller for anything," Ryan sighed. "He seems like a nice enough guy; he doesn't seem all full of himself like you'd expect a big rock star to be. And I understand wanting to get married on the anniversary, and that he has to work—there are other guys in the band, so he doesn't call all the shots...but still. This is really sucking on the tit of every part of my life. I can't stand going to my country club anymore—I'm sick of people asking me if I know when he's coming back in or if I can get an autographed picture for their sick grandmother or something—and now I'm starting to get the same shit at work? It's a bunch of crap!"

Wes's eyes squinted and he nodded his head slightly. "Seems to me like maybe it's the timing that's all wrong, Ryan."

"That's the understatement of the year," he grumbled.

"What if you postponed your wedding? If you got married while the band is on tour, maybe he wouldn't be able to make it— or you could just tell all the would-be wedding crashers that he can't make it and have a legitimate excuse. Then you wouldn't have to worry about any of it."

Ryan's eyebrows rose as he considered it for a moment, but then his face fell just as quickly. "How am I going to get Lexi to go for that? First of all, she has her heart set on a July wedding— she always has. She's got a goddamned fireworks display planned for the reception, for chrissake. Second of all, Tia might be on the tour with Dylan, and she's Lexi's best friend, not to mention maid of honor."

"I think it's matron of honor if she's already married."

"Whatever," Ryan said, waving his hand in dismissal. "The point is, Lexi is going to want her to be there for all the showers, parties, fittings...all that girl shit that they love so much. And, she really likes Dylan too. She spent a couple weeks over in Europe with them on the tour and really got to know the guy. She thinks he's a fucking prince. She'll want him there, and would be pissed if I even suggested having the wedding during the tour. She's probably going to want to invite the whole goddamn band. God knows she's gotten chummy with the drummer..." He closed his eyes and tipped his head toward the ceiling. "It sounds good in theory, but I really don't see any way to get her to agree to that," he said, defeated.

"What if it wasn't your fault?" Wes suggested. Ryan cocked his head in question and Wes continued. "What if you don't *want* to postpone the wedding, but you have to because of say...work?"

"I'm not following you, Wes."

"What if you suddenly got a "big project," he said, making air quotes with his fingers, "and it was going to keep you incredibly busy for the next...oh, I don't know...six or seven months?"

"How am I going to pull that off?" he asked.

"Listen, Ryan. It's no secret that we're all considering you for partnership, but between you and me, the decision has pretty much been made." Ryan smiled wryly—how ironic to get this bit of news when his life seemed to be tanking around him. "There are still some loose ends to tie up, and then a whole lot of paperwork and legal mumbo-jumbo before it becomes official, but we were thinking of springing the news on you around the end of the year. Kind of a Christmas present, if you will. So, if you were to say that this 'project' is so important that it could make or break your partner status, you'd have no choice but to work on it for the good of both your futures, right? And no one would know except for you and me."

Ryan started nodding; slowly at first, then faster as a smile spread across his face. "That could work, you know? She'd be pissed at first, but she'd get over it, right? Especially when the partnership was announced—she'd know that it had all been worth it!" He took a deep breath and exhaled slowly. "You'd do that for me? Keep the secret so she'd never know the truth?"

"I could..." Wes said cooly. "...but at the risk of sounding cliché...I hate to even ask right now, but if I do this, you'll kind of owe me, so..."

"What, Wes, you want to sit next to him at the wedding too?"

InHap*pily Ever After

"Not me, but if he does show up for your wedding, can I bring my niece? She's a big fan—she's got a freaking poster of the guy hanging on the wall in her bedroom. You wouldn't have to feed her or anything, she'd just love to come to the reception and meet him..."

Ryan smiled. "Consider it done," he said. "It's a small price to pay to avoid this little shit storm. I'll be sure to put her on the formal guest list—hell, she can sit in his lap if she wants to. Fuck these primadonnas who think they can bribe or coerce me into bowing down to their every request!"

The two men shook hands to finalize the deal, and Ryan headed back to his office, feeling better than he had since he first saw Dylan Miller with his arms around his fiancé.

Ryan worked on the story he'd tell Lexi most of the rest of the day. She was going to be seriously pissed off, there was no doubt about it, but the whole situation was pissing him off as well, and this was the only way he could keep his dignity as a man. He laughed at himself then. He was dreading telling her, if he was to be honest, and he'd have to tell her soon as he was tasked with picking up wedding invitation samples so they could go through them together over the weekend.

One thing he knew about lying, however—and his experience as an attorney had taught him well—was that you had to keep it simple and consistent. You told everyone the same story, and then you never had to try and remember who knew the truth and who didn't. That was why when Jace called, he decided to set the foundations of the story with him.

293

Chapter 26

"Hey, what's up man?" Jace said when Ryan picked up the call. "Long time no see, my friend. Sorry I haven't been around the club lately…"

"I haven't noticed," Ryan replied. "I haven't been there either."

"Why not?" Jace asked, and then at the same time, they both said, "Dylan Miller."

"Oh man, he got you too?" Jace laughed. "What happened?"

"Long story," Ryan said.

"Well hey; I'd love to hear all about it. I'm glad I'm not the only one who isn't bowing down at his fucking feet. Want to join me for drinks tonight? I was thinking about going to *Skin Tones*, blowing off a little steam."

Skin Tones was a strip club not too far from the office. It was classier than most, seedier than some, but they had a decent selection of top shelf liquor, and Ryan decided he could really go for a drink. He could test out the story on Jace, and avoid telling Lexi about postponing the wedding for at least another day. He accepted immediately, and wrapped up only what was absolutely necessary before calling it an early day.

It felt good to hang with Jace, anonymous in the dimly lit bar, girls working the poles and delivering drinks clad in nothing but tiny g-strings. Jace relived for him again his encounter with Dylan in the locker room. "He knew exactly who I was, man," he said. "He was just fucking toying with me. But because I wasn't a hundred percent sure at the time, I had no choice but to sit there and take it." Ryan voiced his sympathy, and Jace continued. "Then, Bitsy fucking broke up with me. I'd already promised to meet her for lunch, and I grabbed a table that was out of view so he wouldn't see me and have Tia confirm who I was, but Bitsy kept begging to go over there and meet him, and she just wouldn't let up! I said I didn't give a shit if he was God, and she got real bitchy and started saying I was just jealous that I could never measure up to him and that I had to give up my fantasies about Tia." He pursed his lips and shook his head.

"That sucks, man," Ryan said sympathetically, but he knew that Jace deserved it. He'd treated Bitsy like shit in his quest to get Tia to date him.

Jace shook his head. "Wait—it gets worse! I told her she didn't know what she was talking about, and she told me to go to hell. She actually said that..." his voice got high and whiney as he did a pretty good imitation of Bitsy, "'...having Dylan Miller say my name and shake my hand would give me more pleasure than *you've* given me over the past year.'"

"Unfuckingbelievable, man. Really," Ryan said, "but you did kind of treat her like shit, you know. Especially about the Tia thing."

"Yeah, I know," he agreed. "And it's not like I even miss her or anything—she was a pain in the ass most of the time, but now I can't even go to the club anymore," he moaned. "Everyone freaking knows how many times Tia shot me down, and they probably know about me and the Miller thing, and I don't want to deal with the bullshit."

"I know what you mean," Ryan agreed. "I'm not going because everyone suddenly thinks he's my best friend, and that I can get them autographs, pictures, private meetings...I'm sick of it, to be honest, and it just isn't worth it anymore."

"I hear that, brother," Jace agreed, tucking a fiver into the tiny shred of fabric on a stripper's hip. "It's like no one else exists whenever he's around," he said.

Ryan shook his head and tucked a bill into the g-string of a particularly buxom brunette that kept wriggling seductively in front of him.

"Well, I got some news today that'll keep me away from the club anyway. It's great news, but it's going to get me in a lot of shit with Lexi."

"Yeah, what's that?" Jace asked.

"I talked to Wes today," he started, "and he's got a real big project for me. One that could be the deciding factor in my getting a partnership with the firm."

"That's great man! Congratulations!" Jace said.

"That's the good news," he said, taking a deep breath before dumping the lie. He knew he could trust Jace, and that he'd be completely sympathetic of the situation, but he'd made his decision to keep the truth in as few hands as possible— meaning none. He threw back the last of his beer and motioned to the topless waitress with the pierced nipple for another. "The bad news is, unfortunately, it means I'm going to have to postpone my wedding—I'm going to be up to my neck in work for the next few months, and it's going to consume pretty much all of my time— Lexi's going to be so pissed, and I have to admit that I'm deathly afraid to tell her."

Jace exhaled with a whoosh. "Oh yeah, I'd be afraid to tell her too. She's going to kick your ass, bro."

"Yeah, but I'm doing it for our future, right? She has to understand that."

"She doesn't have to understand anything, dude. She's a woman. She's planned her dream wedding, and you're going to tell her that she has to wait for what, months?"

Ryan just nodded.

"Sucks to be you," Jace said matter-of-factly, tossing back the last of his vodka tonic.

"Yeah, and I'm supposed to pick up the freaking wedding invitation samples before the weekend, so I have to tell her soon."

"You have to tell her soon anyway," he said. "She's going to have to cancel a whole bunch of shit. Don't you have deposits down on churches, flowers, limos, food..." Ryan nodded miserably. "Man, I wouldn't want to be anywhere near that volcano when it erupts!"

Ryan's phone buzzed in his pocket and he fished it out, checking the display. He saw Lexi's name and let it go to voicemail. He'd call her later and tell her he was in a meeting about the project, or something, or maybe he'd wait as long as possible before telling her. He still wasn't sure what the hell he was going to do.

They each had one more drink, but neither of them was really enjoying the show as much as they should have been. Ryan made it an early night and called Lexi from the car.

"Hey," she said, "where are you? I've been trying to call you for hours!"

"Sorry," he answered. "I was in a big meeting, and I couldn't get away."

"Did you pick up the invitations?"

"No, I didn't," he said. "By the time I got out of work they were already closed. I'll get them tomorrow."

"Oh, I'm dying to see them!" she said. "Are you sure you'll be able to make it tomorrow?" Without waiting for an answer, she added, "If you can't, let me know by four and I'll just drive in."

"I'll get there," he said, "don't worry."

"Hey, so anyway," she said, changing the subject, "what are you doing right now? Want to meet me at the club for dinner? I was going to call Tia and see if she and Dylan wanted to join us."

"It's almost seven," he replied. "They've probably already eaten." Shit, the last thing he wanted to do was hang out with them and compare wedding notes.

"Well, I'll call them and find out, then. You can meet me anyway, even if they don't come."

He fumbled for another lie. "Not tonight Lex. Wes brought in some sandwiches during the meeting, so I'm not really hungry anyway. Plus, I have to go in early again tomorrow, so I'm just going to head home."

"Want some company?"

"Tempting, but I'm really beat. I was late for this morning's meeting after last night and I need to catch up on some sleep. I'll just call you tomorrow, OK?"

"Are you OK, Ryan?" she asked suspiciously.

"I'm fine—just busy, is all. I'll call you tomorrow."

"OK then," she said, adding, "Love you."

"You too," he answered, and ended the call.

He was torn. He did love Lexi, but ever since the day he saw her in the arms of Dylan Miller, something had changed. Of course he was Tia's fiancé now, and Lexi would never even consider it for that reason alone, but he couldn't help but wonder if she was comparing him to Miller. Bitsy had called that one straight—how could he ever measure up? How could anyone? Ryan made a good living; it would be even better once he made partner; but would she always be wondering why she couldn't travel the world, have designers make her clothes, wear a ridiculously huge diamond on her finger...would she always wish it was her that met Miller first?

And now that Tia was planning to move to Colorado to live with him, would she be constantly wanting to make trips out there to visit her best friend? Would he be excluded from her life, or would he be constantly playing second fiddle to Mr. Celebrity while his own wife lived the life of the rich and famous riding on her best friend's coattails? How would she feel about attending office parties when she could be at the Grammy's or fucking movie premiers?

As if in answer to his question, the sky suddenly opened up under a huge crash of thunder and huge, slushy raindrops began pelting his car like bullets. He went home and poured another beer, sinking into his recliner and closing his eyes.

It had been a real shitty week, and Thursday was no exception. He was running out of time and excuses, and he had to make a decision real quick; he'd have to pick up the invitations by tomorrow at the latest, and he had to decide whether he was going to tell Lexi that they needed to postpone the wedding.

Before noon, he'd gotten two more calls from clients of the firm who sat on the boards of charities that wanted him to get Dylan to appear at their events; or at least provide something autographed for their silent auctions. It got so that he cringed every time his phone rang, and he finally told his secretary to screen his calls and to tell anyone who was not one of his clients or a close personal friend that he was in a meeting.

No matter how busy he tried to keep himself, however, it all kept scratching at the back of his brain, forcing his thoughts in directions he had no desire to go. He'd be studying a client file, and suddenly he'd be transported back to the night he stood quietly in the hallway of his apartment, eavesdropping on Lexi while she was on the phone. She'd never told him the whole story of how she first found out that her best friend was involved with a man she herself had fantasized about for years. She'd never mentioned to him how she'd been sitting in the front row at an Inhap concert, waiting for Tia to show up—how Dylan had come out to perform a song with the opening band and had looked straight at her, smiled, and tossed his head toward the back of the stage, presumably to let her know that Tia was there. Tia hadn't told Dylan that she was keeping him a secret, and she hadn't told Lexi the true identity of the man she'd met at the dumpy bar the night before, so Lexi thought it was an invitation—an indication that she'd be invited backstage.

"You know I'd be all over that," she'd told the caller. "No question! Yeah, Tia knows. She was standing backstage watching and saw the whole thing! She called my cell and when I told her I was going to cash in on my gimme, she just laughed at me and told me not to do anything to embarrass myself." She giggled at something the caller said, and continued. "When she finally got to the seat, and Inhap came on, I told her she was on her own with her cowboy, because I was going backstage to make wicked love to the man...I know! He kept smiling down at us from that big stage, and started rocking the house—Tia kept it up and said that he was looking at her..." she paused and laughed again as she listened. "It wasn't until the third song—when he dedicated the show to her, that I figured it out. I was in a state of complete shock." She listened for a few minutes, while he stood frozen in the hallway, digesting this new information—choking on it, more specifically. "Yeah, but they're so good together, really. He's an amazing guy—easy to talk to, down to earth, fucking hilarious, and obviously gorgeous...she's one lucky bitch, I'll tell you that!"

The conversation shifted, and Ryan snuck back into his office and sat in front of his computer, stupefied by what he'd heard. She would have gone through with it! After all they'd been through, despite the fact that she was engaged to him, she would have spent the night with Dylan Miller and not felt one single ounce of guilt or remorse about it. It was the one secret he knew about Lexi that he wouldn't share, and it ate him up inside.

Sure, he was her best friend's fiancé, but you couldn't turn off attraction. If Tia weren't in the picture, would she still want him? The only conclusion he could come to was that she would, and it tied him in knots. As much as he hated to admit it, the man was blessed by the gods. The mirror would never be as kind to Ryan Stallworth as it was to Dylan Miller. He'd always be second best. Did she ever think of Dylan when she was with him? The thought made him sick in the pit of his stomach.

His phone beeped, and he was jerked back to the present. He'd been staring at the client file for almost an hour while his mind wandered, and he had no clue why he had even pulled it out in the first place. It was obvious he wasn't going to get any work done, so he decided to call it a day.

He sat in his car and came to another realization. If he went through with this big lie, postponing their wedding because of an alleged big project that was going to take up all of his time, he was going to have to find something to do with that time. He didn't need to actually stay at work; and wouldn't want to. He certainly had no desire to fraternize with the custodial staff after hours, and he'd be bored out of his mind. He couldn't go to the club, and his apartment was out of the question—Lexi had a key and could come and go as she pleased. He planned to stick to the story with everyone—Wes would be the only person who knew the truth, and he had a wife and three kids at home—he wasn't going to babysit Ryan for the next six months. He had to find a fucking hobby.

For lack of a better idea, he found himself turning off on the exit that would take him to the printers, and the invitation samples he was supposed to pick up three days ago. He still had no idea what he would do—should he just go through with the July wedding, and deal with the repercussions of Miller's enormous shadow, or follow through with the big project story? Jace was the only one he'd told, so he wasn't yet in so deep that he couldn't get out. He turned up the radio and pounded on the steering wheel—he didn't know what the fuck to do, and he was really running out of time.

The sign was like a beacon. Bright orange over lime green, it advertised a gym—called simply, *Work Out*, a couple miles before he'd arrive at the print shop. It boasted a 30 day free membership to new prospective clients, and additional signs around the building advertised a lap pool, racquetball, and a state-of-the-art weight room. Since he couldn't legitimately work out at the club anymore, and was sorely lacking in his usual exercise routine, he swung into the parking lot to check it out. After the day he'd had, he could really use a chance to blow off some steam, and he always kept a gym bag in the back seat of his Mustang, just in case.

The place looked decent—the front was covered in windows of wavy glass that allowed you to see silhouettes of people working out inside without giving too much away. It was unpretentious, and could be just what he needed to keep up the illusion that he was working on a big project without giving up his entire lifestyle. He could keep in shape and avoid his usual haunts, and Lexi would have no reason to venture into this part of town once he postponed the wedding.

When he walked in, a good looking redhead at the counter welcomed him and offered him a tour. "We've got state of the art equipment, a lap pool, personal trainers, and a lounge," she said, taking him on a quick run of the building. It wasn't the country club, but it did have decent facilities and a hot blonde in a neon pink workout outfit that flashed him a smile as he wandered through. He decided to take them up on the thirty days, and went back to his car to get his gym bag. He changed into baggy shorts and a grey t, and wandered over to the area where he'd seen the blonde. She was just stepping off an elliptical, and preparing the settings on a treadmill as he walked up. She smiled again and tossed her head toward the adjoining equipment. "Care to join me for a little walk?" she asked.

He shrugged. "Sure," he said, "where are you going?"

"About three miles with a seventy percent incline; think you can handle it?" she said, stepping onto the equipment and starting her routine. He programed his treadmill accordingly, and climbed on, matching her stride for stride.

"I haven't seen you here before," she said, barely breaking a sweat. "I'd remember."

"First day," he replied with a smile. "I'm trying the 30-day deal to see if the place is a good fit."

"I'm Tiffany," she smiled back, extending her hand across the gap between them.

"Ryan," he said, shaking her hand. "Ryan Stallworth."

"Wait a minute," she said, the corners of her lips turning up slightly. "You wouldn't happen to be an attorney, would you? Are you the Ryan Stallworth who works for Briggs and Patton?"

Oh shit, he thought. Was there anyone in this damn city who didn't know him now? He gave her a hard stare, but he didn't see the doe-eyed look that usually preceded a question about Dylan Miller—she just looked open and curious. "That's me," he said cautiously.

"Holy crap," she said, smirking. "I know you! Or at least I know of you. I'm Tiffany Truitt." When he raised his eyebrows, she continued. "Truitt Industries? I've seen your name of a lot of paperwork there—you're one of our attorneys."

"Sure!" he said, "you guys keep us pretty busy." When she raised her eyebrows back, he added, "That's a good thing! For us, anyway." He smiled, the first genuine smile he'd felt all week.

"Yeah, whatever," she smirked. "Anyway, it's nice to meet you."

"And you," he said, smiling back.

"I think you'll find this place is a good fit."

"It's looking pretty good so far," Ryan smiled.

Chapter 27

On Friday afternoon, Ryan still didn't know what to do. He'd held Lexi off by telling her he had picked up the invitations, but had to work late and wouldn't be able to see her until tomorrow. Which was now today. He cut out of work early, hoping to get some clarity before he had to face her. The damn gold box was staring at him from the passenger seat, and his head hurt just from looking at it. He tossed a jacket over it and stopped off at the club to work out with Tiffany again, but although he enjoyed her company, her obvious flirting, and that fact that she had no idea that he knew Dylan Miller, it was going to be a long six months if he went through with telling Lexi that they couldn't get married in July. It was going to completely suck, if he were to be honest, and it was all because he didn't want to get married on the heels of Tia and Dylan. He was having a hard time separating the parts of his life that weren't jiving, and although he thought he'd figured it out as he went along, nothing was getting any clearer.

"I'll pick up some Chinese," Lexi told him on the phone. "Pot stickers, vegetable kow and fried rice. Sound good?"

"Sounds good," he managed, without much conviction in his voice. He'd been working on how he'd break the "news" to her all week, but he was still deathly afraid to even broach the subject. Shit, he wondered for about the millionth time, should he just suck it up and go forward? He jumped in the shower and turned the water cold, hoping it would give him some much needed strength, but knowing that this was going to be one shitty night, regardless of the decision he made when he actually saw Lexi.

She knocked on the door, unable to fumble for her keys with her wedding planning briefcase, her purse, and two Chinese take-out bags dangling from her arms. When he opened the door and looked at her, cloaked in shadow, he felt differently than he ever had before—for a second, she was a stranger to him. She leaned in and kissed him, and handed him the bags of food, smiling when she saw the invitation samples that sat on the table in the foyer. She tossed the rest of her bags carelessly on the kitchen table, and went straight for the gold box.

"Oh my God, I just can't wait!" she exclaimed, snatching it off the table and heading for the couch. "I mean, this is huge, right? Picking out our wedding invitations? We can eat after!"

Ryan tried to swallow but found his throat had stopped functioning, and he was unable to say anything. He followed her to the couch as she pulled the samples from the box, spreading them over the coffee table. She stood back and studied the pile from a distance, pulling him over to stand beside her. "What do you think?" she asked, her head tilted in contemplation. "Anything jump out at you?"

Fuck, he thought. He needed to do this thing right now. "Lexi, I need to..." he started, but she interrupted.

"Oh!" she gasped. "Do you see it?" She darted back to the table and shook loose a sample printed on paper that could only be described as an explosion of blue, with tiny stars of white glitter, and fireworks of red, gold, and blue along the edges.

"Oh my God, Ryan," she said breathlessly. "This is the one!" She handed the sample to him, and he could only stare for a moment. "It's got tiny fireworks on it! It's perfect!"

As she reached over to take it back, he put his hand over her wrist and guided her hand away, dropping the invitation back onto the pile. "Lexi, I need to talk to you about something important," he croaked.

"OK," she said, cautiously. "Is it too much? Do you see one you like better?" It was hard not to notice the tension in him, and when she looked at his pained expression, she got a bad feeling in the pit of her stomach. It was impossible to ignore the distance that had come between them over the past couple weeks, and she had grown suspicious about the extra meetings and vague explanations of why they couldn't spend any time together; but she'd been wrapped up in her world too, balancing work with her own new "mini-celebrity," as she called it. Plus, she'd been planning her own wedding as well as starting plans for Tia's. She hadn't thought much about it until now, and her mouth went dry as Ryan led her to the couch and sat down beside her. Something wasn't right.

She waited, looking at the top of his bowed head for what seemed like forever before she finally spoke. "What's going on, Ryan?" she asked. "I know there's something that's bothering you. Spill it already," she said gently.

He took a deep breath. "I don't know where to start," he fumbled. "It's kind of a 'good news/bad news' kind of thing, but …"

She exhaled on a whisper. "Well, thank goodness there's good news—start with that!" she said, relieved. "I was getting worried. You've been awfully busy lately. I've barely seen you all week."

"I know," he said, bowing his head again. His heart was pounding in his chest, and he knew that the next words that came out of his mouth could change his world forever. "The thing is…" he paused, debating one last time about whether or not he'd go forward with the lie. Finally, he decided that he didn't really have a choice. He swallowed and met her gaze. "Wes stopped in to talk to me on Wednesday, and told me that my partnership is looking really good. That's why I've had so many meetings this week."

"Oh, Ry, that's great!" she said, elated. "We need some wine, to celebrate!" She started to get up to grab a bottle, and he put his hand on her arm, looking into her eyes. She immediately sat back down. "Is that not the good news?" she asked.

"That part is," he said. "But he came to me in confidence, so this is between you and me, OK?"

"Of course," she said, confused. "But I'm not really following you. That isn't usually the kind of news that has someone all upset."

"The thing is, Connor is still a bit of a hold-out," he said, working the lie, "You know how the old-timers get sometimes; they think they know everything and that a young partner can be a liability. Of course, he was two years younger than me when he started the firm, but he doesn't seem to remember that." He paused and took another breath. "He gave me a project, and apparently, my success with it could make or break my chances with him. It's a big job…"

"You're up to a big job," she said confidently. "You've never backed down from hard work, and you'll show the old coot that energy and drive are a match for experience any day! Christ, the guy doesn't even have an email address—how can he even expect to compete in today's markets without technology?"

Ryan smiled, feeling guilty that she had so much confidence in him while he was lying to her face. "I appreciate your confidence, Lex, I really do," he said, taking her hand, "but this project is going to keep me incredibly busy for the next several months. Probably six to eight." He paused again.

"OK," she said, confused. "It still sounds like good news to me."

"Oh, Lex," he whispered. He swallowed around the growing lump in his throat and forced himself to continue. "Shit, I don't know how to even to say this to you. Believe me, I've worked it out every way I can think of and it keeps coming down to the same thing."

"What thing, Ryan?" she asked, anxiously.

"Fuck Lex. We have to postpone the wedding. I can't see any other way. I'm going to be working late nights, weekends, holidays, traveling…I can't help you plan a wedding right now, and I sure as hell can't take time off for a honeymoon…until I know how this thing is all going to play out, I can't focus on anything else. I'm going to be stressed out, I'll have constant meetings—I just don't see how I can do both. I'm so sorry Lex," he whimpered, "but I really don't see another option."

For a minute, she just stared at him. He could see confusion, disbelief, and disappointment fighting for room on her face. She shook her head, her features crumpled, and her shoulders hitched.   "I'm sure I didn't hear that right," she said; completely stunned. Her pained look almost made him want to pull the words back; forget he'd ever considered it; but he thought of the alternative, and forced a concerned look onto his face.

"I'm so sorry," he whispered. He reached out to take her hand, but she pulled it out of his grasp.

"For how long?" she asked.

"Maybe November?" he said.

She broke then, and anger took control of all the other emotions. "November?" she yelled. "Fucking November? Are you kidding me?" She jumped off the couch, backing away from him and shaking her head.

"Lexi, I..."

"I have a strapless wedding dress, Ryan—I can't wear that in the winter! And nobody has fireworks in November—it could be fucking snowing!" He opened his mouth to speak; to try and calm her down; but her fury was as hot as a volcano, and he closed it again. "Do you even have a clue about how much money we stand to lose? We've put down deposits on the reception hall, the photographer, the florist, caterers, the limo...and there's no guarantee we could even rebook half of them for four months later—I booked that stuff almost a year ago!"

"Maybe we could do it in Spring, then," he suggested meekly. "When the weather gets warmer..."

"Fuck you, Ryan!" she bellowed. "This is bullshit! I've planning this for almost a year, and you're basically telling me to start over, and plan it for another year? What kind of shit is that?"

"It's work, Lexi!" he yelled back. "This isn't a choice of convenience—I'm doing this for our future! Once I make partner

I'll make more money and we can have a better life! I'm doing it for us!"

"You know," she said, seething, "by then Tia will be living in Colorado—how is she supposed to be here for me when..."

"Give me a fucking break," he said, "as if she won't be able to afford to fly out here to help you with fittings..."

"That a bunch of shit, Ryan, and you know it! There's a hell of a lot more to being someone's matron of honor than showing up for a few fittings. Besides, Inhap's planning a South American tour in the Spring—Dylan might not even be able to be there!"

"Fuck Dylan Miller!" he spat, unable to control his emotions. And before he could reign them in, more words came tumbling from his lips. "Wait, forget I said that," he bellowed. "Because you might actually want to!" He regretted the words as soon as he said them, but the damage had already been done. He felt the sharp crack of Lexi's hand as it connected with his cheek, but the pain and disappointment in her eyes hurt even more. Damn it, this really wasn't her fault, but in the heat of the moment, he needed somewhere to place the blame to alleviate his own guilt.

"What a stupid, chauvinistic, male thing to say!" she cried. "Maybe as a guy you can't turn off your fucking hormones or think with the right head, but I certainly can! I can't believe you would even think that about me, much less say it!"

"I'm sorry," Ryan said quickly, trying to wrap his arm around her. "It was a shitty thing to say. I'm really sorry, Lex." But she wasn't having any of it. She pushed him away, and continued her tirade.

"First of all, I would never, EVER, do that to my best friend! Secondly, Dylan isn't a mystery anymore—a good looking face or an image in my mind—I've gotten to know him as a person, and I consider him a friend. I respect his value system, and I would never do anything to jeopardize that relationship. And I would never, *ever*, fuck one of my friends." She stared at him hard.

"You're right, I know you wouldn't," he said apologetically. "It was a really stupid thing to say." He reached out for her again, but she quickly stepped away, putting the table between them.

"Damn right!" she exclaimed, "but you did say it, so now I guess I finally know how you really feel."

"I don't..."

"Bullshit!" she yelled. "You wouldn't have said it if you weren't thinking it! Thanks for giving me a little credit, asshole!"

"I'm just not running my life on his calendar, is all I'm saying. It's our fucking life, and our fucking wedding, and I'm so sorry if it's going to mess up your plan to have our wedding be a media circus..."

"How dare you?" she bellowed. "He's my friend, and he'll be my matron of honor's husband, and I want him there, simple as that. I'm not trying to make our wedding into a media circus!"

"Then why is your phone still ringing constantly with people who want to talk about it? You love it, Lexi, and if I don't make partner, I'll never have even a ghost of a chance of giving you the kind of life you want; the kind Tia's getting."

"Oh, so that's it," she said deliberately. "You're comparing yourself with Dylan, and you don't think you could ever measure up, is that it?"

"That's not what I'm saying, damn it!" although her words hit a little too close to home, "it's just that I want the best for *us*, and making partner will give us a better life!"

"You really are clueless, aren't you, Ryan? Do you think I'm with you because of what you can give me? You had nothing when I met you—when I fell in love with you. You were a poor struggling student! And Tia's life isn't going to perfect, you know. She's going to have to deal with Dylan being gone for months at a time on tour, with women constantly throwing themselves at her husband...and by the way, she has enough trust in him and his feelings for her to deal with it, unlike your apparent distrust of mine..."

"I didn't say I didn't trust you," he said, "I just said that I'm not entirely sure you've given up on your fantasy to sleep with Dylan Miller, especially since he's suddenly accessible!"

"I am through with this conversation, you fucking idiot. Maybe you should ask yourself if you're postponing the wedding because you don't really want to marry me."

"Ah shit, Lexi, I didn't say that!"

"You apparently don't know what you really want to say," she said, seething. "When you figure it out, let me know." She grabbed her purse and keys off the table and stormed out of the apartment, leaving the Chinese food congealing on the counter and the invitation samples sprawled atop the coffee table.

Lexi was more pissed than hurt by the time she got home. Her first instinct was to call her best friend, to bitch to her about what an asshole Ryan was being and get some sympathy, but she was afraid that she'd let the wrong thing slip and inadvertently spill that Ryan was harboring animosity toward Dylan. One of the things that pissed her off the most was that she could see Ryan's point—at least in some respects. She'd seen the effect Dylan had on people whenever he was in a room; besides the fact that he was a huge celebrity, he was a warm and genuine person, and had a knack of making people feel comfortable as well as mesmerized in his company. It would be hard for Ryan, or any guy for that matter, not to feel at least a little less significant in his shadow. But it certainly wasn't Dylan's fault, and she sure as hell didn't deserve to be punished for it.

The wedding thing was a valid point as well, damn it; there would be a lot of interest in her and Ryan's wedding that had nothing to do with the bride or groom; especially if it fell in such close proximity to Dylan and Tia's own nuptials. She'd had to deal with people like Candy trying to score invitations to her wedding and asking if they could sit at Dylan's table, and because of her television and tabloid interviews, she'd also been approached by strangers on the street wanting to know inside scoops about the celebrity couple. But she knew absolutely that their choice of a

wedding date was not meant to intrude on her own celebration—
if they didn't take advantage of that time window they'd have to
wait nearly another year to get married themselves.

She was pulled from her thoughts by the chirp of her
phone. She saw Ryan's number on the display, and groaned. For a
second, she contemplated picking it up, but then his comment
about her still wanting to fuck Dylan brought the anger bubbling
up again. Instead, she poured herself a glass of chardonnay, and
ran a steaming hot bath with lots of smelly bubbles. When Ryan
called again, she took one look at the display and tossed the
phone back on the table and sank into the tub, hoping the
combination of hot water and alcohol would loosen her tense
muscles.

Chapter 28

Lexi wasn't picking up her phone. Ryan was leaving messages and sending texts, but he was getting no response from either. He was tied up in knots, and he wasn't at all sure what he was feeling. Part of him was actually surprised that she hadn't been a little more understanding—he'd sort of convinced himself that she'd see the merit of putting off the ceremony in order to secure a better future for themselves. He'd known she'd be pissed in the beginning, but he thought that once she'd had time to think about it, she'd see that it was in everyone's best interest. Damn it, he never should have opened up his mouth about Miller, though—he knew that was a stupid mistake—but shouldn't she have seen his jealousy as a compliment instead of a lack of trust? He knew now that she'd never really cheated on him and he certainly knew that she would never be anything but loyal to her best friend. But in the back of his mind, if the situations were reversed and he had the chance to cheat without consequences for one night, would he do the right thing? And because he had the shadow of a doubt about himself, he couldn't help having a shadow about her, as well.

Over the next few days, he kept calling and texting, and even sent her flowers. He went to her apartment twice, but her car was not in the lot. She was doing a great job of avoiding him, and the more she did, the more pissed off he got.

At least the inquiries about Dylan slowed down. The buzz about their engagement was dying off a bit—another celebrity going into rehab after a drunken brawl had taken over the headlines—and his secretary had finally figured out how to handle the calls that weren't business related. He was still amazed that some of these people had the balls to call him up and ask him to hook them up with Miller. They obviously knew that they couldn't get Dylan directly, what with him being such a big star and all, but why the hell did everyone think that he and Miller were best buds?

He was so pissed off by Tuesday that he went straight to the gym to burn off some negative energy. He was twelve minutes into a vigorous run on a treadmill when Tiffany hopped onto the machine beside him. "You look like a man on a mission," she smiled. "I think I see smoke coming off your feet."

Ryan grunted. "Just making it count," he said between gasping breaths. He looked over and saw her leaning on the treadmill next to him in a tight workout outfit of bright purple and lime green swirls that showed off her smoking hot body perfectly. Her hair was twisted into a messy ponytail, and she was smiling at him out of the side of her mouth. He couldn't help it—he slowed his pace and smiled back.

"Want to tell me about it?" she asked sincerely.

"What do you mean?" he asked.

"It's obvious you're trying to run away from something," she observed, "but in case you didn't notice, you don't really get anywhere on a treadmill." She smiled bigger, her head tilted just slightly, and he could see the sincerity in her look.

"Nah, it's nothing," he said, smiling back and feeling his spirits slightly lifted. "Just wondering when you were going to get here—I was getting a head start."

"Afraid you can't keep up with me, huh?" she asked, more than a hint of suggestion in her voice.

"Oh, I can keep up with you just fine," he flirted back. It was harmless, right? And despite the seeming gallon of sweat soaking his shirt and the fact that his calf muscles felt as if they'd turned to lead, he felt lighter than he had in a while. "I like to stay a couple steps ahead, if you want to know the truth."

She set up her treadmill and joined him for the rest of his workout, pushing her pace past his. He laughed, and it felt good. Tiffany was completely neutral territory for him—she didn't know anything about his connection to Dylan Miller or the fact that his life was turning to shit, and he planned to keep it that way. It was a relief to have someone see *him*; instead of seeing him as a way to get to Miller. Although, he thought, neutral territory was a bit of an overstatement. She was beautiful, sexy, and obviously flirting with him, and he was enjoying the only positive attention he'd gotten in quite some time. Dangerous territory might be a more accurate statement, but she made him feel good, damn it; and he deserved it.

"So you think you can stay a couple steps ahead of me, do you?" she challenged, cranking up the speed and incline on her treadmill. "We'll just see about that."

Ryan set his own machine up to her breakneck pace and happily accepted the challenge.

From the treadmill they went into the weight room, and he set about impressing her. He peeled off his shirt and pushed his muscles to the limit, watching her watch him from the corner of his eye. She was easy to look at as well, her well-toned body pulsing and flexing beneath the spandex that hugged her impressive curves in the most tantalizing ways.

"You take care of yourself, Stallworth," she said, smirking. "I like that in a man."

"I could say the same about you, Miss Truitt," he replied, adding, "it is *Miss* Truitt, right?"

"Yes, it is," she said, her eyes blazing into his.

They held each other's gaze for a heartbeat too long, until Tiffany suggested they hit the pool for some laps. "Do you ever quit?" he smiled, exhausted, but finding himself more than a little curious about seeing her in a swimsuit.

"What's the matter," she teased. "Afraid you can't keep up?" And with that, she bolted toward the locker room, tossing back over her head, "I'll see you in the pool...or not. We'll see if you can handle me."

Ryan smiled at her retreating figure and headed toward the men's locker room to change into his suit. At this point, he wasn't at all sure he could keep up with her, but he wasn't going down without a fight.

His breath hissed between his teeth when she stepped out of the locker room. Her suit was a one-piece, but it rode alluringly high on her hips and dangerously low over her breasts, allowing him a generous view of her creamy cleavage. She tossed him a flirty look, and dove neatly into the water.

He really shouldn't be here right now, and he knew it, but the simple fact that she was appreciating him for a reason other than his connection to Dylan Miller was keeping him here. But if he wanted to be honest with himself, that wasn't entirely true. She was a beautiful, successful woman, and she was blatantly flirting with him. That she worked for Truitt Industries, a client for whom his own company was attempting to secure more business, namely in the international market, was also a bonus. Although Wes had virtually guaranteed his partnership, it wouldn't hurt if he could help to increase the firm's bottom line by securing an 'in' within Truitt; plus he could almost justify spending time with Tiffany as part of his "big project." And if he got to do some careless flirting along the way, what was the harm in that? He didn't have to stand in anybody's long dark shadow with Tiffany, and he was more than all right with that part of the situation.

She swam like she did everything else—effortlessly, and with incredible grace. She cut through the water like a knife, barely disturbing the surface, gliding like a mermaid across the length of the pool. Here, no matter how he tried, he couldn't match her pace, and when he reached the deep end, breathless and nearly exhausted, she floated, her head bobbing slightly in the water, smiling warmly at him.

"OK, you got me there," he said. "I'm man enough to admit defeat when I've been bested."

"Four years on the high school swim team," she boasted. "State champs."

"Football," he said, pointing at himself. "Not exactly the same kind of conditioning."

"Well," she said. "I'm glad to know you're not one of those chauvinistic men who can't concede to a woman. The only question now is, are you man enough to let me buy you a drink?"

The word 'chauvinistic' reminded him of his blow-up with Lexi a few days earlier, and he realized he hadn't checked his phone for a message from her since he left the office. He still couldn't understand why she was being so goddamned testy about the whole situation—now that she'd had four days to think about it, couldn't she see that postponing the wedding was best for both of them? She'd been completely ignoring him, and although at first it was more of an aggravation, now it was really starting to piss him off. She was probably off hanging out with Tia and Dylan somewhere, soaking up the limelight and basking in her own quasi-celebrity. She probably couldn't have cared less that he'd been waiting on her call. He felt like he was becoming a liability.

"I'm more than man enough for that," he smiled slyly. "Would you think it was chauvinistic of me to insist that I'm buying?"

"There is a fine line between chauvinistic and chivalrous," she replied, smiling back, "but I prefer to consider the latter." She squeezed water from her hair and hoisted herself out of the pool with almost no effort. "Give me twenty minutes," she said, "and I'll meet you in the lobby." He watched droplets of water drip off her fine ass as she sashayed toward the locker room door.

He followed her out of the city to a little pub off the beaten path. At first he was nervous that she'd take him somewhere where lawyers hung out, and he worried that word would get back to Lexi that he'd been out with another woman. But then he realized that he had a legitimate reason for being out with her. Although they hadn't discussed business at all, nor had he yet questioned the progress of their newly forming international division, he would at some point, and he could always pass off being out with her as work.

She was a regular at the place, which became obvious when she was greeted by name the minute they walked in. "The usual, Tiff?" the bartender called out as they found a cozy little booth in the corner, away from the bar.

"Yeah, thanks, Jimbo!" she called, turning to Ryan. "What's your pleasure?"

For the briefest of seconds, an image of Tiffany naked imprinted on Ryan's mind. He shook his head slightly, and turned toward the bar. "Gin and tonic, with a lime—Hendricks if you've got it," he called. The bartender nodded, and he and Tiffany slipped into the booth.

"So," she began, looking down at his hands. "All cleaned up and no wedding ring. How is it that you're still single, Ryan?"

He felt a momentary twinge of guilt and pushed it away. He wasn't married, so technically he was still single, and Lexi hadn't returned his phone calls in days. He sucked it in, and turned to her. "Work keeps me really busy," he answered. "I'm on the verge of making partner at the firm, and I just haven't had the time to get married." Technically, not a lie, he thought to himself.

Their drinks came, and he squeezed the lime; stirred the clear liquid with the tiny straw before taking a healthy pull. He knew he was treading on dangerous ground here. She was obviously attracted to him, and he'd made no attempt to thwart her advances. She was a client as well, or at least her company was, and he had reason to keep their relationship on a professional level. Still, he was really enjoying being himself with her, and he found it too hard to walk away.

"I understand completely," she agreed. "I've been working on my MBA, spending my time in different departments within the company, trying to get a handle on the whole picture...it doesn't leave much time for a social life, that's for sure."

"So what is your position in the company, actually?" he asked.

"I'm kind of a jack-of-all-trades right now," she laughed. "Daddy believes that when I take over the company, I need to know the ins and outs of all the different departments and how they work together—and I agree with him. It's been a real eye-opening couple of years, and I've really gotten to know how everything connects. I've got a lot of ideas for improvements once I take the helm, and it's really exciting, you know? Of course, I've got a few more years before I get handed the reins, but I'm going to be ready to take Truitt Industries into the next century, that's for sure. Daddy's still kind of old school in the ways he manages some things, so I'm really looking forward it."

Shit, Ryan thought, this really could be a good business venture. She was being prepped to take over the entire company, and he could already see a wide variety of ways they could help each other.

"I can imagine," he agreed, noticing that he'd downed his gin and tonic and was holding up his glass toward the waitress to indicate a refill. "But the important thing is; do you like what you do?"

"Oh, I love it!" she gushed, an excited flush coming up and coloring her cheeks. "I especially like being a woman in power, and showing the men how it's done sometimes." She smiled coyly. "Although I'm sure you don't know anything about that."

"Don't be so sure," he said. "I was kind of the little guy when I came into the firm," he admitted, accepting another drink and taking a sip before continuing. "I didn't come from money or family influence, and I worked my way up against more than a few odds...I think I know what you mean—aside from the 'being a woman' part of it, anyway."

"Ooh, a self-made man—the intrigue grows," she said, scooting close enough to him that their legs were touching. "Where'd you go to school?"

"UCLA," he said proudly. "Graduated second in my class."

"And yet you're in Chicago," she said. "California didn't agree with you?"

"Oh, it agreed with me just fine," he said, noticing that her hand was suddenly resting on his thigh. "But I was born and raised here, and my family's all here, so I decided to come back."

"Very noble," she said, taking a sip of her chardonnay. He took a generous pull of his own drink, and realized that he had a very pleasant buzz going already. He'd completely depleted his body during their workout, and realized that he'd never eaten dinner. The alcohol was going to his head rather quickly, and he found himself covering her hand with his own, almost unconsciously.

By the time he finished his third gin and tonic, he was feeling downright sloshed. Tiffany noticed, and said, "What, I can drink you under the table, too?"

"I didn't have any dinner," he said by way of excuse, "and you did kind of kick my ass tonight at the gym."

"I think you need some coffee before you head home," she whispered in his ear. "I know a little place close by. Walking distance, in fact."

"Lead the way," he said, very conscious of the fact that he was in no condition to get behind the wheel. A little walk might clear his head, and he could definitely use some coffee. It was only Tuesday night, and he had a pretty full schedule tomorrow. He looked at his watch and saw that it was nearly ten. It was going to be a long rest of the week, he figured.

Tiffany took his hand as they walked, and he wrapped her fingers in his; for support, he told himself, as he was a bit wobbly on his feet. When she stopped in front of a large brownstone building and started digging in her purse, his heart skipped a beat. He'd let her lead the way and hadn't paid much attention to where they were walking, but they'd apparently reached their destination, and there wasn't a coffee shop in sight.

"Home sweet home," she said on a breath as light as air, leading him up the stairs to the front door. He followed her up, ignoring the warning bells going off in his very foggy brain. She turned a key in the lock, and led him up another set of stairs to her top level apartment. "I have some great organic Columbian that should do the trick," she said as she swung the door open.

But the moment they entered the apartment, she stopped, and stared at him with drooped lids. "I'll just get the coffee started," she breathed, but then she took a step forward, taking the initiative and pinning him back against the wall, pressing herself against him and stepping up on her tiptoes; rubbing demandingly over his groin. Her mouth found his, and he kissed her back, all his anxiety and anger pushing its way through his tongue and into her mouth, his hands running roughly up her sides, stopping to caress her small but perky breasts through the thin fabric of her sweater. Goddamn, she wasn't wearing a bra, and he felt her nipples tighten immediately under his fingers, and couldn't resist giving them a bit of a tweaking and a rough pinch between his thumb and forefinger. He watched her eyes roll back and her lips purse in the most alluring of ways, and he couldn't help but do it again, just to see her reaction.

"Oh!" she exclaimed, her hand skimming down to cup him between his legs, squeezing gently at the raging hard-on that had amassed there. Before his foggy brain could even assess the situation, she pulled her sweater over her head and granted him full access to the decadent breasts that lie beneath. He reached around and cupped one hand around her tight ass, crushing her hips against him, and caught one swollen breast with the other, tweaking the nipple again with his thumb before bending down to take it in his mouth, reveling in the breathless gasp he heard against his ear as he gently nipped with the edges of his teeth.

She pulled down the zipper of his jeans and shoved her hand into his shorts, grasping him tightly and tugging him by his member toward the bedroom. *I shouldn't be here.* That one fleeting thought crossed over his brain and slid away even as he tossed his shirt to the floor in her hallway. It was like he was watching the whole scene unfold, rather than being part of it, and as much as his mind tried to make sense of it all, his brain was at least three steps behind the instinctive reactions of his body.

They fell onto her bed and his body stretched across hers, her breasts pressed against him and her breath raged in his ear. The alcohol and the anger coursing through him drove him on, and he fumbled with the button on her pants, dragging them down her legs, and then shedding his own. She drove him on with her breath and her words, urging him to "fuck me now!" and he obliged her, driving deep and fast, fascinated by the newness of it all, the urgency of it all, and as he thrust into her over and over he thought, *Fuck Dylan Miller! Fuck the bitch who doesn't take my calls! Fuck the partnership! Fuck everything!* And he pounded on her, frenzied by her gasps of pleasure and the pressure building in his groin, and he drove harder, driven by a crazed need, until he literally exploded, crying out with her on their shared climax and then falling onto her, breathless and utterly drained.

For a minute he just laid there, his brain recuperating and trying to make sense of what just happened. Then the guilt hit him like a brick wall and he was immediately speechless; afraid to move and afraid not to. Tiffany finally whispered, "You keep up just fine, Ryan—I'll go and get that coffee started now," as if he'd just held a door for her or passed her the salt in a restaurant. He stumbled into her bathroom and hung his head over the sink, unable to look at his image in the mirror. He'd seriously screwed up his life in just a few short drunken minutes, and he knew he could never go back. As he splashed cold water over his flaming face, one thought echoed over and over in his mind—oh fuck me, *fuck me.*

Chapter 29

Tia glanced up and smiled as Dylan walked into the kitchen and then stopped; her hand suspended over the platter of cheese and fruit she was artfully arranging. "That's not even funny," she said, stifling a giggle.

"Didn't you say that you'd love me no matter what kind of hair I had?" he teased, rolling the little tail of the mullet around his index finger and giving her a coy smile.

"I may have to retract that statement," she smirked, bumping off his pucker-faced advance with her hip. "You can just go ahead and take it off now—none of us will be able to focus on the wedding menu if you have that dead possum on your head." The chef they'd hired to accompany them to the island was coming over to prepare a sampling of dishes for them to taste, and Lexi and Jessa were adding their palates to the decision-making process.

"You'll be able to concentrate just fine," he said, "because I won't be here to distract you."

"You're not staying?" she pouted, sticking out her lower lip and dropping her eyelids. "Don't you want to taste all the gourmet goodies that Neil will be serving up?"

"I trust you ladies to make exactly the right choices. I can assure you that on our wedding night, the food on my plate is going to be the very last thing on my mind. We could have peanut butter and jelly sandwiches and I wouldn't even notice. All I'll be able to think about will be taking you to bed for the first time as my lawfully wedded wife." He sidled over and pulled her to him, placing a soft and lingering kiss on her lips.

"Then why are we bothering with all this?" she said, sliding her tongue along his lips. "Let's just go for the PB and J, ditch the mullet, and go practice that scenario right now. Just give me five minutes to make the phone calls." She ran her hands down the soft fabric of his shirt and unzipped his jeans, sliding her hand inside.

"Mmm," Dylan moaned, cupping a hand behind her neck and deepening the kiss. "Talk about not playing fair...I'm going to ask you to hold that thought for later on, most definitely. But even though *I'm* not concerned about we'll be eating, I think our guests might be expecting a bit more than a school lunch on our wedding night, and I intend to give it to them. Besides, I won't be able to add much anyway; we both know Jessa's gonna get her bossy on and take over the whole thing."

Tia snickered. Jessa was doing an amazing job with all of the details, big and small, and they were both incredibly grateful for her expertise. "You're right about that," she agreed, "but I'll still miss you. Where are you running off to?"

"I," Dylan said, plucking a fat grape from one of the platters and popping it into his mouth, "am going to poker night." He stuck the grape in his upper lip and made a face before chewing it enthusiastically and flashing her a crooked smile.

Tia laughed out loud. "Poker night—really? You'd rather sit around a musty basement eating potato chips and jarred salsa and drinking beer than hanging out with us and enjoying gourmet food and fine wine? I'm starting to wonder about you, Miller."

"The proper term is crisps, my love, and they just happen to be one of nature's perfect foods. I promise I won't go hungry, and I'm glad I can still keep you guessing." He kissed the top of her head and shrugged into his coat as the buzzer sounded, announcing the arrival of the girls. "So then, you ladies have a great time, and pick us a brilliant wedding feast, right?" He spoke to the doorman through the intercom and hit the button for the elevator. "I'll probably be late, but I'm hoping you'll wait up for me."

"Count on it," Tia said, blowing him a kiss. "Have fun. Enjoy your *crisps*."

"I plan to do just that." He grabbed a duffel bag off the sofa table and tucked the mullet into it, then added a bottle of bourbon. The elevator door opened and Jessa and Lexi stepped off, both carefully balancing a load of bags and boxes. Dylan helped them get the packages arranged on the tables and kissed them both on the cheeks. "Have a lovely time, girls," he said, heading back to the elevator.

"Where do you think you're going?" Jessa asked, hands on her hips.

"I'm going to take some boys to school in the fine game of Texas Hold 'Em," he grinned, waving as the door slid shut.

"Poker night—really?" Jessa said, shaking her head.

"That's exactly what I said," Tia replied. "Guess we're doing a girls' night in."

"Fine by me," Lexi said, tossing her coat over the back of the couch and shaking some blood back into her arms. "Fewer palates means fewer arguments. What time's the chef getting here? I'm starved."

"In about an hour. I've got some snacks in the kitchen to hold us over until then."

"Then let's get this party started, shall we?" Jessa replied.

The driver pulled up to the Wrigleyville brownstone and raised his eyebrows as Dylan reached into the duffel and pulled the mullet over his head. "Inside joke," he said, adding a pair of glasses and checking his reflection.

Trent, one of his regular Chicago drivers/security guards, just shook his head and smiled. "Whatever floats your boat, man," he said. "Want some help with that keg?"

"If you could just get it to the front porch for me, that'd be great," Dylan answered, moving to the back of the car and pulling a five gallon cylinder of Goose Island from the boot. *May have gone a bit overboard with the snacks*, he thought, as he slung a cloth bag over his arm and balanced a party tray the size of a truck tire on his palms. He hadn't been able decide what he wanted at the deli, so he just asked for the works; and judging by the weight of the platter, he got just what he asked for. The girls could have their canapés and petit fours; he'd be more than happy with pastrami on rye and some greasy fried potatoes.

Sean waved through the window alongside the door, his face splitting in a grin when he saw Dylan in the fake hair and glasses he'd been wearing the first night they met. He pressed his lips together in a failed attempt to put on a straight face as he opened the door a crack and said sarcastically, "Yes? Can I help you?"

"Uh, I hear there's some illegal gambling going on here tonight," Dylan whispered from the corner of his mouth with his best Chicago accent. "I've got a few bucks in my pocket…"

"Bloody hell," Sean replied, poorly imitating Dylan's own British lilt. "Sorry dude, but the loser party's across the street. Only cool cats allowed at this shindig. I'm afraid I can't let you in."

"Oh…well that's too bad," Dylan grinned back. "I guess I'll just take my five gallons of Goose Island and my enormous tray of cold cuts and find another party then."

"Now hold on; don't be hasty…did you say five gallons of Goose? Where are my manners?" Sean pushed the door open and motioned him in with an exaggerated sweep of his arm. "Do bring your copious amounts of food and drink into the parlor straight away, won't you?"

"Don't mind if I do."

"About freaking time you showed up for one of these, Miller," Sean said, taking the tray and giving Dylan a friendly pat on the back. "Glad you could finally make it."

"Me too, mate. I've been looking forward to taking your money all day." He pulled off the wig and tucked it back in his bag, shaking out his hair.

"Oh thank *God*," Sean said with overzealous relief. "I was afraid that the hair was part of your strategy. No way anyone could keep a poker face with you wearing that dead rat on your head."

"Ah, feck you, Sean," Dylan said smiling, trying to throw a little Irish into his voice. "Tia said it looked like a dead possum."

"Isn't that just a giant rat anyway?" Sean rubbed his hands together. "Everyone's here. Ready to put your money where your mouth is, my friend?"

"Lead the way," Dylan smiled.

Dave, Tim, Scott, and Brian greeted him with a collective, "Heeeeyyyyy!" as soon as they turned the corner. "So glad you could finally make it. I hope you brought a lot of cash—I'm looking forward to taking it off your hands," Brian added with a smirk.

"We'll see about that," Dylan said, shaking hands with them and taking a seat at the oval table that dominated the center of the room. This was a definite man's space, he thought, as he took in the battered leather furniture, the neutral walls devoid of decoration, and the well-worn wood floors. A long table along the wall held open bags of chips, grocery store tubs full of dips, a stack of paper plates, and a roll of paper towels. Beneath the smell of cigar smoke drifting up from the tip of Brian's stogie it even smelled like a place inhabited by men; fried food, musty laundry, and stale smoke layered under the mask of spray air freshener. It reminded him of his early days in the States, living with Bo and hosting their own poker games on an almost weekly basis, and he inhaled deeply. Ah, how he missed those days sometimes. "Sweet place," he said with a smile.

"Thanks," Sean said as he connected the tap and poured a pitcher of Goose and transferred it into six mismatched mugs and steins that were most likely stolen from a variety of local establishments. Dylan was handed one from Harry Caray's; the familiar face and the words, "Holy Cow!" etched into the glass.

They spent an hour just bullshitting, eating, and putting a damn good dent in the Goose before they even settled down to play. Dylan was having a hell of a time; trading digs with them all and taking a beating over his recent engagement.

"Now why in the hell would you want to go and do that for, Dyl?" Brian teased. "I mean, Tia's a great girl, don't get me wrong, but you know, once you tie the knot, no more 'most eligible bachelor lists' for you!"

"Married or not, though," Scott added, "the girls are never going to stop falling at your feet, man. Damn, I wish could be you for a day."

"Yeah, yeah," Dylan smirked. "That's not all it's cracked up to be, mate, believe me. I really miss nights like this. They don't come around often enough,"

"Well, we're here pretty much every Tuesday," Sean said. "You know you're welcome any time. And for the record? I'm really glad you and Tia are tying the knot."

"As am I," Dylan smiled. "I can't wait to get hitched, actually."

"Better you than me," Dave said, raising his glass for a toast. "Here's to getting off the subject of true love, and getting down to some serious poker!"

"The name of the game, gentlemen, is Texas Hold 'Em," Brian said as he shuffled the cards. The men pulled out their wallets and tossed bills onto the table, exchanging them for chips. Sean stuffed the cash into a cigar box and threw it carelessly onto the couch. "Minimum small blind is a buck, maximum, five." He dealt the hole cards, and turned to Dave at his left to lay down the small blind.

Dylan checked his cards—an ace of hearts and a jack of clubs. Pretty good start. He pasted on his poker face and happily doubled Dave's small blind of two bucks. The first three community cards came up a two of clubs, a five of diamonds, and a king of spades, and Dylan raised two dollars. The third community card popped up a ten of hearts, and Tim raised five bucks, which Dylan raised five more. Scott and Sean folded.

"Got a high card on the table," Brian said as he dumped a burn card and flipped the river; a queen of diamonds; giving Dylan a solid straight.

"Well now," Dylan said, fingering his chips and contemplating the table, "this does make things interesting." He tossed a small pile of chips onto the pile, raising the bet five more dollars. Tim studied Dylan, rolling a chip expertly between his fingers.

"I don't know," he said, "it seems to me that you are one lucky bastard." He drummed on the table for another moment before tossing his cards onto the table.

Dylan grinned. "Read 'em and weep, ladies," he said as he swept the chips from the table and began stacking them in front of him.

"Beginner's luck," Sean said, pouring himself another beer and settling in for the next game. "No way the rich boy takes the next one."

"Oh my God, this lobster bisque is to die for!" Lexi exclaimed as she spooned the last of the creamy broth from her bowl. "This has to go on the menu."

"Agreed," Jessa said, jotting it in her notebook. "But for the wedding soup, or for one of the other nights? If we have lobster on the menu at the wedding, we don't need two dishes with the same ingredient. How about this for Saturday night? That way, all the guests will be there to enjoy this little taste of heaven..."

"Perfect," Tia nodded. "I like this wine, too. It would go perfectly with a lobster main dish, don't you think? It's light and smooth with just a touch of sweetness."

Jessa wrote the name of the wine in her notebook. "Got it," she said, as the sous chef brought out a sampling of cold salads.

Every single dish the chef created in her new incredible kitchen with panoramic views of Lake Michigan; from soup to salad to main dish to dessert; was like a sexy dance on Tia's tongue, and Jessa took careful notes and arranged them into menus for each day. They helped Neil and his assistant chop vegetables and mix sauces, and in between started working out the seating arrangements for the night of the wedding dinner.

"You know, this would be a lot easier if I knew which of the guys were bringing dates." Lexi's ears perked up and she quickly lowered her head before they noticed her interest. She didn't know how she would feel about Bo bringing a date, but she did know that she wasn't relishing having him and Ryan in such close proximity for the long weekend. Ryan had made it very clear that he wanted nothing to do with Bo or any of the other guys, and had been a serious downer at every function they'd attended so far that had anything to do with Tia and Dylan. In the pit of her stomach she was dreading the possibility that he'd ruin her fun by being anti-social and rude. Obviously she wasn't going to be able to spend any time with Bo one-on-one, which meant they wouldn't have a chance to resolve the uncomfortable feelings between them. If anything, having Ryan there would only increase the level of discomfort between her and Bo, and she saw the potential for Ryan to suck the fun out of the whole weekend. She pulled herself out of her thoughts and saw that Jessa had already moved on to another topic.

"It certainly doesn't help that I don't know a thing about the venue," Jessa groaned. "I don't even know if we're indoors or out, I don't know what the weather will be like...what sort of centerpieces are we going to put on the tables? There's a big difference between, say, an elegant dinner in a swanky hotel and an informal meal on the beach."

Tia just smiled. Ever since they'd gotten there, the girls had both been digging for clues about the location, but she refused to give them even a hint. "I guess we'll just have to be prepared for every eventuality, then."

"I'm not used to having so many things outside of my control," Jessa said, "and I have to tell you that the person from the venue is frustrating the hell out of me. I don't know anything about the décor of the place, the china patterns, the stemware—all I keep getting are assurances that everything is 'top notch.' That's just not enough for me to go on. I don't even know if this person is a guy or a girl, because they won't even talk to me—I only have an email address, and 'Sam' has ignored all my requests to speak in person or connect me with someone else who can give me some straight answers. I'm going with guy, though, because a woman would understand how important all those details are. All I've been able to get out of Sam are some hand-drawn maps of the table layout and a fuzzy picture of a place setting. I think he might be certifiably insane, if you want to know the truth. Do either you or Dylan actually know this person?—because I'm really starting to worry."

Tia covered her mouth with her hand and coughed to stifle a giggle. She knew that "Sam" was actually Tony, and that in the interest of keeping the secret for his own reasons, he wasn't even letting his own assistant in on the details. Dylan had told her on a few occasions that Tony was having entirely too much fun messing with Jessa along the way. "It'll be fine," she said. "Let's just worry about the things we can control, OK? Who brought the catalogues with place cards and wedding favors?"

Tia was putting away the last of the dishes when the elevator door opened and Dylan all but tumbled out. "Heeeyyyy baaaby girrrll," he slurred, wrapping his arms around her and leaning against her for support.

"You, my love, are drunk," she smiled. He reeked of cigar smoke and whiskey, and his eyes were spider webbed with squiggly red veins. "I'm guessing you had a good time?"

"I had the bessst time," he smiled, "but I missed you. Did you pick us out a fabulous wedding meal?"

She led him over to the couch and helped him down, pulling off his coat and tugging off his shoes. He swung up his legs and melted into the leather. "I'm thinking we need to hire Neil to cook for us every day. He's nothing short of a magician."

"We could do that," he mumbled, his eyes closing. "Anything for you, love." He took one big breath and began snoring softly.

Tia leaned over to kiss his cheek and covered him with a blanket from the other couch. "Sleep well, baby," she whispered. She put a tall glass of water and a bottle of aspirin on the side table, and smoothed his hair before slipping into bed alone.

Chapter 30

The thing about an affair, Ryan quickly learned, is that you have to become at least three different people who each want to kick the living shit out of both the others. When he finally summoned the strength to walk out of the bathroom, Tiffany was striding around the kitchen, presumably making coffee. It was impossible for Ryan to notice what she was doing, because she hadn't dressed or even slipped on a robe—she was completely naked and she looked really damn good. Every logical neuron firing in his brain was telling him to run—to get the hell out of there before things got really out of hand...*fuck me once, shame on me—fuck me twice, shame on you!* Trouble was, there were only a handful of logical neurons even functioning in his alcohol clouded brain, and they were all firing in different directions. Before he could even form an excuse that would get him out of there she gave him a look that got him hard again and before he fully realized what was happening, he found himself laying on a weight bench in a spare room with her straddled over him and riding him like a mechanical bull. *Shame on me*, he thought even as he came with the power of a pent-up volcano.

His first instinct when he woke up the morning after the "incident" with his second hangover in as many weeks on a work day, was to break things off with Tiffany before he got in too deep. He thought that with time he might be able to justify making one huge and horrible mistake (technically two, but since they happened so close together he was counting them as one) while under the influence of alcohol and a great deal of stress; and Lexi would never have to know. There were other gyms he could join to keep up the façade of the "big project;" gyms that didn't have Tiffany the Temptress playing on his deepest emotions. Problem was, he really was intrigued by the idea of bringing in a huge contract to the firm and solidifying his place at the helm, which would also help to alleviate the guilt he felt for lying to Lexi in the first place. Truitt Industries was that huge, and Tiffany was the perfect ally.

Fucking irony, he thought as he made a strong pot of coffee and tried to put his thoughts into some sort of order. He'd been pissed off at Lexi because he thought, for a few brief yet hellish seconds, that she'd slept with someone else; and now he had blatantly betrayed her trust by screwing the brains out of a woman he barely knew. He gave Lexi all kinds of crap for lying and hiding things from him, and now he was making up a huge and elaborate fabrication that depleted the time he could spend with her, cost him at least a couple grand in lost deposits, and made her postpone her dream wedding. What kind of prick would do that?

He had every intention of calling things off with Tiffany— ending it while he could still hold onto at least a shred of dignity and build on that until he could respect himself again. Of course it would mean another lie—it's not like he could tell Tiffany the truth—that he was a cheating bastard who just needed to feel like he was number one for a little while to stroke his own bruised ego.

When his phone rang at lunchtime and she invited him to her place for dinner he accepted, with the sole purpose being to end it. Somehow, however, he ended up in her bed again, and again the following night.

On Saturday morning he sat nursing a cup of Irish coffee and wondering how he'd become the epitome of everything he hated in such a short time. When his phone rang and Lexi's face popped up on the screen, he immediately felt nauseous and the guilt rose up like bile in his throat.

"Hey," she said quietly into the phone. "You stopped calling me."

Hearing her voice made him realize that he'd really missed her—the last couple months had pretty much sucked, but they had almost five years of building something good together before that—something he thought was worth a lifetime. The guilt slammed down on him like a lightning strike and he realized that he probably didn't deserve her. Not anymore. "Well," he said, "you weren't calling me back."

"I know," she said. "I was really mad. But it was your fault, so you should have kept trying."

"Probably," he replied, sounding genuinely sorry, "but I was really busy at work, too—and your ignoring me was really throwing off my focus."

"I'm sorry, Ryan," she murmured. "I was really hurt that you wanted to postpone the wedding, and I took it personally. But I know how important your career is to you, and I've decided that I'm willing to reset the date."

Ryan rested his forehead in his hand and tried to think. The last thing in the world he expected was a complete turn-around by Lexi. She sounded genuinely sorry, and it wasn't her usual style to let things go so easily—especially not something as big as this.

"I kind of thought you were wanting to call the whole thing off."

"I never said that!" she exclaimed. "Shit Ryan, we've been through too much to let one argument rip us apart. Of course I'm upset—any girl would be. I've been waiting a long time to marry you, and it doesn't seem fair that I have to wait another whole year to make it happen."

"I didn't say a year," he said. "I said a few months."

"It might as well be a year," she answered. "We'll have to rebook everything, and the whole theme, not to mention my dress, won't work except in the summer. I still want a July wedding. But it's OK. I'll wait. I won't lie and tell you I'll be happy about it, but I'll do it for the sake of your dreams and our future."

I won't lie. Her words were like a slap in his face, and he instantly wished he could go back in time and get excited about the freaking firework invitations.

Way too late for that now.

"Really?"

"Really," she answered. "I tried to put myself in your place, and even though I don't like it, I get it. I know it means a lot to you to make partner, and I also know it's been bugging you that Tia's wedding would be so close to ours and that it has the potential to take some of the spotlight off of our own celebration. I guess I just need to suck it up and take one for the team."

Take one for the team? Ryan thought sarcastically. He should have felt relief at her words, but instead, for some inexplicable reason, they pissed him off. If she'd had this epiphany a week ago, he wouldn't be in this shitty situation. Somewhere, in the deepest recesses of his mind, he knew that wasn't true, but it was a hell of a lot easier to place the blame on Lexi's little hissy fit than it was to put it squarely where it belonged—firmly and heavily on his own shoulders. Now that she sounded so sorry, so sincere, he felt even shittier. "I don't know what to say, Lex." At least that was the truth. "I guess I'm kind of surprised."

"Glad surprised?"

"Yeah." What else could he say?

"Want to come over tonight? I'll actually cook," she offered, a huge thing for her since she almost never did more than throw something from the freezer into the oven.

"I'm so sorry Lex, but I can't tonight," he said. "I have something for work..." He couldn't possibly go see her without more warning—he needed some time to get his stories straight in his own head. Lexi knew him better than anyone—she'd see the lie on his face, he was sure of it.

"During the week, then," she said quickly. "How about Monday?"

"Monday's good."

"Come after work. I'll put something together for us."

When she opened the door, she threw her arms around him and buried her face in his neck. "I really am sorry," she breathed. "I missed you terribly."

He hugged her back and took a deep breath. He could do this. He had a lot of time to work with now, and would figure out what to do about Tiffany eventually. Holding Lexi made him realize what an ass he'd been, and what a horrible mess he'd dived into headfirst. "I'm the one who's sorry," he whispered back, meaning it more than she could ever know. "I never should have done that to you—I never meant to hurt you."

"I know, baby," she cried, her tears soaking his shirt. "I should trust that you're going to do the right thing, and I do understand having a more secure future—I'm just being selfish, because I want it to start sooner rather than later."

Holy hell, he thought, her words gnawing at his insides. Here she was, telling him she trusted him to do the right thing, and he had betrayed that trust on more levels than he could even fathom. "It'll be here before you know it," he said, pulling her closer. He hoped to hell that she could trust him to do the right thing. From this moment on, anyway.

She'd really gone all out for the dinner. She made actual lasagna, complete with the spicy Italian sausage from the deli that he loved. The salad didn't come out of a bag, and the veggies were freshly chopped. The Italian bread was crusty and warm, and she'd roasted real garlic to spread on top. There was a bottle of merlot breathing on the counter, and her grandma's good crystal glasses were sitting at the ready. Damn it, she'd put a lot of effort into making a special meal, and he felt so sick to his stomach over how many ways he was lying to her that he didn't think he could eat it.

She tried to keep the conversation light, and didn't bring up their argument at all, which was also very un-Lexi-like. She was usually the one to keep harboring and picking at a situation until he begged for mercy. Finally, he had to ask.

"I'm really glad you did," he started, "but what made you come around a full 360? I never in a million years thought you'd be so calm about this whole thing."

She took a sip of wine to wash down a mouthful of lasagna and smiled at him. "Pretty miraculous, huh? I should be pissed about that comment, but I have to admit that I was ready to be mad for a long time." She wiped her face with her napkin and set it back in her lap.

"I didn't want to talk to anyone after I left. I was furious, and was wallowing in self-pity. After I was through being pissed, I was an emotional wreck, and I finally went over to Tia's to vent. I was even more pissed when they took your side over mine, believe me."

"What do you mean?"

"Dylan said he totally understood how hard it was to put your own life on hold for the sake of your work, but that more often than not, the sacrifice was worth it in the end."

Damn it! Ryan thought. Every time he wanted to hate the guy; he did something that was freaking likeable. He certainly didn't like the fact that Lexi was discussing their goddamn personal life with him, but in this case, he kind of owed the dude. It sucked that Miller was right, that he was cool, and that Lexi trusted him so much. He wasn't sure how to feel about any of it— he felt like he was in a tiny rowboat on a stormy ocean, bobbing and pitching and far from solid ground.

Lexi continued. "He also said that he felt really bad about setting their date so close to ours—the timing isn't his fault, but he's embarrassed by all the media hype and even though he hopes it'll die down soon, he's not terribly optimistic. What hit home the most, though, was when he said that you and I have to make it work for both of us; and that if I forced you to keep the date and then you didn't make partner, you'd never forgive me for it." She took his hand and softly kissed the back of it. "I was being completely selfish, and I'm sorry. It was for good reason, though; it was because I love you and I want to be married to you."

Ryan felt a freaking tsunami of regret crash over him. Dylan had managed to do what he never could—soothe the savage beast that was a pissed-off Lexi. He felt even worse now; knowing that Dylan was standing up for him and the whole thing was a fucking sham. He'd never considered how far-reaching one little lie could be, but now he had betrayed them all. The few bites of food he'd managed to force down started churning in his stomach, and he felt dizzy and nauseous. He'd really fucked this all to hell.

"Honey, are you OK?" Lexi asked, noticing how the blood had drained from his face and jumping up from the table to rush to his side.

"I don't know," he said, feeling even worse now that he'd now managed to ruin the dinner that she'd obviously worked so hard on. "I'm feeling a little sick, actually."

"Come and lie down," she said, helping him up. He actually swooned, and felt like he was going to pass out. "Oh Ry, can I get you something? You want a glass of water?"

"I just need to sit," he said, falling back into the chair. "I'll be OK in a minute." He looked back down at the table, set with the good china and the homemade food. "Damn it," he murmured on breath as thin as paper, "I ruined your dinner. I'm so sorry."

"Screw the dinner," she said. "Are you sure you're all right?"

He took a few deep breaths and put his face in his hands. His head was pounding, but the dizziness was going away, at least. "Can I get a couple aspirins?" he asked weakly. "Then maybe I will lie down for a while."

As the cold winds of February blew into Chicago, Ryan found himself caught in a complex web of lies that had him tied up in knots. Dylan was leaving for Seattle soon to work on the new album, and Lexi was spending lots of time helping Tia with her wedding plans. Since she'd accepted the postponement of her own wedding, Ryan was incredibly impressed with the positive and enthusiastic attitude with which she approached Tia's planning. Plus, the extra time the girls spent together made her even more accepting of his long hours, and that made his guilt gnaw at him constantly. Tiffany, although not demanding too much of his time, was still a regular presence. He didn't really have a lot of extra work to do at the office, so the gym was his only viable escape. He and Tiffany had spent some time putting together ideas for improving Truitt's newly developing International Division, but his self-loathing only got worse when she enthusiastically embraced the idea as something that could accelerate their personal as well as professional relationship. Tiffany had no idea that their entire relationship was based on a lie, and she didn't deserve to be deceived like that either. He threw himself into the work when they were together, hoping to ease back on the intimate side of their relationship until he could figure out how to end it completely without blowing the possibility of landing a big account for the firm. Tiffany wasn't exactly seeing things the same way.

Wes wasn't helping, either. Tiffany stopped in one day to take him for an impromptu lunch, and Wes came into his office to let him know she was there. "There's an incredibly hot woman who isn't your fiancé here to see you on a 'personal matter,'" he said with a smirk. "And if you aren't hitting that, tell me right now, because I'd nail it in a heartbeat."

Flushed and flustered, he stammered for words. "She's a Truitt, Wes, for God's sake. We're putting together a proposal to pitch to the old man. It's work."

Wes wasn't buying it. "She's not dressed for work, I'll tell you that," he said with a sly grin, then he took a step back when he saw Ryan's stabbing look. "Hey," he said, hands raised in surrender, "if you say it's work, it's work. But I say again, if you're not hitting that, give her my number." He waggled his eyebrows and flashed a lecherous smile.

Wes was on his fourth marriage for a number of reasons, one of the main ones being 'hitting' women who weren't his wife. Ryan had no doubt that he'd follow through with it, although he knew Tiffany was smart enough not to get involved with a married business associate. *Only an engaged one who was living a double life, both of which were wracked with lies,* he thought bitterly as he slipped his jacket from the back of his chair and walked toward the doorway where Wes smirked openly at him.

"You wouldn't stand a chance." He forced a smile that he hoped was much more genuine than he felt. "But I'll pass along the invitation."

"Hey, you think you'll actually be able to get face time with Truitt? That would impress the hell out of me. Connor too. Truitt usually only deals with the big guns."

"I'm already halfway there," he smirked, letting the door shut behind him.

"I have a surprise," Tiffany said when they'd been seated at the restaurant. "I was talking to Daddy about you..."

"You were what?" he asked, surprised.

She smiled sweetly. "Well of course, Ryan. You didn't think I'd mention you?"

"I had no idea," he said, his mouth suddenly going dry. If word starting getting out that they were a couple, it could find its way back to Lexi, and his whole life would be blown to hell.

"I did tell him we were seeing each other," she continued, and he felt his face flush, "but I also talked to him about the ideas we've been working on, and I really think he liked what I had to say."

"Thank God," he breathed, glad that the discussion involved work.

"At first he said your firm didn't have enough international law experience under your belts to handle it, but I told him how hard you've been working, and that you'd be willing to get some extra training. I showed him the outlines we drew up and told him about the research I've been doing. He's known for a while that this is going to be my baby and that I really want to separate and expand that division to streamline operations, so he's had some time to open up to the idea. I really think he'll let us pitch it!"

A meeting with Preston Truitt was like a dream—he didn't give up his time unless he really believed there was serious potential for profit. The problem for Ryan was that he'd alluded to doing a lot more work on the proposal than he'd actually done, and he wasn't even close to being ready to present it. He mainly used the project as an excuse to Tiff so he could spend time with Lexi and visa versa. He was going to seriously need to start putting some major effort into this thing.

"I'm hardly ready for a presentation, Tiff," he said, fiddling with the end of his tie. "I've got a lot more to do..." His nerves were instantly on edge, but he also saw one huge saving grace in the whole thing. If he seriously worked on this project—gave it the time and energy it needed and deserved—it would at least temper down his other problems. He'd have an actual project that he could honestly share with Lexi, the time he spent with Tiff would take on a much more professional nature, and if he pulled it off, he'd secure some major business for the firm. "When does he want to meet?"

"You know Daddy," she smiled, "he never does business with anyone unless he knows them personally. He thinks he can tell everything about a person from one meeting, so he wants a chance to get to know you informally first."

Oh crap—as if he needed another reason to make him dread a meeting even more. What if Preston Truitt figured out that he was a two-timing liar who was using his daughter to cover up an elaborate scheme aimed at making his actual fiancé wait another year before he married her in order to soothe his own bruised ego? When he thought about it like that, he really felt like shit. "What did he have in mind?" he asked, trying to look excited, but feeling woozy yet again.

"I have a cousin who's getting married a week from Saturday," she said. "The reception's at the Intercontinental—very fancy black tie affair. I was going to ask you to be my date anyway, and we'll all be at the same table so you'll get a chance to get to know each other over dinner and drinks." She smiled. "I know you'll impress him as much as you've impressed me," she said, putting her hand on his thigh under the table. "And, I got us a room for the night there," she added, sliding the hand up slowly. He caught it just before it reached his package and hitched in a breath.

Shit! This was fucked up on so many levels he couldn't even begin to count them. A hundred thoughts flashed through his mind as he tried to put his life into perspective. He liked spending time with Tiffany, he had to admit that. She was incredibly easy to look at, dynamite in bed, and completely driven in her work; which he both respected and admired. With her, he never had to even think about sharing the spotlight with Dylan Miller. He could enjoy himself and *be* himself, with the one minor exception of the huge fucking lie upon which their entire relationship was based.

But he was engaged to Lexi, and he still loved her; he really did. He'd broken every promise he'd ever made to her, but she didn't know that, and if he could get through the next few months, get the Truitt account and make partner, he'd be a hero, and then he could spend the rest of his life making it up to her.

But as long as he had Tiffany mixed up in his business; professionally and personally; he had to play the right role. They hadn't been "dating," in his opinion—it had only been a few weeks since they'd met and so far he'd avoided taking her out to public places that couldn't be passed off as business meetings. A wedding, however, could be potentially disastrous. There would be hundreds of guests, and there was more than a small chance that he'd know at least a few of them. There would be dancing and he'd be there as Tiffany's date; he'd have to be attentive in a way that would never pass as business; especially in front of her father.

However, a meeting with Preston Truitt didn't happen every day and not only would he be stupid not to take it, but the invitation had caught him so off guard that he couldn't think of a possible viable excuse not to go. He took one glance at her expectant look and realized he'd already waited too long before answering. "That's amazing!" he said, forcing a smile. "I can't wait to meet him!" He took a healthy pull of his gin and tonic and didn't even flinch when Tiffany's hand firmly settled between his legs. *Yeah,* he thought bitterly, *you've got me by the balls all right, and you don't even know it.*

Chapter 31

Dylan had told him that he by no means expected him to show up at their engagement party in Chicago; in fact, he'd pretty much ordered him to stay home and rest. Fat chance. Bo was itching to get out of the house and take his life back and even if his mother didn't agree, the doctors were all for it. He felt like a new man—he looked and felt better than he had in a long time and he'd be losing both the cast and the boot within a week. He was the best man, damn it, and there was no way he was missing the only formal celebration of his best friend's engagement. The guys hadn't been all together since they'd gathered in his hospital room, and it would be great to see them and show them he was not only prepared to fulfill his best man obligations, but he was also more than ready to get into the studio and start on the new album.

Lexi would be there too, he was sure, and he hoped that seeing her in person would help him get to the bottom of the only thing from the accident that was still unresolved. He couldn't have cared less that he didn't remember New Year's Eve, but he damn sure wanted to know what happened during or after the filming of *After Dark* that left him with deep feelings of guilt and regret. No matter how many times he watched the video of that damn show, he couldn't remember any of it; and despite the fact that he and Lexi looked like they really enjoyed each other's company, every time he saw her image on the screen he felt a profound sense of sadness that he couldn't explain.

He had all sorts of fabulous memories of her, but for some reason, he felt some sort of *break*; some separation. No matter what he did he couldn't get clarity, so he hoped desperately that seeing her would fill in some of the gaps.

He strolled into the swanky room and swept his eyes over the crowd. Ty and Angelo saw him first; from behind a bar where they were mixing up one of their famous concoctions; and he waved his casted arm.

"Bobo!" Ty yelled across the room, slamming the metal cocktail shaker on the bar and rushing over to greet him with Angelo in tow. They pulled him into a group hug and then backed up to look him up and down. "Looking good, brother!" Angelo said. "Good to see you up and about. Dyl's going to be so excited you made it."

"Great party," Lexi said when Tia finally had a chance to sit down and have a bite to eat. Lexi and Ryan both had plates filled with delicious offerings; sushi, finger sandwiches, and Mediterranean dips with warm pita.

"It is nice, isn't it?" Tia agreed, plowing into a pile of hummus with a broccoli spear. "I'm so happy for my mom...she really wanted to do this, and it's turned out better than I expected." Tia had been hesitant to let her mother put together an engagement party—she'd already celebrated with her own friends and was worried it might turn into a country club outing with a lot of people vying for Dylan's attention. Instead, it was an eclectic mix of people from all walks of life mingling over cocktails and finger food, and she was really enjoying it. Rock stars in torn jeans chatted with society ladies and college professors; and her teacher friends mixed it up with movie stars and football players. She turned to see her mother laughing with Tony Granger, who'd been circulating the room like he owned it; flirting with the ladies and laughing with the men. Jessa had put out the invitation to a lot of Dylan's celebrity friends, and Tia was surprised at how many of them had actually shown up; some of them coming a long way to be here.

"I'm so glad you could both come," she said, mostly for Ryan's sake. He'd pretty much been sitting in the same spot since they'd arrived, moving only to get more food or refresh his gin and tonic, and Lexi was staying with him out of solidarity. There was a tension there that she couldn't quite put her finger on—she hoped they weren't fighting again.

"Wouldn't miss it," he said absently.

Dylan rushed over and tapped her on the shoulder, pointing toward the door. "Oh my gosh—Bo's here!" Tia exclaimed. "I thought he was supposed to be resting...I'll be back." She jumped up and got to Bo just after Dylan did, wrapping her arms around him and giving him a good squeeze. "It's so good to see you; you look great!" She held him at arm's length and gave him a once-over. "You really do, but should you even be here? Did the doctor say it was OK for you to fly?"

Bo grinned. "Hell, darlin', I'm Superman. No doctor's gonna tell me what I can and can't do. No way I was missing this little party. I'm your biggest fan, you know."

Dylan pulled her close. "Second biggest," he said, "at best. It is great of you to come, mate, but I'll ask the same question. Did you get this trip OK'd by your docs?"

"I'm here, aren't I?" he said, then patted Dylan on the shoulder. "Chill out, Strummer Boy. The docs OK'd it, and I wouldn't have come if I wasn't sure I could do it."

"Why doesn't that make me feel any better?" Dylan mused. "Ah, what the hell, I'm really glad you're here. It isn't the same without the best man."

"I knew you'd miss me," Bo grinned. "So you got anything to eat in this dump? I could use some real food—my nurse has been force-feeding me these horrendous green smoothies, and my body's more than ready for a rebellion."

Tia was tugging him by the hand. "There's tons. But first, I want to introduce you to my parents. I've told them so much about you."

Bo grinned and shook Will's hand, then took Danielle's, turned it over, and kissed it, in his typical style. "Well," he said warmly, "I can certainly see where Tia gets her good looks, Mrs. Hastings." Danielle blushed, and he continued. "I have to tell you that I just love your daughter. She's an incredible person, and she's so perfect for Dylan."

"Bo is Dylan's best man," Tia smiled. "He's the drummer for Inhap."

Recognition lit up in their eyes. "Of course!" Will exclaimed. "I've heard so much about you, Bo," he said, glancing sideways at Lexi, who was watching anxiously from across the room. Bo's eyes were scanning the crowd, and he seemed nervous himself. "All good, of course," he added quickly.

"Well, probably only half of it's true then," Bo joked. "I've heard a lot about you as well. Tia had a real internal struggle about keeping Dylan's true identity from you guys, you know."

"We know," Will agreed, "but we definitely understand why she did it. We also understand that you were a real help to her on a number of occasions, Bo. We appreciate that you've been such a good friend to her."

Bo shrugged it off. "That was nothing," he said casually. "Glad to do it."

"We're so relieved to see that you've recovered from your accident," Danielle said. Are you pretty well healed?"

"Almost good as new. Better even," Bo smiled.

Lexi's heart beat a little too quickly for her liking and she could feel the blood rushing up to flush her cheeks. Ryan had made no secret of the fact that he didn't want to be here, and seemed to be purposefully making sure she didn't have a good time. For the first week after they made up, he'd been attentive and apologetic, but ever since then he'd been edgy and unpredictable. She tried to be the supportive fiancé, not complaining about his long hours and seemingly endless meetings, but something had definitely changed in their relationship, and she couldn't quite put her finger on what it was. He was hot and cold—mostly cold—and she could feel a distance between them that had never been there before. He didn't respond to her texts for hours and often didn't even pick up the phone when she called. God, she couldn't even remember the last time they'd had sex. She knew going in that he was going to be less than thrilled about attending this party and being diminished; in his own mind; under Dylan's shadow, but she hadn't expected him to sulk the whole time they were here.

Ryan had staked out a place in the back of the room as soon as they'd arrived, and only moved to get more food or alcohol. He refused to mingle, and made little snide remarks when she returned after making some rounds to chat with people. He was aloof whenever she introduced him, and barely even said hello to Tia's parents. And now, Bo was here.

She watched as Tia led him over to meet Will and Danielle, and seeing him turn on his usual charms made her feel a sense of relief and lightness. She'd have to say something to him, obviously, but already felt the discomfort of not only the way they'd left things the last time they saw each other, but of Ryan's increased tension. "I see you freaking looking at him, Lexi. I know you're just dying to go over and say hello."

"Damn it, Ryan, you've been a downer all night...what's up with you? He was in a serious accident that almost killed him, and he's a friend. Yes, I want to say hello and see how he's doing. Don't worry; I'm not going to ask him to sneak over to my place later, if that's what you're thinking."

"Maybe not, but if I wasn't here, you'd be running into his arms so he could tell you how beautiful you are."

"You need to ease up on the cocktails, Ry," she snarled between gritted teeth, "and you seriously need to get over yourself. He's a great guy—give him a chance." She hoped that Bo would give her a chance. Maybe seeing her with Ryan would dispel the suspicion that she'd been hitting on him; although Ryan was being a serious an ass and they weren't exactly coming off as the couple of the year. She hated that she felt awkward about seeing Bo—it was the complete opposite of the relationship they'd built in England.

Bo decided he liked Tia's parents right away, especially after they told him how many great things they'd heard about him. He chatted with them for a few minutes, and then excused himself to get something to eat. He stopped in the middle of the room and swept it with his eyes—and then he saw her. The instant their gazes connected it all came flooding back to him and he was back there again—in the hotel room with her in the leopard print outfit, his strong urge to kiss her, his unexpected and uncontrollable desire. Even from this distance he could see the regret in her eyes as well, and he knew then that his asinine behavior had ruined a beautiful friendship. Still, they were the maid of honor and best man, and they'd do right by their best friends regardless of their own shortcomings. He lifted his good arm in a casual wave, and made his way over to their table to say hello.

"Doesn't look like I'll have much choice in that matter..." Ryan mumbled.

Lexi took a deep breath and tried for a casual smile. "Hey Bo, it's great to see you—how are you feeling?"

Every muscle in his body ached to pull her into an embrace; to whisper apologies into her ear and take away the sadness he saw in her eyes. But he didn't know if she'd accept it, and her fiancé was glaring at him with something that looked like a dare, so instead he shook her hand as if she wasn't someone important to him; as if she hadn't permeated his thoughts day and night for the past few weeks. He willed his voice to stay steady and not betray the rush of emotions currently swarming in his brain like a hive of angry bees, and forced a crooked smile. "I'm good, Lex— almost good as new. I think maybe that bump on the head knocked some sense into me," he joked, hoping she might get the hint. He smiled bigger and extended his hand to Ryan. "Bo Collins," he said with a friendly grin. "You must be Ryan. I've heard a lot about you."

"Have you now?" Ryan said, almost suspiciously as he stood and shook Bo's offered hand.

"Don't worry, it was all good," Bo said. "It's nice to finally meet you."

"Forgive me if I don't add 'finally' to my greeting. I kind of just found about you a few weeks ago when I saw the two of you together on TV. I mean, I knew who you were, but I didn't realize that you and my fiancé had...*bonded*."

Bo considered himself to be a pretty good judge of character—and there was something about this guy that just didn't sit right with him. It was impossible to miss the warning in his tone and the fake smile, and although the last thing he wanted to do was cause problems for Lexi, he wasn't going to just slink away with his tail between his legs. Especially when the dude put his hand firmly on Lexi's shoulder and pulled her to his side, placing his own body between them.

"Well, you have yourself a fantastic girl here," he said. Ryan shot an angry look at Lexi and Bo's protective instincts reared up. He stood up taller, looking down at Ryan from his large frame. "You're a lucky man; I know you appreciate how special she is."

The dude glowered at him and wrapped his arm tightly around Lexi's waist. "As if I need anyone to tell me that," he spat.

They continued their silent face-off for a moment longer until Tony walked over and put his hands on Bo's shoulder, breaking the tension. "Bo, Lexi—great to see you two together again," he smiled. "Great ratings for your show, by the way, did Jessa tell you? Thanks again for coming on; especially on such short notice."

"Glad to do it, Tony." Bo forced a smile, and couldn't help but get in one more dig before he made his exit, for the moment, anyway. "I couldn't have asked for a better co-star."

"She's got a face for TV, that's for sure," Tony agreed. "You look great, Lex."

"Thanks, Tony," Lexi said awkwardly. She could literally feel Ryan's anger in the way he was digging his fingers into her hip. "This is my fiancé, Ryan Stallworth."

"Ah yes," Tony said, shaking his hand. "You've got a great girl here, Ryan. Congratulations on your upcoming nuptials."

"Thanks," he replied coldly before practically pushing Lexi back down into her chair and taking a seat himself. "We're very excited."

Tony looked at Lexi with raised eyebrows and she shrugged. He took the hint, and made his exit. "Well, nice meeting you," he said, adding, "Take care, Lexi. See you again soon." Bo followed him, leaving Lexi with Ryan's wrath.

"What's that supposed to mean?" Ryan asked as soon as they were out of earshot. "You running off to California again or something?"

"I'm sure he means at the wedding, Ryan," she said, exasperated. "He and Dylan are good friends."

"How nice for them."

Lexi glared at him, but kept her voice low. "You know Ry, I really thought you were over this whole jealousy thing. This is my best friend's engagement party, in case you hadn't noticed, and you're really sucking the fun out of it. What's up with you?"

"It's all about you, isn't it? You're just soaking this shit up. Pardon me if I'm not impressed that you're on a first name basis with all these celebrities." He slammed the rest of his drink, and pounded the glass onto the table. "Maybe you'd have more fun if I left—then you could do your schmoozing without me getting in your way."

"I want you to be part of my life, Ryan, not exclude yourself from it."

"I don't know what your life is anymore, Lex," he slurred. "But I do know that I'm having a harder and harder time fitting into it."

"That's bullshit and you know it. I've included you in every..."

"Included me?" he interrupted. "You mean put me neatly in a corner so you can go about your business, right? Because that's pretty much the way it feels on my end."

"That's your fault, not mine. You're the one who's behaving like an ass."

"Yeah? Well I'm so sorry that I'm an embarrassment to you."

Lexi sucked in a big breath and let it out slowly. It wasn't that she hadn't noticed that Ryan separated himself from the group when they were out together, but she really hoped that he and Dylan would get to be friends and made a point to try and include him. "Listen, Ry. I understand that you feel left out of the whole equation, I do, and I'm really sorry about that. I also get that I have a history with some of these people and you don't. I know it's hard to understand, but these are real people, regardless of what they do for a living. And they're nice people, the ones I know anyway, so it's not fair that you don't even give them a chance. Dylan's a great guy; so is Bo—and Tony, too. If you got to know them, you'd realize that, and you'd build your own friendships with them."

Ryan mimicked playing a very tiny violin. "And that's where we're never going to agree, Lexi. I'm not going to bend over backward to impress your celebrity friends."

"I'm not asking you to impress them, Ryan—I'm just asking you to be yourself. It's like I don't even know you sometimes, and I don't like it."

"And that, ladies and gentlemen, is what we call irony," he said, tipping his empty glass in her direction. "Do you know how many times I've thought the exact same thing about you?" He stood up to get a refill and left her wondering what the hell was going on. She scanned the room while he was at the bar, and watched with a heavy heart as Bo flirted with Joi Dowling, lead singer for *Sparrows at Sunrise*. Apparently, it was going to be another stressful evening.

Chapter 32

Tia sang along with InHap's first album as she folded laundry and watched the snow fall outside the window realizing, not for the first time, that since she'd met Dylan she found herself drawn to the harmonies rather than the melodies. It felt good to be doing mundane things like sorting socks and folding sweatshirts; it was a nice, normal thing to do on a Friday morning.

Her life was full of harmony lately, and it was about time, in her opinion, The media buzz had dwindled to a low murmur thanks to Hollywood and its seemingly endless supply of marriages, breakups, babies, arrests, and rehab check-ins. Dylan had left for Seattle, but the distance between them was proving to be manageable—there was only a two-hour time difference between them, which allowed them to keep in close contact on a daily basis. Jessa was staying with her on and off, dividing her time between working for InHap and keeping an eye on Tia. She knew that the primary reason Dylan was having her stay was because Tia insisted he ease off the constant security once their story died down, but she didn't mind at all—Jessa was a great friend and was positively invaluable when it came to the wedding plans. Lexi was a great help, as well, and Tia was impressed with the positive attitude she'd maintained since her own wedding had been put on the back burner. It hadn't gone unnoticed that Ryan was a bit of a shit at the engagement party, but for the most part, Lexi and Ryan seemed to be getting along better lately, too, which was a relief after the tension they'd had between them for the past few months.

Her friends had gotten over the initial hoopla over Dylan's real identity and although she was still wary with strangers, she'd fallen back into pretty normal relationships with the people who mattered to her. As normal as they were ever going to be, anyway, she figured.

Harmony was good.

Tia put the clothes away and turned on the television as she started pulling bowls and pans out of the cupboards and placing them on the counter in the kitchen. She had another task to master today, and she was really looking forward to it.

"Hi everyone, and welcome to *Chit Chat*! Please welcome your host...Dottie Miles!" said a disembodied voice as the camera panned over a live studio audience. A lithe redhead appeared at the center rear door and danced down the main aisle, high-fiving and fist-bumping audience members before deftly leaping onto the stage and taking a bow.

"Oh thank you so much, really, it's great to be here today!" She waved at the audience, deep red lips peeling back from impossibly white teeth in a genuine smile. "Please help me welcome my co-hosts...two of the most fabulous people I know, Abigail Cross and Lynne Davies!" Another wave of applause rose as a a blonde and a brunette darted out from the two side entrances and made their way toward the stage, waving and similarly sharing high-fives with the guests. They, too, leapt onto the stage where they joined Dottie in a group bow before taking their seats behind a long table dotted with the usual coffee mugs and several colorful flower arrangements.

"Thank you, thank you very much!"

Tia might have turned the channel if she wasn't up to her elbows in ground beef and spices. God, she hated daytime television with its cornucopia of talk shows sandwiched between quick-loan and injury lawyer commercials; but it was some background noise—a distraction—as she tried her hand at something new. She decided, after a revelation that Dylan had actually never had homemade meat loaf, that she was going to try cooking so that she could make him a proper meal when they were back together again.

"You've never had meat loaf. Seriously?" she had said when they were talking about their favorite childhood food memories.

"It isn't really an Aussie thing and anyway, once I was on my own, the word 'homemade' was very rarely in the name of my usual meals. Now Alicia, my sometimes cook-slash-housekeeper-slash-surrogate Mum in Colorado makes a mouthwatering chicken meat pie and her fried chicken is to die for—can't wait for you to meet her, by the way—but I don't remember hearing the name 'meat loaf' ever mentioned."

"Wow. I can't even imagine making it to adulthood without ever eating a meat loaf. What about hobo steak? Pot roast? How often are you even at the house in Colorado?" It led to a huge discussion of Dylan's favorite foods growing up and things he'd never tried; and Tia decided that while he was in Washington, she would take the time to practice cooking not only foods that she had loved as a child, but Dylan's favorites, as well. She'd spent hours chatting with Kelley and had pages of recipes and tips about how to cook meals Dylan had enjoyed as a boy. She'd even found a couple of places close by that carried some of the meats more common in Australia; and although her mouth wasn't watering over cooking or eating things like kangaroo, emu, and alligator, she looked forward to surprising Dyl with a little taste of home as well as sharing some of her own favorites. Today, she was making meat loaf the way her mom always made it. She scooped the chopped celery off the cutting board and added it to the bowl, mixing it in with her hands.

"Thank you again for inviting us into your living room today," Dottie continued. We've been getting some great feedback about the format of the show, and are really excited to make it what you want it to be! Keep sending us those emails, tweets, and don't forget to like our Facebook page so you can be part of the Chit Chat community. Remember, we like to talk about pretty much everything, so send us your story ideas, too, and we may even invite you to video chat with us live on the show."

Lynne piped in, "Remember, you can also send us your videos, your favorite recipes, your gardening tips...we cover it all."

"Meat loaf," Tia said to the TV. "Two pounds ground chuck, two eggs, lightly beaten, two stalks of celery, finely chopped, one half of a yellow onion, finely chopped..." she dumped the onion into the bowl and continued mixing.

"I 'Dot' the I's," Dottie smiled...

"I Cross the T's," Abigail added...

"And I do whatever I damn well please!" Lynne finished.

"Oh God, really?" Tia groaned, looking briefly at the screen. "Could you be just a little bit cheesier? ...half a green pepper, finely chopped..." She added it to the mixture.

Dottie smiled, and looked at the camera. "We've got big news to talk about today—the earthquake in India, the plane crash in Norway, and the riots in California—but that's all bad news. When I go to a friend's house, I like to start with some light gossip before we hit the heavy stuff. Who's got the gossip?"

Abigail held up a copy of *Person to Person*. "Well, looks like this 'Martini is shaken, stirred, and poured down the drain," she joked, referring to the headline.

"Ah yes, another Hollywood love story with a nasty ending ladies and gentlemen; what a surprise. Seems like Martin Forbes and Tina Provost have filed for divorce, citing 'irreconcilable differences.'"

"Do you think one of those 'differences' might be Jillian Scoretti, perhaps?" Lynne asked. "She and Martin haven't exactly been keeping their affair a secret."

"There was no prenup, either—Tina's going to make out like a bandit."

"What's going on lately?" Dottie said. "It seems like there's been a huge influx of infidelity the past few months. Here's another article just sent to me by Faith Mahoney from Lincoln, Nebraska—thanks Faith!—about yet another politician...people who ask for our *trust*." The headline popped up on the screen and

Dottie summarized. "Senator Paul Husteller was arrested yesterday at his office on charges of fraud and misappropriation of campaign funds. It seems that Senator Husteller needed the money to keep his mistress fed, clothed, and housed in a fancy apartment near his office. His wife of fifteen years hasn't been reached for comment."

"Let's talk about commitment for a minute, can we do that?"

"Sure, why not," Tia said out loud, wiping two fingers on a towel and measuring in some Worcestershire sauce.

"Does it really exist anymore? Do we, as a society, even care?" Dottie said. "I know there are lots of studies out there, but the majority of them average out to half of all marriages ending in divorce."

"Actually, that's only first marriages," Abigail chimed in. "When you start talking about second marriages the number jumps to over sixty-five percent, and it's almost seventy-five for third marriages."

"So, if you don't get it right the first time, you're even less likely to find Mr. Right?"

"Seems so," Dottie said. "Which brings me back to commitment. Do you think that a man in power...that is, a celebrity, a politician, a wealthy business owner...is more likely to cheat?"

"I think a guy like that has more temptation," Lynne said. "Women tend to gravitate toward men with money and power, and I personally think that they believe they're more likely to get away with it. Some of them even think they deserve it."

"Not all men are assholes," Tia yelled at the screen. "I've got a good one!"

"Do you think it's some kind of testosterone power trip or something?" Lynne offered. "Let's face it—you don't see women getting busted for this sort of thing; you just don't hear about women keeping—what would be the male version of a mistress?"

"I'd call it a gigolo," Tia said. She wiped her fingertips on a towel and read, "one tablespoon garlic powder; salt and pepper."

She measured out the garlic powder and sprinkled in the other spices.

"I think that would be a gigolo," Dottie said, "if she's paying the bills."

"What kind of message does this send to young people," Abigail asked, "if these role models—and like it or not, they are—don't model that commitment is important; that you have to keep your promises and work through your problems?"

"I'll tell you what we need," Lynne said, "are more Dylan Millers."

Tia's ears perked up and she turned her full attention to the screen. "Amen to that," she said, "Except there's only one, and he's all mine."

"I mean, there's a guy who went the extra mile to stay faithful to the woman he loves."

"I agree, but that brings me to another point," Abigail said. "It's been big news not because of their beautiful love story, but because of the betrayal by Penelope Valentine that went along with it. If it weren't for that, it wouldn't even be a story. We really need to focus more on situations like that—on men who are worthy of admiration. I think it's incredibly sexy that he got on the first plane to find his lost love after he found out how he'd been played."

"I just think *he's* incredibly sexy," Lynne purred. "But you're right. We don't hear about the beautiful love stories because they don't make for 'interesting news.'"

"You can say that again," Tia said to the TV. "But I repeat; he's all mine!"

"I, for one, don't agree," Dottie said. "In fact, I think it makes for great news!" She looked into the camera. "We want to hear about your great love stories—put them on our Facebook page or our website or email them to us. We'll share some of your stories and pictures on the air over the next couple weeks."

"How about we pick some of the best ones and give them a romantic dinner or something?"

"We can do that! You, the audience, can vote for the winners!"

They high-fived each other, and went to a commercial. Tia patted the concoction into a loaf, placed it in the pan, and put it in the oven. When the show came back on they moved on to the plane crash, and Tia turned off the TV and fired up another InHap album, sinking back into harmony and letting her mind wander over how lucky she was.

When they were in high school, and boys had really started to matter, she and Lexi had planned their dream weddings. Lexi's was going to be on the Fourth of July even then, on a huge boat in the middle of Lake Michigan so she could see the fireworks displays from all directions. She was going to have a famous band playing the music—she couldn't say who, because her favorites at the time changed on an almost weekly basis—and she was going to arrive for the ceremony on a helicopter that would lower her onto the ship as she sat on a swing, the ropes decked out in tulle and ribbons with sparklers lit all along the skids of the chopper.

Tia's was going to be on a white sand beach in a tropical paradise. She'd arrive on a tiny sailboat decorated with the most amazing flowers and palm fronds and pulled by trained dolphins at sunset. She leaned back in her chair and smiled. No trained dolphins, perhaps, but she felt incredibly lucky that she was going to see that dream come to fruition with a man more amazing than she could have ever dreamed.

The details were coming together so well she could hardly believe it; and the best part was that she and Dylan agreed on just about everything. The wedding party was selected; they'd decided that to keep with the intimate feel, they'd each ask two people to stand with them as they made their vows. Tia asked Lexi and Jessa, and Dylan asked Bo and his friend Max from England. They'd finalized the menus for all four days; opting for lots of fresh local produce and seafood, buffet lunches so people could eat at their leisure and enjoy the amenities of the island, a barbecue night on the beach, a surf and turf dinner, and more formal dinners on the rehearsal and wedding nights. The guest list was nearly final, invitations and table cards were ordered, and transportation was in the works. Today, she'd see about the most important detail by far—her dresses.

Dylan had been right when he said there would be dozens of designers wanting to create her wedding weekend wardrobe, and she'd spent hours pouring over sketches and sorting through fabric samples that were sent to her. She knew that whatever she chose would end up being plastered over all sorts of media, and that anyone and everyone would put their two cents into the outcome. Tia didn't care—she was going choose a designer who would give her what she wanted. She wasn't into the super fancy, heavily beaded gowns—she wanted something light and "beachy;" something she could dance in.

After weeks of deliberation, she decided that Gus Vecstrom was just the man for the job. A week ago she'd met with one of his assistants for an initial fitting, and they'd video chatted on two occasions so he could get to know her a bit. Today he was in Chicago for a show, and he invited Tia and the girls to meet with him so he could 'capture their essences' for the final designs of the wedding gowns. He had some samples ready, and she could hardly wait to see them.

The girls were going to make a day of it. Dylan arranged a fabulous dinner and a room at the W, and Tia was positively glowing when the front desk called up to tell her that her car was ready.

She, Jessa, and Lexi arrived at the hotel in the late afternoon and were greeted personally by Gus at the door. He waved to several attendants who efficiently scrambled to pour champagne and place crystal platters of canapés around the seating area. Gus pulled Tia into the room, kissed both her cheeks, and took her face in his hands.

"Best wishes to you, pretty one," he said smiling and nodding his head. He looked straight into her eyes and she smiled at him as he studied her features. "Seafoam green," he said in a low voice. "I was right about the eyes."

"I can't tell you how thrilled I am that you agreed to make my wedding dress," Tia said shyly. "I really admire your work, and it's truly an honor to wear one of your creations."

He waved his hand in dismissal. "I am the one who is honored," he said in his heavy Dutch accent. "I admire your future husband's work, too, and I'm happy to play my small part."

He was seriously under exaggerating. Gus had designed wardrobes for many stars, and was regularly featured in magazines and on television. He had a gift for matching the dress to the person, and his pieces were revered as works of art, not simply clothing.

The girls each took a flute of champagne, and Gus motioned that they sit on the long couch that sat in the center of the large room.

He chatted with them for nearly an hour, asking them about their favorite colors, what they liked, and how they were part of Tia's life. As he talked, he studied their features, their movements, their mannerisms. Finally, he stood and summoned his attendants, who had remained observant on the edges of the room, only moving to refill champagne glasses.

"The bride, she goes last," he announced. "Who is the maid of honor?"

"That would be me," Lexi said.

He turned to Jessa. "We start with you, my dear."

One of his assistants was on her feet immediately, awaiting his instructions. "I think I know exactly what to do," he said smiling. "My instincts usually don't fail me. Monique, start with number two."

The woman nodded, plucked a dress bag from one of the many rolling racks scattered about, and led Jessa into another room.

When she emerged a few minutes later, Tia and Lexi gasped simultaneously. Jessa would be the first to admit that she didn't give her wardrobe much thought; her usual mode of dress was a pair of loose fitting pants and a t-shirt; but she stepped out of that room positively transformed. To say she was glowing would have been an understatement, and she grinned wide when she saw the expressions on her friends' faces. She walked over to the three-way mirror that stood in one corner of the room and took in her image, her smile lighting up her entire face. "Wow. I didn't think I could ever look this good," she said, examining herself from all angles and then spinning on her heel; causing the hem to flutter like a butterfly.

She looked like a sunset, and the soft layers of pale orange fading into orange-red complimented her darker skin tone like they were a part of her. The loose fabric swirled when she moved, causing the colors to shift and blend, and Tia could imagine the sea breezes lifting it just slightly and setting the colors into motion. The jagged hem ended mid-calf, and the long waist made Jessa look taller than her five-foot-two frame. There wasn't really a sleeve; instead the fabric seemed to spill over the top of her arms, leaving her neckline and shoulders bare.

"You like?" Gus asked rhetorically. Tia and Lexi were both speechless for a moment as they took in the sheer beauty of the creation.

"Oh Jess, it's absolutely gorgeous," Tia said. "I know it's silly to say that it looks like it was made for you, because it was, but I couldn't imagine anything more perfect."

"I know—it's spectacular, right? I feel like a dream!"

Gus let them gush over the dress for a few minutes before saying, "OK, now you, Miss Lexi," indicating with his finger. "Number three for her." Monique checked a few tags, took a bag off the rack, and led Lexi into the same room while Jessa continued to contemplate her image in the mirror.

Lexi's dress was entirely different, and just as suited to her. "Ooooh!" Tia and Jessa sighed in unison as she stepped out and did a turn in front of them. Her dress was the sky; several shades of blue swirled together so subtly that it looked like a different color from every angle. It seemed to almost mimic the blue of her eyes, and her blonde hair cascaded down like beams of sunlight. Her dress was strapless, a bit longer than Jessa's, and had a long scarf that wrapped around her neck and fell gracefully down her back. It accentuated all of her best features, and was definitively Lexi. Tia had tears in her eyes when she got up and hugged her maid of honor. "It's so perfect," she whispered. Lexi did another twirl, and Tia again imagined how incredible it would look on the Caribbean beach, set to fluttering by the ocean breezes. Jessa stepped up next to Lexi in front of the mirror, and they marveled at how different their dresses were, but how well they went together.

They all stopped and turned to Tia. "Now," Gus said reverently, "we dress the beautiful bride. Number one, Monique. I should know by now to trust my first instincts when it comes to the bride." He winked at Tia as she followed the slender woman and closed the door behind her.

There was no mirror in the room, and it was lit mainly by a few dozen candles in stands and on the dressing table, so Tia didn't really get a good look at the gown before she put it on. It weighed close to nothing; soft and airy layers fluttered every time she moved, and she didn't feel the least bit restricted. She couldn't wait to get to the mirror so she could see it, but she stopped short when she caught the looks on her best friends' faces. Lexi gasped, and raised her hand to cover her mouth. Her eyes were wide, and brimmed with tears. Jessa's hand flew to cover her heart, and her smile said it all.

"Oh. My. God," Lexi finally said. "Dylan is going to *die* when he sees you in that dress."

"I've never seen a more perfect bride," Jessa agreed.

Gus took Tia by the hand and turned her in a slow circle before walking her over to the mirror. Tia took in her image, unable to believe the gown she was wearing. If Lexi was the sky and Jessa was the sunset, she was the sea; not traditional white but instead the color of the inside of a shell, with the impossible greens and turquoises of the Caribbean subtly swirled in. There was some light beadwork on the bodice that caught every ray of light in the room and tossed it in a different direction. The hem was just past her knees in the front and hung longer in the back where a short train brushed just slightly along the ground. She could picture how it would look skimming the sand; as if the waves were gently rushing up to meet the shore. The simple veil was multi-layered and so sheer it was nearly invisible. It was scalloped at the edges, with tiny 'waves' of the palest sea green incorporated subtly on the lowest layer. It was held in place by a beaded clip that sat at the top of her head and glittered with the muted colors of the fabric. She took one more look in the mirror and then turned back to her friends. "Oh my God, this is my wedding dress!" she exclaimed, her voice breaking. She turned to Gus and bowed her head slightly in thanks. "It's unbelievably perfect," she breathed, and hugged Lexi and Jessa who had jumped off the couch to embrace her.

"I have several other designs," Gus said. "These were merely my first instincts. Would you like to see them?"

The three girls walked to the mirror and stared at their combined reflection. "I think I'm good," Lexi said, pursing her lips. "Jessa?"

"Oh, I'm definitely good," she smiled. "Couldn't be better."

They both turned to Tia. "I'm spectacular," she grinned. "I don't think we need to see anything else."

She went to Gus and lifted her arms to hug him. "It's far from finished," he scolded, gently pushing her away. "Enjoy it for a moment longer, but then you must all stand still while we get them prepared for alterations so I can complete them. Then I'll certainly take that hug."

"I sure hope we're going to be on a beach somewhere," Lexi said. "These are perfect for a seaside wedding!"

"They're just perfect for any wedding," Jessa replied, "but I'd love the beach, too."

Tia just smiled. They took one final look, then reluctantly stood while Monique and another woman gathered and pinned and measured before they shed the dresses and handed them back into Gus's capable hands.

"Thank you," Tia whispered as she wrapped her arms around Gus's neck and planted a soft kiss on his cheek. "They couldn't be more perfect."

"You are most welcome. If I do say so myself, you will be a very beautiful bride."

"I'll certainly have the most beautiful dress, anyway."

"I will call you when they are ready for a final fitting," Gus promised as the girls bundled back into their winter coats. "I have a show in New York next week, but am clear to work on them after that. I'll need three weeks, tops, and then we can get started on the men."

Chapter 33

The girls were positively glowing as they tied their scarves around their necks to ward off the cold and headed into the frigid February evening. They huddled together, waiting for their limo to collect them to take them for a celebration dinner, when Lexi stepped away and stared hard into the distance, cocking her head. Automatically, Tia and Jessa turned to see what she was looking at.

"That looks like Ryan's Mustang," she said, squinting into the dark. "Wouldn't he be furious to know someone has the same paint job as him?" She turned to Jessa. "He actually went to one of those custom places that have their own reality show—he said it was going to be his 15 minutes of fame when he got to pick the car up in front of all the cameras. I think they aired, like, what," she asked, turning back to Tia, "about 30 seconds of him? If that?"

Lexi smiled, remembering, until the car reached the valet station and Ryan stepped out, dressed in a long coat over a tuxedo. She tilted her head again, trying to make sense of it. "What the hell is he doing here?" she said. "He's supposed to be in New York!" She took two steps toward him, but then froze as Ryan opened the passenger door and a very tall, very blonde woman dripping in fur stepped out of the car and into his arms. Ryan smiled and said something, and the woman tossed her head back and laughed, and then took his face in her hands, planting a very sensual and familiar kiss on his lips. Lexi watched, slack jawed, as Ryan popped the back hatch of the car and pulled out two overnight bags, handing them to the doorman. One of them was the bag she'd helped him pack yesterday.

"What the fuck is that?" she spat, a look of pain, confusion, and fury taking turns controlling her features. "*Who* the fuck is that?" Her hands clenched into fists, and she took a few steps toward the couple before the other girls wrapped their arms around her, holding her back.

Tia and Jessa stared in disbelief, and it was a couple moments before either of them found a voice. "Oh my God, Lexi, I'm so sorry," Jessa said softly.

"I just can't even believe this," Tia murmured.

"New York my ass!" Lexi bellowed. "This is why he's been so busy lately? He's got a fucking *girlfriend*? We'll just see about that!" She tried to shake the girls loose so she could confront him, but they held her fast.

"Wait, Lex," Tia said. "Just take a deep breath for a second, OK? Do you really want to make a scene like that here? Maybe there's an explanation..." but she didn't believe it. She'd seen their embrace—they were obviously on very familiar terms.

"You saw him fucking kiss her!" she hissed. "That's all the explanation I need!" But she did take a deep breath of the frozen air and exhaled a long stream of steam that billowed out behind her. She closed her eyes and took a few concentrated breaths before pulling out her phone and punching in his number. "We'll see what kind of game he's playing," she said.

They watched as Ryan pulled out his phone, and motioned to the woman that he'd need to take the call. She continued into the building to get out of the cold, and Ryan came on the line.

"Hey, baby," he said. "I miss you."

"How's The Big Apple?" she asked, her voice dripping honey. Only the girls on Lexi's end could sense the venom beneath the sweetness.

"Lonely," he answered, "but we're getting a lot done. I think I can have the draft finished up by next week if I'm lucky, and then I'll need to work on polishing it and starting on the presentation. Still a lot to do, but at least I think I can see the light at the end of the tunnel."

Lexi immediately thought about how she'd like to make him see some lights at the end of a tunnel…preferably the lights of an eighteen-wheeler carrying a load of topped-off port-a-potties. "How's the weather there? I heard there was a storm. Did your plane land OK?"

"Yeah," he said, caught off guard. "We must have beat it in. We're just coming back from getting some dinner right now, and it's not snowing too much. Hard to tell around the skyscrapers, though."

"Well, stay warm, and I'll see you tomorrow, right?"

"Actually," he said, "just to give you a heads-up, I may need to stay one more night. It just depends on how things go here. We're taking a little nutrition break right now, but we're probably going to be pulling an all-nighter so we can try to get it all finished up, so I'll be turning off my phone here in a little bit. I'm glad you caught me when you did."

"Yeah, I'm glad I caught you when I did, too," she said, anger now evident in her tone despite the tears streaming down her cheeks. "An all-nighter. Well, good luck with that."

"Thanks, I'll try hard to wrap it all up tonight. Love you," he said, and she cut the connection without a reply. They watched as he tapped his phone, and then skipped up the steps and into the arms of the mystery woman who waited for him just inside the entryway.

Lexi stood with her phone in her hand, staring blankly at the space Ryan had just occupied. "I can't even believe this," she whispered, not even bothering to wipe the tears from her cheeks. "I just forgave him for being a complete asshole, and volunteered to postpone the wedding so he could work on his 'big fucking project.'" She exhaled loudly through her teeth. "I guess I know all about the project now, don't I? God, how could I be so stupid?"

Tia rubbed small circles on Lexi's back, her mind trying to find the right words to say but coming up a complete blank. How quickly things can change, she thought to herself. It had been a perfect night—they'd all been having a wonderful time; smiling and laughing and looking forward to a scrumptiously overpriced dinner at one of her new favorite restaurants in the city, and suddenly her best friend discovers her fiancé's infidelity. Just like that, another life changed forever by lies and deception. They continued to stare at the banquet entrance, watching small groups of people drift up the steps and through the glass doors. Ryan and the woman were well inside, but none of them could stop looking and wondering how something like that could have happened. They didn't even notice the limo pull up until the driver jumped out and approached them.

"Oh Lex," Tia whispered. "I don't know what to say. I'm so sorry, and so pissed off, and so hurt for you that I can't even breathe. You just tell me what you want to do, and we'll do it. You want to go home? I can draw you a bath and make you some tea..."

Lexi took one hard look at her friends and stiffened her spine. "Hell no, I don't want to go home," she hissed. "I want to get some fucking revenge, and then I want to go celebrate with my girls. I'm not about to let this ruin your night, Tia—it's been so perfect."

"It doesn't matter," she said, wishing she could put more conviction behind the words. It was most certainly not Lexi's fault, but the festive spirit they'd walked out with had definitely floated away on their sad sighs. "We don't have to go out. There's not a lot to celebrate at this point."

"The hell there isn't!" Lexi said. "I'm celebrating finding out what a snake that bastard is before I married him, and obviously having a famous designer make you the perfect wedding dress is cause for a party," she added. "Just sit tight for a minute. Tell the limo driver to wait."

As she walked toward the parking lot, Lexi admitted to herself that she'd known that there was something going with Ryan for a while now. She wasn't exactly sure when the change had happened, but there had been something off about him. It wasn't something she could put her finger on, but if she fessed up to the truth, she hadn't really been trying all that hard to figure it out. Their relationship hadn't been the same in a while, and although she'd told him she was fine with postponing the wedding, she was still seriously pissed about the whole fiasco. She should have guessed it was something big, but frankly, she'd been kind of wrapped up in her own affairs lately, and had ignored the signs. They were certainly screaming in her face right now, however. Ryan was obviously sleeping with someone else, and the whole "big project" was nothing more than a lie and a manipulation. And she would not be played.

She walked toward the side of the valet parking lot with a sense of casual purpose, her head high and her back ramrod straight. Tia and Jessa watched as she slipped efficiently over the concrete barrier, entering the lot and strolling toward Ryan's parked car.

Lexi reached into her purse and pulled out her keys, heading in the direction of the prized Mustang convertible. She walked past it casually, dragging her keys along the side of the car, the sickening sound of metal against metal piercing the night air. She turned as she passed the headlights and walked across the front of the car, making a deep scratch across the hood and then down the other side. Not a single shard of guilt clouded her mind as she scarred every body panel; in fact, she felt somewhat liberated as she headed back toward the main entrance. Calmly skirting the barrier again, she headed back toward the limo and the waiting girls.

"What did you do?" Tia asked, already having guessed.

"I just made a few custom modifications to his paint job," she said nonchalantly, scraping metallic gold flakes off her keys with her fingernail. "Nothing a few thousand dollars and a lot of lost sleep won't fix."

"Holy shit, he's going to be so pissed!" Jessa exclaimed, unable to control her fit of laughter.

"You have no idea," Lexi said calmly. "Now let's go party, ladies! I may be down a fiancé, but my best friend's still got the sexiest man on earth, so that's saying something!"

"Aren't you Tia Hastings?" the hostess asked.

"I am, nice to meet you," Tia replied, shaking her hand.

"Wow. It's awesome to meet you. I just love your story—congrats on your engagement. You're a lucky girl."

"Don't I know it," Tia smiled.

The waitress was at the table before they even sat down. "Oh my gosh, it's so nice to meet you!" she said to Tia. "You're ring is so gorgeous. Congratulations. Your future husband rocks."

"Thanks," Tia smiled, "and yes he does."

"I'll have a vodka martini—extra dirty," Lexi interjected.

"It's been a bit of a rough night for my friend," Tia said by way of apology. "Thanks for understanding." She took a quick glimpse at the wine list and ordered a glass of merlot. Jessa ordered a chardonnay and the waitress hustled off to fill their orders.

Lexi raised her glass for a toast. "To my best friend, and her InHappily ever after." Tia's and Jessa's eyes met across the table and they shared a knowing look. They tapped the rims of their glasses together and took a cautious sip. Lexi downed half of her drink in one swallow.

"Lex, we don't have to do this. Why don't we just pick up some junk food on the way and go straight to the room? I know how much you must be hurting—it isn't necessary to..."

"You know, I gave almost five years of my life to that bastard," she hissed. "He played me for a fool, but we'll see who's going to really pay in the end. And that's all we need to say about that." She finished her drink, and motioned to the waitress for another, then turned to Tia. "Obviously, this isn't the celebration we all had in mind, but you just found your wedding dress, T, and that's a big deal. It's more than worthy of a little party, and I'm not going to ruin that for you."

"Maybe we'll just get a couple of starters, and then head out." She thought it would be a good idea to get some food in her to soak up the alcohol—Lexi's second drink was delivered, and she took a good hard pull.

"Are you kidding me? We're having dinner on your fiancé's dime. I have every intention of enjoying it."

Tia and Jessa frowned at each other. Neither of them knew quite what to do; this was completely uncharted territory. They asked questions with their eyes—is it better to keep her out so she can at least have something else on her mind? Should we get her the hell out of here and let her get the emotions out?

As much as the girls tried to keep the atmosphere light, the mood was heavy and somber. Lexi tried really hard to keep up a strong façade, but the other girls could see right through her, and neither could really have a good time knowing how much she was suffering. Lexi felt guilty for ruining Tia's day, Tia felt horrible for her best friend, and both Jessa and Tia were very glad that they had a room in the city together—at least Lexi wouldn't have to face the night alone knowing that Ryan was with another woman.

Lexi made it halfway through the main course before she broke apart—the three martinis she'd efficiently slammed likely helped her along the way to a breakdown, but the girls were nonetheless impressed with how well she'd held it together. Her fork was halfway to her mouth when she suddenly looked from Tia to Jessa, and the tears started flowing. She dropped the fork and her shoulders hitched as the emotion took over. "How could he do this to me? To us?" she croaked, trying to control the sobs that took over her body. Tia called for the bill and they cut the evening off, taking Lexi back to the hotel room and letting her cry as they sat by feeling helpless. Tia and Jessa took turns soothing her until she fell into a fitful rest; sitting silently by well into the night just in case she needed them.

Lexi wasn't about to be bested, or played for a fool. She woke up with a wicked hangover—her head throbbed uncontrollably and her stomach rolled like a tropical storm—but she sucked it up and begged off Tia's attempts to come home with her. Downing a couple aspirin on her way out the door, she shot off to the grocery store to pick up as many boxes as they'd give her, then returned to her apartment and cranked up her stereo as loud as she dared. With angry chick music thumping from her speakers, she purged her apartment of all Ryan's belongings—every sweatshirt, his toothbrush; which she gave a little dunk in the toilet for good measure; his favorite CDs, his goddamn Obsession cologne—and dumped them unceremoniously into boxes. Every picture containing Ryan's image was yanked from its frame and tossed into a box that she'd burn later. She ignored three phone calls from Ryan, but wasn't surprised at all when she got a text saying that he was going to spend one more night in New York to 'keep the momentum going.' "Fuck you and your momentum," she said to the phone. Tia called twice and Jessa once—she assured them she was doing fine and refused their offers to come over and babysit her.

On Monday she rearranged her schedule so that she'd be out of work by noon, collected a rental car, and went to Ryan's apartment to do the same thorough cleansing. She tore every picture of the two of them in half, leaving his image with the ragged edges of where her photo used to be in various frames on walls and end tables. She took all her dishes, silverware, mugs, clothes, and everything else she'd stored at his place and took it all back to her apartment. Then she parked outside his office building and waited for him to leave work.

As she expected he left at his regular time, and she followed him in the rental to a gym not far from his office. He jumped out of the scarred Mustang and walked over to another car, tapping on the driver's side window. The same woman from the other night hopped out and greeted him enthusiastically, throwing her arms around him and pulling him in for a passionate kiss. Lexi cringed watching the exchange, but waited for them to enter the building before using her set of keys to open the door of the Mustang. She popped the hatch and unceremoniously dumped all of his belongings into it, pulling the shade over the contents. Then she took her sets of keys to his apartment and the car, hung her engagement ring on the carabineer, and put the keys in the ignition, locking the door with the fob before slamming it shut.

In the daylight she could see the damage she'd done—the gleaming silver scratches, already tinged with rust in a few spots, glared angrily against the custom paint job. Ryan had left several messages on her machine to tell her about the unbelievable vandalism, toting the airport parking lot as a place full of thugs and criminals. She'd ignored every one.

Then she dropped off the rental car, picked up her Beamer, and headed for the country club. Once he realized what she'd done he'd likely swing by her apartment first, then look for her at the club when he found her not at home. She'd turned off her phone so he'd have to go searching for her physically if he wanted to make contact. Considering that he thought that she was completely in the dark about the affair, she figured he'd catch up to her eventually, wanting answers.

She felt him standing behind her as she sat at the bar. There was so much negative energy radiating from him that it was like a wall behind her; something hot and solid. She was willing to bet that he knew she was aware of his presence, but Lexi had no intention of breaking the barrier first. She took a small sip of her mineral water and placed the glass down on the bar top, refusing to acknowledge him. After a short wait she heard the jingle of keys behind her and she smiled to herself, imagining the expression that must have crossed his face when he first saw it dangling from his ignition. She slowly swiveled her stool to face him, careful to keep her face completely impassive.

"Lexi," he said, his hands palms up, the keychain dangling from his middle finger. She could see the engagement ring still swinging from the metal ring. "What the fuck?" he grimaced.

She shrugged, raising her eyebrows at him. "I think *who* the fuck is a much more appropriate question," she answered coolly. "Don't you?"

"I don't know what you're talking about," he croaked, but his eyes shifted just enough to give him away. The jig was up, and he knew it.

"You know exactly what I'm talking about," she said simply. She raised her eyebrows again, and maintained her calm demeanor.

"We need to talk," he hissed, noticing some of the other people at the bar leaning toward them. He tucked the key ring into his pocket. "Let's go back to my place."

"I don't have anything to say to you." she said, loud enough for the patrons around them to hear, "and you don't have anything to say to me either—at least nothing that I want to hear." She started to turn her stool back toward the bar, but he caught the arm of the chair before she could turn her back to him.

"Come on, Lex," he whispered urgently, taking in all the interested eyes that were already focused on them. "We're not doing this here...just come with me so I can explain; please." He squeezed her arm, trying to pull her from the stool.

Lexi raised her voice just a bit. "Get your hands off me you cheating bastard! I'm not going anywhere with you."

"Shit," Ryan muttered, leaning in and trying to shush her. "You can't just leave things like this! We've been together for five years, Lexi. You owe me the right to explain. It's not what it looks like." She smirked at him and shook her head. "I don't know what you think you saw in the gym parking lot, but I'm sure you're making too much of it."

Her stare turned icy, and he felt the chill coming from her. "I know exactly what I saw," she hissed. "I don't need your take on it, but thanks anyway."

"Fuck! You can't just walk away like this—it isn't fair. You cleaned out my apartment; you destroyed all our pictures..."

"Those are pictures of a relationship, you cocksucker—pictures that show a progression toward a future. Since you destroyed the relationship, the pictures mean nothing. Your new girlfriend would have made you take them down anyway, so I just did you a favor."

"A favor?" his voice squeaked. He took a deep breath to hold his temper down and lowered his voice. "She's not my girlfriend, Lexi, it's work, damn it. She works for Truitt Industries, and she's helping me out with the project, that's all. It's the one that's going to help me make partner, remember?"

"It's also the one that canceled our wedding."

"Postponed—it's just postponed, Lex," his words sounded more like a plea than a statement.

"No," she said impassively. "It's definitely canceled, Ryan."

"All you could have seen was a kiss on the cheek in the parking lot. I can't believe you're jumping to conclusions!"

A slow sardonic grin spread across her face. "And on Saturday? When you were in New York? With Wes?"

She watched his eyes shift, his lip twitch; saw his face begin to falter. He looked down at the ground before forcing his gaze back to hers. "What about it?"

"I saw you, Ryan. I was standing there watching the two of you walk into the damned hotel when I called and you lied to my fucking face, all dressed up at the Intercontinental with your goddamn overnight bag that *I helped you pack*. I was standing thirty feet away from you during the phone conversation where you lied and told me you were heading in for a meeting with your boss, you asshole."

"Shit," he muttered, the color draining from his face. Then his expression changed completely; desperation flooding his eyes. Their conversation had become an attraction, and he spoke as quietly as he could. "It's all this goddamn stress, Lexi, that's all!" he groaned. "Please let me explain! Do you have any idea what the past few weeks have been like for me?" he groaned. "What I've been going through?" He felt the heat rising in his cheeks and his voice got more desperate.

Her answer was another shrug and a slight frown.

"I've had people offering me money to attend our wedding, Lexi, just so they can be in the same room with Dylan Miller! I had someone offer me ten thousand dollars just to sit at his goddam table. People are asking me if they can invite their nieces and nephews, their neighbors, and they say that they'll crash the reception anyway if they're not invited. The whole thing was turning into a goddamned circus, and... " He swallowed hard around the lump in his throat. Her expression hadn't changed in the slightest. There was no pity there, no understanding, and certainly no forgiveness. He took a deep breath and finished his sentence. "...none of it was about me, Lexi, or about us—we haven't even picked out invitations yet and it's all about Dylan Miller—it's our fucking wedding!" His breath was coming in ragged gasps now, because he wasn't at all sure that he could pull this off anymore. He couldn't read anything in her expression except for ice—she wasn't buying any of it, and he had nothing else in his repertoire to try and make her understand.

Her expression remained cool, so he raised his voice. "Wes suggested that we hire security for our reception, Lexi—security guards! What kind of shit is that? And people are asking me to get them into Tia's wedding, too. They're asking if Dylan's going to sing at our reception, if he's going to stand up..."

He stopped for a breath, and Lexi finally spoke, her voice sarcastic and condescending. "Poor Ryan," she gushed. "The universe isn't revolving around you and you can't handle it. Am I supposed to feel sorry for you? You don't think I've been dealing with the same shit?" She took a casual sip of her water and turned to him, her expression blank and uncaring. Although she hadn't had anyone offer her money, she'd had a few clients hinting at attending her wedding, and the girls from the snobby clique at work were still falling all over themselves trying to get into her good graces. "I've gotten shit, too Ryan, but I've been trying to balance it all so it fits into *my* life. Your response to it, however, was to go sleep with someone else? That's how *you* dealt with it?"

"It's supposed to be our day!" he howled. "They just got engaged, and they had to plan their wedding for right before ours? There are going to be more pictures of him in our wedding album than there are of us, and no one's even going to care that it's our wedding. Doesn't that bother you? At all?"

Lexi took a deep breath and shook her head. "Dylan can't help who he is, you pompous jackass, and even you know him well enough to know that he doesn't flaunt it in anyone's face. He's my friend, and he'll be my best friend's husband, and he's a damn good person." Daggers flew from her eyes. "I can't even believe you're trying to blame Dylan for you sleeping with someone else. For you lying to me!"

He shook his head. "I was overwhelmed, that's all," he tried desperately to explain. "Even you're out doing interviews, feeding off all the attention, and then there's me, sitting in the background; the asshole who's not privy to all the inside jokes…I feel like I don't even exist when he's around."

"I've gone out of my way to include you, Ryan. I've dragged you to every party and watched you mope around, scowling at everyone. Your piss poor attitude has sucked the fun out of every event, but I never once complained. I tried to be understanding of the fact that it was a bit of a mind fuck to suddenly find out that your fiancé had a secret friendship with a bunch of rock stars; I tried to put myself in your shoes and be patient, hoping you'd get over the jealousy and get to know them like I know them…"

"A relationship is right!" he spat. "I felt the same way watching you with the drummer as I did when I saw you in Miller's arms—there has to be trust in a relationship, Lexi, and you could've trusted me with the secret from the start instead of spending months whispering on the phone and changing your stories every time you told them. I knew you were hiding…"

"You want to talk to me about trust? How dare you?" She clenched her hands into fists and felt the blood rushing to her face. "I never once did anything to jeopardize our relationship, and my word should've been enough. You weren't exactly a prince to be around either, constantly questioning me about where I was going or who was on the phone; tossing in your little accusations about me sleeping with Dylan no matter how many times I told you it didn't happen. And now you have the audacity to talk to me about trust when you really are sleeping with someone else?"

Ryan hung his head. He had nothing else, and he'd picked the wrong choice of words to try and make his last argument.

"So I ask again," she said steadily. "Instead of talking to me about it; trying to work it out together; your solution was to go and get yourself a goddamn girlfriend?"

"Damn it, Lexi," he said, the desperation creeping into his voice, "I just didn't know how to handle it all. I made a stupid fucking mistake and I'm really sorry. Please—we can fix this."

"Oh no, it wasn't a mistake, Ryan," she said, with so much fake sincerity in her voice it made his blood curdle. "Don't you see? It fixed every one of your problems."

Now it was his turn to raise his eyebrows in question. "What the hell are you talking about?"

"Well, first of all," she said, "now you won't have to worry about anyone trying to get an invitation to our wedding, because we won't be having one." He winced at her words. "Plus, you won't have to worry about scoring invites to Dylan and Tia's wedding, because you won't be attending." Her words were like a slap. "And," she added, "you won't have to worry about my imaginary desires to be a fame whore anymore, because nothing I do will ever be your concern again." His head started swimming and he swayed on his feet. "You can just go be happy with your new girlfriend, and forget all about me, Dylan Miller, and our relationship, Ryan," she hissed, looking him straight in the eye. "You disrespected me in the worst way possible, and I can't ever forgive that. So," she said, tossing a quick glance at the door, "you should really just go now." A small smattering of applause rose from the small crowd and Ryan's face burned red. "And you might want to just stick with your new club and give up this one; especially since by tomorrow every person here is going to know what kind of shit you are. I doubt you'll enjoy your usual welcome."

He grasped for something—anything—that might turn the situation around. "I still have stuff at your place," he whined desperately. "Let's just go back there and talk this through!

Please, Lexi, we've invested five years in each other—you can't just walk away!"

"Your stuff is in the back of your car," she answered. "And I have nothing left to say to you, Ryan. Except that I'm glad I figured out who you really are before I married you. Now please just get out of my sight." She turned back to the bar and calmly sipped her mineral water, willing her shaking hands not to betray her. Defeated, and with dozens of eyes staring at him, he finally turned away and slunk out the door.

Chapter 34

Lexi struggled to open the door to her apartment, tears fogging her vision. She'd given Ryan time to leave the club, maintaining her dignity and even getting some reassuring remarks from some of the people who had eavesdropped on their conversation. As soon as she got behind the wheel of her car, though, she broke down, and it was at least ten minutes before she was able to drive home.

It was a lot to absorb, and she fell onto her couch and curled up in fetal position, hugging a pillow and letting the tears come. Once a cheater, always a cheater—she really believed that; which meant that there would be no going back. No forgiveness, no second chances, and no reconciliation—life as she knew it was over.

It was going to take some serious effort to get used to not having Ryan in her life. She'd been with him pretty much since high school, dating on and off for a few years before eventually getting together for good after his second year of college. She'd dated a few other guys along the way, but he was her only serious relationship; they'd planned a future, and now the rest of her life suddenly lay long and empty before her. As she had so many times in recent weeks, her thoughts turned to what Tia had gone through in the past year. She remembered how hard it was for her to start over after Nick died; how she found Dylan because of her concentrated efforts to find ways to ease her way back into life again. What was it she had said? Something about how she was going to have to figure out who she was, just her, because she'd been half of "TiaandNick" for so long that she didn't really know anymore?

Oh God, now that's me, she thought, her heart growing heavier in her chest. Not only would she have to face those same issues, but she would also have to deal with the fact that she'd been betrayed and face the likelihood of running into Ryan out in public with his new girlfriend. At least the five years Tia had with Nick were full of treasured moments and not a complete waste of time that left scars on every memory.

Incidental happenstance, she thought bitterly, a twisted concoction of coincidence and fate. If Tia had fallen in love with anyone in the world other than Dylan...if she'd never started the stupid fucking game with the 'gimmes...' if she hadn't told Ryan that Dylan was the one man in the world she fantasized about...would things have played out differently? What were the odds that out of the billions of people in the world, Tia and Dylan; an unlikely couple, anyway; would find each other? There was probably a bigger chance of getting struck by lightning, being bitten by a shark, and winning the lottery on the same damn day. Vegas would have a field day with those odds.

She also couldn't help the fact that the lawyer in her reared its ugly head and she found herself arguing Ryan's case. In some respects, she could understand where he was coming from. Not the cheating part—she'd never get over that—but she could see how any guy's self-confidence might falter in a side-by-side comparison with Dylan Miller. 'Sexiest Man on Earth' was just the tip of a very big iceberg when it came to defining Dylan. First off, what guy hadn't dreamed of being a rock star at some point in their life; imagined being adored by thousands of fans from atop a huge stage, women screaming their names and worshiping them like gods? And then there was Dylan the movie star—his name in lights on the big screen; playing roles opposite some of the most famous names in the business; attending red carpet premiers and Hollywood parties. And of course, there was Dylan the millionaire—his many talents earned him much more than a comfortable living, and he'd never have to worry about money. He could afford the very best of everything, travel first class, drive fancy cars, and own multiple homes. Plus, Dylan was just a really good person. He treated everyone with respect and never put himself above anyone else. Even without the accolades of fame he would stand out in a crowd. He tried hard to cast a small shadow, but most people felt it looming over them anyway. Still, the fact remained that Ryan had betrayed her in the worst way possible, and there was no excuse in the world for that. *The verdict is in, ladies and gentlemen of the jury; he's guilty on all counts of being a complete prick.*

The flip side of Dylan's situation; the side that Ryan and most other people would never understand; were the sacrifices that Dylan was forced to make because of his fame. She was one of the few people who knew how awkward Dylan's celebrity made him feel…who saw the lengths he went to in order to blend into a crowd, to not call attention to himself. It bothered him that people focused so much energy on his celebrity status, and very little on who he was on the inside. If Ryan could see the internal struggle with which Dylan lived his life, would he still feel the same way? Could he ever truly understand?

Her phone chirped, and she picked it up to see Tia's number on the screen. She broke into a fresh round of sobs as she realized that she could never tell her best friend the real reason that Ryan had torn her apart.

She went through the rest of the week in a fog, avoiding phone calls from Ryan and telling Tia only enough to keep her off her back, hoping that work would keep her busy enough to divert her focus. Although she hadn't intended on talking about the break-up until she was sure she could do it without falling apart, she had a major meltdown on Thursday when Candy started talking about throwing her a shower one day after work. Lexi tried to push it off, but Candy wouldn't let up; asking what her favorite foods were, whether she liked white wine or red, and if they should invite some of the girls from other offices on their floor. Lexi hid out in her own office, but when she ventured out to scrounge up some lunch and saw the invitation; with her name spelled wrong once again; hanging on the corkboard in the kitchen, she lost it. She tore it off the wall just as Candy and her little posse of conceited paralegals walked into the room.

Candy looked at her and winked. "Oh, I get it...we should do personal invitations, right? I absolutely agree...I told Carlie not to put it there." She put her hands on her hips and glared at the brunette, who lowered her head and took the blame that probably didn't belong to her.

Lexi suck in a breath and yelled, "No, you *don't* get it! First of all, we are not friends," she twirled her finger in the air around the little group. "You don't even know how to spell my name! Second of all, I'm not even with the bastard anymore, OK? There isn't going to be a wedding, so you can all stop pretending to like me just so you can score some time with InHap." She tossed the invitation in the trash and pushed her way through the door, crashing into two other attorneys who were coming in to see what all the commotion was about. She ducked into her office and grabbed her purse, telling her secretary as she rushed out that she was going home for the day and wouldn't be in tomorrow. Then she sat behind the wheel of her car until she was cried out yet again, and drove home to get an early start on what was going to be a long and miserable weekend.

Lexi jumped when she heard the key turn in the lock and rushed to hook the chain before the assailant gained entry. The last thing she wanted to do was deal with people right now—any of them. She had plenty of sympathy for herself, and sure as hell didn't need anyone else's. She might have made it if she hadn't cracked her shin on the coffee table and fallen back onto the couch, grabbing her leg and wincing in pain. By the time she stood back up, it was too late.

"Damn it," she muttered, yanking up her pant leg and checking for damage as Tia stepped into the apartment. On any other day she would have been glad to see her best friend; hers was always the shoulder on which Lexi chose to cry. She knew without a doubt that Tia had done nothing purposely to hurt her—knew that she never would—but keeping Tia's secret had apparently been the beginning of the end for her own relationship, and she couldn't help but feel that Tia's now-perfect life came at the expense of her own. Karma was a serious bitch. "Go away."

Tia's eyebrows raised and she gave Lexi an appraising once-over. "You look like hell."

"Fuck you," Lexi answered, plopping back onto the couch.

"You haven't been answering my calls." Tia sat next to her and put her arm around Lexi's shoulders. "I know what you're going through, you know," she whispered. "I gave you some time for your pity party, and now it's time to get back on your feet."

"Again, fuck you."

Tia smiled and shook her head. "Yeah, it hurts; I know. But in the long run, it's better to know now what an asshole he is rather than wait until you have a couple kids and a house in Barrington. You'll get through this, I promise...I know it doesn't seem like it now; but I'm here for you, Lex, just like you were there for me."

Emotion took over and Lexi lost it then, breaking into a fresh round of sobs and letting Tia pull her in; melting into her shoulder and letting the tears come. "It hurts, damn it," she whispered, "I can't believe how much it hurts."

"I know, sweetie, I know it does. It's pointless for me to tell you that you'll get through it, but I'm going to say it anyway. You are one of the strongest people I know, and you won't let this break you." Tia sniffed the air and wrinkled her nose. Lexi obviously hadn't showered recently and her hair was matted into giant knots that bunched at the nape of her neck. Suddenly, it was like looking into a mirror of the past, except that it had been Tia who couldn't be bothered with useless things like getting out of bed, eating, or practicing basic hygiene. She had been pissed at Lexi at the time for forcing her to keep living, but eventually, she appreciated the hell out her tenacity. It could get ugly, but she wasn't going to let her best friend get away with it either. "Come on, you seriously need a shower and something to eat. Better yet, I'll draw you a bubble bath, and call for some take-out."

Lexi shook her head and wiped away her tears. "I'm not hungry. And I'm not that stinky, either, so quit wrinkling your nose at me."

"Oh, you're stinky, alright; but it's nothing some smelly bubbles won't fix. Come on, Lex. Do you remember how hard you had to work to get me out of bed after the funeral? You didn't take no for an answer, and neither will I."

"I'm really not in the mood..."

"I don't care what you're in the mood for, Lex. I'll tell you the same thing you told me. 'You will get in that tub or I'll put you there bodily, girlfriend,' and judging by the fact that you look like you've lost ten pounds, it won't be too much of a struggle for me."

Lexi glared at her, but Tia put her hands on her hips and then pointed at the bathroom door. "Fine. Whatever. It's not going to make me feel any better." She went into her room to get some fresh clothes while Tia started filling the tub.

Surprisingly, she did feel a tiny bit better after a long hot soak; her tense muscles relaxed somewhat, and it did feel good to have her hair clean. She sat and nibbled at a slice of pizza; surprised that she had an appetite; while Tia combed the tangles from her hair. *What a difference a year makes,* she thought; remembering doing the same things for Tia. She felt better after eating, too; living on dry cereal and stale Fritos that she'd found in the back of the pantry had barely kept her alive her over the past couple days.

"Do you want to talk about it?" Tia asked, and Lexi immediately clenched her teeth. God, she really did want to talk about it. More than anything she wanted to pour it out and make it known that the whole thing was entirely Ryan's fault. That he was an egotistical pig who couldn't handle that the world wasn't revolving around him. But damn it, she couldn't. She could never tell Tia; or anyone else for that matter; the whole truth. She could never let Tia or Dylan know that it was the secret she was sworn to keep that cracked the shell and the fact that Ryan couldn't handle being second-best to Dylan in his own mind that broke it open. They would feel guilty; responsible in at least some part; and it wasn't fair to them. It would be another secret she'd have to keep, and it gave her nowhere else to place the blame.

"He's a prick, plain and simple. I packed up all his shit on Monday and cleaned my stuff out of his place. I followed him to some gym, and the chick was there waiting for him."

"No way!"

"Yuh huh. I used my keys to dump all his crap into the back of his car, hung my engagement ring on the carabineer, and left the keys in the ignition."

"Go you," Tia smiled, giving her a high five.

Lexi smiled back. "That did feel pretty good, I must admit. I knew he'd come looking for me, so I went to the club and sat at the bar. No way I was going to give him a private audience, and I knew he'd look there eventually."

"Were there other people there?"

"Oh yeah. It didn't take him long to show up, and we had it out right then and there. He went on and on about the stress of his big project—supposedly, the other woman is part of it. Then he was all pissy about my reaction to postponing the wedding. I didn't return his calls for a few days—you remember, that's when I came to your place—and he said he thought I wanted to call the whole thing off."

"So without waiting to finalize that with you, assuming that out of the blue, as soon as he talked about postponement, after five freaking years together you'd call the whole thing off in the heat of the moment, he was sleeping with someone else within a week? That doesn't make any sense at all!"

"I have no idea when he started sleeping with her. For all I know, it could have been going on for months. We were kind of fighting a lot, and he's been distant for a long time. The signs were there, but I just kind of ignored them, I guess."

"I know what you mean about distant. It seemed like he wasn't even there half the time we went out together—he was really quiet and kind of seemed to gravitate to a corner. Dyl noticed it, too."

"He did?"

"He asked me if I knew why Ryan didn't like him. He said that he got a "negative vibe" from him, or something like that. Especially at the engagement party. It was like he didn't even want to be there."

"So everyone knew he was an asshole except for me? Doesn't that just figure."

"Hey. You loved the guy for a long time, so don't beat yourself up over that. People change, and just as often as not, it isn't for the better. Oh sweetie..." Tia pulled Lexi into her arms as a fresh trail of tears spilled down her cheeks. "I know it doesn't seem like it now, but you'll get through this, and you'll be stronger than ever. You'll realize that you learned some lessons along the way, and you will have some good memories. I hate that he did this to you, I can't stand that you're hurting, and I especially hate that I've put you in the middle of planning my wedding when you're dealing with all this. I'll totally understand if you want to back off for a while; the last thing I want to do is make it harder for you..."

"No way. I'm not going to let this have a negative impact on your wedding. The timing of this really sucks, but I've been your maid of honor since seventh grade and I take that commitment seriously. If I get overwhelmed I'll let you know, and if I need to walk away for a bit I'll do it, but I don't want you tiptoeing around or hiding things from me because you think I'm too fragile to handle it."

"Oh Lex, I didn't mean..."

"I know what you mean, and I appreciate it, I do." She took Tia's hand. "Look, T. I love you, and I love you and Dylan. You guys deserve your fairy tale ending, and I'm not going to piss on that, I promise you. I'm really glad you came over—it felt good to get it out."

"I'm glad to. So what's next?"

"I'm going to suck it up and go back to work. I'm not even going to think about men for a while, but I'm going to move forward."

"That sounds really good. Now what do you say we open a bottle of wine, curl up on the couch, and watch a movie?"

Chapter 35

Dylan was in the sound booth when his phone buzzed in his pocket. He'd been waiting on the call all day; and as much as he hated to hold everyone up, he pulled off his headphones and spoke into the mic. "Sorry, but I gotta take this."

"And so it begins," Ty said, getting a rousing agreement from the rest of the guys.

"And never ends," Tommy added.

"Who would've guessed that Miller would ever be so whipped?" Angelo asked rhetorically.

Dylan gave them the finger as he grabbed his coat and walked out the door into the alley behind the studio. The air was chilly, but at least the little alcove sheltered him from the wind and got him away from the nosey neighbors.

"How bad is she?" he asked, settling in to hear Lexi's story.

"What's wrong?" Bo asked as he watched Dylan walk back to the group after cutting off the call. "You look like you just got some bad news, bro."

Dylan shook it off. They still had at least an hour of recording to get in, and he was determined to get *Forever and a Day* recorded before they broke for the night. "Nah," he answered, forcing a smile. "Nothing to worry about. Let's just get this done so we can get a proper meal, shall we?"

They all wrinkled up their faces at him, but he slipped back into the booth and donned the headphones. It didn't take Dylan long to find his focus—after all, this song would be a wedding gift to Tia, and his entire heart and soul were into getting it right.

"I think that's it!" Dylan finally exclaimed, to the relief of the rest of the guys. They all glanced up at the clock, and saw that it was nearly 10. It had been a long day, and they were pretty wiped. "How about a beer and a burger?" he asked. Ty groaned, and Angelo shook his head. "I'm buying..."

"I'm gonna take a pass," Ty yawned. "I think I'll just slap a sandwich together and call it a night."

"I'm with Ty," Angelo agreed. "But I'll hold you to buying next time—God knows that doesn't happen very often."

"I'm out, too," Tommy said. "Got me a date." All heads turned to him as a smirk spread across his face.

"Who the hell would go out with you?" Bo teased. "Wait...let me guess...you called an escort service."

"Or maybe she's blind," Ty tossed in, raising his palm and smacking Bo with a high-five.

Tommy slowly and deliberately raised his middle finger as he covered the keyboard and grabbed his coat. "She's someone I knew from back in the day," he said, ignoring Bo's double middle fingers. "We went to high school together. It's no big thing."

"Anyone agreeing to go out with you is a big thing, my scrawny friend," Bo chuckled. "Has anyone checked the forecast lately? Bet it's gettin' mighty cold in hell."

"Look who's talking, Collins," Tommy teased back. "When's the last time you even really looked at a woman, much less had a date?"

"Oh, I look plenty, believe me," he smiled. "Just can't seem to find one worthy of everything I've got to offer." He turned to Dylan. "I'll take you up on that burger and beer, Strummer Boy," he smiled, patting his stomach. "Can't remember the last time I had a decent meal."

Ty jumped in. "You are wasting away to nothing, C-man," he smiled. "Thank God the drum kit's in the back—I'm tired of looking at your ass crack all the time. You seriously need to get yourself some new pants, my friend."

"You just keep your eyes off my fine ass," Bo grinned. "You know how I hate clothes shopping."

They finished packing up their things, and Dylan and Bo walked just down the street to The Two Bells Tavern. They'd become regulars over the past few weeks, so were greeted warmly and with minimal pomp and circumstance. They signed a few autographs for some of the patrons who sat at the bar, but since it was fairly late on a Monday night, the place wasn't very crowded. Tammy, one of their regular waitresses, arrived within seconds with a pitcher of Rainer.

"How's that new album coming along, boys?" she asked, her eyes fixed on Dylan.

Bo pulled her into his lap and gave her a friendly squeeze. "Now Tammy," he said, "you know the man's engaged. You can't keep lookin' at him like he's a midnight snack."

Tammy had Bo Collins's number on their very first visit. It was impossible not to notice when Dylan Miller walked into a room—the man was so hot she'd nearly passed out the first time he sat down at a table in her station. All the other girls were incredibly jealous that she got to wait on him, rushing over to fill his water glass whenever they got the chance and finding countless excuses to walk by his table.

He was the whole package—not only was he kind and gracious, signing autographs and taking photos with all of them; his half smile next to a dozen faces sporting shit-eating grins; but he was genuinely nice, and a great tipper. She knew he was engaged; hell, the whole world knew that; but she was a warm-blooded woman, and she couldn't help but feel the flutter of desire in her belly when he was around.

Bo Collins was a character, however; a shameless flirt who made you feel like you were a princess just by smiling at you. She'd come to really like them both—they were so much more down-to-earth than a lot of the other musicians that stopped in for beers or food on their way out from the studio down the street.

"Midnight or any other time of day," she teased back, "unless maybe you're available?" She slid off his lap and handed them menus. "The usual?" she asked, "or you want to try something new tonight?" she wiggled her eyebrows at Bo and smiled. They'd done this dance before, and she'd matched him flirt for flirt.

"I'm always up for something new, sugar," he teased, "but it's been a long hard day." He looked at Dylan. "This man's a task master, I tell you, and I barely have enough strength left in my body to lift my beer." Bo picked up his glass and took a long frosty swallow. "Guess I'll be going with the usual tonight."

Dylan agreed, and Tammy took their menus, heading back toward the kitchen, which she was sure would stay open just a bit later for their celebrity guests.

"She's pretty cute," Dylan said as Tammy tossed one more smile over her shoulder before disappearing into the kitchen.

"Who, Tammy?"

"Yes, Tammy," he said.

"I guess."

"Why don't you ask her out?" Dylan suggested.

"Why don't you mind your own damn business?" Bo snapped back. He picked up the beer menu and started leafing through it aimlessly, feeling Dylan's stare boring into his skull. Finally, he looked up.

"What?" Bo asked, taking in Dylan's smirk.

"I swear," Dylan said, shaking his head. "You could flirt with a stone wall and make it blush, but you never pursue a thing. You know... if there's one thing I've learned over this past year, it's that life is better when you have someone to share it with, and that it's too damn short to keep everyone at arm's length. Don't you think it's about time you put yourself back on the market? It's been almost three years, mate."

Bo took another swig and forced a twisted smile. "That's two things," he said. "I should call goddamn CNN and tell them that you had two epiphanies in the same year. No one will believe it." Dylan Miller was probably the only person in the world outside of his immediate family who would willingly bring up the subject of his second divorce. Dylan wasn't the only one with trust issues when it came to women; Bo had sworn off relationships forever after Shannon screwed him over six ways from Sunday. He'd gotten over it, but it was just easier if no one knew that. The last thing he needed was a bunch of would-be matchmakers trying to fix him up, or even worse, having to admit the truth that he'd only recently admitted to himself. "Hell, I'm just waitin' for the right one, brother," he finally answered. "They don't come around too often, as you well know. It'll happen when it happens, and we'll leave it at that."

"OK, we'll leave it for now," Dylan said. He knew better than to push Bo Collins on the subject of women, but he had some suspicions that he hoped to confirm as he continued. "Speaking of that, though, Jessa's busting my ass about seating charts for the wedding dinner. She's also got to figure out flights, cars to collect everyone to get them to the airports; and with people coming from all over the globe, she's itching to work on the logistics."

"Yeah, that sounds like Jessa. That girl needs to learn how to chill once in a while. You gonna tell me where we're even going?" Bo asked. "You know I'm not gonna spill it to anyone."

"Of course I know that," Dylan replied. "We just decided that it'd be easier if no one knew. That way, nobody has to lie or try to come up with a story when the media comes calling. Plus, we want it to be a surprise for everyone."

Bo nodded. "Yeah, I guess. Just would help me decide what to pack, you know?"

"Jessa's calling it 'resort casual,'" Dylan said. "Warm weather and water. That's all we're telling anyone."

"That's easy enough," Bo agreed. "What about the seating arrangements? I'm not surprised that Jessa's flipping about the details."

"I just need to know if you're planning to bring a date so she can figure out the tables," Dylan said. "Tommy's bringing his new girl, I guess, so if you were bringing someone, we could put them at the same table. Do you have anyone in mind? Looked like you and Joi were doing a happy dance when you saw each other at the engagement party."

"Nah, we're just friends." Bo sat back in his chair and took a deep breath before answering. "I got someone on my mind all the time," he admitted, "but she isn't an option, so I'll just fly solo."

Dylan contemplated that for a minute, his head cocked. He and Bo were as close as brothers, but he'd never mentioned having anyone "on his mind" at all, much less all the time. He couldn't help but wonder why.

"Care to elaborate?" Dylan finally asked.

"Nope," Bo said simply as Tammy reappeared and placed a steaming bowl of garlicky cheese and artichoke dip on the table.

"Well, all right then," Dylan said, grabbing a hunk of the freshly baked bread and scooping up a generous portion. "I guess that'll make all four of you flying solo. It'll keep the numbers even, anyway. Jessa should be thrilled about that."

Dylan popped the bread in his mouth and watched his friend for a reaction. He got it in spades. Bo's ears pricked up, and his eyes widened before narrowing down to slits. "Care to elaborate?" he mimicked, a little too anxiously.

"Nope," Dylan replied with a sly smile, sitting back in his own seat and taking a swig of the frosty brew. God, he loved the Pacific Northwest, no one did beer quite like they did.

"Now come on, Miller," Bo said, leaning forward. "You can't lead off with that and not finish the tale. What four of us?"

Dylan leaned in. Tia hadn't told him not to tell Bo, and he'd certainly figure it out eventually, so he assumed it didn't matter if Bo heard it from him. "The whole wedding party," he said simply.

Bo cocked his head. "Lexi's not bringing her fiancé?"

Dylan shook his head. "Lexi no longer has a fiancé," he said, dunking another hunk of bread and watching Bo's eyes widen.

"You want to say that again?" Bo asked, his voice cracking uncharacteristically.

"You heard me." It was really hard for him to keep a straight face when Bo was trying so unsuccessfully not to jump out of his skin.

"I think you said that Lexi no longer has a fiancé," he said, "but I'm not sure I'm following. What happened?"

"That call I took earlier? The one you guys gave me such a hard time for taking? Tia was filling me in on the details. Lexi found out that the bastard was sleeping with someone else, and she's called the whole thing off."

Dylan felt truly bad for Lexi; she was a good person, and he hated seeing anyone played that way. Bo, however, was waging a sudden battle with his feelings, and Dylan sat back, watching a whole range of emotions playing over his features. From where Dylan was sitting, Bo was putting an awful lot of thought into what he'd just been told.

"He cheated on her?" Bo asked, shaking his head. "On Lexi? How could anyone do that? What did Tia say? How did she find out?"

"The way I understand it, the girls were at the Intercontinental a few nights ago trying on dresses for the wedding." He paused, bowing his head. "Wow, it's probably going to be rough on her being in her best friend's wedding when hers just got cancelled."

Bo held his face with the tips of his fingers and bowed his head. "I can't even imagine," he said quietly.

"No doubt." They were silent for a moment before Bo motioned for him to continue. "So anyway, they were just coming out of the hotel when Lexi saw Ryan's car pulling up to the valet at the banquet entrance—he's got a sweet Mustang with a custom paint job, so it wasn't hard to spot. The way Tia described it he climbed out of the car and into the arms of another woman. He was supposed to be in New York on some big project he was doing for work; Lexi even helped him pack his bloody suitcase the night before, I guess, and then she watched him pull it out of the boot and hand it to the valet."

"Son of a bitch," Bo growled under his breath as his hands balled up into fists.

"Lexi immediately called him and stood there watching while he lied to her—he told her he was in The Big Apple, and that he might have to stay an extra night to get the job done." Dylan pressed lips together. "You'll appreciate this, though...she's one tough chick. After she watched them walk into the hotel together, she took her keys and added some of her own "custom touches" to his celebrity paint job. Then, on Monday, she purged both their apartments while he was at work. She followed him to some gym where he met the other woman, dumped all his shit in the boot of his car, hung her engagement ring on the keychain that held her set of keys to his car and apartment, and left them in the ignition.

"She waited for him to show up at the country club where they both belong and they had it out. Needless to say, she broke it off and says she's never going back. Knowing Lexi, I believe her. I can't see her taking back a guy who would do that to her."

"No way," Bo whispered, and Dylan had a hard time interpreting whether he was agreeing with the statement or contemplating something else entirely.

"So, I guess the whole wedding party will be sans dates," Dylan said. "Tia told me that Lexi has sworn off men forever. Max is hoping to hook up at the wedding, and I can't remember the last time Jessa had a serious relationship."

"Forever, huh?" Bo asked absent-mindedly as Dylan took a swig and watched the myriad of emotions once again play over Bo's face.

Dylan sat back and let Bo absorb it all. The suspicion he'd planned to confirm was that Bo had a real thing for Lexi—not just the innocent flirtation that he made it out to be. He didn't have any solid evidence of the crush; just a gut feeling, mostly. Tia had told him that Lexi's fiancé was jealous of the way she and Bo had greeted each other the night they appeared together on *After Dark*, but Bo had known from the beginning that Lexi was engaged, and he too classy a person to tread on someone else's territory.

"So she says," Dylan smirked, "but who knows? Maybe the right one just hasn't come along yet."

Tammy appeared with their burgers and looked at Dylan with a question on her face when she took in Bo's stunned expression. Dylan nodded her off, and she slipped away without saying a word. He took a bite and chewed slowly, watching Bo's eyebrows do a dance as he processed everything. Finally, he leaned his elbows on the table and exhaled a long breath.

"So tell me," Dylan said sardonically, "this woman who's 'been on your mind all the time...'"

Bo snapped upright. "Damn it, Strummer Boy," he said, obviously flustered. "This is like a punch in the fuckin' head." He looked at Dylan wide-eyed. "How do you do it, man?"

"Do what?" Dylan asked innocently, shrugging and turning up his palms.

Bo slumped his shoulders and rested his chin on his fist. "See right fuckin' through me, man," he said simply.

Dylan leaned toward him and put a hand on his shoulder. "She's the one, isn't she?" he asked. He didn't need to elaborate any further for Bo to understand what he was asking.

"Hell, it's been her since I met her," Bo admitted quietly, as much to himself as to Dylan. In the back of his mind he'd known it all along, really, but he'd managed to push it back for the most part, especially in light of the fact that she was an engaged woman. The first night he saw her, standing there with that doe-like look on her face backstage in Chicago---hell, had it really been almost a year ago?—he'd been flooded with a feeling that he hadn't experienced in a long time. She lit up the room every time she walked into it, and had started more than a few fires in his dreams over the past nine months.

That memory was crystal clear, probably because he'd gone over it in his mind at least a thousand times since that day. He'd just walked into the common room; one of his 'things' was that he was always the last one to leave the stage, waving to fans and tossing drumsticks to random people in the audience. When he walked in, he nearly ran over Dylan and Tia engaged in a smokin' hot PDA. He made some comment about how hot their exchange was and turned his gaze away from the spectacle, which then fell on Lexi. She was a bundle of nervous excitement, and he made some sort of off-hand comment about her being his birthday present.

Dylan and Tia were wrapped up in each other, so he'd made it his personal mission to make sure Lexi was looked after. She'd started out with that doe-eyed look he often saw in the eyes of their fans, but it didn't take her long to jump into the game. They'd started flirting almost immediately, and she matched him dig for dig—which was no easy task. He was working out how he'd ask her for a date, but at some point in the evening she'd dug in her purse for a lipstick or something and pulled out her engagement ring. Bo had no idea why she hadn't been wearing it initially, but the moment he watched her slip it onto her finger, he felt true disappointment. They'd kept up the flirting—in fact, nearly everyone rolled their eyes at the two of them every time they were together during Lexi's visit to Europe—but he put on the brakes damn quickly and tried to put her out of his mind. Fat fucking chance.

He'd thought of her so often that he'd made up some sort of lame excuse that brought him to Chicago in the fall just so he could see her again. The hope was that he'd discover that what they had was nothing more than a friendship, and that he'd be able to reclaim his sleeping hours. Unfortunately, it hadn't had the desired effect. In fact, the moment she walked into the restaurant with Tia, his stomach had started rolling and he found it hard to breathe. And for the next several nights, he'd gotten no sleep at all.

He finally admitted it to himself the night of the *After Dark* fiasco in California, when she innocently cuddled up next to him on the little loveseat in the hotel room and pulled his arm around her. He had wondered later if she would still have sat so close to him if she had even an inkling of how badly he'd wanted to ravage her right there on the little couch. No matter how hard he tried to concentrate on the show, his eyes kept drifting to the way her breasts pushed together as she rested against him and the heat that drifted off her body, consuming him with her intoxicating scent. It affected him to the point that he'd had to pull a pillow into his lap to hide the blatantly obvious tool of his wanton lust, a scenario he'd only recently remembered and still beat himself up over. He'd made a complete ass of himself, and aside from an awkward greeting at the engagement party, they hadn't spoken since. He wondered if she'd ever want to speak to him again.

"I think I knew," Dylan said softly, "but I wasn't sure if you really did. This sure puts a whole different spin on things, doesn't it?"

"Does it?" Bo asked, taking an angry bite out of his burger and giving it a more than thorough chewing. "How so?" he asked around the mouthful. He swallowed, and poured himself a second mug of Rainer. "We're friends, D, and she trusts me completely as a friend," he said even as he wondered if it were still true. "She sees me as flirty ole' Bo; life of the party. Not as a potential boyfriend. She's probably really busted up over the whole situation, and knowing her, she's not going to be willing to jump into another relationship any time soon. Especially not with someone like me…"

"Someone like you?" Dylan pressed. "What the hell is that supposed to mean?" He tucked a strand of hair behind his ear and leaned toward Bo. "At the risk of sounding like a bloody woman, I can tell you that you are one of the most honest and decent people I know, and you know I wouldn't bullshit about something like that. Lexi sees *you,* my friend," Dylan said, "and she of all people knows you're the real deal. I'm not saying you should ask her to marry you tomorrow or anything…I'm just saying that if you were looking for a chance, it seems you might get one. Of course it's all fresh right now, the whole break-up thing, but in the future, who knows? If you really want something to happen…"

"The life we live isn't conducive to lasting relationships, Miller…" He stopped. They'd had this conversation at least a thousand times over the years, but things had certainly changed for Dylan over the past nine months. He believed that he and Tia would make it, and Bo was sure they would, too. They had something incredibly special, and it was obvious to him, as someone who'd known Dylan for a very long time, that he'd found the right person to spend his life with. Could he dare to hope for the same kind of happiness? He spoke again as Dylan raised his eyebrows at him, waiting for him to figure it out for himself.

"Don't even say it, man," Bo warned, taking another bite of the burger and chewing contemplatively.

Dylan shrugged. "I wasn't going to say a word. You'll figure out what's best for you." He bit off a chunk of his own burger and let Bo roll things around his brain for a minute. "Oh, bloody hell—I have to say it," he continued. "A semi-wise man once told Tia, when she was feeling like a relationship between a rock star and an average person couldn't work, that it was pointless wasting the time you did have worrying about time you might not get later, or something to that effect. Those words helped her put things into perspective, and helped get us through what might have been our last night together."

Bo smiled wanly and shook his head. "I said that?"

"You did."

"Ah, shit, man, this is fucked up."

"Nothing fucked up about it, mate. You think about it for a bit, work on getting over your commitment issues, and follow your heart. I'll be rooting for you, either way."

"I don't have commitment issues," Bo said, but there was no force behind his words. Dylan just looked at him hard, his head tilted to the side, until Bo surrendered. "Maybe a little. But there's reason behind it. Two ex-wives and a half dozen ex-girlfriends..." He shook his head.

"Bloody hell, Bo, are you still worrying over the ex-wives? You were nineteen for the first one, and the second one was a money grubbing whore...neither was your fault. God, I'd like to think we've grown a little bit over the last decade, I can tell you that. You can't think that because those relationships didn't work out that nothing will."

"Damn. I don't even know what to think about the whole thing right now. But I think it's pretty safe to say that I won't be sleeping much tonight." He took another pull of his beer and bowed his head. "I really want her to be OK."

"She's a strong woman," Dylan stated. "It sucks, but if there's anyone who can bounce back, it'll be her."

Bo smiled. "Now that, I know," he agreed, raising his glass for a toast. "Listen, Dyl," he added, "I don't need to ask you to be on the down-low about this, do I? I wouldn't want her getting scared off because she heard I was something different than what she thought before I get a chance to assess the situation…"

Dylan smirked, and raised one eyebrow. "So it comes full circle, does it? Lexi had to bear the burden of hiding my and Tia's relationship for months, and now you want me to hide from Tia that you've got the hots for her best friend?" Bo looked perplexed for a moment, but Dylan jumped back in. "Don't worry; I'm just messing with you, BoBo. It's not any of my business, and it isn't Tia's either. You don't need to worry about me mentioning a word. I just find the whole thing a little ironic, is all."

"Yeah. Here's to fucking irony," Bo smirked, topping off their glasses with the last of the beer.

Chapter 36

He wanted to call her. More than anything, he wanted to tell her that he was sorry and that he was her friend. He'd gone so far as to get her number from Dylan; something he'd not trusted himself to have before. Oh, who the hell was he kidding? What he really wanted to do was to hear her voice, to tell her he was sorry about the way things had gone down between them since that damn television appearance, and find out if she'd see him. But every time he took the crumpled piece of paper out of his wallet and started punching in the numbers, his mind went blank and his fingers started shaking.

He'd screwed this up in more ways than one. First, the whole fiasco at the hotel that had never been dealt with loomed over him—she'd either left thinking he wanted nothing to do with her, or she noticed his 'indiscretion' and had gone running for the hills. Then he had his accident and was out of everything for weeks; and it was even longer before he finally remembered the reason why he felt sad and guilty every time he watched the recording of the damn show.

Then another thought crept in...what if that was part of the reason her fiancé strayed? Thoughts of the leopard print outfit jumped back into his mind. The dude could had been pissed— and after watching back the tape of the show, and the way the mic picked up his surprised and excited greeting, he might've been too if it was his fiancé leaping into another man's arms on national television.

Dylan kept his word though, and as the days passed, he never asked if he'd gotten around to calling Lexi. He also wasn't saying much about how things were going with her, except to say that she was still in the dumps, but moving forward. At this point Bo had no idea if she'd even take his call; and he had absolutely no clue about what he would say; *'So hey, sorry I had such a boner for you—want to get some dinner?'* so he put it off and put it off and before he knew it weeks had gone by and the guys were taking a few days off to let the producers do some mixing while they took a little break from recording. Dylan was meeting Tia in Colorado to finally take her to the house in which she'd soon live, Tommy was taking his new girlfriend to Disney World, of all places, Ty was going to visit his parents in Philly, and Angelo was going to some meditation retreat in Sedona to "get his chakras in balance." Bo hadn't really made any plans—he'd spent the last three weeks thinking about Lexi and checking the weather in Chicago. It sucked, as it usually did in March.

"You should come with me, man," Angelo said as they were checking out of their hotel. "I've never seen you so out of balance, bro. Seriously, you sit in one of those vortexes and you can just feel the positive energy of the planet coursing through your veins. They do Reiki, too—it'll heal up any residuals left over from the accident."

Bo tried to picture himself sitting in a vortex with his legs crossed and palms up chanting a mantra, and laughed out loud. "I don't need a bunch of hippies trying to balance me. I'm pretty sure it's an impossible feat, anyway. I'm going to be in charge of my own meditation, thanks."

"Suit yourself, but I think you'd get a lot out of it."

What Bo really needed was some absolute solitude, so he decided to take his good friend Joi—one in a long line of exes but on a short list of those he still considered a friend—up on the offer she'd made him at the engagement party. She wintered somewhere warm; The Florida Keys, if he remembered correctly; and her place in Puget Sound on Orcas Island was secluded, quiet, and vacant. Maybe he could actually sit down and think some things through.

He said goodbye to the guys on Friday afternoon and headed north. Three hours later, he turned down the dead end street and snaked his SUV down the drive. Already he could see that the house had spectacular views of the Sound, and it was nestled among plentiful trees and foliage. An older gentleman was in the driveway, waving him into the garage.

"I'm George," he said, extending his hand once Bo hopped out of the car. "Folks around here call me Big G. Welcome to the island—first time?"

"Bo, and yes, it is. Beautiful place."

"Indeed. I'm the caretaker here. I've stocked the kitchen with some staples; eggs, milk, cheese, pop...things like that. There are some steaks in there too; enough to last you a couple days, at least. The nearest grocery store is just a couple miles away..."

"Yeah, I passed it on the way in."

"Oh good. Joi asked me to give you a little tour; show you where everything's at."

Bo followed him into the house, feeling more relaxed already. The smell of the air was different here; heavy, cool, and tinged with the salt spray that came off Puget Sound. "These here are the controls for the hot tub," George pointed out, "and the steps off the big deck lead right down to the beach. Not too many folks around here this time of year, so you'll pretty much have it to yourself, I imagine. There are a couple kayaks in the garage, and the keys to the boat shed are in the drawer here. There's a little private sitting area down there with a fire pit; wood's in the shed; and fishing gear too, if you're so inclined." Bo jotted a few notes, so he could keep everything straight. "Oh," he added, reaching into his pocket, "here are the keys to the house. I'll just let you get comfortable, but my number is on the fridge if you need it. Don't hesitate to call if you have any questions about anything here or island related. I've lived on this little slice of heaven for going on 25 years now, so I can give you insider information about pretty much anything."

"Thanks, I appreciate the welcome and the tour. I'm sure I'll be fine."

As soon as George's Buick rolled out of the driveway, Bo slipped on his jacket and walked down to the beach. It was just a small bit of sand, really, and aside from a scarcely-used path he could see in the trees behind him, he didn't see any other way to get to it. The solitude he had hoped for surrounded him like a blanket, and he kicked off his shoes, letting the icy water rush up to greet his feet as he walked along the little stretch of shoreline. Out in the distance he could see several rocky outcrops and thought that later on he might squeeze his ass into a kayak and check them out. It was just the start of orca season, and he hoped he might get lucky enough to catch a glimpse of them.

For tonight, though, he was going to fire up the grill, sear a steak to perfection, and watch the sunset from the expansive deck that overlooked the calm water. Then maybe a soak in the hot tub, a movie, and a good night's sleep. He'd start on figuring things out tomorrow.

✳✳✳✳✳

"Thanks again for barging in on me, and for spending the night; I'm sorry I was such a bitch when you first got here, but I really do feel better."

"Already forgotten, and you're welcome." Tia pulled Lexi into a tight hug. "I've always got your back, right? Don't hesitate to call if you need me, OK?"

"You've already done so much. Really, Tia, I was seriously dreading making all those phone calls—nothing says 'loser' more than having to cancel your wedding over and over again."

"I hate that I had to repay that debt, but I'm glad that you don't have to face it." She remembered, a lifetime ago, hearing the soft voices of Lexi and her mom on their separate phones explaining time after time that the groom had passed away suddenly and that they had to cancel the wedding. She couldn't imagine leaving Lexi to do it on her own.

"You'll be back in a week, right?"

"Yes, but like I said, call me if you need to talk, or if you need anything."

"I will. You better send pictures—I want to hear every detail. I'm really happy for you, you know, but I do hate the fact that you're going to be moving so far away." She knew Tia was both apprehensive and excited—she was going to see her new house for the first time, and Dylan was meeting her there. Part of her, a part she didn't like very much, resented the fact that Tia was skipping off to Colorado when she needed her best friend the most. She'd never left Tia's side after Nick died, and even canceled a trip to the Caymans to take care of her. Damn it, she shouldn't feel this way; she knew that the whole band was taking a week off and that Dylan couldn't just take a break whenever he wanted to; she knew that it was planned long before the whole catastrophe with Ryan. Lexi suddenly feared that she would have nothing once Tia moved away permanently; no best friend, no fiancé, and, the way things were going at work, maybe no job. Bryce, her boss, was none too happy about the blowup in the kitchen and her outburst at Candy. Then she'd taken the rest of the week off without officially informing him. She dreaded going back, and was far from feeling ready to do so. "Oh God, I don't know what to do next," she whispered.

Tia was at her side in an instant. "What you do is get back to work, stay busy, and show the world that you aren't so easily broken. Call some people— go out...go to Paddy's. You know everyone there, and they certainly know how to have a good time."

"I really don't feel like being social right now; I just need a break."

"I've got an idea...why don't you call Bo? He's a champion at making people feel good. He always brings a smile to your face, that's for sure."

"Oh, right. Like he wants to listen to me bitch about my shitty life." *Or like he'd even want to talk to me at all,* she added in her mind.

"Oh honey, you don't have a shitty life; you had a shitty boyfriend. Believe me, I know that it feels like he was your whole life; like every part of you was tangled up in him; but once you unravel all that, you'll see that who you are hasn't really changed." She put her arms around Lexi's shoulders and gave her a squeeze. "I also know that there are good guys out there; guys who are actually worthy of you; and when you find one, you'll see that all this happened for a reason."

Lexi dropped her head. The rational side of her knew that it was true—Tia had lost the love of her life and still managed to find Dylan—but the emotional side of her wasn't ready to even think about the possibility of another relationship and the chance that she'd be hurt again. "Whatever. I can't even think about that right now."

"I know," Tia answered quickly, glancing at her watch. She reached into her purse and pulled out a notepad. "I'm going to leave you with his number anyway, just in case," she said, scribbling on a fresh page. "I know I don't have to tell you that this isn't public, so I'd suggest you tuck it away somewhere, just to be on the safe side. And you know I'm a phone call away, too." She took a long look at Lexi's drawn face. "Do I have to worry about you?" she asked. "Maybe you should call your mom; see if she can come stay with you for a while."

"That's the last thing I need. She'd probably tell me to forgive the bastard and try to make it work. You know she forgave my dad when she found out he was sleeping with one of his nurses. I'll pass on that option."

"Just promise me you're not going to sit here for the next week and mope around. I know it sucks, but dwelling on it doesn't make it any better. I've always been jealous of how strong you are, you know. You can't let this break you." She glanced at her watch again. "Listen, honey, I'm so sorry, but I've really got to go. I have a plane to catch, and I still have to stop by my place to pick up a few things..." She pulled Lexi into a hug as she headed for the door. "Promise me," she said again, holding out her pinkie.

Lexi groaned, but linked her little finger around Tia's and gave it a limp shake. "Have fun."

"I'll call you."

"OK," she said as she closed the door and the emptiness enveloped her.

Going back to work was no piece of cake. She held her head high, put on her best stoic face, and did her best to shrug off all the condolences and faces that held pity, but she was having a hard time concentrating, especially when her boss chewed her out for her behavior of the previous week.

"I understand that you had a rough time," Bryce said, "but you need to keep your head in the game when you're at work. I won't have you berating your coworkers; especially in hearing range of clients. You owe Candy an apology, and I expect we won't have any more similar outbursts."

She didn't think she owed Candy anything—Bryce was only bothered because he was currently sleeping with the office slut— God, did the cheating never end? He was a married man. Her plan was to avoid Candy completely, but there she was, hovering outside her office when she went back after her ass chewing.

"Hey, Lex," she said. "I'm really sorry about what happened last week...I had no idea. Major bummer."

Ya think? Lexi thought, but she forced a thin smile. "I'm sorry, too," she said, for the sake of office peace. "I overreacted."

Candy seemed unphased, and Lexi was immediately suspicious. "No problem," she said brightly. "I was thinking, since you've got some free time now, that you'd come to this month's progressive dinner. The theme is French cuisine, and we're having it at Denise's on Thursday. Seven o'clock. You don't have to bring anything for your first time," she added quickly, "just show up and have fun."

What was her deal? Lexi thought. No way Candy really wanted to hang out with her; there was always an ulterior motive. "I don't think so," she answered. "I'm really not into it. But thanks anyway."

"Oh, come on, it'll be fun! You need to get back out there; trust me, I know." She put her hand on Lexi's in a fake show of sympathy. "You can bring Tia too, if you want, we'd love to have her!"

So that was it. She was still trying to find a way to get to InHap. "Tia's out of town."

"Oh, that's too bad. Will she be back next week? We could postpone it."

Lexi groaned inwardly and held her breath for a ten-count. "Look, Candy, I'm just going to say it. Again. It's really nothing personal, but you and I don't really have anything in common. We've worked together for three years, and we've never once done anything socially together besides office parties. Tia barely knows you at all, and she's got to be careful about going out in public these days. You wouldn't believe how many people suddenly want to be her friend just so they can get close to the band. It's pathetic, really." A small part of her hoped Candy would get the hint, but Lexi wasn't at all surprised when she didn't even bat an eyelash.

"Oh, I believe it," she said, eyes wide. "She's such a sweet person, though...I've always liked her. I can't believe we didn't think to invite you guys before; we've talked about it a lot."

I just bet, Lexi thought. "I think I can speak for Tia when I say she wouldn't be able to make it. She's got a lot to do with planning the wedding, and packing up stuff to move out to the new house in Colorado."

"Oh my gosh, the wedding!" Candy exclaimed as if it were the first time she'd considered it. Lexi knew better, though, and her scheme was coming into focus. "Obviously they had planned on you bringing a guest, and now Brian won't be going with you." Lexi didn't bother to correct the name—she saw the question coming, and couldn't believe she'd have the gall to even ask. "I'd do anything to go to that party," she said wistfully. "I'd be a really fun date." She winked and turned the corner of her mouth up in a sly smile.

Lexi tried to tighten her tenuous grip on her self-control, but it was a lost cause. She balled her hands into fists and kept her voice low, although her tone was menacing. "Oh my God, you just don't quit, do you?" She clenched her teeth and fought to keep from yelling. "You are not my friend, Candy. You've made it a point to exclude me from your little clique; not that I ever wanted to be a part of it; so you can just stop pretending right now, OK? I'm not going to introduce you to Dylan or any of the other guys in the band, I'm not going to get you tickets, and I'm sure as hell not getting you into the wedding. Period. End of of story. So just go back to looking down your nose at me and talking about me behind my back and quit trying to worm your way into my life just so you can try to get one of the guys from InHap into your bed. Not. Going. To. Happen."

Candy's face reddened with fury and her eyes narrowed to slits. "You are such a bitch," she spat. "You walk around like you're big shit while you ride on your friend's coattails. You're nothing, Lexi. No wonder Brian cheated on you—who could stand to be around you and your newly-inflated ego? You deserved it, you condescending fame whore."

"Ooh, a four syllable word," she yelled as Candy stalked out of her office into the lobby. "That's a stretch for you, Candy. Better to be a whore for fame than the kind you are—everyone knows you're fucking Bryce, so you'd best be careful about the accusations you toss around."

Candy's face split into an evil grin and she slowly and deliberately raised her middle finger. "Fuck you, Lexi," she snarled. Then she turned and marched toward the boss's office, just as his wife walked out. She collided with Candy and grabbed her arms before she could make a getaway.

Time seemed to stop, or at least go into some sort of slow motion phase that Lexi couldn't quite make sense of. Bryce burst into the lobby, and Lexi saw the warning he shot at Candy with his eyes over his wife's shoulder.

"Are you sleeping with my husband?" her voice was low and level, but the tone was downright menacing. Candy squirmed in

Cecile's firm grip, and Bryce put his arm around his wife, trying to pull her back into his office. Cecile shrugged him off and turned to him without loosening her hold. "Get your filthy hands off me, Bryce, and tell me right now. Is this your mistress?"

"Don't be ridiculous, Cecile. Lexi is pissed off at the whole world right now, aren't you, Lexi?" He shot her a similar warning as he tried to take Cecile's hands off an obviously pained Candy. "Her fiancé cheated on her, so now she thinks all men are snakes, that's all. She's projecting…"

"Shut the hell up, Bryce, and tell me the truth for once in your pathetic life." She turned to Lexi. "Is my husband a snake?"

Lexi nodded. "I'm afraid so."

Cecile's flaming eyes turned immediately to her husband's and then to Candy. All around the office doors started opening and people either stepped out to watch the spectacle or peered through cracks so as not to get hit with any of the backlash. Bryce threw Lexi a hard look and tried to cover his tracks by berating her.

"We cannot have this sort of bullshit happening in our office!" he bellowed. "You were supposed to apologize to your coworker for your unacceptable behavior, not start some ludicrous office gossip!" He turned back to his wife and his mistress. Candy was visibly shaking now, whether from the physical pain of Cecile's vice-like grip or the emotional pain of being busted, and the black streaks of tears and mascara that were running down her face were dripping onto her too-small and too-low-cut perky cream colored sweater. Bryce once again tried to separate the two women. "Come on, Cecile, darling," he whined, "This is nothing but a pack of lies and misconceptions invented by a depressed woman. I love you, and would never be unfaithful. Come in and talk to me."

"He's lying," Lexi said quietly. As much as she hated being the one to give Cecile the news, no one deserved to be treated that way. And as much as she hated that Ryan cheated on her, knowing was better than playing the clueless fool.

"I will deal with you later," Bryce growled, his face reddening and his eyes narrowing to slits. "Not one more word. It ends here, Lexi."

Lexi had done some research during her sabbatical, and knew that the stages of grief after a break-up were similar to those that followed a death. She actually felt herself cross the plane from sadness to anger, and it roared through her blood like a beast. She stepped out of her doorway and into the lobby, and closed the distance between her and the lying piece of crap that was her boss. "Does it?" Does it really? What ends here, exactly, Bryce? Candy harassing me to try and get an invitation to my friend's wedding so she can attempt to get one of the guys from InHap into her bed?" His eyes widened like he'd been slapped. "Oh yeah, that's right. You think you're the only one? She tells everyone she has a sex addiction, but she has a power addiction, too—you think she sleeps with you because you're an Adonis? Ha!"

"You are out of line Miss Summers, and are treading on very thin ice."

Lexi threw her head back and laughed. "Am I? Maybe you should check the ground you're standing on, Bryce, because I think a sinkhole is about to open up under you." She looked at Cecile with sympathy in her eyes, but turned daggers back on her boss. "How about the lies and manipulation? Maybe *they* can end here, *Mr. Southerton*. Oh, come on, Bryce," she hissed, "You're going to sit there and defend an underproductive para against one of your attorneys because she gives good head?" She turned to Cecile. "I'm really sorry, Cecile. I've very recently been on the receiving end of that kind of news too, and I know it's not pretty. I hate that you had to find out like this, and hate even more that I had to be the one to break it to you, but I'm sure as hell not going to cover for his cheating ass."

"I figured as much," Cecile said, releasing her grip on Candy, who immediately made a dash for the restroom.

"Get out," Bryce growled, turning his beet red face to Lexi. "I've tried to be patient with you while you went through your little celebrity encounter and your break-up, but this is beyond inappropriate, and I won't tolerate it."

"Are you firing me, Bryce?" She was hepped up and ready for a fight—she felt alive again for the first time in weeks.

"Yes, Lexi, I guess I am."

"Fine. Screw you, Bryce. I hope your wife dumps your worthless ass."

"You know what? *You* get out," Cecile fired back at her husband. "You might want to remember that my father owns this building, and I guarantee you a quick eviction notice." Bryce tried to put his arm around her, and she efficiently stepped out his reach and thrust her finger at his chest. "You are finished," she hissed. "Everything you have is because of my family, and it's gone, Bryce; all of it."

"Cecile, please. Just talk to me. We can work this out."

"All of it," she said again, touching the tips of her fingers together in the air and then splaying them open in one quick motion. "Poof. Just like that." She grabbed her coat from the hook on the wall and walked out the door with her head held high.

Bryce's eyes swept around the room and took in the sea of faces that witnessed the scene. "Get back to work!" he bellowed, turning his stare on Lexi. "Except for you. You get the hell out of my sight!" He strutted back into his office and slammed the door.

Lexi spun on her heel and stormed into her office, dumping a case of copy paper on the floor and tossing her personal things into the box. Just for fun, she opened her filing cabinet and grabbed a huge handful of client files, turned them upside-down, and let the contents flutter to the floor. She knew it would be Candy's job to have to clean them up; if she even had a job anymore; and that with her piss-poor filing skills, it would probably take her days to get them all sorted out. She strolled out of her office with her back ramrod straight, accepted the praise or looks of pity from a few people that she'd likely never see again, and walked out the door.

Lexi hadn't taken two steps into the parking garage when the sleek red Jaguar pulled up and the tinted passenger window slid down. "Hop in," Cecile said. "I'd really like to have a chat."

Lexi leaned down and peered inside, the words, 'don't kill the messenger' rolling through her head. When she made eye contact, however, there was no threat in the woman's eyes. She didn't know Cecile well, but they'd attended their fair share of office parties together and she'd always been kind and easy enough to talk to. "I'm really sorry for you," Lexi said as she plopped her butt on the warm leather. "I just found out my fiancé was cheating too, and I'm having some trouble dealing with it— obviously. I swear I didn't know you were there—it's not my place to bring you that bit of news, and I'm really sorry. I guess I already said that, but I am."

"I've suspected it for quite some time now," she said, "but I couldn't bring myself to face it. Oh hell, I've known it all along. She's not the first." Lexi put her hand on Cecile's arm in a show of support. "I didn't want it to be true, but I had a feeling the bastard only wanted me for my family's money from the start. Don't apologize—I'd rather know than be in the dark. And you just saved me from a costly divorce. Now I'll make sure it's Bryce who pays." She rolled up the sleeve of her coat and glanced at her watch. "I know it's early, but can I buy you a drink? I sure could use one."

"Why the hell not?" Lexi said, tugging the seat belt and enjoying the throaty sound of luxury engineering as Cecile gunned the engine and headed for the exit.

*****

It had seemed like a good idea at the time, but by Tuesday, regret settled in like like a flood. She didn't feel bad about walking out—at least she could say she maintained her integrity—but she suddenly found herself with no fiancé, no job, and a best friend who'd be moving halfway across the country in just a few months. A best friend who was, unknowingly but at least partially, responsible for the mess her own life had become. Damn it. She'd never considered herself a jealous person; or a vindictive one; but the downward spiral had really started with the damn secret. Ryan lost his faith in her loyalty, lost his sense of self-worth in Dylan's shadow, and found solace with another woman. She'd foolishly thought that her life would get better after the secret was out—she'd certainly never anticipated the landslide that had effectively buried her entire future.

She went into the kitchen and took the paper out from the back of the silverware drawer. She stared at it for a long time, even picking up her phone twice and starting to punch in the number. Bo did have a way of making her feel good, but after the way they left things in California, there was a chance that she was the last person he wanted to hear from. Frustrated, she tossed the paper and her phone on the counter and went to lie down.

By Tuesday night though, she was getting sick of herself. There were only so many hours a person could sit and stew in self-pity, and she'd well exceeded that. So she'd lost her fiancé. And her job. And soon, she'd probably lose her best friend. Once Tia moved out west, things would change. They'd been inseparable since they were twelve, but soon there'd be a thousand miles between them, and Tia would forge a new life for herself. A damn good one, at that. She couldn't help but worry that, through no fault on either part, they'd slowly lose touch; which made the loneliness that pushed down on her even now feel like an ever-growing chasm.

What she really needed to do was to reinvent herself. She needed to start looking at the possibility that there might actually be a silver lining above the dark cloud that currently hung heavy over her life. She had been complaining about the weather in the Midwest for years; maybe it was time for a move. At least if she was in a different city, she wouldn't have to worry about running in to Ryan and his new freaking girlfriend. It was an exciting yet daunting prospect. She was still young, newly single, and she had enough in savings to keep her afloat for at least a year while she was settling into a new place and looking for a job. She pulled a road atlas out of the drawer in her home office and studied the US map. For the next hour, she crossed out states. Too cold, too hot, too crowded, too expensive, too rural...and her eyes kept falling back to the same place. Colorado. Damn it.

She needed some clarity—some perspective—to get her mind off her issues. Finally, after giving herself a huge pep talk, she punched in all eleven digits, and hoped that Bo wouldn't hang up on her.

*****

He felt so much better. In the four days he'd been on the island he hadn't had a single headache, his arm hadn't ached despite the vigorous workout he'd dealt himself on the kayak the past few days, and his tension had nearly melted away. The days were already starting to fall into a pattern; he woke up whenever he wanted, usually by 7:30, walked down to the beach to greet the day, and then hiked up the steep path that led to a crumbling roadway and a forest trail. It was a good couple miles round trip, and the exercise and fresh air were doing wonders for both his physical and emotional states. When he got back to the house he made himself a smoothie with tons of fruits and vegetables, a little bit of yogurt, some protein powder, and some chia seeds. He'd sit on the deck and watch the water for a while; letting his body process the nutrients, then he'd kayak out to one or two of the little outcrops that dotted the bay. It took him a while to get the rhythm right with the vessel; the first day he came back soaking wet from leaning too much with his body as he tried to steer the thing; but he was really getting the hang of it now. It was an incredible feeling, being so close to the surface of the water and skimming silently across its glassy surface. Twice he'd seen harbor seals almost close enough to touch, and he'd followed the flight of a bald eagle back to its enormous nest in a dense clump of trees just above a rugged shoreline. The place was rich with life, and it made him feel alive just being part of it.

Usually after his kayak trip he'd nap on the swing on the deck, then take a soak in the hot tub before showering and grilling up something for a late dinner. He was barely five minutes into his soak on Tuesday when he heard his phone ringing from inside the house. That was one thing he didn't miss when he was out in nature—he left the phone behind, and only checked for messages while his dinner was sizzling on the grill—he ignored it and sank deeper into the heat and pulsating water.

Not another five minutes passed, and he heard the drone of an engine, the slam of a car door, and then the front door creeping open.

"Bo, are you decent?" Joi's voice rang through the screen door.

Bo sat up, surprised. "I'm on the deck," he called back, standing up and reaching for the towel that hung over the back of one of the patio chairs.

Joi slid open the screen door and stepped out, looking him up and down. "Not only decent, but looking mighty good, my friend. You been working out?"

Bo ignored her question and asked his own as he rubbed the towel over his body. "What are you doing here, Joi? I mean, it's your place, and you have every right, but I thought..."

Joi collapsed into a chair and took a deep breath. "Ah, there was a fire. Electrical, they think, but I won't know for sure until they do their investigation. Talk about an interruption to my winter holiday."

"Holy shit," he said, wrapping himself in a robe to ward off the chill and taking the seat across from her. "No one was hurt, were they?"

"No, no," she said with a dismissive wave of her hand, "but I couldn't salvage anything. I had to come back and regroup—get some things and figure out where I'm hiding out for the rest of the winter. It's going to be a bitch trying to find a rental at this time of year, but my assistant is working on it. God, I could use a glass of wine. Will you join me?"

"Uh, sure." He took the couple minutes she was gone to recover. He'd been pretty much in isolation since he'd gotten here and aside from a quick call to his mother to tell her that he was doing just fine without her nursing him, he hadn't talked to another person in days. In fact, the only human voices he'd heard, aside from his own when he was talking to the seals and the little crabs he found on the beach—and they were damn good listeners, he thought—were Dylan's and Ty's; and those were only recordings of songs to which he was trying to work out some beats before they went back into the studio. He always enjoyed Joi's company, but it threw a bit of a kink in his proverbial chain.

She strolled back onto the deck with a huge smile on her face; two glasses and a frosty bottle of chardonnay cradled in her arms. "Don't look so panicked, Bo—I'm going to pack some things up and I'll be out of your hair by tomorrow afternoon at the latest."

Bo grinned. "It's not panic, darlin'; it's just surprise. It's always great to see you. But it's me who should get out. This is your place, you certainly shouldn't..."

She waved her hand again, a dozen bracelets clinking together and reflecting the late afternoon sun. "Are you kidding? I can't work on my tan here—not at this time of year. No, this is my summer destination, not my spring one. Whether you were here or not, I'd pack some things and make a quick exit." She tilted her head and narrowed her eyes. "Didn't you get my messages? I've been calling you all day to let you know I was coming."

Bo shrugged. "I like the quiet here; helps me clear my head. I heard the phone ring a bit ago, but I'd just gotten in for my soak."

"So you're feeling pretty good then? No more headaches?"

"Not since I got here," he smiled. "Something about the air, I think."

"Glad to hear it. What I want to hear now is that whatever's cooking on the stove is enough for two. I'm famished."

"Then you are in for a treat, my friend, because those are my special recipe ribs tenderizing in the pressure cooker and my nearly famous homemade barbeque sauce infusing on the counter. I've got hickory chips soaking, some potatoes we can bake up, and I picked up some fresh asparagus this morning. Plenty for two."

"Now you just made my day," she smiled, tipping her wine glass in his direction.

Bo stood and hung the towel over the back of the chair to dry. "They'll be ready for the coals in about a half hour or so. I'll just hop in the shower real quick, and we can catch up while we feast."

"Anything I can do?" Joi asked.

"There're salad fixins' in the fridge...you could put that together if you want."

She gave him a warm smile. "It's good to see you back to your old self, Bo," she said. "You really had us worried for a while there."

He kissed her cheek. "Thanks. I'm glad you're here. It'll be nice to have some company tonight."

Joi was slicing a green pepper when she heard drum beats thump against the counter. Smiling, she picked up Bo's phone and tapped the screen. "Hello...Bo's phone...he's, um, indisposed at the moment...this is Joi; can I take a message?"

"Oh, uh, I'm sorry...I must have the wrong number," Lexi said, punching the screen to end the call and then collapsing onto her couch. "Well, there you go," she said out loud. "So much for Bo making you feel better." She crumpled up the paper with Bo's number on it and tossed it in the trash, grabbing a bottle of wine from the fridge and yanking out the cork. Oh God, it was going to be a long week.

Chapter 37

"Oh my," Tia breathed as they turned another bend in the road and the house came into view for the first time. They'd rolled through a winding wooded drive, past the "Big D Ranch," sign and through an ornate gate that opened when Dylan hovered his finger over a print reader. She'd expected the place to be magnificent, but she wasn't prepared for the incredible structure that would become her new home.

"Welcome home, baby girl," Dylan said, stopping in the curved driveway. Tia was out of the car before Dylan could even undo his seatbelt, and she just stood and stared at the immense log cabin with floor to ceiling windows and wrap around decks.

"This is a house?" Tia joked as Dylan reached her and wrapped his arm around her waist. "I would've guessed 'hotel,' or 'ski lodge,' but not house."

"Home sweet home," Dylan replied with a half-smile. "I have a makeshift studio here, and some rehearsal space, so when we're getting ready for the tour, the guys come stay here. Believe me, it doesn't seem so big when they're all here taking up space." He swept her into his arms and carried her toward the walkway that led to the front door. "I know it's not official, but I'm planning some consummating in the very near future, so..."

Tia threw her arms around his neck and giggled, kissing the tip of his nose. "Funny, I was thinking exactly the same thing." They hadn't been together in nearly a month, and she'd been thinking a lot about making love for the first time in what would be their marriage bed.

Dylan turned the knob and swung open the unusually tall front doors, setting her down to stare gape mouthed at the interior. She was only in the foyer, but a sparkling chandelier hung on an incredibly long chain from three stories up, passing two levels along the way that looked over the entryway. Dylan put his hand at the small of her back and led her into the living room and her breath caught immediately. It wasn't the three story stone chimney or the view of the mountains through the enormous windows that caught her eye first; it was the painting that Kelley had given her at Christmas hanging over the fireplace that took her breath away. It was perfectly at home there among the rustic stone, as the vineyard had been staggered on a hill with vines separated by stone much the same color. It was at home there, and instantly, Tia knew she would be, too. "It's perfect," she smiled, pulling Dylan into her arms and resting her head on his chest. "I don't need to see anymore to know that I'll love it."

"I can't tell you how relieved I am to hear that," Dylan smirked, scooping up her legs to cradle her in his arms again. "I was worried I was going to have to do the whole five dollar tour before I got you to our bed."

"The tour can wait," she winked, "take me to our bed."

It was good to be home. Even better, it was good to have Tia home. Life on the road wasn't all it was cracked up to be, and although they were making a base in Chicago, after months in hotel rooms and tiny trailers, it was good to be in his own bed, especially with the love of his life opening her arms to him. Ah, how many times had he imagined her right here, her dark hair splayed over his pillow, languid limbs awaiting his caress? "So beautiful," he said softly as he ran his hands up from her waist to the curve of her breasts, releasing the buttons of her blouse with one hand while running the other through her her hair.

Tia's lips parted slightly and her eyes rolled back as he slipped his hand beneath the fabric and stroked a nipple with the pad of his thumb. He separated the fabric and unhooked the clasp of her bra, gently kneading the flesh and taking one of the hardened nubs between his lips. He felt her moan resonating in her chest, and pulled away just long enough to tug his shirt over his head so that he could press against her body.

"I missed you," she smiled as she nuzzled his neck and raked her fingernails gently down his bare back.

"Prove it," he murmured back, sliding his hand down to undo the button on her jeans. She lifted her hips to shrug out of them, and he quickly slipped out of his own, tossing the clothing to the floor and stretching out beside her.

She took his hand and kissed each of his fingertips, taking the middle finger into her warm mouth before moving it between her legs and pressing his hand against the heat of her mound. He moved his hand upward until he found the velvet folds, his own growl vibrating in his throat as he slid into her drenched opening. "I'll take that dare," she smiled, reaching down and wrapping her hand around his urgency, gently stroking the tip with one finger.

"You know," he said with a half-smile, "Every single time I tell myself I'm going to take it slow, make it last, tease you until you beg for mercy; but then you're naked and I lose all control and want to ravage you like a beast. You have me under a spell, love, and I can't keep my head."

"I don't want you to keep your head, baby," she said as she tightened her grip on him, "I want to bury it deep inside me."

"Bloody hell," he croaked, sliding his slick finger out of her and rubbing small circles while bringing his lips to hers. He reveled in every gasp that he took into his mouth and the way she swayed her hips as he brought her closer to climax and when her hips shot upward and he felt the shudder through her entire body, he dipped his finger into her again and felt her tighten around him. "You are an incredibly sexy woman, Tia Hastings. I can't wait to make you my wife."

She swung her leg over and straddled him, raising up and then sliding onto him, her back arching and a groan escaping her as she took the full length of him. She began to rock slowly, rising and falling as he ran his hands up her stomach and over her breasts. Finally, he could take no more, and he pushed his hands beneath her, flipping her over and driving deep in one swift motion. Her mouth made an 'O' of surprise, and she cried out as he pushed faster, bringing them both to the edge and then tumbling over.

She pulled him to her, taking his full weight and nuzzling his neck. "I can't wait to be your wife," she whispered.

"This place is amazing, Dyl," Tia said as they walked through the many rooms of the incredible house. It was a huge space, but the layout made it feel intimate. Several bedrooms were in a separate wing of the house; complete with a second kitchen and its own entrance from the outside, so they could still live in relative privacy when the rest of the guys showed up for rehearsals. Every room was homey and filled with comfortable furnishings, and the kitchen absolutely took Tia's breath away. She looked forward to cooking for the two of them and for InHap when they came in late July. "I really think I will love it here."

"Come on, I want to introduce you to Denny and Alicia," Dylan said after showing her the gardens and the secluded pool area that would be great for hosting summer parties. "They're the caretakers of the place, and they run the ranch. Alicia's an amazing cook, and Denny has the greenest thumb I've ever seen, as well as being something of a horse whisperer."

Dylan grabbed a backpack and they walked down the winding, wooded driveway, then past a pasture where four majestic horses and two foals, still shaky on their spindly legs, were grazing on the spring grass. "Oh, look at the babies!" Tia exclaimed, running for the fence and jumping onto the bottom rung of wood to get a better look. "They're beautiful, Dyl; are they yours?"

"Ours," he answered, smiling. "I thought you'd like them. The gray one is Murphy; he's a bit ornery and thinks he owns the place, the brown one with the white markings is Angel; she's a sweet gentle soul. The brown one with the black patch on his nose is Brutus, and the black one is Shadow. I haven't met the foals yet...you can name them once you've had a chance to get to know them."

Dylan dropped the backpack and unzipped the top, pulling out some apples and making a snickering noise in the direction of the majestic creatures. They were already on their way over, but they quickened their steps when they saw the treats Dylan held up for their inspection. He handed two of them to Tia, who happily fed them to Angel and Shadow. "Aren't you a beauty," she said as she let them sniff her hands and then rubbed between their eyes. "Are those your babies?" Angel snorted an answer, then nuzzled Dylan's arm.

"Hey there!" A man's voice rang out. Tia looked up to see a man perhaps in his fifties complete with cowboy hat and boots striding out of the barn. "Bout time you showed your face around here again. They've missed ya," he tossed his head toward the horses, "and frankly, so have we." He turned his head and called out for Alicia over his shoulder.

"Great to see you, Denny," Dylan said, pulling the man into an embrace. "It's always good to be home; especially this trip." He turned to Tia. "I want to introduce you to my fiancé, Tia. She'll be moving in here in a couple months; after the honeymoon. Where are the boys?" he asked, looking around.

"Jake took them in to the vet for their shots. They should be back soon."

"We've got dogs?" Tia asked excitedly.

"Two," Dylan answered, "Jasper and Murphy."

"Don't tell them they're dogs, though," Denny added. "It'll hurt their feelings. Well I have to say, it'll be great to have a lady of the house," Denny said, wiping his dusty hands on his even dustier jeans before extending his hand to Tia. "Pleased to meet ya, ma'am."

"Tia, please, and I'm glad to meet you, too." She heard another excited greeting, and saw a heavy-set woman jogging toward them. She wrapped Dylan in a warm hug and kissed his cheek.

"It does my heart good to see you, Dylan," she said with a huge smile. "I've been reading the papers and seeing you on TV..." she turned to Tia, "...and this is the lovely Tia. Best wishes to you both on your engagement; and I'll tell you, it'll be so nice to have another woman around this place."

"Tia, meet Alicia. She's my mum away from home, and they're both part of my family."

The woman pulled Tia into a breathtaking squeeze. "I've been hoping for a long time that Dylan would find the right woman," she said warmly, "he's a great catch, but I'm sure you know that already."

"I certainly do."

"Now you know I've stocked the place," Alicia said to Dylan, "but I'm cooking up a fabulous supper—homemade fried chicken with all the fixins', and I'm hoping you'll join us."

Tia hadn't thought about it, but as soon as food was mentioned, her stomach growled in response. She smiled at Dylan and gave him a slight nod.

"I'm going to take Tia for a ride to see the rest of the place," he said, "and then we'd be happy to. We've got some catching up to do." He turned to Denny. "Can you help me saddle up Angel and Murphy?"

"You bet." Denny let out a shrill whistle, and the horses headed for the barn.

The property was incredible, and Tia couldn't believe that she'd be living in such a magnificent place. They meandered through some forest trails, and galloped across open spaces with the mountains rising up behind them. There was a large pond down a hill from the back of the house, and they scared up two herons as they approached on horseback. They left the horses to graze, and walked across a curved wooden bridge to a gazebo that sat on an island in the middle of the pond. Dylan reached into a cooler that was already sitting there and pulled out a bottle of champagne. "Alicia's the best," he said as he popped the cork and poured two glasses. "She knew I'd bring you here."

"I'm really blown away by the whole thing," Tia said. "I can't even believe that I'm going to be living here. It's just amazingly beautiful; and so private. I can see why you chose this place."

"It's going to be more amazing once you're here. I'll really have something to come home to then."

She heard the barking before the dogs came into sight. From the top of the hill, a Golden Retriever and a chocolate Lab mix came bounding down the hill, tails wagging and back ends practically dragging on the ground as they put on the speed to rush over to see Dylan. "There's my boys!" he said happily, and they skittered across the bridge into the gazebo wriggling uncontrollably and wagging their tails as Dylan scratched them all over. "Jasper," he said, touching the Golden, "Murphy," he said, pulling his face from the Lab's tongue, "this is Tia. Your new momma. Put on your manners and say hello."

"Hi, babies," Tia said, putting out her hand for an introductory sniff. Dylan snapped his fingers and they both sat and offered her a paw. She took one in each hand, and scratched them both behind the ears. "I love dogs," she said with a smile. "I think I just might like it here."

"Wait until you try Alicia's homemade fried chicken. You'll never want to leave."

They ate in Alicia's homey kitchen, Tia smiling as they traded stories and the couple gave her the rundown of the place. After the meal, Denny and Dylan went into an office to discuss ranch business, and Alicia and Tia donned their jackets and sat on the front porch to watch the sunset over the mountains.

"How long have you been here?" Tia asked.

"Oh, going on thirty years, I guess," Alicia answered.

"Then you were here even before Dylan?"

"Oh, yes." She cocked her head at Tia. "He didn't tell you, did he?"

"Tell me what?"

"I figured as much. That's the kind of guy he is. You're one lucky lady, Tia, I'll tell you that; although I think you already know."

"I definitely do."

"This place was Denny's dream. We'd just been married a couple years when the property went up for sale. His whole family went in on it—his parents and two brothers—and started the ranch. They each built here, and ran the ranch together. For a long time it was a huge success; we'd have folks paying to have a real dude ranch experience, we bred horses, farmed a bit...it was a great life. You probably saw the cabins on your ride." Tia nodded. "One after the other, his brothers moved on and Denny bought them out, and then his parents passed on and it was the two of us; until Denny had his accident."

"What happened?"

"He was working on a tractor, and it fell on his leg, shattering his femur. Long story short, he had to have a number of extensive surgeries; he has a metal rod in his leg now."

"Oh, wow."

"He was out of commission for almost a year. The medical bills were astronomical, and there was physical therapy...he couldn't ride or work the land. We hired people to come in, but that just about eliminated our profits, and we were in a hole that we couldn't get out of. We sold off the horses and the farm equipment, but it wasn't nearly enough with all the bills coming in. It was the hardest thing in the world for him to do; we held on as long as we could; but we had to put the ranch up for sale. The real estate market wasn't so good at the time, so we were forced into a really low asking price; much less than we thought the place was worth. We were an eyelash away from bankruptcy, and Denny was falling into a depression. Then, lucky for us, Dylan came along. He'd apparently been looking for some acreage in the general area; it was his assistant who came to see us first; a lovely little spit of a woman."

"Jessa," Tia smiled.

"That's her. Is she still around? She was such a nice girl."

"Oh yeah, she's the best."

"She said she was sure that her 'client' would love the place, and she gave us some earnest money right away and set up a meeting. We had no idea who he was at the time; we didn't follow music or movies too much, and I don't go in for those tattler magazines. We just thought he was a nice young man. Our hearts were breaking at the thought of giving up our dream, but we didn't have much of a choice at the time. He came by twice to check the place out; once with Jessa, and once with a team of folks; architects, builders, and the like. Then he asked to speak with us. We sat down right here with some lemonade, and he asked us point blank why we were selling for such a low price. I kind of broke down and told him the whole story; told him it broke our hearts to leave the place; told him about the dude ranch business...he absorbed it all, and told us he'd stop back in a couple days. When he came back, he made us an offer we couldn't refuse.

"He told us that the land was worth much more than we were asking, and insisted on paying a fair price. That in itself was a blessing; at least we'd be able to get another place and pay the hospital bills. But then, he told us who he was. He said that he'd like to build a house further back on the property, but that he wouldn't be living there full time because of his job. He needed caretakers, he told us, and offered to let us stay in our home in exchange for looking after the place when he was away, and for some light cleaning and cooking duties. Dylan said he wanted to keep the ranch operational, and planned to not only rebuy the horses we were forced to sell, but to get a couple more. Then he told us about his charity, and said he had some ideas for developing camps for sick and underprivileged kids in addition to the dude ranch experiences we were already offering." Her eyes teared up as she recalled the memory.

"So Denny's actually 'Big D.'"

"Depends on the day, I reckon. They rib each other about that a lot, arguing about whether it should represent 'big' in size or reputation. Guess I don't have to tell you which one's which," she giggled. "In the beginning, though, Denny was thrilled that the ranch would keep its name, even if a new 'D' was the real namesake. Denny's a tough guy; a cowboy in the real sense of the word; but I tell you when Dylan made that offer, he completely broke down in tears. He'd kind of given up on his therapy at the time, and was still walking with a cane. He believed that he'd never ride again; never work with the horses he'd come to love like his own children. We didn't even need a minute to think about it—there was something about Dylan that made us feel completely comfortable with him right away, you know? We agreed on the spot. Denny's depression was lifted, and he worked on getting back into shape, ditching his cane within a month.

"Then Dylan surprised us yet again. About a month later there was all kinds of heavy equipment rolling in to start construction on his house. He said he felt bad about all the noise and disruption, and sent us away on a two-week cruise. Denny and I didn't want to accept, but he insisted—we hadn't been on a vacation in years, and it was the most amazing time. When we got home, Dylan had taken the liberty of having this amazing porch added on to the house, and had added on to the barn, as well. Denny's horses were back, and it was like a dream, you know? That man saved us, he did, and we're forever indebted to him. Over the years, he's become like one of our own; we love him like a son. We're so glad that he found someone to share his life with, and I want you to know that we'll consider you family, too."

Tia wasn't at all surprised by Dylan's generosity; but it always touched her heart when she was reminded of how humble he was. "I appreciate that so much, Alicia; it'll be so nice to have a friend when Dylan's away. I was a teacher up until a few months ago, and I'd love to get involved in the programs that bring kids to the ranch. I don't know a whole lot about horses, but I'm definitely anxious to learn."

"Oh, Denny would love to teach you!"

"You know, I was actually a bit worried about moving here to a new place, out in the country, where I didn't know anyone; especially knowing that the place was secluded and that Dylan would be gone a lot of the time. I just feel so much better about that part of it, knowing that you guys are here."

Alicia took her hand and smiled. "I'm so glad," she said.

The boys came out onto the porch with beers in their hands, and each went to kiss their ladies on the cheek before sitting in one of the rockers. The sun was just dipping below the mountains, turning them incredible shades of purple and orange. They rocked for a while in comfortable silence, and just as the last crescent of the sun disappeared behind the Rockies, Dylan took Tia's hand. "Welcome to your new life," he whispered.

"I'm going to love it here," she answered.

*****

By Wednesday Tia started to worry. She wasn't totally freaked out that she hadn't heard back from Lexi over the weekend; and frankly, she was so busy getting acclimated to the house and the land, getting to know Denny, Alicia, the horses, and the dogs, that she didn't have a whole lot of time to think about it. She was constantly snapping pictures and taking video; sending them in texts and emails to a long string of people, and hadn't particularly noticed that Lexi was the only one who never responded. When she figured it out and called Lexi's office only to be told she no longer worked there, she got a sick feeling in the pit of her stomach and called her mother to ask her to check in on Lexi. When her mom reported that Lexi's car was in the parking lot but no one answered the door, Tia felt like she had no choice. She asked her mother to call the police to do a wellness check on her.

She knew Lexi was still depressed when she left, and she felt a pang of guilt for leaving her alone. Lex was always the strong one; the one who couldn't be tamed; the one Tia looked to for support time and time again over the years. Normally, she didn't let anything get her down—she laughed at adversity and faced life head-on. Tia knew all too well how it felt to sink into that dark pit of self-pity, that place where no one and nothing could touch you, but she never would have imagined that Lexi had a hole that deep. The Lexi she knew was the one who took her keys to Ryan's Mustang and hung her engagement ring on the carabineer while he was working out with his mistress; the one who insisted they go on with their celebration plans after she'd discovered his infidelity.

All Lexi had to do was return a phone call and say she was OK. Instead, Tia was a thousand miles away and suddenly conjuring up images of a lifeless body lying on the floor of her apartment.

"OK, the police are here now," her mom said, and Tia hung on the line listening to her give the story to the officers. Why hadn't she thought to leave Lexi's key with her mom? The flutter of a second thought roiled in her stomach but at least this way, if Lexi was sick, they'd be able to help her right away. She heard the sharp knock and the bellow of the cop's voice as he pounded on Lexi's door. "Police, ma'am, open the door, please." He pounded twice more, and Tia heard the jingle of something metallic. "Are you sure she's in there? We may have to break the lock if she..." then Tia heard the familiar squeak of Lexi's door as it swung open.

"What the hell is going on?" she heard Lexi's shocked and groggy voice, and her shoulders slumped in relief. "Mrs. Hastings?"

"Oh Lexi, thank God you're OK."

"Is everything alright, Miss?" a policeman said.

Now Lexi just sounded agitated. "Of course everything's alright. What is all this?"

"Oh honey, Tia's been trying to call you for days, and you weren't answering. I came by to check on you and saw your car, but you didn't come to the door, and she got worried and asked me to call."

"Wait a minute," another male voice said. "Would that be Tia Hastings, Dylan Miller's fiancée? I thought I recognize you—you were on *After Dark* a while back, right?"

"Oh God," Lexi groaned, "does it never end?"

"Thanks so much, officers," Tia heard her mom say, "I'll take it from here." She came back on the line and said, "I guess you probably heard. She's fine, but she looks like she's been on a three-day bender. Let me help her get cleaned up, and I'll call you back."

"Tell her to call me," Tia answered. "She may be fine right now, but I'm not so sure she will be when I get a hold of her."

It was almost 45 minutes before Lexi's number popped up on her screen. "What the hell was that? You don't call back for days, don't answer your phone or your door until the police show up?"

"What the hell was *that*," Lexi replied snidely, "that you didn't notice for four freaking days?"

Tia felt like she'd been slapped. Lexi was right; she should have realized it right away, and been more diligent about getting someone to check in on her sooner. She mentally kicked herself for being so selfish; she'd been so caught up in seeing Dylan, exploring her new home, getting to know Denny and Alicia and the animals; that she'd let Lexi's problems slip to the back of her mind. "You're absolutely right," she said softly, "and I'm so sorry. It was really shitty of me, and I feel horrible."

"You should feel horrible," Lexi bellowed, and then softened her voice. "Oh, damn it," she said, "it was shitty of me, too. I really thought at first that I'd be able to pick myself up, brush myself off, and get on with it, but it's all hitting me harder than I thought it would. I'm sitting here like a zombie, drinking way too much wine, eating nothing, and shutting out the world." She paused and took a deep breath. "How did you ever get through it? How did you learn to smile again? It hurts so much..."

"Oh, sweetie, I'm so sorry. I wish I could tell you that it'll be alright tomorrow, but it takes time. I know that's not what you want to hear, but it's the truth."

"It sucks," she sobbed. "I lost my job."

"I heard. I called the office. How in the world did that happen?"

"Long story, but basically, I finally had it out with Candy, and Bryce took her side, of course. Helps that she's sleeping with him, I'm sure." She left out the part about the previous meetings with her boss when they'd discussed the distractions her new status brought to the firm; the phone calls from non-clients, people who set up meetings just so they could narrow their connection to a celebrity down a few degrees, calls from media types hoping to get a comment about the celebrity love triangle; things had been bad for a couple months, and she had to admit that she was having a hard time keeping her head in the game.

"But he just fired you on the spot? He can't do that! Doesn't there have to be a process, or something? You can probably fight it."

"Yeah, I could; but considering Bryce's wife heard the whole thing and is going to shut him down—her father owns the building—there won't be a firm for much longer. She's making sure I get a decent severance package, and I've got all the money I had saved up for the wedding and the honeymoon...so I'm OK for a while. Believe it or not, I actually did do some soul searching over the past few days, and decided that I could use a change; maybe it's a chance to start over."

"It still sucks. Why didn't you answer when my mom came by?"

"Honestly? I was kind of passed out—I didn't even hear the door."

"Oh honey," Tia said, feeling the guilt punch her in the gut.

"I'm better. Really. I'm sorry I had you worried. I did see the pictures—the place looks amazing. I can't wait to hear all about it. It's great to hear your voice, but you should get back to Dylan and enjoy the rest of your vacation."

"Are you sure you're OK?"

"I'm sure."

"And you won't ignore my calls?"

"Cross my heart."

"I was really worried, Lex. I love you, you know."

"You too." She cut the connection.

Dylan wasn't happy about her leaving early, but he was understanding. He even offered to come with her, but she declined. "She's kind of hating men right now; she just needs to have someone to vent to. Trust me, it wouldn't be any fun."

She said her goodbyes to Alicia and Denny, and nuzzled with the dogs and horses in turn, promising them that she'd be back soon to stay. She left with very little; much of what she'd brought with her had found a place in her new home.

"Oh, God, are you serious?" Lexi moaned when Tia opened the door to her apartment and walked in with Chinese carry-out bags hanging from her arms. "What are you doing here, Tia?"

"I had to come and make sure you were really OK," she answered, "plus, I felt really guilty for leaving you when you needed me."

"Damn it, all I needed was a few days to wallow in self-pity and cry myself out. I didn't mean for you to miss out on your trip....now *I* feel guilty."

"Well then, we can feel guilty together." She looked Lexi up and down and nodded. "You look better. You're clean, at least."

"Yeah, nothing like the police showing up at your door when you're at your absolute worst and then having them recognizing you as someone they saw on TV to put things in perspective." She lifted her nose in the air and gave an appreciative sniff. "Do I smell pot stickers?"

"Of course," Tia answered, pushing aside a half dozen empty wine bottles to make room for the bags on the kitchen table. "You weren't kidding when you said you went on a bender. You drank all these yourself?"

"All by my lonesome," she said, "and believe me, I paid the price. Don't want to do that again."

"I would hope not," Tia scolded, scooping some fried rice onto two plates and bringing them to the coffee table in the living room. Lexi quickly picked up the mountain of tissues and chip bags that littered the table so Tia could put them down. "Are you all cried out, then? Looks like I should've bought some stock in Kleenex."

"Not only that, but I'm actually on a reinvention mission. I think I'm going to move—a change of scenery might be just the ticket." The changes were coming anyway, she'd decided, and she figured she could at least be the master of her own destiny. Her days of hanging with the boys were over; she didn't begrudge Bo his happiness—he of all people deserved it—but now that he'd forged a relationship with Joi, they'd never again have the same relationship and it would just be awkward.

"Reinvention is good," Tia agreed, and they dug into their meal while Tia filled her in on her adventures in her new home.

Chapter 38

"I really wish you were here."

"Me too. It's below zero outside, and no matter how high I turn up the heat, the bed is still cold when I climb in it."

"Actually, if you want to know the truth, I'd rather be there. Or back in Colorado. It's going to be an interesting night, that's for sure."

"I can't wait to go back to the ranch and stay. I could really go for Alicia's fried chicken right about now. So who's going to be at the party tonight?"

"I don't know," Dylan sighed. "It's Skip's deal, and he has a tendency to go overboard at times. I kind of wish I could bug out, but I'm going to have to hang for a bit, anyway."

"Sounds like it's a big accomplishment for him, though," Tia said, curling up against the arm of the couch under a blanket. "How many albums that he produced have sold?"

"A hundred million. And you're right, it is a big deal. He's a great guy and a fantastic producer, too; he's just a little over the top. It'll be fine—I'll text you some pictures."

"Looking forward to it. Have fun. Miss you, baby."

"Love you, baby girl."

"*Day*-yam," Bo said when they walked into the the studio. "Are we in the right place?"

Dylan handed his coat to a woman in the lobby who looked as if she'd been dipped in latex while two ethereal brunettes in red and black bustiers and fishnet stockings rushed up to offer them a colorful concoction in a test tube. "Ah, so it's going to be this kind of party," he said to Bo from the corner of his mouth and immediately knew which persona he was going to need to get through the evening. A fair number of people mingled in the small lobby dressed in everything from evening gowns to lingerie; torn jeans to tuxes; sipping from glasses that were lit from below with neon rings.

Angelo whistled between his teeth. "Hard to believe we were making a record in here just yesterday," he said as they entered the studio from the hallway, his eyes roaming around the transformed room. Big enough for an entire orchestra complete with chairs, music stands, and a conductor, the room now housed a makeshift DJ booth, a long table full of food featuring a gigantic record album-shaped cake with the number 100,000,000 sprawled across it in neon blue icing, two portable bars, and a couple dozen tall round tables where people could stand and mingle. The can lights were dimmed, but there were strings of tiny twinkling LEDs draped around the ceiling panels and spilling from corners. Candlelight flickered through a wide variety of funky glass votives on the tables and from artistic pieces around the room. "Check this out," Angelo said, drawn to a stand where four saxophones were mounted to a stand. Huge pillar candles were jammed into the bells and blue flame licked from the ligatures.

The boys walked around the room, taking in the artwork and stopping to chat with some of the other guests along the way. There were some people that they knew from the business, some people they knew of, a few celebrities from genres other than music, and enough model-types to round out the mix. Skip spotted them and broke away from a small group to greet them. "A hundred fucking million," Ty said, shaking his hand, "quite a number, my friend."

"And I'm counting on you guys to get me to a billion," he winked, greeting the rest of them and motioning to a scantily clad waitress who sidled her way over to take their drink orders.

"We'd like nothing better than to make that happen for you," Bo agreed.

Dylan ordered a Maker's and Coke and had the waitress take a picture of the group with Skip so he could send it to Tia. They chatted for just a couple minutes before a high-pitched voice called out Skip's name from across the room. "Oh, I need to take this," he said with a sly grin, and he left the boys to go and greet an attractive woman who'd just entered the studio.

Not what I expected, Tia texted in response to the photo and Dylan couldn't help but chuckle to himself. Skip did more than neglect his appearance—it seemed like he actually put effort into looking like a homeless man who'd been on the streets for a fair amount of time. His hair was long, shaggy, and unkempt, and he had a full reddish beard with streaks of premature gray. He wore faded jeans with an assortment of holes, Chuck Taylors, and faded flannel shirts that gapped between the buttons over his ample middle. Beneath that modest exterior, however, lay the mind of a musical genius. InHap had hooked up with him after Bruce, their original producer, had met his untimely death at the age of forty-two under mysterious circumstances that involved a call girl, a poodle, and large amounts of blow. Skip was still an apprentice at the time, but there was something about him that all the InHap boys liked right away—and they paired up with him to do a single based on a recommendation from one of Ty's friends. The rest, as they say, was history. Skip worked only with a select few, but those bands had taken him to the top in just a few short years.

"*Looks can be deceiving, especially in this case*," Dylan texted back.

Ty waved to someone across the room and tapped Tommy on the shoulder. "Hey, Mike Wilmont's here." Tommy looked over and raised his hand in greeting and the two of them disappeared into the crowd.

Dylan, Bo, and Angelo wove their way through the horde of attendees, but it was slow going. They hadn't moved more than a few feet when Dylan heard a familiar voice. "I was hoping I'd see you here, Dylan," Susannah Atwald said.

Dylan turned and smiled. It was a lifetime ago that he last saw her—he'd been a completely different person when he worked with her in one of his early films and dated her for a few months. She had been one of his hard lessons about the ugly side of celebrity and the way it blurs the edges of any relationship. Much as Gina had dumped him early in his musical career for the guitarist of a group perched to hit the big time, Susannah had gotten stars in her eyes as well. Dylan had thought she was different, and liked the way the relationship was going—until he was confronted with a tabloid picture, ironically enough, of her cozying up to a star whose "name in lights" was considerably taller than his was at the time. But that was ages ago, and he harbored no ill will—not when he was currently in the best place life had ever taken him. "Great to see you, Susannah," he said, lightly kissing both her cheeks and taking her hands in his. "It's been a long time."

"Yes indeed," she said. "Best wishes on your engagement. She's a lucky girl."

"I'm the lucky one," he said with a smile, "but thank you. I'm very excited."

"You deserve to be happy. You're a good person, Dylan; too rare a thing in our line of work." Like so many other Hollywood romances, hers and Dirk Sanders' had ended in disaster, and he was currently in rehab somewhere, trying to get his life back on track.

"I appreciate the kind words, and I am incredibly happy," he smiled, shaking hands with her friends and moving on. Once they'd made their way to the back of the studio, Dylan, Bo and Angelo finally parked at a table and wordlessly tipped their glasses toward each other.

"So, how about those Broncos," Angelo said smiling, purposefully starting a seemingly normal conversation in the surreal atmosphere of the transformed studio. There had never really been a time when this sort of bash was in Dylan's comfort zone, but Angelo had once kept the party scene as a fickle mistress— seeking out the limelight and partying so much that the boys had been forced to give him an ultimatum about changing his ways or leaving the band. Thankfully he'd seen the light; and often hung with the other guys making light conversation when the scene got too crazy.

"Tia's trying to convert me into a Bears fan," Dylan moaned, waving non-committally at a trio of girls who sashayed by their table and blew kisses in their direction.

"Oh, the horror!" Bo exclaimed sarcastically, lifting his beer for a toast. "Here's to the mundane, normal, everyday things that keep us from turning into *that,*" he offered, pointing at an up and coming singer wearing hot pink skinny jeans and sporting a dyed blue mohawk and chains hanging from multiple piercings in his face and ears. Angelo and Dylan raised their glasses and tapped their rims against his. "Oh, hell yeah," they agreed simultaneously.

"Son of a bitch, wha 'appen?" Dylan turned to see a figure cloaked in shadow sporting long dreads, shredded bell-bottoms, and a Bob Marley t-shirt.

"Bloody hell," Dylan smiled, "Dozer Cane." They exchanged a series of greetings that included a variety of handshakes and chest bumps. The Jamaican shook hands with Bo and Angelo and bellied up to their table. "What rock have you been hiding under?" Dylan asked him. "I haven't heard your name in a while."

"Ya mon, but I be 'earing yours a lot. Dey say you're no gallis no more—dat you're gettin' marry," Dozer grinned, showing off a few gaps in his smile. "Dat sick, mon."

"It is, and thanks, mate. It's put quite a different perspective on things, that's for sure."

"Ya mon. I know what you mean. I got hitched last year…"

"Hey, that's great--congratulations!"

"Ya, everyting irie. She straighten me out. We started a name bran together—Rasta wear, mostly; like hemp sandals, tie-dye…shit made out of bamboo. All eco-friendly. She da artist and I run tings."

"We'll just give you two a chance to catch up," Bo said, motioning to Angelo with a slight shake of his head. Dozer was from Dylan's pre-InHap days, and neither of them knew him all that well. "Let's go check out the buffet." The two of them grabbed their glasses and headed off through the crowd.

"That's great mate, really," Dylan said after the boys wandered off. "You still making music?"

"Just at the local wells mostly. Selina—dat my main squeeze—is going pop me out a bwoy in a few weeks. Can you believe it? I'm going to be someone's *fadda,* mon."

Dylan grinned and hugged him. "Fucking brilliant, mate. You'll be great at it, I'm sure." He surprised himself by feeling a passing twinge of jealousy, and thought, not for the first time, about what it might be like to a father. "Is she here?"

"Nah, she home. I 'ave business here and wanted to get it done before he's born. You be makin' a new album, den?"

Dylan nodded. "We're recording here, actually. This just kind of popped up in the middle of it all…"

They passed about an hour standing at the small table; shooting the shit and reliving old memories. Lots of folks stopped by; expecting them to follow the standard protocol of greeting everyone who approached their table like long lost friends; and Dozer couldn't help but notice that a lot of them were women. "You still got da ladies fallin' at your feet mon," Dozer said. "I was always a bit jealous of dat, but it could be a curse too, ya?"

"More often than not," Dylan said as two blondes who'd been eyeing them for quite a while grabbed the boys' drinks off a waitress's tray, turned away for a moment and whispered to each other, and glided up to their table. They were practically carbon copies of each other—big blonde hair, huge fake tits, legs that went all the way up to their chins, unbelievably high heels, and micro-dresses that left absolutely nothing to the imagination. Dylan rolled his eyes slightly and tipped his fresh Maker's and Coke in Dozer's direction to punctuate the statement.

"Good evening, Dylan Miller," the taller of the two said. Her voice was smoky and had a heavy Swedish accent. "My name is Sonja." She put both her hands out to Dozer who took them and brushed her cheeks with air kisses. When it was Dylan's turn, she connected with the kiss and breathed into his ear, "I've been a fan for a long time."

"Thanks," Dylan said, shaking the other girl's hand across the table. "This is Dozer Cane."

"Melena," the second girl smiled, her accent just as heavy. She turned to Dozer. "I know your work. Reggae, right?"

"Da only true music," he teased, poking Dylan in the arm. "I also have a clothing bran name." He tilted his head and squinted at the ladies. "Are ya models? You look kind of familiar."

"We are actresses," Sonja said, tipping her head and looking up at them through thick dark lashes.

Dozer's expression didn't change. "Dat mus be it. What movies?"

"We make adult films," Melena smiled, biting the corner of her lower lip.

Dylan closed his eyes and rolled them behind his lids. He took a sip of his drink while Dozer smiled wide and looked them slowly up and down. "Ya mon I tink I've seen you in action. Didn't recognize you with your clothes on."

"We maybe can fix that," Sonja grinned as the girls stepped closer and leaned seductively over the table in almost perfect unison, giving the boys an excellent view of their ample cleavage. Dylan inhaled some of his drink and nearly choked, and Dozer gave him a good slap on the back. He took another slug to ease the cough and shook his head.

"Oh, wow," Dozer said, shaking his head. "It's too bad, but you see, you're too late for both of us." He held up his left hand. "See, I'm marry, and he's engaged, so it's not good timing right now."

"That is not important," Sonja said seductively. "We fuck lots of married men. Engaged, too," she added, running her tongue slowly over her upper lip while locking her gaze on Dylan.

Dozer opened his mouth to speak, but his phone suddenly started playing something that could only be described as a reggae lullaby. His eyes went wide and he yanked the phone from his pocket, staring at it in disbelief. "'Oly shit," he breathed. "Da baby's comin'!" His eyes darted around the room, but he didn't focus on anything; he hopped from foot to foot, but he wasn't going anywhere.

"Congratulations, mate!" Dylan exclaimed, pulling him into an embrace.

"I'm going to be a fadda!" He lifted his drink for a toast, and they both drained their glasses.

"Best get to it then, eh?"

"Oh. Oh yeah. I 'ave to get 'ome!" He gave Dylan a hug, planted a big kiss on Melena's cheek, and headed for the door.

Dylan turned back to the table and gripped the sides for support. A sudden wave of nausea and dizziness took hold of him, and he shook his head to try and throw it off. His brain was suddenly swimming and his eyes refused to focus. He looked at the empty glass on the table—only his third the whole evening. They were making them strong, sure, but still…his knees went weak and he squeezed the sides of the table harder and looked at the girls. "These must be going to my head," he slurred.

"You should sit down," Sonja said, taking an arm. Melena grabbed him from the other side and they led him through the door at the back of the room. "I know just the spot."

Dylan looked around once for Bo but didn't see him in the crowd. He remembered walking through two sets of doors and sinking into a couch, and then nothing.

Tia was asleep when the text came in. She hadn't gotten anything from Dylan in a couple hours, the last being a picture of him and a man with long dreads and deep wrinkles in his dark face tapping his glass against Dylan's in a toast. She reached over in the dark and grabbed her phone, catching the time on the digital clock as she did. It was only past midnight in Seattle, but it was after two in Chicago, and she forced her eyes to focus on the backlit screen as she pulled up the message. It took only a couple seconds for it to register and for her to sit straight up in the bed, her heart pumping wildly and her consciousness at full alert. It was a picture of two women—beautiful women—lips together in a sensual kiss as they looked at the camera seductively. The message beneath the picture read, *dude look what I found!* She tilted her head and clicked off the picture, her breath catching when she verified that it came from Dylan's phone.

She checked her surroundings to make sure she wasn't dreaming, and then tried to rationalize the photo. Someone probably found Dylan's phone lying somewhere and took the picture, she reasoned. That had to be it. They must have tried to send it to someone with a name or number close to hers and the phone automatically inserted her as a recipient. Still, panic squeezed at her heart, restricting its beat, and she found herself swinging her legs over the side of the bed and shuffling to the living room to fall onto the couch. No way was she going to be able to go back to sleep after that. It was only a minute before her phone chirped the sound of another incoming text. Tia felt a sense of dread as she tapped on the picture and enlarged it on the tiny screen of her phone. She couldn't be absolutely sure it was one of the same women, nor could she be sure the other person in the picture was Dylan; although her brain clearly leaned toward both being true. There were no faces clearly identifiable; one was completely invisible, buried between the breasts that filled much of the screen. All she could see was the hair; long, blonde, and wavy. A hand with long manicured fingernails was pushed through it as if holding the face in place.

She took a deep breath and held it, unable to look away. She stared for what seemed a long time, and then the phone vibrated once again in her hand. She closed her eyes and willed the next text not to be what she feared it might be. Her prayers were not answered. The picture showed the same man lying on a couch with one of the women straddling him. His shirt was open to the waist and her breasts were out. One of the naked breasts was pressed into the man's face. The message beneath said, *between u n me man. obviously!* Tia gasped and dropped the phone, hearing it buzz again against the floor. "Oh God," she breathed, feeling panic rise up to wrap around her lungs and give them a good squeeze. She gasped for breath as the phone buzzed again and she bent down to retrieve it. She didn't want to look—it scared the hell out of her, actually—but she couldn't help herself. She clicked on the picture and saw the woman on top of the man on the couch, his hand resting on the place where her dress had been hiked up to expose her buttocks. The other woman leaned over his face, her lips pressed to his. Tia's eyes were drawn immediately to the Chinese symbol for younger sister tattooed between the man's thumb and forefinger. She moaned in pain as she sunk to the floor and curled into a fetal position, her breath hitching in sobs.

"What the hell is going on?" Bo roared when he walked into the tiny lounge next to the kitchen. He flicked on the light, and the women just smiled at him.

"Want to join in?" one of them asked.

Bo shook his head in complete and total disbelief. "No, I don't want to join...I want to know what the hell is going on in here." He directed the question at Dylan, but there was no response.

"I think that would be obvious," a blonde hissed in a Swedish accent. "We'd be happy to invite you to our private party if you want to join, or you can go away. Or maybe you just want to watch?"

"You've got to be trippin' on something," he mumbled, pushing his way between the near-naked women and pulling Dylan by his wrists to a sitting position. "Dylan. Are you OK?" The only response was a low moan from deep in his chest, barely audible over the muffled beat of the music that resonated through the open doors. "Dude. Talk to me." He nudged the women—who still made no effort to cover themselves—aside and yanked Dylan up from the couch. Bo's eyes widened when he sank right back down without so much as a glimpse of recognition or consciousness. Bo turned him so that he'd fall onto a loveseat away from the women and knelt on the floor in front of him. "Shit. Dyl—look at me." He slapped his friend's cheeks and Dylan opened one eye and looked at him without focus.

"What the fuck did you do?" he growled, glaring at the women, who shrugged innocently.

"He invited us to come back here," one of the women said.

"Said he would make us sing," the other smirked.

"The hell he did." He lifted Dylan's chin and tried to get him to make eye contact, but his eyes just rolled back in his head and then closed. "Holy shit," he muttered to himself. Then he turned back to the women. "Go get me some water from the kitchen—and for fuck's sake, put your goddamn clothes back on." The girls looked at him blankly. "NOW!" Finally one of them moved, and brought a punch bowl half-full of water and a towel. He dunked the towel and squeezed the cold water over Dylan's head, then slapped his face again.

"Hey Bobooooo...whassup?" The words were barely audible, and Dylan's eyes were looking in two different directions at once. Bo pressed Dylan's face with his hands and shook him.

"What's going on, Dyl?"

"My head's tooooo drunk. They took pictures. Bad pictures."

Bo's head jerked toward the women. "What's he talking about?" He watched as one of the girls tried to slide Dylan's phone onto the table next to the couch. Bo reached over and snatched it, tapping the photos icon and gritting his teeth at what he saw. "Was this consensual, Dyl?" he asked, holding the camera in front of his face. Dylan squinted, and then his eyes widened when he finally managed to see it well enough to know it for what it was. He shook his head, and his eyes closed again.

"Unfuckingbelievable," he snarled. "You sick bitches. Get the hell out of here right now, before I call the cops."

The shorter of the two women flinched just a bit but the taller one just smiled. "Nothing illegal about a little foreplay between adults—now either you want to join, or you let us finish in peace."

"I said get out!" Bo grabbed their bags off the couch next to Dylan and tossed them to the floor, sending the contents of one or both skittering across the tile. He watched a lipstick roll toward the door, a packet of condoms slide across the granite, an assortment of pills bounce in all directions, and glass from a compact shatter against the wall, dusting the dark squares of tile with a fine powder. The taller of the two got to her knees, trying to scoop the contents back into the bag as Bo shook with fury. He stood to his full height and glared at them both, clenching his hands into fists and shooting daggers at them from his eyes. "Right. Fucking. Now." The message finally registered—they left the rest of the contents and ran from the room.

Bo turned back to Dylan and swung his friend's legs up onto the couch, trying to make him comfortable, and took stock of the situation. His jeans were unbuttoned and unzipped, but thankfully still on his body. Bo buttoned up Dylan's shirt and grabbed a blanket off an adjacent chair; tossing it over him. He sat in the chair and blew out a breath, thankful that he'd appeared to have found him before the little orgy had gotten to the point of no return. He'd been looking for Dyl for a while—if it hadn't been for the flustered waitress who shot him a guilty look as he'd walked past the door that led to the kitchen, he may have been too late. "I didn't want to do it," she'd whimpered. "I don't think he knows what he's doing." She rushed off then, disappearing into the crowd. Bo had seen the guilt and the recognition in her eyes and pushed through the door immediately.

"Son of a bitch," he muttered as Dylan groaned, and he fell to his knees and pushed his index finger to his friend's wrist to get a pulse. The bastard's heart was beating; at least for now. He was smashed off his gourd, but he was going to live to feel the wrath of what promised to be a very nasty hangover. "Drink this," he demanded, holding a cup of water to Dylan's lips and tipping it back. Dylan sputtered and coughed, but managed to get some of the liquid down the right pipe.

"Sleeeep," Dylan hissed, laying his head back onto the arm of the couch.

"Yeah, buddy, you need to sleep it off all right." He picked up Dylan's phone and started deleting the photos, gritting his teeth as each new image popped onto the screen. The fury bubbled up in him as he realized how much Dylan stood to lose if these pictures got out, and cursed himself for not smashing the bitches' phones as they were sliding across the floor along with the rest of their bags' contents. He'd known Dylan plenty long enough to know that there was no way in hell he consented to any of this. Even if he wasn't engaged he would never have given those fake trashy whores the time of day. He deleted the last photo, shut off the phone, and hoped to hell that he'd averted disaster. God knew Dylan didn't look like he was going to remember any of this in the morning. Bo shoved Dylan's shoes back onto his feet, led him through a back door, and somehow managed to drag him the few blocks to the hotel.

Chapter 39

Tia awoke with a feeling of dread in her gut that she prayed was from a bad dream. It was still dark and she shivered under a thin blanket on the couch instead of in the warm cocoon of her bed, which pretty well dashed her feeble hopes that the horrendous pictures that still burned on the backs of her eyelids were conjured up by her own mind.

No way she was going to fall back to sleep, so she dragged herself off the couch and slipped into her favorite thick robe before stumbling into the kitchen to make some coffee. She sat at the kitchen table with her face in her hands as the pain settled into her consciousness. There had to be some logical explanation; there just had to be. She had complete trust in Dyl—it had taken her a hell of a long time and a lot of concentrated effort to rid herself of the jealous feelings every time she saw a picture of Dylan smiling next to another woman. She had learned to bite her tongue and smile when women flirted with him unabashedly— but she had gotten there; or so she'd believed. Dylan had told her long ago that pictures could be fabricated and doctored to look real, and the Penelope situation had proven it beyond the shadow of a doubt. They'd even had a number of discussions about how she'd have to be more trustworthy than the average girlfriend, and he'd never given her the slightest reason to doubt him. Until now.

Unable to help herself, she dug her phone out from under the couch and opened the texts, wincing out loud as the first one popped up on her screen. After having seen the final picture just a few hours ago, she could now positively ID Dylan as the man in the previous photos. Although there were at least two different women in the shots, it was the same man—she could tell by the shirt and the backdrop—a plaid couch against a beige wall. A wave of nausea rolled through her stomach as she realized three things. First, they were all sent from Dylan's phone, most likely from the party where she knew there'd be plenty of willing women. Second, although the texts came to her, the messages attached were directed toward a guy. Did he inadvertently tap her name on his contact list; actually meaning to send them to someone else? Tim, maybe?

The third realization was the one that made her heart break in two. The texts had come in quick succession—she'd gotten five pictures in the span of less than half an hour. There was no way they could have been doctored. The only conclusion her mind could reach was that she was witnessing Dylan breaking every promise he'd ever made her.

The coffeemaker beeped behind her and she numbly made her way over to the counter and poured, falling back onto the chair and wrestling with the images in her head. She stared blankly at the rainbow swirls that spun lazily atop the dark liquid until it went cold, and didn't bother to pour another cup. It was over an hour before she could even process that she needed to go—she needed to get somewhere safe where she could work out what to do next—she was so full of conflict at the moment that she couldn't even see straight. *Once a cheater, always a cheater,* she heard Lexi say over and over in her mind. She stood up and paced around the apartment that had only recently become her place of residence; she'd given up her little house and it now belonged to a young couple with a toddler, so she had no place to call her own. God, she'd given up her career, her home, her life... All those years, all that work to become independent—to take care of herself and build a life of which she could be proud, and she'd thrown it all to the wind for Dylan. He was once the man of her dreams, but now she feared he would haunt her nightmares; the man who texted her pictures of himself in various stages of undress with at least two beautiful women at a music producer's party. No matter how hard she tried, she couldn't see another explanation.

The walls started closing in on her, and she felt cold panic rise up from the ground to swallow her whole. She needed to be anonymous for a few days; to figure things out. Unfortunately, there were precious few, if any, places where she could hide away from it all. No way she was sharing the pictures yet with anyone— she wasn't about to deal with the pity she'd get from her loved ones, and she didn't know how long it would be before she'd be willing to hear Dylan's voice; if he even had anything to say to her. She tossed a few things into an overnight bag and picked up the phone.

"Hey, it's Tia," she said when the familiar voice came on the line. "I really need to get away for a couple days. Can I come stay with you?"

"You know you're always welcome here."

"I know, and thank you. Could you be ready for me in about an hour?"

"I just pulled a coffee cake out of the oven. If you get here sooner, it'll still be warm."

Tia let out a long slow breath. "I'm on my way right now."

"Damn, dude, you still in bed?" Bo plopped himself less than gracefully at the foot of Dylan's bed and watched him nearly jump out of his skin. "I expected you to be hung over, but I didn't think you'd still be asleep at ten o'clock."

Dylan shook his head and glanced over at the digital radio on the bedside table. 10:06. He looked back and forth between Bo and the clock a couple times and ran his fingers through his tangled hair, stopping with his palm on his forehead and wrinkling his face in confusion. "I'm not hanging at all," he answered. "Should I be? I don't remember drinking that much."

"What do you remember?" Bo asked cautiously. His friend had been really out of it—if Dyl didn't remember the incident with the ho-bags then he sure as hell wasn't going to point it out. Bo had destroyed the evidence, and hoped to hell that if there were other pictures, the bitches only took them for themselves. He had a really bad feeling about the whole thing, but time would tell, and Bo wouldn't.

"Shit," Dylan said, his eyes gazing upward as he tried to recall the previous night. "Not much, really. I remember talking to Dozer...he told me he's going to be a dad. You and Angelo took off and then I never saw either one of you again the rest of the night."

Bo sat patiently as he watched Dylan try to put the pieces together. He was glad at least that he had no recollection, at least not yet, of the little tryst in the back room. As his best friend, he would have stood behind Dylan no matter what, but he would have definitely lost a lot of respect for him if he'd knowingly played Tia that way. It left a bad taste in Bo's mouth that he'd done it at all, but he'd seen how out of it the man was and knew that the porn stars were taking advantage of it.

"I walked you home, brother," Bo replied. "It was no easy task, either—I practically had to carry your sorry drunk ass."

Dylan laughed. "Damn, I knew they were mixing them strong, but I had no idea I had that much. Thanks for looking out for me, mate." Dylan hit the button to power up his phone, and Bo held his breath. "Oh, we've got that bloody photo shoot today, don't we?" Bo nodded. "Let me just shoot Tia a quick good morning— it's past noon by her. I can be ready to go in fifteen minutes." He was already multi-tasking, setting up the espresso machine with one hand and texting with the other.

Bo exhaled when he heard the swoosh of the outgoing message. "I'll just hang out here, then, and we can ride over together."

"You suck for doing that to her." Dylan did a double-take at the girl who was trying to tape a light box to the floor of the ferry.

It was not shaping up to be a good day. He'd started it running from behind and it had just gotten worse as the day went on. A storm blew in (*Really? Who knew that it might rain in Seattle?* he thought) and they'd had to spend more time on the boat than they'd originally planned. The water was rough and they'd already soaked through two changes of clothes from either the rain or the spray, and they still had two more locations to visit before they called it a day. He was getting concerned that Tia hadn't returned any of his texts—he'd sent at least a dozen since this morning and tried calling twice, and now he had to deal with one of the minions from 'Penelope's Posse' hassling him at a photo shoot. "Whatever. She deserves that and more."

"I can't believe you would even say that!" she yelled, throwing down the roll of duct tape in disgust and marching off. A minute later, a guy came out to finish the job and they completed the shots on the ferry before heading toward the dry land of Bainbridge Island. Dylan was grateful for the clouds when the photographer decided they should match their expressions to the weather. He didn't feel much like smiling.

Tia was pretty sure the taxi driver didn't recognize her, but she wasn't taking any chances. She had him drop her at Hilton, and promptly jumped into another cab just in case. The day was dismal; cold, windy, and with clouds that looked positively pregnant with snow. The forecast was calling for six to eight inches starting around noon and although Tia often remarked about how being a weather person was the best job in the world because you could be wrong ninety percent of the time and still get paid, she could almost taste the storm brewing in the air. Or maybe it was the vile taste left in her mouth after seeing the horrendous pictures. Either way, a storm was going to dump over her head. Why not two?

The further she got from the center of the city, the more her heart settled into a normal rhythm. The roads were quiet for a Saturday morning, and they made good enough time that she decided to take a little tour of her old life. She guided the driver past her school and then her old house, in front of which stood a regal snowman with a carrot nose and a hot pink scarf. They drove down Main Street, past her favorite old café and the boutique where she always knew she'd find something that she just had to have. When they got to the park where she used to take her neighbor's dog, Bonnie, she had the driver pull in. "I haven't been here in a long time," she told him, getting out of the car to take a quick walk to the wooden bridge that spanned the creek.

She stood there and realized that it had been longer than she'd thought since she had been here. It had been in another lifetime. Already these places felt...*separate,* somehow, and she no longer belonged. This wasn't her world anymore, and no amount of wishing would make it any other way.

Tia took a big gulp of the frozen air and exhaled it slowly, watching her breath swirl away on the softer breezes that sifted through the park. For a couple days, at least, she would sink into the mundane normalcy of her old life. She had the driver make one more stop where Tia ducked into a store and bought a pay-as-you-go cell phone so she could let everyone know that she was fine; she was just taking a bit of a sabbatical. Not wanting to see any texts from Dylan, she'd left her phone in the drawer of the nightstand at the apartment.

"It is so good to see you!" Lilly opened her arms and Tia walked right into them. She'd considered on the way whether or not she'd tell Lilly the real reason for her visit, and decided that she would not. Getting away from it all for a couple days was the ultimate goal, and she knew that Lilly's company would do just that.

"You too," Tia said warmly, wrapping her arms around her friend in a tight embrace.

Lilly pushed her back and held her at arm's length with her hands on Tia's shoulders. "You look the same. At least your head hasn't gotten any bigger. Yet."

Tia couldn't help but laugh. "That's a relief. I've been worrying about my hat size a lot lately."

Lilly smiled and Tia thought, not for the first time, that her facial expressions reminded her of Bo. They had the same cocoa skin, the same expressive eyes, and almost the exact same laugh lines curling alongside lips that were almost always curved in a smile. "Some things never change," she said, taking Tia's hand. "Come on, best get to that coffee cake before Marcus finishes it off."

"I'm savin' her a piece, don't you worry your pretty little head!" Marcus popped out of the kitchen, wiping his mouth with the back of his hand. "I saved you a *big* piece," he smiled at Tia, pulling her in for a hug.

"How are you, Marcus? You're looking as handsome as ever, I see."

"Retirement agrees with me," he smiled, patting his stomach. "I live the life of leisure and my woman won't stop working. I'm a kept man, and I like it."

Lilly grabbed a wooden spoon from the breakfast nook between the two rooms and swatted him on the backside. He howled in fake pain and ran back into the kitchen. "You sure you want to get married, Tia? They seem so charming when you first get hitched, and then they turn into something else entirely."

"I was a something else entirely when you met me," Marcus teased. "You were just too charmed by my good looks to notice."

Lilly just rolled her eyes. "Men," she whispered. "Can't live with 'em and you can't live with 'em."

"Don't you mean, 'without 'em?'"

"I know what I said. Now how about some coffee and warm strudel?"

"I won't say no to that."

"Then you can tell me all about the world of the rich and famous. I've been following you, you know—life is good, huh?"

"First I want to hear all about how things are going at school. Is Drake staying out of trouble?"

"Oh, I got stories, honey. You really want to hear them?"

"I do," Tia grinned. "I really do."

They got so caught up in story telling that it was almost two hours before Tia took a break to make her calls. "I'm fine," she told her mother. "I'm just taking a little break from it all. Some peace and quiet. I'll be in touch soon." To Lexi she added, "Call

Jessa for me and relay the message. I left my phone behind, so I'm borrowing one, and it doesn't have texting. Have her tell Dylan that I'm fine and I'll be in touch soon. He's really busy the next few days anyway."

"Where are you, T?" Lexi asked. "You know Dyl's going to freak if he just hears from Jessa that you're on 'sabbatical.' You gotta give me more than that."

"Then it wouldn't be a sabbatical, would it? I'm fine, Lex, and he will be, too." She wondered about the truth of her last words even as they escaped her lips. "I've got to go." Tia cut the connection over Lexi's protests and powered down the phone.

As promised, the storm hit at about 3:00. Thick, heavy snow fell so fast that they actually watched the driveway disappear under a blanket of white, and they couldn't even see all the way to the street. Tia helped Lilly in the kitchen as she prepared the perfect meal of homemade chicken soup, salad, and freshly-baked bread, while Marcus watched his alma mater sock it to Purdue. Tia was struck by how comfortable they were with each other, and by how much they still loved each other, even after all these years. She'd really believed that she would have that with Dylan, and she pushed back the crushing sadness that she was planning to deal with later. Spending time with Lilly and Marcus made her feel better; lighter; and she just wanted to enjoy the feeling for a while.

When the power went out around 7:00, Marcus started a roaring fire and Lilly placed candles all over the house. They challenged each other to identify the different scents of the candles in the potpourri of odors and played Monopoly by the fire. Tia was reminded of her childhood and the joys of the simple, normal life that she'd probably never get to have. Those were her last thoughts as she cried herself to sleep later that night.

"Holy shit, Dylan, I've been trying to get hold of you for hours! Were you hiding out on me? We've got a disaster to try and avert, and I can't reach you!"

"I was at a shoot all day, Jessa, and I didn't have…what are you talking about? This whole day's been a disaster. I don't think I could take another one." He jammed his thumb and forefinger into his eye sockets to try and push back the headache that was pounding there. He'd sent over thirty texts to Tia with no answer, and had called Lexi to see if she knew why Tia wasn't answering her phone. "Um, didn't you talk to Jessa?" she asked. When she explained that Tia was 'on a break' and wasn't taking any calls, he snapped at her.

"What the hell is going on? What do you mean, 'she's taking a break?' From what?"

"Don't shoot the messenger, Miller. She hung up on me before I got any details, and she doesn't have her phone. I tried calling the number back a little bit ago and just got a message that the voice mailbox hasn't been set up; so I can't even leave her a message. I don't know what else I can tell you." Shortly after that his phone died, and he didn't have a charger, so he had to wait until he got back to the hotel to plug it in and retrieve his messages, and there was still no reply from Tia.

And now there was another disaster to avert?

"Well, there isn't going to be much of a choice in this matter. Where the hell were you last night, and what the fuck did you do?"

Dylan could hear the anger in her voice, and could almost feel her shaking through the connection. "I was at Skip's party at the studio, and I had a few drinks with some old friends. Apparently, I had a bit too much, because I don't really remember anything after Dozer left, and that was about midnight, I think. Bo walked me back to the hotel, and we went to the shoot in the morning. What's up your ass, Jessa? Why do you sound so bloody pissed?"

"Oh gosh, I don't know," Jessa said sarcastically, her voice venomous, "maybe because I love Tia almost as much as I love you and I can't believe you'd hurt her like that. Did you think the pictures wouldn't get out, Dyl? Did you really think you could do something like that and blame it on being drunk and get away with it? Holy shit, Dylan, I just don't even know what to think about you right now."

"You're going to have to back up, Jessa, because I have no bloody idea what you're talking about. You're saying I did something last night that might hurt Tia?"

"I'm sending you a link, Dylan. You need to have a look at it, think about it for a very short time, and call me back so we can figure out if there's any way to spin it. I don't think so, but maybe you can come up with something. In the meantime, I'm supposed to tell you that Tia is fine. She's left her phone at home and gone on a short trip to a place that no one knows about, apparently. That says to me that she's already seen them and it may be too late."

Dylan felt icy fear swirl through his gut just from the tone of her voice. "Seen what?"

"Sending the link now. You might want to sit down." Jessa hung up.

He didn't take her advice, but within seconds of the words appearing on the screen, he was on the floor, leaning against the wall for support. "*Our Menage-a-trois with Dylan Miller,*" the title read. The O's were made with little handcuffs, the I with a dildo, and the S was a whip that had been curled into shape. The words beneath the title were too small to read on his phone, but he could sure as hell see the picture—it was his own face, pressed between two sets of very large, very naked breasts.

He crawled across the floor to where his laptop sat at the desk in the corner of the room. Unable to trust his legs, he reached up and grabbed the computer and brought it down to his level on the floor. He tapped his fingers nervously as he waited for it to boot up; there were other pictures, but he couldn't make out any detail on the tiny screen of his phone. There had to be an explanation for this—he had no memory of *ever* being sandwiched between two pair of fake tits, and he sure as hell didn't recall being there *last night*. More doctored photos? And pornographic ones at that? He'd sue their asses off if that were the case...and it had to be.

He finally got the link open on his laptop and he froze, his hand holding his heart in his chest while it threatened with every beat to bust out through his rib cage. The air was eluding him and he fought for breath. He recognized the women immediately, and also recognized the shirt he'd been wearing and the couch in the little lounge off the kitchen where he'd had lunch at least a dozen times over the past few weeks. It was like watching someone play him in a movie, he thought, looking at picture after picture of him *doing things* with these women...kissing them both at the same time, their tongues touching each other as they slid over his lips; his hand holding one unnaturally large breast, his telltale tattoo like a bloody name tag; one of the women on top of him, his hand firmly on her ass... His life flashed before his eyes—not his past, but his future—and it was looking mighty fucking grim at the moment.

She must have seen these. Somehow, Tia must have gotten a glimpse and run for the hills. And who could blame her? She'd already dealt with the fake pictures Penelope had put out there, and those had nearly crushed her. He'd promised her that he'd never put himself in a situation that would hurt her like that again. He'd promised that he'd always have her best interests at heart. And she'd seen these pictures. Dylan felt the explosion coming and he scrambled to his feet, barely making it to the toilet before throwing up violently until only bitter bile crept up his esophagus. Because at the bottom of it all he had an explanation for Penelope's pictures—they never happened. For these, though, he had nothing; no way of salvaging the situation. No matter how hard he tried, he couldn't remember any of it, and that explanation was going to go over like a fucking bull in a china shop.

He tore off his clothes and jumped into the shower, turning the water on cold and shocking himself back to full consciousness. Not even bothering to towel off, he pulled on a pair of lounge pants and called Jessa. She picked up the call, but didn't say a word to greet him.

"I don't know."

"You don't know? You don't *know?* That's a great answer, Dylan. I'm sure Tia will be fine with that."

"Bloody fucking hell, Jessa, it's all I've got! I don't remember a single minute of it! Bo said he had to walk me home because I was so drunk—I didn't remember that either. I know I was with Dozer Cane, and I do remember those women stopping by our table, but I swear to you, I don't have a single memory that matches any one of those damn pictures! You need to make them take them off their site. Threaten to sue or something."

"Already in the works, but they have almost a million followers, Dylan, and if even ten percent of them—*five* percent even—shared the link, it could be viral within hours. And did you read the comments? Some girl said she was at a photo shoot with you today, and that she told you that you were a shit to do that to Tia and that your response to her was that she deserved that and more."

"Bloody fucking hell, I thought she was one of 'Penelope's Posse,' or whatever they call themselves."

"How much did you have to drink last night?"

"I don't know. Way too bloody much, obviously." All the strength drained out of him and he fell defeated onto the couch.

"You know what, Dylan? Good luck with Tia, because I'm already getting sick of this conversation."

"I'm sorry; I know it isn't what you want to hear, but I haven't got anything else. They were making them strong; and Dozer and I tossed back a few; but I know my limits, Jessa, and you know I rarely pass them. It's been a hell of a long time since I was shitfaced at a public gathering. It just kind of hit me all of a sudden, and I must have blacked out. I swear to you on my sister's grave, Jessa, that I am telling you the truth. I. Don't. Know."

Jessa inhaled deeply and let the breath out on a long, sad sigh. That was a game changer. She'd known Dylan for a long time, and she knew beyond the shadow of a doubt that he would never *ever* swear on Shelby's grave unless he meant it. He really had no memory of cheating on Tia with a couple of porn stars. Fanfuckingtabulous.

Would his word be enough? Would the fact that he didn't remember fondling some Swedish sluts be enough to make up for the pain and suffering that Tia was probably already dealing with? How about the additional pain and embarrassment that was still to come? Should she even tell him that the tabloids already had the pictures and that they'd hit both the airwaves and the covers within hours?

She loved Dylan *and* Tia, and she loved them even more as a couple, but she had some serious doubts. After all, she hadn't been able to believe Derek when he told her the same thing seven years ago, and she hadn't been able to trust a man with her heart ever since. This was bad. Really bad.

She could hear the tears in Dylan's voice. "What do I do, Jess?" he asked weakly.

"I don't know, Dyl. I don't know."

Chapter 40

When Tia awoke, she could see her breath in the room. She reached down to the floor where she'd left her sweatpants and hoodie and pulled them under the relative warmth of the covers, letting them get at least to her body temperature before pulling them on.

"Whoo whee!" Lilly shivered as she came running out of her own room wrapped in a thick robe and wearing fuzzy duck slippers on her feet. "Marcus, you got one minute to get that fire blazing, or I'm kicking you to the curb!"

"Yes, your majesty," he said with chattering teeth.

"I can't believe the power's still out," Lilly said, handing Tia a flashlight. "Come on and hold that for me. I knew there was a reason I kept that old coffee percolator. Marcus kept telling me to throw it away, said it was an old piece of junk...we'll see what he has to say about it when he has hot coffee in his belly this morning!" As usual, she said it plenty loud for her husband to hear every word.

By the time they got back up the stairs the fire was roaring and the candles were flickering again.

"And this is why I'll never own an electric stove," Lilly said, turning the switch, striking a match, and putting the pot of water over the flame. "You can't live in Chicago and not expect your power to go out a few times a year."

They huddled around the fire and drank their coffee, Marcus praising Lilly with overzealous adulation about the incredible intelligence she must have to keep the old fashioned coffee pot. Tia loved watching them interact—they teased each other constantly, but they both knew each other so well that they saw it for what it was—an expression of love.

When they finally warmed up, and the sun peeked out from behind the clouds, they decided to venture outside to check out the snow and shovel the driveway. For once the weatherman was right—the storm had dumped about eight inches, and the wind had sculpted it into drifts that were in some places well over a foot deep. Marcus fired up the snow blower while Tia and Lilly grabbed shovels and started in on the front porch. Tia was glad for the mental distraction and the physical demand on her muscles—it took her mind off her troubles for a little while. She'd come to no conclusions; in fact, she'd been working really hard to push it way to the back of her mind, and she knew that she wouldn't have been able to do that anywhere else but here; wrapped up in the warm embrace of a loving family that didn't question her motives for running away.

Marcus dug out a crank powered radio from the basement and they listened to it as they sipped hot chocolate and warmed their frozen toes and fingers by the fire. They learned that the storm had done some major damage, and that there were a lot of trees that had fallen, which was the primary reason for downed power lines. Clean-up crews were working 24/7, they said, but it still might be a couple days before the power was restored to all customers. People were urged to stay inside and to check up on their elderly neighbors—roads weren't being plowed because the plows couldn't reach them and stores and restaurants were closed. They were already announcing school closings for the next day, fully aware that busses wouldn't be able to get through. Lilly did a little victory dance when they announced that Jefferson was on the list. "Hooray, snow day!" she sang.

Tia helped Lilly move all the food from the fridge and freezer to the garage or the back porch, where she filled a bucket with snow and dumped things in. They decided to make a huge pot of beef stew and share it with some of the neighbors who might be unable to cook. Smooth jazz played on the radio as they chopped carrots, onions, celery, and beef by candlelight, filling a huge pot and setting it on a slow simmer. While it cooked, Marcus worked his way down the street with the snow blower, clearing other driveways and meeting up with neighbors who were doing the same. While Lilly and Marcus made the rounds with containers full of hot stew stacked on a sled, Tia made some phone calls.

"Dylan's pissed, and Jessa wants you to call her," Lexi said without emotion. "Of course, they don't believe me when I tell them that I don't know where you are. Thanks to you, they think I'm the world's best liar."

"Sorry about that, Lex, I don't mean for you to be in the middle. I just know that Jessa will give me the third degree and I'm afraid I'll crack under her interrogation."

"Wait, are you saying that you're more afraid of Jessa than you are of me?"

"Unequivocally."

"But she's like, four foot nine, or something. I could squash her like a bug."

"Five foot one, and you wouldn't stand a chance."

"OK. Seriously. Something's going on, and I think I'm the only one who doesn't know about it. Jessa's frantic when she calls me, and Dylan's downright unhinged."

"Dylan called you?"

"Like four times already today. He says to tell you that, 'appearances can be deceiving, and that he loves you more than anything.' What does that mean, Tia? It's all cryptic, and I don't like to be caught in the middle but out of the loop. What's going…" her voice cut out, and then she was back on the line. "That's Dylan on the other line. Again." Tia's heart started pounding. "Hold on a sec." Tia pulled the phone from her ear and hovered her finger over the end button, but couldn't bring herself to hit it. She heard Lexi's voice again, and put the phone back to her ear. "He says he needs to talk to you. I don't know what's going on, but I don't like it. If you two are fighting, let him apologize and be done with it. You know that you're going to make up eventually, and all the two of you are doing is irritating me and Jessa. I gave him your number. I love you, goodbye—work this out with Dylan."

The phone was already beeping when she hit the button to end her call to Lexi. Her hands were sweating, her heart was thumping like a jackhammer, and she was shaking all over. She was fighting a battle with herself, and neither side was going to win. Part of her desperately wanted to hear Dylan's voice, to hear him say that it was all a horrible mistake and that none of it actually happened, but she knew it wasn't true. The phone rang six times before it cut off mid-ring and fifteen seconds later, it started ringing again. Tears fell from her eyes as she held it in her hand until finally she punched the pillow on the guest bed, jammed her finger onto the power button on the phone, and tossed it onto the comforter, backing away from it as if it were alive.

She knew it would only be a matter of time before he got the number, which was the main reason she didn't set up the voice mail. The phone would only be turned on when she needed to use it, and he wouldn't be able to leave her any messages that she'd probably be too weak to ignore. Lies, all of it, anyway; although looking back on her last few conversations, especially the one with her mother where she told her everything was fine, Tia was starting to think that maybe *she* was the best liar in the world.

The power came back on about an hour later, just as Tia was handing over an obnoxious amount of Monopoly money to Marcus for landing on the Electric Company. "Well, how about that?" he mused. "I think maybe I need to charge you double."

They cheered as the heat kicked on and the first blasts of warm air pumped out of the vents. They ran around and blew out the candles, and then reset clocks around the house. Layers of clothing were shed as the house warmed up, and the television was turned on. Marcus wanted to watch Sunday night football, but Lilly insisted that they watch the news. "We've missed out on almost two days of news, Marcus. The world could have ended, and we wouldn't know a thing about it." He rolled his eyes at her.

"Besides, we should see about any damage that's been done from the storm. Go watch football in the bedroom."

"The news doesn't look better on the big screen," he pouted, but he grabbed a bowl of chips from the table and headed down the hall.

Com Ed says that it still has around 130,000 customers without power; most of those are in the southwest suburbs where the wind speeds gusted to seventy miles an hour and knocked down a lot of trees, which in turn fell on power lines, the news anchor said. *They hope to have power restored to those customers by the early morning hours, but urge customers to be patient and to check in on their elderly neighbors.* They switched over to a reporter who was out in the field standing on a dark street interviewing people who still didn't have power. Then they switched to a segment called 'Hometown Heroes,' and highlighted the police and firefighters who were going door to door to check in on residents in low income areas and delivering hot soup to families with children. Tia wanted to smash the TV when she heard the start of the next segment but she sat there frozen, instead.

In entertainment news, Kendra Kirby is back in rehab after a judge sentenced her to no fewer than ninety days after her third arrest for DUI in as many months. The star of "Midnight Express" gave a statement through her lawyer that she would 'use this time to regain my focus so I can shine my light on the world again.' That comment has prompted a social media buzz and a Twitter hashtag #lightsoutforkirby. Social media is also buzzing about a series of photos that allegedly show the recently engaged Dylan Miller engaged in some less than wholesome acts with a pair of Swedish adult film stars. Sonja and Melena—that's right, they don't use last names—had the pictures on their website with the title, "Our Menage-a-trois with Dylan Miller," but were required to take them down or else face legal action from Miller's camp. The pictures have been removed from the actual website, but they are still all over the internet and will likely be appearing on a tabloid near you. Neither Miller nor his fiancé, Tia Hastings, could be reached for comment, but Sonja and Melena are talking to our own William Brody tomorrow morning, so don't miss it.

Tia turned to Lilly with tears in her eyes. Lilly simply opened her arms and Tia slid over the couch and into them, pressing her face into Lilly's shoulder and letting the tears come. She'd been here before but had hoped to never need that kind of support again. When Nick died, no one knew quite how to handle her. Sometimes she got so much pity from people that she couldn't stand it, and she looked for ways to be alone rather than deal with it. Lilly was different. She'd lost two sons; one in a car wreck and one in a random shooting at his school; and she knew that pity wasn't the answer.

Lilly helped Tia to come to terms with what happened and to move on, and her quiet strength and strong faith had given Tia a component that no one else had been able to give her. Tia hoped that the strength would carry her through her life and help her face any adversity that came her way. Apparently, adversity had a way of breaking down even the most reinforced walls.

"Oh sugar," she said, her voice vibrating against Tia's skull. "I'm so sad for you. I can't imagine how you must feel. I take it you knew about this?"

"I knew, but I didn't know that anyone else did. I should have, though. That's the worst thing about this kind of life—everything you do has the potential to be a news story, and everyone thinks they have the right to judge you. What are they going to think of me now?"

Lilly stroked her hair and let her cry. What could she say? That people would mind their own business, or even that they would feel bad for her and give her space and support? It wasn't going to go down that way, and trying to sugar-coat it wouldn't make anything better. The majority of the public seemed to support Tia and Dylan as a couple, and to cheer for Tia's transformation from average Joe to a celebrity in her own rite. She'd handled herself with class, stood tall in the face of adversity, and didn't let the pressure break her. Lilly could only imagine how hard it would be to deal with everything that had been piled on Tia's plate, and she was proud of the way Tia maintained her quiet dignity and didn't let things go to her head.

But like most things in life, there was a flip side to that coin, and it was considerably less shiny. Tia had already paid a price for her new life; she'd had to give up her career, her house, and her ability to be normal; Lilly knew that the reason she'd begged out of helping to deliver the stew to the neighbors last night was the fear that she'd be recognized. She knew now that Tia had come to her because she could remain anonymous, and no one would think to look for her here. The pressure cooker was over full heat, and she felt like she was about to blow.

There were those who envied Tia's new life, and even those who took pleasure in talking about how she didn't deserve it. That horrible Penelope woman seemed to be recruiting them, and they'd verbally and even physically attacked Tia for nothing more than falling in love with a particular man. They were going to be all over this, and they would definitely make it news.

"Oh honey, what can I tell you? I wish I could say that they will feel sorry for you and that most of them will understand that you're hurting over it, but you know as well as I do that some them will judge you, and that a few will even take pleasure from your pain. I know it's futile to tell you that it doesn't matter what they think; that it only matters what you think and how you handle it with Dylan; but you and I both know the truth."

"I honestly don't know what to think," Tia sobbed. "It hurts so bad that I can't think past it; not right now, anyway."

"Is that why you're here? To avoid dealing with it?"

"Partly. Mostly. I just needed to get away from it for a while, to think things through I guess."

"And what conclusions have you come to?"

"None."

"Look Tia. You know I love you and that you are welcome to stay with us as long as you need to...but you can't hide away from the whole world forever. Take a little bit of time, but at some point, you are going to have to deal with it. What does Dylan have to say?"

"I haven't talked to him. I just can't right now."

"He doesn't know where you are, does he?"

"No."

Lilly pulled back and took Tia's face in her hands, forcing her to meet her gaze. "I don't know anything about this situation, but I do know that man loves you and that it has to be killing him not to be able to explain himself. You need to at least let him tell his side of the story."

"How can he explain it? What can he possible say that's going to make this go away?"

"It isn't going to go away, honey, but you know from past experience that there are two sides to every story, and things aren't always what they seem."

"I know I'm going to have to deal with it eventually, but I'm not ready to do it right now. I just need some time to figure things out for myself, to see if there is any way I can go forward. I've given up so much, Lilly—my dignity is one of the few things I have left; and even that's taken a big hit. I just don't know how I can face him—or anyone—right now. Not until I get my own head straight. It's just been so nice being here; feeling normal again."

"So be it, then. If he did this thing willingly, he deserves to stew in it for a while. Maybe he even needs to wonder where you are and what you're doing and feel what it's like to lose you. We'll kick Marcus out of the house tomorrow and have a girl day. We can bake some cookies and watch some TV and drink wine for lunch and forget about the rest of the world for a bit."

"Thanks, Lilly. You really are the best."

*****

"This is fucked up sixty ways from Sunday, mate. I really need to know what the hell happened last night." After he got off the phone with Jessa, Dylan scoured his phone for anything that would help him fill in the gaps. He went backward through all the texts he'd sent to Tia, and found the pictures that had been sent to her from his phone. Did he do that? He couldn't think of a possible scenario in which he'd put himself in that situation, and he sure as hell would never send pictures like that to the woman he loved more than anything in the world. She was obviously devastated, and had no intention of talking to him. He couldn't blame her, but he needed desperately to find out what really happened. It was almost a blessing that she wouldn't talk to him—he had nothing that he could tell her that would come close to explaining his disgusting and disrespectful behavior. He waited for the nausea to pass, and called Bo to come to his room.

"Shit brother, I hoped it wouldn't come to this," he said, hanging his head sadly.

"Bo, did you know about this?" Bo just nodded, never taking his eyes from the ground. "What the hell, mate?"

"I had no idea what was going on dude. I saw this waitress coming out of the back room looking all guilty, and she said something like she couldn't be a part of it and that you didn't know what you were doing. When I got back there, those chicks were all over you like flies on shit. They asked me to join in, and I kicked them out. It was obvious to me that you didn't know what the hell was going on—you were so smashed that you could barely open your eyes to acknowledge me. I got rid of them and deleted the pictures off your phone and brought you back here to sleep it off—when you didn't remember it the next day, I hoped that would be the end of it. All I could do was pray that they didn't have pictures of their own and that it would never go any further than that room. I sure as hell wasn't going to dump it in your lap the next morning."

"Fuck!" Dylan got up and paced the room, putting his hands to the sides of his head and fisting them in his hair. "I swear to you that I have no memory whatsoever about any of this! I would never do that to Tia—I would never do that at all! What the hell happened?" He took a swing at the wall hard enough to leave a mark and send a spike of pain radiating up his arm. It was a small fraction of the pain that Tia must be feeling, and he felt he deserved that and more.

"They were pretty smug about the whole thing, I'll tell you that."

Dylan dropped his head. "How far did it go, Bo? Do you think that I..." he was unable to finish the thought as his stomach threatened to upheave again.

"No," Bo said immediately. "I really don't think it went that far. You still had your pants on, and I don't think that you'd have been able to get them back on yourself if they were off. They still had their clothes on too, although they weren't fully covered. I'm pretty sure it didn't cross that line, at least."

Dylan let out a huge sigh that held only a small amount of relief. "Thank God for that, but it still crossed my line. And it damn sure crossed Tia's. I don't even know what to say to her, and that's even if she'll ever speak to me again. Nothing sounds more like bullshit than 'I don't know.' But I don't. No matter how hard I try, I don't remember anything after Dozer leaving."

"Do you think he would know anything? Maybe he would remember something that you don't. Can you call him?"

"Ya, tanks mon. 'E is a beautiful bwoy. Jus a beeny bwoy."

It was Sunday afternoon before he'd finally been able to get him on the phone, and Dylan was thankful to hear his voice. "Congratulations again, mate. To both of you. Listen, I've got something to ask you. I fucked up, Dozer, and I don't even remember it. I'm hoping you can tell me if anything strange happened before you left. How drunk was I?"

"No, not much. You had a clear head."

"Do you remember when the blondes came to our table?"

"Ya mon. Dey bring us some drinks an talk about getting naked wi' us. Dey really like you."

"Anything else? Was there anything strange about the way they were acting? Or the way I was acting?"

"You brush dem off, tell dem dat you not interested. I don't tink dey like dat answer."

"Obviously," Dylan said wryly. "Listen Doze, if you think of anything else—anything at all, no matter how small it might seem, will you call me? It's really important."

"Ya mon, no problem."

There was nothing else he could do. He dragged himself into the studio on Monday morning, but he was completely useless as far as recording went. All he could think about was Tia, hiding out somewhere where he couldn't get to her; suffering alone. He'd talked to Lexi again—or more like gotten his ass thoroughly chewed out by her, and he got no further with Sean. He was afraid to call Will or Danielle, and equally scared to call Paddy. In their eyes he had betrayed Tia in the worst way, and how could he expect forgiveness from them when he couldn't forgive himself?

Tia would have to go back to the apartment eventually, and it might be the only chance he'd have to talk to her face-to-face. Not that he had anything he could say to make things better. He could only throw himself at her feet and beg forgiveness, and hope to hell that she'd give him another chance.

He'd laid down enough vocals that the guys could work on things without him for a little while, and he booked the next flight out to Chicago.

*****

Bo was really feeling it. They were doing the best they could with the music, and were making some headway with a couple of the new songs, but he couldn't help but worry about Dylan. He was pretty much a wreck when he left, and the texts he'd sent over the past couple days were downright depressing. He'd had no word from Tia, and Lexi refused to speak to him, too. He was holed up in the apartment waiting for her to come back. Bo hoped she was coming back.

When his best friend was hurting, he was hurting, and he just felt completely drained. He decided to stay behind while the rest of the guys went out to grab some lunch and he made his way to the kitchen to throw a sandwich together. As he ate without tasting, he found himself standing in the little lounge where the now infamous photos had been taken. They'd been featured on a handful of tabloids, and were all over the internet; painting Dylan as a louse and Tia as a victim. Tabloid TV was talking about it like crazy, and so-called experts were speculating that Dylan probably had commitment issues and didn't really want to give up his life as the world's most eligible bachelor. He'd never really dealt with bad press before, but he could take it. He was one person who truly didn't care what the rest of the world thought of him, but the fact that it was hurting Tia, and that he couldn't do anything to protect her, was killing him. Bo had never known him to be so down.

He shoved the last of the sandwich in his mouth and lay down on the couch that had become almost like a crime scene. The drum sticks he had in his back pocket were jabbing into his back and he pulled them out and laid them on the back of the couch so he could stretch out and close his eyes for a few minutes. He wished to hell that he'd kept those damn bitches in the room and questioned them—there had to be something that could cast at least a faint glimmer on what the hell went down.

Bo went over it in his mind again and again and there was just something that didn't add up. Maybe it was the smug look on their overly made-up faces, maybe it was the way the one was so sneaky about the way she tried to slide Dylan's phone onto the...Bo sat up and hit the back of the couch with his fist, his drumsticks clattering to the floor. That was it. It had to be. There was no way Dylan would ever be stupid enough to text those pictures to Tia and even if he was drunk enough to be that stupid, he didn't even have enough coordination to button his own damn pants, much less maneuver his way through his contacts and send a series of texts with attached photos. And the messages that were sent didn't sound like Dylan at all—he was a Brit; he didn't use the term 'dude,' it was always 'mate.'

Dylan was beating himself up over being insensitive enough to send those pictures to Tia but Bo saw now that he hadn't sent them at all—the whole thing was orchestrated to make him look like a complete prick, and once again, both Dyl and Tia were paying the price for someone else's bullshit lies.

He dashed out the room to grab his phone—he needed to call Dylan and share his suspicions. His head was swimming with the possibilities, and he thought maybe he should call Jessa and run it by her first; try to make sense of the whole thing. Was it possible that the bitches had planned the whole thing ahead of time and had every intention of putting Dylan in a compromising position and then documenting it? Absofuckinglutely it was; and the more he thought about it, the more he knew that he needed to document everything that he saw that night. He went back into the kitchen and rummaged through the drawers until he came up with a pen and some paper and sat down at the table to write it all down.

Bo reached for his back pocket; he thought better when he had a stick in his hand. When he came up empty, he pulled the couch from the wall so he could collect them from where they had fallen. As he reached down, something else caught his eye. The first thing was a piece of candy; what might have once been an M&M, except that it was covered with a fuzz of dust that indicated it had been there for some time. The second thing was a pill—an oblong-shaped, olive green colored tablet with the number 542 stamped into it that was devoid of dust, so must have been only been there for a short time...only a few days, perhaps? An image from the night of the party filled his mind—the purses of the women spilling onto the floor, scattering a variety of contents including some pills from a plastic bottle that rolled off in all directions.

"Gotcha, bitches," he smiled, feeling lighter than he had in days. He took a baggie from a cabinet and dropped the pill inside, pulling the zipper shut. He was headed out the door when he spotted the phone book on a little table in the corner of the room. He grabbed it and his phone, and called for a taxi. He texted Ty on his way and told him that he was taking the afternoon off.

Chapter 41

Dylan sat in the apartment for the third straight day. He'd showered once, yesterday he thought, but he was afraid to leave the couch for fear that Tia might come and go while he was away or otherwise occupied. He had sighed a collective breath of relief when he saw that she hadn't packed up all her things before she left, and he was determined to be here when she returned. *Oh God, please make her return*, he thought.

He'd ordered take-away once, but had been surviving mostly on what was in the fridge and the cupboards. It certainly wasn't like he had much of an appetite, anyway.

He desperately wanted to turn off his phone, but couldn't in case Tia called. Bo had rung him twice a day and Jessa even more often, and he nearly jumped out of his skin every time it rang only to feel the brief hope that rose with every chirp collapse when it wasn't Tia's new number on the display. He had nothing new to tell them, and their words of pity and encouragement did little to make him feel better. His soul appreciated their support, but his nerves were getting damn tired of it.

Sleep was pretty much eluding him altogether. He couldn't bring himself to even lie in their bed, afraid that Tia's scent on the pillow might send him on a downward spiral from which he couldn't climb back out.

How could he have been so incredibly stupid? He had thought of nothing else for the past three days, but still couldn't understand how he could have even allowed himself to fall into that kind of a situation. Even before he'd met Tia he wouldn't have given those women the time of day—they were trashy and self-indulgent, and that had never been his style.

All he could do as he sat and faced the elevator door so he could see her the second it opened; if it opened; was fight with his failed memory and kick himself in the arse for being the epitome of everything he despised and swore he would never become.

He'd pretty much given up on finding the right woman; the one who he could love without worry and give himself to completely. And then, Tia crashed into his life. God knew he wasn't looking for anything to happen that night, but he fell for her quickly and he fell for her hard. She was his everything, and he may have lost her and didn't even understand why.

The hour grew late and he lay back on the couch, pulling a blanket over himself and hoping that pure mental exhaustion would bring him some much needed dream-free sleep.

*****

"Rohypnol," Bo said to Jessa's image on his phone. "Otherwise known as a date-rape drug. The cops knew what it was the second they saw it."

"Oh thank God," Jessa breathed. "I mean…that's not what I mean…it's just that I knew Dyl would never…"

"I know. I can't tell you how relieved I was when they told me. I just know it came out of one of those bitches' purses—there were pills bouncing all over the damn floor, but I didn't make the connection at the time. I just wish I'd grabbed one of them that night so we could prove it."

"Holy crap. Do you think it might still be in his system? Could he go and have a blood test or something and maybe get some proof?"

"The cops don't think so, but it might be worth a try anyway. They said it usually only stays in the system for about 24 hours, and 60 would be the max. It's already been almost five days."

"Have you told Dylan yet?"

"I tried calling him, but he didn't pick up. I haven't heard from him since last night and frankly, he didn't sound too good. I'm worried about him. I'm going to try him again right after I hang up with you, but what if he doesn't answer? He needs to know this, like, yesterday."

"OK. I'm going to get on this right away. We may not have solid proof, but I can certainly get it out there as a strong suspicion at least and maybe sway some minds. I'm going to do some digging into the porn stars, too. Maybe I can find something there that will give us a motive."

"As if people need a motive when it comes to Dylan Miller," Bo said sarcastically.

"I agree, but this thing has the stink of Esther Caglio all over it. It wouldn't surprise me a bit if she had a connection somewhere."

"I thought exactly the same thing."

"Listen, if you can't get through to Dylan, you need to get through to someone who can. Maybe you could explain the whole thing to Lexi and she could go over there."

Bo's heart skipped a beat at the sound of Lexi's name. He'd really love to hear her voice, but wondered if she'd even take his call. Then he wondered if he'd be able to talk to her at all once he did hear her voice or if he'd trip over his words and make an ass out of himself yet again. He had so much he wanted to say to her, but this sure as hell wasn't the time for it. "Maybe you should call her. I don't know if she'd really want to hear from me."

"Why wouldn't she? Did you two have a fight or something? Why don't I know anything about it?"

"It's not that, exactly…"

"Whatever it is, get over it. You just need to take care of this, OK? Dylan needs this news *right this freaking minute,* and if he doesn't answer, you need to find a way to get it to him. I have to get on this thing and try to diffuse a bomb that's already exploded."

"Yeah, OK, whatever. What's the number?"

"You don't have it?"

"No I don't have it," he said, the agitation clear in his voice.

"OK, I'm texting it to you now. Text me back and let me know what happens—I'm going to be on the phone trying to get some answers."

Dylan didn't pick up. Damn it, he'd thought about calling Lexi at least a hundred times, but could never figure out how to even start a conversation, much less say what he wanted to say. Hell, he didn't even really know what he wanted to say. He tried Dylan's line once more, but it just rang and went to voice mail. Bo guessed that he wouldn't answer for anyone but Tia, and she probably wasn't calling. There was no other choice; he needed to get Lexi to do a wellness check on Dyl as well as to fill him in on the new revelations. It would be an enormous relief for him to know that he hadn't betrayed Tia, and it wasn't fair to make Dyl wait for the news because his own palms were sweating over talking to the woman he was crushing on. He would just make it all business, and deal with his own shit at another time; if the time was ever right.

"Damn it, Miller, I told you that I don't want to hear any more of your bullshit..."

His number would appear on Lexi's screen just like Dylan's would—all zeros. Bo couldn't help but smile at her matter-of-fact greeting and lack of pleasantries. "It's not Dylan. It's Bo. How're you doin'," God help him, he almost said, 'beautiful,' "Lexi?"

"Oh." There was a moment of silence as she let that register, and then she was all back to business. "If you're calling to tell me that I should take that bastard's calls, you can just forget about it. I don't know where Tia is, and even if I did, I wouldn't tell him."

Bo couldn't help but chuckle. Damn, she was one feisty woman. "I figured it out. I know what happened, and Dylan isn't a bastard."

"Like hell he isn't."

"Listen Lexi, he isn't picking up his phone, and I'm really worried about him."

"And I should care because..."

"Because I found one of the pills that the bitches dropped when they were making their quick exit. It was a date rape drug."

There was a beat of silence and Bo could hear the intake of Lexi's surprised breath. "Say that again?"

"I'm positive that they not only drugged him, but that they planned to take the pictures and make it look like Dylan was steppin' out on Tia."

"Oh my God." He could clearly hear the sadness in her voice.

"I walked in on them in the middle of it all and kicked their asses out; and when I tossed their purses off the chair, some pills went flying across the room. Dylan was so out of it he couldn't even stand up. I thought that he was just drunk at the time, and I carried him back to the hotel so he could sleep it off. I had no idea about the texts until later the next day, and even then, he couldn't believe he sent them. Now I know he didn't. I didn't believe him at first either, because all he kept saying was that he didn't remember anything. I found one of the pills today under the couch and took it to the cops; and they confirmed that it was a date rape drug. I can't prove it, but I know in my gut that it went down that way."

"I believe you," she breathed. "God, I had such a hard time believing that Dylan would do something like that, but the evidence was kind of overwhelming. I feel like such a bitch. I was so mean to him."

"I didn't cut him a whole lot of slack either, but none of it sat right with me. The important thing is that they both need to know this information, and I can't get through to either one of them. Dylan isn't answering his phone, and I'm really worried about him. He's really fucked up over the whole situation, and he still thinks that somehow he's the one to blame. He's gone back to Chicago to wait for Tia to show up at the apartment, and I just know he's sitting there stewing in this whole mess and blaming himself for hurting her."

"Oh God. Poor Dyl. Poor Tia!"

"You need to help me fix this, Lexi. Can you go to the apartment and fill him in on this information so he can stop kicking the shit out of himself? And if you do really know where Tia is, she needs to know that he never did anything to hurt her. I don't know a whole lot of people who deserve each other like they do, and I can't stand that they're both doubting that right now."

Lexi was already shrugging into her coat and heading for the door. "I'm on my way to him right now," she said breathlessly. "I'll make them let me in. I'll call the cops if I have to." The images of the cops busting in on her own pity-fest were still fresh in her mind, but she wouldn't hesitate to do the same for Dylan if it would help resolve the situation.

"Thatta girl," Bo said, cheering her on.

"I honestly don't know where Tia is, but she calls me at least every other day and tonight should be a call night. Oh shit, I hope it's a call night. I really can't believe this, Bo. No matter how many crazy things happen to them, I can't help but wonder how people can be so shitty to each other. I feel horrible for the way I treated Dylan, and once again, he didn't do anything wrong."

"Tell him that. It'll mean a lot to him, I promise you."

"I'm leaving now." She paused, and Bo held his breath. "Thanks, Bo. Once again, you're the hero."

His heart melted just a bit at her words. "Thank you, Lex, but I think you'll get the hero status out of this one."

He heard the click as she cut the connection and he sat there with the phone in his hands for a long while, praying for miracles.

*****

"Welcome to *Chit Chat*!" The familiar voice of Dottie Miles filled the living room, and Tia sat back with a cup of tea. She'd been avoiding watching the television, preferring instead to hide in books and prepare meals for Lilly and Marcus. Curiosity had finally gotten the better of her; but more than that, she really needed to get a grip on her life and make some hard decisions. She needed to see if people were still talking about the pictures and find out what they were saying. Did the whole world think she was a complete loser who couldn't hold onto her man, or that Dylan had decided that Penelope had been right all along and that a relationship between a rock star and a teacher could never last? Were they right?

She couldn't keep hiding out at Lilly's. She and Marcus had been wonderful to her and hadn't mentioned a word about her leaving; even when the snow was under control and Lilly had to go back to work on Tuesday. Tia had done some hard thinking that day and every day since, but her brain was still clouded and the pain was still too fresh to come to any definitive answers. The time had come, however, and even though the apartment in the city still didn't really feel like home, it was hers and she missed it.

It was nearly halfway through the show before Dottie brought it up. "OK, can we go back to the Dylan Miller story for just a bit?" she asked her co-hosts. "Now you know I've been a fan from the start—and I still am—so I just have to say that I think people are making entirely too much of the whole thing."

"I don't agree," Lynne said. "I think it's another case of a man who couldn't keep it in his pants and never even considered the consequences."

Tia felt as if a giant hand was squeezing her heart.

"I know that's what people *say* it looks like," Dottie argued, "but really. I did some research last night, because I just couldn't get it out of my mind. I've been rooting for him and Tia since the word go, and I couldn't make myself believe that he'd really do that to her. The man's been in the spotlight for a lot of years, and never once has there been a situation where he's been caught in such an insanely inappropriate scenario. He's kept his life pretty private, and hasn't even dated extensively. I know a lot of people are saying he's a complete idiot for getting caught like that, but a lot of people are coming to his defense, too; some of them are ex-girlfriends who say that Dylan was not only faithful and trustworthy, but also devoted and much too classy to mix it up with a couple of low budget porn stars."

"Well, he obviously did, or we wouldn't have the evidence," Abigail chimed in.

"I think someone threw him under the bus." Her co-host opened her mouth to protest, but Dottie cut her off. "You've seen him with Tia; you've heard the way he talks about her and seen the way he keeps her close. He loves that girl, but there are an awful lot of people who aren't happy about that, and I'm not just talking about *'My Bloody Valentine.'"*

"You can't argue with the proof, though, and the fact remains that something went on between him and those women."

"But did you actually see the pictures? Does he look like a man who's enjoying himself? Most men, if put in that same situation, would have huge grins on their faces and would be hamming it up for the cameras—Dylan just looks out of it."

"I'm going to need more proof than that," Lynne said.

They moved on to other topics and Tia turned off the TV and sunk into the couch, wondering how her life had come to this.

*****

"We need to have a talk," Lilly announced on Thursday when she got home from work.

Tia had been expecting it; in fact, she'd already come to the conclusion that it was time for her to take her life back. She'd spent the past couple days weighing her options, and realized that she couldn't make a final decision until she'd heard Dylan's side of the story, even if it wasn't what she wanted to hear. No matter how many ways she turned it in her mind, she was sure that Dylan loved her and even more sure that she loved him. Life without him wasn't something she could even consider at the moment, but until they talked, she would be stuck in this limbo. She knew that she was hiding from the possibility that he'd decided that a life with her wasn't worth his time, but in her heart of hearts, she just couldn't believe that to be true, and what Dottie had said kept tugging at the back of her mind. "I know."

"Listen, darlin'. I know you're still hurting, but I've been thinking about this a lot. I was watching *Chit Chat* on my break today and that woman, Dottie Miles, made some good points. Have you seen the show?"

"I saw it today. I was afraid to see what they would say before and I..."

Lilly took a deep breath and pulled her carry-all bag onto the table. "Tia, have you seen the pictures?"

She looked down at the floor, afraid to look at what Lilly was pulling out of her bag. "They were texted to me."

"I know, but have you really seen them? After the show, I couldn't get them out of my mind, and I had to go buy the magazine."

Tia's stomach churned instantly. "No Lilly, please. I don't want to see them. Absolutely not."

"Answer me this," she said, looking deep into her eyes. "Do you love that man, Tia?"

She hitched in a breath and a tear spilled from her welling eyes. "More than breathing."

Lilly put her arm around Tia and gave her a squeeze. "Do you believe that he loves you?"

"Yes."

"People aren't perfect, Tia. Sometimes they fuck up, plain and simple. Hopefully they learn a lesson from it and go about making it right. Do you think Dylan would want to make it right?"

Tia was transported to the day Dylan came back for her, the day he walked into a staff meeting and told her he had never stopped loving her. He hadn't done anything wrong, but the hurt on his face and the pain in his eyes nearly broke her heart. She remembered the way he looked at her hard when he insisted on apologizing for not seeing through Penelope's lies; how sorry he was that she was hurt because of him, even though he wasn't the one who caused the pain. God, the love she saw in his eyes was almost too much to bear, and she thought her heart would explode with the sheer intensity of his sincerity. She did believe that he wouldn't intentionally hurt her—had to believe it before she made the decision to make a life with him. *You have to have a lot more trust than the average girlfriend,* he'd told her on more than one occasion, *they try to fabricate relationships, try to sensationalize the simplest things to sell their rags. It might get hard at times—really hard.*

She cried out then, breaking down completely and sliding to the floor, pulling her legs to her chin and curling up as small as she could get. Dylan had never once given her a reason not to trust him—and at the first sign of something hard, she'd run away and not even given him a chance. She hadn't once considered what her leaving may have done to him; the thought that he might be hurting, too. She hadn't given him a chance to do anything.

"I'll take that as a yes," Lilly said, pulling Tia's head into her lap and cradling her while she sobbed. "Dottie said that no matter how much evidence there appeared to be, she couldn't believe that he'd do that to you. She said that she could see how much he loved you, and that she believed someone had thrown him under the bus. I love how she uses that expression. I had to see for myself if what she said could be true, and I think it is. You need to look at the pictures, Tia."

"I can't," she whimpered.

"Dottie said that most men in the position of being with two porn stars would be loving life; hamming it up for the camera and smiling big. Dylan doesn't look like that at all. He doesn't look *anything*, baby. It's almost like he doesn't even know what's happening. I can see it, and I've only met him a few times. I think you'll know when you see them that he didn't make it happen. I don't even think he was a participant."

She didn't want to. God, she just wanted to crawl back into last week and make the whole thing not happen, but if what Lilly was saying was true, it might settle her heart just a bit. Being drunk was never an excuse for bad behavior, but maybe she could find a way to live with it. She nodded, and Lilly reached into the bag and pulled out the magazine.

She tried not to see the whole picture; whether Dylan was out of it or not, she didn't want to see the man she loved in the arms of another woman. Her whole focus was on his face, and she could see instantly that the face she was looking at wasn't

Dylan...at least not the Dylan she knew. There was no expression whatsoever; not pleasure, not victory, not disgust; just a kind of noncompliance that really did indicate that perhaps he wasn't fully aware of what was going on. His eyes were closed and his mouth was open slightly like he was asleep. Looking closely at one of the pictures, she could actually see manicured fingers holding him at the wrist in what appeared a way to keep his hand in place. Oh God, Lilly was right and so was Dottie Miles. Dylan wasn't any more present in the scene than she was was—physically he was there, but there was no awareness in any part of him. She felt the guilt pour over her like a waterfall and knew instantly that he was here, in Chicago, waiting for her to come home; hurting and suffering once again for her pain that he hadn't intentionally caused.

His first text of the evening flashed in front of her eyes. *Looks can be deceiving*, he'd said, *especially in this case*.

"Oh God Lilly, I'm such a fool. I have to go to him."

"I knew you'd see it, too," she said. "I just knew it. For what it's worth, my money's on you two making it."

Tia planted a kiss on Lilly's cheek. "Do you have a phone book? I need to get a cab."

"I'll drive you. I would be happy to."

*****

The elevator door opened, and he was exactly where she knew he'd be; sitting on the long black couch in the living room waiting for her to come home. Her heart nearly melted when she saw him—his eyes were red and rimmed with dark circles and a shaggy beard shadowed his face. His normally silky hair hung limply over his eyes and he looked gaunt and tired, but his eyes widened with surprise and relief when she stepped off the elevator and into the dimly lit room. She thought she'd never seen him look so beautiful.

For a moment they just stared at each other, and then he slowly got off the couch and made his way to her, falling to his knees and wrapping his arms around her legs and burying his face in her stomach. She could feel the shaking of his sobs and he fought to keep his voice steady as he whispered, "I've never been so sorry about anything in my life, Tia. I know I don't deserve you, but I'm dead without you, baby girl, and I hope to God you'll find a way forgive me. You are my whole world, and I love you more than I can ever tell you. Please..." He nearly choked on the last word, and he clutched her with his whole being.

Tia fell to her knees and wrapped her arms around his neck. They cried together like that for a few moments, each desperately holding on to the other, before Tia was even able to form words. "I'm so sorry I ran away, Dyl. I'm sorry I didn't even give you a chance to explain. I love you more than life, and we'll get through this. I can't live without you, either."

The hitch of his breath was enough to tell Tia that she'd made the right decision; that no matter how hard it was, they'd come out on the other side of this with their love intact and maybe stronger than ever.

"Oh God, baby girl, I was so scared I'd lost you again. I was worried that this time I wouldn't get you back."

Through her tears, Tia said, "I told you, Miller, you aren't going to get rid of me that easily. You're stuck with me forever."

"I wouldn't have let you go, you know. I would move heaven and earth to keep you in my life."

They held each other for a long time, holding each other like life rafts in stormy seas. Dylan stroked her hair and wiped her tears, and she wrapped her legs around him so she could press against him with as many cells as possible. They cried together and whispered mutual sentiments of relief, forgiveness and love.

They both jumped when they heard the buzzer, and looked at each other with confusion. No one knew Dylan was here, and Tia hadn't told anyone but Lilly that she was coming home. "I'll get rid of them," Dylan whispered, pulling Tia to her feet and walking over to the intercom. "Yes?"

"Dylan, thank God. It Lexi. I have to talk to you right now—it's an absolute emergency. Buzz me up."

*****

Tia and Dylan stared at each other for a few moments as the elevator door closed on Lexi, heads reeling from the information she'd just given them. Finally, Dylan took her hand gently and pressed his lips to the back of it. "You forgave me before you knew," he whispered. "When you believed I'd betrayed your trust." He leaned over, putting his head in her lap.

Tia pressed her lips together in a thin smile. "No, Dylan, no." She fisted her hands in his hair and gently pulled him up to meet her gaze. "I just had to realize that there was nothing to forgive." He raised one eyebrow in question and she pressed a kiss there. "I have to believe that you would never betray me—otherwise we'll never make it. I know you love me…"

"More than you'll ever know."

"…and that you'd never willingly do something to hurt me. I'm sorry it took me so long to figure that out; but I promise you I'll never forget the lesson I learned. It just hit me like a truck, and then I worried about what other people would think of me…I still have to work on that one, I guess."

"That's the hardest one to get used to," he admitted. "It doesn't matter how much you tell yourself it doesn't matter; it still hurts when people who don't know you pass judgments without knowing even a fraction of the truth. I wish it wasn't that way, baby. I wish you never had to hurt because of me."

"I just need to figure out how to let it roll off my back, like you do. I'm not there yet, obviously, but I'm working on it."

"It never rolls off your back. It sits there like a weight until you shrug it off; but you do shrug it off eventually because it gets too much to bear. But you can trust me, Tia, always. I'm going to fuck up sometimes; God knows I'm not perfect; but I will never, ever, do anything to hurt you. I know it's hard, but you can absolutely trust that."

"I do know," she whispered, "I'm so sorry that it took me so long to figure it out, Dyl. I never should have doubted you."

"So you'll still marry me, then?" he smiled.

"Try and stop me."

He laced his fingers through hers and lifted her hands over her head, bringing his lips to hers. "I love you, Tia Hastings. Nothing and no one will ever change that."

"Show me how much," she breathed against the soft brush of his lips.

"Oh my sweet, sweet, baby girl." He pressed his lips to hers and smiled. "I desperately need a shower."

"I'll wash your back if you wash mine."

"Always and forever," he whispered, taking her by the hand and leading the way.

Chapter 42

"Great to see you, Dylan, although I wish it were under better circumstances."

"Indeed," Dylan said, shaking his hand. "Bradley Erikson, meet Tia Hastings, my fiancé."

"Now there's a good circumstance," Bradley said, shaking Tia's hand. "Best wishes to you both."

"Thank you. It's good to meet you."

"I assume you're in LA for the premier?" He looked at Dylan and tipped his head. "Congratulations on the release, right? I mean, in light of the whole situation...she isn't going to be there, is she?"

"She sure as hell hasn't been invited, but frankly, I think she's gone a bit off her rocker lately, so I wouldn't put anything past her. I thought about skipping it myself, but it turns out that Tia really wants to do it, so here we are."

"Do you have a restraining order against Miss Caglio?"

"No. I didn't see it necessary."

Bradley frowned. "Considering the fragile nature of her...psyche...and her connection to those porn stars, I'd advise you to be extra cautious. She could use this as another platform to spew her BS, and showing up would give her the national audience she's been so desperate to get."

"We're both prepared for that scenario, I think, and I've been assured that there will be extra security on hand, just in case."

"I'm glad to hear it." Bradley turned to Tia. "I've followed the story; with Dylan being my client and all; and I have to say that you've really handled this whole thing well. You've got class—a lot more than she's been showing lately."

Since she'd been out on bond, Penelope had been making the rounds of the talk show circuit and posting frequently on social media. She continued to insinuate that she and Dylan had more than a professional relationship, and that it was only a matter of time before he got bored with the choices he made. It was getting old, but Tia was way past the point where her words had any sting. If anything, her pathetic attempts at gaining sympathy made her look even more desperate.

"Yes, well, retaliating only brings me down to her level, and means I have to interact with her in some way, which I'd really like to avoid as much as possible."

"Which brings us to the point of this meeting; to discuss your options for a civil suit. The buzz that I hear around town is that her lawyer is going to enter some sort of a mental health plea— and her behavior lately is making me think that maybe he's right. I'll be honest with you; I don't think that the prosecutor is going to push very hard to make an example of her—she's young, famous, and let's face it—a bit unbalanced. She wasn't stealing Social Security checks or credit card numbers; they were love letters. The Feds don't really stand to gain anything by going for prison time. I think they'll go for a stint in a psych facility and some fines; probably some community service of some sort. Of course, she won't be able to profit from the situation, either—that option will go to the two of you."

"What does that mean?" Tia asked.

"It means that she can't write a book about her ordeal or secure any film rights for the story. If it were made into a movie, she couldn't star in it or even have a minor role, for that matter. She can't consult, and she can't be paid for interviews related to what happened in New Zealand."

Tia's eyes narrowed. "Made into a movie? Our story?"

"Why not? It's got intrigue, adventure, a great love story—it would be a film about making a film that has a perfect villain and a love triangle tossed in for good measure. Sounds like Hollywood to me."

"Don't forget a happily ever after," Dylan added with a smirk.

"Wouldn't be a chick flick without one," Bradley winked. "Speaking of chick flicks, I also hear through the legal grapevine that she's been pretty much blacklisted. No one wants to work with her until they figure out the whole legal mess and frankly, a lot of them are worried about her state of mind. She's kind of teetering on a rail right now, if you know what I mean."

"Do you know how much she ended up having to pay in New Zealand?" Dylan asked.

"I think it was somewhere around one-fifty."

"Thousand?" Tia asked, her eyes wide.

"Yes, ma'am. I imagine she'll face even more here. New Zealand wanted to get rid of her."

"That seems like an awful lot."

"Well, there was a long list of offenses, and each of them held a penalty. Plus, she wanted to get out of there, so was willing to pay it. Which brings us back once again to why we're here." Bradley slid a thick folder from his desk and opened it for Dylan and Tia. "She imposed on a lot of your civil rights and caused you both a lot of very public pain and suffering. The fact that she documented so much of it for herself, which will be on display for all the world to see, is going to make it pretty open and shut. Just the pain and suffering alone could..."

Tia held up her hand to interrupt. "I don't want to press charges."

The men stared at her. "Excuse me?" Bradley asked.

She turned to Dylan and let out a huge sigh. "I don't want to do it, Dyl."

"Why the bloody hell not?"

"Believe me, I've thought about it a lot, and I just don't see what it's going to accomplish."

"It's going to accomplish justice, Tia, pure and simple."

"It tastes a little more like vengeance to me, and it's really sour. It isn't me, and I don't think it's you, either."

"Either way, she needs to pay for what she stole from us."

Tia took his hand and looked into his eyes. "What's the right price, Dyl? She's already paying, and not just with money. She's lost her credibility, maybe her career, maybe even her mind—and I know from personal experience how it feels to lose you."

"Oh, Tia…"

"I mean it, Dyl. She really thought she loved you; maybe she even did. Her own family has dragged her through the mud and disowned her; she could be looking at jail time and another big fine…how much more should she pay?"

"You know, you could get a pretty penny; especially since you can both sue her individually," Bradley tossed in.

Tia's eyes didn't leave Dylan's. "We don't need a pretty penny, or any amount of pennies, baby. Suing her isn't going to prove her guilt; she's already done that to herself. It isn't going to change anything that's already happened; it's only going to rehash it. I don't want to have to appear in court to repeat what I've already said at least a hundred times, and I sure as hell don't want to relive it all again. I don't even want to give her the chance to tell her side of the story, much less have to hear it. Whether we sue or not, we've already won—and she's already lost. A lot, if you ask me. I just want to put the whole thing behind us and move forward. We're planning a bright future, and I don't want a single minute of that joy getting tarnished by Esther Caglio."

Dylan pushed his fingers through his hair and dropped his head, cradling it in his hands and murmuring to himself. Finally, he sighed and looked at Tia, nodding slowly and smirking with a half-smile.

"Bloody hell. You're right; of course you are; about everything, and I couldn't love you more for it." He leaned over to kiss her cheek and whispered, "You have the most beautiful heart, baby girl."

"I love you, too—I knew you'd understand," she whispered back.

Dylan sat back in his chair and contemplated a moment longer before speaking. "You're sure? This is your final decision?" Tia pressed her lips together in a thin smile and nodded, and Dylan turned to Bradley. "OK then, I concur. She certainly isn't getting away with anything, and it would be a breath of fresh air to put it behind us once and for all." His eyes met Tia's again and he smiled. "There you have it, then. I want it firmed up that she can't profit from any of this, but aside from that, we won't be pressing charges. This whole thing is officially over."

Bradley pressed his lips together and alternated between nodding and shaking his head. "As your attorney, you know I need to advise you of what you stand to lose if you don't go through this, but as your friend, I have to say that I respect your decision. You've got yourself a great girl here, Dylan. Penelope didn't stand a chance."

"Not even for a second," he smiled at Tia, pure adoration in his eyes.

They spent nearly another hour signing papers and going over details with Bradley before he stood to shake their hands. "Until next time, Dylan, it's always a pleasure. Enjoy the premier, and best of luck to both of you."

"You're going to rock that red carpet tonight," Dylan said as they left Bradley's office. "You ready to turn some heads?"

"Oh, I'm more than ready," she smiled.

Three hours later, Tia glided out of the bedroom of the suite and did a slow twirl in front of a waiting Dylan. "Wow," he whistled between his teeth. "Stunning doesn't seem an adequate word for how incredibly sexy you look, but I can't think of a better one. You are one gorgeous lady, soon-to-be Mrs. Miller."

Gus had designed her dress; and it was a knockout. The blues and greens captured the colors of both their eyes, and it fit her perfectly, accentuating her best features and flowing in soft layers from her waist to the floor. The borrowed teardrop diamond rested just above the gathered bodice, and made her neck look long and lean. She felt like a dream, and Dylan's eyes concurred.

"You clean up pretty well yourself," she smiled as she ran her eyes over the man she loved, taking in the perfectly tailored tux and the careless tumble of his wavy hair. "Talk about turning some heads."

"We are pretty damn good together, aren't we?"

"In every single way," she smiled, moving into his arms.

"Oh my God," Tia breathed as the limo took its final turn and slowly approached the theater. "It's like Disneyland."

She'd seen it on television, of course, but that didn't even come close to preparing her for a Hollywood movie premier; especially when she'd actually be walking the red carpet. Searchlights tossed beams into the fading sky, the theater was illuminated in a full spectrum of colors, photographers stood at the ready to get the first photos of them exiting the limo, and hundreds of fans stood along the velvet ropes and spilled into the street waving and cheering. There were hoards of people stepping off busses parked down the street, and one of those open-air tour busses slowed, people on the upper deck waving and snapping pictures. A few of Dylan's co-stars were already on the carpet, some chatting briefly with fans and others posing for photo ops or interviews. The whole thing had been orchestrated so that Dylan would arrive last, and the fact that Bruce Dinsmore, his character's kidnapper, was just starting his walk, allowed Tia to breathe a little sigh of relief. She wasn't nervous about tonight— well, maybe now she felt a flutter in her stomach—but she had worried that the star who should have hit the carpet right before Dylan might show up, and the last thing she wanted was a public confrontation with Penelope.

He tipped her chin up and kissed the tip of her nose. "As usual, the best view is through your eyes." he smiled. "I just want to fall into them and see the world as you do, love."

She snuggled into him, and let out a little squeal of delight. "Oh, Dyl, never in a million years did I ever picture myself doing something like this. I feel like Cinderella at the ball." The constant flash of cameras and the swing of the searchlights gave everything a strobe-like effect—it was like being inside of a dream.

"Cinderella couldn't hold a candle to you." Dylan took her face in his hands and planted a soft kiss on her lips. "You look every bit the part, but I'm glad that at midnight, you'll still still be in my arms."

"I'm so glad you're my prince, Dyl."

A valet in a tux with tails stepped over to open the door and Tia could almost feel the anticipation of the waiting crowd. Dylan raised his fist and Tia tapped it with her own. "Let's do this thing, shall we?" he smiled, stepping out of the car and offering a quick wave to the gathered crowd before reaching in for Tia's hand. The voices from the mostly female fans were unbelievable—Dylan was the one many of them had come to see, and he turned on his rock star charm. Tia assumed her own public persona, and arm in arm, they started their stroll toward the entrance.

"Dylan, Dylan, will you sign my book?" "Dylan, can I get a picture?" "Dylan, I love you!" "Tia, you rock!" "Tia, can I get your autograph?" The very atmosphere was crackling with electricity and Tia swept her eyes over the crowd, feeling easier when she took in the number of security guards that perked up to full attention and scanned the swarm of people as they exited the vehicle.

They started their journey down the red velvet mingling with the audience, as it should be, singing autographs and pausing to take photos with a few of the fans. Then, they wound their way through the various stations manned by TV personalities and photographers, stopping for brief interviews and more pictures. They ended up near the entrance where the rest of the cast and crew had gathered, catching up with each other and mingling with other celebrities who had shown up to take in the premier or get a little time in the spotlight themselves. They worked their way around the group, making introductions and accepting congratulations on the movie and their engagement.

"Great to see you, Dylan." Stan separated himself from the crowd and gave Dylan a short hug. "You must be Tia. I certainly have heard a lot about you. Congratulations to you."

Tia shook his hand. "Thanks so much, it's nice to meet you, Stan. I've heard a lot about you, as well. I owe you a huge thank you for being so understanding when Dylan had to leave on such short notice."

"Yeah, well, I wasn't too happy about it at the time, I have to admit, but things came together surprisingly well, I think. I'm pretty happy with the end result. I imagine it will be a bit of a mixed bag for the two of you; watching it. I'm really sorry about the whole situation—Penelope's really been...vocal."

"Now there's the bloody understatement of the year. Please tell me she isn't here."

"Not that I've seen or heard. We certainly didn't invite her. Some of the studio reps thought it would be great press if the two of you were seen in public together for the first time since the shit hit the fan, but I didn't agree. I put my foot down on that pretty hard."

"I'm glad for that, and I owe you another one."

"You're both coming to my after-party, right?"

"We'll definitely be there."

Tia was introduced to the rest of the cast and a lot of the crew, all of whom greeted Dylan warmly and seemed genuinely glad to meet her. "His whole trailer was covered in pictures of you and he talked about you all the time," Sadie said, pulling her into a warm hug. "It was so sweet. I'm really glad things worked out for the two of you."

Finally, Tia watched her parents walk in with Bo, their eyes wide as they took in the spectacle. She ran over and threw her arms around them. "Pretty cool, huh?" she whispered to her mom. "Did you ever imagine you'd be on the VIP guest list for one of these? I know I never did."

"Not in my wildest dreams," Danielle said. "It's a trip, isn't it? Don Pradinski interviewed us on the way in!"

Bo took Tia's hand and lifted it over her head, spinning her in a slow circle before pulling her into his arms. "You are the best looking thing in this whole room," he said with a smile. "Strummer Boy better know how lucky he is!"

"He knows it all too well," Dylan agreed, joining them and greeting his best man. "You look beautiful too, Danielle. I'm so glad you could be here with us." He kissed both her cheeks and shook hands with Will before lifting a finger to summon of one of the servers and handing each of them a flute of champagne.

Tia was thrilled to see the spark in her mother's eyes. Dylan had given her the option of inviting whomever she liked, but she decided to be a bit selfish and keep this first one mostly for herself. There would certainly be others, and she could invite other friends then. Her parents, though, were a given.

They hung out for about another half hour in the VIP lounge, sipping champagne and chatting before they were waved inside and ushered to their seats. Stan made some opening remarks about the 'interesting circumstances' surrounding the making of the movie, and the house lights dimmed.

I should be in there, Penelope thought as she watched the scene from across the street. *That's my red carpet, too, damn it. I earned it!* She'd spent the better part of the past two days; ever since Ben had called her warning her against showing up uninvited; weighing her options. She was one of the stars; she had every right to be strolling the red carpet and basking in the applause and adoration of her fans. The last time she'd gotten a public reception was when she was brought back from New Zealand; and to say that it had been less than glamorous would be the understatement of the century—she'd been given the same shabby clothes she'd been wearing the night Dylan walked in on her in her trailer, and they wouldn't even give her any make-up or let her do her hair properly. They refused to provide her with any decent hair products in jail, and her crown had lost its shine and luster. Much like her life these days.

The scene had been a very mixed bag. She had expected fans to show up in support of her and they had; but there were more than a few hurtful, negative remarks hurled in her direction by the small crowd, as well.

Watching Dylan, looking incredibly sexy in his gray tux, his wavy hair falling past his shoulders in casual disarray, was downright painful; but watching his date strutting around in her expensive gown—God, she could see the fucking rock on her finger from *here*—was like a punch in the gut. How dare she walk around like she *belonged* there, posing for pictures and signing autographs. She was nobody!

Ben told her point blank that it was a bad idea—the last thing she needed was more negative press, he'd said, and her showing up expecting to get the star treatment was likely to end badly. "You need to lay low for a while, Penelope," he told her. "Give it a couple months for the spotlight to fade, and then you can start thinking about your comeback. Consider it a gift Miller and Hastings aren't pressing charges—that'll get this thing finished a lot more quickly and with a lot less fanfare."

But the spotlight wasn't fading, and she was tired of waiting. First it was their reunion, then their engagement, her arraignment, and now the wedding was in the news; especially since no one could nail down the actual location of where the ceremony would take place. It wasn't going away any time soon, and she desperately needed to do something to get her life back on track. God knew she'd been at the bottom before, and she'd always managed to find a way to claw her way back up to the top.

She looked down at the ticket her agent was able to get and felt the hot coil of anger twist around in her gut. No way in hell she should have to sneak into her own movie premier; no way she should have to watch from across the street, a hoodie covering her head and glasses over her eyes—not when her name was second on the goddamn bill. She had earned the right to walk that fucking carpet and she needed to see the film; needed to be in the same room with Dylan even if he had no idea she was there. But, maybe if she could catch him alone, she could finally get a chance to explain her side of the story.

She showed her ticket to the guard at the front entrance and slipped into a seat just as the lights were dimming.

✶✶✶✶✶

Maybe she was biased, but Dylan was nothing short of amazing. He played the role perfectly and he looked damn good on the enormous screen. It was hard at first watching him interact with Penelope's character and she had some minor personal issues with the love scenes, but she had anticipated it and it only took a spin of the ring on her finger to remind her that it was all an act. She recognized some of the backdrops from the tabloid pictures that had been burned into her brain and could see how they had so easily convinced the public that Dylan and Penelope were a couple. As much as she hated to admit it, Penelope was a good actress, and they looked like the real deal. Her character was much softer than she was in real life, so she was actually likeable. Somewhat.

She reached over to pluck a few kernels of popcorn from the tub in Dylan's lap and he grabbed her hand, snatching them with his mouth and then licking the butter from her fingers. Tia giggled and grabbed another handful, leaning her head on his shoulder and whispering, "You're amazing, as always—how is it that I'm constantly impressed by you?"

"It's not bad so far, is it?" he said modestly. "You can never tell when you're filming, and I've never been so nervous about an end result as I was with this one."

"Quit talking to me," she smiled, "I'm trying to watch this amazingly hot guy on the big screen, and you're throwing off my focus." He squeezed her hand and then brought it to his mouth to press a kiss against the back of it.

Penelope's soul broke into pieces. She'd seen them on television, of course, thanks to that bitch of a prison guard who played it over and over and over; and she couldn't resist watching their other appearances, just so she could see Dylan's smile and hear his sexy, accented voice; but seeing them together in person was like having her heart ripped out and crushed by a steel-toed boot. He loved her. It was painfully obvious in the way he touched her, the way he smiled at her, and even the way he kept taking popcorn from her fingers. He really loved the bitch—even her friends in low places weren't able to pry them apart. He wasn't going to listen to her explanation; wasn't going to give her another chance to be even a small part of his life. She went back and forth between watching them and watching herself interact with Dylan on the screen in front of her, and the juxtaposition was almost more than she could bear.

Why didn't she get a happy ending? Why was it that she had to struggle and fight for everything she got and that little skank of a school teacher got to live the life Penelope herself deserved? She'd paid her dues and her overdues and still she came out in last place. She watched as the final love scene played out—the one she should have done but that was instead filmed using a double shortly after she was taken to jail just for loving someone too much—and the anger boiled up inside her until it threatened to erupt. The credits rolled and the lights came on...

...and Tia was the first one on her feet, clapping enthusiastically. She wiped tears from her eyes, both from the emotional ending of the film and the tremendous sense of pride she had in Dyl. He and the rest of the cast stood and took a bow, and the audience rose to its feet. It was going to be a hit—they could all feel it. There were a lot of handshakes, hugs, and back slapping, and the cast members pulled the production team up to the front of the theater so that they could get their own round of applause.

"Speech!" someone called out, and Stan held his hand up for silence.

"I have to say, I had my doubts about this one," he smiled wryly, "but I will also say that I've never worked with a better group of professional people, and that no matter how tough things got, they never lost focus." He looked at Dylan. "We lived and worked in some pretty primitive conditions, and as most of you know, our filming schedule was cut short by...unforeseen circumstances. I owe a big thank you to Dylan for toughing it out another couple days when all he really wanted to do was reclaim the life that was nearly taken from him, and to the editors for piecing together an ending worthy of the film with precious little to work with." He paused, and swept his arm toward the screen which showed an image of the promo poster—a shot of Dylan, soaking wet, dragging himself out of a raging river. "I think we have a winner!"

Stan handed the mic to Dylan, and he stepped to the center. "I want to say thanks to Stan, for his patience and understanding, and to the great people I got to know during this little adventure. I also want to reiterate Stan's comment to the editing department—brilliant work, my friends." Gary gave him a thumbs-up. "This is a little unconventional, but I want to thank all of you for your love and support during the past few months...it's really meant a lot. And I'd be remiss if I didn't thank Tia; for sticking with me through some tough times and for keeping the faith. I love you, baby girl."

Tia waved shyly at the audience and blew a kiss to Dylan.

"Thank y'all for coming out this evening and sharing this with all of us." He held out the mic and looked around at the other members of the cast and crew. "Anyone else want to say something?" he asked. They shook their heads shyly and looked around at each other.

"I should've been invited here, you pompous jackasses! I should have been *included*!"

All heads turned to where Penelope stood glaring angrily at the group lined up under the screen. The rest of the audience fell quiet, waiting to see what would happen next. Reporters scrambled out the exit doors to get camera crews that weren't allowed inside the screening and banged into security personnel that were simultaneously rushing in to deal with a potential situation.

Stan put his palms out in an attempt to calm her, giving an almost imperceptible shake of his head to the guards who were making their way down the aisle toward her.

Dylan put his arm around Tia and led her toward the aisle furthest from Penelope. "I think this is where we make our exit," he whispered.

"Hi, Penelope," Stan said. "It really is good to see you. Can we talk privately? I wish I could have explained all this to you ahead of time, but…"

"Is it? Is it Stan? Is it good to *fucking* see me?" Stan nodded, trying but failing to put some sincerity into his smile, and Penelope raised her middle finger. "You know, I really don't need to hear your bullshit explanation, thanks anyway. And this *is* bullshit. I am the star of this goddamn movie and I did a hell of a job. I should have walked the carpet—I deserved that!"

"You're right. Come on, let's go somewhere quiet and talk it through, OK?"

Penelope turned her head and narrowed her eyes at Dylan and Tia as they made their way up the aisle. "And you! You think you're better than me because you dropped the charges? You are not better than me! You are nothing, understand? He'll get tired of you so fast it'll make your head spin!"

Dylan tightened his grip around Tia's waist and led her quickly toward the nearest exit. "Ignore it, baby, it means nothing," he whispered as he hustled her up the aisle.

"You are not better than me!" she yelled again.

Something in Tia snapped. Her vision went foggy around the edges, her hands clenched into fists, and she felt all the anger and frustration that Penelope had forced her to endure bubble up to the surface and threaten to explode. She held her breath and willed it to simmer, but it wasn't going to happen. She turned, pulled out of Dylan's grasp and stormed down the aisle and across the front of the theater to face Penelope.

"I don't think I'm *better* than anyone," she said, her eyes glaring. Dylan put his hand on her arm, and she shrugged it away, punching her hands to her hips and walking over to the end of the aisle where Penelope stood.

"Let her go, Dylan," Stan said, putting his own hand on Dylan's arm. "She's never really had a chance to deal with this. Let her have her say." Dylan fell back into the line, eyeing the security guards that had already positioned themselves between the two women. They nodded at him to indicate that they'd have the situation under control if it got out of hand.

Tia stopped at the aisle entrance, with Penelope only a few yards away. "Oh, you know, wait—maybe I need to rethink that. I know I'm a better *person* than you, *Esther,* because I don't look down my nose at everyone else in the world. I don't lie, I don't steal, and I would never intentionally try to destroy someone else's happiness."

Penelope took two steps forward and Tia matched them. "Don't try and make yourself out to be some sort of fucking martyr, because I'm not buying it. You dropped the charges for yourself, not for me, and don't think I don't know that."

"You don't even know kindness when it's staring you right in the face, do you?" Tia answered coolly. "I'm not trying to be a martyr, Penelope. I didn't press charges because I thought that you'd been through enough. I know what it's like to lose someone you love, thanks to you, and I thought that spending time in jail, facing charges here, and the hit on your career and your personal life were enough punishment. Add losing Dylan to the whole mix—because I believe that in your deluded little mind you really think you did—and I thought that was punishment enough. I really don't expect your thanks or your admiration, but I sure as hell deserve some respect. I've never done one thing to hurt you, despite everything you've done to me."

"I don't owe you anything, you conniving little bitch. You didn't earn any of this and you don't deserve it. You've orchestrated this whole little nice girl routine to make the public take your side."

"I don't have to orchestrate anything—there's another big difference between you and me. I don't pretend to be anything I'm not, and I..." Tia's eyes widened and she turned and caught Dylan's eye before continuing. "Speaking of orchestrating, would you happen to know anything about the little situation at the album party?"

Penelope's lips peeled up in a sneer. "Prove it."

"That's pretty much what I thought," Tia said softly, turning back to Dylan with an apology in her eyes. She was done here—done with letting others have control over her feelings, her self-confidence, and her faith in the most wonderful man she'd ever known. She took two more steps toward Penelope and looked her straight in the eye. "I am not better than you, but nor are you better than me. The sooner you realize that, the sooner you can get on with a life that's real and has some sort of meaning. I really do feel sorry for you, Penelope."

The fog cleared, and Tia looked around at the stunned faces and the backs of cell phones that had recorded her entire rant. She held her head high and faced them before turning slowly and walking into Dylan's waiting arms. The audience burst into thunderous applause.

"Let's get out of here, baby. I'm done."

He pulled her in tight and brushed his lips against her ear. "You were fucking brilliant," he whispered; and then, wrapping his arm around her shoulder, he led her back up the aisle.

"Why is there never a bus around when you need one?" Tia asked, her eyes sweeping the street as they ignored the constant click of the cameras and the shouts of the paparazzi and climbed back into the limo.

"What do you mean?" Dylan asked.

"Oh, it's nothing," Tia replied, wrapping herself into Dylan's loving arms.

*****

Welcome to *Chit Chat*! Dottie Miles said on Monday's show. Tia knew that the scene between her and Penelope had hit social media even as she was walking out the door, and she knew that Dottie would have something to say about it. Even in hindsight Tia thought she'd handled it pretty well, but wanted to see what the media take was on the whole thing.

"Well, it isn't surprising that Penelope Valentine's back in the news," Dottie started. "And it's even less surprising that she's made a complete fool of herself—again." She looked over at Abigail and narrowed her eyes.

"OK, OK. I've been trying to give her the benefit of the doubt; mainly because no one else

would; but she effectively lost any sympathy votes with her latest performance."

"That's the understatement of the year," Lynne agreed.

"In case you missed it, we've got the video of her latest rant—and if you weren't a Tia fan before, you will be after you see this. That lady has style."

"Thank you very much," Tia said with a smile.

They rolled the whole video, and Tia felt a touch of pride as she watched how well she handled the situation. She couldn't help but giggle when she saw the part she had missed— Penelope's less than graceful exit out the back door that included a trip and an awkward roll down the aisle.

"Now that goes straight for the jugular, doesn't it?" Lynne said, stifling her own giggle.

"I can't believe that Tia didn't go straight for her jugular," Dottie said. "I don't know that I wouldn't have."

"And what about the evil grin and the 'prove it' statement when Tia called her out about the record party? She pretty much admitted that she was behind it."

"Yes, I would say that it puts Dylan firmly in the clear, that's for sure."

"That's what we call 'throwing *herself* under the bus,'" Lynne mused.

"Now I don't say this often, and I don't say it lightly," Dottie said, "but I'd love to be the one behind the wheel of that bus!"

"You'll have to get in line for that," Tia said, clicking off the television and picking up her phone to call Dyl.

Chapter 43

"Good morning, ma'am," the driver said, tipping his hat, as Lexi handed him her bags. He swung them into the trunk, and then looked at her, his eyes widening as recognition settled in. "Wait, I know you," he said, surprised. "You're Tia Hastings's friend...you're on your way to the wedding, aren't you?"

Lexi nodded, smiling, and held out her hand. "I'm Lexi," she said.

"Wow, the Maid of Honor. It's my pleasure to be driving you today." He held the door open for her, and she climbed in. Once he got behind the wheel, he turned. "OK, I'm really out of line here, but I just have to ask. I mean, it's been all over the news, right? The girls back at the office have a pool going to see whose guess is the closest. Do you know where you're going?"

"I honestly don't," Lexi replied, kind of glad that she didn't. Besides the anticipation for the wedding, she was actually enjoying the element of surprise about where she was going. The speculation had been out there for weeks, and like everyone else lucky enough to be on the guest list; and at least half the free world; she'd wondered openly about where the wedding would actually take place. As expected, the media had managed to get hold of an invitation; but since it gave away no clues—just telling guests to pack "resort casual" and to bring passports—they were all in the dark, which was exactly where Dylan and Tia wanted them to be. Locations all over the world were being tossed around; and there were numerous pools and contests giving people the chance to win prizes by guessing the actual location. *Chit Chat* was even promising one lucky winner a trip to the city that was the closest to the guess of the actual venue. Tia and Dylan were having some good laughs watching the media people scramble to try and figure it all out, and were feeling pretty confident that they'd be able to have the intimate wedding they both wanted. "If you had any idea how many times I've been asked that question..." she smiled. "I'm glad I don't know. I've had enough of keeping secrets."

"I understand," the driver nodded and he fired the engine, pulling away from Lexi's building and heading toward the little airport where she'd meet the plane.

She was looking very forward to getting away for a while; far from the hot mess her life had become over the past few months. A fresh perspective was in order, and hopefully some sun and sand between her toes would be part of the deal. She leaned back in her seat and let her mind run over all that had happened in the past year of her life—the events that changed so many things she could hardly believe them. This weekend was going to be monumental—not just because her best friend was getting married to the man of a lot of people's dreams; not just because it was being called the "event of the year;" but also because of what it held for her personally. It would bring some sort of closure to the current chapter of her life; which was very near the end; and allow her to turn a fresh page in her own saga.

It was hard to put into perspective, actually. At this time last year, she'd been a completely different person with a solid future and a sense of direction. It was almost as if she and Tia had swapped roles—a year ago, Tia was struggling with trying to get her life back together after Nick died. She was going through the motions of a normal life, but wasn't really living it. Lexi was her support system; making sure she didn't hide out in her house feeling sorry for herself, dragging her out to the country club, and trying to help her heal. It was Lexi who was planning the wedding of her dreams and Tia, God love her, never once complained about sitting through bridal shows or accompanying her to shop for dresses, flowers, or wedding cakes. Lexi had known it was hard for her, and that, even though Tia was genuinely happy for her best friend, the little trips had to serve as countless reminders of what she herself had lost.

In the past couple months, it had been Lexi fighting the internal battle—trying to focus on her best friend's happiness rather than wallowing in self-pity. At times it had been hard— twice she'd found herself at the same restaurant as Ryan and his new girlfriend, and had fought the urge to pay an informative little visit to their table—but she'd managed to hold her head high, give Tia the full support and enthusiasm that their friendship deserved, and plan her own reinvention along the way.

She had two more months on her lease, and she didn't plan to renew it. Once the wedding was over she'd have an obscene amount of free time, and she was going to narrow down a location and start looking for jobs and new places to live. She was even considering hanging out her own shingle and starting up a small firm. Although she hadn't nailed down a final destination, she had decided that she'd go west; somewhere with better weather and fresher air for her new life. It felt good to finally be in a place where she was really looking forward to it.

Just four more days, she thought, *and I can work on making my own happily ever after.* She had dubbed Tia's romance her "InHappily Ever After," and the thought now gave her heart pause. The thought of the wedding thrilled her; but she was apprehensive about seeing Bo, and it reminded her that she'd never have an InHappily ever after of her own. Even though Tia had told her that Bo wasn't bringing a date, and had even laughed at the idea that he had a thing going with Joi, Lexi was still saddened about the way she'd royally screwed up her relationship with him. At some point over the weekend she knew that she was going to need to at least clear the air with him, but no matter how many times she'd tried to picture it in her mind, she still had no idea how to even approach the conversation. She had no doubt that they would both handle things with all the appropriate pomp and circumstance, but Lexi hoped deep in her heart that they could fix things between them; or at least make amends. Either way, she couldn't help but look at this weekend as her last hurrah;

at least where InHap was concerned. She took a deep breath and reached into her bag, fingering the custom drum sticks she'd gotten Bo for his birthday. *We'll always have London*, they read.

Lexi hoped that the sun and fun of the weekend would also help her burn the dark spot from her heart—she hated once more having to carry a secret that threatened to make things difficult for her best friend. She had decided from the start that she could never tell Tia the real reason Ryan had thrown away their relationship—could never allow her to know that it was because he couldn't handle the daunting depth of Dylan's shadow and the fact that he'd never be able to give Lexi the life her best friend was getting. People would ask, she knew, and she really didn't have a good answer. She'd just have to tell them she didn't want to talk about it. Almost as much as she wanted this weekend to get started, a part of her looked forward to it being over, and she hated herself for that.

She took a deep cleansing breath as the car turned onto the frontage road that led to the little airport and pushed the thoughts from her mind. Her demons were her own, and she planned to keep them that way. Ah well, she was going to enjoy the hell out of this weekend, and now that it was finally here, she couldn't wait to get it started.

She saw the small group standing around the tarmac as the car pulled up, and she hopped out to hug Tia's parents and grandparents. "So, what's the final prediction?" she asked with a smile.

Danielle grinned. "I'm going with Hawaii, and Will's thinking St. Lucia. How about you?"

"I'm going to go with Aruba," Lexi said. "I'm definitely thinking Caribbean—or maybe I'm just hoping, because I really want some palm trees and crystal blue water." She turned to Tia's grandparents, Russ and Loretta. "Do you have a guess?"

"I haven't even tried," Loretta said. "I'm still trying to get over the fact that I'm getting on an airplane! Seventy-three years I've been on this earth," she said, "and my feet have never left the ground. I thought I'd keep it that way, but I wouldn't miss this wedding for the world."

They all looked up anxiously as the small jet touched down and taxied up the runway toward them. Lexi bounced restlessly on the balls of her feet as she grinned at Tia's parents and shared in their mounting excitement. When the plane came to a stop, the steps came down and Ty stepped through the open doorway.

"You folks need a ride?" he asked excitedly.

"Ty!" Lexi exclaimed, dropping her bag and running over to hug him. "It's so good to see you!"

Tommy hopped out next and then Angelo, both pulling Lexi into friendly hugs. "Thought we'd stretch our legs for a few before the second part of the trip," Angelo remarked, pushing his palms toward the sky and stepping up on the balls of his feet.

Lexi looked to the stairs once again, hoping, but Bo did not appear.

"Ah, Bo went out yesterday with Dyl and T," he said, interpreting her look.

"I thought he might," she said with a forced smile and she wrapped her arm around Ty's waist and turned to introduce the boys. "Ty Waters, Tommy Fletcher and Angelo Isely," she said, indicating each man in turn, "these are Tia's grandparents, Russ and Loretta. You remember Will and Danielle."

They exchanged greetings and turned as they heard the clatter of feet on the steps once more. "Good morning," a petite brunette in a flight uniform said brightly, "and welcome aboard. My name is Leigh, and I'll be taking care of you today." She held a plastic tote in one hand, and a box of storage bags and markers in the other. "As you know, I'll need to collect your cell phones before you board; just a formality; they'll be returned to you when you head for home."

They'd already been told that this would happen, and had their devices in their hands, in bags already labeled with their names. Each of the guests introduced themselves to Leigh, and handed over their phones before stepping onto the plane.

The jet was opulent—that was the only word Lexi could conjure as she took in the interior of the Gulfstream. There were several plush leather chairs and long couches along the sides to accommodate groups of people. Tables of heavily polished dark wood shone like glass, and a well-appointed bar was set up just inside the door. She heard the low whistles of Tia's parents as their eyes swept the interior of the aircraft.

"Well, it sure ain't United," Will said. "This is some serious first class!"

"If you'll all take your seats," Leigh informed them, "we've been given clearance for take-off. I wish I could tell you where we're going, but they haven't shared that information with me just yet. Once we get in the air, I have champagne for all of you—I understand this is a celebration!"

The excitement on the plane was palpable—the champagne flowed freely, they nibbled on hors d'oeuvres, and the group enjoyed getting to know one another. The layout of the plane made it easy—all the chairs swiveled so that they could all be involved in conversation, and the chatter never stopped. The boys turned on their natural charms, and Lexi felt all the stress slide from her body as she enjoyed the company of some of her favorite people in the world. They were just over two hours into their flight when Loretta exclaimed, "We're over water!"

They all turned to the windows and peered out. Sure enough, there was nothing but blue below them, with tiny whitecaps that could only be waves.

"So we are leaving the country, it seems," Will said. "I can't wait to get another stamp on my passport—but really, I can't wait to find out where we're going."

"Oh!" Lexi exclaimed. "I'm so hoping for palm trees, turquoise water, and warm sand! Now that's a perfect setting for the wedding of the year."

Danielle smiled wide. "I still can't believe my baby's getting married—and in such grand fashion—I'm positively giddy!"

Will laughed and put his arm around her. "You don't think that maybe the champagne has anything to do with that, do you?" he asked rhetorically.

"Oh, maybe," she answered, "but who cares? I am just loving life right now. Here we are, on a beautiful private jet, sipping Moet, heading for an unknown tropical destination—who wouldn't be at least a little bit giddy?"

"Here's to that!" Angelo offered, holding up his glass. They toasted the happy couple, and watched the window for the arrival of what they hoped would be a lush island rising up from the ocean.

"Welcome to the Islands of the Bahamas!" Leigh said as the plane touched down. They'd watched in anticipation from the windows as the island came into view—the indescribable colors of the Caribbean Sea swirling below them and the palm trees taking shape. "You can just keep your seats—immigration will come aboard and clear you all, and then there's a van that'll take you the rest of the way," she explained.

"Where exactly is our final destination?" Will asked.

"I honestly don't know," Leigh answered, "but I sure wish I was joining you. Along with the rest of the world, I'll be watching the TV, hoping to catch a glimpse of the wedding—I imagine it'll be spectacular. Could you please give my best wishes to the happy couple? Not like they'll care, but it's kind of cool only having two degrees of separation between me and Dylan Miller."

The van dropped them at a long pier that jutted out into the ocean, dotted on both sides with spectacular vessels. Several Bahamian men in white suits rushed over to take their bags, and led them down the pier to the end, where the most amazing yacht of them all was docked. "No way!" Lexi whispered to Ty. "Is that for us?"

Tommy shook his head. "Leave it to Dyl to make sure his guests arrive in style."

Sure enough, they were led up the ramp into what could only be described as complete and utter luxury. It was almost unbelievable—absolutely no detail was spared. There were three decks, and as they wandered around the incredible spaces, it was hard to believe they were on a boat. They made their way up to the top deck, where a group of people were already chatting and nibbling from platters of fresh fruits, shrimp cocktails, and other culinary delights.

"Hello there!" A beautiful blonde woman with a heavy Australian accent broke from the group and rushed over to them. Lexi guessed that she must be Dylan's mother; she could see the resemblance immediately. She headed straight for the boys and pulled them into a warm group embrace as the rest of the group turned to welcome them. Lexi hadn't expected to feel such a rush of emotion, but her heart soared when she saw Dylan's friends from Northampton waving frantically and making their way over for hugs and hellos. They all gushed over introductions and raised their crystal glasses in toasts as the boat pulled away from the dock and made its way out to sea.

They had barely left the port when a local band fired up some pure Caribbean music and they were dancing within minutes; laughing and changing partners as the mainland grew smaller and smaller in the distance. It was nearly an hour before they approached another, smaller island, and the yacht glided effortlessly up to the pier. They hung over the deck railing to read the sign that greeted them: "La Bienvenida a Isla Lujoso." Below that, in smaller letters, it read, "A. Granger, Proprietor."

"I should have known!" Ty mused. "Why didn't I think of it?" He knew that Granger had his own freaking island, and that he and Dylan were good friends—why hadn't he guessed that the secret location of the wedding might be here?

By the time they made their way down to disembark, Tia and Dylan were jogging down the pier hand in hand to greet them, with a woman balancing a tray of fruity tropical drinks following behind them. Cameras on floating rafts were on either side of the pier, capturing the reactions of the first group to arrive.

"Welcome to my wedding in paradise!" Tia exclaimed, rushing to hug everyone and welcome them to the island. "It's so amazing here, I can't wait to show you!"

"It's just breathtaking!" Danielle gushed, taking in the
scenery. A powdery beach sprawled off to the left of the main
pier; dotted with cabanas, palapas and colorful beach chairs.
Tropical flowers burst from artistic pots, and lush foliage rose up
over rolling hills in the background. To the right, a number of
smaller piers jutted out over the turquoise water, playing host to
jet skis, kayaks, paddle boats, small sailboats, and several other
vessels. Many of the piers featured little gazebos at the ends,
overlooking the sea, and Lexi tried to gauge in which direction the
sunset would light up the sky. In the distance they could see the
rise of a few buildings, thatched roofs that blended beautifully
with the surrounding landscape. There was a feeling of seclusion
and privacy here, and they were all excited to see more.

"Come and have a tour!" Tia exclaimed. "Paradise is the only
word for it—I couldn't have imagined a more perfect place for my
wedding!" Dylan pulled her to him and kissed her tenderly.

The place was nothing short of spectacular. Tony met them
on the main plaza; a huge open-air deck that would play host to
the wedding reception, and took everyone on the grand tour.
"Everything on the island was designed to blend into the natural
environment," he said, "and the entire resort is self-sustaining
and ecofriendly. It has its own desalination plant on the far side of
the island to provide pure water, solar panels to generate
electricity, and gardens to provide all the flowers and organic
fruits and vegetables. The workers are all locals, and have their
own comfortable living quarters on the other side of the island.
They're paid a fair wage, and are sequestered here for the
duration of any stay to assure the anonymity of the guests; plus
there's uncompromised security—cameras all over the island are
monitored constantly so anyone can stay here and maintain total
privacy." He smiled. "At least that's the plan. This is the first test
of the whole place, really." A cameraman wearing a Travel
Channel shirt recorded Tony's words as well as the reactions of
the guests.

"Every part of the wedding is Tony's gift to us," Dylan
explained. "He's planning to open this place next month to paying

guests, and wanted to do a test run to make sure everything's working the way he wants it to before he starts taking exorbitant amounts of money from people."

"Yeah, well, there's a little more to it than that," Tony added, waving off the looks of amazement from the little tour group. "This is a business venture, too, and I'm going to get a lot more out of it than I put in. I consider it a personal favor to me that Dylan and Tia agreed to have their wedding here. It's obviously the event of the year, and I get first dibs on all the pictures and videos for my show and a magazine where I hold a majority interest. Then, when the Travel Channel approached me and wanted to do a show about the island, I knew I couldn't do it with paying guests, but that it would be a lot more interesting if there were actually people here. This is a big deal—the fact that they're letting me film some of the wedding—which will keep their fans happy and still let them have a private celebration; plus the fact that Dylan and his new bride are the very first ones to stay here; it will make this a sought-after destination for a long time to come. Dylan and Tia maintain control not only of their wedding, but of any images or videos that go out. Everybody wins."

"Everyone but me," a voice behind them said as Tony turned toward the main building.

"Jessa!" Lexi exclaimed, wrapping her arms around the tiny woman and lifting her off the ground.

"About time you got here, Lex, I need another strong woman to help me control this asshole," she teased, pointing at Tony. "The man doesn't want to do anything but work, and he thinks I'm at his beck and call. Tia's hopeless—no help whatsoever. Now that you're here, I can finally relax a little bit. Where'd you get those frosty drinks?"

Tony looked surprised, just for a moment, before he got the joke. "I'm a task master?" he laughed. "I can't even keep up with you! Really," he said, turning to Dylan, "how do you put up with her? She's bossier than all my ex-wives put together." He shook his head at Jessa, but in the same motion, waved to an employee behind the desk who rushed to get Jessa one of the frozen concoctions.

Tony led them then through the main building, well-appointed with marble, chandeliers, and comfortable seating, glaring once more at Jessa before continuing. "Now if I can pick up where I left off before I was so rudely interrupted..." Jessa scratched her cheek very deliberately with her middle finger, making a face at Tony before graciously thanking the stunning woman who'd appeared with a pina colada. "The Wi-Fi can be turned on or off, depending on the guests' preferences, but there's a hard-wired computer in here and phone communication with the main islands. Dylan and Tia have opted not to allow the use of cell phones to make sure there aren't any breaches of the location before the wedding."

They walked out a set of French doors back onto the huge wooden deck; where the beach and Caribbean Sea greeted them.

"Well, that concludes my tour," Tony said, smiling. "I really hope you all enjoy your stay here, and remember—you're kind of my test audience. I want to know if there's anything that isn't perfect—any little thing at all—so I can make sure everything's in working order before I open next month. It's great to have all the rooms full so that everything can be put to the test, and I want to know if there's not enough hot water for the showers, if doors squeak, if your towels aren't the softest ones you've ever used—seriously, anything. It'll really help me a lot."

He lifted his hand and spun his index finger in a circle, and four Bahamian men appeared within seconds. "These gentlemen will show you to your rooms," he said, "and will bring your bags up right away so you have a chance to freshen up. Feel free to explore the island at your leisure; there are some brochures in your rooms that tell about the many amenities of the resort, and you're free to use all of them. You can ask any of the staff if you have questions; in fact, I encourage you to. They've all been trained, of course, but it would be great practice for them to interact with the guests.

"We've set up a spot on the beach under one of the cabanas to do some preliminary interviews for the Travel Channel show. It's completely voluntary, of course, but I sure would appreciate if you'd consider it...you can go as couples, if you want to. Since it's a small group tonight, we're going to have a barbeque on the beach in a few hours. Until then, they'll be setting up a little buffet here in just a bit. I hope you enjoy your accommodations, and I'll see you all back here for lunch."

As Tia and Dylan's families waited for everyone to gather on the comfortable deck, Jessa breezed through with a notepad and a pen, scribbling notes and then tucking the end of pen in the corner of her mouth. She was in her business mode, and didn't stop to make small talk; telling Lexi and Tia she'd be done in about a half hour. She orchestrated the placement of silver trays laden with fresh tropical fruits, cold salads, fresh breads, and deserts, and then buzzed out with a look of concentration on her face.

Tony turned to Dylan and asked, "Does she ever quit?" Dylan just laughed and shook his head.

"She's the best there is," he stated simply. "I'm lucky to have her."

Tony watched her retreat, and smiled. "I could use someone like that, you know."

"Don't even think about it," Dylan said. "She's mine."

Lexi was just scooping some crab salad onto her plate when she heard his voice. "It's about time you people showed up for this little shindig!" Bo said as he strolled out from the main building.

Her heart skipped a beat; it wasn't just the sound of his voice that sent a shiver down her spine—the man looked *good*. Bo had always been a big guy—Lexi often described him as being "built like a football player," but the Bo who strutted onto the deck looked more like a Marine drill sergeant; except for the pencil thin dreadlocks that framed his face and just brushed his shoulders. Broad shoulders, she noticed, which led into thickly muscled arms that threatened to bust out of his shirt. *Buff* was the first word that came to her mind.

His face though, was the same old Bo—big genuine grin, dark chocolate eyes that crinkled when he smiled; skin the color of a perfect cup of morning coffee. Four months ago she would have been the first one to leap into his arms but now she held back, unsure of her place.

Dylan's mom was the first to wrap him in an embrace. "Bo Collins," she said after a warm hug and a loud smack on the lips. "You had us worried for a while there." She stepped back and looked him up and down. "I don't know why. We all know you're the most stubborn man ever born and that you would pull through. It does my heart good to see you looking so well. I've missed you."

Bo pulled her back into his arms as Steve shook his hand and other members of the group lined up to say their hellos. "It's been too many years," he said fondly. "I missed you, too."

Lexi stood at the back of what could only be called a receiving line feeling like an idiot as her heart threatened to burst out of her chest. Something she couldn't explain shadowed Bo's eyes when they finally fell on her. "Good to see you, Lexi," he said.

"You too, Bo. I'm really glad to see you fully healed." He didn't call her beautiful, or princess, or any of the other pet names he'd had for her in another lifetime, and his embrace was awkward, at best. It was just as she'd feared it would be, but she pasted on a smile.

"It's gonna take more than an earthquake to keep me down," he said. He opened his mouth as if to say something else, but Margo jumped in and wrapped her arms around his neck.

"I'd say you healed brilliantly," she smiled, fluttering her eyelashes just the slightest bit. She tucked her hand into his elbow and led him toward the spread of food and drink. "Join me for lunch? I'm dying to catch up with you."

He looked at Lexi once more, the shadow even more pronounced, before she turned away and he let Margo lead him to the buffet table.

They spent the afternoon catching up, hiking the beautiful grounds, and splashing in the crystal sea. As the sun began to dip, they enjoyed an incredible dinner at elegantly-set tables on the beach, overlooking the water and a near-perfect sunset. Tomorrow would bring the rest of the guests, and there would be a flurry of activity. For tonight, they had a small intimate group, and they enjoyed an evening sail and local live music; and of course, the company of friends and family. Dylan pulled out his guitar and played enthusiastically with the local musicians while the group danced around the bonfire; the sea breezes blowing gently and the full moon hanging heavy in the sky. Tia saw Dylan whisper something into the singer's ear, and they shared a laugh before bursting into "Brown Eyed Girl." Tia giggled, remembering the evening they'd spent in Northampton when Dylan had shimmied over to her and pulled her into a seductive dance. Dylan remembered it as the night he'd finally realized that he was hopelessly in love. Lexi and Jessa let out little squeals and ran for the bonfire to join in the dance. Margo grabbed Bo immediately and Lexi found herself paired up with Max, who turned out to be a pretty good dancer. Everyone else found partners and spun around the beach—even a surprised Jessa found herself in Tony's arms.

As the evening wound down, the music got softer until it was just Dylan with his guitar. Tia sat in the sand near his feet, always ready to enjoy the smoky tones of Dylan's unique voice. "I've got something for my fiancé," he smiled, plucking a few strings to check the tune before strumming a low chord. Then he sang the first words, and Tia found herself mesmerized by the lyrics.

Across a crowded room like great romances

First eyes then smiles then halting glances

From the very first tentative hello

I'm wrapped around your finger...

got nowhere else to go.

You danced with me around the world

The universe was ours

And even in the brightest day

You filled my head with stars

So now we make a solemn vow

Here beside the sea

No hesitation, dive right in

It's not too deep for me

Always and forever girl ...your dreams I will fulfill

And even at the end of time, I will love you still

You are my forever girl...The good in everything life brings

Imprinted now upon my heart...You're every song that my soul sings

From now until the end of time, I pledge to you my love

Its depth is like the sun and moon, and universe above

Forever you will be my girl—you give yourself to me

And with you by my side I'll be the man I want to be

The group broke into a round of applause, and Tia wrapped her arms around Dylan's legs, resting her head in his lap as he stroked her hair. "It's beautiful, baby, thank you," she whispered.

"You're beautiful," he whispered back, leaning down to rest his lips on her head. "I have to say, it's incredibly easy to write songs about how much I love you."

The fire burned down, and couples started wandering in, heading for some much-needed sleep after their long days of travel. Tony stood back, sipping his scotch and smiling— everything was just as he'd hoped it would be.

Bo couldn't sleep. He should have been exhausted—he'd spent most of the previous night walking aimlessly up and down the beach much as he had on Orcas Island; more anxious to see Lexi than he was comfortable with. Their first meeting had been disconcerting, as he figured it would be, but as the music pulsed and the booze flowed freely, he actually found her in his arms for a dance and couldn't help but pull her close. Oh damn, she smelled like coconut and rum and smoke from the fire, and he thought he'd never smelled anything more intoxicating. With her body pressed against him, he couldn't help but wonder if she could feel his desire pulsating through every tense muscle, and just as he was about to lean in and whisper into her ear, Kelley cut in and Lexi spun away with Dylan's dad, her hair tossed back and her musical laughter drifting off to sea.

"Isn't this just brilliant?" Kelley smiled as Bo put his hand on her waist and dipped her low.

"Pretty close to perfect," Bo grinned back, watching Lexi over Kelley's shoulder. It would be absolutely perfect if things with Lexi would go the way he dreamed they would; but the flip side of that was that he could completely shatter their already cracked relationship.

He wondered if he could really give Lexi what she needed— he'd had had more than his share of failed relationships, and wouldn't be able to live with himself if he hurt someone like her.

Too many questions and not enough answers invaded his thoughts. Would it be better to just hope for a return to their light-hearted, flirty, and fun friendship, and not take the chance on something more? It would certainly be easier.

The song ended and Kelley kissed his cheek before wandering off to find Steve, leaving Bo to stand and watch as Tia grabbed Lexi's and Jessa's hands and pulled them into a huddle.

Oh hell, taking the easy route had never been his style. Besides he couldn't stop imagining what it would be like to kiss her; to press his lips against hers and taste her sweetness...he imagined it would be like pineapple; sweet and tangy with just a little bit of bite. *Sweet Baby Jesus*, he thought, feeling himself going hard just thinking about a kiss, *I really got it bad for this girl*. He didn't know if the time was ever going to be right, but he did know that he was going to put it out there, and that it was going to have to be this weekend.

He threw the sheet off and stepped out onto the balcony that overlooked the sea, enjoying the soft breeze that cooled his skin. He took a deep pull of it, and looked up at the incredible array of stars that blazed in the night sky. Sinking into a soft chair, he leaned against the railing and looked out over the beach, letting his mind wander. Lexi in a bikini...Lexi in the hot tub...Lexi in his bed...and when he saw her there, he thought at first that he'd conjured her up from his imagination.

His heart knew it was her...the solitary figure walking along the shore, kicking up little splashes as gentle waves rushed up to meet her feet. She wore tiny shorts and some sort of flowing camisole top that fluttered out behind her in the wind that also tossed her long blonde hair. His gaze was focused intently and he positively ached to go to her; to make sure she knew she wasn't alone; to tell her that he would give her whatever she needed to make her life happy again. God knew his dick wanted desperately to go to her—it felt as if it were actually jutting in her direction, reaching out for her in a way that was well beyond his control. But he couldn't think with that head, he knew.

Lexi was still hurting; he could see it in her eyes every time she looked at him. She was doing a great job of hiding it, but she wasn't fooling Bo. He knew from personal experience how hard it was to get over a betrayal like the one she'd been dealt. She deserved so much more—could he give it to her? What did he have to offer her, anyway? She was a smart, sophisticated woman—a lawyer—and he'd dropped out of his second semester of college to pursue his music. It had done well for him, sure; extremely well; but she deserved more than money and a lot of empty hours while he was out on tour. *Unconditional love,* he thought, *that's what I have to offer,* and it hit him like a punch in the gut. Oh shit, he was in love with Lexi. What the hell was he going to do about it?

As if she'd heard his admission she turned in his direction, her face washed by moonlight, and scanned the buildings. He sank back into the chair and melted into the shadow, wishing that she didn't see him as lovable old Bo, the laughing jokester with the flirting complex.

He contemplated again going to her, but it wasn't the right time—not yet. So instead he watched longingly as she turned back, heading for what had become the girls' building, and he slipped back inside, falling into the bed and tossing and turning on all the words yet unsaid between them.

Chapter 44

"Ah," Lexi moaned as she took a delicate sip of her frosty cocktail. "Life doesn't get any better than this—sand, surf, sun, and some incredible eye candy to go with my frosty umbrella drink!"

"I'll drink to that!" answered Gina, who held up her own glass for a toast.

A group of the boys was engaged in a spirited beach volleyball game: Dylan, Bo, Ty, Sean, Tony, and Dylan's cousin Cameron on one side, and Max, Leroy, Collin, Chad, Brett, and Dex on the other. You could almost smell the testosterone in the air, and the men were sweaty, flexing, and scantily clad. The girls were sunning themselves, sipping their frozen concoctions, and very much enjoying the view.

"I'd forgotten that European swimwear left so little to the imagination," mused Alana, "but I'm not complaining! Who's the one in the tiny little red shorts? He's yummier than a chocolate bar!"

"That would be Max," Gina answered with a smirk. "I'd warn you off that one."

"Really? Is he taken?"

Gina laughed. "Just about every night," she said. "He's a bit of a playboy, if you know what I mean."

"Hmmm," Alana hummed, "now you've only gone and made him more intriguing." She licked a bit of foam from her drink off her lips and smiled.

"Seriously," Gina giggled. "You take your chances with that one. He's good looking, but he knows it—and he's not shy about using it, either. When Dylan moved to the States, he openly joked that he was happy to no longer be the second-best looking guy in the UK. He was always jealous of Dylan's..." Gina caught herself and her eyes went wide as she turned to Tia. "Oh, bloody hell," she said. "I didn't mean..."

Tia waved her off with a smile. "Don't worry about it," she said casually. "I mean, you'd have to be blind not to notice how sexy the man is." As if he'd heard her, Dylan turned toward her as the other team rotated and blew her a kiss. His long hair was pulled back and carelessly tied with a rubber band and he was gleaming with sweat and covered in sand. As so often happened when she looked at him, she felt a warm spot in her stomach roll over and giggled like a schoolgirl with a crush. She blew a kiss back, and turned back to Gina. "I mean," she joked, "*bloody* hard not to notice!"

"But he loves you so much, you know that, right? I'm still absolutely amazed by the way he looks at you."

"Me too," Tia agreed. "I lose my senses sometimes, I swear I do."

"Yeah, yeah," Lexi groaned. "The world's perfect couple; we all know it!"

"What about the guy with the spikey dark hair and the tattoos?" Gina asked. "I could put him on my ice cream, but he's so hot it would just be a puddle in no time." She fanned herself with her hands in an exaggerated show.

Tia answered, "That would be Sean. An Irishman, so doesn't that make you mortal enemies or something?" she teased.

"Oh, I might be able to put aside our differences for the weekend," she smirked. "Seriously, what can you tell me about him? Is he related to you or Dylan?"

"He's one of my best friends," Tia said, not wanting to get into the whole story of how she and Sean were connected, "and he's a great guy. Single too. He's an audiophile—he designs home theaters, plays guitar..."

"Oh, now you've done it," Margo teased. "She's always had a weakness for guitar players!"

As soon as the words were out of her mouth, she regretted them, and shot another quick apology to Tia, who waved her off.

"Quit apologizing already, girls," Tia said. "It's no big deal, honestly. Everyone has a past." She turned to the other girls. "Gina and Dylan dated for a while when he lived in England," she explained.

"About a thousand years ago," Gina interjected. "Listen Tia," she said sincerely, swinging her legs off the chair and leaning in her direction. "I want to tell you how much it means to me that you wanted me to be here. Dylan told me that he'd written me off, but that you insisted I come. Just for the record, I do consider him one of the most incredible people I've ever known and a good friend, and I feel the same about you. I'm truly happy for you two, and I'm just thrilled that you included me."

Tia reached over and patted her on the arm. "I feel the same way—and I know. It wouldn't feel right if you weren't here, and I'm really glad you came."

Just then, the volleyball came flying at them, landing at Gina's feet. A very sand-covered Sean stood up from where he'd landed when he dove for it and tried to brush the grit from his sweaty body. Gina winked at Tia, scooped it up and sidled over to him, smiling coyly as she held out the ball.

"Thanks," Sean said, shooting her his best smile. "Should've had that one."

"It was a good try," Gina said brightly.

"I'm Sean, by the way," he said, holding out his hand.

"Gina," she answered, putting her hand in his.

"Thanks again, Gina. I'll see you around later, I hope?"

"I'm counting on it," she purred.

Tia could almost see Sean's heart skipping a beat, and he stood just a moment too long, staring at her. Tony called out, "Hey, Sean, you playing the game, or flirting with the bikinis?"

A flush crept up his cheeks and he turned, jumping back into the game with renewed energy, looking back to make sure Gina was watching.

"I think you better talk to Alana, my friend," Tia smiled. "Sean's her brother, so she could give you the inside scoop."

Gina studied Alana for a moment before saying, "I do see a resemblance. So, think you can hook me up?" She waggled her eyebrows and rubbed her hands together in exaggerated interest.

"I don't think that would be too hard," Alana exclaimed. "Especially since the minute he stepped off the boat, he spotted you and said, 'Will you look at that, this island just got even more interesting...'"

"No way—really?" Gina giggled. "Well then, I think you and I really need to have a chat. How about I buy you a drink?" They headed over to the little tiki bar toward the back of the beach and put their heads together.

"I'll tell you who impresses me," Margo cooed. "I have to say that Mr. Bo Collins is sure looking good for himself. Who would've thought he looked like *that* behind the drum kit?"

Lexi's ears perked up at the mention of Bo, and she turned her attention away from the game to join in the conversation. She'd had a hard time keeping her eyes off him, too—at six-foot-four he was easily the tallest player in the game, and she couldn't help but appreciate how his muscles rippled every time he spiked the ball on the other team. It gave her a bit of a twinge to see the scars that were still healing on his left leg, but he had an amazing six-pack and huge arms, and, sheened with sweat, seemed to glow like polished marble.

She hadn't yet figured out how to get some time alone with him so she could try to set things right, but even though there was still a curtain of doubt between them, she was sure she felt the same old Bo coming through when they'd danced together the previous night. However, she thought she'd seen him later on when she was walking the beach, but when she turned toward him to wave, he faded into the shadows and disappeared. She just didn't know what to think.

"I was going to say the same thing," Jessa chimed in. "It's been a little while since I've seen him, and my, a lot has changed! When did he get so buff?"

"He is gorgeous," Margo agreed, "like a Greek god or something. I remember meeting him in England—he was such a flirt, and so much fun to be around. I might just have to explore that a little further…"

Lexi felt a twinge of jealousy pluck at her heart. Bo had always been her flirting partner, and the thought of him behaving that way with someone else bothered her on some subconscious level that she couldn't explain. She had no claim on him, of course, but she somehow felt that they had something…exclusive between them. She tried to shake the thoughts away—after all, it wasn't like they had a relationship, or anything. They were just friends, right? And these days, maybe not even that. He could flirt with—or be with—anyone he wanted. Besides Tia and Jessa, she was the only other woman around during the tour, so he didn't exactly have a choice of flirting partners. Still, she felt a rush of heat creep up her neck as the girls continued to talk about him like he was a piece of chocolate. A creamy, delicious piece of chocolate that would melt on her tongue…

"Ladies and gentlemen," Margo crowed, "I think we've just found the world's next sexiest bachelor."

"Now it's too bad he isn't wearing one of those tiny little swim trunks—you know what they say about black men with big hands, right? And that boy has some serious big hands." Gina added.

Margo giggled. "Something like, walk softly, and carry a big stick?"

"And we're not talking drum sticks, either!" Gina giggled.

The girls burst into peals of laughter, and Lexi held her drink to her forehead to cool the flush that burned her face. She'd had the same thought, actually, but hearing it out loud from the other girls made that jealous streak rise up again.

Jessa stood up frowning. "I think this is where I take my leave, ladies," she said with exaggerated annoyance. "I have to spend way too much time around those guys to have that picture in my head. I think I'll go grab another round of drinks. Anyone?" She waved her empty glass in the air, and several of the girls lifted theirs in response. Jessa plunked them onto the tray and headed for the bar.

"Sorry ladies, but I'm afraid you're going to have to forget about Bo," Tia joked. "He's only got eyes for Lexi."

All heads turned in her direction. "Seriously?" Margo asked. "You and Bo are an item? I'm so sorry, I didn't realize…"

Lexi blushed. "No!" she said, perhaps too quickly. "We just have this flirting thing, that's all. Tia has a tendency to over exaggerate."

"You're sure?" Margo asked, "I wouldn't step on on any toes…"

"Positive," Lexi mumbled, grabbing the bottle of suntan lotion and squirting some into her hands. She lowered her head so none of them could see the flustered look on her face, and rubbed the cream vigorously onto her legs. What could she say? That she was feeling things for Bo that she couldn't explain? That her life felt all kinds of empty if he wasn't in it? She felt a prickle on the back of her neck; had the sense that someone was watching her, and she turned her eyes toward the game and saw Bo standing stock still and looking at her.

Damn, thought Lexi, *these boys must have some kind of telepathy when we're talking about them*. They locked eyes for a moment and there was something in their exchange that confused her; something about the way he stood frozen on the court, even as the ball sailed over the net and smacked him in the head, providing the game winning point for the other team. The Brits exploded—it was their first victory in three games, and they were letting the other team know it.

"Nice shot, Collins!" Tony yelled, picking up the ball and tossing it back at Bo. "Maybe next time you can keep your eye on the ball instead of your forehead." He glanced over and looked at the group of bikini clad girls and waved, adding, "Oh, hell, you're forgiven. That view is enough to divert anyone's attention."

Bo stood for a moment longer and smiled, then turned and trotted to the water. As though an alarm had sounded, all of the boys followed, diving into the sea to cool their hot—in every sense of the word—bodies. They met in a little huddle and laughed at their exchange, then ran back up the beach to shake the cool water on the girls, who giggled and squealed with delight.

Dylan grabbed Tia's hand, pulled her up, and carried her to the water, unceremoniously dumping her in. The guys shouted encouragement to the rest of the girls, and they all ran into the sea, laughing.

"Let's take out the wave runners!" Margo exclaimed. She turned right to Bo. "Would you take me out?" she asked. "I don't know if I can handle all that power between my legs." She smiled suggestively, and took his hand.

Bo was taken aback by her tone and the way she looked at him as she wrapped both of her hands over one of his. He tossed a sideways glance at Lexi, but she was focused on something in the other direction and seemed not to notice. Or maybe she just didn't care. "Um...yeah, sure," he stuttered.

"Who wants to join us?" Margo called.

Tia spoke up. "I can handle the power just fine," she said, taking Dylan's arm and heading for the pier. "Let's go."

Sean looked at Gina and shot her his best smile. "What do you say?"

"I say, lead the way," she smiled back.

Lexi watched as the group jogged over to the pier and Margo climbed on behind Bo, wrapping her arms around him tightly and laying her head against his back. She was suddenly overwhelmed by a confusing array of emotions that seemed to assault her all at once. The spark of envy flared up in her again, and for one brief second she pictured herself yanking Margo off the back of the wave runner and tossing her out to the sharks. She shook her head to clear the image—she had absolutely nothing against Margo—she was sweet and friendly and had a dynamic personality; there was no reason at all to harbor ill-will toward her.

When she heard Margo's shrieks of laughter as Bo spun the machine around the waves, she decided that maybe what she needed was to take a walk and clear her head a little. She had to try and get to the bottom of the odd feelings she'd been having ever since she got to the island.

Tony saw Jessa sitting at the bar, looking out over the beach, watching the wave runners race back and forth with amused interest. He left the water and grabbed a towel, rubbing it vigorously over his hair and chest as he approached her.

"Hey," he began, "do you have a few minutes? I was thinking of going over some of what we have so far, and making a list for some interviews at sunset..."

Jessa scowled at him. "Tell me you're kidding, Tony," she said flatly, as if the question was ridiculous. "I'm not an employee today; I'm a member of the wedding party. This is the best part of the day, everyone's having an incredible time, the sun is shining, and you want to go work?"

He was completely taken aback. It hadn't occurred to him that she wouldn't go, and he didn't know what to say, so he just stood there, dumbfounded.

"Lighten up and have a little fun, Tony," she added. "Everything's going beautifully—you've already put in the work to make that happen. Now you need to sit back and just enjoy it for a bit." And with that, she stacked the drinks on the tray and balanced them on her forearm as efficiently as a waitress, and walked back over to the girls' cabana.

Jessa could feel Tony's confused eyes on her as she walked back to deliver the drinks. The look on his face was priceless—she figured that he was used to people jumping every time he lifted a finger and didn't often get no for an answer. *Get used to it, Granger,* she thought. *I don't take shit from people either, and I'm not afraid to butt heads with anyone. Bring it on!*

It took Tony a minute to come to his senses. He'd just been shot down by a little bit of a woman—she couldn't stand more than five foot two, and she'd left him completely speechless. He tried to remember the last time he was put in his place, but he couldn't come up with anything in recent memory. She was on his island as his guest and was technically his assistant as far as the wedding plans and filming went—then why did he suddenly feel like she was actually the one in control? He thought he should be insulted, but instead, he was intrigued. There was really no need to work on anything at the moment, he realized, it was just an excuse to spend some more time with her. Why, he couldn't say, but there was no doubt about it—Jessa had piqued his interest.

He strolled over to where she'd taken a seat in one of the oversized beach chairs, surprised that his heart was pounding faster than he'd expect. "How about a sail, then?" he asked as casually as he could muster. When she looked at him over the top of her sunglasses, he shrugged. "What? You just said I should enjoy myself, and you're absolutely right. I'd love to get a view of the festivities from the water; see the whole beach from a different perspective. Care to join me?"

For a moment he held his breath, worried that she might say no. He exhaled when he saw the smile spread slowly over her features. "Why not?" she said, grabbing her beach cover and pulling it on. "Let's go."

From the water they did indeed have a completely different view. Around the beach, clusters of guests were scattered about, taking part in a variety of activities. A group of musicians was sitting around with guitars and bongos, sharing musical interludes, a few older guests took shelter under palapas, sipping concoctions made of the local dark rum, and a number of snorkels poked up from the water over the little reef that hugged the island. Dylan's and Tia's families were sitting together getting to know each other, and by the way their laughter rang through the air, they were getting along just fine. A few guys were tossing around a football, and another group was sailing a Frisbee through the air. A group of girls was building a sand castle, and a few couples were simply floating in the water on inflatables, enjoying the combination of sunshine and calm sea. As they flew by on the jet skis, Dylan raised his hand in a wave, but his arm froze halfway up when he saw Jessa sitting with him on the sailboat. He pointed a finger at Tony, likely to warn him again that Jessa was his, since Tony had already hinted; maybe too many times; at how much he could use a person with Jessa's skills and work ethic on his team. Or maybe, he thought for a fleeting second, a flash in his mind of her peeling off her cover and pulling the string on her bikini, he could come up with a much more interesting use for her.

As he cut the power and slid the water craft onto the beach, Bo looked automatically for Lexi. He thought maybe he could talk her into a little ride—the whole time he was on with Margo, he was thinking about how it would feel to have Lexi pressed up against him as Margo had been; breasts flattened against his back and her hands tight around his middle. He thought he'd talk her into taking the controls for a while as well, so he could have a valid excuse to sit behind her and wrap his arms around her smokin' hot scantily clad body. As his eyes swept the beach, he noticed that she was no longer there and handed the machine over to Leroy, who climbed on with his wife and headed out into the crystal blue waters.

Then he saw her in the distance...just turning around the curve of beach that led to the gardens and hiking trails. He took a deep breath to summon his courage and was about to start heading in that direction when Margo came over with a glass in her hand.

"You're a beer drinker, right?" she asked, handing him a frosty mug topped off with a foamy head.

"Um, yeah," he said absently, taking the glass. "Thanks."

"No problem. Hey, want to get a bite to eat? Gina told me they were setting up the buffet for lunch."

Bo watched as Lexi turned the final curve and disappeared from view. He wanted to ask her about the look she'd given him at the end of the volleyball game—about the confusion he saw in her eyes. It was maddening, really, the way he was feeling. Now that he'd fully admitted to himself that he was more than crazy about Lexi Summers, he found it hard to even talk to her—he wasn't at all sure that he could even look her directly in the eyes without her seeing the truth. He feared that it must be written all over his face, but the suggestive hints that Margo was throwing his way gave him some confidence that his secret was still safe. She'd been pressed up against him much more than necessary on the wave runner, and the way she was smiling at him right now left little confusion about her intentions.

It was painfully clear that Lexi still had a lot on her mind. She'd been quieter than usual, and now she was obviously looking for some solitude. Who knew? Maybe being here, watching her best friend about to get married, reminded her of what she'd lost in her own relationship. Perhaps she was missing her ex, wishing he was here to share the romance of this place. Either way, it seemed pretty obvious that she wasn't in the mood for his company, which really bothered him. Things were uncomfortable between them, and no matter how hard he thought about it—for the past four months, truth be told—he couldn't figure out just how to fix that. He glanced in the direction she'd disappeared, wondering if the timing would ever be right, or if he'd get up the nerve to tell her how he felt about her. It sure as hell wasn't now. "Let's go," he said, as Margo linked her arm in his and led the way to the main porch.

Lexi picked her way over the little peninsula that served as a breakwater for the beach and wandered into one of the gardens that sat just a small walk into the tree line. It was blissfully quiet; just the songs of birds, the chatter of a couple resident monkeys, and the sounds of the waves rolling onto the shore behind her filled the air. She plucked a blossom off the hibiscus and absent-mindedly pulled off a petal, nibbling at it. She'd read that the flowers had medicinal properties; that they helped with stomach problems and helped soothe the nerves. God knew her nerves could use more than a bit of soothing. She took a deep breath through her nose and held it for a three count before pushing it out through pursed lips slowly and deliberately. Yoga breathing wasn't going to make this any easier, but at least it might settle her thoughts enough that she could put them in some sort of order.

"Hey," the soft voice made her jump, and she turned to see Tia balancing a plate of food as she made her way up the trail.

Lexi gathered herself and sat up, flashing her a warm smile. "Hi!" she said brightly. "Is that for me?" she asked, motioning at the plate. Tia handed it over and Lexi picked up a tiny sandwich and popped it in her mouth, chewing enthusiastically. "Oh, thanks, I was starving!" she lied.

"You can't bullshit me, you know," Tia said, cocking her head. "I know you way too well for that. Something is bothering you. Want to talk about it?"

Lexi opened her mouth to protest, but quickly realized the futility of a lie. She and Tia had shared way too much over the years, and could read each other better than a lot of sisters she knew.

"I don't even know what it is," she said with a sarcastic giggle. "I honestly don't."

"Are you thinking about Ryan?"

Lexi looked her best friend right in the eye. "I'm really not," she said. "I haven't thought about him much at all." It was true. She'd given him one fleeting consideration at the bonfire; and it wasn't to miss him. She'd looked around at the crowd gathered— her InHap boys, her best friend, the new friends she'd met along the journey she'd hopped on and off of with Tia—and she knew instantly that Ryan didn't belong. He wouldn't fit in here, and if he had come, she'd have had to spend most of her time running interference for him or placating his wounded ego.

She realized, too, that if Ryan were here, she wouldn't be free to be herself—and that it had probably been that way for longer than she cared to admit. He had lost trust in her the minute he'd heard that she had met Dylan. Nothing she did or said made the situation any better, so she found herself downplaying the whole thing for his benefit, to the point of avoiding all conversation involving InHap so he wouldn't make a big deal out of it. She'd been furious with him when he postponed the wedding, but sucked it up eventually and put everything she had into supporting his career. *Yeah*, she thought bitterly, *and how did that work out for you*? She had put herself in a self-imposed holding pattern for the past year, and wasn't even sure who she was anymore. Sure as hell not the same, though.

Without a doubt she wouldn't have been able to spend any time with Bo if Ryan were here; not that Bo seemed to want her company anymore either. There were a lot more woman here to catch his eye than there'd been on the tour, and it appeared that maybe Margo had.

Tia took a seat next to her on the bench and took her plate, setting it on the little table next to the bench. She took Lexi's hands in hers and looked her straight in the eye. "Oh honey," she said sadly, "is it the wedding? Is it too much? I'm so sorry."

Lexi jumped off the bench, pulling Tia up and into a crushing embrace. "NO," she said firmly. "Absolutely not." She put her hands on Tia's shoulders and held her gaze. "I am happier for you than I've ever been for anyone in the world," she said honestly. "You've found your soul mate and you're going to have the most amazing life together...this is the most incredible location—the perfect place for the perfect wedding of the perfect couple." She smiled, and the corners of Tia's lips twitched up in a grin. "And I couldn't say that more perfectly." They sat back down, and Lexi threw her arm over her best friend's shoulder and gave her a squeeze. "I honestly don't know what's bothering me exactly," she said. "It's like..." she looked hard at Tia. "Oh hell, can I just say that I've learned a whole new respect for you over the past few months?"

Tia's eyes narrowed. "What do you mean?"

"I've always admired you, Tia, but the strength you've had over the past couple years has made me appreciate you more than I can even explain. I never really knew how hard you had it after Nick died." She hurried to explain. "I mean, I understand the grief, the mourning, the sense of loss...but what I didn't get until just recently is how hard it is to try and reassume your identity once you're on your own. I guess I'm still trying to figure out how to reinvent myself."

"You're always going to be amazing to me," Tia whispered. "You know that, right?"

"I do," Lexi nodded, "and like you, I'll figure out eventually who I want to be now that I'm on my own." She wrung her hands in her lap, choosing her words carefully. "Maybe it's just so many changes all at once," she said. "I just have to figure out how to juggle them, is all." She rested her forehead against Tia's and smiled. "And you know what? This little pity party is over! I just came out here to clear my head a little and try and get some perspective; not to set off an alarm that I'm in pain or something. I'm really not, I promise, and I also promise that I am having a really fantastic time, and that I couldn't be happier! Now, let's head back, shall we? There's a party going on over there, and I want to be part of it!"

"You know what you need is a little Bo," Tia teased. "He always puts you in the right mood." She felt Lexi stiffen.

"I think Bo's found himself a new flirting partner," Lexi replied, trying to keep her voice casual. Tia, of course, saw right through her.

"Oh my God!"

Lexi scrambled. "Oh my God, what?" she said, standing and turning away so Tia couldn't see her face.

"You're jealous!"

Lexi stiffened her spine and turned back to face Tia. "What?" she said, shaking her head. "That's ridiculous." She tripped over her words, and didn't sound at all convincing, not even to herself.

Tia put her hands on her hips. "Not from where I'm standing. It's pretty clear from here."

"I have no claim on Bo. He can flirt—or be with—anyone he likes, and it looks like he's made his choice already."

Now Tia's eyes widened as a realization sunk in and she turned her hands palm up. "Holy crap. You're hot for Bo."

"What are you talking about? We've never...he's never...you have no idea..." She walked over to the tree and plucked another hibiscus, rolling it nervously between her fingers.

"Sit back down here right now, Alexis Marie," Tia ordered. Lexi sat, defeated, and tried to meet her friend's gaze. "Are you?"

"Are I what?" Lexi mocked.

Tia stared at her for a minute, waiting for her to speak.

"You're asking me if I'm 'hot for Bo?'" she asked, making air quotes around the words. Still, Tia didn't speak. "I mean, he certainly is hot," she added with a smile, "but that's not the kind of relationship we have. Shit, we flirt, we joke around…admittedly we say a lot of vulgar things…but that doesn't mean…"

"What does it mean?"

Lexi's shoulders slumped. "I honestly have no idea."

And there it was. *Leave it to Tia to see right through her and hit the nail on the head*, she thought. The jealousy was there, no doubt about it. At first she tried to tell herself that it was just because she felt like her and Bo's flirting was their own; that they had something unique that neither of them shared with anyone else. Watching him dance and laugh and ride jet skis with Margo, however, made her think things that she'd never pondered before; mainly, could what they shared go deeper than either of them had even considered? Had he ever considered that they could be more? Could they be? She felt more comfortable around Bo than anyone else in the world; except for lately, after what happened in LA. She missed what they had together but it was more than that. She missed *him*. More than once over the past two days she longed to go into his arms and she had to admit that it was more than comfort she was seeking. Oh God. She *was* hot for Bo.

Tia put her arm around Lexi's shoulders and pulled her in for a hug. "I can't think of a better time or place to figure it out."

"Believe me, I'm working on it."

Paddy, Siobhan, and Lexi's parents joined Dylan's and Tia's, and the eight of them volunteered to wander the grounds and cut some flowers from the many gardens on the property. Kelley hosted a little flower arranging class, using her artistic eye to create gorgeous displays that would serve as centerpieces for the reception, as well as the girls' bouquets.

"Let's go for a little sail, mate," Dylan said to Bo after lunch. "I need some time with my best man," he added for Margo's sake as she was opening her mouth to invite herself along.

"Of course," she said, running her hand down Bo's arm. "See you later?"

"Um...yeah," he said, grateful that Dylan was saving him. Margo was a great person, but she was really turning it on thick and he wasn't quite sure how to brush her off.

"You actually know how to control this thing?" Bo asked, slipping into a life vest and climbing onto the catamaran.

"I guess we'll find out pretty quickly," Dylan teased, smiling as Bo's face twisted into mock fear. "Just don't forget to duck when I say 'boom,' and we'll probably make it back alive."

"Oh, well, that makes me feel a whole lot better."

Once they'd cruised out a distance, Dylan let the sails slack and handed Bo a beer.

"This is one hellova party, Strummer Boy."

"It's even better than I dreamed."

They sipped for a while in companionable silence as they watched the various parties on the beach and bobbed in the gentle water.

"OK, so I have to ask. I know it's not any of my business, but what's going on with you and Lexi? And you and Margo?"

"Nothing, on both counts," he sighed.

"Neither of them look like nothing."

"Margo's a great girl, but not for me."

"And Lexi? There's something off between the two of you. Did she turn you down?"

"Haven't even asked." Bo sighed, and took a healthy swallow from his bottle. "I'm not going to go into any detail, but something happened back in California the night we appeared on Tony's show. Something I should have fixed a long time ago, but I just didn't know how to do it. I'm not sure I even can anymore."

"Well, it ain't gonna fix itself, mate."

"I know. This is gonna sound pretty stupid, and I wouldn't say it to anyone but you, but ever since I figured out that there were these crazy feelings there, I get all tongue-tied when I'm around her."

Dylan patted him on the back and smiled. "I totally understand."

"I'm going to figure it out. I have to figure it out."

"I'm sure you will."

"Damn, I hope so, brother. I'm running out of time."

Chapter 45

Tia and Dylan weren't the only ones ready to scrap the bachelor and bachelorette parties—the whole group agreed that they were having entirely too much fun together, and decided to forgo the separation of the sexes in favor of another bonfire on the beach. A makeshift stage was set up, and the many musicians in attendance played together, sharing musical styles and genres. When InHap hopped to play a little set, the group sent up a cheer.

"I'm going ask the love of my life help us out with this one," Dylan said, reaching out his hand to Tia. Most of their guests hadn't heard them sing together live, and she was proud and honored to join them on *I'll Pull You Up*. "This one's for all of you who could join us for this special time, and especially for those who can only be with us in spirit." He looked to the stars, touched a kiss to his index and middle fingers, and held them up to the sky. Tia did the same, sending her thoughts to Nick as Dylan sent his to Shelby. Their guest sang along with them, and Tia felt more power in the song than she ever thought possible. They clapped together when the song ended, and Tia jumped from the stage as the boys jumped into a more upbeat tempo. "This one's for you, Tia," Dylan growled with an obnoxious grin as the guitar jumped in to match Bo's beats.

Hot summer sun sweat drips from naked skin

Got some nice cool shade to pull you in

Make my mouth water bring your appetite

In my enchanted garden you'll find every delight

Want to squeeze ripe melons so firm and sweet

You've never seen so many tempting treats

Come and take a stroll through my garden

A myriad of flavors sure to tantalize

You've never seen a place like this Eden

Here we can get downright uncivilized

Come and climb upon my magic beanpole

Don't even need a green thumb to make it grow

Once you've spent some time in my garden

I'm hoping that you'll never want to go

Close your pretty eyes and open wide

I'll slip a tempting flavor right inside

Like a delicate flower you open for me

Lapping up the nectar like a honeybee

My garden's got it all to fill your every need

Won't you come right in and help me plant the seed

Leave your inhibitions run wild and free

Come and spend time in Eden with me

The repeated the chorus, Dylan's smile growing as he took in the grins of their guests. It was just a silly, obnoxious song, and the audience of friends and family were having fun with it, razzing Tia and laughing out loud.

"Now that's one hell of a wedding song!" Sean exclaimed when they finished and took an over-exaggerated bow.

"I got more where that came from," Dylan laughed. "Why don't you come up and join us, Sean—I know you know this one."

Sean jumped up eagerly and grabbed a guitar, nearly beside himself to play alongside his favorite band and have the chance to impress Gina with his guitar skills. Other musicians jumped up to join them and Dylan stepped down to dance with the love of his life. The crowd danced under the moonlight of another perfect Caribbean evening.

Tony tipped his glass toward Jessa. The mood was festive, the music was incredible, and everything so far had gone off without a hitch. He was feeling damn good about the whole thing, and part of it was because of the interesting woman who sat beside him. He stood and put his hand out, bowing. Jessa took it, and they joined the group to dance beneath the moon.

When they finally wound down, Dylan moved from the little stage to a chair and picked up his guitar.

"This is the last day in my life I'll have a fiancé, and I couldn't be happier about that. I have a little something for my soon-to-be-wife," he said, and everyone got immediately quiet as he began to strum. Tia sat beside him, mesmerized as always by her fiancé's talent as well as his thoughtfulness.

Under the moon and the stars, he sang his wedding song for her.

In my mind, I'm back in gay Par-is,
serenade upon the tower, new love for you and me...
I look at you, and moon glow fills my eyes,
Hand in hand we skip upon the stars
And swim through starry skies...

You...wrap me in your heaven—
Blue skies and sunshine
Good God you take my breath away
You...make me a new man

Oh baby, we're so good together, but even though we'll have forever...
I'll still need another day

So now we pledge our lives forever more...
There's a promise in the whisper of every wave to kiss the shore
Enchanted by the smallest things you do
When I look into your eyes, I have the greatest view

Wrap me tight in your heaven
bright shooting stars
Good God you take my breath away
You make me a better man

Baby I know we're so good together
But even though we'll have forever...
I'll still need another day...

Hold me close in your heaven...
Float in the clouds
Good God you steal my breath away
I'm yours, I am only your man...

We're best when we're together,
But even with forever...
I'll still need another day...

When he strummed the final chord, there was an audible gasp; an intake of the wind by every silent guest that sat on the beach. Tia couldn't speak—she could only smile at her perfect man as tears of joy burned in her eyes. Dylan set his guitar on the back of the chair and pulled her to him, wrapping his arms around her waist and looking deep into her eyes. "I love you, baby girl" he whispered, "I'll always love you."

"Always and forever," she whispered back, and he kissed her so reverently, so sweetly, that she swooned.

One clap sounded, and instantly, the rest of the crowd joined in an enthusiastic round of applause. Tia turned to Dylan with a tear in her eye. "I can't even begin to tell you how you complete me," she smiled, and Dylan took her mouth with an intimate kiss.

"I mean it, you know. Forever isn't long enough to give you all the love I have."

They took a moment with each other before turning toward their audience—their true friends and family—and taking a little bow. "Hey," Dylan said to the crowd. "I just want to tell you all how happy we are that you are all here to share this incredible time with us." Tia nodded her agreement. "This is the most special time in my life, and I want to thank you all for your support, your love, and your friendship—it really means the world to both of us, and we couldn't imagine a more perfect wedding. Each of you has been there for one or both of us over the course of this crazy year, and we will continue to need your love and support as man and wife." He paused, not having planned the little speech. "So, ah, anyway, thank you very much."

People started separating from the crowd to come up and hug them both, and only Bo saw Lexi slip away after embracing the couple. *Ready or not*, he thought, giving his friends a hug and slipping off in the direction she'd gone.

He caught up with her around a bend on the beach, out of sight from the bonfire. "Come on," Bo said, putting his hand on the small of her back and steering her further away from the roaring bonfire and toward the breakwater. "Let's take a walk. Tell your old friend Bo all about it."

She wiped away a tear and turned to him. "That's sweet," she said, her voice nearly lost in the wind. "But it's nothing, really. I'll be OK."

"Not taking no for an answer," he said simply, keeping pace with her.

They found a little secluded spot away from the partygoers and took a seat on a fallen palm that had been smoothed by the waves. The light of the bonfire didn't reach here, and overhead a million stars splattered the dark night sky, and gentle waves lapped up on the shore just a few steps away.

They simultaneously sucked in huge breaths and said at the same time, "I'm so sorry about what happened in California..."

"You don't have anything to apologize for, Lexi, that's all on me," Bo said.

"I came to your room before I left—I didn't want to leave things uncomfortable between us—but you didn't answer the door..."

Bo felt relief and hope settle in his bones. She hadn't run off because of him—she'd actually come back! "I went down to the gym to burn off some energy—I came up to your room after, but you were already gone."

Lexi's heart lightened at the news. "Oh God, that's a relief. I thought you never wanted to see me again."

"Now that's never going to happen."

"I'm so glad. I really missed you, Bo."

"I missed you too." *Oh I want to tell you how much.* "Well, I'm listening," he said gently. "It's obvious you've got a lot on your mind—why don't you dump the burden?"

"Oh Bo," she started, her lips pursing and her eyes going distant. "I just don't think I can really talk to anyone about it," she exhaled slowly, then turned to meet his gaze. "Is it really that obvious that something's bothering me?" she asked, trying to force a wan smile.

"It is to someone who knows you," he replied, then added, "but you're doing a good job of hiding it, don't worry. I've got insight, though, you know. Mad skills."

The ghost of a smile touched her lips. "It's not a big deal, really," she said wistfully. "Just something I have to deal with."

"You don't have to deal with it alone, you know," he said. "I'm a good listener, and it might help to just get it off your chest. Is it your ex?"

"In a way," she said, taking a deep breath and letting it slip back out through clenched teeth. She made a decision then, and figured there was no one she could trust more than Bo Collins. He waited patiently for her to continue, and she finally took another deep breath and stared off toward the sea.

"I know I can trust you, Bo, but I don't ever want Tia or Dylan to find out," she said softly. "I don't want them to feel guilty or responsible in any way."

"That's not my style," he said sincerely. "I would never betray your confidence. I hope you know I really mean that."

Her shoulders dropped, and she turned her head slowly, stretching the muscles she'd been clenching so tightly over the past few days. Finally, she spoke.

"It might be a long story," she said. "I have to start at the beginning."

"I've got nothing but time," he said softly, reaching over to pat her sweetly on the shoulder.

She inhaled deeply, and pushed the breath out through clenched teeth. "OK," she said. If you're sure you want to hear it, I'd appreciate a sympathetic ear." He nodded, and she continued. "It all started, I guess, when Ryan and I were watching a movie one night—oh, a couple years ago or so. I don't remember the title—it wasn't that good of a movie, really—but it starred Alexis Janice."

"Mmm hmm," Bo murmured.

"There was this one scene where she was running along the beach in a bikini with a 357 magnum in her hand—she was dirty and her hair was a mess, but it was hard not to notice Ryan noticing her. I made a funny comment, about chicks with guns in skimpy bikinis, and he admitted he found her 'sizzling,' or something like that. So I said, 'OK, I'll tell you what. If you ever meet Alexis Janice on the street, and she wants to sleep with you, go for it. One night for free; no questions, no consequences. A freebie.' I called it, his 'one gimme.' Of course, we both knew that the chances of that happening were slim to none, so it just became a stupid game, a private joke. He said that if he got a gimme, it was only fair that I got one, too." She paused, absently twirled a lock of hair around her finger, and stared down at the ground. "Mine was Dylan," she said slowly.

"I see," Bo said. "You know, I have a pretty strong suspicion that he's at the top of a lot of those lists, wouldn't you agree? Is that what you don't want them to know?"

"Oh, Tia knows...she knew from the beginning and could have told Dylan for all I know, but that doesn't even matter anymore at all."

"Are you worried that she still thinks you..."

"Oh no!" she cut him off. "Now that I know him, I like him as a person. A lot. I could never think of him that way—at the time I objectified him; just like every other fan does. Now that I call him a friend, I could never, ever, think about him that way again. Even if he wasn't with Tia," she added. "But they're so perfect together anyway, and I'm incredibly happy for both of them. They belong together, and I love them as a couple."

Bo nodded. "Me, too. It's great seeing Dylan so happy, too. It's been a long time comin' for that dude, and I can't think of anyone who deserves it more than he does."

"I feel the same way about Tia. The whole 'gimme' thing crashed down the first time I saw them together—at the show that first night. And it's never once entered my mind again."

"I think I see," Bo said, the realization dawning on him. "Ryan couldn't see that, could he?"

She shook her head. "The trouble with Ryan," she continued, "started when I got home from Europe, I guess. I couldn't tell anyone about Tia and Dylan, but I also couldn't keep the whole story to myself. Tia was going to tell people that she'd met all you guys at the first Aid for Africa concert—her secretary at school had a mad crush on Dylan and Tia wanted to give her an

autographed picture of him as a little gift. It's Lilly, you know, she's here, and she looked after Tia a lot after Nick died—sending her home with meals, dragging her out to social gatherings, stopping over with groceries and helping her with yard work; things like that.

"I mean, Tia did tell people Dylan's first name, and that he played in a band; she just gave the impression that he was playing on one of the smaller stages and managed to meet you guys. She didn't figure that anyone was going to assume that she'd won the heart of Dylan Miller, and she was right. No one even gave it a second thought. So even though I couldn't say much, I could tell people that I'd hung out with Inhap."

"A bit of an understatement," Bo chuckled, remembering their trip, the shows, nights out, spa days for the girls, shopping sprees, the night in Northampton...

She smiled thinly back. "It gave me a bit of celebrity status for a little while," she said, "but Ryan couldn't get past the fact that I'd met my gimme face to face. He was pretty agitated, and asked me point blank if I'd slept with him. Of course I hadn't, and I told him that, and he got really snotty—started saying things like, 'What, he didn't want you?' and 'What a disappointment that must have been.' I told him the same thing I told you—that I'd had a chance to get to know him as a person and that I didn't think of him that way anymore—that I'd have to find a new gimme—but he wasn't buying it. Of course, I couldn't tell him about Tia, so he didn't believe that I'd have any reason not to try.

"He knew I was hiding something too—something big—and of course it was the secret that Tia and Dylan were dating, and shortly after that, the secret that they were in love. Paris was the next stop after I left you guys in Amsterdam, so it was just a few days after I got home that she called me and told me about her birthday dinner on the Eiffel Tower.

"When I told Ryan that Tia and her new boyfriend were in love and shared some of the story with him, his immediate response was to tell me that I probably wished it was me up there, with Dylan Miller. We fought that night—he was so jealous and convinced that something had happened between Dylan and me, and things were just never the same after that. I could feel the distance growing between us from then on, even though I didn't fully realize it at the time. I was pissed that he didn't trust me, and maybe more so that he didn't believe me—that he really thought I'd lied to his face. That just isn't me—I have a bit of a reputation for telling it like it is..." her voice trailed off, and Bo interjected.

"Ya think?" he said sarcastically. Then he added, "It's one of your better qualities, Lex."

"Thanks, I think," she said, smiling thinly. "He finally stopped talking about it constantly; stopped accusing me, but it was always there, hanging out in the background, waiting to rear its ugly head. One night there was a rerun of some late show on where Dylan was the guest, and he called me into the room to tell me; in not so nice a tone; that my boyfriend was on TV. Then, when the second Aid for Africa festival was televised, he asked if I wanted him to make me some popcorn so I had something to do with my hands while Dylan was on the screen—little jabs like that that he said in a joking manner, but the sarcasm and accusation were always there. Of course I wanted to watch you guys! It killed me that I couldn't sit down and enjoy it live; that I couldn't explain to him what was really going on." She paused and sighed. "I'll have you know that I stayed up until two that night to watch the recorded version of the concert.

"It certainly wasn't Tia's fault—after seeing how the media descended on her after they went public; I knew she'd made the right decision not to tell people about her and Dyl. I knew it at the time, even though it was really hard to keep it all a secret. I wanted to tell people my part, but I couldn't do that without telling hers." She was quick to add, "And it wasn't Dylan's fault either. He can't help who he is, and anyone who knows him knows he never shoves it anyone's face. It's just always there."

Bo nodded. He understood completely. He wasn't the 'sexy front man,' and didn't make movies so didn't have the same amount of public exposure, but Dylan made damn sure that they were a band, not a solo act, and Bo got his fair share of the same treatment. It had certainly created problems for him on more than one occasion, and he was actually thankful that Dylan was willing to deal with most of the attention, sparing him and the rest of the guys the bullshit that went along with the constant glare of the spotlight. "But do you think that if you had been able to tell him the truth, things would have been any different?"

"I don't know. He probably would've been even more jealous if he found out I'd hung with you guys for almost two weeks—that I'd been in the front row for all the shows, hanging out backstage...looking back now, it might have made things worse."

Bo raised his eyebrows in question. "What do you mean?"

"Let's just say Ryan has a bit of an inferiority complex when it comes to Dylan," she said. "I would guess a lot of guys would, I mean, let's face it, even if you erased the entire celebrity thing—forgot the fact that women are constantly falling at his feet—he's still incredibly successful, wealthy, well-traveled, kind..."

"Don't forget damn good-looking," Bo teased.

"Well, there is that," Lexi said with a half-smile. "'Sexiest Man on Earth,' and all that."

"Kind of hard to ignore," he smirked.

"When Dylan came back—after the whole Penelope thing—he went with Tia to the country club to meet her parents, and I was waiting for Ryan by the locker rooms so we could have lunch. Dylan was hiding out in there so Tia and her parents could have some time to debrief a little as a family—they'd just found out the truth about who Dylan was, and he figured they needed a little time. When Dylan walked out, I was shocked and surprised, and so glad to see him! Tia had left me a message the night before to meet them there, but I'd lost my phone...whole other long story that doesn't affect the outcome...and when he told me that they were back together, I threw my arms around him and gave him a huge hug—just as Ryan walked out the door."

"Oh, boy," Bo said.

"Yeah. He nearly went ballistic seeing me in Dylan's arms. He was sure that Dylan was there for me, and his first reaction was *pissed off*. Of course, I immediately explained that he was Tia's Dylan, and he relaxed some—we even joined them and Tia's parents for lunch, and then for dinner, a few nights later. He came with me to Paddy's, where Dylan and Tia went the first night they met, and to the engagement party, obviously, but he was pretty much a shit at every single outing."

"I think he wanted a piece of me that night," Bo said. "He certainly wasn't happy to meet me."

"That was all on him—please don't take it personally. It bugged the shit out of me when he acted that way, always putting himself in the corner and refusing to have fun and then giving me crap about it later; but I tried to put myself in his shoes—what if he had spent ten days with Alexis Janice? Would I feel the same way? The conclusion I always came to, though, was that I'd have to trust him, and that I'd have to let it go. He couldn't let it go."

"I'm really sorry, Lexi," Bo said gently.

"You know what Bo? I don't know if I actually am sorry. I'm glad I found out who he really was before I married him, and I was already wondering if I could spend my life with someone who didn't trust me. I'm sad that we couldn't make it work, but looking back, I don't think we ever could have."

"So that's what ended it then?"

"That was the beginning of the end," she said, looking off into the distance at nothing in particular. "Once Tia and Dylan went public, he started getting hassled at work. I'd been interviewed a couple of times, as you well know, and people who knew Ryan and I were engaged started crawling out of the woodwork."

"Isn't that the way it always happens?" he asked rhetorically.

"People started offering him money for an invitation to our wedding—and offering pretty big 'bonuses' if they could get a seat at Dylan's table."

"Oh man," he sighed, shaking his head.

"Oh yeah, the shit hit the fan, let me tell you. Some people went so far as to tell him, point blank, that they'd crash the wedding if they weren't invited. One of his co-workers suggested that he hire a security firm to handle the reception, and he about went off the deep end."

"I can imagine."

"They were hassling him for other things too; you know how it is; and it irked the living crap out of him that he was always second fiddle to Dylan. It was obvious when we were out with them too—Dylan always got so much attention and Ryan was just kind of in the background. He wasn't used to being invisible. It pissed off his world that people who barely knew him would come up to the table and act all happy to see him, then turn all their attention to Dylan as soon as he'd made an introduction. Again, it wasn't Dylan's fault, but Ryan just couldn't handle it."

"That can be a tough situation to be in, you know."

"I do, and that's why I tried to be understanding; tried to give him plenty of attention so he wouldn't feel inferior. But that's exactly how he felt, and there was nothing I could do or say to make him feel otherwise. He pretty much told me that he'd never be able to give me the kind of life that Dylan was giving Tia, and that he'd always wonder if I was comparing him to Dylan and that he knew he'd never measure up."

Bo put his arm around her shoulder and gave her a gentle hug. "It wasn't your fault, either, Lexi. You have to know that."

"I do know now, but things weren't quite so clear at the time," she said wistfully. "When he told me that we had to postpone our wedding because of a "big project" he was working on for the firm—one that he told me could guarantee a position of partner—I was the one who went ballistic. We fought hard, and I stormed out and didn't return his calls for over a week.

"Ironically, it was Dylan who helped me put the whole mess into perspective. He pointed out how tough it had to be for Ryan to deal with the fact that I'd been internationally jet setting over the summer and that he'd just found it out. He said it would take a while for him to realize that it hadn't changed me. He also apologized for planning his and Tia's wedding so close to ours—of course he didn't have much of a choice, but he felt guilty anyway. He told me to try and understand how it must make Ryan feel to suddenly have the celebrity shoved into his life and to see Tia's wedding being talked about on TV and in the papers, while his own seemed to be on a back burner.

"Dylan was right, of course, and I sucked it up, called Ryan, and told him I was OK with the postponement; I tried to be a fucking cheerleader for his "big project," and was being completely understanding of his late hours, his sudden inability to return my calls, his mysterious trips out of town..."

"And that's when you found out that he..."

"Yeah. Apparently, she didn't know about his connection to Dylan, and so when he was with her, he didn't feel covered by Dylan's shadow, or some shit to that effect. He could 'feel like a man again,' he said, as if I hadn't been jumping through fucking hoops to make him feel that way every day."

"Dyl told me about that. I'm really sorry. I can see why you don't Dylan and Tia to know the whole story."

"Exactly! I don't want them to feel guilty or responsible—it isn't their fault at all, it's just the way it all worked out. Ryan couldn't deal with it, and that's his own fucking problem. But knowing Tia and Dylan the way I do, they'd feel at least partly responsible, and I would never do that to them.

"So that's my story," she sighed. "He'd broken every shred of trust I had in him based on his own delusion that I'd done the same thing to him. Or it just wasn't meant to be in the first place. Either way, I realized that all the nights he'd been "working late" were just excuses to not see me. Or to see her. Probably a combination of both."

They sat in silence for a while and Bo tried to process it all in his mind. He could understand every side of the story—except for the cheating part—and poor Lexi came out the loser from every angle. She was carrying a heavy burden in order to protect the ones she loved, and he respected her tremendously for it. But damn it, she shouldn't have had to suffer, not for a minute. He took a few deep breaths to try and calm the fury that bubbled up inside him that she'd had to bear that burden alone for all this time. Finally, he burst. "He's a complete ass who didn't even come close to deserving you," he snarled, the anger evident in his voice. "I mean, to make you feel guilty for something you didn't even do—for not trusting you—for hurting you like that..." He'd been keeping his own feelings in check, but he lost control of his emotions and the words tumbled out before he could reign them in. "I mean damn—if you were my girl, I'd be looking for excuses to come home early. Every day."

"Thanks for that," she said softly, staring off at the dark sea, the breeze lifting her blonde hair and sending it tumbling around her face. She reached for him without averting her gaze and he took her hand, holding it tight. "Maybe I should be your girl then, Bo."

"Yeah, Lexi, maybe you should," he said, the words low and gravelly.

She was struck by the timbre of his voice but when she turned, she still expected to see the usual humor on his face, the smirk he often wore when they flirted. What she saw was completely the opposite—a look she'd never seen before. His lips held not even the hint of a smile, and his eyes were intensely focused on hers. She felt the heat rush up to her face in the intensity of his gaze and a flutter rose in her stomach. There was no doubt about the seriousness in his eyes, and at that moment, she felt she could simply fall into them and stay forever, cocooned in the warmth and safety she saw there.

"I really think I could do that," she whispered on breath as light as the ocean breeze.

He held her gaze a moment longer, waiting to see if she would break into a grin, laugh it off like it was one of their usual jokes. He would have gone along with it, laughed with her, because he wouldn't ever want her to feel uncomfortable around him knowing he felt something she didn't. But she didn't look away, didn't laugh, and he could read it in her eyes—she wanted this, too.

He brought his hands up to cup her face, and slowly lowered his mouth to hers, hearing the soft sigh slide through her lips just before they touched his.

His soft, full lips closed over hers, and one of his hands slipped behind her neck, pulling her in closer. She fell into the kiss, fireworks exploding in her mind and her stomach flipping over and over and she slid her own hands around his strong frame and scooched closer until their legs were touching and leaned into him. His beard tickled her cheeks and chin and she sighed again as his tongue requested entry and she immediately granted it. This felt so warm, so comfortable, so right, and she couldn't believe that they hadn't done it sooner. Couldn't believe she hadn't admitted to herself before now that what she felt for Bo Collins was not just an innocent flirtation but something more—something deeper.

When the kiss ended and he backed away, she could only look at him for a moment through eyes lidded with desire, her breath quick and shallow. "Wow," she finally managed to whisper, a slow smile lighting her face. "Mad skills indeed."

"Wow doesn't even begin to describe it," he croaked back, his voice thick as honey. "I think I need to do it again just to make sure I believe it."

She smiled, and straddled the log so she could press closer into him, moving in to kiss him again. As their bodies pressed together, she could feel the strong pull of desire and anticipation coursing through her veins. She'd wanted this, she admitted to herself. A part of her had wanted it all along.

When they broke the kiss, she rested her head against his chest and heard the pounding of his heart against her cheek. He enveloped her completely in his huge arms, and rested his lips on the top of her head.

"Damn, woman, talk about some mad skills!" he joked softly. "Why didn't you tell me you were such an incredible kisser? It's even better than I imagined, kissing you."

"Well, you never asked...wait a minute, better than you imagined? You mean you've imagined kissing me before?" She tilted her head up to meet his eyes.

"You want to know what happened in California?" He didn't wait for an answer before continuing. "You were sitting there, looking so damn sexy in that little leopard outfit, and images that had no right being there started playing in mind. I lost my head for a minute, and almost kissed you. Just the thought of it got me...well, *overstimulated*."

Lexi put her hand over her mouth to stifle a giggle. It explained everything—and to think, she had thought all this time that he put the distance between them because he didn't want to be close to her...

"Yeah, yeah, laugh at it now; but at the time, you were an engaged woman."

"So when you didn't hug me goodbye..."

Bo chuckled. "I don't think I could've gotten close enough to you to hug you goodbye. Not with my...well, you know...getting in the way."

Lexi laughed out loud. "Totally the opposite of what's been going through my head over the past few months. Oh my."

"Hell, if you want to know the truth, I've had it bad for you since the first time we met," he admitted. "When I saw you backstage and asked if you were my birthday present, I kept hoping you would be. And the more I got to know you, the more I liked you."

"But you never..."

"Again, you were an engaged woman," he reminded her, "and I never go there. I've got more class than that."

"You are the epitome of style and grace," she teased. "And I respect you for that," she added more seriously. She paused, letting her breathing return to normal. "Oh my God," she said, "what does this mean? I mean, what are we..."

"It means," he said with a smile, "and correct me if I'm wrong here, but I like you and you like me, and we're going to spend some more time together, see if we can make a go of things."

"A go of things?" she giggled, and he knew that he could listen to the sound of her laughter forever. "What are we, in high school?"

"Well, I guess I am asking for permission to be your boyfriend," he smiled slyly, cocking his head to one side and shooting her a crooked grin.

"Oh, I'll have to think about that," she teased, tilting her own head and sizing him up with her eyes. "I have some pretty high standards when it comes to boyfriends." She loved this about Bo from the start—they could go right from an intimate moment to their usual teasing, and both felt as comfortable as a favorite pair of slippers.

"Try me," he smirked. "I am the epitome of high standards, as well as style and grace, as you so eloquently aforementioned."

"Well," she began, touching her index fingers together to begin a counted list. "First of all, any boyfriend of mine has to be honest and trustworthy at all times."

"Ah hell, that's easy! Give me something harder than that!"

"OK, here's a good one. He has to be emotionally available and talk about his feelings."

"I wear 'em on my sleeve, sweetheart. Try again."

"That's about it," she said. "Oh, except for one other thing."

"Shoot."

"He has to treat me like the goddess I am and love all my quirky attributes."

"Now that's the easy part! And, the part I'm going to enjoy the most," he said, taking her hand in his.

She looked down at their joined hands, loving the blend of cocoa, cream, and moonlight she saw there. She looked back up at Bo and whispered, "I guess you pass, then," and tilted her chin up to meet his lips once again.

After a long and smoldering kiss, Bo held her face and looked her in the eye. "Well, since I'm your boyfriend and all," he smiled, "I got an invitation to the wedding of the freaking century. Will you be my date?"

"I'll have to check my schedule," she smiled, "but I think I just might be able to squeeze you in."

He pulled her in and held her for a moment, whispering, "Best birthday ever!"

Lexi jumped. "Oh my God! It is your birthday! Today!"

Bo smiled. "Yep. And I finally got the present I've been wanting since my last birthday." He pressed his lips to her forehead and whispered, "Definitely worth the wait."

"I didn't forget, Bo—I got you a card and a present and everything! It's in my bag on the beach."

"I just told you, beautiful," he said sweetly. "You have given me the very best present I could ever wish for. Did wish for."

She pulled him up. "Come on—we've got to go celebrate! We can't just let something like that go!"

"I'm fine with a little private celebration right here," he smiled, trying to pull her back down into his lap.

She shook her head with determination. "Let's go, birthday boy," she insisted. "All our friends are here, and it's your special day. I insist we sing to you. You love birthdays!"

"Don't worry," he smirked. "Dylan's got it all planned out. I overheard Jessa talking about it to Tony yesterday—they've got a big cake and everything." He looked at his watch. "Oh, and actually, I think they'll be looking for me right about now. I guess we'd best head back." He got up almost reluctantly—at the moment he wanted to just stay right here, where he could have Lexi all to himself, but it was true—he was a kid at heart when it came to birthdays, and he had been looking forward to the attention all day. "Oh, alright," he moaned, allowing her to pull him up and wrapping his arms around her for one more lip lock before they made their way back to the bonfire.

When they rejoined the crowd, as Bo had predicted, Dylan was looking for him. Dylan's old band from England, Slingshot, had been playing, and as soon as he spotted Bo and Lexi, he curved his index finger toward them and gestured to Max. When the song ended, Max snapped a note while Dylan brought everyone to attention.

"Hey, everyone," he began. "This has already been the best weekend of my life, and I haven't even gotten to the best part yet!" He pulled Tia close and smacked a loud kiss on her cheek. "But Tia and I aren't the only ones with something big to celebrate this weekend, and I'd be remiss—plus I'd never live it down—if I didn't call attention to that fact..." He looked toward the portico, motioned with his hand, and a trio of staff members walked onto the beach, holding an enormous cake covered with sparklers and lugging a gigantic tub of ice cream. Two more people balancing plates and bowls on giant platters followed, hustling to a massive table that had been erected for the occasion. "Ladies and gentlemen—and in some cases I use the term lightly," a murmur of laughter and some good-natured punches on the shoulder moved through the crowd, "today is Bo Collins's birthday. He's my best man in every sense of the word, and I'm thrilled to be celebrating yet another milestone with him—especially when it isn't on the road; and we can actually share it with our family and friends. This day last year was my and Tia's first date, and he knew even more than I did that night just how much she'd come to mean to me." he glanced over at his best man, who had his arm firmly around Lexi's hip and smiled. "He's really a big baby when it comes to birthdays—he loves the limelight and the singing—so get your voices tuned up, and help me wish Bo a happy day!" Max jumped into a rousing rendition of the birthday song, and the entire group joined in. Bo hopped up on the stage, pulling Lexi with him to bathe in the adoration, a huge grin on his face. When the song ended, and the cheering fell to a dull roar, Dylan exclaimed, "Make a wish, and blow out your candles!"

"My wish," he said with fanfare, "already came true." He smiled, pulling Lexi to him, lowered her into a dip, and kissed her enthusiastically. The crowd cheered louder, and he let her up, smiled, and made a big spectacle of extinguishing the candles. "Let's have cake, and eat it, too!" he proclaimed, planting another kiss on Lexi's cheek and handing her the first slice.

Tia and Dylan stared at each other for a moment, a look of pleased surprise on both their faces. "About damn time," they said in unison.

"Oh, they'll be so good together!" Tia exclaimed. "God knows no one else can keep up with her, or put her in her place."

"Funny," Dylan smirked, "I was just thinking the same thing about her for Bo. They just may be able to keep each other in line."

Tia grabbed his hand and pulled him toward the couple. "Well come on, let's go find out!" she exclaimed.

Dylan conceded, laughing. "OK, my bride. I'm with you."

They made their way to the table, where Bo and Lexi were happily handing out pieces of cake and scooping enormous globs of ice cream into bowls. Bo started up before they even reached them.

"Oh, here come the nosey neighbors," he joked. "I know, I know, you want to know why I planted a big juicy one on her in front of all your company, right?" He punched Dylan playfully on the arm. "Don't worry, Strummer Boy, I'm not trying to steal your limelight or anything—I just couldn't help myself."

Tia turned to Lexi, who couldn't keep the blush out of her cheeks or the smile off her face. "I couldn't help myself either," she giggled. "Seems Bo's got this idea that we should..." she made air quotes with her fingers, "...make a go of things, and since I didn't have a proper date for this shindig, I figured, what the hell?"

Tia shrieked in excitement and ran up to hug them both. "Seriously?! You two are a couple?"

Lexi shrugged. "Seems I just might have it in me to give him a shot," she said solemnly, holding the look for only a second before a huge grin split her face.

"I'm so excited!" Tia yelled, grabbing Lexi's hands and spinning with her around the beach while Dylan pulled Bo into a rough hug.

"It's about bloody time," Dylan joked. "I couldn't stand seeing the tension between the two of you for another minute!"

Bo shot him the finger. "Screw you, Miller," he said. "As if your mind has been anywhere but on your girl here for the past...oh, I don't know, months?"

"Still hard to miss you moping around like a little lost puppy, Bobo," he joked back. "I'm glad I figured out that Lexi was the one who was 'on your mind all the time.'"

Bo nodded, grinning slyly.

"What?" Lexi asked, looking back and forth between them.

Dylan looked at her and smiled. "When I asked Bo if he was bringing a date for the wedding and he told me no, I asked if he even had anyone in mind."

"I'll finish this little story, thank you very much," he said, turning to Lexi. "I told him there was someone on my mind all the time, but that she was spoken for, so I had to keep my hands off. It didn't take Mr. Genius here long to figure it out."

"Aww!" Lexi said, putting her arm around him and stretching up on her toes to kiss him. Then she took a step back and put her hands on her hips. "Wait a minute," she scolded, grinning. "You meant me, right?"

"Of course I meant you, you crazy woman!" he laughed, pulling her into his arms and spinning her around, kissing her full on the lips.

Tia clapped her hands together and jumped in place. "Yay!" she said, truly thrilled for her friends. "Now we have even more to celebrate! Love is in the air, and I think we all need some champagne!"

"We can definitely make that happen," Dylan said, pulling Tia back to his side and calling over one of the staff members.

"Oh, your present!" Lexi exclaimed, running off to find her bag and returning with the package, wrapped in gold foil. Bo handed her a glass of champagne, and they touched the rims of their glasses together.

"I told you, you've already given me the very best present." He grinned, though, as he peeled off the paper. "We'll always have London," he said, reading the inscription and remembering when she'd said those words to him as they watched her TV debut. "Oh, princess, we're gonna have a lot more than that," he smiled.

"I certainly hope so," she said, wrapping her arms around him. "Happy Birthday, Bo."

"Best birthday ever," he whispered.

They had their cake and then strolled back to the bonfire, the couples arm in arm, and Tia holding Lexi's hand affectionately, swinging their arms between them. In the distance, they saw Sean and Gina, hand in hand, walking along the water's edge. Love was definitely in the air, and it was a beautiful thing.

Chapter 46

The day of the wedding dawned bright and clear. Tia watched the glorious colors of the Caribbean sunrise spill over the turquoise waters of the sea, and hugged herself. Today she would marry Dylan! She'd barely slept a wink all night, but nonetheless, she felt wide awake and invigorated. She couldn't imagine a better setting for her wedding, and she could still hardly believe that the soundtrack of her life had turned into the man of her dreams.

"I know you're happy for me, Nick," she whispered on the cool morning breeze. "I know I have your blessing." She did know, too. If Nick could have hand-picked the man she'd eventually marry, it would have been Dylan Miller. They'd both idolized him when Nick was alive, and she could almost feel him smiling down on her.

Tia inhaled the salty air and went over the past year in her mind. She never even imagined that the night, so long ago, when she was going to be a fly on the wall at a little dumpy bar and try to figure out how to ease back into life again, could lead to this perfect, beautiful day. There had been more than a few bumps in the road along their journey, but she wouldn't trade any of it; because it led her here. As she looked out over the inexplicable blues of the Caribbean, colors that reminded her of Dylan's eyes, she took the calm sea as a sign that they'd have smooth sailing for the rest of their amazing journey. Today she would pledge her love to Dylan in front of the people they loved most, and they would begin the next adventure of their lives—their InHappily ever after. Everything was as it should be, and all was right with the world.

She and Dylan had agreed to follow tradition and not see each other on the day of their wedding, but they had lingered on the beach the night before after the last of their guests had retired for the evening to steal a few private moments together. The next time they'd see each other would be when Tia was walking down the aisle—combed beach lined with tropical flowers—on her way to become his wife. They came together and he held her tightly, neither of them speaking for several moments. Finally, Dylan broke the silence.

"Any cold feet?" he whispered.

She looked down at her bare toes, buried in the cool sand. "Nope. Nice and toasty," she replied. "You?"

"Not even a little chill," he smiled. "All I can think about is tomorrow, and you walking down that aisle and into my arms. About you being my wife. Finally."

Tia smiled and snuggled into his embrace. "Me, too," she said. "This is the last day I'll be Tia Hastings."

"Tomorrow, it's Tia Miller. Always and forever."

"You know, hanging with your mom and cousins and Gina—I kept wishing I'd met you sooner. I just don't know if the rest of our lives will be long enough to spend with you."

"The kind of love we have, baby girl, goes on for eternity."

"I could do eternity," she whispered. "I could easily do eternity."

"Plus one more day."

They walked the beach for a bit, stopping in front of the completely secluded bungalow where they'd spend their first night together as man and wife. As they'd been in separate housing since they got to the island, it was going to be a much anticipated reunion for them both.

"I wonder if we should go in—check out the bed and make sure it's...comfortable," Dylan whispered, raising one eyebrow at her.

She punched him playfully on the shoulder. "Mr. Miller," she began. "As much as that idea entices me—and believe me, it does, I think we should wait until we can christen it as husband and wife."

"Wow," he said. "We really will be christening it. We'll be the very first couple to spend the night there—that's kind of crazy."

Tia leaned into him and sighed. "We'll give it good luck," she said. "Just think of all the other couples who'll spend their wedding nights or honeymoons here."

"Tony told me that there's a guest book in there that he wants us to sign—so every couple who does come here will know that true love was the first guest."

They held each other for a long while before Dylan walked her back to her building, kissing her long and slow before sending her inside. "Until tomorrow, Mrs. Miller," he said softly.

"I can't wait," she whispered in reply as he turned to go.

And now the day was here. In just a few short hours, her wedding day would begin. The girls would have breakfast together in the grand dining room of the main house, and then the spa crew was coming in to provide some incredible pampering at eleven. They'd have a light lunch around three, and then, at six, to capture the start of the sunset, she'd be stepping out of the main house for the last time as Tia Hastings. She'd be walking toward her future as Mrs. Dylan Miller.

She smiled at the thought—she couldn't possibly be more in love with Dylan, and although there would be challenges, especially when he was out on tour, she relished the thought of every minute she could spend as his wife.

She was thrilled for Lexi, too—her new romance with Bo seemed so genuine, so unexpected yet not surprising—so, *Incidental Happenstance*, once again. Tia really thought they could make it. Neither of them was going into this blind—they'd seen what could happen by watching her and Dylan go through it, and they were both at a point in their lives to know what they wanted, and to go after it. She imagined how nice it would be for her and

Lexi to be world tour widows together—they'd always have each other when their men were away, doing what they loved and earning their paychecks. They could travel together to meet them at shows, and support each other when they were missing their boys. Everything would be easier if they had that in common, and she said a selfish silent prayer that things would work out between the two of them.

She went back into her room and poured some coffee, and stepped back out to watch the sun rise over the calm water, filling it with hues of red and orange. She jumped when she heard the whispered, "Good morning, bride!" from the next balcony, and motioned for Lexi to come and join her. Lexi ducked into her room and then appeared at the open door, pulling Tia close.

"I guess it's true what they say," she beamed. "You are positively glowing this morning, Mrs. Miller!"

Tia smiled, loving the sound of her new name. "I think it's more because I just got up," she said, "but thanks anyway. I am beside myself. I can't believe I'm getting married today!"

"I am so incredibly happy for you, you know that, right?" she whispered. "You and Dylan are a perfect couple, and I'm just so glad you found each other."

"And what about you and Bo?" she asked. "Not that it came out of left field, but I have to say, I was a bit surprised."

"So was I!" Lexi said. "I mean, we flirted constantly…"

"Obviously," Tia broke in.

"…Obviously," Lexi repeated, batting her eyelashes, "but I had no clue he felt that way about me for real. He said he's wanted me since the first time he met me—backstage at the first show, when I was make a babbling ass of myself."

Tia laughed, remembering. "You were in fine form that night, you're right about that!" she teased. "It was kind of obvious that there was something going on there, but I didn't imagine it would lead to this. Although, I must admit, when you and Ryan ended, I kind of hoped in the back of my mind that you might see Bo as something more." She looked her best friend right in the eye. "He's an incredible guy, Lex. The real deal."

"I know it," she sighed happily, falling into one of the soft chairs and looking out over the ocean. A few puffy clouds floated gently through the sky, and the soft ocean breeze lifted her hair. "I guess part of me knew there was something there from the beginning, but of course I didn't think about it, or act on it. Until last night, that is," she said with a sheepish grin.

"Tell me how it happened," Tia prodded, and Lexi happily recalled the story for her. "Incredibly romantic," Tia said when she finished. "And I can't imagine a more perfect setting for the start of a great romance."

"I've said it at least a few times before," Lexi grinned, "but I'll say it again. You get me into all the right parties. I'm so glad we're buds."

The two friends exchanged another hug before going to rouse the other girls. It was time to get ready to marry the man she loved.

One of Dylan's favorite musicians and good friend, Austin Renault, sat at the ready with his acoustic guitar, waiting for the signal. When it came, he wound into a beautiful and unique melody as the guests began to arrive to take up seats on the beach before the platform under the archway that was covered in silk, tulle, and tropical flowers. Dylan walked his mother up the aisle, and led her to her seat before taking his place at the base of the platform. He couldn't stop tapping his foot. He wasn't nervous, not in the least, but while the girls were kept busy with spa treatments and pampering, he'd been pacing the beach, wishing the minutes would tick away more quickly so he could make Tia his wife. Now he was just moments away from making that a reality, and although he relished the family and friends who had joined them for this momentous occasion, he was truly looking forward to spending some time with her alone, especially on this, their wedding night. Serious quality time.

He heard the change in the music and watched as Jessa came walking down the aisle. She immediately caught his eye and smiled. They'd been through a lot together; the two of them; and

Jessa was one of only a handful of people who really knew what this day meant to him. He owed a lot of it to her—there was a lot of her handiwork in this week's events, and she'd done a bang-up job. But her involvement went much deeper than that. She'd been Tia's companion during the European tour when he was working, and they'd become fast friends. Plus, of course, she was instrumental in helping him to find her again once he uncovered Penelope Valentine's bullshit scheme. He was looking forward to presenting her with her thank-you gift later that night; a week at a spa resort on Virgin Gorda, where her mother would be joining her as an extra surprise. She'd fight it tooth and nail at first—she wasn't one to relax very often—but he knew that she would enjoy every minute once she got there, and she certainly deserved it.

She was spectacular in a dress that looked like a sunset, and he smiled back as they shared a knowing look. He was lucky to have her, and he knew it. He was thrilled that she was such an integral part of his big day. Not as his employee, but as his friend.

Lexi swept down the aisle next, and Dylan raised an eyebrow as he took her in. She was dressed like the sky—all blues and yellows—and she looked dazzling. She winked at him and tossed him an approving look, then turned to catch Bo's eye. It wasn't hard, since his eyes were practically bugging out of his head at the sight of her. Dylan smiled at the thought of his best friend finding love, and was secretly thrilled that Tia could have someone to turn to on those long lonely nights when he was on the road.

Austin's melody effortlessly slipped into his own rendition of the wedding march. He'd expertly matched it to the occasion, putting in the sound of the ocean and chords that he knew were Dylan's favorites. Dylan hopped from foot to foot in anticipation of the appearance of his bride.

When she turned the corner and he caught his first glimpse of her, he thought he'd stop breathing. She was incredibly beautiful, her sun-lightened hair spilling in soft waves around her face, which was positively glowing. She looked like the sea rolling slowly toward shore, and the late-day sun caught little jewels on the dress that made her look like a mermaid gliding back toward the ocean. There was a halo of light surrounding her, and he thought, *here comes my angel*. His smile lit up his entire face, and the second she met his stare, he saw a tear of joy glistening there. She smiled back at him, and he saw his future flash before his eyes. *Never*, he thought, *has anyone loved as much as I love this woman!* He touched his fingers to his lips and blew her a tiny kiss as she walked toward him, on her way to be his. Forever.

At that moment, no one else on earth existed except the two of them. Tia looked at Dylan, her man, her love, and couldn't turn away. He was incredibly sexy in a light gray suit that was perfect for the occasion, his wavy blonde hair dusting his shoulders and blowing carelessly in the ocean breeze. It was the look on his face that nearly stopped her heart, though. There was something so pure and honest in his smile, something so raw that it was exquisite, and it positively took her breath away. He always made her feel like the only woman on earth, but this day, she could see that it was true. She couldn't wait to get to him, to hold his hand and say her vows, to slip the ring onto his finger, to hear the preacher pronounce them man and wife. She felt all the eyes on her; felt the presence of her family and friends, but it was only her and Dylan now; just the two of them as she made her way toward her future; her husband.

The sun was just starting to sink and the sky was an explosion of color as she reached Dylan's side. He took her hand, barely able to take his eyes from hers to acknowledge her father as he lifted her veil, ready to hand her over to him. Tia looked at him, and her smile nearly melted his heart. The waves gently lapped at the shore, and the colors of the sunset melted into the sea beside them as the preacher spoke the first words of their wedding ceremony.

"Friends and family," he began, his voice clear in reverence to the setting, the moment, the obvious love between the couple, "we have gathered here today to witness one of God's greatest miracles; the love between a man and a woman that causes them to pledge themselves to each other, forsaking all others, to further His grace. It is with great honor that I officiate over this ceremony; this sharing of hearts; this pledge of undying love."

Tia and Dylan stared into each other's eyes, so much said but yet unspoken, a promise made long before the formation of any words discernible to the loved ones who had gathered to witness.

Dylan nodded to Tia's father as he officially gave his blessing and placed her hand in his, never taking his eyes off his beautiful bride. The preacher continued with his speech, but neither of them heard it, really. They were completely engrossed in each other, and it wasn't until they were prompted to speak their vows, the words that would bind them together forever, that they were pulled back from their private celebration. Both had written and rewritten their words, determined to get it right on this one day, this one chance, to make it count.

Tia held Dylan's hand in hers, and looked deep into his eyes, amazed and humbled by the love she saw there.

"Oh, Dylan," Tia began, "I've gone over and over what to say to you today; how to put into words the way you make me feel, the way the sun shines more brightly when you're beside me, the way your hand fits so perfectly in mine. I don't think love is a strong enough word, but I honestly don't think a strong enough word exists to explain the way you light up my world, the way you complete me." She paused and met his eyes, his smile saying it all as he gently wiped away a rogue tear of joy with the rough pad of his thumb.

"There hasn't been a day since you came into my life that I haven't thanked God and all the lucky stars for you; that I haven't wondered how I could be so incredibly fortunate to have your love and devotion. And I know there never will be.

"I love you with everything I am, with every breath I take, and with every beat of my heart; and I can easily promise that I will love you until the end of time. I look so forward to sharing my life with you, and to sharing in yours. You have my undying pledge that I will be a good and faithful and understanding wife, that I will put your needs before my own, and that I will spend the rest of my days loving you beyond comprehension. I promise you this before God and all these witnesses, and I so happily take you to be my incredible and amazing husband until the end of my days."

There was a moment of collective silence among the guests, and more than a few wiped away a tear as she finished her heartfelt vows. The preacher turned to Dylan, and he squeezed her hand, taking a breath before beginning his own.

"My beautiful and amazing Tia," he started, smiling. "I, too, struggled to find words that could even begin to explain what you mean to me, but so much of what we share goes so far beyond words, so beyond explanation, that it seemed an impossible task. You are my music, my muse, the most beautiful melody I've ever heard. You're the part of me I didn't realize I was missing until I found you, and the part that I now can't live without.

"I would go to the ends of the earth just to see you smile; stop time just to hear your laughter. I promise you before God and these witnesses that as long as I have breath in my body you will want for nothing—it is my personal mission in life to make you as happy as you make me just by being mine. Words cannot express how elated I am to take you as my wife, my partner, my best friend, for all the rest of my days and beyond."

The preacher waited for the words to lose their weight on the ocean breeze before continuing. He took the rings and said a blessing over them, handing one first to Tia. Her hands shook as she slid it easily onto Dylan's finger, and her voice wavered with the intensity of her emotion. "I give you this ring, Dylan, as an undying symbol of the love and devotion that fill my heart to bursting. With it, I call you my husband, and put my full trust in you and our love for a long and happy life together."

Dylan smiled and put out his hand for her ring without ever taking his eyes from hers. He held up her shaking hand, and slowly slipped the ring onto her finger. "I give you this ring, Tia, as a symbol of the promise I make to you to be a good and faithful husband, a life partner, and a best friend. No matter what life throws at us, I know that together we can conquer any challenge, and I look forward to meeting each and every one with you by my side. I am so happy and proud to call you my wife." He choked up a bit on the last words, and a tear slid from Tia's eyes.

Lexi's and Bo's eyes met, and they shared a knowing glance, a happy smile. They were both filled with happiness for their best friends; and with their own promise for a possible future together.

"Tia and Dylan," the preacher said proudly, "may you find love and joy in all of your days, and be faithful partners to each other." Dylan glanced over him expectantly, and urged him with his eyes to hurry things along. The preacher smiled knowingly, and quickly continued. "So now, by the power vested in me, and by the generous love of God, I now pronounce you husband and wife." He smiled down at Dylan, whose grin had taken over his face. "Dylan, you may kiss your bride."

"Come here, Mrs. Miller," he growled from the back of his throat, pulling her in and wrapping his arms tightly around her waist. He smiled at her, and brought his lips to hers, picking her up off the ground and spinning her in a slow circle.

What a kiss! Tia was breathless with the thought that Dylan was now her husband; that their future together was assured and promised to be full of all the best that life had to offer. The rest of the world fell away, and it was just the two of them in their shared embrace, their testament of love fulfilled, their amazing kiss sealing the vow.

When he finally set her gently down, he moved his lips to her ear and whispered, "I love you so much, Mrs. Miller."

"I love you more, dear husband," she whispered back, pulling him close for a loving embrace.

"Ladies and gentleman, friends and family, it gives me great pleasure to introduce to you, for the very first time, Mr. and Mrs. Dylan Miller!"

A cheer rose up from their guests, and they turned to accept their congratulations as Dylan walked Tia, finally his wife, back down the aisle. Bo grinned at Lexi and took her arm, following the couple, pressing his body against hers as they went.

Jessa and Max followed them, and they formed a line in order to receive individual well-wishes from their friends and family.

"That could not have been more perfect!" Lexi exclaimed. "Oh guys, that was the most gorgeous and romantic wedding ever!"

"I especially liked the ending," Dylan said with his famous half-smile. "The pronouncing us man and wife and the kiss the bride part were by far my favorites."

"Yeah, well that was pretty obvious," Bo teased. "I wanted to yell out, 'get a room!' but I was afraid you might just run off and miss the reception!"

"You mean we have to go the reception?" Dylan joked. "Getting to our room is exactly what's on my mind." He grabbed Tia and dipped her down, kissing her long and deep.

"Now, now, dear husband," Tia laughed, loving the sound of the word and thrilled to be able to say it, "we'll have the rest of our lives together, but we only get to do this wedding thing once."

"Oh, alright," he conceded with a smile as their parents made their way over to the happy couple. "I guess we can hang out for a little while. If we absolutely have to. But later, lovely wife, I have plans for you."

"I sure hope so," she said under her breath so only he could hear.

The reception was exactly what they'd hoped for—the final throes of the sunset cooperated with their photo session, and they got some amazing shots. The weather was perfect, the food was amazing, the wine flowed freely, and the music was incredible; thanks to Dylan's many musician friends. There couldn't have been a more perfect night for any of the guests, and everyone was having a fabulous time.

Tony smiled as he took it all in. It couldn't have been more perfect for him, either. The wedding had gone off without a hitch, there had been no breach, no paparazzi, and the reception was going perfectly. He'd had a chance to review the film from the interviews and the overview of the place, as well as some of the afternoon's wedding pictures, and he couldn't have been more thrilled. Not only had he been able to give his good friend and his lovely bride the wedding of their dreams, he stood to make a fortune on the pictures and film rights of the wedding. He'd already sat down briefly with Jessa, and she'd approved nearly everything he'd selected.

His plan was to show some of the pictures and video from the wedding on his show tomorrow night, a bit more of the wedding video on the tabloid show the next day, and sell off some others. He knew that the public would want to see the entire wedding, and he thought he might be able to convince Dylan and Tia to let him air the whole thing once they saw how tastefully it had been filmed and how much they all stood to gain; as well as appeasing their fans, who seemed insatiably hungry for more of the beloved couple.

The rich and famous would be lining up to vacation and get married on his little slice of paradise, and he could almost hear the money rolling in.

But tonight, love reigned supreme. The bride and groom couldn't get enough of each other, and both Dylan's and Tia's parents were spinning across the dance floor. Bo and Lexi cuddled up as they swayed to the music and stole away for some private moments on one of the swings in the garden. He decided it was the perfect time to ask Jessa, who had more than piqued his interest, for a dance.

Lexi sat curled up under Bo's arm beneath a beautiful array of tropical flowers and palms that seemed to dance in the gentle breeze. The moon swelled in the sky, and the stars were out in all their glory. The sounds of frogs and crickets mixed with the music in the background and she added her sigh to the harmony; a mixture of contentment, joy for her best friend, and a new sense of hope for what tomorrow could bring.

Coming here was so much more than she'd expected, and she had known it was going to be incredible. She was so thrilled to see her best friends in the world find the happiness that they so deserved; especially in light of all the pitfalls they'd encountered along the way.

What she hadn't expected, though, was that she and Bo would realize that there was more to their unabashed flirting than either of them had been able to admit; that there were real feelings there. She felt the flutters of a schoolgirl crush in her stomach as she smiled and snuggled closer to him, feeling his strong and capable arms pulling her in. They hadn't talked yet about what would happen next, after this incredible weekend, but they both knew that what they shared was not just a little fling. She smiled at the thought, and hummed deep in her throat.

"Mmmmmm," she sighed. "This feels really good. It was such a gorgeous wedding—I'm so happy for Tia and Dylan."

Bo pulled her up onto his lap and kissed her. "It was pretty awesome," he agreed. "You're pretty awesome, too, Lexi, and this thing with us..." his voice trailed off as he searched for the right words.

"...was a happy and unexpected surprise for me, Bo. It feels so natural, so easy." She smiled back at him. "It's made an incredible weekend even more incredible than I could have ever dreamed possible."

"I was thinking," he said. "Do you think you could get another week off of work? I don't have anywhere I need to be right now, and there are a lot of very romantic islands around here where we could explore the whole thing further..." he waggled his eyebrows at her, and she couldn't help but laugh. She loved that they could still joke about pretty much anything, and was thrilled that he wanted to extend their time together.

"Didn't Tia tell you? I'm currently unemployed, so I've got all the time in the world. I hear The Virgin Islands are nice this time of year," she said.

"Hey," he teased, "if we do this, I don't want there to be anything virginal about it. I was thinking more of Aruba, or maybe Trinidad—something sexy—you know, worthy of the two of us."

"I like the way you're thinking, handsome," she smiled, leaning over and pressing her lips to his.

"I wonder if Jessa might look into a few things for us— she's got the magic touch when it comes to things like that. Should we head back to the party and see if we can talk her into it?"

"Mmmm," Lexi moaned. "I like it right here, thanks." Bo tilted his head and raised his eyebrows. "Oh, all right," she groaned, "I guess we are the maid of honor and best man—we should go join in the celebration."

Just then, Jessa came around the corner and made her way into the garden. "There you are!" she said, out of breath. "They're going to toss the bouquet and garter soon, and they both want you to be there!"

Lexi peeled herself off Bo's lap and smoothed her dress. "I'm coming," she said with a smile. "We were just headed that way anyway."

"You are going to make a try for that bouquet, right princess?" Bo winked at her. "Couldn't hurt to have a little luck on our side, right?"

"I will do my best. You're going for the garter, then?"

"Are you kidding me? I've been visualizing it all night," he swirled his hands around his head, his fingers wagging. "It's in the bag, sister."

Lexi giggled and wrapped her arm around his waist, while Jessa shook her head and groaned. "Oh hell," she said. "One of you InHap boys in love is hard enough, but two of you will be impossible!"

Bo detached himself from Lexi and wrapped his arm around Jessa. "Now, now, little one," he said smoothly, "you know I never ask for much. I'm always easy to please!"

She stopped and turned, looking at him suspiciously while Lexi giggled. "OK, Collins, what do you want?" she asked, hands on her hips. Bo shrugged and pasted an innocent look onto his face. "Spill it," she insisted.

"Well, now that you mention it—speaking of mentioning, did I tell you how stunning you look tonight? Positively gorgeous!"

"I don't need any of your sugar, Bo. Just ask. You know I'll help you if I can. I can always squeeze in some time for you, you know that." Bo kissed the top of her head affectionately. "So, what do you need?"

Bo pulled her into a friendly hug. "You're the best, you know that? We're all lucky to have you. I mean that."

"Uh, sugar?" she reminded him. "Don't want it, don't need it. Give me something to do."

Lexi broke in and took Jessa by the arm, leading her back to the reception. "Bo and I are thinking of extending our little vacation, and were hoping you might be able to get us some info on some good destinations."

"I see," she said with a knowing smile. "I can definitely help you out with that. Tony's been impossible; I can't wait to see the look on his face when I tell him I have to steal away for a bit and find some stuff for you. You want to stick in the Caribbean?"

"Might as well; we're already here," Bo said. "I want something quiet and romantic; private, and with a view."

"You want activities and excursions, or just something...with a big bed?" She smirked and shook her head. The two of them together wasn't a big surprise—not to her at least. She'd guessed a long time ago that there was more between them than a casual flirtation. It was overpowered when Dylan and Tia were in the room, but it was there—she'd seen it.

Lexi and Bo shared a devious smile. "Maybe both?" Lexi said. "I don't know that we'll make too many excursions..."

"I'd like a private sunset cruise," Bo interjected, "and maybe something a little adventurous—horseback riding? Zip lining?" He looked at Lexi. "How does that sound?"

"I'm up for it if you are," she said, smiling.

"I'll see what I can do for you in the morning," she said. "But for now, you go work on catching that bouquet!"

They climbed the stairs to the enormous open air deck where the reception was still in full swing. Lexi caught Tia's eye and made her way over.

"I didn't miss anything good, did I?" she asked.

"It was pretty interesting watching Tony and Jessa on the dance floor, that's for sure," she smiled. "But other than that, I haven't noticed much besides my incredibly fine husband," she giggled, and knew she'd never get tired of saying that.

"He does look damn amazing," Lexi agreed, "and so do you. Marriage agrees with you both already."

"It does, and I know it's terrible of me, but I want to get the formalities out of the way so we can sneak out of here a little early and…" a grin spread across her face. "…you know."

"I do," Lexi agreed, "so just toss me that freaking bouquet and get it over with already. Eat some cake, make a toast to thank everyone for coming, and get out of here. There's not a single person here who isn't going to understand that."

Dylan sidled up and wrapped his arms around his bride. "I missed you, sexy wife," he said, kissing her on the cheek. "I'm ready when you are."

"I'm working on it, husband," she smiled. "We have to do the bouquet and garter, cut the cake, and make one more round of goodbyes, and then we'll be done."

"Not done," Dylan said with a sly smile. "Just getting started, baby." He leaned over and nibbled on her ear.

Tia grabbed his hand and started for the stage. "Let's hurry, then," she said breathlessly.

She climbed the steps and took the mike, and Dylan joined her. Immediately, the silverware started clinking against dozens of glasses, and Dylan happily obliged.

"Whew!" she said into the mike. "I will never get tired of that!" The guests cheered, and raised their glasses. "So listen," she started. "We want to thank each and every one of you for sharing this incredible time with us. We both feel so blessed to have you all in our lives, and couldn't imagine this day without you. Many of you came halfway around the world to be here, and we are so grateful. It's been the best day of my life so far, and we are both looking forward to starting our married lives together…"

"As soon as possible!" Dylan called into the mike, a few whistles and catcalls coming from the floor.

Tia punched him playfully on the arm. "So we're going to toss the bouquet and garter, cut the cake, have one last dance and then make our exit—since we won't see you again before we're off on our honeymoon, we wanted to say goodbye, we love you all, and we have loved every minute we've spent with you! So, with that, if I can get all the single girls over here…"

It was Jessa who ended up with the bouquet, much to the delight of the crowd. She stood there dumbfounded—she hadn't had a real romantic interest in anyone since the horrible break-up she'd had shortly before she'd started working for Dylan; and getting married was the furthest thing from her mind. She felt a blush rise up in her cheeks as she stood there holding the beautiful bundle of tropical flowers, and she looked over to see Tony Granger smirking at her. Who the hell did he think he was, anyway? Mr. High and Mighty, reigning over his little kingdom here, calling meetings with her at his whim to go through pictures and videos so he could profit from this whole event? He did put on a hell of a wedding, though, and it had been incredibly easy to put it all together with his help. He was a pretty good dancer, too, and they'd actually shared a few light moments. Maybe she was being a little too hard on him.

A thin smile touched her lips before she decided to roll with it, and held the bouquet over her head, doing a little victory dance.

Dylan made a huge deal out of diving beneath Tia's dress to retrieve the garter, and although the guests saw the humor in it, Tia shivered as she felt his tongue slide deliciously up her thigh past the garter belt to the edge of her panties. She felt the vibration of his moan between her legs, and had to work hard to keep a light expression on her face.

Bo did manage to grab the garter, but it wasn't too much of a struggle for him, since Dylan practically threw it right at him. He waved it in the air, and then pulled Lexi over for a hug, telling her, "Looks like the luck's all on my side tonight, sweetheart!"

The music started up and they took to the dance floor once more, Dylan with Jessa and Tia with Bo.

Bo smiled down at Tia. "You take good care of my man, there, you hear me?" he said.

"No worries there. You take care of my friend, too, Bo. She's had some tough times this past year too."

"I know it, and I will," he assured her, and she knew his word was golden.

"I trust that you will," she smiled, adding, "I couldn't be happier, you know, for the two of you. How awesome would it be for this to work out for all of us?"

"Well now, don't be getting ahead of yourself now, little missy," he said with a sheepish grin. "Or I guess now I need to say little missus. I'm very hopefully optimistic, though, you know? She brings something out in me that I didn't even know was there. I feel like I'm back in grade school with a major crush. It's a little disconcerting, to be honest, but it feels really good."

"I like the two of you together," Tia smiled, "although I wouldn't want to be within a five-mile radius if you get into an argument. Neither of you would ever win."

"Ah," Bo said smiling. "The answer to that is to always let her win. I definitely know that."

"Well, in that case, there shouldn't be any problems," she laughed. They both watched as Tony Granger strolled confidently onto the dance floor and approached Dylan, requesting to cut in on his dance with Jessa.

"I was hoping to get one more dance with my bride anyway," Dylan smiled, handing her over as Jessa frowned at him jokingly. Dylan cut in on Tia and Bo, and Bo motioned for Lexi to join him, twirling her around the floor and laughing with her. It was a hell of an end to the evening for all of them as the other guests joined them for their final dance.

They cut the cake, posed for the obligatory pictures as they fed it to one another, and ran around to hug their guests one last time before heading out and down the path that led to the romantic little villa where they'd be spending their wedding night. Dylan grabbed her hand and tugged her along, and Tia kicked off her shoes in an attempt to match his pace.

"Are you in a hurry, Mr. Miller?" she asked slyly as they hurried down the path.

"You better believe it, Mrs. Miller," he answered breathlessly. "It's not official until we consummate, you know."

Tia picked up her pace and they nearly ran to the bungalow, stopping just long enough for him to pick her up and carry her over the threshold into the well-appointed villa. They stood staring at each other for a moment, getting one more look at their wedding attire, and they both smiled.

"You are my wife!" he exclaimed, reaching out to run his fingers down her cheek. "Finally."

"And you are my husband," she replied, her eyes lidded. "I can't tell you how happy I am to say that."

He pulled her close and slowly undid the zipper on the back of her dress, letting it fall to the floor. She smiled as she watched him take her in, loving the lustful look in his eyes. "You like?" she whispered. The matching bra and panties were a gift from one of her showers, and she wore them as her "something new."

"Oh yeah," he growled back. "I really like."

She slipped off his jacket and threw it over the back of a chair, taking her time with the buttons on his shirt. Frustrated, he yanked it off over his head, and pressed his bare chest against her. "Mine," he said. "All mine."

"I've been yours all along, Dylan," she said, repeating what she'd said to him nearly a year ago. "Didn't you know?"

They fell onto the bed, and he kissed her, long and deep, his hands sliding slowly up the length of her body to cup her face in his hands. "And I yours, my love." He brought his lips down to hers and they made love, slow and easy, for the first time as man and wife.

The music kept playing, and the guests kept partying, long after the bride and groom had left. It was an unreal experience for most of them; a private island in the Bahamas, witness to one of the weddings of the century, and a chance to let loose and have some fun in the beautiful Caribbean. Bo and Lexi danced the night away until they could barely stand, and then, as the night was winding down, Bo whispered, "Stay with me tonight."

"I packed the leopard outfit," she whispered.

"Oh, hell yes," he growled, pulling her closer.

Tia had the best room on the property—the master suite in the main house. It had been cleared out after she'd gotten dressed for the wedding; her bags packed and moved to the villa. She'd told Lexi at the reception that she was welcome to it that evening, if things moved to that level, and that was where she led Bo now.

She was full of anticipation and nervousness—their relationship would never be the same after this, but she found herself looking forward to the changes it would bring. The air grew heavy—they both knew that this was a game changer—no longer would they be harmlessly flirting; this made them a solid couple. And since their respective best friends were now married, they'd be part of each other's lives regardless of how their own relationship worked out. They were both willing to take the chance, however, and neither was naïve about how it could affect the ones they loved most.

Lexi lifted the little rug outside the door and took the key Tia said would be waiting, and turned the lock. She'd been in this room just this morning, but somehow it all seemed new. Tia had obviously anticipated they'd be here—the giant four poster bed was turned down and sprinkled with fragrant petals, and there was a bottle of champagne chilling on the nightstand. Candles were placed strategically around the room and Lexi set about lighting them, creating an ambiance much different than the room had previously assumed. Bo popped the cork on the champagne bottle and poured two glasses, handing one to her as she lit the last candle. The ambient light flickered over his features, and she took them in one by one as they spoke to each other without words. The thin dreadlocks that fell just below his shoulders, his thick, full lips, chocolate brown eyes rimmed with long lashes, the rich cocoa of his skin, the shortly trimmed beard and mustache, and of course, the mere size of him—six foot three at least, she thought, and bulging muscle.

He looked deep into her eyes. "Are you sure this is what you want, Lexi?" he asked softly, his own eyes literally dancing. "You know what they say—once you have black…"

She chuckled in spite of herself, and looked at him. The humor was in his voice, but his eyes told a very different story. This was serious business, and she tried to come up with an equally corny cliché. "Yeah? Well," she said giggling, "maybe once you have cream, I'll haunt all your dreams."

"You crazy woman," he breathed. "You've been haunting my dreams for a year now. Are you finally gonna make them come true?"

She felt the heat rise into her cheeks. "I'm going to be yours tonight, Bo, and hopefully for many nights to come."

"Then all my prayers are answered," he whispered, coming to her and pulling her gently into his arms. He took her face in his huge hands, and kissed her gently. She felt her limbs soften as other parts of her throbbed intently, and kissed him back, intensifying the contact. She pressed against him, molding her body to his, and felt her stomach turn in anticipation.

She wondered for a moment how his kiss could be so soft when every part of him was so hard—and she slid his jacket from his shoulders and dropped it to the floor. As she fumbled with his shirt buttons, he slowly slid the zipper down the back of her dress, and she stepped out of it as it pooled at her feet, kicking it behind her.

She shivered as his hands ran over her bare skin; down her arms to her waist, then up to cup her breasts, and cried out softly as he deftly released the front clasp and bent to kiss them, taking each nipple into his mouth and swirling his tongue over the hard peaks.

"You are so beautiful," he groaned as he shrugged out of his shirt and pulled her against his bare chest. She could only growl low in her throat as she ran her hands up his back, around to his tight stomach, and down to the waistband of his pants. She undid the button and slid the zipper down, letting them fall to the floor with the rest of their expensive and exclusive clothing, pressing her body to his and letting her hands wander where they liked. And it seemed that wherever they wandered, she liked.

His hands were wandering, too, and when they found their way beneath the thin material of her panties; when he slowly slid one long finger into her, she gasped. "Oh God!" she breathed, grinding against him to hold him there. She felt an urgent need to connect with him, to make their bodies one, and her breathing quickened as she reached around to stroke him. He slid her panties down with his other hand, and pushed her onto the bed where she lay breathless. Without hesitation, he hooked his thumbs into the waistband of his boxers and yanked them down. She moaned as she took him in.

She'd seen him in swim trunks, and had appreciated the intense masculinity of his form, but this was something entirely different. He stood in front of her, and she could only hum low in her throat. He was huge. Every single delectable part of him was huge. She wondered why they hadn't made statues from his form; carved his likeness in marble; because he was absolutely perfect.

He couldn't help but snap his trademark grin as he gauged her reaction to him. For the past year, since he'd first fallen for her, she'd been an unattainable prize; an engaged woman. But she'd gotten into his head, and many a morning he'd wake with a painfully swollen erection that wouldn't be satisfied, and her face burning into the back of his eyelids. He had to do something to deal with the frustrations, especially after their encounter in LA, and he'd taken to working out on a regular basis to try and release some of the pent up anxiety. He'd done push-ups in the mornings, run the treadmill in the afternoons, and finally made use of all the gym equipment he'd purchased over the years that he'd always promised himself he'd start using.

Sometimes in his fantasies he'd meet her again and she'd see him as more than the amiable jokester; good old Bo; and more as the man he felt inside. The results had been remarkable. Without making a specific plan, he'd become incredibly fit—a nice six pack, strong arms and shoulders, a narrow waist. And the way she was looking at him right now made every single bead of sweat, every aching muscle, and every grueling work-out more than worth it.

Damn! He wanted to take her—to possess her—so badly, but he'd waited much too long for this dream; unbelievably realized; to hold her in his arms, and he wanted this night to last forever. Their first night. Hopefully, the first of many.

He came to her slowly, stretching out beside her on the enormous bed. She could feel the tension in his coiled muscles, but he moved patiently, slowly, tracing the outline of her face with his fingers and staring deep into her eyes. "You have no idea how many times I've dreamed of this," he whispered as he brought his mouth to hers, starting slow and then intensifying the kiss with a swipe of his tongue. She melted into him, turning to press her body against his but he pushed her back, nibbled his way down her neck, and explored her reverently, kissing her toes, kneecaps, belly button, and all of the places that made her cry out in pleasure. When he finally came back to her mouth she could only whisper his name, over and over, as she pressed against him, molding her curves to the hard lines of his body. The smile he gave her then was not his usual boyish grin, but something more—something deeper, and it made parts of her absolutely come alive.

She ran her hands along the contours of his chest, his hips, and stroked him urgently, groaning in pleasure at the way his eyes rolled upward as he growled in the back of his throat. Too soon, he pulled her away, entangling both of her hands in one of his and stretching them out over her head. He used his other hand to set her on fire, and she moaned in pleasant agony as he took his time, teasing at her entrance until she writhed beneath his touch.

"Perfect and beautiful in every way, just like I knew you would be," he whispered, and before she could answer, before she could tell him he was perfect, too, he plunged inside her and she cried out his name, pushing against him as she rode the unbelievable wave of ecstasy all the way to the end and was breathless.

"Oh Bo—that was…" she searched for the right word—incredible? Awesome? Amazing? And then settled on, "perfect."

He rolled over to kiss her once more, and smiled. "It was even better than I imagined," he whispered, "and I imagined it would be pretty close to heaven." He traced the contour of her breast with his finger, and slid his hand up to stroke her cheek. "You've just made me a very happy man, Lexi," he groaned. "A very happy man indeed."

"You rank pretty high on the happy scale, too, I must say."

"Yeah?" he smirked. "Well, I hope that means we'll do it again. Soon."

"Definitely," she murmured against the hammering of his heart. "Most definitely."

And after a fabulous weekend, an exhausting day, and an incredible night, they fell asleep, tangled in each other, and listening to the sounds of the sea.

Monday dawned bright and clear; another perfect Caribbean day. Tia awoke in the arms of her husband and snuggled closer to him. In just a few hours they would leave for their honeymoon—she had no idea where they would be going, except for a few days in Paris where Dylan would keep his promise to play at the mayor's daughter's wedding in payment for the private birthday dinner at the top of the Eiffel Tower. The night that he'd first told her he loved her.

As she listened to the waves rushing the shore and the calls of the birds that flitted about in the trees to greet the day, she was filled with a light—a pure joy at what her future held. She rolled over and kissed Dylan on the cheek.

"Good morning, Mrs. Miller," he mumbled with a smile, pulling her close and wrapping her in his arms.

"Best morning of my life. So far."

"And they lived happily ever after," he whispered, stroking her cheek.

"InHappily ever after," she smiled, bringing her lips down to meet his. "Always and forever."

ABOUT THE AUTHOR

Kim DeSalvo is the author of Amazon Best-Seller, *Incidental Happenstance*. She holds a master's degree in education, and works as an elementary teacher. Kim lives in the Chicago area with her husband and her hairy mutt.

This is a work of fiction. Any resemblance of characters to actual people is pure happenstance.

30162603R00331

Made in the USA
Lexington, KY
22 February 2014